Hyenas & Lotuses

A Novel from the Time of Ancient Egypt

Hyenas & Lotuses

A Novel from the Time of Ancient Egypt

by Prof. Andrzej Niwinski

All material contained herein is
Copyright © Andrzej Niwinski 2020 All rights reserved.

***

Originally published in Poland by Publishing House Pro-Egypt in 2010 as Hieny I Lotosy

***

Translated and published in English with permission.

***

Paperback ISBN: 978-1-7348606-1-0

EPub ISBN: 978-1-3867450-0-6

***

Written by Andrzej Niwinski

Published by Royal Hawaiian Press

Cover art by Tyrone Roshantha

Translated by Arkadiusz Gil

Publishing Assistance: Dorota Reszke

***

For more works by this author, please visit:

www.royalhawaiianpress.com

***

Version Number 1.00

For my children

INTRODUCTION

The people whose names appear on the pages of this novel, really lived and left traces of their activities, sometimes in carefully executed carvings or monumental hieroglyphic inscriptions in temples and tombs, and sometimes just scratched out with a sharp stone on a rock or written on a piece of papyri or a shell of a broken vessel.

They lived in Thebes - the largest center in the south of Egypt, several hundred kilometers up the Nile from today's Cairo. Their time fell on a particularly turbulent episode of history, including a period that can be compared to the "martial law" introduced by several generals to restore order after the tragic civil war that shook the foundations of the then Egyptian state. It all happened around 1082-1070 BC, during the time of King Ramesses XI, as well as High Priest (and King) Heri-Hor.

Both of these figures have already appeared in Polish literature once: Bolesław Prus placed the action of the historical novel "Pharaoh" during this period. However, one should be aware that this wonderful work was a study of the political power in Poland at the end of the 19th century, set in ancient Egypt, but does not fully reflect the historical realities of the time of Ramesses and Heri-Hor. "Hyenas and lotuses" have a different idea.

The author has been exploring various groups of monuments from that period for nearly 40 years, and this novel is an attempt to reconstruct them. The real picture of events resulting from this research is the background here. It is where the dramatic fate of the protagonists, animated with full respect for the cultural reality of Egypt in the eleventh century BC, takes place. This respect makes it necessary to show their lives from day to day and from holiday, based on the original sources, but it also makes the names, geographical names or measures and weights given according to the terminology used then.

Therefore, not once do the names Egypt, the Nile or Thebes fall here, because they are much later. The novel is addressed to everyone, regardless of their knowledge about Egypt. In situations where, according to the author, the reader may feel lost, there are short footnotes at the bottom of the page. More complete information about the different Egyptian names can also be found at the end of the lists.

Inviting you to this trip in time to ancient Egypt about 3100 years ago, the author hopes that after its completion, the Reader will understand the Pharaoh's culture better than school textbooks allow, and maybe feel the connection with people of that era. In their lives, despite the passage of millennia, we can recognize quite current problems of our time.

CHAPTER I

There was white-yellow silence under the pure blue sky. The sand mixed with limestone dust and small stones, like a huge coat, covered the undulating plain stretching from the green fields visible away to the hill covered with a jagged rock mane. On its slopes lay numerous boulders with uneven shapes which gave the area a taste of wildness evoking the beginnings of time. At the foot of the hill, the old tombs of the Kings, crowned with brick pointed pyramids which have been damaged for centuries, froze in dignified oblivion. Here and there were also smaller pyramids, under which were chapels of the family tombs of various dignitaries, sometimes colorfully painted and carved. However, they were all closed and gave the impression of being forgotten. High in the sky, falcons circled slowly and majestically – the natural eternal guardians of this vast area called Horizon of Eternity, or the Place of Maat, that is the great necropolis of the City.[1]

Hyenas & Lotuses

Royal Scribe of the Necropolis, Djehuty-mes, a man to whom His Majesty King of the Both Countries, Ramesses, entrusted the supervision of the mysteries of the City of the dead, slowly climbed the hill, leaning on a cane. It was usually a sign of dignity, but here it fulfilled its basic function of support for this gray-haired old man with a face covered in numerous wrinkles. Djehuty-mes still felt strong, but it was time to start handing over duties to his son and successor Buteh-Amun, who had recently graduated from the scribe school at Ipet-sut and had already begun his first months of priesthood at the House of Eternity of Amen-hotep Djeser-Ka-Re, justified[2], in Khefet-her-neb-es.[3]

That is why Djehuty-mes, when inspecting the cemetery, more often than not took Buteh-Amun with him, showing him, in turn, all the recess of the necropolis, including those furthest away and almost forgotten. Today, Buteh-Amun also accompanied him.

"Maybe you would like to rest a few moments, father?" he asked. "It is not so hot today and the wind brings a nice breeze from the river, but Re is already high[4] and it's hard to get up the hill."

---

[1] That's how the Egyptians called Thebes (today's Luxor). The alternative name was: Waset (see City Map, map of Egypt marked with all the cities listed in the book, as well as List of geographical names and names of individual parts of ancient Thebes).

[2] I.e. the deceased who obtained justification at the judgement of Osiris.

[3] Temple of the posthumous worship of King Amenhotep I in the western part of the City (see List of royal names and a table of outline of the history of ancient Egypt).

[4] The Sun was defined by this divine name (see List of divine names).

"Not yet. Today, I want to show you one place that is not far away; we will rest there," Djehuty-mes answered. "But as long as we go up, let us refrain from speaking and not waste our strength."

They overcame the first haughtiness, and then the second one, invisible from below, and found themselves on a vast highland, full of unevenness and protruding limestone rocks, between which the whole area was covered with yellowish-brown and black small stones clearly distinguished against the background of yellow sand. There was no path here, and Buteh-Amun stared with admiration at his father, who walked confidently, circling among the rock bulges that seemed to be absolutely identical to someone who was here for the first time. At last, Djehuty-mes stopped, then sat down on the sand and reached for the leather water bag he carried which was hung on his back, and after tipping it, he drank water for a moment. Buteh-Amun did the same; he knew that his father would soon begin the teaching that he had prepared for him today.

"You saw down there the very old tombs of Kings that ruled here hundreds of years ago. Everyone has a pyramid because in those days it was a sign by which the place of eternity of the pharaohs was recognized. You know that this has not been the case for a long time, on the contrary, the presence of the pyramid shows that the grave with which it connects does not belong to the King, but only to some official. All the Kings from the Amenhotep or Ramses family, who rest in the Great Valley, are under one great pyramid. Oh, this one," and Djehuty-mes pointed to the highest peak of the nearby mountains rising far away, which really resembled the pyramid in its shape.

"And although those dead Kings are like sacred amulets for the City and the surrounding area, it is this mountain that is the source of power and provides protection to all living and the dead, like a mother and we turn to her in prayers as to Hat-Hor, mother of God, as well as every divine Pharaoh who rests in a grave invisible to humans. Only one tomb of the King, the patron of our City and our family, which has served him for many generations, is, as you probably know, visible from afar and known to all – the Horizon of Eternity of Amen-hotep Djeser-Ka-Re."

"The one above the ruins of the temple of King Djehuty-mes Men-kheper-Re?"

"Above the ruins is only his grave chapel, which can be seen from afar. The tomb itself was located under the floor of this temple, or rather temple was built there to protect this tomb - King Djehuty-mes Men-kheper-Re, justified by a voice, honored the grave of his great-grandfather, whom he particularly adored."

"But is this Amen-hotep grave safe now that the temple is gone? After the destruction of the temple by the collapse of rocks, it was deconstructed."

"Unfortunately, not really. Admittedly, the whole area is protected day and night by several guards, but if they were lacking ..." the old priest suspended his voice.

"Father," Buteh-Amon asked, "but here, not far from place where we are now, above the graves with the pyramids is also a place that is called the grave of Amen-hotep?"

"Yes, also his mother Ahmes-Nefertari, justified. Although none of them are lying there, but in that temple below, "Djehutymes pointed to the rectangular outline of sacred precinct surrounded by a clay wall," there is still a statue, which is called the Amen-hotep from the Courtyard." The new tomb of the King was carved elsewhere, but the cult chapel associated with the old one remained and still serves people. But son, I brought you here to see where the entrance to the grave of someone is who lived at the same time as our holy patron Amen-hotep."

"One can't see anything here..." Buteh-Amun looked around helplessly.

"Exactly, and you are sitting ten cubits[5] from the entrance. Until now, we only talked about such graves that can be seen from afar, but most are well hidden. Can you see this rock? Below it is the shaft leading to this grave. It was carved out just under the hanging rock, but after the funeral, the rock was collapsed, and it covered the entrance. The workers who worked here were brought from afar, I suppose from Ta-mehu, and then taken there. Even if they told someone about this rock because they certainly talked about it when they returned home, tell me, is it possible to someone who came from the Northern Country to guess which rock they were talking about? Even all the stones that were excavated from inside the mountain during the carving of

---

[5] Length measurement unit, approx. 52 cm.

this grave were carried away so that no one could guess that there was a grave nearby!"

"Father, how do you know it is like that?" Buteh-Amun asked in awe and slight disbelief.

"These are the secrets that royal necropolis scribes have been passing on to each other for generations. I learned about it from my father, he from his and so on, and now I am talking about it to you. You just need to remember the path so that in the future, when you make a check, you can easily find out if nobody was looking for anything here or breaking a rock. If you see the same view we see today, it means that everything is fine, and inside are intact mummies and everything they have been given for eternal life. And remember, even if you want to help your memory with a note scratched on a rock, do not write it right next to the grave, but a little further from where you have a good enough view, and besides, do not give any details! Oh, just your name alone, and at most an additional mention that you came here "to see the mountain."[6] Unfortunately, we must remember that the days we live in are difficult. Good times of peace and safety are long gone, and customs are generally declining."

"Do you think there are people who could commit the sacrilege of violating the peace of the dead kings?"

"Yes, son, this is already happening, unfortunately," Djehutymes got up, dusted his white tunic from the sand, funneled sand

---

[6] In the Theban necropolis there are several hundred such inscriptions scratched on the rock, the so-called graffiti, among which more than 120 are connected with the name Buteh-Amun.

out from the sandals and added, "We must return, but on the way back, we will pass the royal tomb, one of those with pyramids that was robbed quite recently; you were a small child then…"

They slowly began to descend from the hill and soon they could clearly distinguish all the old circles of the royal tombs they were talking about. Djehuty-mes stopped for a moment, looked around and pointed to his son the grave he meant.

"This is the one. One of my tasks, and soon your duties, is to look after the royal archives regarding necropolis, which, as you know, is in the building between our house and the Great Gate. There is a document written during the robber trial in the days of His Majesty Ramesses Nefer-Ka-Re justified by voice. Well, the accused, I don't remember his name, described there in detail how he got to the burial chamber and then that he found the gilded sarcophagi of the king and queen there. Then he described how he opened them, stripped sacred mummies from bandages to get to precious necklaces, rings and all other amulets, how he finally hacked the gold from wooden coffins, and finally, how he set fire to everything that was left there. It's terrible, even when you only read about it…"

"And what happened to him?"

"Of course, he ended up at the stake, but this event showed that for some people nowadays there is no such sanctities which they would not be afraid to defile to get a few gold items. Since then, I have been constantly afraid that something like this will happen again. The only place that does not threaten anything is the Great Valley – at least the holy mummies of kings are completely safe – *medjayu*[7] guard the valleys and no unauthorized person has the right to enter there. But even if someone got to the grave, which seems almost impossible, after all, no one can open all the chapels and sarcophagi and remove the mummies! The Amen-hotep's horizon of eternity is also rather safe because it is guarded. Similarly, the graves in Ta-Djeser and on the Hill of Wedding Rites, because too many people are still hanging around there. But the necropolis is large and those fragments that are far from everyday paths, such as Ta-set-neferu, where there are numerous royal spouses and children, or even the part where we are now, raises my constant fears! Look at these numerous graves – can you see someone who would be around them? People come here only once a year, during the Beautiful Valley Festival, they bring a sacrifice, they eat a meal, rarely anyone will stay overnight to put out the torches in the milk in the morning[8], and then everything is closed again. Unless someone in the family dies and you must bring another casket into the chamber. This is an ideal situation for thieves, and I will not be surprised when one day..." Djehuty-mes stopped talking and Buteh-Amun did not ask for anything anymore, because he saw that the old father was already tired.

They were coming back in such a perfect silence that they could probably hear their hearts beating. It was then that they heard a strange sound like the crying of a child and the howling of a jackal at the same time, but it could be neither child nor

---

[7] Policemen, most often from Kush, a land to the south of Egypt (in today's Sudan).

[8] Allusion to the old ritual associated with the said holiday.

jackal. They stopped to uncover the source of this sound and found that it was coming from the temple of His Majesty Sethi Maat-Men-Re, justified. This old house of God, opened only on holidays, was almost at the end of a long line of buildings along the road leading to the center of Khefet-her-neb-es, running along the canal separating the fields from the desert. The sound repeated, but now it was accompanied by lower tones, as if groaning, which meant that it was probably made by man.

"Whatever it means, I have to check it out!" Djehuty-mes said and he headed for the temple, but Buteh-Amun overtook him and entered first into the temple courtyard through the open side wicket between the two high gates.

"This wicket should probably be closed," he thought, and his surprise rose a moment later when he saw the wicket open at the other gate of the temple; only a few men entered this way, and between this gate and Saint of Saints there were only several dozen steps. Buteh-Amun heard groans again; they came from inside the temple, so he entered between the columns into the shadow twilight of the Hall of Appearances[9]. He saw an elderly man sitting on the floor only 10 cubits in front of him. He was dressed in the usual linen kilt that the villagers and service wore and constituting the clothing of the vast majority of the inhabitants of Khefet-her-neb-es, except on public holidays. The seated man had his face hidden in his hands and alternately gave low moans or higher tones of tearful wailing. When he heard

---

[9] Column hall in the central part of the temple, where during the procession the eyes of the people gathered in the courtyard appeared a holy barge with a statue carried by priests.

footsteps and saw Buteh-Amun coming in, he jumped up and made a move at first, as if he wanted to run, although he didn't have anywhere to go. He looked at the unknown newcomer in a priestly dress with horror in his eyes and only a moment after he saw the Djehuty-mes coming in, relief on his face appeared, though he did not stop lamenting. With a groan, he threw himself at the Necropolis Scribe's feet and for a moment he was shaken by crying.

"Help me, Lord!" he said, still lying down, "Because I have suffered a disaster I have never experienced before!"

Djehuty-mes scooped the miserable up and looked at him more closely. He had bruises all over his body and visible swollen traces of fresh scratches and bumps, in which droplets of frozen blood were still pearling. On his head was a reddish-blue tumor; meaning that the man had been severely beaten quite recently.

"What is your name and what happened here that you look like this?!" the Necropolis Scribe asked, and the questioned man began to speak quickly, gesturing violently.

"I am Nes-Amun, the guardian of this temple of His Majesty Sethi Maat-Men-Re, justified. I have been working here for 30 years and I have not gone away from here for a day, watching over the house and all equipment entrusted to me. I cleaned the sanctuary and opened it only on days intended for holy activities, especially on the day of the Beautiful Feast of the Valley. I live in the house next door. When I finished cleaning the Sethi House today and went out, they attacked me, tied me up – look, Lord, I still have rope marks on my hands!" and he stretched out his hands, on which the bluish imprint of the rope weave was clearly visible. "The attackers dragged me here and beat me, made me show them the place where the sacred equipment for priests to perform sacrifices is hidden, and when they saw the end of the rope at the door[10] of this side chapel in the Hall of Appearances, where these things were closed, they took my door opener by force, opened the chapel and took everything away! Oh, here they were: a *hes*-vase and a copper bucket with a bowl, two silver dishes *nemset*, a bronze censer decorated with ivory, dishes with natron[11] and incense and a silver tray!" Nes-Amun stretched out his hand towards the emptied niche, which was hidden in the wall and after closing almost invisible in the dim light. "I shouted that they should leave these holy objects, because God would punish them, but then they hit my head so that the night came to me during the day. Only recently I woke up and I was able to shed those cords, but it was better not to wake up! What will I do now? Where will I get these vessels when priests come to perform their sacred duties?! They'll charge me with theft! It has never

---

[10] The Egyptians used an interesting way of closing the door. They opened inward, and when closed, they were blocked by a round bolt with a cord attached at the end, the pull of which pulled the bolt out of its socket in the wall and blocked the door. The end of the cord was led through a fairly large track in the door and dangled outside. To open the door, a kind of universal "key" was used - another similar bolt, pierced through on one side, and terminated with a cord on the other. The end of the cord hanging at the door was passed through the hole in the "key" and the entire "key" was transferred to the inside of the closed door, then, manipulating both cords caused the main screw to was pushed through the "key" into the wall socket and the door opened. The "key" was only for opening the door; to close it, all you had to do was pull the door towards you and pull the cord from the locking bolt, sliding it out of the socket again.

[11] *Hes* and *nemset* vases - names of ritual vessels often used during religious ceremonies; natron - a type of soda, a substance used for ritual purification, also during mummification.

happened to me before! Even at a time when bands were prowling here, no one took anything from the temple, and now..."

He began to moan again, but Djehuty-mes did not allow him to lament again.

"Nes-Amun, your words are true, and Maat lives in your eyes and voice. You don't have to worry, I will tell His Majesty First Servant of Amun, Amen-hotep, about everything I saw here. Nobody will accuse you of theft; we are witnesses: me and my son Buteh-Amun. Did you recognize anyone among those who attacked you?"

Nes-Amun looked down and fell silent. Djehuty-mes looked eloquently at his son; this man was obviously afraid.

"You know, Nes-Amun," Djehuty-mes continued, "that there are still people in the City that others are afraid of. It would be good if His Majesty Amen-hotep could know the name of the villain if you are sure you know it."

"Lord," Nes-Amun whispered, as if afraid that someone else might hear his words, "I know it and you know it too, but if I say it and he finds out, he'll come here and hurt me even more!"

"I told you, Nes-Amun, that you don't have to worry about anything in giving your testimony," the Necropolis Scribe repeated.

"It was Aa-neru," Nes-Amun whispered even more quietly, "And several other soldiers, but he gave them orders."

"Nes-Amun, rest assured that nothing will happen to you, and thanks to you, perhaps this robber will finally be punished," Djehuty-mes said, and then took off from his hand a bracelet made of silver wire, on which small faience scarabs were threaded and gave it to the guard.

"This is a reward to you for good service. Keep doing it as before!" he said, not letting Nes-Amun fall to his feet again.

"I expected to hear the name Aa-neru," Djehuty-mes turned to his son when they were away from the temple, heading toward the center of Khefet-her-neb-es. "He is a real bandit, but he is protected by the title of an army officer, and even more by the friendship of General Pa-nehsi."

"Father, you meant to say Vizier Pa-nehsi," Buteh-Amun added ironically.

"Yes, of course, and also the Head of the Granaries Pa-nehsi and the Royal Son of Kush[12], Pa-nehsi," answered Djehuty-mes. "He only lacks the title of Amun's First Servant and would have everything an official can gather in one hand. But this lack is a bother to him, which is why Pa-nehsi hates Amen-hotep. The paths of the Son of Re's[13] activities are unknown, but His Majesty Ramesses probably entrusted too much power to one man. When he sat on the throne 16 years ago, the City was a little restless. People still remembered the bands of robbers that Nes-Amun had mentioned, invading nearby villages, which made the people working in the Great Valley afraid to go to work and leave only women and children alone in the town of workmen. Sometimes

---

[12] Vizier - the highest position in the Egyptian administration, comparable to the office of prime minister. Head of the Granaries - a high official title, like "the Minister of Economy". The Royal Son of Kush - the head of the territory to the south of Egypt, acting on behalf of Pharaoh.

[13] Son of Re, One of the five titles of Pharaoh preceding his own name.

those workers also refused to work because they did not receive payment. Even the royal tomb we had talked about earlier was plundered. His Majesty learned all this and sent an army to the City and Pa-nehsi to clean up."

"But now his army is causing widespread unease," Buteh-Amun added, "And because they are actually dark-skinned people from the south, people are not only afraid of them, but they treat them almost like invaders.

There is a lot of scenes on the walls and high gates of the temples, where those Kushites[14] along with Asians and Tjehenu people are treated by the pharaoh as enemies? Will it ever lead to something bad? And instead of coming here and talking to City officials, the King sits far away in his palace in Pi-Ramesse and probably doesn't know anything about it."

"Son," the Necropolis Scribe replied, "You're right about the Kushites, but only a little. The Both Countries have long been strongly associated with the lands to the south of Abu, and the Kushites are our brothers whom God created on an equal footing with us – the people of Kemet[15], and also with Asians and Tjehenu people.

---

[14] Kushites - dark-skinned inhabitants of the territories south of Egypt; Tjehenu - population living west of Egypt (= Libyans). At the time when the takes place action of novel many Kushites and Lybians lived in Egypt.

[15] Term of Native Egyptians, as well as Egypt itself. Another term for the country was: Both Countries, which means together the areas of the Nile Valley (the so-called Southern Country), as well as the areas of northern Egypt, including the so-called the Nile delta (so-called Northern Country).

In the royal tombs in the Great Valley, in the texts that cover the walls of corridors and chambers, there are also such words and are accompanied by images of all these people, including foreigners, walking in ceremonial dresses,[16] not bound and waiting for the royal sword's blow; I saw in the archives that I look after, papyri with examples of these scenes and these texts. Anyway, times are changing. Once upon a time, Tjehenu were called "strangers" and feared as enemies. Today, they live in numerous settlements in the land of Kemet, especially in the Northern Country, and we even know those who descend from them and are as good subjects of the King as you or me. There are also decent Kushites who differ from us, only a little darker-skinned, but they would give their lives for this country and Pharaoh, like many *medjayu* who keep order in the cities of the Both Countries. Finally, some have lived here for many generations and are by no means related to any foreigners, and yet they have a terrible temper and we avoid them as much as we can. Such as police chief Pa-Shu-uben, for example, who made a career because he reported to the Vizier about everything that was said in the City and is still doing the same, hiding behind the title of the Knowing City Secrets and being in the service of Pa-nehsi. And Pi-ankh? He is a simpleton, though a general. On the other hand, look, Pi-nodjem and Nodjmet - his children - are completely unlike him... Indeed, everyone must be measured with the measure that his actions deserve: the measure of Maat," Djehuty-mes concluded.

---

[16] It is about one of the scenes in the so-called *Book of Gates* - a composition created for the king's use in the 14th century BC.

They did not even have the favorable conditions to continue this conversation, because they came to the more densely built-up central part of Khefet-her-neb-es, where on narrow streets people were still passing by who met them and greeted them, and sometimes, even had to squeeze between the market stalls and sometimes stop to someone riding the opposite way on a donkey. They were also slowly approaching the southern part of the Western City, which was dominated by the huge, 20 cubits thick and 36 cubits high, brick walls of the district of His Majesty Ramesses User-Maat-Re Meri-Amun's temple. Both main stone gates leading to it from the east and west, which protruded in both directions beyond the line of walls, were even more powerful. These enormous fortifications surrounded a large area where, apart from temple buildings, there was also a royal palace, numerous office buildings and several houses of important officials. The house of Djehuty-mes stood out there, occupying together with the royal necropolis archive, a vast area in the southwest corner of the district.

The entire district of Ramesses served as a fortress capable of giving shelter to the inhabitants of this part of the City. When its walls were rising, they might have seemed very necessary. The country was only recovering after the great war that had to be fought first with the Tjehenu people, and then with the invaders who attacked Kemet from the north, arriving as if "from the sea," but also from the east, from which the Asians have always tried to invade. On the walls of the great temple, which occupied the center of this walled area, there were numerous scenes of battles with these attackers, as well as scenes of the final triumph of His Majesty Ramesses User-Maat-Re Meri-Amun.

However, since then, the borders of the kingdom have never been threatened, and the great fortress has turned into a vibrant office complex, in which until recently the view of a man carrying a scroll of papyri was certainly more common than the view of a soldier with a spear or bow. However, the situation has changed in recent years. General Pa-nehsi, who lived in the former fortress residence of the King at the eastern gate, has just surrounded himself with his officers and Kushite soldiers from the southern corps of the army of the Both Countries and again the area that Djehuty-mes and Buteh-Amun just entered had begun to resemble a barracks atmosphere. All its eastern part was separated from the rest by a wall with a narrow gate, at which the guard checked who wanted to enter the palace or general's section of the fortress, and what the scribe was scrupulously writing down. For this reason, at this transition, it was almost always swarming and even some regulars, or residents of the palace part, who wanted to get to it from this side, had to wait for their turn at times.

Buteh-Amun was the first to notice Aa-neru, who was apparently in this situation. The officer spoke to a woman who was sitting in a litter carried by four black servants. They both recognized her immediately: she was Nes-Mut, the wife of all-powerful by the grace of King Ramesses dictator, Pa-nehsi. Djehuty-mes hesitated for a moment; he had no sympathy for both and rather avoided all conversations with them, but today's event at Sethi's temple prompted him to behave in an unusual manner. Leaning on his cane, dignitary walked to the Nes-Mut and Aa-neru who were busy with lively conversation.

"...I think five *debens*[17], as usual in silver," the woman's last sentence came to him before he bowed to her, greeting her.

"Forgive me, Lady, that I interrupt your conversation, but I saw Aa-neru and I wanted to ask him about something," he said. Then turning to the officer, he asked if today, he had by chance been in the temple of His Majesty Sethi Maat-Men-Re, justified? "I passed that way and had such an impression, but I couldn't recognize the face well," he added, staring intently at the officer.

Aa-neru opened his mouth to say something, but at the same moment Nes-Mut did it for him:

"It is impossible, august Djehuty-mes because this young man worked here all day for me," she said, making a sweet smile.

"I must be imagining things," the old man said, "But I would like to remind you that even officers must get my permission each time to walk further in the necropolis. There are break-ins and then it's easy to be accused." he added and smiled.

He was about to leave when Buteh-Amun interrupted suddenly, "My Father is already old and may not always be strong enough, but he introduces me to my duties, and I will make sure that everyone who steals temple equipment from the necropolis is captured and punished!" He turned firmly to Aa-neru, "His Majesty Amen-hotep will be notified of everything."

---

[17] A measure of weight corresponding to a weight of 91g of copper, silver or gold; it was also a measure of value that was also used in barter trade, comparing the value of goods sold and bought.

"Are you accusing me?" Aa-neru replied defiantly.

"There are probably those who could accuse you, so I don't rule it out," Buteh-Amun said, staring at Aa-neru who was confused.

"It looks like a threat against this officer. I will have to complain about you, Buteh-Amun, to my husband," Nes-Mut interjected and gave a sign to the servants carrying her litter to move, as the gate was free. Aa-neru followed her without saying goodbye.

Djehuty-mes turned and walked towards his house, which vestibule leaning on two high columns clearly stood out from the neighboring buildings made of gray mud brick. He climbed a few stairs, then entered the larger room just behind the entrance, which's roof was supported by four high, plastered white columns topped with palm-tree capitals. There was a comfortable chair on a small platform by the wall, on which the Necropolis Scribe sat with great pleasure; the long path he had today tired him.

"That was not smart, son," he said to Buteh-Amun, who followed him, "You have a too direct way of talking to criminals. Even if you didn't say anything, we would get the same valuable information that the General's wife, Nes-Mut, covered this robber, Aa-neru. Your words, arising from a noble reflex, were unnecessary because now Pa-nehsi will certainly receive the "right" version of events. Of course, I must inform the First Servant Amen-hotep about everything, but because tomorrow is the tenth day of the month, so it is time for prayer and rest, I cannot go to him until the day after tomorrow," he said, looking through the open door of the vestibule at the sky, which was already turning red with the fact that Re, tired just like him, was already taking his boat to the western horizon.

CHAPTER II

It was still early, and the City was awkwardly coming to life when Suti-mes reported to the guards at the Great Gate in Ipet-sut, saying that he was going to Khefet-her-neb-es today, then got into his small boat and began to row, heading for the opposite bank of the river. It was the second month of Peret's season[18]. Hapi rolled its waters slowly, a slight wind wrinkled their surface. It was still quite cold, but the work of the rowing was warming up so he did not take with him even the outer woolen coat that the inhabitants of Kemet used to protect against the cold at this time of year. The opposite shore was slowly approaching, and along

---

[18] The Egyptian calendar year was divided into three seasons, each covering 4 months of 30 days: Akhet (= season of the overflow of the Nile, also called Hapi or simply the River), around from mid-July to mid-November, Peret (= Growth) from mid-November to mid-March and Shemu (= Drought) from mid-March to mid-July. Between Shemu and New Year, on the first day of the Akhet season there were 5 days "out of year". During the period of the novel, the names of months were not yet used on a daily basis.

with it were slender palm trees and spreading sycamore patches. Finally, he floated between the green plates lifted by the water, where the lotuses were smiling at him, and already parting their white arms, greeting Re and enjoying his warmth. He still had to bypass a thicket of coastal papyri and flowed into a long narrow canal, which, crossing the spreading fields on both sides, headed perpendicular to the river towards the sacred Ta-Djeser valley visible from afar, enclosed by a high wall of vertical rocks at the feet of which lay three magnificent temples of which two: King's Mentu-hotep and Queen's Hatshepsut are already time-bitten, and the third - King's Djehuty-mes Men-kheper-Re was completely ruined by the collapse of rocks and deconstructed. The same path that Suti-mes' boat now took, once a year, during the Beautiful Feast of the Valley in the second month of the Shemu season, beautifully decorated barges flowed with all the holy images of God that Ipet-sut inhabited to visit the temples of the Western City. Behind them, hundreds of boats of residents who, on that day, visited their close relatives living in the tombs of the Necropolis. At that time, the canal was so crowded that it was necessary to row and, even more so, sail very carefully so as not to hit one of the neighboring boats. Around there were loud conversations, shouting, laughter, sometimes singing and rhythmic clapping or sounds of tambourines. Today, it would be completely quiet here, were it not for the croaking of frogs and the various voices of birds that created a real concert of creation's joy. After all, it was the time of Peret, when after the floodwaters subsided, nature exploded with a passionate need for growth and reproduction.

Suti-mes directed the boat to a transverse canal that ran along the lofty desert shore, on which successive precincts of temples of long-dead rulers rose, and between them the houses of some residents of Khefet-her-neb-es. He finally arrived at the shore and moored his boat to one of the many stakes driven into the ground here for this purpose. He reached the fortified shore by the nearest jetty and, bypassing one of the temples, headed straight for the hill visible against the background of white vertical rocks densely covered with dark skewers of pyramids. At its top stood a small chapel; it is not known when and by whom it was built. However, for a long time, the local people associated it with Osiris – the patron of the dead and with Amun-Min – the embodiment of invisible power, thanks to which man could pass on life. This eternal mystery of the inseparable relationship of death and new life took the form of a traditional joyful custom which young women willingly followed on their wedding day. They went up the hill and circled the top of the hill, which was called the Hill of Wedding Rites, after which they sacrificed to Min-Osiris, praying that they would soon receive the grace of conception, and descending they would take away a small stone that would become an amulet. The ceremony was reserved for women, and Suti-mes, going up the hill, he only sighed and wished that perhaps Henut-netjeru – his love and source of all life hopes - will soon reach the top for the same purpose. Henut-netjeru, or rather: Henut, because everyone called her that, was 16 years old and was the living embodiment of the Peret season: a pretty flower that has just developed from a bud, multiplying the beauty of the world. Suti-mes might have felt really lucky that this wonderful girl, who all the men were interested in, had chosen him. Their hearts had already decided, and if it were to depend only on them, they would have merged even today. But in order to make Henut "the mistress of the house," firstly one must build this house, equip it and be sure that any gust of wind will not break the roots of this jointly sown plant.

Unfortunately, none of them belonged to a wealthy family. Henut's father was the leaseholder of the temple land belonging to the House of Amun in Ipet-sut; her mother, a weaver in Amun's workshop in Khefet-her-neb-es. What they earned was barely enough to support a family of four, because Henut had a brother who was several years younger. The girl was only learning her mother's profession and could only count on the future income that she would make in order to spend on her own contribution to the marital community. However, most important was Henut's parents' good attitude towards Suti-mes, so he believed that one day, he would receive their consent for his daughter's hand in marriage with parental blessing. His parents, unfortunately, could not give such a blessing. Suti-mes just approached the grave where they both were resting, looked at the stone stela built into the hillside and read aloud:

"Let the king sacrifice Re-for-Both-Horizons-Atum, Lord of Both Countries, Osiris, Lord of eternity, First of the West, Lord of Abju, the One who is good and reigns over the living, Anubis Lord of Ta-Djeser, First in Place of the Truth, Isis – the great mother of God, who is the Eye of Re and the Lady of the West, Nephthys, the divine sister and the Divine Nine of the south, north, west and east, in the sky and in the underground world! Let them give thousands of loaves and jugs of beer, a thousand portions of beef and a

thousand birds, a thousand robes, a thousand alabasters and oils on all feasts of the year, as all good and clean, beautiful and sweet things for the Ka of Father of God, listing sacrifices for God at House of Amun in Ipet-sut, Pa-di-Amun, justified and for Ka of Musician of Amun, Lady of House Ankh-iri, justified by voice."[19]

Suti-mes took from a small bag strapped to the waist a small faience vessel in the shape of a slender *hes*-vase on a wide round foot and took out an equally wide stopper closing it and poured all the contents onto a small stone sacrificial table in front of the stela on which the bread, head and leg of an ox, as well as several vegetables and a beer pot were imagined. "Let Amun give you a life!" he said and hid the empty dish.

His parents' grave was much more modest than most of the graves around. He had neither a sacrificial chapel with colorful religious performances, nor a pyramid. The burial chamber and a short corridor leading to it were located directly behind the stela, but the entrance to them was perfectly masked with hard mortar. Its color imitated the natural rock, and besides protected the grave against the waters of any rain that would be deadly for the mummies. "Why did you die so quickly?!" he couldn't get answers to this question, and he always asked it when he came here. He still remembered his most recent cheerful and carefree times, when he was the same age as Henut today. His father had a good position in the temple and as a family not only did they feel no hassles, but Pa-di-Amun could afford to send his son to the best scribe school in Ipet-sut, where Suti-mes met his best and

---

[19] The text quoted here is one of many versions of the so-called offering formula saved in the tombs.

closest friend Buteh-Amun. The misfortune came suddenly when Ankh-iri died during childbirth, taking also with her the little brother of Suti-mes to the Underworld. He remembered the despair of his father, whose tragedy hit when he was on a business trip outside Waset. Suti-mes had to take care of funeral matters. Thanks to his friendship with Buteh-Amun, he obtained from his father, Royal Scribe of the Necropolis, Djehuty-mes, the right to use a small grave carved in the slope of the Hill of Wedding Rites, and Djehuty-mes covered the costs of mummification and coffin, which later, naturally, the father of Suti-mes returned. Suti-mes also remembered that before closing the coffin with his mother's mummy and the baby laid at her side, he put two pairs of sandals there: one belonged to Ankh-iri, and the other – the child's one which the owner, who was expected at home with great joy, never got to wear. Suti-mes did not want their sight to be a source of pain for his father. As if one misfortune was not enough, in the temple when the group of the Fathers of God had their duty, to which Pa-di-Amun belonged, a silver ritual vessel was stolen, and some suspicion fell on him. Not only did he have to give back the value of this object, which he did not steal, because of someone's jealousy, but he was also suspended in the activities of the Scribe of the Victims, which after a while caused them to run out of their livelihood. The poor father of Suti-mes had been so worried about it that he began to behave strangely, he became distrustful of people, and finally, he began to suspect that his dead wife had brought all these troubles on him.

Suti-mes sighed and looked at the small vessel dug near his parents' grave. There was a small scroll of papyri on which was the text of the letter that his father had written to his wife at the time. Suti-mes knew the letter well – proof of his father's love for his mother, and also a testimony of the illness that soon joined Pa-di-Amun with Ankh-iri for eternity. Now, Suti-mes couldn't help himself but read it again.

To the perfect spirit of Ankh-iri. What have you done to me that I found myself in this bad condition? What have I done wrong against you? Here you stand against me, even though I did nothing wrong to you since I lived as a husband with you, to this day. What have I done to you? I will complain to you against the gods of the West and you and I will judge based on this letter. I married you as a young man and you were with me when I held various offices. You were with me and I didn't cheat on you nor let your heart get angry. I have not let you suffer what I have done with you, and you have never found me lying to you like some villager who goes to another house. I have not fooled you, but look, you do not know the good that I have done for you. I am writing to you so that you would know. When I left, and you found yourself in the condition that befell you, I spent eight months, eating or drinking almost nothing, almost unlike a human. When I finally came back, I came to where you were, and I cried a lot with people outside my apartment. Look, I have been living alone for three years now and I have not even gone to the "sisters" house[20]. I did it for you, but you do not distinguish good from evil. That is why they will judge us![21]

---

[20] It is about a brothel, whose existence is confirmed by various sources.

[21] The text of the authentic so-called letter to the dead, kept at the Museum in Leiden (Netherlands).

Suti-mes rolled up the papyri and put it in a dish – it belonged to this grave and no one had the right to take it away. "Do the dead read such letters? Do Pa-di-Amun and Ankh-iri affect my life?" he thought. Maybe, because many of the prayers which he brought to them were fulfilled. After the death of his father, the invaluable Djehuty-mes got him a position in the temple of Amun, in the service of Amun's First Servant, Amen-hotep. Then he came here when he saw Henut and fell in love with her from the first moment, asking his parents to look after this love and for the favor of the girl and he has it all!

"I will come to you someday and ask for a blessing for my relationship with Henut," he said loudly, and the last word spoken became a balm to soothe all sad memories. Suti-mes turned his gaze towards the temple of His Majesty Mentu-hotep, justified, near-visible from there: "I think they will move soon," he thought, "and Henut will be there, then I will see her!" He looked again at his parents' grave and again, this time he read the sacrificial formula silently, then began to descend from the hill to the plain, which was full of people.

Today was the holiday of the tenth day of the month, i.e. a day off from work, which had to be celebrated by participating in the "departure of God." For nine days, all His paintings remained inaccessible in the depths of the temples and only the duty priest, who performed a sacrifice on behalf of the king every day, could visit them. On the tenth day, priests took these holy images from the temple, and then, although still hidden in the portable chapels and veiled, they became closer, more accessible. In front of the old temple of His Majesty, King Mentu-hotep justified, hidden among sycamore and tamarisks planted in large pots carved in rock, stood a small building. In there were three chapels next to each other in which lived three such statues, surrounded with special worship by the inhabitants of Khefet-her-neb-es, because they represented the patron of the necropolis: His Majesty Amen-hotep Djeser-Ka-Re, his dignified mother Ah-mes-Nefertari and his wife, Queen Merit-Amun, justified, several hundred years ago. Usually, only the Amen-hotep figure was carried out in the procession, which everyone called the "Amen-hotep from the Garden." When Suti-mes came down the hill and mixed in with the crowd, four priests were just taking the holy Amen-hotep's barge from the temple with a chapel surrounded by a white veil. They crossed dozens of cubits along an avenue running between the middle rows of trees and here they crossed the low wavy brick wall that separated the two worlds. The one in the garden was a sanctified land, and to enter there one had to cleanse himself with a special rite; in fact, only priests who were entitled "those who enter" could do so, although sometimes they could bring special guests with them. On the other side of the wall was a world tainted with worldly matters; here all the other participants of the procession were waiting for the holy barge. The first of the singers intoned the melody of the hymn in honor of Amen-hotep and the procession began to form. At the head was a priest carrying on a high pole a figure of Up-uaut - "Opening the Way" in the shape of a jackal. Behind him in two ranks, followed women in white solemn robes and elegant wigs decorated above the forehead with fragrant lotus flowers. Each of them was carrying a decorative frame embedded in a handle, in which wires with loosely plated plaques were stuck; which shaken, it made a rustling sound, from which this instrument took its name: *sesh-sesh*[22].

Henut was also with these musicians. He noticed her right away, not only because she was one of the first, but above all because of her wonderful, distinctive and eye-catching beauty. From under the wig, on the white of the dress flowed her gorgeous jet-black braids, which harmonized perfectly with the color of the girl's eyes. Her face was thin, oblong, her nose was small, but outlined with a clear straight line, her lips were full and marked with noble red, and the slightly outlined cheekbones formed a whole that one could only admire. The girl also saw him and smiled flirtatiously, revealing the whiteness of her teeth, and as she passed him, she waved her *sesh-sesh* right next to his ear, what for Suti-mes sounded like: Do you want? Do you want? And evoked a smile on his face as the obvious answer.

Behind the white of women's dresses, the white of priestly tunics now appeared. The two Fathers of Gods on duty with their shaved heads advanced seriously, repeating the following phrases of the hymn to Amen-hotep, which were chanted by a "singer from among singers:"

The gates of the holy chapel are opening
The temple gates are opening
The City is celebrating, Iunu is enjoying it
Shouts of joy continue in heaven and earth
Joy overwhelmed both banks of the river

---

[22] This instrument is today widely known under the later name sistrum, derived from the Greek language.

Everyone sings hymns, praising God
Amun-Re, Lord of Ipet-sut!
Heaven and earth are filled with your beauty
Flooded with gold of Your rays
When two scepters touch and enliven this perfect God
Lord of Both Countries
Amen-hotep Djeser-Ka-Re, whom you loved![23]

The last few priests of this group carried various equipment necessary during the rites that were to be celebrated at subsequent procession stations: *hes*-vases with water, censer and incense vessels. Behind them, immediately preceding the holy barge with the image of Amen-hotep, was the main celebrant dressed as all priests in white puffy robes but girded from his right shoulder to his waist with a red sash; and unlike others, he had a wig on his head. Everyone who passed the holy barge fell on their faces, then got up and joined the procession. Behind the Hill of Wedding Rites, the procession turned off the procession avenue of Mentu-hotep and Amen-hotep, framed by trees and stone statues of both rulers depicted as Osiris – ruler of the Underground World and Necropolis, with arms crossed on his chest. Now, everyone was walking along the edge of the cemetery, passing numerous graves visible on the slopes of the hills and heading towards the wall of the fortress and at the temple district of His Majesty Ramesses User-Maat-Re Meri-Amun, to turn right in front of it. They were soon to join the main road passing through Khefet-her-neb-es, along which stood the houses of

---

[23] There are cited here an authentic texts of hymns written on papyri, among others from the Egyptian Museum in Cairo.

residents of the western City built between the sacred precincts of subsequent temples, in which, among others, the memory of the great deceased rulers of Both Countries were worshiped. At this point, the number of participants in the ceremony doubled, as some of the people who lived here waited for the retinue to arrive at their homes and now joined the procession to accompany it on the way back to the temple of Amen-hotep from the Garden. Some did not care much about the orders of religion, but they were guided by mere curiosity because traditionally, events that were particularly important for the life of the Khefet-her-neb-es community were to take place only now.

Here a man came up to one of the priests carrying a writing pad in hand, and behind the ear, a reed to write and he talked to him for a moment. The scribe looked around, picked up one of the countless and crumbling potsherds of broken clay vessels from the ground, and wrote something on it, then handed the potsherds to another priest, who handed it to the chief celebrant. At that moment, he raised his hand and the entire procession stopped.

The priest stood before the holy barge, then bowed and asked, "O Great God, our Lord and guardian, dignified Amen-hotep! Would you like to hear the case of Seseh-nofru, your servant of Khefet-her-neb-es?" The priests carrying the barge took one step forward at that moment, "Oh, our Lord, the Great Amen-hotep, since you have agreed, show Seseh-nofru your grace and tell him whether he should buy a cow from his neighbor, Iah-mes?"

Now, the scribe lifted two more potsherds from the ground, on one he wrote quickly: "yes," on the other: "no," and then placed one of them on the left side of the road, and the other on the right. The chief priest turned, and the procession started again, and after a while, everyone saw that the priests carrying the barge turned to the left of the road. The celebrant again signaled, the retinue stopped, both potsherds were raised, and again placed a few cubits by the road, but this time switching them. After a while, the procession started and again everyone could see the holy barge turn clearly, but this time to the right. There was no doubt: the holy image of Amen-hotep twice made the same decision.

The selected potsherd was given to the ceremony leader, and he turned and said loudly to the participants of the procession, "Seseh-nofru! Be thankful to your God and patron, Amen-hotep, who deigned to tell you not to buy a cow from your neighbor, Iah-mes!"

Seseh-nofru stepped out of the crowd and fell on his face in front of the barge, touching the ground with his forehead, his face expressing obvious satisfaction. The barge was incensed, and the sweet scent of myrrh spread far away, carried with a light breeze. The procession continued, and the priests began to sing the hymn:

O mighty Power, Lord of all phenomena!
Maat is with you, power is yours,
Your voice has magical power.
Joyful uproar resounds when you act through your good
Oh, Amen-hotep Djeser-Ka-Re,
Everything you do is desirable and glorious!

However, they did not go far, the chief priest again raised his hand stopping the march.

"Oh, our Lord," he exclaimed, "Good and fair Amen-hotep, you who distinguish between good and evil, you are Maat, please show your grace to Your Servant, Amun-em-uia, who asks you, who stole five tunics from him?"

The priests carrying the barge took another step forward again. There was a murmur of excitement. There were also those who, first of all, went with the procession to be witnesses of such events, for example, the sentence that would be given in this accelerated trial, much faster than the usual procedures that could last for months. The barge was again incensed, and the procession started again, and the "singer among the singers" chanted the next part of the hymn:

Oh, luminous God, Amun, Lord of Ipet-sut!
Heaven and earth shine when they see your beauty
The storm is dying of fear of you,
Everyone worships you when you do justice.

Subsequent houses were slowly passed, and tension increased among the participants of the ceremony: it is impossible for Amen-hotep to refrain from giving the oracle. As a moment later, the barge stopped unexpectedly, even though the High Priest gave no sign. That was God's answer! At that moment, the barge was exactly in front of the house of the temple landlord, Pa-chau-em-di-Amun, who was called: Pa-chau, for short. Of course, he was walking in a procession with everyone, and now everyone looked at him. Pa-chau turned red and began to complain loudly that it was not he who stole the tunics of Amun-em-uia, but he was gridlocked to the entrance to his house. He was pulled aside and two dark-skinned police officers along with an inspector of the local judiciary who assisted in the court of God, on behalf of the mayor Khefet-her-neb-es, Pa-uer-aa, entered the home of the accused, and soon returned from there, carrying tunics that Amun-em-uia recognized as his own.

"Do you admit you stole those tunics?" the inspector asked, at which Pa-chau lowered his head and quietly confirmed. "So, you'll get 100 beats by a palm branch, and if it ever happens again, you'll be thrown to a crocodile!" The court was over, the *medjayu* with the inspector took the offender to punish him immediately, and the procession with the barge went on, surrounded by incense smoke, the sound of *sesh-sesh* and singing:

Oh, Amen-hotep Djeser-Ka-Re, who are alive!
Make the king last forever,
sitting on the throne of Horus and Seth!
Accept this sacrifice, Amun-Re, King of Ipet-sut...

Soon the procession was again on the avenue leading to the temple of Mentu-hotep and Amen-hotep from the Garden and, having arrived there, dissolved. Priests "with the right to enter" collected all the equipment used during the ceremony, including all the *sesh-sesh*, and carried them to the temple's closet, counting exactly whether their number corresponded to what they had issued before the procession and the barge soon disappeared into the inaccessible depth of the unauthorized eye of the Amen-hotep House. The ceremony was over, but people were moving slowly, and some, gathered in smaller or larger groups, stayed where they were talking about the events of the morning, and other topics as well. Actually, this was the only day off from daily duties and the need for rush.

Henut and Suti-mes did not have to look for each other, because they both knew exactly where they would be. For a long time, they had designated a meeting place, which was a broad acacia growing at the foot of the Hill of Wedding Rites. Acacia, like a sycamore tree, was considered a tree dedicated to Hat-hor, the patron of love and lovers, and young couples who were under the cover of the branches of such a tree could kiss freely, without causing any scandal, or rather the opposite, which was, arousing feelings of sympathy in those who saw it. Henut and Suti-mes often and willingly exercised this privilege, so now they also fell into each other, enjoying their eyes and lips with their mutual existence. Previously, they also saw each other on the tenth day holiday; daily chores ruled out more frequent meetings, and a 10-day break seemed like an eternity. So, they assured each other that they missed each other so much and counted the hours separating them from the meeting and that these continuous breakups were terrible. Finally, they took their hands and walked slowly towards Henut's house.

"I thought that today's procession would never end!" Henut's voice sounded like a complaint. "Say, dear, is it serious to ask holy Amen-hotep a question like this villager did today: "Should he buy a cow?!"Next time someone will stop the barge to ask if he should clean the house or can he wash his cloths…"

"Don't laugh," Suti-mes looked at his girlfriend with a smile, "At least when it comes to the last one, it's a real problem and always a matter of courage. Is it by chance a place where they do the laundry, i.e. Launderer's Bank also called the Crocodile Backwaters? If I'm not mistaken, in Khefet-her-neb-es, only men do the laundry and they usually arrange to go there in two: one washes, and the other strikes with a stick in the water and repels these beasts. I also would ask Amen-hotep if my sister sent me with the laundry..."

"Coward!" Henut replied, feigning indignation. "Prepare today because I will send you!"

"So, I'll ask the oracle if I should love Henut..."

"What if she says you shouldn't?"

"She won't say it like this, she will definitely "confirm very strongly," I already know that!"

"Exactly, Suti," a note of genuine curiosity was in Henut's voice, "How is it that God "confirms" or "does not confirm?" You are wise and you are a priest, then tell me, how did Amen-hotep know, for example, that this Pa-chau stole the tunics?"

Suti-mes felt slightly embarrassed.

"Henut, I have only recently been in the priesthood in Ipet-sut and I know very little. You would have to ask the one who bears the title 'who knows the secrets of heaven, earth and the underground world' or 'who is great with secrets.' God is Creator, but in such small matters He certainly leaves the decisions to people. I know one thing that before the oracle takes place, there are those who thoroughly examine each case. There are a lot of such questions, and Amen-hotep answered only two today. Certainly, his priests got to know these two matters well. Maybe they knew, for example, that a neighbor wanted to fool the peasant who had asked for a cow and prevented fraud. And this Pa-chau was probably well known to many people, or maybe someone saw him with these tunics? In ordinary courts, this case would drag on for months, and here the perpetrator was surprised and did not manage to hide what he had stolen. Amen-hotep, with all his holy power, in which we also believe, announces only what his priests know, and they strive to do the best of Maat for all whom Amen-hotep protects. So, if I really asked the oracle for love for you, the priests would talk to your parents who, after all, agree to our future relationship, would probably reach my friends, for example, Buteh-Amun, who knows the secret of my heart, and maybe send someone to watch us, what we do under the acacia and after all, they would know that our love is real and honest, that we do not hurt anyone. Then, Amen-hotep could publicly confirm this. Fortunately, we don't have to ask the oracle, just have some patience so I can finally say:

My sister's mouth - a lotus bud,
her breast - is the fruit of mandrake,
her arms are decorative like branches,
her eye and forehead - is a willow trap.
I am a wild goose,
my fingers are tangled in her hair,
which is bait in this trap."[24]
"And you probably want me to say too:
I loosened my hair from the side,
when I was running for a tryst with you.
I spread my hair,
when I took off my dress...

---

[24] The texts quoted here are authentic ancient Egyptian love poems of the New Kingdom.

Henut couldn't read, but she remembered the poems Suti-mes had once read to her. She squeezed his hand harder and added quietly: "You know that one day I'll take it off for you, but now...

Your hand in my hand,
my body shivers,
my heart is joyful,
when we walk together.

Suti-mes looked with undisguised admiration at the girl who could remember in her memory so many words of love songs heard once, so, not wanting to be worse, he remembered the song he once heard at a funeral feast, sung with great affection by a harper:

So, celebrate the day joyfully, Father of God!
Take resins and oils that please you,
neck and shoulders of your beloved sister,
who rests at your side,
bedeck with a wreath of lotus!

Then he leaned over Henut and whispered passionately, "When will it finally happen? When will you be my sister and rest at my side? Waiting for this day is suffering!"

"You think I don't want it? Both of us, must suffer a little more," Henut sighed and turned her gaze to the small house, visible from afar, where she lived with her parents and younger brother.

The house was built on a small sandy hill among fields lying on the opposite side of the road that ran towards the river along the ruins of the huge temple of His Majesty, Amen-hotep Neb-Maat-Re, justified. From the road, one could reach it by a narrow path running along the dike here. For most of the year, this dike and house were surrounded by arable fields, which Djed-Mut-iuf-ankh, father of Henut, rented from the temple of Amun in Ipet-sut. During the Peret season, the fields planted with wheat greened, in the Shemu season, turned yellow – at first with lush grass, then after the harvest with a short crop, but during the Akhet season there was water here, and both the hill and the causeway fulfilled their necessary protective functions. Every year, when the flooding waters fell, it was necessary to repair both the road and the artificial sandy elevation on which the house stood, but if one day Hapi came too abundantly, the whole house could be destroyed. It was the constant concern of Djed-Mut-iuf-ankh and the topic of conversation and prayers of the whole family in the first weeks of the Akhet season; these prayers have been answered, so far. After sowing, there was waiting time for crops, the size of which could be estimated initially. From the words of her father, Henut learned that this year promised to be poor and the reserves they would have, after paying the obligatory taxes, would be small. For the young, it could only mean even longer waiting time for the wedding, because there was no indication that the income of Suti-mes would increase significantly in the near future. That is why the girl's face became a bit sad when she looked at her poor house growing out of young wheat greenery. However, now, she noticed something strange, which was glistening strongly in the rays of Re next to the house.

Suti-mes noticed this too, covered his eyes with his hand and looked at the glowing object for a moment, then answered the silent question in Henut's eyes, "There is a chariot there; your parents have some distinguished guest. Maybe some prince sent a matchmaker to ask your hand in marriage?"

They both laughed. Firstly, no prince would send matchmakers to the poor farmer's tenant house, secondly, even the king himself would not have the slightest chance, because Henut was in love and her parents knew the secret of her heart. However, the presence of the mysterious chariot was a surprise and the young people increased the pace of their walk to solve this riddle. When they were nearby, they heard raised voices and something like crying from within the house; whoever was the mysterious guest, his visit was not very friendly. In the chariot, which they could now see, stood a coachman whose outfit and features indicated that he was a Kushite soldier. Henut and Suti-mes were already in front of the entrance to the house, when suddenly, the door opened and a powerfully built, tall and fat man stood there with a huge bald head and a red face on which drops of sweat were pearling. A precious chain on a short oily neck and double bracelets on thick hands indicated his high position in the City, but neither Henut nor Suti-mes had ever seen him before. He also didn't know them either, because he was looking at both of them for a long time. The sight of Henut brought to his face the expression of undisguised lechery and lust, with which he reconstructed the shapes of her body hidden under the dress. Then he jealously looked at Suti-mes, looked at him again thoroughly, and then without a word got into the chariot, throwing the coachman a short order to leave.

When the young people entered the house, they immediately noticed that the just-finished visit of the unknown dignitary had fatal consequences. Hereret, Henut's mother, loudly wailed, cuddling the weeping little Nes-Mut. Father Djed-Mut-iuf-ankh sat gloomily with his head in his hands.

Henut ran up to him, started stroking his hair, and her question was obvious, "What happened, Father? Who was this scary man?"

Djed-Mut looked at his daughter with love, but, at the same time, also with pain. "It was the eminent Pa-Shu-uben," he said, "The right hand of the great Vizier, General Pa-nehsi. He came to inform us that saintly Amun's First Servant, Amen-hotep gave the order that all temple tenants give away not two sacks of wheat from the *setjat*[25] after the harvest, as it was since my father's times, but six sacks and the harvest will be small this year; I don't even know if I'll collect enough to pay this tax. How are we supposed to live? I thought that the First Servant, Amen-hotep, was a good man, that he had Maat in his heart and would not hurt those who work in the fields of the House of Amun. Now, I know that all of them – these dignified people – are equal and do not care about our fate. How is he different, this Amen-hotep, from General Pa-nehsi? Nothing! Let the plague catch him!" Djed-Mut spoke louder with every sentence and, at last, he stood up and threw both hands up, casting his curse.

Suti-mes was astonished and terrified: he had never seen father of Henut in such a condition before but, at the same time, he could not believe what he heard. Amen-hotep, who once supported the protest of workers from the town where craftsmen

---

[25] Unit of area measurement: 100 x 100 cubits (= approx. 2756.5 m^2).

working in the royal necropolis live, because he learned that they were not getting the remuneration due to them, the same Amen-hotep would now raise taxes from temple lands three times in a year when the stroke was weak, and the harvest promised to be worse than usual?

"Don't say that, please," he said to Djed-Mut-iuf-ankh, "I know more about the First Servant because I work for him. He is very loved by his subordinates; he looks after them... He is a really good man and observes Maat."

"Are you defending him?" Djed-Mut stood right in front of Suti-mes and started shouting. "Sure, you are defending him! You serve him! Every dog is barking in defense of who is filling his bowl!"

"Father, how can you speak like that to Suti-mes?!" Henut stood by her boyfriend with fire in her eyes. "What did he do to you?"

"What he did? He showed that he was holding the Amen-hotep's side, this thief, and since Amen-hotep is our enemy..."

"Djed-Mut-iuf-ankh, you cannot talk like that about the High Priest, I forbid you, do not hurt our ears with such accusations!" Suti-mes raised his voice too, though he regretted it a moment later.

Djed-Mut-iuf-ankh pointed two fingers at him, making a gesture with which the magicians ward off all evil creatures and shouted even louder, "And what right do you forbid me to? Because you like Henut? Forget about her! I will not give my daughter to a thief's servant! Get out of my house!"

Suti-mes heard the painful moan of Henut, who hugged him crying, assuring him that she loved him, in the background the loud cry of her mother Hereret and little brother Nes-Mut, and in the foreground the dominant shout of Djed-Mut-iuf-ankh, who, after all, was the head of this family:

"I said, get out and never come back here! I swear to Seth that there will be no wedding as long as I live!"

Suti-mes staggered and half-conscious left the house, which an hour before he considered as harbour of his happiness.

CHAPTER III

The afternoon silence fell on the fields densely covered with blue flowers of flax, and then also with green shoots of young barley, enjoying the warmth of the rays of Re. Colorful weeds blooming on the edges of crops, but also often mixing with them in the middle of the field, also benefited from this heat. Suti-mes walked very slowly, unknowingly following a beautiful, colorful butterfly that fluttered happily from one flower to another, spreading and folding its delicate wings and grabbing them with successive portions of hot glow flowing from the cloudless, clear blue sky. In this joyful insect dance and the green hope of young grain, which invariably accompanies each spring, there was the beauty itself, which could constitute the natural background of the hymn which praised the Creator, who in such an obvious way multiplied the good, making millions of himself according to the myth of the creation of the world. Meanwhile, for Suti-mes, all this was only a source of pain, all the more so that it was in stark contrast to the cool darkness of his thoughts and feelings in which there was neither beauty nor hope. The pain was even more painful because it appeared suddenly, in the least expected moment, caused by a mysterious demon whose name Suti-mes did not know. The blow was terrible, and its cause was incomprehensible. Wasn't he, Suti-mes, even yesterday, accepted as the future husband of Henut by her parents? Didn't Henut love him and didn't he loved her? Should anything other than their beautiful, pure love count? She was now the only bright spot, like Sopedet in the night sky before the appearance of the Re's barge on the eastern horizon. But will this rising ever happen? After all, they cannot connect against the will of the girl's father, and he solemnly swore that he would not give his consent, as long as he would live.

"He swore to Seth, and it was certain that Seth was in his heart," thought Suti-mes, "But he said these words with his hand raised and they went straight to the divine throne. An oath is a sacred thing, and Henut's father's life is sacred too. So, there is no future for us?" A wave of despair hit him and took away all the joy of life. With every step he felt, he was overwhelmed by doubt and hopelessness. He came out of the fields onto a road running from Khefet-her-neb-es to a river distant from here by about 40 measuring ropes[26], then turned left. He was now walking along the long wall that surrounded the ruins of the huge temple of His Majesty Amen-hotep Neb-Maat-Re, justified, having on his next left, fields and floodwaters where terrible crocodiles lived. He

---

[26] Length measurement unit: 100 cubits (= approx. 52 m).

came to the place where launderers used to come, but today, due to the holiday, there was no one here, while from the coastal thickets of papyri came all sorts of trills and twitters of birds, attracting in their flirtatious intentions, or those booming at the building of their nest. This view depressed him even more because he often saw himself in his dreams as a father who would take care of his family nest, and now this vision had fallen apart like a house built of wet sand. For a moment, he wondered whether to find his boat and return to Ipet-sut, but then he would have remained completely alone. While in reality, he subconsciously felt a great need to share his misfortune with someone if only to not go crazy from the rush of his heavy thoughts, in which he was surprised to discover the recurring motive of death as an escape or rather a liberation? Weren't the considerations of this unfortunate man who complained to his Ba in a certain story, which Suti-mes discovered while studying at the scribe school in Ipet-sut, not similar:

Death is like a fragrance of odorousness for me today,
like staying under a sail on a day when the wind blows,
death is like a lotus smell to me today...[27]

Suti-mes thoughts moved for a moment to the school days of carefreeness and meeting friends. Suddenly, he was dazzled: Buteh-Amun! Of course, if he was to confide in anyone, it was only to that with whom he had strong affectionate bonds! Suti-mes stopped hesitating and started toward his friend's house. While he had dragged his feet heavily before, he now accelerated

---

[27] Quote from a writing called *Tired of life* from the Middle Kingdom, from the Berlin Museum.

very much, wanting to dump as soon as possible, and thus to drop from his heart even a little bit of, this enormous weight that was unbearable. He passed a few passers-by who were still on the streets of the now deserted Khefet-her-neb-es, where it was time for a meal. Finally, he reached the great gate of the temple district of His Majesty, Ramesses User-Maat-Re Meri-Amon, justified, and entered the courtyard. There was much lesser traffic here today; the dictator Pa-nehsi went somewhere to spend a day off from both clients and religious ceremonies, which painfully made the General aware that he was not omnipotent in this area at Waset.

When he entered the house of Djehuty-mes, he found him with Buteh-Amun and his young wife Shed-em-dua sitting at the meal. In the dining room, which was directly behind the main hall with columns, a mat lay on the floor with various dishes on plates and bowls, and household members sat on low stools, reaching for those plates and dipping pieces of bread that they ate, drinking milk. Today, due to the holiday, there was even a bowl with cooked meat on the mat, accompanied by broad beans, onions and lettuce. On the side was a tray filled with *cucu*[28] and dates. As Suti-mes stepped into the dining room threshold and uttered a greeting, an expression of undisguised joy appeared on Buteh-Amun's face. He jumped up, opened his arms wide and exclaimed:

---

[28] The fruits of the palm tree called by the ancient Egyptians *mama*; today's Arabic name for this palm: *dum*.

"For Amun! Suti! You don't even know how happy I am that the wind has blown your boat here!"

"Hello, my son's friend, so also my friend!" Djehuty-mes joined the greeting, "Sit down with us for a meal!"

Suti-mes stood perplexed: the effusive warmth of the hosts and their joy, too, practically like the whole world around them, stood in stark contrast to the mood he had in his heart. He knew that in a moment he would spoil this good atmosphere and sadden his friends, and he felt even worse with it. He did not know what to say, but he certainly did not want to eat. On the contrary, he was certain that he would not be able to swallow anything, so he only said, "Thank you, I'm not hungry." He replied in such a discomposed voice that both hosts immediately realized that something had happened to him.

"I see; indeed, you do not come to eat, but rather you have something in excess, and you would like to share with us confidently." Djehuty-mes became serious, but looking at the guest with a cordial look, he emphasized, "Speak, because you need it, and in this house, you don't have to worry about choosing your words or your listeners!"

Shed-em-dua got up and discretely left the dining room, not wanting her presence to restrain the guest. Suti-mes noticed her strongly rounded belly, "You will be a father..." he asked his friend, once again discovering today that all normal phenomena of life cause him unspeakable pain.

"As Khonsu will allow, in two months," Buteh-Amun confirmed, who at that moment saw that Suti-mes' eyes had glazed and sensed that the woman could be the cause of the sadness that was visible from the face and the whole form of his friend.

"Forgive me, Suti, for asking directly: has something bad happened to Henut?"

Suti-mes looked at him with great gratitude: if he was the first to say the name, he would probably roar with a loud cry, and now it was already present, hovering gently around them, filling the entire space of the world.

"Henut, thanks to Amun, flourishes like a fragrant lotus, but this lotus grows in a pond to which I have closed entrance," he whispered, finally shedding his weight, "And without it, my life does not make sense," he added and bit his lips, fighting again with a wave of despair; indeed, at that moment, he felt a ridiculous regret that he was not born a woman who is allowed to cry always.

"Let's go to the hall with columns, there are comfortable chairs." Djehuty-mes realized that they were waiting for a longer story and was the first to enter the room in which he usually received visitors, sitting on a comfortable beautifully carved chair on a platform by the wall. The chair itself resembled, thanks to its decorations and armrests, a royal throne, and indeed, it was a gift he had received years ago from His Majesty, King Ramesses Nefer-Ka-Re in proof of his merits in explaining the mystery of the robberies of royal tombs. Everyone who came here, seeing this dignified old man sitting on such furniture, was extremely respectful and rarely dared to question his words, which undoubtedly helped him in the office. At the sidewalls between the columns, there were also two other chairs with woven seats and backs, but less ornate and without arm supports. Usually, distinguished guests and officials sat on them. Now, the Djehuty-mes also sat in his chair, but before that, he took it down from the platform and moved them to the others closer, and Buteh-Amun was indicated that he would put a table with dates in the middle.

"Their sweetness," he said to Suti-mes, "will not remove your bitterness, but it can make it easier to bear!" and indeed, Suti-mes ate some fruit, which was his only meal since the morning. He might not have felt much better but eating these dates, he calmed down a bit and it was easier for him to reconstruct all events from the Henut house and put them in the right order. He immediately began his story, seeing great tension and curiosity in friend's eyes. So, he talked about his arrival, visit to the grave of his parents, about how he saw Henut in the procession and how the ceremony seemed too long to him. He even mentioned that on their walk after the procession, they caught up in a place where acacia grows, and both listeners just smiled and nodded with understanding.

"Suti, your story is like a breath of invigorating wind," Buteh-Amun couldn't stand, "That's for sure this girl loves you. But have you not exaggerated with caresses under this acacia?"

"Defend me, Amun! You know me, and you know that the last thing I could do was to hurt Henut. Also, I am a priest and I can be the master of my heart – have they not taught us in Ipet-sut?"

"Forgive me for asking, but the flame in heart sometimes defies the school teachings. What happened then? Has anyone else come your way, sending a matchmaker?"

"It wasn't a matchmaker, though I felt disgusted at him just for looking at Henut. Djed-Mut-iuf-ankh said it was Pa-Shu-uben."

Djehuty-mes, who has not spoken so far, moved uneasily, "He's always a harbinger of bad news, and he's ready to commit any meanness. Because of my duties, I have to talk to him sometimes, but after that, I always want to wash and cense. This man does not speak or do Maat. But I don't understand what he has to do with you and Henut at all?"

"He came with an order from Amen-hotep that temple land tenants would pay three times more tax, and Djed-Mut was so upset that he began to say terrible things about the First Servant, and when I tried to defend Amen-hotep, he insulted me and kicked me out of the house, swearing that as long as he is alive, he will not let us get married..." Suti-mes felt despair again. Djehuty-mes shook his head while muttering:

"That's bad, very bad, but also very strange. Pa-Shu-uben came with an order from Amen-hotep? He hates the First Servant even more than Pa-nehsi! Besides, how could the Amen-hotep suddenly make them pay more taxes, since it has long been established that from such land as Djed-Mut-iuf-ankh cultivates, a field long and wide by one measuring rope, everyone gives two sacks and it doesn't matter if this land belongs to one temple or another, King, Queen or someone else! And since the time of His Majesty, Ramesses Nefer-Ka-Re justified, together with the scribe, Di-Amun of Ipet-sut, I represent Amen-hotep in the group of those who, after the harvest, share the crop and send their due part to the King. There is also among us the wife of General Pa-nehsi, Nes-Mut, and there are his other people: Scribe of the Army, Ka-shuti, inspectors Ini-naht and Amen-hau – I would not trust them – but there is also Pa-uer-aa, who represents the City and whom I saw two days ago. He was here and was sitting exactly where Buteh-Amun is now sitting. We talked about many important matters, but he didn't say a word to me about any new tax ordinance. So, either I don't know about something that I should know first, or..." the old Necropolis Scribe was deep in thought, and both young men did not dare to interrupt his reflection. Suddenly, Djehuty-mes raised his head, looked at Suti-mes and said in a firm voice, "You bring very important news, Suti-mes. If your pain today had not covered your ears there, in the house of Djed-Mut-iuf-ankh, then His Majesty, Amen-hotep, should know about it immediately, and also His Majesty, King Ramesses himself, may he live! Are you sure of everything you said about Pa-Shu-uben and are you ready to repeat it to His Majesty the First Servant of Amun?"

"I swear on Amun, it's all true! At that time, when Djed-Mut was talking about taxes, I wasn't stunned by pain yet, so I remembered everything well and of course, I can repeat it even in front of His Majesty," Suti-mes said and looked at Djehuty-mes straight in the eye, and the thought that the old Necropolis Scribe may have doubted his account even for a moment, caused him pain. However, almost immediately, he realized that thanks to what Djehuty-mes said and the seriousness with which he said it, Suti-mes lost the urge to cry and ponder his regret. Suddenly, he realized that the mysterious matters that separated him from his beloved girl are important, perhaps even to the whole country, since the King's name was given and, in this situation, it is not appropriate to feel sorry for oneself.

Djehuty-mes confirmed it as if he was reading his mind, "Don't think I don't believe you. Your pain is real, and your problem is serious, and for you probably the most important in the world. But time will solve it, and your love will overcome all obstacles and one day you will be together with Henut – trust me, the old man who knows life. However, now things are happening in the City that matter to many people, not just you. Do you know how many temple tenants there are for whom this strange tax news is just as painful as for Djed-Mut-iuf-ankh? You will help them all if you testify Maat to His Grandness Amen-hotep. You will go there with me immediately, you both will go," he looked at his son. "Today is a holiday and nobody should interrupt somebody's rest or do business, but in this case, time can play a role. You mentioned that you came here by boat from Ipet-sut, didn't you?"

"Yes," Suti-mes replied, "Only that I moored it, quite a long way from here..."

"That's fine, we'll go there and use your boat. Mine is standing in the harbor on the opposite side of the walls of this district, where we are now, just two ropes from here, but going there we would have to report to the guards at both gates and someone would know too early that I went to Amen-hotep; I prefer it to be different."

Djehuty-mes got up and headed for the door. He was known for implementing his decisions immediately and all persuasion would be of no avail. Buteh-Amun only took a step back into the house to find his wife and tell her that they were sailing to Ipet-sut and it is not known when they would return, probably already in the evening. When he left, he saw his father and Suti-mes already far away. He also knew that the matter was very important since the old priest was walking so fast, despite his age.

They passed through the very center of Khefet-her-neb-es, but they did not meet anyone; at this time the meal was followed by a time of rest and probably most of the residents enjoyed the privacy of the bedroom. A bustle was coming only from behind the door of the beer house - there was always someone sitting in there, and there were those who stayed there from morning to evening. The road leading over the side canal, which connected the main waterways running from the river to the most important Temples of Millions of Years[29], built on the edge of arable fields for the worship of subsequent pharaohs, was completely empty. Suti-mes saw his boat swaying slightly on the water.

"Forgive me, Lord," he turned to the Necropolis Scribe walking next to him with a note of embarrassment in his voice, "But the way to Ipet-sut on such a small boat will not be comfortable for you; three people fit on it, but you can't compare it with yours, which you probably are used to. I had no idea this morning that I would be accompanied by such an important person on the way back."

---

[29] This name included large temples where the cult of the Creator was combined with the posthumous cult of the founder ruler and his ancestors.

"Come on, young man," Djehuty-mes waved his hand, "There comes a time when this important person, as you wanted to say, has become very problematic for others, more important, is being observed and reported on.   Using your boat, as well as the time of day when nobody does anything, I hope that I will avoid such a report once and get to Amen-hotep before these 'more important' find out."

They got in and Suti-mes began paddling, but after some time, at the insistence of his friend, he gave him the oars. The boat sailed quickly, they did not meet any other one, and soon they reached the river. Here they saw several smaller and larger sailing barges, but there were no fast courier boats *tjesem*[30], or any marked with special colored ribbons of ships belonging to the dictator Pa-nehsi and dignitaries associated with him. However, at the shore from the side of Khefet-her-neb-es stood several large and even huge military boats, capable of accommodating entire troops of soldiers, and on some of them, there were high shields from which archers could shoot at defenders in places where they could reach in high water season. The very sight of these powerful floating vessels aroused due respect and the inhabitants of the City could probably think that they were safe, if not for the general knowledge that no enemy was expected. There were several houses close to the bank on this side of the river. They saw several children in front of one of them. The smallest ones were completely naked, older girls wore, like their mothers, simple

---

[30] A type of small maneuverable sailing boat used for fast travel on the Nile.

linen dresses, and boys' wide bands covering the hips. Djehuty-mes stretched out his hand toward the busy group, then turned his eyes to the ships of the war fleet.

"Look, Suti-mes," he said, "All these children were born and grew up while Pa-nehsi's army has been stationed in Waset and these ships are for them a natural part of the world they live in. They can't even imagine it differently, although their parents remember the City without these ships. Do they feel safe now? Maybe there are some of those people, but I can't get used to this view, I'm afraid of it. The war fleet is needed and always has been, but it should be kept somewhere further from here, not just opposite the great House of Amun in Ipet-sut!"

Everyone looked towards the temple, still distant by a wide strip of river, but clearly visible in the clear air and especially at this time of day wonderfully illuminated by the rays of the Re, which has already traveled more than half of its daily path to the western horizon. The golden glow from the sky radiated the gilded decorations on the Great Gate and the visible ends of the slender obelisks covered with gold metal, visible from behind, flashing gold, as if signals sent from God's earthly headquarters to his heavenly boat.

"Re and Amun are talking in gold, creating the golden unity of divine majesty," Suti-mes could not resist commenting on this view.

"You put it beautifully in words and it would be great if everyone looked at the house of God like that, but there are, unfortunately, those who only see gold there..." the old Necropolis Scribe again returned to his miserable considerations, then turned to the rowing Buteh-Amun, "Go not to Ipet-sut, but to the right, to the marina at Ipet-resit. We will go on foot. I suspect that Pa-nehsi also has his man at the Great Gate, because whenever I come to the first servant, the General immediately finds out."

Soon, they reached the shore and, having anchored the boat, set off along a long street running through the City along a procession avenue, on which both trees were growing, and between every ten cubits lay stone lions with the heads of His Majesty, Ramesses User-Maat-Re Sekhep-en-Re. This alley came alive especially in the second month of the Akhet season, during the great holiday when Amun of Ipet-sut visited the temple in Ipet-resit to ceremoniously connect with the King's Great Spouse and remind him that Pharaoh is his son. The whole City was lying on the streets at that time, and they were all wedding guests of Amun: they ate, drank, and rejoiced. Today, as in Khefet-her-neb-es, it was empty here, only sometimes did they pass by groups of playing children, who, unlike adults, did not feel the need for a peaceful rest in the comfort of the home bedroom and whose parents did not stop at home, enjoying more freedom during their absence. They rarely encountered a passerby, but on this side of the river only a few could recognize them, and absolutely no one would expect to see the dignified Royal Necropolis Scribe walking down the street dust. Such officials were carried in litters, or they rode a chariot, and most often sailed with their ships to the harbor in Ipet-sut, almost to the very gates of the temple. That is why the Djehuty-mes plan succeeded completely and when after a long walk, having traveled almost 40 ropes, reaching the southern gate of the Ipet-sut district, he was sure that none of the General's people noticed his unexpected visit.

The gate built by His Majesty, King Hor-em-heb, justified, where they had just arrived, was a place where even more people reached unlike the Great Gate from the riverside, but just like it, only a few could get the right to go further. Most often, residents of the City, who expected help in the form of an oracle appeared here; they brought their requests written on papyri and passed them on to priests on duty at the gate. There were also newcomers who did not even dare to ask Amun to intervene during the procession but entrusted him with their troubles, hoping that God would solve them as soon as he knew about them. They also brought papyri but asked that the priest who had the right to enter the rooms adjacent to the Holy of Saints, carry them and put them as close to the place of the statue as possible. These people most often supported their request with a gift: a sweet cake, a pitcher of milk, a few duck eggs, or some handmade object. Everyone who wanted to go through the gate was meticulously asked about the purpose of the visit, and their names were recorded in the papyri journal. Of course, the priests had the right to pass, although their names were also recorded. A separate group, which was passed through, were pregnant women who consulted the doctor at the temple of Khonsu. Once, this temple and the adjacent area called Nefer-hotep, or Good Rest, was a separate sacred complex located near the temple of Amun, but not covered, as today, by the wall of the district of Ipet-sut and thus more easily accessible. Khonsu as the patron of the moon and time was also a guardian of a different state and births, so many residents of the City came here to find out if the pregnancy was going properly, and some to give birth to a child under the watchful eye of experienced midwives and spend the first difficult days after birth. When Djehuty-mes with Buteh-Amon and Suti-mes were already entering through the door in the gate, they passed by a young woman who was carrying her newborn baby. The mother's face radiated joy and that happiness filled her so much that she clearly felt the need to communicate this to the whole world. She smiled at those entering, and Buteh-Amun, seeing that his father was completely absorbed in his thoughts, returned the smile and asked if the bundle hides a boy or a girl?

"Girl," the young mother said, and without waiting for further questions, she added, "Khonsu told me long ago after seeing wheat and barley[31], that it would be a daughter and that she would live, so I called her Djed-Khonsu-ius-ankh!"[32]

"Let Amun, Mut and Khonsu look after you!" Buteh-Amun replied and quickened his pace, as if afraid that the woman would want to tell something more about her child or anything else, while Djehuty-mes was already impatient to go on. Behind them came the reciprocal greeting of a happy mother, entrusting them to Amun's protection.

---

[31] It was believed that it was possible to predict the sex of the child by sprinkling grains of wheat and barley with urine of the pregnant woman. Faster germination of wheat was interpreted as the announcement of the birth of a girl, barley - a boy.

[32] This name means "Khonsu said she would live".

"It's nice to look at such a joyful face and it's good that the Kingdom of Amun has welcomed a healthy new citizen," Suti-mes added.

But today, the extremely cloudy Necropolis Scribe said something that this woman certainly would not want to hear, "May she live to see the day when she knows and influences her fate."

"Why are you saying that, father?" Buteh-Amun was surprised by what he heard.

"Because I'm afraid for the City and its inhabitants, I'm just afraid!" Djehuty-mes replied and said nothing more.

Walking toward another of the three gates that separated them from the great Hall of Appearances of the House of Amun, on the left, they now saw a perfectly built temple of Khonsu, most of which was covered by a high, rough wall reaching the roof, and a long transport ramp[33] sloping sideways from that wall transport; this part of the temple was under construction for a long time.

"Have you been there lately?" Buteh-Amun now turned to Suti-mes, "because I have the impression that since we went to the scribes' school, nothing has changed there."

"It has changed a bit," he replied. "In the Hall of Appearances, virtually everything has already been built, even the roof is already there, and now the sculptors have started decorating. The holy barges, as well as the figures of the king and first servant of Amun are ready, also most of the inscriptions. As you know,

---

[33] All vertical transport of heavy stone blocks was carried out using ramps. They were placed on wooden skids, which teams of workers pulled with ropes upwards, ascending the slope.

names are written at the end, even cartouches are filled just before the end of all work so that you don't have to change anything if the King unexpectedly dies. In this case, there is rather no doubt that the Hall of Appearances will be sacrificed on behalf of His Majesty, Ramesses Men-Maat-Re, may he live forever, and the First Servant Amen-hotep, but recently the pace of work has slowed down, and the King has not been in the City for a long time. Maybe there are any problems with the House of Silver[34]? I do not know, I am only God's child and such matters are far from me."

Talking like this, they went through another gate and approached the High Priest's palace. Suti-mes reported to the guards that he had returned from Khefet-her-neb-es and told his friends that he would wait for them in the palace courtyard between the two high gates; after leaving Amen-hotep they had to pass this way. Djehuty-mes was known to everyone here, so the guards had no objections to let him and his son into the part of the residence where the First Servant welcomed the guests. It was a great place, where just being present was very pleasant: a fairly large room was closed on three sides with beautifully carved scenes showing various great moments in the life of the High Priest, while the fourth one went out to the terrace by the Holy Lake. Guests sitting here could admire the finest parts of the temple. To the left was the gigantic wall of the Hall of Appearance decorated with huge war scenes from the pharaohs' expeditions, hiding behind an incredibly large space completely covered with a

---

[34] The name of the royal or temple treasury.

forest of carved large columns and, to the right, gilded the ends of the same obelisks that they admired from the river, but here, they were much closer and larger. White walls covered with colorful images of reliefs painted red, yellow, green, as well as other colors and these golden pyramids carried by granite obelisk needles were reflected wonderfully against the natural background of the blue sky, to which they climbed in a great act of adoration of the Creator. Closer, on the holy lake itself, the trees and shrubs covered with flowers created a different richness of colors, harmonizing with that. Anyone who has seen this amazing accumulation of colors would think that before his eyes there was a kind of competition between nature and man in the multiplication of beauty.

"I have never been here, I have not seen the House of Amun from this side," Buteh-Amun said, delighting and admiring the vastness of the building. "It is an eternal work, unsurpassed in wealth and indestructible in its power."

Djehuty-mes made an indefinite movement of his head, "Maybe, as you say, the House of Amun is incomparable in wealth, but is it indestructible? Today there are those who, if they could, would tear these gold sheets from gates and obelisks and one should only hope that such a misfortune will never happen, and nobody dares to raise their hands on the Majesty Amun and the sanctity of the House of God..."

He wanted to add something else, but in the door was appeared the one they came to. Amen-hotep was once a tall and well-built man, but now well advanced in years, he was gray and slightly stooped. He was wearing a plain white tunic, so nothing pointed to his position, except maybe the big gold ring on his finger. He cordially greeted Djehuty-mes, and then Buteh-Amun, whom he had known mainly from stories so far. Once or twice he saw him at his father's side, but he never had the opportunity to talk to the young man directly. Although he was the head of the state of Amun for many years, he did not behave like a great dignitary who, with every word and gesture, lets his interlocutor know that he is in a much higher position. He even started with an apology that the guests had to wait for him because he was not expecting anyone's visit today, he was taking a nap. Djehuty-mes replied that he owed Amen-hotep an apology because he violated the holy day of prayer, but he did it only because...

"There are others who use this day for activities that are not only incompatible with Maat but can seriously shake the foundations of the Kingdom of Amun. I was not going to Your Grandness until tomorrow, so as not to disturb your rest, although with Buteh-Amun yesterday, I witnessed events that you should know about."

Here he told about the assault on the guard in the temple of His Majesty Sethi Maat-Men-Re and about his suspicions about officer Aa-neru, as well as about the unclear role of Nes-Mut, the wife of General Pa-nehsi.

Amen-hotep listened to the worried relation with a troubled face, "There have been no temple break-ins for a long time; this is a new and dangerous phenomenon," he said when the Djehuty-mes was over.

"You know how bad relations are between me and the dictator, who is insolent in his brashness, and my letters to His Majesty

Ramesses have found no resonance. I try to avoid all irritations and sometimes pretend I don't know about some things, but there are limits beyond which I can't let him. The offenses of the soldiers of the Kushite corps against the City's female residents, of which, unfortunately, sometimes occur, thefts in private homes, and even assaults on the streets are a curse of our days, which Pa-nehsi acknowledges with the mocking remark that it is the price for protecting the City from bandits... Maybe bandit times are back, I do not know. Craftsmen working in the tomb of His Majesty Ramesses, may he live, would not go to work many times and remained in town, fearing that the soldiers of the General would rape their wives and belongings here while they were in the Great Valley. But there have been no break-in temples yet, which is the raising of hand for holiness! This is an insult to Amun! In this situation, I must initiate an official investigation and bring to trial, even this Aa-neru. What you say about Pa-nehsi's wife is even worse: did Pa-nehsi know all this? I don't think good about him, but I do not believe that he stoops so low to organize burglaries after several ritual vessels. Of course, I will order that the missing vessels be taken from the warehouse and handed over to that temple, otherwise, the guard may be in trouble at the next Beautiful Valley Festival. It's good that you came to tell me about it and even interrupted your celebration because of it..."

Djehuty-mes sensed that Amen-hotep scolded him gently that he had not waited until tomorrow, so he decided it was time to tell about the second, much more difficult case.

"Noble Amen-hotep," he began, "I would not allow myself to violate the holy day of rest of Your Grandness just for such a reason. The second one is much more serious, although what I want to say I know from someone who learned about it from someone else, and a third person told that one. But the third one is well known to us: it is Pa-Shu-uben who visits, and today, tenants of the land of Amun and tells them that Your Grandness has given the order to increase the tax threefold."

Amen-hotep's face turned pale, he started shaking his head in disbelief and finally, he jumped up and shouted, "It's a lie! This bastard and his band want people to hate me!"

"I am afraid that the feeling of Your Grandness is right, and we even know that it is already happening, hence our visit at the wrong time and the wrong day. I do not know how many tenants have already received such a message, but those who it reached think badly about you, and this leads to personal tragedies. My son's friend, who is the Father of God in your service, has a fiancée – a daughter of such a tenant. When he heard what the man said about you, he stood up for you, and then he swore to Seth that he would not let them get married. The boy is depressed and I'm afraid that he would hurt himself."

"Who is this noble young man?" despite the agitation caused by the disastrous news, Amen-hotep felt he should know his defender.

"His name is Suti-mes and he can confirm what I said to you. He is waiting for us in the courtyard," the Necropolis Scribe answered.

Then the First Servant turned to Buteh-Amun, "Let him come here; I'd like to meet him, and I owe him something."

After a while, Buteh-Amun returned, leading a completely surprised friend who did not expect that he would have the honor of talking to the Chief of State of Amun, to whom he was subordinate, but whom he saw only from afar during the processions.

"Come here, young man!" Amen-hotep encouraged and reached out with an inviting gesture towards the stunned Suti-mes standing in the doorway. "So, you stood up for me today, even though you didn't know the truth. Of course, you were right, and Pa-Shu-uben was lying. I see you love Maat and it guides you. I need such people. From today you will be in my personal service if you want of course."

Suti-mes fell at his feet without a word. An unexpected promotion meant a significant improvement in salary and he could bring closer the dreams of his own home, Henut, if... painful consciousness pierced his heart again and took away the momentary joy that the words of the First Servant brought him.

Amen-hotep again spoke to Suti-mes, "Stand up and don't be overcome with sadness; it will pass. That's what Amen-em-Ipet always says; I would like you to make friends. He sees everything farther than others and I asked him to write what he says because it is just as wise as *the Teachings of Ptah-hotep* or *Teachings of Ani*, which you had to learn at the scribe school."

He walked briskly across the room, reached the door, opened it a little and spoke quietly to the servant who waited there. After a few moments, an older man dressed in white festive robes entered the chamber. His dignity and sobriety were felt in every gesture. Suti-mes, of course, knew the name of this high-ranking priest who, on behalf of the First Servant, often celebrated various ceremonies and even the greatest rituals as one of those who knew the secrets of the earth, heaven and the underworld, but this dignitary was not available to him on a daily basis, as he stayed in the palace part of Ipet-sut. Now he came to Amen-hotep, who took his arm and led him to his guests.

"I present to you the Father of God, Suti-mes, who has Maat in his heart and courage on his tongue; today, he denied the lies that Pa-shu-uben personally distributes among the tenants of Amun's fields so that they would hate me and pay hard for it; because father of his girlfriend swore, he wouldn't allow marriage. I entrust him to you, because his heart and head need relief, and you know the words that heal!"

Amen-em-Ipet turned his wrinkled face towards the young man, smiled and said in with a gentle voice, the sound of which introduced soothing calm, "The words that people speak pass away; only God's works are completed! Indeed, you do not know God's intentions, so you also cannot know what will happen tomorrow[35]. Trust in the divine arm, then you will calmly defeat your opponents, and these are your worries and unhappiness today. You have shown today that you are righteous and remember that justice is a great gift from God. You have this gift; think that this is a reason for joy, not sadness!"

Suti-mes had a strange impression as if he knew this voice and this man for many years. Father Pa-di-Amun, justified, once

---

[35] Amen-em-Ipet's statements are woven with real fragments of a didactic work from the genre of *Teachings* that arose during the novel's time and whose author had the same name.

spoke to him so calmly and warmly, and he also often said that one always has to trust God. Amen-em-Ipet, because of his age, could also be his father, maybe even grandfather. Suti-mes felt the warmth he needed so badly flowed from that old man, and he knew that Amen-hotep's wish that he would make friends would come true.

"Thank you for your beautiful words," he said, looking at the furrowed face of Amen-em-Ipet and returning a smile, "I believe that my joy will come back someday, but I'm just a weak man."

"You are right, man is clay and straw, and God is a builder. Man uses his tongue as the rudder of his boat, but it is the Lord of Everything that is its helmsman; we can never forget that. Perhaps what happened to you today was your destiny of Shay, but you will probably also meet your Renenet. Be strong in your heart!"

Suti-mes looked with surprise at Amen-em-Ipet, then at Djehuty-mes, whom he also always admired for wisdom, and finally at Amen-hotep, who was the authority for both these wise men.

"It's really difficult to meet so many good and wise people at once," he whispered.

"Do not lose hope. After all, you are in the service of the best possible," Djehuty-mes said.

"But not the safest," Amen-hotep said. "Remember that I have many enemies in the City, and when they find out that you are serving me, they will also become your enemies, and they are ruthless."

"I am not afraid of them, Lord, and I ask you to entrust to me the most difficult tasks that will allow me to repay you for your grace and goodness!" Suti-mes said this very solemnly, looking directly into the eyes of the High Priest.

"Thank you for this sincere readiness! Who knows, you may receive such possibility soon," Amen-hotep said and signaled to Amen--em-Ipet that he would go with the young man because he still wants to talk to Djehuty-mes. Suti-mes bowed low and went out with his new friend.

"Your Grandness, please accept my gratitude for accepting my friend into your service," Buteh-Amun said. "I know him, and I know that he will not only faithfully fulfill all tasks, but he will put his whole heart into it, otherwise he simply is not able."

"I read it from his eyes and I'm glad that I found such a helper in these hard days to come. I can see that these people here are already going to do everything; His Majesty Ramesses must be notified at all costs. Do you have among your people," he turned to Djehuty-mes, "trusted servants, but also those whom Pa-Shu-uben does not know?"

"I think Kari and Kasaya could do this – the *medjayu* who are guarding the path in the mountains above the Great Valley. They will not attract anyone's attention, even though all roads leading north are under the control of the people of Pa-Shu-uben, who also uses the *medjayu* police."

Amen-hotep sat on a cushion lying on the floor near the window, crossing his legs in the same way scribes do. He cut a piece of papyri from a thick roll and, opening his writing tool, began to write a letter. It lasted a long time; On the water clock standing on a high stone table, above the level of slowly flowing water, appeared another concavity[36], the guards at the temple gate changed, and Amen-hotep was still writing while guests waited patiently, knowing how important the letter was. Finally, the First Servant finished, read everything again and rolled up the roll, then stuck the letter with clay and pressed his ring in it.

"Let your *medjayu* go with it to Pi-Ramesse immediately. From the City, they can get to Gebtiu on donkeys, and from there on one of my boats straight north. In Pi-Ramesse, they only need to reach one of the Fan Bearers[37], who will forward the letter to the King. They should be back in two months, as long as they don't encounter any problems..."

Amen-hotep reflected, looking at the sky, where the multicolored clouds already announced the end of Re's daily journey. He handed the letter to Djehuty-mes, said goodbye to both Necropolis Scribes, then washed the face and hands in the bowl and went up the long stairs to the roof of his palace. He turned toward the bloody sky on the western horizon, raised both hands in a gesture of adoration and began to hum quietly:

Hail, Re who lives by going to bed

---

[36] The water clock resembled a water-filled pot with a small hole at the bottom; its inner surface was divided into 12 parts corresponding to months, and each such part contained a vertical row of 12 circular cavities corresponding to hours. The Egyptians divided each day and night into 12 hours, regardless of the season. As a result, in summer the hours of the day were long and the hours of the night short; in winter the situation turned around. Since each month the length of the hours was different, in the water clock this proper one was recognized by the level of water remaining in the vessel.

[37] High court rank destined to some of the highest dignitaries; in practice, it meant close and direct access to the Pharaoh (originally the person holding the fan stood right next to the king, fanning him).

and joining the heavenly horizon![38]
Here you appear on the west side
as Atum in the red of evening colors,
full of power, not stopped by anyone!
You enter the body of Your mother Nunet,
and your father Nun greets you with a nini[39] *gesture.*
All the powers of the Mountain of West welcome you joyfully,
and those who are in the Underground are enjoying,
seeing their Lord, Amun-Re, Lord of humanity!
Oh, Lord of All, who can do everything!
Send a good night for your servant Amen-hotep!
Let me see your beauty tomorrow too
in full health and well-being,
that I could greet Your view with the morning prayer...

---

[38] This is the authentic text of the hymn to the setting sun from one of the Egyptian tombs.

[39] This gesture consisted of extending both hands in front of each other with the hands turned upside down and marked: "Come to me!"

CHAPTER IV

Several weeks passed, during which the daytime hours were getting shorter and night hours were getting immeasurably longer. It was cold, so cold that the oldest inhabitants of Waset did not remember a similar year. It was the coldest on the threshold of the day, when only the brighter sky on the eastern horizon announced the appearance of the Re's barge. It happened then that from the lips of a man, who wanted to give a hymn to welcome God and spoke or sang his next calls, apart from words he emitted a kind of bright smoke, like a sacrificial oil lamp filled with noble fat, which did not blacken the walls of the chapels. Some people read it as a special sign of making a double sacrifice and got up very early to experience it. Because when Re, already clearly visible in the sky, had already warmed the world, the mysterious phenomenon disappeared.

The second and third months of the Peret season were not easy for the inhabitants of Both Countries, mainly because of the cold. They did not have to protect themselves against it for only a few hours during the day and their usual clothes, mainly short kilts, were sufficient. But when Re disappeared in the west, it soon became chilly and then cold, and the wind on the river was not a pleasant breeze, but it penetrated deeply. Extensive linen tunics, very densely woven and covering the whole body, protected from the cold, but not everyone could afford it. Woolen robes were even rarer. Most people put on regular tunics, with an additional covering on their heads. At home, some people had sheep or goatskins that could cover themselves, but the best way to protect themselves from the cold was to set fire often, not just to cook the food, but simply to warm up with it. So, in the evenings, in many places of Khefet-her-neb-es, as well as in the eastern part of the City, one could see burning bonfires, where entire families from several neighboring houses gathered. Everyone brought with them anything that could be burned. Sometimes, though rarely, they were branches, more often palm leaves, dry reeds and even dried donkey manure. Such meetings were also an opportunity to tell each other various news, and topics were provided by both nature and its phenomena, as well as recent events. There was indeed always something to talk about.

It seemed that for unknown reasons Amun decided to punish the inhabitants of Waset and send them one plague after another. Not only was the day short, but it was understandable at the time of Flow and returned every year, making each of the 12 hours between sunrise and sunset twice as short, as in the last month of the Shemu season, there were also those days when the Re's barge in it was not visible at all in the sky obscured by clouds. What's more, from these clouds sometimes a piece of the sky in the form of water[40], fell to the ground, which some considered the inevitable announcement of the approaching end of the world, announced by Atum[41]. Usually, this water was scarce and it fell in single drops, but on the fifth day of the second month of the Peret season, i.e. the day after the feast of the joyful coronation of Mut – the divine wife of Amun, a completely black giant cloud appeared over Khefet-her-neb-es and the mountains closing the west horizon and burst it with lightning and a terrible roar of thunder, pouring out all its contents. Streams of water, flowing from the mountains from all sides, began to fill the Great Valley and it happened so quickly that the *medjayu* guarding the royal tombs barely managed to escape, climbing with great difficulty to the top, from where the streams of water fell at a great speed, trying to take the guards and drag them back to their posts by force.

Unfortunately, the four craftsmen: Ken-Amun, Un-nefer, Bek-en-Mut and Pa-Shedu, working in a room intended for the sarcophagi of His Majesty, Ramesses Men-Maat-Re Sechep-en-Ptah, may he live forever! were not so lucky, When the water burst into the room, two ropes down the entrance, it was too late, and the poor men had no chance to escape against the current of the river rushing down the grave corridor. A few days later, when

---

[40] It was believed that the world was surrounded by water, which was expressed by the blue color of the sky. The end of the world was to take place when heaven reunited with earth (i.e. it would flood it)).

[41] In the so-called Chapter 175 of the *Book of the Dead* is the phrase spoken by the Creator Atum: „I will destroy all that I have made; the earth shall return to the surging flood, as in its original state."

the water left the Great Valley, their bodies were found lying in a corner, covered with still standing there water and four cubit high embankment of limestone dust, stones and mud, which the water brought with it to the grave. Ken-Amun was still holding a chisel and Pa-Shedu a lamp; probably, fleeing the element, they also wanted to save valuable tools so that no one would later accuse them of causing a loss. So, not Pharaoh, but mere mortals: a carpenter, two stonemasons and their assistant who lit their workplace, they were the first to rest in this tomb. This was a bad omen, both for the King and his burial place, so before resuming the work, cleansing rituals had to be performed to remove the evil destiny from the Lord. In the shaft forged for this purpose, where the royal sarcophagi were to stand in the future, special wax figures were placed, showing His Majesty Ramesses Men-Maat-Re, may he live! He was made a magical gesture in front of the image of the Lake of Flames protected by four baboons. In addition, several small items belonging to the pharaohs, who had been resting in the Great Valley[42], for a long time, were brought along to bring with them protective power. The work was to continue, but the workers were afraid and preferred to lose their pay rather than work in a cursed place. There were also those who dared to prophesy that the King – let him live forever! - will never rest here. In fact, the tomb was still far from complete, and not a single sign of the holy scripture was still carved on the walls of the unfortunate sarcophagi hall.

---

[42] These items were found during excavations in the tomb of Ramses XI in the Valley of the Kings in 1979.

In the town of craftsmen, there was a special mourning for the loss of colleagues, not to mention the despair of the families of the unfortunate victims of the downpour. But this terrible event, which was the flood from heaven, also brought death to the homes of Ahauti-nefer, Bak-en-Iseth and Pa-nakht-resi, built in the vicinity of the temple of His Majesty, King Maat-Men-Re Sethi. When the water, like a swollen river, fell out of a narrow rocky isthmus leading to the Great Valley and spilled around, it not only destroyed several of the nearest old royal tomb districts with their pyramids but also hit the row of clay houses with great force and caused that six of them dissolved and collapsed [43]. The building belonging to the main priest of a nearby temple with a statue called Amen-hotep from the Courtyard fell apart, but the host was not there, fortunately. Su-em-bah-Amen and Pa-ua-Amenhotep were in their homes, but they managed to escape, and their women were shopping at the market and they were not there at the time. Unfortunately, Ahauti-nefer's wife lay sick and could not run away, and the small children of Bak-en-Iseth and Pa-nakht-resi were sleeping when the water came raging.

Their funeral gathered the whole community in Khefet-her-neb-es and everyone later talked about it for a long time, remembering terribly screaming unhappy mothers, especially the wife of Pa-nakht-resi, who at that tragic moment was nearby, milking a goat and threw herself to help, but she didn't make it: before her eyes, the walls and roof of the house collapsed, and the water covered everything. The poor woman wanted to go to the

---

[43] The author had the opportunity to see personally in the same area the effects of the downpour that hit Luxor in November 1994.

crocodile alone and her husband and neighbors had to hold her by force.

A familiar sculptor made a grave stela out of a piece of limestone, and the father of Aseth-em-Akhbit - the tragically deceased daughter - carved a text on it that, read aloud in the cemetery, touched everyone so that even some men had red eyes:

I greet you, Amun, Lord of Gods!
Hear the harm that has happened to me, child without guilt:
You said the word and here it was that I sleep in the valley,
although so young and thirsty,
although the water is next to me.
You took me out of my childhood,
although the time has not yet come
and I left home without being satisfied with it.
Darkness, which is something terrible for a child,
enveloped me high, placing a breast on my lips.
The guards of this gate are taking the world away from me,
And yet I don't have time for loneliness!
My heart would like to see people: I loved cheerfulness!
Oh, King of Gods, Lord of eternity, who all the faces follow,
give me bread, incense and water from your sacrifice table!
I am a child who has not committed any sin...[44]

The terrible downpour did not improve the situation in the fields. Akhet season this year brought little moisture; Hapi spilled but reached a level three cubits lower than usual and the water

---

[44] This is an authentic text found on the stela, which today is in the Museum of Antiquities in Leiden.

remained in the fields too short to properly soak the soil burned with the heat of the last year's season of Shemu. Farmers plowed and sowed, as they do every year, and worked more than usual because the land was more resistant to the plows. Despite this, the cereals grew meager, were much lower than ever, and the ears were frightening with their thinness and the additional hard work of watering with water laboriously extracted from the canals using cranes did not help at all. At present, the fields have already turned yellow everywhere and in a few weeks in the first days of the first month of the Shemu season, the harvest preceded with the Renenutet festival – caregivers of fields and abundance and ended with the Great Exit of Min on the eleventh day of that month should begin.

Usually, both celebrations were welcomed happily, especially the festival of Min, when the tiredness of heavy work with sickle mowing was only a fresh memory and one could enjoy the crop, a significant part of which was to remain in the home granaries. However, this year, despite the harvest, and with the Great Exit of Min, fast approaching, no one was happy. The collections promised to be meager, and a new tax ordinance was to be in force, which Pa-Shu-uben and several other officials reporting to General Pa-nehsi have been proclaiming for a long time, visiting all temple tenants in turn. It was this that the people around the bonfires talked of mostly now, and all these conversations ended in a curse against the First Servant Amen-hotep.

It was imagined that this dignitary would, during the Great Exit of Min, cut off the crop ears at the stairs of Min, when he would happily release the birds and, with a clear face, proclaim the good news: "Horus, son of Isis and Osiris possessed a white and red crown." How will he be able to look people in the eye? He'll take the last supplies from everyone and give them back to Amun, but are the grain stores short at the temple? Is there little gold in Ipet-sut? There was no need to answer this question; the gilt tops of the obelisks could be seen from afar, and some could boast of knowing priests who had the opportunity to see other riches inside the House of Amun.

"There are places where even the gates and floors are made of gold and silver, and there are gold-covered stelas on them," they said. They are so heavy that the earth bends under them, and if you had at least a few *kedet*[45] of this gold, you could buy warm material and not freeze..."

Here again, conversations returned to the topic of weather, waiting for warmth, with which inevitably will come harvest and tax collection, and yet Amen-hotep...disgruntled people used increasingly strong words, among which "thief" was not the worst term. There were even those who explicitly wished the High Priest to die, convinced that he was doing wrong despite the good King, who probably knew nothing about it. Slow anger grew among the tenants of Amun's land, and hatred of the First Servant made them see hope in the army that was already here. News of the course and topics of the evening conversations reached different ears because strangers often sat at the bonfires,

---

[45] A weight measure of approximately 9 g, equivalent to one-tenth of *deben*.

who were allowed to warm themselves, and who were interested not so much in the heat of the fire as in all the conversations.

Pa-nehsi and Pa-Shu-uben were overjoyed to see the wonderful harvest reaping of their rumor. The High Priest Amen-hotep, although he had great confidence in the Djehuty-mes, at first did not believe that he could be dealing with a planned and systematically carried out lie or that people would believe it so easily. With time, he began to ask his people to listen to the conversations of farmers and only then realized that the situation was extremely serious, far more dangerous than he had imagined. He eagerly awaited the return of his messengers to the King, hoping that in the face of open abuses, Ramesses would dismiss General Pa-nehsi from positions that made him a dictator, binding the hands of the High Priest.

All Amen-hotep's actions were now limited only to temple and religious matters, although in the eyes of the inhabitants of Waset, he still remained the head of the State of Amun, that is, he exercised supreme power in the Southern Country. If Pa-nehsi ceased to be even the Vizier and Administrator of the Granaries of the South, the High Priest could announce, even during the Renenutet festival, that all taxes would be charged as usual, and maybe, due to the expected crop failure, he could convey Amun's will that every tenant this year can leave one more sack of grain with him. The people would forget the gossip in an instant, and their love for Amun and the First Servant would become even greater.

Unfortunately, both *medjayu*: Kari and Kasaya returned without bringing back any response from Pharaoh. At the same time, they gave a report to the Djehuty-mes about their expedition, which should have been successful. Well, not disturbed by anyone and without arousing suspicion of numerous guards deployed by Pa-Shu-uben on the roads leading from the City to the north, they reached Pi-Ramesse and there they were looking for someone who, as the Fan's Carrier, could give the letter to His Majesty. They were directed to General Pi-ankh, who received them, asking thoroughly about the situation in the City, recent events and people's moods, and finally about the health of the High Priest himself. When they had answered all the questions, the General took the letter, but did not make them wait for an answer, but immediately return to Waset, which they did.

When Djehuty-mes told Amen-hotep everything, they both agreed that, unfortunately, the delicate mission failed. *Medjayu* Kari and Kasaya fulfilled their duties unobjectionably, but they hit as badly as they could. Amen-hotep and Djehuty-mes knew Pi-ankh well. He was a man sickly jealous and eager for power, if not royal, which he could only dream of, at least a High Priest and personally hated Amen-hotep. Although it was difficult to suspect that he might dare not give the letter to the King but knowing who had sent the letter, he could keep it. It was strange that he had the messengers come back unanswered. Messengers coming from such a distance were usually ordered to take various letters and instructions in a solitary way. Apparently, Pi-ankh did not take the *medjayu* seriously. Thus, it was still uncertain whether King Ramesses knew what was going on in the City; only

General Pi-ankh found out and Amen-hotep did not have much hope here.

Meanwhile, in Ipet-sut, preparations were being made for the burglary trial of Sethi's temple, which was to take place on charges of the High Priest. In this area, and this was the property of the House of Amun, his First Servant did not have to have the consent of the dictator, although it was Pa-nehsi who, as the Vizier, was to preside over the trial. That is why Amen-hotep prepared the evidence very carefully, being in constant contact with both the Mayor of Khefet-her-neb-es, the distinguished Pa-uer-aa, as well as with the Necropolis Scribe, Djehuty-mes, who had, among others, an archive on cases of Khefet-her-neb-es, including the files of the high-profile case of a robber who, in the 16th year of the reign of His Majesty, Ramesses Nefer-ka-Re, violated the inviolability of the royal tomb. Suti-mes became the special messenger of Amen-hotep, who constantly carried letters and transmitted confidential oral messages, as well as documents necessary to organize the trial. The High Priest thought that only intensive work could save this young man from breaking down.

His drama continued, although frequent meetings with Amen-em-Ipet mitigated its effects. The old priest tried not to let Suti-mes have too much time to think, and kept finding jobs for him, entrusting him with various tasks that the young man did very well. He gained more and more recognition in the eyes of this experienced and wise man whom he treated as his own father. Amen-em-Ipet introduced him to the secrets of rituals, explained the sense of various scenes engraved on the walls of Ipet-sut temples and explained how oracles operate. He often brought old papyri scrolls from temple libraries and read the hymns and technical instructions written there, usually read by the priest-lector, and intended for the celebrant. Amen-em-Ipet taught him how to use the scrolls and at the same time read strange instructions invisible to people contained in the performances carved on the columns and walls of the rooms through which the procession passed. There were also some places in Ipet-sut that Suti-mes was not allowed to enter, and Amen-em-Ipet explained that he himself was not allowed there without proper preparation and dress, which makes the priest the deputy of the King himself. In addition to teaching rituals, Suti-mes received numerous instructions on how to manage groups of people employed in the temple and in numerous places outside the walls of the district where, for example, artists performing liturgical equipment worked. Every day, his knowledge of the temple's affairs and the organization of the entire House of Amun grew, as did his respect and sense of friendship towards Amen-em-Ipet.

However, when the ten days passed and another feast was coming up, Suti-mes was going into his boat. He was crossing the river to participate again in the local service and procession of the divine Amen-hotep Djeser-Ka-Re in Khefet-her-neb-es. After the procession, he was waiting under the acacia at the foot of the Hill of Wedding Rites for Henut, later they were kissing each other and enjoying for a short time, with the illusory feeling that nothing had changed. Yet it had changed! The joy of the meeting lasted briefly and soon turned into a torment of shared regret that the fulfillment of their mutual love went beyond the horizon of the desert – the land of Seth, which Henut's father invoked, casting his curse. Once, their meetings were full of laughter, joyful Henut chatter, banter, when the lack of words usually meant only a break for a kiss. Now, they mainly remained silent, clutching to each other, like defenseless owl chicks, when the mother leaves the nest, going on a hunt. Henut's eyes were full of tears, which Suti-mes kissed with great tenderness, but could not say much consolation.

In addition, these shared moments were short now, because Henut's father strictly ordered her to come home right after the procession. The farewell was harder every time, and though they repeatedly said that only death could interrupt their feelings, every moment they lost sight of each other to begin the next 10 days of painful longing seemed to them like death. So, the whole second month of Peret passed and the third began. When the tenth day came and they met again under the acacia, Suti-mes with the usual sadness on the face of his beloved saw the shadow of something worse: despair.

"Dear, we can't see each other in ten days," the girl whispered, cuddling up to him, "There will be the festival of Amen-hotep Djeser-Ka-Re and even he will come here then!"

"Your father? Maybe I'll talk to him then, kiss the land before him and beg him to undo what he said..." Suti-mes tried not to let himself think that he might not see Henut and he would have to wait 20 days for the next meeting.

"Don't even try... As if you didn't know him! Even if he were to regret it, he would not undo what he once said, and he is more and more sinking into his hatred of the First Servant. He can threaten with a fist at Ipet-sut and says such terrible things, for example, that the army should throw the High Priest that he would gladly take part in such an expedition. He also talks about you and I always run away to the field, I don't want to hear it. And he knows that I love you and he knows that we are meeting here and said that he would talk with Pa-nehsi's soldiers to watch over me, and if they see me with you, let them attack you, beat you or do something worse. I would die then! And he really can do it, because now he often meets those Kushites and lets them use him, and you know that they are scary, and everyone is afraid of them. Suti, my love, we'd better stop meeting now, I don't want to lose you, I will always love you, I..."

And Henut burst into tears. Suti-mes pressed her head to his chest, stroked her hair and just said:

"Don't cry, Henut, please don't cry!" but he himself suppressed himself not to cry. The world around has blackened. Their beautiful feeling, which they cherished, like the greatest treasure, not only lacked hope for tomorrow, but it took away that of the present day. They had only what was left yesterday and they both knew that beautiful memories would have to replace dreams and plans, at least for some time, if not forever. They said goodbye with a long kiss and a mutual promise that nobody and nothing would kill their love, even if destiny separated them for a long time.

When Suti-mes returned to Ipet-sut, he was told that the High Priest wanted to talk to him. He went immediately to the reception room, where he also found Amen-em-Ipet. The old priest with a glance at Suti-mes's face guessed everything.

"I know your suffering. Djed-Mut-iuf-ankh, your girlfriend's father, repeats around what he once told you about His Grandness. We are very worried because a lot of people listen to him, and Pa-nehsi and Pa-Shu-uben use it and apparently often send a boat for him, take him somewhere, and then drive him away; he is also seen in the company of Kushite soldiers."

"We have to ask you not to meet his daughter now because it can be dangerous for you," Amen-hotep added. "I heard he supposedly threatened to defend her with the help of soldiers."

"Henut told me the same today, but how does Your Grandness know about this?" Suti-mes was completely surprised.

The High Priest just smiled and Amen-em-Ipet replied, "The First Servant must know what is being said about the bonfires in Waset. People like Djed-Mut-iuf-ankh are blinded; they don't even understand that they are victims that they have become like pawns on the *senet*[46] board. His Grandness has no hard feelings toward them, but he must know everything; we must also anticipate the effects of various events. If this poor father of Henut sees her with you and actually sends soldiers to you, and if Pa-nehsi's Kushite soldiers beat the priest in the service of the First Servant, then a very bad wind will rise, which can easily start a fire. Think also about Henut, because then, you can really lose her.

Suti-mes listened to it with his head down. He understood that by a strange twist of fate he found himself like a grain of wheat between the quern stones and nothing could save him from

---

[46] Popular board game of the ancient Egyptians.

grind into flour. What exactly did he do that all this happened to him? He loved the girl and tried to honestly and properly fulfill his duties in the priesthood service in Ipet-sut. After all, both are in agreement with Maat... Now it turned out that not only one became the enemy of the other, but that both bring threat not only to him but also to those whom he loves and respects.

"I can't change my heart. What can I do?" he asked quietly.

Amen-em-Ipet paused for a moment, but seeing in the eyes of the young man a focused expectation, he continued: "The heart is the seat of Maat, God's Law. Don't change it. Your love is good and will survive your Shay, the time of trial that Amun has set you up for. Trust him. If your faith is weak, like a flame of a lamp, the opposite wind that blows in your face will extinguish it and then your troubles will overcome you and overcome you completely. If it is strong like a bonfire flame, the same wind will only strengthen and enlarge this flame and give you the power to win. I've been with you long enough that I have no doubt about your faith and the strength of your heart and told the First Servant about it. His Majesty wants to entrust you with an important task."

"Well, some officers and people of Pa-nehsi dared to raise ungodly hands to one of the houses of eternity. We are afraid for other Temples of Millions of Years, which are now very rarely a place of sacred rites. If we don't stop impudence, they can even reach out for ownership of places like Ipet-sut or Ipet-resit. The High Priest wants to sue them, but many materials need to be collected. Djehuty-mes and your friend, Buteh-Amun, take care of the House of the Scrolls, where documents from previous processes are stored. The mayor of Khefet-her-neb-es, the eminent Pa-uer-aa, knows all the residents there well and knows at least as much as Pa-shu-uben or more. You will be the special messenger of His Majesty Amen-hotep, who will give you a special ring: if someone interrupts you in your work, you will show him this ring and he will withdraw. You will also have the right to enter those temples – everywhere except for Saint of Saints – and check, together with the priests who look after them, that all the equipment is available. We know for sure about the burglary in the house of His Majesty Maat-Men-Re Sethi, but you must also visit other places. You will notify us of everything you learn, and you will bring back these scrolls and letters that you will receive from Pa-uer-aa and Djehuty-mes. We hope that you will not refuse the High Priest and not have anything against visiting your friend more often?"

All this long speech by Amen-em-Ipet and his cordial tone, as well as his eyesight, which gave fatherly firmness and warmth, made Suti-mes not only feel immense relief but even wanted to immediately start a new task. Therefore, without waiting for what Amen-hotep would say, he fell at his feet, thanking him for the trust he had been given by the dignitary, and the next day eagerly began to fulfill the duties entrusted to him.

Although he was now the official envoy of the High Priest and all the guards immediately let him go, seeing his ring, he did not use the official Amen-hotep boat, but every day he sailed to Khefet-her-neb-es in his small boat so as not to draw attention. Djehuty-mes retrieved several papyri scrolls from the archive, which contained descriptions of the process of burial robbers during the reign of His Majesty Ramesses Nefer-Ka-Re, but also other interesting documents about the control that was carried out in those years in the West City, visiting various royal tombs. Since then, no one had examined whether these graves and houses of God have lost any of their possessions. This led to the discovery that Suti-mes made when he came to the great Temple of Millions of Years for His Majesty, Ramesses User-Maat-Re Sekhep-en-Re-Khnemeth-Waset,[47] to make a great check.

This building, famous for two giant statues of this king made of stone mined near the Sunu, 40 cubits high, was surrounded by a common wall together with large warehouses in which the grain was gathered, collected as a tax paid by the tenants of the land of Amun as well as all other goods that came to the City from both lands. People were still hanging around the granaries, while the central part of the district in which the temple was located was separated by an internal wall. Anyone who wanted to get to it from the farmland, had to overcome the narrow passage, having previously performed a special rite of cleansing consisting of washing hands and face with water, wiping the sandals on the sand hill accumulated here and saying the prayer. Like most old temples in West Waset, the shrine of Millions of Years of Ramesses the Great came to life mainly on the occasion of the Beautiful Feast of the Valley, when the rite of greeting of Amun arriving on the western shore from Ipet-sut to visit various

---

[47] It is the funerary temple of Ramesses II in Western Thebes, known today as the Ramesseum.

houses of God was celebrated. Apart from these ceremonies, hardly anyone came here.

Suti-mes wanted to come in personally and also asked about liturgical vessels, since they were of interest to thieves. In the presence of Suti-mes, the priest taking care of the temple, Ramesses-nakht, opened the hiding place in one of the walls of the Scroll Hall lying behind the large Hall of Appearances filled with 48 columns. It was the last room to which Suti-mes had the right to enter; then there were only holy chapels with statues that either the King or a priest who could replace him could stand. All the dishes were in place. The young priest, shining a lamp, now began to look into other nooks drowning in the deep twilight of the Hall of Appearances, and he did so mainly out of curiosity. He knew the various rooms in Ipet-sut and wondered if this temple looked similar.

Walking along one of the sides of the room, beyond the last row of columns, he passed other closed entrances leading to the side chapels, and the flickering light of the lamp caused golden reflections in them. Suti-mes thought that the days of Ramesses the Great had long since been a period of prosperity in the City and in this temple since there were so many walls upholstered in gold. He crossed over and saw the same thing again. He passed first, second, the third chapel, then walked along a long wall decorated with a bas-relief; behind this wall, there must have been an elongated room. The entrance to it was in the very corner of the Hall of Appearances, but first, one had to turn into the darkest corner, to a narrow vestibule.

"What room is this?" asked Suti-mes.

The priest Ramesses-nakht who accompanied him replied, "This is the Golden House of this temple, there are valuable images of the ancestors of His Majesty Ramesses the Great, which are raised in processions at the Great Exit of Min, Beautiful Feast of the Valley and several others.

Suti-mes raised the lamp to illuminate another gilded entrance that must have led to that Golden House, and at that moment both, he and the people who were accompanying him gave a cry of wonder and awe: the solid high door was closed, but the gold sheet that was upholstered, it was mostly detached, and its uneven, jagged edge ended at the height of Suti-mes's head. What's more, the threshold of the elevated floor of the Golden House, which was made of precious wood and upholstered in thick silver sheet, was also destroyed: the sheet was ripped off completely, and the cedar boards sawed off.

"For Amun!" the pale Ramesses-nakht shouted, whose care this temple was entrusted to, "Mind you, during the last Beautiful Feast of the Valley I put the images of the divine pharaohs here and everything was as it was at the beginning! It must have happened recently! What will happen now? Amun, save me!"

With shaking hands, he opened the door to the repository. Fortunately, all the gold-plated statues were in place, but the destruction of the entrance was reason enough to immediately inform the Mayor, Pa-uer-aa. Suti-mes was very sorry when he looked at the terror in Ramesses-nakht's eyes. He certainly did not lie, but he will probably be arrested and testify in court. Soon the mayor, and *medjayu* who accompanied him and the scribe, arrived and began the investigation, wanting to know the names of everyone who had access to this part of the temple on a daily basis. Ramesses-nakht remembered that in recent months he had seen several priests several times who came here, although they did not belong to people associated with the House of Millions of Years of Ramesses the Great. One of them, a Sedi, a scribe responsible for supplying grain to all who worked here, always appeared in the company of priest Hori or Neb-nefer or Tuti, and this Tuti was employed in the Amun's workshop as a goldsmith.

The same names were mentioned by the gardener, Kar, who also worked here in the temple garden. Summoned before the mayor, he wanted to run away, but he was brought back and threatened that only telling the whole truth would save him from the painful interrogation. He not only confirmed that he knew about the burglaries but admitted that he once showed the place in the temple to Sedi, the Scribe, "because he really wanted to see something like that up close and touch real gold." Of course, Pa-uer-aa arrested the gardener and then all the priests he indicated, and then interrogated them in the presence of the Necropolis Scribe. Then the scribe Sedi said that he was entrusted with everything by the captain of the archers, Pa-Minu, an officer of General Pa-nehsi and "it would be better if Pa-uer-aa and Djehuty-mes forgot everything because as Lady Nes-Mut finds out, they'll both be in trouble."

It was unbelievable insolence, but it fully confirmed that some officers of the Kushite army corps stationed in the City were committing crimes against the sanctity of the house of God, and the dictator's wife also plays a vague role here. Pauer-aa and Djehuty-mes prepared a comprehensive description of the results of preliminary interrogations of all suspects and witnesses and Suti-mes took the scroll to the High Priest Amen-hotep along with a letter from the mayor, in which he also mentioned the insolent words of Scribe Sedi. Everything was prepared for the trial, but the situation was difficult because it was Pa-nehsi as the Vizier to preside over the trial and it was not known how he would react to the news that some of his officers would also be among the accused. In the meantime, even to the astonishment of the High Priest, the dictator did not make any troubles. He even ordered Pa-shu-uben to arrest both the commander of the archers, Pa-min and the Army Scribe, Aa-neru, but also those who accused them, including Nes-Amun – the guardian of the temple of His Majesty Seti, whom Djehuty-mes promised protection. Having learned about this, the old Necropolis Scribe immediately went to Pa-Shu-uben and told him about how he saw Nes-Amun shortly after the attack, beaten and with traces of a rope on his hands, which he did not put on himself. Pa-Shu-uben listened, then said that in the guard's house some valuables had been found, which certainly came from theft, and if he was innocent, he would be cleared by a court where, after all, Djehuty-mes would be present. The old Necropolis Scribe was very dissatisfied, but he achieved nothing more.

The day had arrived for the trial, which, like all lawsuits regarding the violation of the ownership of the House of Amun, was taking place in the small Maat Temple in the northern district of Ipet-sut. This building, preceded by two courtyards, was adjacent to the temple of the ancient patron of the entire Waset region, the falcon-shaped Montu, as people called the

Creator here, before Amun, i.e. the Hidden, was worshiped on his behalf. Only one wall separated the room with the statue of Montu from the statue of his daughter Maat, who first appeared in the world, to right rule it, not the dark ocean of chaos. Before the court began, a sacrifice of bread, beer and incense was made in front of the Maat statue, the sweet aroma of which filled the entire room. The priest also incensed the members of the tribunal who sat under one of the sidewalls of the room.

The main place was taken by the chairman of the court, General Pa-nehsi, who played the role of Vizier today. He sat on a highchair in the middle. On the sides, other members of the tribunal sat on the lower stools. The High Priest, Amen-hotep, was represented by Amen-em-Ipet, the management of the Western City - Mayor of Pa-uer-aa and Djehuty-mes, the Scribe of the Necropolis. The representative of the police and police authorities was Pa-Shu-uben, and the military - the Scribe of the Army, Kashuti. A scribe sat at the side to record the process. On the other side of the room were several *medjayu* policemen and several Pa-nehsi soldiers; some of them kept reed sticks and palm branches and wooden stocks –they were dangerous tools, which often during the trials were used to "extract the truth" from the accused. All those arrested were gathered in the courtyard, where surrounded by soldiers stood waiting for a call.

Pa-nehsi gave the sign and Amen-em-Ipet, who represented the prosecution and the aggrieved party, i.e. House of Amun, stood up and began to talk about how burglaries were found in two Temples of Millions of Years: His Majesty Ramesses the Great, and his father, His Majesty Seti, justified.

"From the first one," he said, "A total of 300 silver *debens*, 89 gold *debens* and seven boards of precious cedar wood were taken. On the other a silver tray, two silver *nemset* vases utensils, a *hes*-vase, a bowl, a bronze bucket and censer, and vessels with incense and natron. The investigation initiated on the order of His Majesty Amen-hotep, First Servant of the House of God and Amun in Waset, led to the names of those who took part in or persuaded those hideous acts of theft. These people are waiting in the courtyard. Among them, unfortunately, are also priests and temple scribes who used the benefits of working for the House of Amun. There are also officers of the southern corps of the army of Both Countries, who were supposed to protect the City and all its goods. Today it will be necessary to judge them and make Maat..."

At this point, Pa-nehsi interrupted impatiently, "Amen-hotep makes a very serious accusation. Your priests may be thieves, but I find it hard to believe that my soldiers, especially officers, were involved. Who are they?"

"Your Dignity knows, because he has been notified, it is about the captain of the archers Pa-Minu and the Army Scribe Aa-neru."

"So, bring them in!" Pa-nehsi gave a short order.

After a while, the soldiers brought the two accused who had their hands tied but did not look like people who were charged with a serious crime and were on trial. They walked freely and quietly exchanged comments with each other, which must have been witty because Aa-neru laughed aloud. Pa-nehsi also smiled at them, then told to untie them and tell them to say what led to their names being mentioned there?

"How should I know?" Pa-Minu answered with a question. "I've never crossed the threshold of any temple!"

"Neither have I!" Aa-neru added. "We faithfully serve Your Grandness, General, and you and your wife, Nes-Mut, know about our everyday activities. I don't know anything about the things Amen-hotep accuses me of. If I'm telling a lie, let them send me to Kush!"

"Let them also send me to Kush!" Pa-Minu added, and he made such a funny face again that Aa-neru laughed again.

"Respect the seriousness in this place!" outraged Ame-em-Ipet shouted. "I believe you both would love to go back to Kush where you come from, but probably not to work in a mine as slaves with their nose and ears cut off!"

"I am the one to conduct the trial," Pa-nehsi interrupted, and, turning to the accused, added, "Amen-em-Ipet is right: you haven't done the full formula and you are behaving inappropriately. Now, we will see if others will confirm their accusations," he signaled the soldiers to lead the two men back into the courtyard, though without any ties. The gardener, Kar, had now been introduced. This one was truly terrified, especially since Pa-nehsi had him make a slightly different oath formula: "I swear by His Majesty King that if all I say is not true, I will be impaled."

"So, tell us everything you know about how you and your associates broke gold from the door of the Golden House in the

Temple of Millions of Years of His Majesty, Ramesses the Great," Pa-uer-aa said to him.

Kar began to speak in a trembling voice, already knowing he was in danger if he concealed something[48]. "Temple Scribe Sedi came along with the Goldsmith Tuti and they stripped some gold from the door, maybe one *deben* and three *kedet* and took it to the Captain of the Archers, Pa-Minu. Then we went there again with Sedi, Tuti and Neb-nefer; it was the four of us and again we tore off three *kedets* of gold, and then five *kedets* and we shared it. Again, we went to this door, with Sedi, Neb-nefer and priest Hori and we broke off five *kedets* of gold and in the City we bought the grain we shared. Then Sedi and the others went there twice more, took some gold and brought it. But a few days later, Pa-Minu began to complain that he hadn't got anything, so we went to that door again, we broke off five *kedets* of gold and we bought an ox and we gave it to Pa-Minu. But the Scribe Suteh-mes overheard us and threatened to tell the High Priest of Amun about everything, so again we brought some *kedets* of gold and gave it to him, but it was not enough for him and again we had to go to that door to give it to Suteh-mes. That which was in our possession, we melted and this time it was three *debens* and three *kedets*, the Prince of the West City, Pa-uer-aa, sent *medjayu* to arrest us." Kar finished and waited in horror for what would happen next.

"I listened to what you said," Pa-uer-aa said. Indeed, we have recovered so much gold from your home. But I counted what you

---

[48] The following statement by the gardener Kar is a quote from an authentic text on one of the papyri containing the trial court report from the time in which the novel is taking place.

mentioned: together, no more than 12 *debens* of gold. But 89 *debens* were stripped of those doors. Who took the rest?"

"I swear to Amun that I said everything I know!" the pale Kar cried.

"So, you accused Captain Pa-Minu. Bring him!" Pa-nehsi ordered.

Reintroduced Pa-Minu was no longer so sure of himself and everyone saw that he paled when he saw the gardener.

"Is it true you got an ox from this man?" the General asked.

"Indeed, I remember he brought me an animal and left it for safekeeping," he mumbled.

Pa-nehsi blushed, "I didn't think you were so stupid. Indeed, I will send you far out of town; here you bring me shame!" he said but did not even order that the officer be re-tied, as everyone expected.

"I think that Pa-Minu would have more to tell us…" Pa-uer-aa tried to protest, seeing how clearly pleased Captain of the Archers walked away quickly. "You can question him differently…"

"I'll decide on it!" Pa-nehsi cut off and told them to summon the priests mentioned by the gardener. Everyone admitted that, in fact, forced by Pa-Minu, they visited a dark corner of the Temple of Millions of Years of Ramesses, User-Maat-Re Sechep-en-Re, and took a little gold sheet from the door of the Golden House. Who took the cedar boards and 300 *debens* of silver from the doorstep in front of this door – no one knew, and Pa-nehsi – exceptionally gentle in this case – did not want to order "interrogation with a stick," which usually brought the truth closer.

"You will all be imprisoned and sent to Kush!" he finally pronounced, and when the accused were led out, he turned to Amen-em-Ipet, "So, we've already investigated the Pa-Minu case. And who accused Aa-neru?"

"The guard, Nes-Amun, was attacked by him and beaten-up in the temple of His Majesty Maat-Men-Re Seti, but he..."

"Enough!" the General interrupted, "Introduce the accused!"

In a moment, pale and terrified, Nes-Amun, with his hands tied, stood before the tribunal with a pleading look at the Djehuty-mes, who spoke for the first time at the trial, "Vizier, the guard Nes-Amun is not charged, untie him!"

Pa-nehsi pretended to be surprised, "What? I heard that valuables were found in his house, which certainly is not evidence of his innocence. Pa-Shu-uben, you told me about it..." he said neither the question nor the statement to the silent Chief of Police.

"Yes, Your Majesty! We found a precious silver wire bracelet with images of sacred beetles." confirmed the Inspector of the City Hidden Affairs. "It doesn't belong to him!"

"It does!" the Necropolis Scribe said, "I gave it to him myself."

"But, Djehuty-mes, do you want me to believe it? I see you have a special reason to defend this thief," Pa-nehsi replied and, without waiting for what the old man would answer, turned to the guard in a menacing voice, "Tell me how you stole these items from the temple, because if you lie, you'll end up on a stake!"

"Let it be away from me, Lord!" Nes-Amun cried, pale as canvas, and began to talk about the day he was attacked and beaten-up, how the attackers found a storage room for ritual equipment, and when he cried that God would punish them, they beat him even more so that the night came to him at day. Aa-neru was also among the attackers.

"So, you're saying you didn't steal these things, even though you knew where they were?" the General asked, and the poor guard rapidly denied.

"Lord, I served as a guard in this temple for 30 years and I always knew where they were, but I never had such a thought!"

"Until that day," the dictator said, and ordered for the first time today to investigate the accused with a stick. Djehuty-mes wanted to protest again, but Pa-nehsi with the red face shouted loudly at him, "Would you like to challenge my right as a Vizier to conduct the trial and establish Maat? If he tells the truth, we'll find out. Begin!"

Four Kushite soldiers pulled the guard down, and two others beat him with hard palm branches. The man began to scream in pain, calling for Amun and swearing that he had told the truth, but Pa-nehsi did not interrupt the examination.

"Stop it, on Amun!" Nes-Amun shouted in a waning voice and then the General signaled to interrupt.

"So, will you start telling the truth now?" Pa-nehsi asked.

The poor guard began to conjure again, "Lord, I swear to my mother and all gods that I was telling the truth. It wasn't me who stole the equipment, but Aa-neru and his band!"

"Are you saying my officer is a bandleader and you, miserable worm, are innocent? Examine him with a stick and *menen*[49]!" he commanded.

Djehuty-mes and Amen-em-Ipet got up from their seats and began to protest loudly, but Pa-nehsi didn't even want to listen.

"You act, august priests, as if you wanted Maat not to be discovered and you do so in front of her statue at the Maat Temple. Perform!" he said to his soldiers, and the torture of Nes-Amun began again, but this time he would have worse torture. The poor man was knocked with wooden beams, in which a stick was inserted, and the massively built Kushite began to slowly, but constantly twist the stick. To the blows still received on the back, buttocks and legs came the terrible pain of the hands, which now threatened to break. Nes-Amun no longer shouted, but howled, and in this howl, one could hardly hear a cry for help to Amun. Pa-nehsi watched the interrogation calmly and even clearly, satisfied and allowed it to be interrupted only when the torturer gave him a sign that the bones were about to break.

"Will you finally decide to admit that you stole the dishes from the temple?" Pa-nehsi asked.

A clearly reluctant surprise appeared on his face when he heard the guard whispered, "It's not me, it's Aa-neru, I swear to the gods!" and then he fainted.

"Take him to the dungeon and question him again tomorrow with a stick and *menen*!" Pa-nehsi ordered and wanted to end the court session.

---

[49] Type of instrument of torture used during interrogation of criminals; a similar sounding word means "twist, wring" which is the basis for the interpretation of the tool in the novel.

Then, however, Djehuty-mes stood up and pronounced the oath so loudly that even the farthest soldiers heard it, as well as those who stood in the courtyard, "I, the Royal Scribe of the Necropolis, Djehuty-mes, I swear that what the guard Nes-Amun says is true! I saw this man with my son Buteh-Amun right after the robbery. He still had rope marks on his hands, and he didn't tie himself. I told Pa-shu-uben about this when I found out that Nes-Amun had been arrested. That bracelet you found, I took off my own hand that day and gave him as consolation because he was very unhappy. And what you have done with him now is wicked! You only ordered the torture of an innocent because he recognized Aa-neru. And did you order Aa-neru to be examined with a stick or *menen*?"

Djehuty-mes stood upright and looked down at the still sitting dictator.

"Aa-neru is my officer and has my trust, and besides, my wife claimed..."

"So, maybe one should also interrogate your wife with the help of a stick, because she had already lied once, saying that Aa-neru was with her just when he was hacking!" shouted Djehuty-mes and added even louder, "In the name of His Majesty the King, to whom I am subject as much as you are, I call you to free Nes-Amun, who did not change his testimony even in torment. Aa-neru should be in the dungeon. Indeed, this process is *isefet*[50] at the House of Maat! I will complain about you to the King!" At the moment, Amen-em-Ipet stood beside the Necropolis Scribe, "I

---

[50] Evil, wickedness, the opposite of the divine law of Maat.

also heard what Djehuty-mes said about the burglary to His Majesty, Amen-hotep. Nes-Amun is innocent and should no longer testify. This Aa-neru is not telling the truth."

"I agree with Djehuty-mes and Amen-em-Ipet words," Pa-uer-aa added, who was the third to stand over Pa-nehsi, who blushed and became blue. He would have liked to arrest all three, but they were independent representatives of three important offices, practically untouchable, and raising hands on them would be a crime that could not be hidden.

Searching for a convenient solution, Pa-nehsi turned to Pa-Shu-uben. "Did the Necropolis Scribe tell you something about Nes-Amun?" he asked. "I don't remember," Pa-Shu-uben muttered ,"Maybe he was saying something..."

Pa-nehsi stood up and, trying to calm down, said, "Well then, I will free your hero, but since I have no convincing evidence of Aa-neru's guilt, I will not punish him as you all want. He will be moved to another place outside of Waset so that he cannot be harmed with suspicion anymore!" He narrowed his eyes and fixed them on Djehuty-mes, then came very close to him and with hatred, he mouthed, "Djehuty-mes, called Chari! You insulted my wife and me. I will not forgive you. And to the King, may he live in happiness and health, naturally, send complaints..." and leaning down he whispered in his ear: "...if you can..."

The court session was over.

CHAPTER V

On the same day, the First Servant of Amun, Amen-hotep, in the reception hall of his palace at the Holy Lake in Ipet-sut, heard the report of Djehuty-mes and Amen-em-Ipet from the trial. Both senior priests were deeply moved by what happened and by the very eloquent behavior of dictator Pa-nehsi.

"There is no doubt at all," the Necropolis Scribe said, "that he covers for his people and knows perfectly well what Aa-neru or Pa-Minu are doing. He did not allow them to be interrogated with a stick, although both were directly accused. That who worked for them – those Kar, Sedi, Hori and someone else there, and even that Suteh-mes who threatened to denounce them and forced their share in profits, got a very small part of what we lacked in the Golden House – The Temple of Millions of Years of His Majesty, Ramesses the Great. What happened to the rest? If Pa-nehsi ordered an examination with a stick, which he should do in that case, they could admit to larger amounts of this stolen gold and silver, but they would also tell whom they gave most of the loot. And these names could be embarrassing for the General."

Djehuty-mes paused for a moment, trying to remember what Nes-Mut, Pa-nehsi's wife, had said to Aa-neru when he and Buteh-Amun had met her the day of the robbery. She was talking about kind of sum… At the time Djehuty-mes closed his eyes and effortlessly replayed that conversation. Suddenly he found what he was looking for in the recesses of memory.

"Perhaps, this has nothing to do with the burglary, but that woman, Pa-nehsi's wife whom he protected so much today, said to Aa-neru on the day of the robbery at Seti's temple, "As usual, five *debens* in silver." For what did the General's wife usually receive five *debens* in silver? And didn't scribe Sedi say that we might be in trouble if she finds out? I think that today's dissertation has revealed as much as a young plant when it shoots a green sprout: what remains in the ground is much larger, although hidden…"

Amen-em-Ipet nodded and added, "Pa-nehsi showed how everyone who learns anything about crimes supervised by his people will be treated. Of course, all of today's witnesses of what happened in court will tell about it, and that unfortunate guardian of this temple will be a living confirmation that this process – organized on the order of Your Grandness, in which the High Priests of the House of Amun participated has nothing to do with Maat. It can have similar effects as this unfortunate tax rumor."

Amen-hotep, who had not spoken so far and was sitting sadly, resting his head on his hands, at the memory of the innocently tortured Nes-Amun raised his head and asked, "What's the matter with him now?"

"Pa-uer-aa gave his litter and told me to take him home and appoint another guard before Nes-Amun gets better: he probably won't be able to walk for at least half a moon," answered Djehuty-mes.

"But does anyone look after him?" the High Priest insisted.

"His wife is dead, but his son is there, almost an adult boy who turns ten[51], who can feed him."

"Let them bring this poor man here. My doctor will cure him, and I will reward him for loyal service!" Amen-hotep ordered and sent several people with a litter to Khefet-her-neb-es, ordering them to take an official High Priesthood boat. The Necropolis Scribe farewell and said that he would lead them to the home of Nes-Amun, and from there he would come back.

When Amen-hotep stayed with Amen-em-Ipet, the conversation turned to other topics. Amen-em-Ipet began to talk about what various servants in the temples, workshops and various places belonging to the House of Amun had told him about the conversations they overheard. The news was more and more disturbing because simple people, tenants of the land, were already familiar with the rumors about taxes throughout Waset, and the harvest was approaching quickly. Not only Pa-Shu-uben and his people walked from house to house, spreading the untrue

---

[51] In Egypt, accountability began after the age of 10.

news, but they also used tenants themselves who's hearts had been poisoned, like Henut's father's heart. They were taken to further villages and later brought back, using military boats.

"Now everyone knows that additional sacks of grain will be taken away from him," Amen-em-Ipet said, "And certainly the inspectors of Pa-Shu-uben with the help of Kushite soldiers will actually do it. Since this will not enrich the King nor the House of Amun, it is easy to guess, whom. We also need to prepare the feast of Min; I don't know if Your Grandness should take personally part in the procession this time because there will be regret and bitterness in people, not joy and I am afraid that something bad will happen."

The conversation lasted a long time, while it was getting dark and Amen-hotep ordered the lamps to be lit.

"I'm sure everything will be explained soon. I have to talk to Pa-nehsi to let him know that we're not blind and deaf. This trial today, although it did not lead to the conviction of major criminals, was very much needed. It should stop the burglary because now everyone will be very vigilant. It's good that I have people like you and Chari with me!"

Amen-em-Ipet bowed respectfully, "I'm worried about the Necropolis Scribe. Today Pa-nehsi told him that he would not forgive him that he mentioned Nes-Mut, which, as Chari said, "could be interrogated with a stick."

"What a story!" Amen-hotep laughed honestly. "I knew his courage, but he had to sting the General well with something like that. After all, he is not in danger, he is too important a figure in Waset and, moreover, directly subordinated – except for me –

only to the King. Pa-nehsi knows well that there are boundaries that he cannot cross unless he wants to declare war on the Both Countries."

"However, I would like to draw Your Grandness attention to what he said at the end, although in a whisper, but I stood close enough to hear it... I conclude that the reaching the King with a complaint he considers impossible. We both know that even in Pi-Ramesse, Pa-nehsi has friends who do not facilitate the delivery of the letter to Ramesse."

"You are right, but there are other ways to reach Pi-Ramesse than by the routes along the river. There is no way that they can all be controlled..."

At that moment, a servant appeared at the door, announcing that Prince Khefet-her-neb-es, Pa-uer-aa and the Necropolis Scribe, Djehuty-mes, had arrived.

"What is Chari doing here again?" Amen-hotep asked the question aloud, though he felt that his visit did not bode well.

After a while, he saw the Necropolis Scribe, even more agitated than after the trial, and at the same time in his gaze, he read the expression of tragic helplessness:

"Nes-Amun is dead," Djehuty-mes said in a strangled voice, "And I did not defend him not only from the pain and suffering of the interrogation but also from death, although I promised him protection and I assured him that he was safe. It turned out that he was right in saying that when he confesses the name of the attacker, he will take revenge on him."

"How did this happen?" Amen-hotep asked quietly, knowing that he was actually asking only about the way Aa-neru carried out the murder.

"After the trial, I ordered to take him home in my litter," Pa-uer-aa said, "And my people left him there on the bed. They left him food and drink, and sent his son, a 10-year-old Aha-nefer-Amun, to get a doctor who would prepare herbs for the compresses of the beaten places. When he came with the doctor – he wasn't at home, maybe an hour – they found Nes-Amun lying in bed, but he was dead: his head was cracked with a stone, and it had not been wounded in court. The doctor sent Aha-nefer-Amun for me, and right after I had come there, Chari and the people of Your Grandness came. We wrote the protocol and sent for embalmers from the Clean Place. And I dared bring the boy here: without mother and father, he could easily go on the wrong path of life."

"You did well. Tell the servant to call him," the High Priest commanded, and a moment later a weeping Aha-nefer-Amun stood in the chamber, scared and intimidated by the sight of so many important people in priestly dresses.

"What's your name?" The First Servant addressed him.

"I am Aha-nefer-Amun, son of Nes-Amun, and they call me Pa-khar," he said quietly, with bowed head.

"Boy, it's very difficult for all of us to understand why Amun called your father to the Hall of Both Truths. We all highly respect Nes-Amun, who gave his life in defense of Maat. At the expense of the House of Amun, he will be buried in the coffin and buried in a grave at the foot of the Holy Mountain in Khefet-her-neb-es. You will be proud of him by visiting this grave where you and your children will also rest. But first, you will go to the school of priests and scribes in Ipet-sut and you will never run out of bread."

"Can I eat something now?" the boy asked, looking eagerly at the date bowl on the table.

"Of course!" Amen-hotep replied and took a full handful of fruit from the bowl, which he gave into the child's greedy hands.

"Take care of him, please," he said quietly to Amen-em-Ipet. "I see that not all Waset residents are doing well. I will help him, but I would like to know if supplying all employees of the House of Amun, even in such workplaces as guards, gardeners and cleaners, is going well and whether they are also being robbed by the army and people like Pa-nehsi or Pa-Shu-uben, not to mention ordinary thieves. When Amen-em-Ipet and the little Pa-khar left, the First Servant, turning to Djehuty-mes and Pa-uer-aa, said seriously, "The goblet has been fulfilled. I can't wait any longer with my reaction. You will take both a letter to General Pa-nehsi, that tomorrow morning I will await him here to discuss important matters of the City and Waset." after which he struck out a few sentences on the papyri card, rolled it up, stuck it with wax and pressed his ring in it.

"Take my boat again and go straight to the harbor in front of the temple of His Grandness Ramesses User-Maat-Re Meri-Amun, and let my heralds use trumpets and officially announce my messengers!"

Djehuty-mes and Pa-uer-aa bowed respectfully and left.

The next day, when the fourth-hour guards[52] at the Great Ipet-sut Gate were just changing, General Pa-nehsi's boat entered the marina. There were trumpet sounds and the herald shouted in a loud voice.

"His Grandness, Pharaoh's Army General, Head of the Granaries of the Southern Country, Vizier of the South, Royal Son of Kush, Pa-nehsi visits His Grandness the First Servant of Amun, Amen-hotep!"

The General got off the boat, then took his place in his own litter and carried by his four soldiers, preceded by a herald and two duty priests from Ipet-sut, set off along an avenue framed by statues of ram-headed lions towards the Great Gate of Amun district visible in the distance. Here the herald trumpeted again and made the same announcement. Immediately, a small door in the gate was opened and a guard stood there, who, bowing low, took the place of priests and led the retinue through the great Hall of Appearances towards the gate leading to the palace of the High Priest. Here for the third time, the herald repeated his activities and after a while, the litter was brought to the palace courtyard. Here Pa-nehsi got off, his soldiers and herald were shown a place where they could sit waiting for the return of their Lord, and a servant priest led the distinguished guest to the Admission Hall, showed him a comfortable chair, and left him alone. While waiting for the host, Pa-nehsi looked around this spacious room, open to the Holy Lake on one side, on the other

---

[52] The day began at sunrise; at this time of year, the mentioned change of guard could take place around 10 am.

one decorated with a beautifully painted magnificent bas-relief, showing Amen-hotep standing with hands raised in a gesture of joy, receiving a precious necklace from His Majesty, King Ramesses Nefer-Ka-Re. The figures of the High Priest and Pharaoh were almost of the same size, which gave Pa-nehsi a derisive smile, shaking his head slightly. At the moment, he saw the host himself - the head of the State of Amun, dressed much more modestly, in a simple tunic and without any decorations, not counting the gold seal ring on his finger. Amen-hotep greeted him, thanking him for coming.

"I am always ready to come if important matters require it, and from the invitation you sent to me, I conclude that such have appeared, isn't it?" Pa-nehsi replied, scanning the face of the High Priest, who was completely devoid of the smile with which the First Servant of Amun usually greeted his guests.

"Yes," the Amen-hotep also looked very thoroughly into the General's eyes, "I would like to know who murdered the guard Nes-Amun, the same whom you interrogated so stubbornly yesterday?"

"Ah, so he's dead? Probably the reason was remorse…"

"Really? Unlike you, Nes-Amun had a clear conscience and, in addition, remorse does not crush the skull."

"Then it had to be an accident; there are many rocks in the Necropolis and a stone must have fallen on his head."

"Undoubtedly, after which the poor wretch got to his bed, even though he could not walk yesterday at all, he lay down and only then died…"

"Apparently, God wanted it, Amen-hotep."

They were keeping their eyes on each other all the time, saying the successive sentences calmly, but now Amen-hotep burst out: "Don't comment on topics you don't know about!" It was an accurate blow because the only supreme function in the City that Pa-nehsi lacked was related to religious matters.

The General searched for an equally accurate answer for a moment, and then his eyes went to the scene he had previously looked at, "Well, yes, I see," he clearly emphasized this word, "That the First Servant of Amun, who has this knowledge, is equal to the King…"

"You are wrong again," Amen-hotep followed Pa-nehsi's gaze, "Because the figure in the royal crown is not the king himself, but his statue, and in addition standing on the platform, so Pharaoh is taller, and secondly, this scene shows the reward I received for properly delivering temple taxes due to the ruler. It was always my pride that I did not overburden the people, and the King got what he should get and his temple…"

"And you and your family also…" Pa-nehsi came in his word. "Do not make me laugh, Amen-hotep, because it is no accident that all the functions related to counting grain or cattle, which I took on the order of His Majesty King Ramesses, were in the hands of your family before?"

"And what does it mean? I entrusted those positions to whom I trusted, and they performed their duties well. I have never deceived the tenants of Amun's land and told them not to give away more grain than has been established for many, many years. During the time of His Majesty Ramesses Meri-Amun, justified, tenants gave two sacks of grain from the *setjat* and during the reign for Ramesses Nefer-Ka-Re, justified by voice, they were only two sacks and I don't know that His Majesty Ramesses Men-Maat- Re, may he live forever, changed anything here. And I know that Pa-Shu-uben goes from one tenant to another and says that they have to give back three times as much, and at the same time he cites my command, which I never gave. Unfortunately, since you are the Vizier and Granary Head here, he is subject to you and I cannot stop the *isefet* which is being made against the tenants of the land of Amun. Of course, the King will find out and will certainly react in the right way, he will restore Maat. Can you tell me who will get these extra sacks of grain because it's not the temple?"

Pa-nehsi did not deny. He reached into the bowl with dates, put the fruit in his mouth and for a long time absorbed his sweetness, finally spit the stone onto the painted floor and only then answered.

"You know perfectly well that the army has big needs and that for too long not much has been flowing from the royal magazines. I have even heard that the workers who should work on the tomb of His Majesty King Ramesses often remain in their town and refuse to go to the Great Valley because they do not receive remuneration, i.e. obligations towards Pharaoh are neglected in your area, which the King should probably also learn."

Amen-hotep was almost speechless with indignation and stared in disbelief at his interlocutor, who was calmly eating another date.

"Do you consider me blind and deaf, whom no news reach, and in addition as a fool to whom you can speak any absurdity?

After all, you as the Vizier are responsible for supplying the town and you know why these people don't go to work sometimes. They are afraid of your soldiers, whom you cannot keep in check, they are afraid for their wives and daughters, as well as their belongings, and therefore they prefer to stay at home so that they can defend them all. Well, but since you have officers like this Aa-neru... Ah, how this name fits him perfectly![53]

The seed of another date fell to the floor. "Aa-neru has exaggerated a bit, but I said I would transfer him to the service outside the City," Pa-nehsi replied calmly, and the High Priest shouted again:

"But now he has even committed a murder!"

Pa-nehsi stopped eating dates and stood up, "I'm tired of this conversation, Amen-hotep. I see that it doesn't make sense. Take care of what belongs to you, talk to the gods and offer them Maat, and leave me the matters that the King entrusted to me with full confidence…"

"…which you are abusing, General!" Amen-hotep concluded and added, "I think His Majesty does not know what is going on in Waset."

"You really think so?" Pa-nehsi started toward the door. "I assure you that I often and extensively inform the King of the City's peaceful and prosperous life, and I do not bother him with the foolishness with which you send your emissaries. Am I wrong? General Pi-ankh recently mentioned to me, writing from Pi-

---

[53] Aa-neru means: "Great terror," which was one of the terms of Mut (se. List of divine names).

Ramesse, that some ragamuffins had come to him, claiming that they had a letter from you to His Majesty. So, the High Priest sends letters to the living Horus, using shabby tatterdemalions? Of course, no one will believe it... I wish you a good day, and then a quiet night in the City of Amun, which thanks to me and my soldiers is safe for its inhabitants!"

"I wish you a peaceful heart in which Maat will live!" The First Servant answered dryly and called out the duty priest who appeared immediately; it was Suti-mes today. At the sight of him, Amen-hotep's face softened and some tension disappeared from the unpleasant conversation, "Escort His Grandness to the marina," commanded the High Priest.

"Oh, what a kindness! I'll get there myself, I have my people," Pa-nehsi said, crossing the threshold, but then he heard Amen-hotep's strong voice.

"But here, General, I am the host and have confidence in my people!"

The meeting was over. Suti-mes led the noble guest out of the palace into the courtyard, where Pa-nehsi's soldiers with the litter and herald were waiting. The General sat down in the litter, the herald stood in front of it, but it was Suti-mes who now led the retinue, passing through the Hall of Appearances to the Great Gate and further along the avenue of stone lions to the marina. Pa-nehsi got out of the litter and headed for his boat. At the edge of the waterfront, he stopped and looked at Suti-mes, who was walking beside him to accompany the visitor, ready to fulfill the wishes of the dignitary, if he wanted something.

"So, His Grandness, Amen-hotep, trusts you... It's good to have such trusted slaves," he said, and a fleeting smile appeared on his face.

"I am not a slave, Lord, but the Father of God in the service of the High Priest," Suti-mes replied calmly.

"What, so you haven't yet been promoted to the position of the Servant of God?"[54] Pa-nehsi did not ask, nor said and immediately added, "Because you probably know, of course, if you can read that this priesthood title and the word meaning slave sound the same, and the scripture used to express both these concepts, after all, presents a tool, which is used by the washers. Once you get this promotion, you will probably have the honor and pleasure of washing dirty Amen-hotep's garments and cleaning his muddy sandals..."

He grinned like a smile and got into the boat without waiting for an answer that Suti-mes did not intend to give.

"So, a man who speaks such crude things has been endowed with so many dignities," he thought in surprise, feeling a distinct disgust. "How he is very different from such people as Amen-em-Ipet or Djehuty-mes..."

---

[54] All officials living in Thebes associated with the temple of Amun bore the title "father of God", which was the lowest rank in the priesthood hierarchy. The higher rank was represented by priests described as "pure" or "clean" ones. The elite group were "God's servants," and the strict leadership of those who received the hierarchical terms "fourth," "third," "second," and "first" servant of Amun. The latter - the high priest - was the head of the entire extended structure of the State of Amun. He was chosen by their priests themselves and even Pharaoh could not undermine such a choice.

Of course, Suti-mes did not even intend to repeat the General's words to anyone, much less go to the High Priest when he suddenly summoned him again. The First Servant was walking slowly through his chamber, arms folded back, while wandering a 20-cubit space between the front door and the terrace overlooking the Holy Lake. Suti-mes stood for some time near the door, but the High Priest seemed to not see him, though he approached him several times, no more than two cubits.

Finally, he stood just before the young priest and said, "Suti-mes, you once asked me for the most difficult tasks; today I have one for you. This is a unique challenge, very dangerous, but if you do it, you will help me a lot, as well as your friends and your girlfriend. I want you to go to Pi-Ramesse with my letter intended for His Majesty King Ramesses, may he live! There, you will find General Heri-Hor and give him the letter personally: only to him, nobody else. You will tell him that along with my greetings, I send him a message that the barge of Re no longer appears in the City and has disappeared on the western horizon. Let him immediately take the letter and this news to the palace of Pharaoh and pass them to King Ramesses, may he live! And let no one but the King find out! You will leave today."

The High Priest paused and was silent for a while, and Suti-mes was not dare to break the silence.

"Because," Amen-hotep continued, "I am afraid that most of the roads leading north and maybe all of them are controlled by my enemies, you will go in a completely different direction than they expect. First south to Djeret, then to Sumenu and then through the desert and oases. I will provide you with a seal that should make your journey easier everywhere. In every town, starting from Djeret, you will go to the temple of Amun, and there, look for a priest *setem* or a priest *hery-khebet*[55]; they will direct you to people who will help you to overcome your journey as soon as possible. When you reach the river again, there will be others who will show you my fast boat, waiting with its captain for instructions. You will sail to Pi-Ramesse. Of course, you must bring an answer from the King. You can take the entire route back by the river, but with my boat you can only reach Khemenu, and then you should change to any other ship, many of which come from the north to Waset. They probably don't control them so thoroughly, and my marks on the barge could arouse suspicion. Were you able to remember everything I told you?"

Amen-hotep ended with a question, but he knew the answer immediately, seeing the flash in the young man's eyes. Suti-mes understood that he was uniquely distinguished, and the importance of the task entrusted to him testified to the great trust the First Servant of Amun gave him. He confirmed warmly, and then Amen-hotep took his arm and led him to the next room, where he used to work and write letters. On the table, there was a small wooden box decorated with ivory inlays, from which, lifting the gable lid, the High Priest took out a ring with a faience image of a holy beetle framed in gold, on the underside of which there was an inscription repeating the title and name of Amen-hotep, as well as a stamped roll of papyrus. "Here is the seal and letter to Pharaoh. Let God lead you as Re during the day, and Khonsu at

---

[55] Titles of high-ranking priests directing ritual ceremonies.

night, let him open your path as Up-uaut, let him grant you a happy return as Ini-heret!"

Suti-mes fell to the feet of Amen-hotep, and in a sense of immense joy and worship for the High Priest, he wanted to kiss his sandal, but at that moment the dignitary withdrew his leg and raised the young man, saying, "I won't let you touch my dirty sandals! It is unworthy of the Servant of God which you are from today!"

CHAPTER VI

The time has finally come, which was very much feared in the City and throughout Waset, as well as in other districts of the Southern Country: the harvest season. For several weeks, ears of wheat or barley took on a noble gold color and became ripe, absorbing from the sky, the heat that previously lacked as much grain as people. Now, this heat was even in excess. From the beginning of the Shemu season not only the hours of the day were extended, but Re sent such hot rays from his barge as if it was the last month, not the first month of the drought season. However, in the fourth month, all work usually ceased in the hot-burned fields, where the earth with thousands of cracks opened its interior, waiting for the invigorating chill of the flooding, and people protected themselves at home or tried not to leave the shade. Now, on the contrary, without the slightest heat shield from the sky, everyone was waiting for a huge effort to cut the sickle of the ears, bind them, transfer them to the concaves next to the houses, then the more demanding process of beating the crop to separate the precious grain from the straw, and finally load it into sacks...all this not only took place in the heat, but the ever-shorter nights gave less time to rest. However, the heat was not the worst. Every year, when the hard work of the harvest was coming to an end, the sadness of fatigue gave way to the joy from the prize, which was knowing that the collected grain is not only enough for bread and beer for the whole family for the whole year, but that it will be possible to exchange part of it for other products brought to the market by animal breeders or various craftsmen. This year, almost all tenants of Amun's fields lacked this joy. The harvest was meager, the grains tiny and compared to previous years, each obtained at least two bags less. The same would be enough for men to seriously care for the next year and, from women's lips, would be moan and complaints, which could be accompanied by tears, especially when a group of children ran around the house, happy with their ignorance. However, for several months everyone knew that they were to give back not two, as they had done since time immemorial, but six sacks of grain from *setjat* as tax due. For all Peret season, everybody was talking about it every time and feared it, but many tenants did not believe that this terrible announcement could come true. They couldn't believe it all the more when they saw the exceptionally small collection this year.

"It is impossible," they were saying, "That His Grandness, Amen-hotep should not have mercy over the people of the State of Amun when he sees what low crops have yielded in Waset this year. The temple is rich!"

They repeated it to scribes and officers who, in the company of soldiers, appeared in every house to collect the tax due, and they confirmed that "...the temple is rich and the harvest is small, but apparently His Grandness Amen-hotep does not want to show mercy" and ignoring the women's laments and men's curses, they unceremoniously ordered the porters to carry six bags from the *setjat* from each farm to the nearest harbor, where transport boats were already waiting, taking grain to storage. Two sacks, as usual, were sent to the great granary at the temple of His Majesty Ramesses the Great, who was under the authority of the High Priest, Amen-hotep, and that was where these barges first headed, slandered by insults, which were often accompanied by a handful of ground thrown at them by desperate people. Hardly anyone had the opportunity to follow the way of the same boats on which the remaining grain was taken from each tenant. They were usually transported to two huge military barges moored together with the entire Pa-nehsi fleet on the west side of the river and poured into cavernous boxes of these floating warehouses. It happened sometimes that some tenants defended themselves against giving away the required number of sacks, but then ruthless and brutal Kushite soldiers usually were entering the action, who not only forcibly were ripping the tax from the peasants but also were stretching them on the threshing floor, were beating them with sticks, until the poor wretches and their families pleaded for grace, ensuring that such resistance would never happen again.

The hard days had barely ended, after which the entire Waset District remained sore and recollecting the unhappiness that had not been remembered here since the time of the forefathers when the eleventh day of the first month in the month of Shemu came the day of the Great Exit of the Min. This was usually when the finished harvest was celebrated joyfully, and besides a colorful procession full of attractive events the participants anticipated a funny contest of the "climbing for Min."

All residents of the City usually had a great desire to watch an unusual procession, in which, apart from the usually carried divine images, unusual guests participated. So, there was a black man from the land of Punt, whose color resembled the color of Min – the patron of fertility, followed by a white bull – also a picture of life-giving reproductive power, imported for this purpose from the temple in South Iunu. Further off 22 priests, hidden under a curtain decorated with stars, carried a wooden platform with a statue of Min covered with a feathered canopy. The procession came to a specially built platform called Stairs of Min, where the statue was erected. At that time, the High Priest who was replacing the King first released a bird in each of the four corners of the world, proclaiming the joyful news of confirmation of royal power, and then he cut off a few ears of barley with the sickle that he sacrificed to Min.

Everyone was also waiting impatiently for the annual competition in which strong youths participated – representatives of various towns from all over Waset. In the middle of a special square, a tall mast made of cedar wood, from which ships were built, was dug into the ground, and several thick sailor ropes descended from the top of this pole. At the sign, the contestants started climbing on these ropes, racing who would be the first to reach the top of the mast, where the prize was waiting for a winner: a beautiful faience scarab with the name of Amun-Min. The competition was accompanied by cheers of encouragement issued by the acquaintances and friends of each participant, and sometimes laughter and moans when one of them slipped or even fell to the ground without achieving his goal.

The Great Exit of Min was one of the many permanent events of the year that determined the rhythm of the City's life, so it was difficult to imagine that the ceremonies would not take place. It was organized by the First Servant of Amun, Amen-hotep himself, who knew that this year he would face an extremely thankless task. Amen-em-Ipet even advised against personal participation. Knowing what was happening during the collection of taxes, the old sage was even worried about the safety of the High Priest during public celebrations of the holiday, all the more so that it was impossible to count on the favor of the army.

"Pa-nehsi would be delighted if one of these deceived poor wretches did something that would also harm Your Grandness personally and would also break faith in Amun. Better not risk. I can lead these ceremonies, and I will tell that Your Grandness feels bad," Amen-em-Ipet said, but he encountered strong resistance from the First Servant.

"I appreciate your concern, my friend, but I have not done anything wrong to hide from Amun's subordinates. On the contrary, I will stand before them with a clean face, and then I am convinced no one would dare disturb the ceremony. Maat will be with us," he decided and Amen-em-Ipet already knew that any further attempts to convince the head of State of Amun to change this would be unsuccessful. Everything was prepared, as every year and at the same time as a year ago and in the past a solemn Min procession set off from Ipet-sut towards the temple in the southern part of the City, where the "Stairs of Min" was set up in front of the great Ipet-resit gate.

The procession moved, as always, in the middle of the avenue of lions, stone guards, between which stood the real guards from Ipet-sut, and the preventive Amen-em-Ipet this year ordered to double their number so that between one and the other two pairs of watchful eyes stared into a crowd gathered on both sides of the avenue. However, it turned out, that Amen-hotep was right when he said that he did not expect problems from the residents of the City. The dignity of the procession and the presence of sacred objects worked soothingly, and no one was found who, even with an offensive word or an improper gesture, would spoil the magnificent view, liked and still awaited in the City at this time of year.

However, something has changed. Usually, a colorful procession with a white bull and a black Negro from Punt triggered joyful reactions in the people and the gathered crowd greeted them with shouts and applause. This time, fewer people were watching the procession, and they showed much less excitement, and there were times when a cheerful procession moving through the City with music was walking among a motionless and silent crowd, as if deprived of the ability to feel joy. And when the High Priest, Amen-hotep, released jays to the four corners of the world, ordering them to inform everyone that here... "Horus put on a white and red crown," which in the past was always welcomed with applause, complete silence answered him as if it suddenly became quite indifferent to the happy ending of the myth about the battle of Horus – a good son and successor of Osiris – with the evil uncle Set. However, the worst was the same silence and immobility of the crowd when Amen-hotep cut a few ears of grain with a sickle and offered them to the statue of Min, then began humming the hymn to this patron of fertility and abundance, doing dance moves with raising hands and throwing forward the left and right legs alternately, which was varied by the additional rotation of the whole body.

Welcome, Min to your superior place![56]
Welcome, Min, who fertilized your mother!
Oh, how mysterious is what you did to her in the dark!
The High Priest wiggled, sang and danced,
And the crowd surrounding
The Stairs of Min stood silent and still.
Oh, you, the only God whom everyone worships loudly...

In the silence, every Amen-hotep's word could be heard, but today none of those watching this scene wanted to loudly worship the one who was usually profusely thanked for a good harvest. Then Amen-em-Ipet joined in singing the hymn, repeating his words and imitating the movements of the First Servant of Amun, and after him other priests in the procession did the same, but only them: the inhabitants of Waset remained motionless, although usually, from that moment all the City was

---

[56] Authentic words of the hymn to Min, preserved on Egyptian monuments.

transforming into an anthill vibrating with dance, and everyone carried this dance home, where they continued to celebrate. Today, people were getting sad and the return route of the procession to Ipet-sut was something almost nobody wanted to watch.

"Really, the night is falling over the City," the High Priest said when he could finally rest after this very difficult and painful day. "I don't know what will happen if Pharaoh, may he live, does not change his mind about Pa-nehsi. Do you think our Suti-mes succeeded?"

"I don't know, Your Grandness," Amen-em-Ipet replied, "But if so, we should find out soon enough. It is good that this holiday is already over, although in a month it will be the Beautiful Valley Feast and a great trip to the west bank awaits us, and it can be even more difficult and equally dangerous. I would advise you to stay in Ipet-sut!"

"Ah, you're starting this again! As you can see, nothing happened."

"Praise to Amun, but Pa-nehsi must have been very happy today..."

Of course, Amen-em-Ipet was right. Although Pa-nehsi himself did not see the Exit of the Min, he avoided all religious ceremonies and now also remained in his palace - but the procession did not have time to return to Ipet-sut when Pa-shu-uben gave his superior the exact account of the ceremony and atmosphere, which was more like a funeral and mourning after someone's death, rather than the joy of multiplying life, for which the Feast of Min was to express itself.

"It is a pity that Your Grandness did not see how miserable Amen-hotep looked, romping in front of the statue of Min and singing the hymn against the grave silence of the City's inhabitants," the Chief of Police said. "I was wondering if any of them would say aloud what they were shouting about the First Servant to our soldiers at the time of Peret season, when they were gathering at these bonfires, or recently when they had to give more sacks of grain than usual... Unfortunately, today there were too many temple policeman."

"Cowards, Pa-shu-uben, they only used to tell the truth when asked with a stick. But you say that they didn't clap, they didn't dance, as they used to do, they just kept silent...that's a good sign. In a few months, they will start to miss everything, Amen-hotep will not give them anything, because he will not have anything, and we, perhaps, will help...under certain conditions. And then again, the harvest and taxes will be the same as this year. Who knows, maybe they will show Amen-hotep that they have enough of him and that they know that the temples are very rich... senselessly rich, which we already know. All those silver floors, gates and obelisks covered with gold metal... Really, Amun does not need it all..." Pa-nehsi paused and raised a beautifully carved faience cup to his mouth, drinking cool water with a mint aroma.

It was very hot, and the General felt overwhelming drowsiness. Pa-Shu-uben noticed this, bowed and discreetly backed out, not wanting to disturb the head's nap. He felt that Pa-nehsi, who had been so openly talking about him for the first time about the treasures of the Temple of Amun, would need his knowledge as head of police and the Inspector of the Hidden City Affairs and would undoubtedly call him again soon.

A few days later, he received the news that the General wants to speak with him and for this purpose invites him to his palace for a midday meal and wine. Although Pa-Shu-uben enjoyed the trust of the dictator and their relations were the best, he never forgot that he was only a subordinate and the gap between him and the position occupied by Pa-nehsi, after all, of personal acquaintance of King Ramesses himself and in The Southern Country's head of almost anything that could be managed, except temples and cemeteries. When Pa-nehsi was calling for him, it was always a matter of brief exchange of words: the General was asking questions, listening to the answers, and then most often giving an order. Usually, the dignitary would sit then, and Pa-shu-uben would stand by him, and only rarely would he be offered a date or other fruit if Pa-nehsi was eating something like that. Now, they were supposed to sit down together for a meal, and then drink wine, which meant that the conversation was important, and so Pa-shu-uben became more important. Therefore, when going to the palace, Pa-Shu-uben put on his festive robe, hung a rich pectoral around his neck with ornaments made of colored glass paste embedded in golden compartments, and bracelets on the wrists and arms. Behind his belt, he placed a decorative dagger, which he liked to wear as a personal weapon, although his huge body and big fists were enough to discourage any potential attacker. Probably there would be no one in Waset who could beat him in wrestling, although of course, Pa-Shu-uben was too high a clerk to take part in such competitions. He usually arrived at Pa-nehsi's palace on a chariot, entered through the western gate of the district of His Majesty Ramesses Meri-Amun and continued on foot. This time, he ordered to take his boat to the main harbor from the eastern side of the palace, i.e. the road that the messengers and guests came to the General. He expected this visit to be of a special nature and would not be disappointed.

Pa-nehsi greeted him with great cordiality, and before he invited him for a meal, he told him that in recognition of the very well done action of "preparing" the inhabitants of Waset, and especially the temple tenants for the "new tax system" and for efficient collection of taxes, he also appoints him to the position of Army Scribe Supervisor. Of course, this was to be accompanied by a significant reward in all produce provided by the lands of Amun. Pa-shu-uben was happy because, in addition to his function as police chief, he now had extended control rights not only on the inhabitants of Waset but also on a significant part of the army. He felt that he was now becoming the powerful right hand of the dictator.

They sat down on low stools and in a moment the servants set up a table mat in front of them with a bowl of boiled lentils mixed with oil and onions seasoned with salt and herbs, and they dipped in it pieces of bread torn from flat cakes and carried them to their mouths, putting a second hand with bread, so that nothing falls and does not dirty the white of the tunics. Then there were roasted duck and sycamore fruit, and when they were saturated, they moved to another room, where high pitchers of wine were standing in special stands. This time they sat on highchairs lined with soft papyri mat, and the servants handed them long cane stems hollowed out in the middle, one end of which they put into the pitcher, and the other, covered with a faience mouthpiece with many holes, served directly for drinking.

"Unfortunately, Pa-shu-uben," the General said, when they had satisfied their first thirst, "we must be content with wine produced in Kemet. One makes it much better in the land beyond the Great Green[57], but it reaches Both Countries in a small amount through intermediaries, mainly the prince of Keben, and they are capricious, and we have had difficulties for years to get more important things from them, such as cedar wood, so nothing to tell about wine! Maybe His Majesty Ramesses, may he live forever, more often has the opportunity to enjoy the taste of wines from abroad, because he is a king, and besides, he is closer to commercial ports. Unfortunately, this rarity does not reach us here, although it used to be different. Apparently, in the old tombs are representations of the emissaries of the Keftiu people[58], who bring such wine, but then the king resided here. Have you seen these scenes?"

"I didn't see," Pa-Shu-uben had to admit. "I don't like walking around the cemetery, especially among those old graves. Now, the tombs present something different from everyday life paintings that were painted in the past. The only themes of today's paintings are life in the Underworld, which is the same as they also show on the papyri of the *Book of Going Out by Day*. I had the

---

[57] The name of the Mediterranean Sea.

[58] The name of the inhabitants of Crete, with which the Pharaohs State had commercial contacts.

opportunity to see it myself during several funeral ceremonies in which I participated, saying goodbye to my friends."

"Exactly," Pa-nehsi took up, "how good you reminded me... Probably because of your position, which you had before you came to Waset, you also had the opportunity to attend the funeral ceremony of Ramesses Nefer-Ka-Re, justified. Have you been inside such a tomb? Have you seen what is in it?"

"Indeed, I attended the ceremony and stood so close to the entrance that I saw a large fragment of the first corridor. There, the decoration is as colorful as in the houses of eternity of dignitaries in which I was, but all the images that are there look completely different; from the hymn that was sung there, I conclude that they depict various forms of Re…"

Pa-shu-uben paused, because at that moment Pa-nehsi put the reed away from his mouth and, leaning back, started laughing loudly, "Forms of Re! But, dear Pa-shu-uben, I don't ask what is painted there! I don't care! I would like to know what they brought there during the funeral, that is, they brought and left it and where does it all lie?"

Only now Pa-Shu-uben realized what his superior was aiming for and what the purpose of the whole conversation was.

"Your Highness, I am asking for forgiveness, but apparently, the wine has suppressed my thoughts. I understand, of course. I know what was being brought there, because I had to take care of the porters' safety during the whole journey to the Great Valley! And there were probably a thousand of them, they walked in long ranks, carrying various chests, gilded statues, beds on which the king's mummy had previously lay, a lot of things. Others carried the walls and roofs of several chapels that were to be built around the sarcophagi - all this was upholstered in gold. Of course, the coffin of Osiris itself – even richer. The largest group of porters carried the small coffin and they changed frequently; it had to be very heavy, probably whole made of gold..."

"Gold from Kush," Pa-nehsi said. "What else did they bring there?"

"I can't name everything, I don't know what was in all these boxes. But all this was very, very valuable. I don't know exactly where it is, because I couldn't enter the tomb anymore – the temple police, who was subject to Amen-hotep, guarded everything there. But I remember that I once saw a part of the archives that the Royal Necropolis Scribe looks after. Chari was looking for some papyri, took them one by one from the shelves, partially unrolled and watched. I stood by - we talked much more often than we did now. At one point, when he unrolled another scroll, he looked it and showed me. There was a plan of a royal tomb, one of the Ramesses[59]. I remember that he even explained to me how to read this plan. A long straight corridor ran there, it could have 100 cubits or more, and then a large hall with a marked sarcophagi and those wooden chapels all around. Several smaller rooms, that's all. If all the graves look the same, then everything that was brought into the grave of Ramesses Nefer-Ka-Re must be in these corridors and halls. Osiris-shaped coffins certainly lie one inside the other inside a large stone sarcophagi covered with a heavy lid. I remember maybe a year before the

---

[59] At the Egyptian Museum in Turin there is a plan of the tomb of Ramesses IV sketched on papyrus.

funeral, these stones were transported to the grave. It lasted at least 10 days, and probably 200 people pulled the ropes. They are so big and heavy that it is hard to imagine that they could be broken; it would probably take an entire army. Indeed, royal mummies are perfectly protected."

Pa-nehsi took a larger sip of wine, moved and repeated something indistinctly, and when Pa-shu-uben paused, directing a questioning look at the General, he said loudly, "You say very interesting things, Pa-shu-uben. So, the entrances to the tombs resemble gates in temples?"

"Not all of them, Your Grandness. The Great Valley is vast. I was only in its front part, where there are tombs of several Ramesses and where also now they are preparing the tomb for His Majesty, may he live forever! Older graves are hidden in further parts of the Valley, from the south. I haven't been there, but most of the *medjayu* of Djehuty-mes hangs there. He certainly knows about everyone, of course, but he won't say anything, even interrogated with stick and *menen*. His son Buteh-Amun is probably already well versed. He is also a very faithful servant of Amen-hotep, but he has a young wife and he recently had a child…"

Pa-nehsi looked at the speaker appreciatively, but mischievously asked, "Do you see, Pa-Shu-uben, any connection between the location of the royal tombs and the family happiness of Buteh-Amun?" and they both began to laugh.

Further conversation was interrupted by a Kushite soldier who announced that the messenger had just arrived, who brought from Pi-Ramesse a letter from His Majesty King Ramesses to General Pa-nehsi.

"This is probably another letter of greeting and words of concern, is everything going well in the City and are the works on the tomb of His Majesty going well?" Pa-nehsi didn't seem worried. "From what you tell me, I conclude that all roads north are well guarded and that only the right messengers with the right news go to the King from here?"

"I assure you, Your Highness, that since General Pi-ankh wrote that the two men with the letter from Amen-hotep arrived at Pi-Ramesse, I tripled all the guards that guard the roads day and night and check all those who depart from here north by ship."

"But Amen-hotep is also clever and has very loyal people," Pa-nehsi murmured as Pa-shu-uben headed toward the exit to meet the messenger. When he saw him, he had the impression that he had seen this young man once. He quickly was running with his thoughts through the nooks and crannies of his memories – he had the talent to remember the faces of everyone with whom he had contact even for a short while.

"I think he was accompanied by that pretty girl, the daughter of the tenant Djed-Muth-iuf-anch," he said, thinking about meeting quite distant in time. He asked the messenger for a letter, checked the address and found that the royal titles imprinted on the clay had not been violated.

"Wait here," he commanded, "Maybe His Dignity Pa-nehsi would like to ask you a question," and without delay he took the scroll to the dictator. The General once again read his name and inspected the seals, then tore them and unrolled the papyrus.

The first four lines were filled by the official titles of Ramesses, listing all five names, which was very rare even on temples. This fact disturbed the General, and when he read the next words, his face changed: *"Royal order for..."* here was the enumeration of his own titles. There was no greeting, no awaited gracious inquiries about how he was doing, the City and its inhabitants, only the official command! Pa-nehsi read the whole thing again and again, rolled up the papyri, stood up and began walking nervously around the chamber. He stopped, read the whole letter again, and threw it furiously on the floor:

"So, it is like that, okay, wait..." he said to himself through clenched teeth.

Pa-Shu-uben stood pale, afraid that by some reckless word he would cause another burst up of this man, whose height reached only to his shoulder, but his position exceeded his head and that this burst up could turn against him, if only because that no one else was here.

Finally, the General remembered his existence, stood right in front of him and glared at him with reproach, "Triple guards, day and night...and yet someone had to get to the King!" Then he picked up the papyrus and once again, this time loudly, read the entire letter:

"Horus: Mighty-Bull Beloved-By-Re; Two Patrons: With-Mighty-Strength-Which-Smites-Hundreds-Of-Thousands-People; Golden name: With-Great-Strength-He-Who- Revives-Both-Countries,Majesty-Whose-Heart-Enjoys-Presence-Of-Maat-And-

Which-Provides-Peace-In-Both-Countries; King of Both Realms: Re-Which-Maintains-Maat, Chosen-By-Ptah; Son of Re: Ramesses-Shiny-In-Waset, Beloved-By-Amun, God-Who-Rules-In-Iunu, may he live in happiness and health!"

Royal order to the Royal Son of Kush, Royal Army Scribe, Granary Supervisor, Pharaoh's Troop Commander, Pa-nehsi, regarding the following:

This letter with a royal order was given to you to tell you that I had sent Ines - the Head of the Palace and faithful servant of Pharaoh - and that he had been entrusted with tasks from Pharaoh, his Lord, with whom he was sent to perform it in the southern districts of the country. As soon as this letter from Pharaoh, your Lord, reaches you, you will join him to carry out these tasks from Pharaoh, his Lord, with which he was sent. You have to see this wooden portable platform for the Great Goddess, to finish its processing, to load it on a barge and to make that under his supervision it would come to the place where I am. You also have to make that the following things will come: the colorful decorative stones herset, khenemet, iunkhur, ismair, as well as katcha flowers and khesebedj[60], in great numbers here to the place where my person is, that the artisans would be provided with all this. Don't be reluctant to this task I'm sending you! Look, I wrote to you to instruct you. This letter is to make you know that the King and my Palace are in good shape and healthy.[61]

---

[60] The names of the various minerals listed in this (authentic) letter; among others *herset* means red cornelian (carnelian), *khesebedj* - blue lazurite (lapis lazuli), and *khenemet* some type of jasper.

[61] This is a literal quote from the original letter of King Ramesses XI to the dictator Pa-nehsi, preserved on papyri at the Egyptian Museum in

Pa-nehsi finished, then rolled the papyrus neatly into a roll this time and added, "All clear! Pharaoh simply recommends me to leave the City, naturally with the army, which I will not leave alone, and only to help Ines near Abu with the transport of some barge and decorative stones! What a nonsense! Really, Ramesses could come up with something smarter! Craftsmen work constantly and everywhere, and no one has ever needed my help to supply them with stones! I have no illusions: this faithful smoothie of Ramesses, Ines, never liked me...after all, he had to sail through the City to Abu, but he did not even bother to visit me! Now, he is waiting for me with another letter from which I will probably find out that I am no longer the Vizier or the Head of the Granaries, and maybe I am no longer the Royal Son of Kush! Certainly Amen-hotep is behind all this; I swear to Horus from Miam and Behen that he will pay me for it!"

Pa-nehsi raised his right hand in a gesture in which priests used to call the magical power during religious ceremonies and held it for a long time, moving lips as if uttering a terrible spell. Finally, he lowered his hand, controlled himself and looking at Pa-Shu-uben, he asked:

"Who and how could take the Amen-hotep's letter to Pi-Ramesse?"

"Maybe this messenger knows something," the other one said. "I told him to wait just in case!"

"You did it perfectly, bring him right now!" Pa-nehsi was <u>completely calm and sat down again, still holding the King's letter</u>

Turin.

in his hand. The messenger should not guess that this letter made such an impression on him. However, when he saw Suti-mes coming in, he grew slightly pale: he immediately recognized the young priest whom he had once honored by conversation. Therefore, now, trying to smile, he asked him friendly, "I think I've seen you before. Weren't you the one who escorted me to the gates of Ipet-sut recently when I was a guest at the August First Servant Amen-hotep? How are you called?"

"I'm Suti-mes. Yes, Lord, it was me."

"Ah, how nice to see you again!" Pa-nehsi exclaimed and smiled again. "Just tell me how is it possible that we met in the eastern City recently, and today you brought a letter from the King from Pi-Ramesse? It's so far…"

"His Highness the High Priest of Amun wanted to send me with his letter to His Majesty and I went that same night," Suti-mes said.

Pa-nehsi, with an eloquent look on Pa-Shu-uben, said, "Oh, yes, of course, I understand. So, you saw His Majesty Ramesses, may he live forever! How is he?"

"I was not lucky enough to see the Majesty of Pharaoh himself, but I passed the letter to the General, Fan Bearer, who assured me that he would pass it on to the King and from whom I later received the letter that I brought here."

Suti-mes this time looked directly into the eyes of Pa-nehsi, therefore he noticed that the General exchanged quick glances with Pa-shu-uben, and this immediately put in his question, "Was it General Pi-ankh?"

"No, it was General Heri-Hor."

"Ah, Pa-Shu-uben, what's the difference which of the Fan Bearers forwarded this letter to?" Pa-nehsi looked rebukingly as if to indicate that he was in charge of this conversation. "It is important that His Majesty deigned to answer. Thank you, Suti-mes, for your effort and the favor you gave me, and of course the High Priest Amen-hotep, at whom you have probably already been?"

"No, Your Eminence, I was told that the letter is very urgent, and I should go straight to Your Grandness with it," Suti-mes replied, but at that moment he understood that he had made a mistake, for apart from a quick exchange of glances between Pa-nehsi and Pa-shu-uben he saw the smile of relaxation on the dictator's face.

"If so, it's great, you'll take to Amen-hotep a letter from me. Wait!" General said and at his sign Suti-mes left the room.

"Is Your Highness really going to write to Amen-hotep?" Pa-Shu-uben asked.

"You must be kidding me," Pa-nehsi looked clearly disappointed at the lack of guesswork from his subordinate. "Amen-hotep will get an accurate message from me in time, much better than a letter. Now I will write only to our friend Pen-nesti-tawy, because..."

"Your Grandness reads my thoughts," Pa-shu-uben said.

"...Amen-hotep shouldn't know too soon that I got a letter from the King." Pa-nehsi finished.

Meanwhile, the duty soldier led Suti-mes to the courtyard, where there were many similar half-naked Kushite archers and javelinists, probably the entire unit. Some were squatting in groups, eating bread, onions and some fish laid on the mat. Others, apparently after the meal, were sitting or laying in the shade of the nearby temple. There were also those who were apparently on duty at the moment, as they stood motionless along the walls of the palace with their arches and spears prepared for use in the event of an alarm. Suddenly Suti-mes noticed how from the inner gate separating the western part of the district, where, among others, the well-known house of Djehuty-mes and Buteh-Amun was situated, several soldiers were approaching, leading a donkey laden with travel bags and some poor-looking old man who was brandishing with his hands and he seemed to be strongly protesting against something. As they approached, Suti-mes heard the man shouting that he had been assaulted and asking for a just judgment, "...to restore Maat, which the soldiers do not know," he pointed to those who led him. Suti-mes came closer, like many Kushite soldiers who were in the courtyard and from the broken sentences still shouted by the old man understood that he was arrested when on a narrow path where he was riding on his donkey to exchange his goods on the market, he drove across the tunic of one of the Kushite archers, whom he had previously begged in vain to free him and remove his tunic for a moment.

"He was detained for such foolishness?" Suti-mes said, convinced that everything would be clear in a moment and old man would leave.

Pa-Shu-uben appeared in the doorway, holding a papyrus letter in his hand. At the sight of the concourse, he stopped and listened to the accounts of the old man and the soldiers who brought him.

"He said that the Kushite soldiers did not know Maat," one of them said.

When Pa-Shu-uben heard it, he said, "Then show him how the accusation of soldiers ends. Take his donkey, give him 50 strokes of a palm branch and banish him!"

After which, ignoring the old man's screams, he began looking for Suti-mes. Seeing him and seeing that he had witnessed the whole incident, he turned to him with a smile, "Of course, this old man was right, but now there are times that one can't annoy Kushite guests, because the City owes them peace and Maat."

Suti-mes stood speechless: this dignitary mocked justice...

"As a priest, I do not agree with this understanding of Maat: it is wicked to beat and rob an innocent man and rely on Maat - God's law that protects every man!" he burst out.

"But Maat is also the patron of a state that guards everyone else. And soldiers and dignitaries stand guard over the state. For them, Maat is different," Pa-Shu-uben replied with a smile, then added seriously in his voice, "Like all the inhabitants of Waset, this old man is officially assured Maat, having the right to go to a complaint, even to the King himself."

"And how will he get there if they took his donkey?" Suti-mes was very agitated.

"He probably won't make it, he will probably die soon and meet his Maat. For some people, it's even better because they have less trouble. Anyway, does anyone know the day of his death? Even you, though young, cannot be sure if you will see Re tomorrow...here is a letter to the High Priest Amen-hotep, rolled up with a command to the Great Gate guard in Ipet-sut to let you pass quickly; His Eminence Pa-nehsi told me that he cares so that you don't waste time, therefore you will take my boat."

Suti-mes felt very disappointed because he did not intend to go to Ipet-sut immediately. From the two important writings he had with him, it was only because of this that he first decided to hand over the letter to Pa-nehsi, because here, in Khefet-her-neb-es, Henut lived, to whom his heart wanted to get. He thought that he would give it to someone from the dictator's people, and then stand near his beloved's house, hoping that he might see her for a moment, though from afar, and only then cross the river and go to Amen-hotep. Now, Pa-Shu-uben spoiled all these plans for him. The dignitary also saw Suti-mes hesitating.

"What, you probably wanted to go to the girl?" he asked, as if reading his thoughts. "Is this the beauty I've seen you with? Indeed, Suti-mes, God rewarded you... but you understand that Maat, which you spoke of with such expert knowledge today, requires that you postpone your private affairs. So, hit the road and don't forget to send Amen-hotep the words of my love..."

Suti-mes thought the word "love" in this thick-skinned brutal man sounded very false, and he felt a great urge to move away from him now, which he could only achieve by going to Ipet-sut. In addition, he unfortunately, had to admit that what Pa-Shu-uben said about the need to postpone private affairs is somewhat right: he was a royal messenger.

"I will go near Henut's house tomorrow," he thought and allowed himself to be led to the marina, where next to the long-unused royal barge, elegant ships belonging to Pa-nehsi and several important dignitaries living on this side of the river, like Pa-uer-aa or Djehuty-mes, the Pa-Shu-uben's boat stood, always ready to go. The soldier who escorted him instructed the captain to sail straight to the main harbor in Ipet-sut and they would move on shortly.

They sailed for some time along the canal, after which the refreshing wind, which blew out the sails, made the thoughtful priest aware that they were already on the river. The harbor at Ipet-sut was approaching quickly. Holding in one hand a rolled and sealed papyrus from Pa-nehsi, Suti-mes instinctively checked with the other whether a leather case with King Ramesses's letter to Amun's First Servant was still lying safely in the inside tunic pocket. After a while, the boat moored to the waterfront, the Captain and Suti-mes stepped up the gangway onto a stone bridge, from where a road framed by ram-headed lions led straight to the Great Gate visible from far away, from which peaks of the huge colonnade of the Hall of Appearance was visible. Temple guards stood outside the gate, but Suti-mes saw no one of his acquaintance among them. When asked about the purpose of the visit, the captain announced that a messenger had arrived from His Grandness the Royal Son of Kush, General Pa-nehsi with a letter to His Grandness the First Servant of Amun, Amen-hotep, and added that he had the order that the gatekeeper of the Great Gate Pen-nesti-tawy personally accompanied the guest.

After a while, the door in the Great Gate opened and a short man with Kushite features appeared, whose small and bloodshot eyes indicated a passion for wine. Pen-nesti-tawy was clearly dissatisfied, because at this time he was just resting, so he barely responded to the greeting of Suti-mes, who gave him the papyrus received from Pa-shu-uben. Pen-nesti-tawy found his name in the place where the recipient was mentioned, opened the scroll and began to read. If Suti-mes looked closely, he would probably be surprised, for there was no other letter inside and everything he brought was solely addressed to the guard of the Great Gate. However, the young man was with his thoughts on the other side of the river, and he was not in the habit of watching someone read a letter addressed to himself. Facing Khefet-her-neb-es, he looked at the sky covered with bloody light today and the darkening strip of arable fields on the other bank, behind which the village hid, and in it one particularly important house for him...

It was only the dry voice of the doorkeeper, who ordered Suti-mes to follow him that pulled him out of his dreams. As the young priest walked, he was still thinking about Henut, and that is probably why he did not wonder why, after passing through the second door in the Great Gate instead of going straight through the large Hall of Appearances filled with columns to the right towards the palace of Amen-hotep, Pen-nesti-tawy turned into left, where the high wall of the district blackened, completely shaded at this time. Right at the gate, Suti-mes saw another narrow passage in the wall toward which the doorman apparently led him. It was only now that he was awake, and he wanted to ask Pen-nesti-tawy walking in front of him why they were actually moving away from the target but at the same time that one turned round and Suti-mes felt the narrow blade of the dagger sticking into his side, and soon in the chest at the height of the heart. Pen-nesti-tawy pushed him so that, losing his consciousness, Suti-mes fell on his back, hitting his head against the base of the wall, and then he froze. Pen-nesti-tawy walked over him, then panting, dragged him to the end of the passage in the wall, and kicked the low wooden door open, then pushed the still body through it. There was a splash of water in the narrow branch of the canal that ran along the wall of the precinct forming a kind of moat. The Overseer of the Great Gate quickly backed away, wiped the bloody dagger on the patch of grass, and hid it again in the folds of his tunic. The captain of Pa-Shu-uben's boat was waiting at the crossing. Pen-nesti-tawy took a letter from Pa-nehsi and wrote underneath: "It was made according to the order," then folded the papyrus, stuck it with clay and stamped a seal on it with his ring.

"Please, send to Pa-Shu-uben my greetings and say that I led the messenger to the right place."

When the boat sailed away, Pen-nesti-tawy slowly climbed the stairs inside the Great Gate, heading for his room, then returned quietly to the not finished jug of wine.

CHAPTER VII

At the same time, the High Priest was walking around his chamber in the palace not much more than 100 cubits away from the Great Gate. It was getting dark, so he ordered to light a few lamps, which cast flickering light on the walls, bringing the characters there to life. His gaze instinctively wandered to the wall where the scene was, which evoked Pa-nehsi's comments, and of which he was particularly proud: raising his hands in a gesture of joy, he receives a magnificent gold necklace as a royal prize.

Amen-hotep delved into memories. It was certainly the greatest day of his life, a great triumph and payment for the many works he did in the Temple of Amun, above all for the magnificent gate in the southern wall of the Great Column Hall, through which processions were going to and from the distant temple in Ipet-resit, as well as the nearby precincts of Mut Lady of Asheru and of Khonsu in Waset Nefer-hotep. Then, in the tenth year of his reign, His Majesty Ramesses Nefer-Ka-Re as the first pharaoh himself passed through this gate during the Feast of Ipet, and a few days later, he also wanted to see how the work on his tomb in the Great Valley was progressing. He, Amun's First Servant, Amen-hotep, not only accompanied the King every day of his long visit to the City. As the host, he was also responsible for the peace of his sleep and the pleasure of his meals. Moreover, he also had to take care of the good mood of all very high dignitaries who came with Pharaoh and their servants as well as servants of those servants. His Majesty also wanted to know if the warehouses in the City are well stocked, whether the inhabitants are not, as before, harassed by the desert attackers, whether the crop harvesting system is efficient and whether there is no problem with transferring the part due to Pharaoh to Pi-Ramesse. If His Majesty stated that any of these tasks were improperly supervised, he would have the right to punish him, express his dissatisfaction and, after returning to the residence, send him orders that would result from this dissatisfaction. Meanwhile, in the third month of Akhet, when His Majesty had returned to Pi-Ramesse, his emissaries and high servants of the Palace came to the City: Nes-Amun, Nefer-ka-Re-em-Per-Amun and the Royal Treasurer Amen-hotep who in the courtyard in front of the Great Gate of Ipet-sut to all residents of the City announced that the King sends to Amun's First Servant a great reward: gold and silver vessels, gold necklaces, gold nuggets in bags and vessels with the best grade of oil and that Amen-hotep is to continue to oversee the collection of taxes due and their proper distribution between the temple of Amun and the royal palace…

"It was a great King and great times," the High Priest sighed. Then it was only worse. Worse harvest came, unfortunately also reappeared bandits attacking residents in the Waset region. People talked about them incorrect "Tjehenu" but only because here in the Southern Country no one saw the real Tjehenu and those unknown foreigners, often depicted in scenes where the pharaoh kills enemies, could easily personify all "bad" and "strangers" of which these bands consisted. In the Northern Country Tjehenu were well known, and no one was afraid of them, while the term: Kushites could foment fear there, although it was certainly easier to find a Kushite in Memphis or Pi-Ramesse than a Tjehenu in Waset. Because of the fear of those bands that the temple police could not cope with, craftsmen working on decorations in the King's tomb often stayed in their town, which upset Vizier Kha-em-Waset very much. He decided to limit and even temporarily suspend the payment of their food rations. Famine began to face unhappy people. Amen-hotep remembered how one day the mayor of Khefet-her-neb-es Pa-uer-aa came to him and showed him a complaint from the town:

"Year 13, the first month of the season of Akhet, day four. We did not work today, although there is no one around Tjehenu, because we have not received our rations yet for the third month of the season of Shemu, nor for the fourth month of the season of Shemu, nor for five days at the end of the year, nor for the first month of the season of Akhet!"

Amen-hotep settled the dispute at that time, the workers received their overdue remuneration, but the Vizier Kha-em-Waset did not like the First Servant ever since, and he hated the

Mayor Pa-uer-aa, whom Amen-hotep asked for more frequent visits to the town of craftsmen and reporting on the moods prevailing there. When Kha-em-Waset found out about this, he appointed the scribe Pa-Shu-uben as his representative in the town, who now kept a special book there, scrupulously recording who and when went to work in the tomb, as well as who and what said, especially about the Vizier. Amen-hotep decided that since the workers were working in the royal tomb in the Great Valley, which, together with all the temples, was under the authority of the High Priest, it was him who had the right to order them to work or, when he deemed it necessary, release them from the obligation to go to the Great Valley. On the other hand, Vizier Kha-em-Waset believed that since he, on behalf of the King, pays them food rations, he also has the right to decide about their work. Out of sheer malice, he was stopping payment from time to time, to which the craftsmen responded with a strike, and the High Priest supported them. The Vizier, who received continuous reports from Pa-Shu-uben, then sent letters to the King complaining about Amen-hotep, while the High Priest was mentioning about the malice of Kha-em-Waset in his letters. The king saw that senior officials in the City did not like each other, but he did not react. So, the years went by, and in the 16th year of the reign of His Majesty Ramesses Nefer-Ka-Re a new row broke out. Vizier Kha-em-Waset learned from Pa-Shu-uben that he overheard the conversation of several workers, which showed that some royal tomb was reportedly a victim of robbers. Kha-em-Waset triumphantly notified the Major of the Western City in whose territory this crime was to take place. Pa-uer-aa did not believe that such a thing could have happened, but he set up a special commission that visited ten royal tombs lying outside the Great Valley, especially on the northern edges of the cemetery, where people rarely hang around, and also *medjayu* rarely visited. The result of this trip was an unpleasant surprise for both Pa-uer-aa and Amen-hotep: Kha-em-Waset was right! One grave was found to be completely robbed and, in addition, burned, and the thieves were already approaching another tomb with the help of a tunnel that was boring from one of the neighboring graves of officials. A vigorous investigation was initiated and, of course, the guilty parties were found, brought to justice, convicted and executed, and many Waset residents watched the execution. Vizier's name, Kha-em-Waset, became a terror since then, and Pa-shu-uben benefited most of all, because the Vizier appointed him as the head of police and Inspector of Hidden Affairs in Waset. His Majesty Ramesses Nefer-Ka-Re was already very sick then and soon died. His solemn funeral in the Great Valley after bringing the embalmed body from Pi-Ramesse was the last great ceremony involving the King, though already dead, which the City saw. None of his successors: neither His Majesty Ramesses Kheper-Maat-Re, justified, nor His Majesty Ramesses Men-Maat-Re – may he live forever – never came there. When the first one took the throne, the workers began, as usual, to carve out his tomb in the Great Valley, but immediately afterward, Kha-em-Waset stopped their payment again and it all began from the beginning: workers strike, letters of complaint... the High Priest Amen-hotep was very nervous because he had the impression that the Vizier even wanted the work on the royal tomb to be completely stopped. Workers complained, as before:

We are weak and hungry, because we do not receive our rations, which we have granted from Pharaoh!

Amenhotep again asked the Vizier for charity, but Kha-em-Waset insisted that the workers were on strike for no reason. When they finally got persuaded and resumed work, although they did not obtained due products, Amen-hotep told them to stop and not let be exploited. Then Pa-shu-uben appeared in the town, asking why they were not listening to the Vizier.

"Let the Vizier carry the beams alone!" one of the carpenters shouted, and something like this had never happened before! It is not known what fate would befall the miserable who dared to say and even shout such a thing, if not for unexpected news came, that surprised everyone, "Pharaoh died!" Vizier Kha-em-Waset went to Pi-Ramesse as soon as he found out.

This time there was no question of the King's body resting in the Great Valley: his grave was very far from the condition in which it could be quickly prepared for the funeral and even 70 days needed for embalming the body would not be enough to finish even the necessary decoration. So, the funeral took place at Pi-Ramesse, and then the young successor appeared on the throne of the forefather, Son of Re, Ramesses Men-Maat-Re Sechep-en-Ptah, may he live! Probably Kha-em-Waset had the opportunity to discuss the situation in the City with him before the solemn coronation took place. Amen-hotep had no doubt that during this conversation Vizier accused him of everything that was wrong in the City and what had happened in recent years: artisan strikes, not completing the royal tomb and robberies in cemeteries. He had to add to this many other accusations, which were false and resulted from jealousy: Kha-em-Waset could not bear that it was not him, but Amen-hotep and his family hold the most important posts: tax collection and grain inventory management. He obstructed him as much as he could, probably hoping that he would obtain from the new Pharaoh the position of the Granary Manager of the Southern Country and for this, he went to Pi-Ramesse. Meanwhile, the new King also surprised him and chose the General Pa-nehsi, who led the entire southern army corps, consisting almost exclusively of mercenary Kushites. Pa-nehsi came to Waset as the Head of the Granaries, the Vizier and the Royal Son of Kush, and an army came with him.

"His Majesty made a terrible mistake then," Amen-hotep said to himself loudly, "But it was already 17 years ago and then Pa-nehsi and his soldiers did not feel so unpunished. And today, truly, the barge of Re has disappeared on the western horizon, there is less and less hope, and Ramesses is still doing nothing. At least to know if Suti-mes reached him with my letter..." Amen-hotep returned to his daily thoughts about today, how different from the one shown on the wall of the palace and shining with the light of its former splendor!

A sudden noise, unusual for the peace and quiet of this chamber, especially at this time, roused him out of the consideration. He heard someone running around here, someone's voices were raised in the background. The chamber door opened and the running man almost bumped into the High Priest.

"My lord!" the priest on duty shouted, catching his breath. "A murder has been committed in Ipet-sut! One of the priests went out of need beyond the walls and then heard someone falling into the canal, several dozen of cubits from him. He ran there and saw a corpse in the water, which he pulled ashore. This man had to be killed a moment earlier because he was bleeding heavily. With the help of the guards, he brought the body to the temple and then another priest met this man and said that it was our Suti-mes! They brought him to the palace courtyard and there he lies…"

"Amun!" Amen-hotep moaned and ran out of the room. When he reached the courtyard, he saw a group of guards and priests bent over a lying body. One of them was kneeling, putting his ear to the lying breast. When Amen-hotep arrived, he saw that it was his personal doctor, Sunu, who was happily there when the body was brought. For a moment, the High Priest stood motionless, pale and alone on the verge of fainting, waiting in great tension for the verdict that the investigator's first words were to bring. Everyone else did not even speak in a whisper, and in this absolute silence, only the high boring cicadas singing from the Holy Lake was heard.

"He's still alive," Sunu finally said, raising his head, "But he lost a lot of blood and I don't know yet if he can be treated!"

At the words that left a little hope, Amen-hotep felt that life was coming back to him as if he had lifted his leg from the abyss at the last moment. Now, he only noticed that he had for this young priest not only sympathy but even paternal affection. "Sunu," he turned to the doctor, "Please do everything…"

He didn't have to say that at all: Sunu was one of the best specialists in his profession throughout Kemet. The wounded one was moved to the nearest kitchen room, where a longitudinal wide bench stood, and besides, there were numerous vessels with water. A soaked and bloody tunic was cut and removed from him so that the doctor could examine the wounds thoroughly and then found a thick leather papyrus case hidden in the inside pocket. This pouch saved Suti-mes, for the dagger, which was very accurately pointed and held with a skilled hand, pierced him, but did not reach his heart, only inflicting a shallow wound. The second wound at waist height was much worse, deep, and it caused such heavy bleeding. Although the blood stopped already flowing, the doctor examined it for a very long time, silently uttering some mysterious words only known to him.

Finally, he stood up and said a formula that brought everyone real relief, "This is the disease I will treat.[62]", but he added, "It's too early for joy, though there is hope. If he survives, he will have to lie down for a long time; the treatment will last for several months if," Sunu repeated the word with emphasis, "the patient survives. Everything in Amun's hands."

The High Priest breathed a sigh of relief. He believed that since God had put an obstacle in the path of the assassin's dagger, he would also direct the head and hand of an experienced Sunu and strengthen the young body of the sick one.

However, referring to what his doctor had just said, he addressed everyone present with a clear order, emphasizing that this was a matter of great importance, "No one is allowed to say

---

[62] The doctor, after examining the patient, spoke a formula that included an assessment of the chance of recovery; when the patient was in a hopeless condition, the doctor stated that "this is a disease that I will not treat".

that Suti-mes was found and he is alive. Let those who wanted to kill him think that this is what happened, and his friends should not know the truth yet, especially those who live in Khefet-her-neb-es: Buteh-Amun, and also Henut, a girlfriend of Suti-mes. Especially she, because her eyes could tell someone that suffering does not live in her heart. Besides, we don't know yet if he will recover! It is a miracle that he lives at all…"

The High Priest again remembered how close it was that the crime had been committed and how little it would have been that nobody would have discovered it. It was only at this time that Amen-hotep reached into the leather case and took out only a slightly damaged letter, on which was a well-known royal seal. So Suti-mes brought Ramesses' reply, by which he was to die, and which actually saved his life. But what was the answer? The High Priest once again turned to Sunu to entrust him with all efforts for Suti-mes, and then went to his chamber, ordering the servants to inform Amen-em-Ipet that he wished to see him immediately. Holding in his hand the letter for which he had waited so long, he realized that this letter may carry a message that would completely change the situation of the City, and perhaps his own. He expected this and was afraid that the King would once again disregard his appeals; did he not inform Ramesses in previous years that the situation was getting worse and that the great power of Pa-nehsi was becoming dangerous? But is it possible for Pharaoh not to react to the last letter? Amen-hotep delayed tearing the seal. He wanted to know the truth, having a trusted advisor beside him and waited impatiently for his coming. Finally, Amen-em-Ipet has come, who had already found out about Suti-mes in the palace of the High Priest: he was passing through the courtyard when a wounded one was carried from the kitchen to a special chamber and Sunu gave him a brief account.

"So, this expected day has come!" Amen-em-Ipet said the words instead of the greeting, and Amen-hotep already knew that he did not have to spend time explaining.

Amen-em-Ipet looked at the letter, still sealed but pierced with a dagger, nodded and added, "Really, man is clay and straw in God's hands! This boy is enjoying the special grace of Amun! Someone was very involved that he could not get to Your Eminence, and this letter will probably reveal to us why," and gave the papyrus to the First Servant, who first looked into his deputy's eyes for a moment, as if seeking confirmation for the act of courage, which the breaking the royal seal was, and finally with one move he tore it and began to read. King Ramesses acknowledged receipt of the letter, and with him news that saddened him and prompted him to send to Pa-nehsi an order to leave Waset and go to Abu. There, the Head of the Palace Ines will give him another letter, which will only leave him the function of General and Royal Son of Kush. Soon new officials will come to the City: Un-nefer, who is to take over the duties of a Vizier, and the Treasurer Men-Maat-Re-nakht, who will act as Head of the Granaries. In addition, the King instructs Amen-hotep to ensure that work on the royal tomb goes smoothly. Pa-Shu-uben and the *medjayu* police are to watch over the safety of the inhabitants after the Kushite army's departure. The letter ended with an assurance that the King was healthy. Amen-hotep finished reading and looked at Amen-em-Ipet again:

"It seems that Ramesses has no idea who Pa-Shu-uben is, and there is neither the time nor the conditions to send another letter in this matter. We will have to tolerate this man!"

"I think," replied Amen-em-Ipet, "that after Pa-nehsi's departure he will become small, despite his height and weight. The only question is, will Pa-nehsi really go away?"

"He will probably not risk the war with the King?" the High Priest asked this question, though he knew he did not know the answer. "His hatred towards me can drive him to do terrible things. Indeed, as long as he is in the City, Ipet-sut is not safe, despite its magnitude…"

He looked through the window at the majestic columns of the Hall of Appearances lit by the cold moonlight and he felt permeated chill.

CHAPTER VIII

The next days passed peacefully as if nothing had happened. Amen-hotep even began to wonder whether the announced letter of His Majesty Ramesses to Pa-nehsi has even arrived. Maybe the king sent him through someone else and the other messenger is still on his way? This was unlikely, and besides, if Suti-mes was going straight to Ipet-sut, who would care if he died? He must have known something that Pa-nehsi wanted to hide from the High Priest, so it was probably he who delivered the letter to the dictator. Unfortunately, Suti-mes was still unconscious, on the verge of life and death, and Sunu did not hide that he is probably closer to death. The wounded one lay feverous, it was not known if his heart and head would withstand this fever, and if so, would he not starve because he did not eat any food. Amen-hotep was also tormented by the question, who in Ipet-sut dealt a traitorous blow to Suti-mes? The place where the wounded one was found indicated that he had already passed through the Great Gate and therefore, someone had to attack him in the Hall of Appearances. The thought that the murderer was hiding so close to the High Priest's palace did not give him peace, but he could not order an investigation, because it would immediately come out that he knew about the assassination, and it was necessary to pretend that he was unaware.

Meanwhile, Amen-em-ipet instructed trusted people to observe all marches of the Kushite units, as well as the ships of Pa-nehsi's fleet. Indeed, after a few days, he was reported to have intensified traffic around these ships: smaller boats were still floating there, and then various things were carried from them to the big vessels: sacks, boxes and chariots from which the wheels were removed. This view greatly pleased Amen-hotep as it was a clear sign of preparations for the departure of the army. If they wanted to use these chariots for some military action in the City, they would not have been dismantled. Ten more days passed and then it was noticed that Pa-nehsi's infantry began to get on the big boats, which then moored and began to slowly flow up the river. When they disappeared, Amen-em-Ipet immediately ordered the guards at the great gates of subsequent temples south of the City to report as the fleet passed them. He suspected that Pa-nehsi would only be able to leave nearby to come back unexpectedly. However, incoming reports, which the guards from the high gates transmitted successively using conventional signs, confirmed that Pa-nehsi and his army were moving away. When he passed the temple of Horus in Behdet, Amen-hotep breathed a sigh of relief: the General apparently obeyed the King's orders. On the same day, Pa-shu-uben arrived to the High Priest, assuring him of his readiness to carry out all orders and emphasizing that he was the humble servant of Amun's First Servant. Amen-hotep had to control himself so as not to laugh out loudly; he remembered what Amen-em-Ipet had told him. He thanked for the visit, expressing the alleged regret that General Pa-nehsi had left without saying goodbye. He ordered the Police Chief to ensure that nobody disturbs craftsmen working in the Great Valley and to check if any overdue payment was owed to them. Finally, he asked if Pa-Shu-uben knew anything about the royal messenger that the High Priest had expected and who had not yet arrived from Pi-Ramesse. The Inspector of the City Affairs regretted that, unfortunately, he had no idea, but asked who the messenger was to be? When he heard the name: Suti-mes, he tried to remember something for a long time, finally, he said that he never met anyone with such a name, and because the name is rare, he would certainly remember such a man, because he has a very good memory. The High Priest agreed with this last statement and the conversation was over. Since Pa-Shu-uben received the news that Suti-mes had not arrived from Pi-Ramesse, it was also impossible to investigate the assassination attempt.

"I hope Suti-mes tells me everything if he recovers," Amen-hotep thought, and stopped working on the subject, especially since the Beautiful Feast of the Valley was approaching and he wanted to give it a particularly solemn character. Amen-em-Ipet still reminded that the departure of the army had changed little in the lives of most Waset residents and that they still consider the High Priest to be unjustly taking their taxes this year, leaving too little grain at home. Therefore, the High Priest decided to return to the tenants at least part of the unjustly imposed tax in the form of a "feast prize". The Beautiful Feast of the Valley was an excellent opportunity for this. Of course, he first had to discuss how to conduct this difficult and quite unusual operation with the new Head of the Granaries of the Southern Country, Men-Maat-Re-nakht, who, along with the new Vizier Un-nefer, just arrived in the City. Men-Maat-Re-nakht has ruled out the possibility of moving the royal grain that has entered the warehouses in the same amount as each year.

"Since the grain taken away from the peasants by force is not available and sailed away with Pa-nehsi's army, Your Grandness may, if he has the will, give the taxpayers the supplies from the temple warehouses," he said. Amen-hotep already knew that he would not be able to return to the tenants more than one sack of the four that were taken from them by force. Despite this, he ordered preparations for this operation. The Beautiful Valley Festival was, as usual, very joyful. With the hymns and sounds of thousands of *sesh-sesh*, a flotilla of colorful boats crossed the river and through the channels cut out among the arable fields, moved towards the rocks visible from afar, at whose feet, in Ta-Djeser, were the oldest great temples of the Western City. The main purpose was the chapel of the guardian of the dead and the lady of love Hat-Hor, but Amun's barge spent the night in the Hall on the Barge preceding the shrine of Amun in the temple of Djeser-Djeseru[63].

---

[63] That was the name of the building known today as the temple of Queen Hathshepsut.

From the harbor, sacred images in veil-covered shrines on portable barges were already carried on the shoulders of priests. Along the way, they were joined by local processions from other temples of the Western City. A human river flowed along with the official procession. On this day, probably all residents of the City took part in it because many had some deceased close relatives whose graves they wanted to visit in the Necropolis. Those whose deceased family members had no graves and were buried in the river[64], on that day also connected with them in memory and consumed with them a meal, because the holy images of God present on this side of the river embraced all the dead, both dignitaries and the poorest servants. That night, the Western City was teeming with unique life flashed with thousands lights of torches that were to be extinguished in milk the next morning, was resounding with the echo of tambourines, flutes and pipes, clapping hands, singing and laughing. Although this time there were no special attractions, such as climbing for Min or the participation of acrobatic half-naked dancers during the Ipet festival, the Beautiful Feast of the Valley was very much liked by the residents. The days when Pharaoh himself participated are gone, but the Amun's First Servant also represented him. This time, quite unexpectedly, when the procession was approaching its destination and when it was

---

[64] The number of graves carved in the rocks is very small compared to the entire population of ancient Egypt. Like the mummification process, such graves were limited to the elite layers of society. The local climate perfectly preserves the bodies buried in the sand in the desert, but also such finds are among the exceptions. Everything seems to indicate that the funeral of the vast majority of Egyptians consisted of ceremonial throwing of an unmummified body into the river, which was in line with the popular myth of the death of Osiris - the patron saint of all the dead.

accompanied by the largest crowd, Amen-hotep stopped Amun's great barge and asked in a loud voice whether he could ask God a question. Those who were closest fell silent, but in further groups, the tambourines and clapping were heard for some time until they were silent. Amen-hotep told Amun that this year's harvest was worse, and people had less grain. In this situation, will the Great God agree that from what was collected for him, every tenant of the land of Amun received one sack of grain? At that moment, the priests carrying his barge took one step forward, which meant that God agreed. Amen-hotep thanked Amun warmly, saying that soon after the feast day, his priests would start delivering grain to the homes of tenants. A murmur of wonderment combined with joyful surprise rang out through the crowds. That day everyone was thinking well about the First Servant, but the next day, when the great action of transporting grain sacks from the warehouses at the temple of Ramesses the Great and leaving them in individual homes began, this good mood disappeared. Everyone remembered that he had been taken "out of Amen-hotep's orders" four sacks excessively, and now only one of these four was given back. Few appreciated the gesture of the High Priest and enjoyed the unexpected gift. Many more people were dissatisfied that they get so little, and there were others such as father of Henut, Djed-Mut-iuf-ankh, who cursed Amen-hotep even more, accusing him of "playing with unhappy people, not only robbing them but even expecting them to be grateful." When news of such reactions reached the First Servant, it hurt him and made him realize that the whole idea of at least partial reparation for what Pa-nehsi had done was successful only to a very small extent.

On Amen-em-Ipet's advice, when large warehouses were opened, and grain reserves were taken out, grain was also transported to Ipet-sut.

"Maybe it will never happen, but if someone attacked the temple, we could not defend ourselves for a long time, because our warehouses would be cut off from us," said the old priest to Amen-hotep. On his question, does he allow the thought that someone would raise the sacrilegious hand on the House of Amun, he replied that it had already happened before and not only the temples were robbed of jewelry and their treasuries were emptied, but criminal hands destroyed images and divine names everywhere.[65]

"We should be prepared, and even increase the ranks of our temple police, and ensure that they have adequate supplies of arrows, bows and stones for slings," he added, which seemed exaggerated to Amen-hotep at first. However, he valued the old man's wisdom and insight too much to disregard his comments, so he gave instructions and Ipet-sut was soon better equipped than ever before.

Meanwhile, another month has passed, and people were eagerly awaiting the next flood, hoping that this time Hapi would be abundant, enabling better harvesting. This was the main topic of conversations, but also the prayers addressed to Amun, Min, Osiris and all the divine powers patronizing the abundance

---

[65] Allusion to the so-called Great Heresy during the reign of Akhenaten in the 14th century BC (see table of the history of ancient Egypt).

during the New Year's holiday, which culminated in the five-day preparation period "off the calendar," between the time of Shemu and the season of Akhet. In fact, everything soon began to show that Amun had listened to the people in Waset. Hapi came on time and the water level began to rise steadily, flooding larger and larger areas of the fields. Finally, in the second month of the season of Akhet, it reached the much-desired 16 cubits. In all the houses, there was joy and a great feast of Ipet with a wonderful procession of Amun, who was united with his bride, had a true wedding mood. The construction of the Khonsu temple was resumed with greater willingness. In accordance with Amenhotep's recommendation, the City's residents engaged in agriculture were obliged to work for the King, and a time when the water standing on the fields made agricultural work impossible. Meanwhile, all conversations began to center around the topic of plowing and sowing, which were approaching slowly, although they could only begin after the floodwaters subsided. Then a disaster came suddenly, which not only thwarted all these plans, but was to plunge the City into the abyss of misery and change its fate for a long time.

At dawn on the third day of the third month of the season of Akhet in the 18th year of the rule of His Majesty Ramesses Men-Maat-Re Sechep-en-Ptah, the guards at the top of the Great Gate in Ipet-sut suddenly saw the approaching huge warships sailing straight toward the harbor. They seemed even larger, for they were flowing in the river waters raised a few cubits. In the distance, other ships were sailing straight towards Khefet-her-neb-es, towards the great temples of Ramesses the Great and

Ramesses User-Maat-Re Meri-Amun. As the first ship approached a distance of one rope, from the towers of the gate one could easily recognize the Kushite soldiers standing in full combat readiness, with strung bows, as if preparing to attack. Undoubtedly, the guards of the temple of Amun could ask themselves why their colleagues from the high gate of the temple in Ipet-resit had not sent them signs announcing the approaching of the enemy fleet, which, after all, had to sail from the south for several days. They could also ask each other how they should behave in this situation: raise an alarm. Get ready for defense? There could be even more questions, but all the answers were given by a cloud of arrows that knocked down all of men from the top of towers. The screams and moans of the wounded put the rest of the defenders on standby, and from the walls one answered with equally accurate shots. After a short time, the Kushite ships retreated slightly and moored at the stone pier where the holy barges usually were arriving and from where they were leaving. The gangplanks were lowered, and a group of archers equipped with a large shooting shield took a position in the procession alley between ram-headed lions, blocking the main road leading to the Great Gate. At the same time, numerous infantry troops disembarked from other transport boats, which were deployed by their officers along the walls of the precinct of the temple of Amun, so that they soon formed a tight ring around the precinct, but out of range of arrows from the defenders' bows. The walls of the temple district of His Majesty Ramesses User-Maat-Re Meri-Amun were also surrounded, while the army entered the temple of Ramesses the Great without any problems, killing a few guards and temple servants. In this way, Amun's large warehouses were captured and the same day, the wine accumulated there was distributed among the troops of Pa-nehsi's army.

Pa-nehsi was living himself on one of the ships and was giving orders from there. He was receiving also there his officers and first guests who decided that a visit should be made to the General to assure him of their devotion. Pa-Shu-uben appeared among the first ones. The Inspector of Waset Secret Affairs assured the General that he and many City residents were happy about what had happened, and especially that the old order would return and Amen-hotep would have nothing to say anymore. He also ensured that his subordinate police will stand faithfully on the side of the army.

"There are also many men here who will join your Eminence eagerly because they hate the High Priest," he assured, then added with a smile, "This fool Amen-hotep gave back to every tenant one sack of grain from taxes but did not get back their love."

"I will give back the other three sacks to those who want to be with me. Make all the inhabitants of Waset learn about it as soon as possible," decided Pa-nehsi.

The next morning, the *medjayu* of Pa-Shu-uben, walking from house to house and shouting in the streets, as they always did, when one of the poorer residents of the City died and was to be buried without mummification, they announced that everyone was to be today at noon on the vast grounds in front of the Great Gate of the temple in Ipet-resit. Residents on the west side of the river were to gather in the vast space between the hills and the back of the district of the temple of Ramesses the Great, where all processions usually went. The middle of the day, when it is the hottest time, small children sleep most often, and women prepare a meal, was a very uncomfortable date for meetings, but all the inhabitants of the City have already learned that one shouldn't take chances with the *medjayu* of Pa-shu-uben, or with the Kushite soldiers, so all of them went there: men and women, sometimes leading children by the hand or with babies in scarves next to their breasts. Only the elderly and the sick remained at home. When they came to the designated places, armed soldiers stood around. Pa-nehsi's officers, standing on prepared elevations and surrounded by several army scribes, then read a message prepared by their leader. The General greeted everyone, expressing joy that he is again in the City as a Vizier, Head of the Granaries, King's Son of Kush and Army Commander, and came to bring Maat, that was missing here as a result of the enemy of the Both Countries and the enemy of the beloved King Ramesses, may he live forever! That enemy is Amen-hotep, who sneakily took from people, even the poor ones, four bags of grain beyond what was necessary tax so that there could be even more gold in his palace and temple in Ipet-sut. Now, this enemy is under siege by the army, but to defeat him, everyone needs to help. Everyone who volunteers to join the ranks of Pa-nehsi's army will receive three sacks of grain and a measure of oil. Any woman whose husband or brother serves in Amen-hotep's temple police should report it and she will receive help. The scribes will write down the names of these volunteers, as well as the names of those poor women left behind the walls by those who were tempted by the evil Amen-hotep and serve in the police in Ipet-sut. When the message was read, the scribes began to work, creating name lists of those who applied. There were not many volunteers enrolling in Pa-nehsi's army. Even if someone had a grudge against the High Priest, he didn't have to risk his life right away, even for the price of three sacks of grain and a jar of oil. Some did not consider Amen-hotep at all as an enemy and did not want to participate in the private war that Pa-nehsi declared to him, using foreign soldiers. But there was also a group of fierce opponents of the High Priest, and Djed-Mut-iuf-ankh, father of Henut belonged to it. Despite the pleas of his wife and daughter who did not want him to leave home and family, the man insisted that he wanted to fight Amen-hotep and was taken to the barracks the next day by the same soldiers who brought the promised grain and oil to his home, and on the wall of the house they painted a big *ankh*[66] mark with red paint, meaning "life." Similar signs appeared on every house of those who helped Pa-nehsi in any way. No signs were left on the houses where the families of those men who served in the temple in Ipet-sut lived. There were a lot of such houses and only women and children lived in them. Those women came in large numbers, encouraged by the promised help, and indeed, the Kushite soldiers visited their homes, bringing there only one *hin*[67] of grain, which was hard enough to prepare several meals. Nevertheless, the gifted women judged the General's act as very noble.

---

[66] Hieroglyph used to write the words: "live", "life", "alive" etc. Shows the knot tied on the umbilical cord of the baby.

[67] A measure of volume, corresponding to approx. 0.5 l of grain (one hundred and sixty part of a bag).

Surrounded by a ring of Kushite troops, the defenders of Ipet-sut and the temple-fortress of Ramesses User-Maat-Re Meri-Amun of course did not know what was happening in the City. The sudden attack and killing of several guards standing at top of the towers of the Great Gate said everything about Pa-nehsi's intentions: he began fighting to gain the only power in the Southern Country, which meant practically declaring war on the entire kingdom of Kemet. There was no doubt that his first goal was to defeat Amen-hotep, under whose orders was the only military force with which Pa-nehsi had to reckon in the south: Amun's police concentrated in two temples, currently under siege whose high gates and thick the walls resembled strongholds. These police were even well-armed and well-stocked, at least in Ipet-sut, thanks to the cautious transfer of supplies from warehouses in the district of Ramesses the Great, but it was created mainly to guard the order and protect the procession, not to face the professional army considered invincible: the army of the Both Countries. Amen-hotep and Amen-em-Ipet realized that without the help of the second part of the army, which was now stationed near Pi-Ramesse, they would not be able to defend themselves long. However, both hoped that Pa-nehsi would respect the holy place. The shooting of the guards on the towers had the obvious purpose: preventing them from passing north to the temples that an enemy was coming from the south. Therefore, Pa-nehsi made sure that all the guards on the towers of the temples lying between Abu and the City were killed when he set out with his war intentions; all that was needed was the small squads of archers who reached near each temple and at the appointed time attacked the guards standing there. The plan was apparently successful, and the surprise was complete. Amen-hotep had no doubt that in the same way the guards were removed from the temples further north to Qift. Anyway, in most small temples only a few guards served, and the Kushites could easily control them, which effectively interrupted the news passed from the gate to the gate.

Since Ipet-sut was surrounded by the Kushite army, an attack was expected at any time, but days passed, and the attack did not occur. For the defenders who waited in suspense, it was very difficult, because they practically did not leave their posts on the walls, but it aroused the hope that Pa-nehsi may indeed intend to stop only at the siege of the Temple of Amun. Amen-hotep also expected that sooner or later a messenger from the besieging troops would appear. After 10 days from the beginning of the siege, it was noticed from the Great Gate that the Kushite soldiers stationing opposite stepped aside to, let two people pass, one of whom was holding a military trumpet. Its distinctive high tone announced that the long-awaited messenger had arrived. What a surprise for Amen-hotep was....was played by Buteh-Amun, son of the old Scribe of the Necropolis Djehuty-mes! The momentary joy of the High Priest gave away immediately to the sad reflection that since he was here, it means that the temple of Ramesses User-Maat-Re Meri-Amun[68], which was the main seat of the authorities in the Western City, and the walls of which also

---

[68] It is about the temple of Ramesses III in Medinet Habu.

protected the house of Djehuty-mes, fell! And this temple-fortress was considered to be impregnable.

Indeed, this temple became the first object of the assault of Pa-nehsi's troops. Three days after the General's message to the inhabitants of Khefet-her-neb-es had been read, the trumpeter who stood at the eastern defensive gate of the fortress, announced the arrival of the messenger "from His Highness Vizier of Waset, Overseer of the Granaries of the Southern Country, Son of the King of Kush, General of the Army of His Majesty Pharaoh, may he live forever! Noble Pa-nehsi." Then Un-nefer, recently sent to the City by King Ramesses, appeared in a window on the second floor of the stone tower, which was the central fragment of this gate, and replied that the one who sends the message is no longer either the Vizier or the Granary Supervisor, nor noble one since he attacks the temples and should not refer to the King, for it was not Pharaoh who sent him here. In this situation, he, Waset's Vizier, Un-nefer, does not want to talk to the messenger of somebody who usurps the titles of other people, and if Pa-nehsi wants to talk to the Vizier, let him come alone!

"Then maybe I will give him the audience!" The deputy left without a word, and among the defenders there were voices of joy: "He well said him! Our Vizier is a brave man!" But others were silent.

Pa-nehsi felt deeply hurt. For many years of his power in the City, he became known as a ruthless man who will not hesitate to do everything to achieve the goal. Besides, he commanded a select army many time larger that defenders. But is it possible that he could have managed the double wall of such a powerful fortress?

After all, neither siege ladder can't reach the top of these walls! So maybe he'll step down without a fight? The next day Pa-nehsi dispelled all doubts and ordered to start the assault. Both gates: the eastern one and the western one, provided with stone towers and bastions, were very powerful fortifications, but access to the walls from the east was additionally hindered by a water harbor, so Pa-nehsi concentrated the attack on the western wall. This wall was also enormous: 36 cubits high and 20 cubits wide, and protected by a second, but a much lower and narrower wall, and a dry moat lying between them, but despite this, the approach to the fortress from this side was easier. Pa-nehsi chose as the main attack site a fragment of the fortifications no longer than 30 cubits, located near the western gate. The first task of the attacking troops was to remove a bottom part of the outer wall topped with decorative, semi-circular stone slabs. Behind these slabs in the real strongholds could have been defenders, but here this wall mainly adorned and added splendor, as did the moat in which there was no water. It was only the second, high internal wall along with the gates that formed a real fortress, although it had never happened before that it had to be used against a real enemy. Besides, there were too few besieged temple guards to take up positions on both walls, though they could defend themselves for a long time. From the top of the high wall, and especially from the bastions of the western gate, they had within reach of their bows the entire foreground of the lower wall. Before the destruction of the wall began, a group of soldiers ran up to him carrying a huge leather shield of the size equal to at least twenty normal shields, from which two extremely long spears protruded. The soldiers stuck these skewers into the wall of dried bricks so that the shield remained fixed there. Then another similar gigantic shield was attached on the other side of the selected section of the wall. While the archers' protected by these shields began intense fire on the gate and the entire length of the walls, not giving respite to the defenders, a special brigade of "breakers" began to work, consisting of people armed with stone hammers, sharp hoes and heavy copper crowbars. This group was striking the bottom of the brick wall. Every now and then, people carrying jugs of water were coming there pouring their contents onto the wall, weakening and softening the brick.

From the top of the high inner wall, defenders shot at the smashing ones, while Kushite archers hidden behind both guards hurt them and from time to time a temple soldier hit with an arrow was falling on the wall, or sometimes straight from it into the moat. On the other hand, numerous accurate shots were reaching the workers. However, immediately the bodies of the dead were removed, and next "breakers" were coming undertaking the work of destruction. Shouts of commands and moans of the wounded were piercing the air mixing with the clatter of tools that falling on the brick wall raised a cloud of thick dust carried by the wind.

The crumbling of the wall lasted all the day and was not interrupted even by the arrival of the night. In the dark, one could continue to strike a brick obstacle, while temple archers had a difficult task, all the more so as the workers having made a huge breach in the wall were now protected by its upper part.

In the morning, the outer wall was finally pierced through and now the work of its destruction began to resemble work in quarries: the workers, standing in a hole they had knocked, now were removing bricks from above their heads one by one, throwing them under their feet and thus moving more and more upwards, while a pile of brick debris was growing beneath them. Finally, the highest parts of the wall collapsed, and above the workers' heads, the sky appeared again, from which deadly missiles were falling. They were not protected by any shields when they were pushing the embankment of gray-black debris into a moat yawning with a deep chasm between the walls. It took two days and a night between them to cover it, and it was a time when a group of workers carrying out this thankless task was decimated by shelling from the high wall of the fortress, despite the protection of the Kushite archers. Finally, the moat on the attacked section was filled in and the whole operation of breaking the wall began again, preceded by mounting the same large leather shields on the sides, from behind which the attacking archers could smite the defenders. They now had directly under them the "breakers" trying to break through the wall, so they not only were striking them with arrows from the bows but also were throwing heavy stones from the top of the wall and pouring boiling water with oil. This was boiling in huge vats set on the top of this 36 cubits high wall and so thick that two chariots could pass on it, each drawn by four horses. It would seem that it is impossible to break such a mighty wall, but after a few hours, the workers managed to make a deep breach in it so that they could feel safe there, shielded from all death carriers that were thrown at them from above. However, before this was achieved, the brigade of "breakers" made a very high blood sacrifice, even though Kushite archers also decimated the ranks of the defenders. When the workers were already covered by the same wall they were breaking, the defenders learnt that it remained a matter of time when the attackers would break through the wall, even if it was so thick. In this case, it did not even have to be completely demolished, but only cut through at the bottom, with which something like a gate would be made, giving passage for assaulting troops.

The Vizier Un-nefer, who was living in the upper floor of the western gate modelled on the palace, and was watching the fight from there, was terrified when he saw Pa-nehsi's stubbornness. When he had not received his representative a few days ago, he was convinced that the General only wanted to show his strength, but he would not dare to act militarily against the legal authority established in the City by His Majesty Ramesses. "However," Un-nefer concluded "even if he tried despite everything, he probably would not be able to conquer such a powerful fortress, against which the assault ladders remained harmless, able to reach almost half the height of the walls." Now, when the Vizier saw that the war art of the Egyptian army could overcome even such an obstacle, he decided to send a message to Pa-nehsi to propose the surrender. His deputy, accompanied by a trumpeter, left the fortress through a loophole in the gate and headed for the Kushite units, which were moved away to a safe distance and whom, apart from archers protecting the work of the "breakers," did not participate in the fight. However, as soon as he approached them, he was shot, and one of Pa-nehsi's officers ordered the trumpeter to come back and tell "this dog Un-nefer" that he had decided to surrender too late because the price for the blood of the soldiers of His Vizier's Dignity could be only blood, and Un-nefer himself can get ready to die. Un-nefer thought again that Pa-nehsi would not go so far as to raise his hand to one of the highest dignitaries in the Both Countries, but he thought that further resistance could only bring an even more bloody harvest. Therefore, without waiting for the brigade of "breakers" to finish the work, he decided to surrender the fortress. Archers on the walls were ordered to stop shooting and go down, and the great western gate was opened, as trumpeters announced. Pa-nehsi did not hide his surprise, but in this situation, he also ordered to stop work on breaking the wall, after which he ordered all defenders to leave the fortress, leaving their weapons there. Temple guards began to leave, and then they were captured and tied up by Kushite soldiers. Finally came Un-nefer himself, who met the same fate. The dignitary began loudly demanding the unknotting and the leading him to the General, and then the Kushite officer, who was Pa-Minu, having been tried some time ago for burglaries in the cemetery, hit him with a reed stick. Seeing this, several defenders who were just leaving the gate, backed up screaming and, grabbing the bows abandoned there, ran out and started shooting. Pa-Minu hit with two arrows fell dead to the ground. Now, however, the Kushites raised a scream and, with their spears and swords raised, rushed towards the open gate through which the defenders of the fortress were still coming out. Those who were nearest, among them already bound Un-nefer, became the first victims of this attack, others managed to retreat and were looking for any weapon in panic. An unequal battle began, where the Kushites had a huge advantage because a handful of surprised and most often defenseless temple policemen had no chance to fight with bloodthirsty brawlers, more and more of whom were falling into the fortress. The attacked people dispersed and began to flee and hide in the recesses of the area and the houses that filled this part of the temple precinct, but almost everyone was caught and killed, not sparing the inhabitants of these houses, including women and even children. The slaughter was stopped only by Pa-nehsi, who appeared in the entourage of his guard just when the Kushite soldiers, having tasted blood and destruction, wanted to break into those houses that were still untouched to deal with their inhabitants, regardless of whether they resisted or not. Several soldiers were just trying to force open the solid door of the largest house standing near the western gate. Seeing their leader, they stopped, and then someone opened the door from the inside and stood in them and a dignified old man in white priestly robes stood in them. The appearance of this figure so different from the half-naked warriors covered with dust and blood surrounding it was so unusual that suddenly an also unusual silence fell in the war scenery.

Djehuty-mes looked around, incredulously looking at the area so well known to him, which suddenly turned into hell. On the threshold of the neighboring house lay one of the policemen of the State of Amun and the defenders of the fortress, with the head almost cut off by the sword, and right next to him a woman holding a small child in her arms – both of them pierced with a single spear blow. This morning Gat-seshen – this young neighbor and friend of the daughter-in-law of Djehuty-mes was at his home and Shed-du-dua, who was terrified by the war, asked her if she was afraid of herself and her son, only a year older than her own child. Gat-seshen said at the time that neither women nor children carry weapons and are not dangerous to anyone, and besides, Pa-nehsi was the City's Vizier, so he would not hurt the inhabitants...

Djehuty-mes slowly raised his eyes and looked at the one about whom Gat-seshen spoke with confidence, "So, you came here to perform the duties of Vizier and to officiate Maat. Tell me what crime this woman committed that you carried out a great death sentence on her? What did this child, who was not yet old enough to judge it?[69] You came here as a military commander who should know the art of war. Is it okay for a soldier to kill a man, even his opponent who does not hold a sword, or a spear ready for battle, or even a bow or arrow and who cannot shield himself? What are you waiting for? Order to kill me and then my son, his wife and his little child who are in this house. We don't have weapons, so we'll be easy opponents for your brave soldiers!"

A murmur passed among the Kushite warriors, "He really deserves to die for what he said! He insulted us!"

But Pa-nehsi raised his hand and said loudly, "Let no one dare to hurt the inhabitants of this house! Let someone paint the ankh on his wall!" After which, to reward disappointed soldiers, he said,

---

[69] The period of "adolescence" in which you could already be accountable began when the child turns 10.

"You can enter the palace above the western gate and take everything you find there. Arrest the servants from the palace, but don't kill anyone else, unless he fights!"

Then he turned to Djehuty-mes: "I have saved your life; there is no danger for you and your family any more. Your archive is also safe. You should be grateful to me. I will talk to you again!" and left.

CHAPTER IX

The following days brought some calming down in Khefet-her-neb-es. Pa-nehsi moved into his former palace over the eastern gate, from where he had taken away Men-Maat-Re-nakht; of course, he thought that, as before, he holds all offices himself. On the advice of Pa-Shu-uben, the Granary Supervisor, sent by the King, was placed in the house of the Mayor Pa-uer-aa, and the house was now guarded by the *medjayu* and both dignitaries could not leave him, although their service was free and could care for normal supply. Pa-nehsi was aware that the death of Vizier Un-nefer, though not a direct result of his command, would always incriminate him and decided to pretend to be correct towards other high royal officials, and even surround them with some protection against the savagery of his own soldiers who in the conditions of war felt completely unpunished.

Even they knew, however, that the *ankh* sign painted on the wall of any house ensures the inviolability of its inhabitants.

The house of Djehuty-mes and Buteh-Amun was also marked, and they could freely move around Khefet-her-neb-es. The Necropolis Scribe even considered it as his duty and the very next day after the fall of the fortress he went out to the rounds of the entire Western City to see what damage the war had brought here. To his joy, combined with some surprise, he could find that beyond the damaged walls of the fortress of His Majesty Ramesses User-Maat-Re Meri-Amun and several houses within its ward, there was no other damage. The bakery and beer house were open, and a few brave women even appeared on the street with their products for exchange: eggs, onions and other vegetables.

The corpses were cleared. Now embalmers had a lot of work in the Clean House, where the body of Vizier Un-nefer was also brought, as well as a dozen or so bodies of those citizens of the State of Amun, i.e. the Fathers of God, who came from wealthier families and had tombs at West Waset cemeteries. The remaining fallen ones were to be buried without mummification with no delay. Pa-nehsi agreed to organize a funeral ceremony common to those killed ones on both sides and even allowed to use one of his warships for this purpose, because only on such a large boat could it be possible to fit together over 200 bodies accompanied by several priests from the temple of His Majesty Amen-hotep Djeser-Ka-Re, justified. On another smaller boat was a group of weepers partly consisting of women who were actually mourning for their fallen husbands and brothers. Both boats sailed along the canal to the river, then turned south and, unrolling the sails, headed up the river towards the Crocodile Island near South Iunu. Throughout the way, priests recited numerous texts from the *Book of Going Out by Day*, and also sang hymns to Osiris – after all, each of those dead ones became just him and was to share his fate. As the holy tale, known to everyone, proclaimed, Osiris was killed by Set and thrown into the river. All those who rested on this great boat, driven by the force of numerous oars and carried additionally by the wind, were really killed as a result of violent actions that Set undoubtedly patronized, and in two hours they were also to be thrown into the river. According to the myth, Isis – Osiris's wife and sister mourned him after his death; were the laments that came from the other boat, not from their wives and sisters? The story described in the holy legend ended happily: Osiris rose from the dead and lives forever, he reigns in the Underground, but during the day he unites with Re and provides life to the world. Most of the words read from papyri scrolls by the priests circling laboriously between lying bodies, bending over them, touching them with various powerful objects contained just assurance that the same fate awaits them all, if Maat was obeyed in their lifetime. A quasi-judgment of the dead carried out during the funeral by the priests made everybody believe that they would be admitted before God.

Finally, the shore of the Crocodile Island was seen in the distance. The oarsmen stopped rowing and the boats were only moving in the wind. Soon, everyone could see the familiar view, because of which the island got its name: on its shore were many crocodiles, which seemed as if they were expecting the arrival of funeral boats. At the sight of them, some reptiles began to move towards the water, and then they submerged in it, ready to accept the prey. The rowers got up and started throwing the bodies into the water, which was accompanied by the shrill scream of women on the other boat and the low choir of voices of priests reciting the prayer:

You who make the perfect Ba-souls enter the House of Osiris,
Make their Ba also enter the House of Osiris,
So that they can hear as you hear, see as you see,
Stand as you stand, sit as you sit!
You who give souls bread and beer at the Osiris House,
Also give bread and beer to their souls!
You who open roads and gates in
The House of Osiris for the souls,
Open the roads and gates for their souls,
So that they could enter and leave
The House of Osiris without hindrance,
And their instructions were carried out...[70]

On the third day after the battle, the Royal Necropolis Scribe received a summons to appear in Pa-nehsi's palace. He went there reluctantly, although he hoped to learn something about the situation in Ipet-sut. He was worried about the High Priest Amen-hotep, but also about the temple. Although it was surrounded by a wall it was inconspicuous, in comparison with

---

[70] This is a fragment of the so-called Chapter 1 of the *Book of the Dead*.

the huge fortifications around the temple of Ramesses User-Maat-Re Meri-Amun, and to break that wall would be a child's play for Pa-nehsi's professional army. In Ipet-sut, the number of Amun police guards was many times greater than here, yet the forces were uneven. Amun remained the main defender of Ipet-sut: it would be sacrilege to attack the walls of the temple. But did Pa-nehsi consider it at all?

"I know you have already done an inspection of the West City," the General has not used to spend time giving welcome formulas. As you can see, it has not been destroyed and everything works in it, as in the old days. Do you still think that I am fulfilling my duties as a Vizier improperly?"

"The City functioned in the same way before your invasion, but there were not so many widows and orphans," Djehuty-mes answered.

"They would not have been, Chari, was it not for Un-nefer's mindless resistance, whom I had only to show that he was dealing with a real army who knowing how to conquer fortresses. You must admit that I did well," Pa-nehsi smiled at the unquestionable military success.

"Until the slaughter of defenseless people began. Your hands are soiled with blood," the Necropolis Scribe touched a sensitive place and Pa-nehsi stopped smiling.

"These are Un-nefer's hands that are soiled with it. My soldiers are easily getting upset, and he caused it. In addition, one of your supposedly defenseless man after surrendering the fortress, killed my officer, Pa-Minu."

"So, this thief is dead?" Djehuty-mes was surprised, but he couldn't hide that this news wasn't particularly painful for him. "As you can see, the punishment he deserved was only suspended. Is the other "hero" of that trial, Aa-neru, also with you?"

"Aa-neru is doing well. I'll tell him you're worried about him. You see, Chari, such a hotheads like them, though they are great officers, can be dangerous for the inhabitants of the City if they are provoked and only I can stop them, as I did in front of your house. That's why you should help me in the Eastern City." Pa-nehsi looked piercingly at the Necropolis Scribe and Djehuty-mes sensed that their conversation was beginning just now.

"I don't know what's going on behind the river," he began cautiously, "but if you besiege Ipet-sut, you are committing a rape against Maat. This is holy and untouchable place and any raising of hand against it would be an unforgivable crime!"

"But, Chari, that's the thing, this place should be intact! My troops are standing around Ipet-sut, but I do not intend to raise my hand against the holy abode, although I think that it is not as sacred to all soldiers of the Free Kush army as it is to me. It is not my fault that Amen-hotep chose Ipet-sut as his headquarter. If his palace stood elsewhere, it would probably be all over now, and I could leave..."

Djehuty-mes felt the blood draining from his heart, "Free Kush Army – so, this is a coup d'état and it is not just about regaining lost positions. Pa-nehsi does not wage a private war against Amen-hotep, but using the royal army, over half of which he once received power from Pharaoh, he declared war on Both

Countries! What can an old royal clerk in charge of the cemetery do in this situation?"

"I'll tell you what you can do," said Pa-nehsi, as if guessing the old man's thoughts, "Go to Amen-hotep on my behalf and convince him not to fight me, because he will lose and will endanger Ipet-sut. Let him, take his police out of the temple, and let him surrender himself to me. He will be arrested, but no one will hurt him, and as my prisoner to whom I will provide royal conditions, he will be an important argument in my conversations with His Majesty Ramesses, may he live forever!, and then, of course, I will send him away with the honors and gifts to Pharaoh from the King of Kush..."

The Necropolis Scribe sat with his head down and remained silent. Here he learned the whole plan of Pa-nehsi, which, unfortunately, seemed well thought-out, and completely feasible. It is true that surrender of Ipet-sut would save the blood of his defenders, and perhaps of other residents of the City, too, and having such a distinguished prisoner as Amen-hotep would make it easier for Pa-nehsi to negotiate with the King. But High Priest of Amun in captivity with barbarians – that would be the end of the world! Both Countries survived many wars and invasions, but they always emerged victorious from these fights. The Kushites are usually shown at the temple gates and on the footstools of royal throne as prisoners with bound hands, remaining in the power of the King, or are offered to Amun. This has always been the case since the time of the forefathers, and every child in the Both Countries knows that the Nine Bows[71], and therefore also the Kushites, are as dangerous as the lions or wild buffalos in the desert, but Amun causes their terror shrinking in the glare of the royal power. Would this picture to be reversed now? Maybe Pa-nehsi would even order to carve the scene as he leads by cord the First Servant of Amun and the children in Kush would learn such a message.

"It's unbelievable, Amun won't let it happen," he thought, and added loudly:

"You hate Amen-hotep and want to triumph over him. But Amen-hotep is only Amun's First Servant and even the King has no power to appoint or dismiss him. You want to use the person of the High Priest as a tool for your battle with the King, but you have to fight Amun first, and He is invincible! Recall how Amun saved Ramesses the Great in a battle with the barbarians of Hatti[72]; you can't beat God!"

"Ah, really, Chari, stop telling me fairy tales about the miracle at Kadesh! You priests may believe it, but we generals know what it looked like and I assure you that no miracle will save Amen-hotep if he rejects my offer. You can help him, but if you don't want to, I'll send someone else there, so decide, because I don't have time to listen to sermons!" Pa-nehsi began to show

---

[71] A symbolic designation of all the foreign potentially hostile people surrounding Egypt from the South (Kushites), the West (Libyans) and the East (Asians). Each group was symbolizing by three strokes meaning the plural which makes the sum: nine; the bow was typical weapon of these warriors.

[72] A reference to the famous episode of the battle with the Hittites at Kadesh (around 1275 BC) described and illustrated at many Egyptian temples.

impatience, and Djehuty-mes thought that only by agreeing to go to Amen-hotep, he would learn the truth about the situation in Ipet-sut. At the same time, he recognized that such knowledge could be much more useful to the future Necropolis Scribe than to an old man of his age, so he replied, "I see I can't convince you, so let it be as you wish. However, because I am not feeling well, I will send my son Buteh-Amun with your message to Amen-hotep; I think it won't make a difference to you."

Pa-nehsi admitted that he did not care, and the conversation ended there. Surprisingly, however, it was not easy to convince Buteh-Amun to the idea of representing Pa-nehsi and to take the role of his messenger. The young man was resisting for a long time and only gave in to the firm demand of his father.

When he found himself in the chamber of Amen-hotep, he emphasized that he had come here forced by Djehuty-mes, because he is ashamed of such an unusual role of a representative from someone like Pa-nehsi.

"Your father is a very smart man. This is the last opportunity for us to talk, then all contacts will become impossible," the High Priest replied. "Djehuty-mes understood that I may need a help of someone young and energetic who is outside of Ipet-sut, because everything seems to indicate that I will have to get out of here and go personally to Pi-Ramesse, and then you will help me. But first, show me what Pa-nehsi sends you with and tell me what is happening in West Waset."

"I have no letter from the General and I can only repeat what my father told me," the young priest said. He began by telling about the assault and the terrible day when the Vizier Un-nefer was killed and they were saved, about the fact that life in Khefet-her-neb-es goes almost unchanged, even the damage is minor. Everywhere there are Kushite soldiers, but they behave calmly. At every step you can also see the *medjayu* of Pa-Shu-uben, although he has not seen him, just as he doesn't know what happened to Men-Maat-Re-nakht and mayor Pa-uer-aa. There's something else he doesn't understand. On some houses are painted the signs *ankh*, and there is nothing like that on other ones. Finally repeated the demands of Pa-nehsi, to which the High Priest just waved a hand.

"Since he attacked the State of Amun, he declared war on the Both Countries. There is no other way than to give his soldiers a vision of the Kingdom of Kush, but these are fantasies: he would have to defeat the northern army, but he probably won't make up his mind about such a madness. Yes, he would also like to become High Priest of Amun, and maybe that is what he mainly wants. He counts that after my death the Amun's barge surrounded by the Kushite troops would then name him to be the First Servant. He really underestimates the divine power. And as for this "royal prison" for me, I am sure he would kill me on the first day, that is, one of his people would do it "by accident". However, from that moment on, everyone who condemned him: your father, Pa-uer-aa and others, would no longer be protected by anyone. Who knows, if in such a situation Ramesses would not reconcile himself to the facts and choose a peaceful path and cooperation with Pa-nehsi instead of war? Unless Pa-nehsi would declare himself King, what he is capable of. I shudder to think, what would happen then. I can see clearly that the unity of the Both

Countries can be saved only if Pa-nehsi fails to capture me. We may pay a high price, but we can't give up."

Although Pa-nehsi transmitted his message orally, Amenhotep decided to reply by letter. Handing it to Buteh-Amun, he said, "Listen carefully and make a note in your heart of what you hear now. I know Pa-nehsi and suppose that several months will pass before he makes a decision to act. He knows that launching an assault on the House of Amun will ruin his plans to become High Priest. Therefore, he will renew his messages, although he will never use your services again. First of all, he will want to defeat us with hunger, hoping that Ipet-sut will surrender when stocks run out, but we are ready for a long siege. However, one day his patience will end, and he will have to decide: he will either withdraw or go to Kush or attack. There is no infinitely long time, because His Majesty Ramesses, without receiving any letters, neither from me nor from Un-nefer or Men-Maat-Re-naht, and these are certainly expected, will guess what happened here and can send an army. I still do hope that Pa-nehsi will stop short of the ultimate sacrilege, but if... We can withstand a maximum of two days of assault. Watch and listen if the battle begins here and if so, go immediately to Southern Iunu, even if with a funeral procession that, after all, often heads towards the Crocodile Island. Then cross to Sumenu and go to Sobek's temple there. Let the priest *setem* of this temple prepare for us a few horses and provisions for the journey."

Buteh-Amun looked at the High Priest with admiration, but also with amazement. "Forgive me for boldness, but how will

Your Grandness reach Sumenu?" he asked and Amen-hotep replied with a smile.

"You want me to reveal to you one of the most kept secrets of Ipet-sut, which apart from me only Amen-em-Ipet and two other priests know about... But let it be so, maybe it will be useful to you someday. Well, from Ipet-sut leads a well-masked underground passage to the district of Mut, which they do not besiege. From there, I will go on foot to Madu, from where along the edge of the desert, I will reach Djeret in front of Sumenu and cross the river there. I think that someone will accompany me then, someone you know well, although it is not the time to talk about it now."

"Someone I know well?" Buteh-Amun repeated like an echo, "Could Suti-mes have returned from Pi-Ramesse?"

"Yes, he came back a long time ago, but someone attempted then to kill him, and it was only because of Amun's miracle that he is alive, and is quite well now, though he was very ill. Go now, boy, look after your father, wife and son...what's his name?"

"Ankh-ef-en-Amun, Lord"

"Amun... If we were to escape, we would be completely left on his protection. So, see you. Here or in Sumenu!"

An hour later, Buteh-Amun handed over to Pa-nehsi the letter of Amen-hotep.

"So, His Grandness deigned to answer me in writing..." sneered the General, then opened the letter and began to read aloud:

You are raising your hand against the City and Ipet-sut, and therefore on God. Re sees it during the day, Khonsu at night, and

Amun is everywhere, so nothing will escape God's knowledge and Djehuty will write it down... You mocking Maat. You talk about great works for the Kush people, but you are guided by low desires for power and wealth. Come to your senses, come back to where you came from or go to Kush - you are the Royal Son of Kush. Maybe then the King will forgive you and maybe God will forgive you the blood you have already shed. Remember that raising of hand on Ipet-sut is a crime that would require re-creation of the world, although you would not be among created ones!

Pa-nehsi began to laugh; of course, he didn't expect anything else.

"You were a witness, Buteh-Amun, that I wanted a compromise. Now you can see yourself that Ipet-sut is very tightly surrounded and even a mouse will not get out from there unnoticed, not to mention rats like Amen-hotep. But let's wait until hunger chokes him..."

"So, as the High Priest expects, Pa-nehsi is planning a siege," Buteh-Amon thought and having bowed, went out to report his message to Djehuty-mes, and to enjoy him with news of Suti-mes – maybe the only ray of light in the dark of night that would soon fall over the City of Amun.

The season of Akhet was ending, the waters of the river had already subsided, leaving the wonderful fertile silt in the fields. At this time of year, farmers usually grabbed plows and seed for sowing, and intensive work began to ensure that the seed would benefit from the moisture accumulated in the soil. Usually, whole families stayed in the fields for most of the day. Men harnessed cows to plows if they had cows, but the poorer peasants used only the hoes. The women followed their husbands directly, carrying bags of grain that spilled into the freshly cut furrows. Children took grains from bags in small bowls and poured into bags carried by their mothers to improve their work. The fields were coming alive with bustle and conversation. This was the case a year ago, even though the poor flooding and dry soil did not bode well. This year the land was well prepared for plowing and the harvest could have been very good, but complete silence and stillness in the fields announced that they would not be at all. Most men were conscripted into Pa-nehsi's army besieging Ipet-sut. Initially, only a few tenants came forward and they immediately received "payment," which was practically a refund of what Pa-nehsi received as allegedly "increased tax." They now lived in a military camp, but, despite the wives' fear, they did not participate in any battles, creating only a siege ring around Ipet-sut. They were well-fed, did not have many duties throughout the day, although they were cleaning the camp and serving the Kush soldiers. The news of how well it was doing for those who had appealed to the General quickly spread throughout Waset and since then every day more volunteers were coming to the camp who were also welcomed, although payment for their delay in their readiness to fight against Amen-hotep was already smaller; at first, they got two, and then only one sack of grain.

When the time of plowing and sowing came, it turned out that only a few peasants appeared in the fields, and sometimes they were only women with hoes, who tried to sow at least some grain. Season Peret saw only small islets of green ears among the vast black, not even plowed land. The grain reserves from last year's miserable harvest ended early, so grain had that been intended for sowing but not used was now consumed. It also ended before long. The famine first came to those houses where people associated with the temple of Amun lived. Weavers, carpenters, sandal makers, even potters did not earn, because the besieged temple could not order their services. Wives and children of all who were locked up in the besieged Ipet-sut, serving as duty priests, guards, temple police, servants or employees of those workshops that were located in the temple were completely deprived of supplies. The neighbors, were sharing what they had, some of them out of the goodness of their hearts, others meticulously writing down all the loans. Everyone was hoping that the war would end soon. At the beginning one was thinking with some degree of jealousy about these families who joined as a volunteer in Pa-nehsi's army and received payment for it. However, the siege was prolonged, and the famine also reached the families of even most faithful Pa-nehsi's allies. Most residents of Waset no longer had enough flour to make bread and beer, so mainly vegetables from the home gardens were eaten.

The latest dictator's order was announced that all families in the City are obliged to donate their cows, rams and goats to the army without murmuring. In times of peace, the army used its own herds, which the soldiers themselves were breeding. Now the army was besieging Ipet-sut and the burden of its maintenance fell entirely on the shoulders of the unhappy people of Waset. The Kushites were coming to different farms every day and were taking all the livestock away, and every attempt at resistance ended in heavy flogging at best and forced recruitment of men if they were still at home. There were also executions of "rebels". In this situation people decided to kill even the last cow or sheep to break the hunger food for at least a few days with a "meat feast," redeemed with lamentations. There was more and more crying. In the situation, when there were no cows nor goats anymore, the milk became almost unobtainable rarity.

When most of the cows and geese from the household were eaten, the time came for dogs and cats. Almost every day one could see the funeral boats sailing towards the Crocodile Island, but it also happened that the people whose hope had died out went to their own death at the Crocodile Backwaters, also known as Launderer's Bank. Others were seeking the desert and did not return from it. Piercing human-like laughter of hyenas which were sniffing blood and not buried corpses could be heard closer and closer to the settlements of the inhabitants of Waset who called this terrible time the "year of hyenas"[73].

---

[73] This name comes from some court testimony preserved on papyrus. One woman says that she sold some barley to someone "in the year of hyenas when hunger reigned."

CHAPTER X

On the edge of the desert plain, near the northern wall of the great temple of His Majesty User-Maat-Re Sechep-en-Re of Ramesses the Great, three old patulous sycamore trees were growing close each to other, leaning over the verge of arable lands. Their branches were interweaved, forming a shady cover. At fruiting time, hoopoes and other winged amateurs of sweet figs were flying here in and the opportunity to eat these fruits was also used by women sitting in the shade of trees. Apart from the House of Sisters located on the opposite side of West Waset, on the road to the craftsman town, the sycamores were the second place in Khefet-her-neb-es, where men used to come to buy a moment of oblivion. However, while in the House of „Sisters" comfortable beds and girls smelling with fragrant oils and adept in their services were waiting, here under the sycamores they could only find a cheap equivalent of "sisters", very poorly dressed and not always clean, and only passively accepting their fate. These women were as if dead artifacts borrowed from here to be sent back after the use. Of course, in the House of "Sisters" one had to pay well, so only a few, mostly regulars, were going there. Women under the sycamores counted only on a few loaves, a pitcher of beer or milk that is why their customers were also undemanding. Although the place under the sycamores as a marketplace of cheap love was as old as Waset, especially the female inhabitants of the City were despising it and those who were passing the nearby road tried not even to look in this direction. In the "year of hyenas" everything changed. Hungry women began to come to the sycamores more and more often, even those who previously, while replete with food, had been thinking about this place with superiority and condemnation. Because now in the role of customers mainly those were calling here in who had enough bread: the soldiers of Pa-nehsi's army. They were bringing a camp language and customs with them, but the women returning from their tents had the food that could satisfy their hunger as well that of their next of kin, making easier the surviving of the next two or three days of waiting for the miracle of ending the war of which they were victims.

The day 20 of the fourth month of the season Peret promised to be hot. Not a single cloud obscured the eastern horizon of the sky, so when the barge of Re appeared there, the slopes of the mountains above Djeser-Djeseru became covered with purple, which slowly turned into gold.

Aset came under the sycamores as the first one, as usual. She was a plump, not very pretty girl in full bloom of mature youth, who had been fruitlessly waiting for years to be completed. For the first time, she appeared under the sycamores, not so much forced by hunger as guided by curiosity and since then she was coming here almost every day. She also cared to be men's liking a little, so she wore a colorful dress, and in her carefully combed hair she weaved some yellow acacia flowers, which were blooming now. She also greeted customers with a smile, while the other women, waiting to be chosen and feed by somebody were sitting moody, with expressionless faces on which fear was easier to appear than joy. That is why Aset soon felt like a lady of this place and a spontaneous guardian of a group of women the composition of which was different every day. Aset was showing the incoming girls where to sit and was advising how to behave. Sometimes she could shout at a girl, but it also happened that she was reviving and watering one fainted of hunger or heat.

"You should work at the House of "Sisters"," they were saying to her, and she was answering with a sigh, not denying it:

"With such an ugly face? Who would want me? Anyway, they have a full house for now..."

Aset took a good place, from where she could see a large part of the road between the temple of Ramesses the Great and the old and already partially ruined funerary temple Heneket-ankh of His Majesty Djehuty-mes Men-kheper-Re. Everyone who went to the sycamores had to follow this way and then enter the path leading here from the road. Aset could see how the women were appearing one after another, all of them were supposed to be her rivals today. Aset did not like the morning time when they were gathering here; each subsequent woman was reducing the chance of the earning, so she was accepted with greater reluctance. When Shebti, Heryt-uben and Nesi-Khonsu came, Aset even greeted them, though she assessed that the first two, albeit thinner, did not look better than she. Shebti had messy hair, and Heryt-uben a dirty dress. As she wondered what could be criticized about the third one, two more young women came, both looking decently, not ugly, and in addition similar to each other as two leaves from the same tree. Ta-shed-Mut and Bak-en-Mut were twin sisters, and their husbands belonged to the service of Amun and were locked in Ipet-sut. The girls were coming here rarely, but when they came, they were usually chosen first, so Aset looked at them reproachfully and without a word she showed them a place to sit. However, when she saw another woman walking towards them, she could not stand it and "greeted" her aggressively:

"Are you stupid? Are you hoping that a granddaddy will come here?"

The woman was clearly older than all of them, her first wrinkles were appearing, and several gray hairs could be seen on her head.

"Greetings!" she turned to everyone, taking the last shaded place, then looked at Aset and added:

"Are you afraid that someone will choose me and not you? Maybe it will happen, and it does not have to be a granddaddy, only someone who will prefer a woman with experience than heaps of young fat!"

Aset wondered what to say, but at the same time she looked at the path and an immeasurable amazement overwhelmed her:

"For Amun and Hat-Hor!" she said quietly, "Is this really happening? Is she here too?"

Henut walked down the path towards the sycamore, walking carefully between the tufts of grass, as if afraid of each subsequent step. Dressed in a simple white dress, on which her long hair fell in a wave, she walked with her head bowed and eyes fixed on the ground. She came up to the sycamores and looked uncertainly around, seeing seven pairs of eyes fixed on her and seven motionless figures sitting there. Not knowing what to say, she raised her hand in a silent gesture of greeting. At that moment, Aset awoke and poured out all her discontent. Not only as many as eight women came today to the sycamores, but also the girl considered one of the most beautiful in the West Waset is now among them.

"Ah, welcome princess!" she said. "What an honor! When she was embracing under the acacia with her beloved from Ipet-sut, she was noticing anyone, and now, well, we're equal!"

"Please, Aset, stop it! I'm hungry!" Henut threw out, while feeling that she would cry soon.

"Hungry? So, your lover is no longer interested in you, or is he still afraid of your daddy?" Aset attacked mercilessly. "Besides, there is no place here!"

Henut covered her face with both hands and began sobbing spasmodically. Then Ta-shed-Mut shifted a bit and said: "Come here, there is enough shade for everyone! How can you say that!?" she shouted at Aset. "Maybe her boyfriend is locked up in Ipet-sut just like my Pa-du-Amun. Do we come here for pleasure? I think you are the only one!"

"It's not your business why I come here!" Aset shouted back. "I want, like you, a man to take me to his tent today and feed me, but if she is here, we can both wait!" Then she threw at Henut, threatening her with a fist. "Remember, you pretty one, that if you take my client away, I will cut your face with those claws so that nobody will want you later!"

Silence fell, only Henut was crying loudly, lying between Tashed-Mut and her sister.

Three soldiers appeared then on the path to the sycamores.

"They're coming!" Aset warned, and the women froze in suspense. Henut was still sobbing, covering her face with her hands, but she was doing it in silence. The men, however, behaved noisy, laughing every now and then. Despite the rather early hour, they had to be in the beer house before, because they brought with them a strong beer smell.

"Well, get up, flowers, show yourself!" One of them said and all women rose from the ground. The men came up to them, and started looking at the "goods", sharing their comments with each other. One immediately chose Nesi-Khonsu and told her to wait by the path, after which he decided to help a colleague and, pointing at Henut, threw, "This one is nice!"

The other one looked at the girl, was reflecting for a moment on the suggestion, and said: "Maybe not the worst, but I can see that she will howl all the time, which I don't like!" and nodded at Ta-shed-Mut, then turned to the third one, "You, I remember, you like fat women, take that one!" and pointed to Aset, who smiled and wanted to go out on the path when the third man shook his head, saying, "Leave, this is Pentu's favorite, and he goes here too, I'd rather not get hit... But look, this one here seems to be identical as the one you chose. I'll take her and then we shall see if they are really the same!'" Both of them hooted with laughter and, having nodded at Bak-en-Mut, left with the other two girls.

"Your prince is also coming here, as I heard," Shebti turned to Aset not without malice. "You will have a man, as you wanted, this Pentu. You are not happy?"

Aset was sitting sulky in silence.

"What's wrong?" Shebti was surprised.

"I will have Pentu..." Aset replied as if speaking to herself. "Pentu and his five colleagues from the tent..." she added and none of the other women wanted to mock this unhappy girl.

They were waiting, however, a long time before the announced Pentu appeared, along with another soldier who even from afar seemed drunk. Pentu did not even reach the sycamore trees but being halfway down the path stood and waved a hand at Aset, then shouted, "And one more!"

Then Aset nodded at the oldest one, "Come, you, that one is boozed up, he will not notice that you have wrinkles!"

Shebti, Heryt-uben and Henut remained alone.

"Did you hear that?" Shebti turned to her friend, apparently the men from our street found metal...[74] For this, you can also buy bread from Pa-nehsi's soldiers."

---

[74] During the famine, some residents of Thebes robbed tombs in the necropolis; all metal objects had high commercial value. The British Museum keeps a papyrus with the preserved testimony of those

"But remember that you can also run into the stake," answered Heryt-uben and looked at the sky. It is long past noon. "There are still chances. Some are eating now, and then sometimes they want a woman, but they are the worst," she added and nudged Henut, who for a long time was sitting as if petrified, afraid to move or even speak.

"You'd better get out of here, this is not a place for you."

"I see you are here for the first time," Shebti added. "It would be a pity to give you to these shady characters who come here. Maybe your boyfriend can still be found somewhere."

Henut awoke and looked at both girls, then smiled. They were right, she probably couldn't go with just some random guy, often drunken soldier who wags his finger at her. Hunger is terrible, but such a life is probably even worse.

"Thank you, indeed, I will go!" she said and got up.

At the same moment, they heard the wheel rattling and a chariot appeared on the road. On the path leading towards the sycamore, a coachman stopped the horses, and a man got out of the chariot, who started toward three women.

"Amun, not him!" Heryt-uben whispered, looking at the approaching huge figure with the whip on the horses in hand. When he was quite close, Henut also recognized him: he was leaving her house when she came with Suti-mes, he brought the terrible news that destroyed her happiness and then looked at her just as he does now with lust on his red sweaty face.

---

interrogated persons during the trial, including a woman: "I was sitting under the sycamores, and the men were trying to sell metal because we were hungry."

"Well, that's a real surprise!" Pa-Shu-uben muttered to himself, and in the direction of Henut he said short, "Come on!" waving with the whip, like at the horse. He didn't even look at the other girls whose eyes were expressing the real joy that their prayer had been answered. Henut stood petrified like a statue.

"You probably don't want me to be angry!" the Waset Secret Affairs Inspector asked menacingly and, taking a step toward her, grabbed her with his giant paw and started walking toward the chariot, almost lifting the flimsy girl who had no chance to break free.

Horror took her voice away, so she was repeating more in her thoughts than with her frozen lips: "Amun, save me! Suti-mes, forgive me! Mom..."

When they came up to the road, Pa-shu-uben picked up the kidnapped girl and set her on the chariot next to the coachman, he stood himself on the other side, hugging the girl in the waist and ordered to move. The chariot turned with a rattle and it ran ahead while stirring up dust on the road. They passed the great gate of the temple of Ramesses the Great, and then several more temple precincts and houses, then turned right and after a while entered the courtyard of a spacious newly built palace, which was full of Kushite soldiers, *medjayu* and all kind of servants. Everyone was now looking at the superior and his booty, some were smiling significantly and exchanging comments with each other. Pa-Shu-uben helped the girl down off the chariot and pushed her in front of him into the palace, and there up the stairs to the first floor, where reception chambers, offices and private rooms werc located in which he was living and resting. After a while, Henut found herself in one of them. When they entered, two robust Kushites stood at the door that Pa-Shu-uben closed behind him on the staple. The chamber was not large nor richly equipped; the Police Chief liked soldier's simplicity. The main piece of furniture here was a low bed with legs carved in the shape of a lion's paws, woven with reeds and covered with several sheepskins. Next to it was a tall woven chair and a large wooden chest, and there was also a high table with a pitcher of water and a mug. The light coming through the narrow window seemed to create a wide beam diagonally cutting this chamber.

Pa-Shu-uben placed the girl paralyzed with terror so that these light rays brought out all the details of her beauty: a beautiful face with large eyes as if enlarged with fear, long lush black hair falling on the chest and shoulders, a slim body with a beautiful waist and hips line hidden under a simple white linen dress reaching to the ankles. Pa-Shu-uben was standing without saying anything, was looking at this beautiful phenomenon, which a fortune allowed him to enjoy unexpectedly. He brushed a strand of hair back from Henut's face, finding her beautiful long neck, looked into her eyes, absorbed the horror that filled them with great pleasure, then smiled with complete satisfaction and in a quiet voice told her to remove her dress.

Henut didn't move; she was standing speechless, unable to make the slightest motion. Pa-Shu-uben repeated the order, and when it was not fulfilled again, he approached the girl and unceremoniously ripped her robe from top to bottom, revealing a perfectly shaped body and all its secrets. Henut reflexively covered her face with both hands, and the man was taking for a long time delight in the sight of her nakedness, then suddenly turned her over, pushed her onto the chest and while pressing the girl's head against the furniture, having moved away the torn dress, he took her brutally. Henut screamed painfully and began sobbing excruciatingly. Pa-Shu-uben finally was satisfied, picked up the girl from the chest and turned her back to look at her face again. Unable to bear the sight of his satisfaction expressed with a foul smile, Henut covered her face with both hands again, but Pa-shu-uben tore her hands off with strength and with cynical satisfaction looked straight into her tearful eyes.

"Well, your Suti-mes really lost a lot," he said, drawling his words, "But, you see, he's dead, so someone had to make you a woman. You should be grateful to me..."

Having no news about her beloved for a long time she was suspecting intuitively that something most terrible may have happened to him, however she was brushing aside such thoughts from herself. And now this horrible message was given by the one who knows all the secrets of Waset, and therefore it must be true. But, how could he... He was still looking at her, and Henut felt, how aside from the pain and despair, a terrible hatred is building up in her heart to the awful man who just at that moment approached his red sweaty mug to kiss her. Henut managed to free her hands for a moment, then pushed him with the utmost disgust and spat in his face. Pa-Shu-uben stopped smiling, his face turned from red to bluish and the rage obscured all other feelings. At first he just intended to strangle the girl and he was already raising his enormous hands, but suddenly he stopped, changing his mind. He moved away the staple in the door, opened it and called the guards standing there.

"Take these rags off her and tie her!" he said, and the Kushites carried out this command with skill, which indicated that it was nothing special in this house. The ropes were prepared and lay in the same chest that Pa-Shu-uben had previously used, and after a few moments, the naked victim was laying on the bed with arms and legs tied, each separately, to those lion's paws that supported the furniture, trying unsuccessfully to get at the fetters with her teeth and throwing her head left and right.

"Have some fun with her!" Pa-Shu-uben ordered, turning to the Kushite guards, "The boyfriend of this bitch served till his death to Amen-hotep, the enemy of Kush, and she spat on the deputy of the Royal Son of Kush!" he added with a cynical smile, watching as the first of his subordinates begins to carry out this order, while the second grabbed the girl by the hair, holding her head.

"My father serves in your army and there is the *ankh* mark on my house!" Henut shouted then and the Kushite hesitated, looking at Pa-Shu-uben. This one gave, however, his soldier a sign that he should continue, and for some minutes observed then the scene taking place in front of him.

"I didn't take from her home," he added as if to excuse that she knew Pa-nehsi's order, "Only from under the sycamores tree, and she went there because she wanted to get a customer. Well, she is extremely lucky today, because she will have three!" He laughed out loud with the second guard who had just swapped places with his colleague.

Henut understood that she had lost everything and began shouting at her rapists the words of execration that have formed a terrible, though untrained curse, "You abominable ones for God, let Sekhmet catch you in the year of plague, let the donkey rape your mothers and sisters, and the flame will destroy your homes! Amun, you see my harm, become Montu for these scabby dogs, for these pigs of Seth, that they never see the Fields of Reeds, that they walk upside down and eat their own shit!"

"Boss, to silence her?" asked the one who was holding Henut by the hair, waiting until his colleague satisfies his needs.

"No, it's pleasant, excites me," Pa-shu-uben answered. "But for what she says now, one has to punish her and I'll do it..." he added and closed the door again behind the outgoing guards. He poured water into a cup, sat down on the chair and, drinking, looked at the still lying and silent naked girl, whose eyes showed only indifference.

"You say nothing? We'll wait, you will speak soon..." Pa-Shu-uben finished drinking, put down his cup, looked around and found his whip for the horses with which he came here, but which he had not needed so far. He lifted it and, standing above her, looked once more at the details of her beautifully shaped body.

"Elegant whores have durable patterns on their skin that adorn them and excite men[75]. You don't have anything like that, but I will decorate you!" He shouted the last word, wildness

---

[75] On the skin of some mummies of women, as well as on some figurines of the so-called concubines some decorative tattooed rhomboidal patterns made of numerous crossing lines consisting of points have been discovered.

appeared in his eyes and began to whip the girl's body, putting all his strength into every blow. Each stroke was leaving behind three red welts on the skin, which turned bluish after a while. Sometimes they were so strong that the delicate skin was cracking and drops of blood were appearing on the welts. Pa-Shu-uben was whipping Henut's breasts, then her belly and thighs, which gradually became covered with parallel blue marks of the straps, and then he positioned himself differently and began to "decorate" the same places with welts made at an angle in relation to the previous ones, creating bloody-bluish "squares" and "diamonds". Henut, who from the moment when the Chief of Police stood over her with his whip, knew what awaited her, clenched her teeth and bravely endured the first few plagues so as not to give to the degenerate the satisfaction he hoped for. But this resistance only increased the strength of the strikes and finally, the girl started screaming, filling the whole house and the courtyard with this cry, which, however, in the palace of the Waset Secrets Master was nothing new or unknown, so it did not arouse much interest of the soldiers and servants who were hanging around there.

"Oh," only one of them said, looking at the upstairs window, from where the terrifying sounds of the tortured were heard, "The boss has what he likes!"

Anyway, these screams became weaker in a while and then quieted down completely: the girl fainted. Then Pa-Shu-uben finished the beating, but the course of the punishment and reaction of the girl, combined with her nudity, so excited him that he entered her again, crushing with his huge bulk the surfaces of her body that had just been injured. The violent pain caused that Henut regained the consciousness but only to recognize her extreme humiliation, which together with terrible suffering lasted an unusually long time. Finally, Pa-Shu-uben stood up, drank some water, and then he called the maid service and ordered to untie the girl, as well as to re-attire her in her own torn dress.

"She can't walk naked, because someone could hurt her," he said cynically and added: "Take her to the sycamores, because one should not deprive her of a chance to earn again. Of course, give her normal payment for the service, even triple one, in bread and beer – let her remember that I am always honest and obey Maat!"

The same chariot that Pa-Shu-uben had used while bringing Henut to his palace served now to drive her away, but the accompanying soldier had to hold the half-dead girl all the way so that she would not fall off the chariot. But when they arrived, the soldier released her and told her to dismount, and in view of her awkwardness he simply pushed her with his foot to the ground, throwing behind her a piece of cloth with bread and beer for which she came today under the sycamores. One of two clay vessels with this drink crashed while hitting against a stone. The chariot drove away, and Henut was laying by the path, not even having the strength to stand up.

Two women jumped up from under the sycamores and ran to the lying woman. They were: Heryt-uben, who was the only one not chosen by anyone today, and Aset, who had already returned from the tent of Pentu, where she earned a double portion of bread, but as she had expected, for the repeated service. When she returned, she was long execrating the harm she had encountered, and other women comforted her that although there are people like this Pentu, others are fine and give what is due, although it is better not to listen to what they say about their "booty" among colleagues.

"You are lucky," Heryt-uben said, "That you left with Pentu because soon after you left this big fat pig, Pa-Shu-uben came. I was at his place once: it is not enough for him to take a girl, he still has to beat her. Today, he took the new one – I do not envy her..."

As if to confirm these words, a well-known chariot rolled out from behind the bend and in a moment drove away, raising clouds of dust, leaving Henut lying by the roadside. The women helped her to stand up on her feet and carefully brought her to the shadow, placing on the grass. Trickles of tears were flowing from under Henut's closed eyes. Shivers were shaking her wounded and burning body covered with freshly congealed blood and the terrifying "patterns" of bluish swollen welts on which flies were now alighting. The girl was moaning softly, and every movement and touch intensified that moan. All women under the sycamore chambers were united in their compassion and indignation. Aset has already completely forgotten her morning resentment and was speaking gently to Henut as if she was a child, and she did a lot to ease her suffering. She ripped a large piece of cloth off her own dress and, after having soaked it with water she laid it on Henut's wounded breasts, belly and legs, and gently lifted her head, giving her a cup of cold water, and pouring it into the thirsty lips of the girl. Heryt-uben wept; Henut's fate brought back her own painful memory of the day when she was also in the house of Pa-shu-uben, but what this cruel man has done today was many times worse.

"He's an animal!" she said. "He should die for that. You'll see that your boyfriend will come back from the war and kill him!" she added, wanting to comfort Henut.

However, Henut only whispered with trembling lips, "He is dead..." and a sudden sob began to shake her body, increasing the pain from the wounds that were nothing in comparison to the one – in the heart.

The day was already over and the whole Western City was wrapped in twilight. At this time no one would come to the sycamores anymore and there was no point in sitting here. The women were leaving, taking their precious bundles with earnings, which at home were to sate the hunger not only their own but most often of other household members: children, parents, siblings...

Aset stayed for a longer time beside Henut, but she was preparing to leave, too.

"I will walk you home," she said, "You can't stay here, and if you go alone, you'll faint along the way!"

"You are so good, Aset," Henut said, "But I can handle it. I'm better; I'm strong, I've been resting for a long time. I will stay here for a while - this wind from the fields is so pleasant - and then I will go; I don't have far to go home."

"It's up to you, but don't stay here tonight, because you smell of blood and you may lure a hyena," Aset took her bundle and left.

Henut looked at the linen bundle soaked with beer poured from a broken jug but hiding one more whole dish and a few loaves – she didn't even want to count them, but certainly, it would be enough for today's meal for mother, brother and herself, although actually she was feeling no hunger.

"I'll take it to them," she thought, but immediately imagined that for Hereret the most important topic of the first conversation would be the price her daughter paid for this bread. If she knew that Henut was going to the sycamores, she would probably stop her, but Henut hid it from her mother and, doing so, for the first time, she betrayed Maat. Now, she has been punished. Pa-Shu-Uben was right in telling his servants that she had gone to the sycamore trees voluntarily: in the house protected by the *ankh* sign nothing would threaten her. It means nothing except that awful feeling of constant hunger. But the worst crime she had committed was the betrayal towards Suti-mes: the crime of the unbelief that he would come back and that she would be able to connect with him as she had promised him. She did not betray the feeling, because she never stopped loving him, she still loves him, even though...The terrible truth returned to her at the same moment as the terrible memory of the cynically contorted face of Pa-Shu-uben saying that Suti-mes is dead and being pleased that he learned the secrets hidden for her beloved. Well, that's sure, it's the end of dreams of a shared home, the end of hope for a better life. Since he is dead, her life has no value either. Should she live only to wake up with a feeling of hatred every morning, not only towards the one who hurt her so much today, but first and foremost towards herself, and also with the feeling of hopelessness, lack of future, and a powerlessness even in the face of hunger?

Henut dragged herself off the grassy bed, which had given her the illusory feeling of comfort for several hours and started to walk straight ahead with unsteady gait, not even having taken her bundle. Every her step was causing an unspeakable pain. The linen wrap Aset gave her fell as soon as she got up and stayed under the sycamores, so she walked in her dress torn at the front, and the two halves of it being blown with the wind so that she was walking actually naked. The cool air was slightly appeasing the burning wounds. At this time of day, the road along the temple districts was completely empty, so there was no one who could help her, but also no one who could take advantage of such an unexpected meeting with a beautiful naked girl.

Henut's thoughts were after all far from reality. While walking she was recalling memories of her walks with Suti-mes, which were often – in a happy past – following the same paths. She was hearing his voice, feeling the touch of his hand, which she was holding firmly, so as not to release it even for a moment. She past an intersection of roads, where, going left, she would soon reach her home, and going right, she would walk toward the terrible place she was driven to today. Henut went straight, squeezing Suti-mes's hand. The wind from the fields brought now also the rustle of reeds and the smell of water; she was passing the Launderer's Bank. "Is it by chance that this place is also called the Crocodile Backwaters? I also would ask Amen-hotep if my sister sent me with the laundry..." Suti-mes's voice was full of warm contrariness, as it was then. "Do not be afraid, Suti, your sister will not send you with the laundry, I have to wash this dress myself..." Henut stopped at the edge, looking at the slightly wind-wrapped surface of the water, after which she carefully entered the pond, moving toward the rushes growing nearby and surrounding a small sandbank. The cool water first eased the thighs until Henut smiled: therefore, she was still pleased. Something moved in the reeds and Henut heard a splash of water. Will she still have time to cool the burning belly? She took a step forward. Can the death inflicted by a crocodile hurt more than the blows of Pa-Shu-uben's whip? There is nothing to be afraid of, but it's better not to look. The girl closed her eyes.

"Amun, accept me as I was after birth. Tell my mother that I had to, I wanted... Suti, I really loved you, forgive me... What else can I say, is this crocodile here at all, and maybe even it doesn't want me?"

Suddenly something milled violently around in the water. Henut unwittingly opened her eyes, next to her she saw a gaping mouth with a series of sharp teeth. At the same time, she felt someone pulled her sharply back and she saw a large branch of a tree pushed into the mouth of the beast. Her feet stopped touching the sand at the bottom and she understood that someone was carrying her. She has even felt regret that she was not allowed to part with earthly suffering, and then she did not care: she fainted.

The first sound of life that reached her again was the whimper of a small child that after a while calmed down soothed with her mother's breast. Henut recognized this woman; after all, they both repeatedly were participating in processions, while shaking *sesh-sesh*. It was Shed-em-dua, the wife of Buteh-Amun, whom Suti-mes talked about so often that she was almost jealous, though she never had the opportunity to talk to him.

"What is its name?" she asked, looking at the baby.

"Ankh-ef-en-Amun," Shed-em-dua answered. "But the most important thing is that you woke up because when Buteh-Amun brought you here, we all thought you were dead."

"It's a pity that I hadn't died," Henut replied quietly and all the terrible events of that day appeared before her eyes again.

"Don't say that Henut," Shed-em-dua looked at her seriously. "We are young, and life is the most valuable. Gat-seshen was living here next door, she wanted to live very much and had a small child, like me. They're gone and you're alive. Appreciate it, even if you can't enjoy it right now. I will boil milk for you and tell my men that you have come to life."

Shed-em-dua left, and during her short absence, Henut realized that she was lying on a comfortable bed covered with a linen bedspread, and the wounded parts of her body were dressed and smeared with something that was not only to heal but removed the pain from her. So, it was Buteh-Amun who saved her from the crocodile, a friend of Suti-mes – Henut did not yet know if she had more regret or gratitude in her heart, but the fact that she was among people closely associated with Suti was soothing.

At the moment, the curtain separating this room, where she lay, from the neighboring room (probably the kitchen, because a wonderful and almost forgotten smell of the cooked broad bean was coming from there) opened slightly and two smiling men came in. Henut guessed that the younger of them was Buteh-Amun, and the older one was probably his father, the famous Djehuty-mes whom she had seen several times from afar.

"It is rare in these terrible days to hear the good news," he said as he approached the bed, "and you're coming here and coming back from the condition you were in is such piece of news! I know you wanted to go to the crocodile, but Amun decided differently and persuaded Buteh-Amun to be there at the right time."

"It was rather my father," the younger man corrected. He insisted on sending me to the Launderer's Bank with his slightly soiled tunic, even though dusk was approaching, and I thought that the tunic could wait until tomorrow. But I went because the one who knows my father also knows that it is impossible to oppose him" he added with a smile, and the old Necropolis Scribe has only shaken his finger at him.

"Don't believe in what he says; he is stubborn like a donkey, but with this tunic it is true: he did not want to go, but apparently, Amun spoke with my mouth because he went. He didn't wash the tunic, so he got his way and he will do it tomorrow, but when he brought you, we both knew that it was your good destiny, Renenet[76]."

"Thank you for your kindness and sacrifice," Henut said quietly, and lowering her eyes she added: "But I think that all that

---

[76] The Egyptians believed that everyone is assigned a certain portion of good fate in life - Renenet and bad - Shai. But sometimes it was possible to prevent the bad destiny through prayer.

happened to me today is my Shai. If I have to live and remember – this is my bad destiny."

"That's not for us to judge," Djehuty-mes looked at her warmly but seriously. "Remember that God can change a man's destiny if he wants. Don't you know the story of the Enchanted Prince?[77] The crocodile, which was the prince's destiny and was to kill him, gave him a new life..."

At that moment, Shed-em-dua entered, carrying a cup of milk.

"Here, have a drink," she said and handed it to Henut, and the girl grabbed it and began to drink greedily, emptying it in the blink of an eye.

Then, seeing that everyone was looking at her, said as if excusing herself. „I didn't eat anything today nor yesterday; I was only drinking water, that's why I went to the sycamores..."

It was only at that moment that she realized that she had confessed in front of these people everything, although no one had asked her for anything.

"Poor child," Djehuty-mes stroked her head with a paternal movement. "I didn't know that in the families of those who are with Pa-nehsi, like your father, it's already so bad. I did not know that women from under the sycamores can suffer so much. Your wounds will heal soon, but the one who inflicted them should be brought to justice. You have to tell Pa-Shu-uben about him..."

---

[77] Allusion to a well-known story preserved on a papyrus dated to the New Kingdom (Papyri Harris 500) actually in the British Museum, London.

Hearing this name, Henut jerked, sitting on the bed, and her dressing slipped off her breasts, revealing their cruel "decoration" again.

"No!!!" she shouted, "I prefer a thousand times to go to the crocodile than to go there again! It was him who did it to me, and he told me... he said..."Here, she burst into tears and for a long time, both men unsuccessfully tried to calm her down. Finally, exhausted by the attack of spasms, the girl sank down on the bed again.

Shed-em-dua corrected her compresses and gave her milk again. Buteh-Amun and his father waited patiently for Henut to drink, after which the old Necropolis Scribe said with utmost seriousness, "Maat died in the City when things like this happen. You have told us about very important matters. In this situation, you cannot go home, because your mother would certainly do what I was thinking, and then the *ankh* on your house could no longer protect you. Pa-Shu-uben would not accuse himself and Pa-nehsi would not hurt him. It will be much better if everyone thinks you went to the crocodile. Buteh-Amun will take your dress to Pa-shu-uben and say that he found it on the Launderer's Bank, which is true anyway. I will take care of your mother and will give her my clothes for repair; neither her son nor she will feel hunger anymore. You will stay with me as my daughter. You will not go out anywhere. My home is so close to Pa-nehsi's palace that no one will look for you here; anyway, on my house is *ankh* too."

Henut looked at both men in disbelief. What Djehuty-mes was talking about meant a complete change of the fortune of her mother, her brother and herself.

"How will I repay you?" she whispered.

Buteh-Amun replied, "Shed-em-dua has a lot of work with little Ankhef now, so you'll be able to help her, and besides, it's good to have a friend at home to talk to. Anyway, I think Suti-mes will repay us one day even more."

Henut looked at him with suffering and in a cracking voice she said what she could not say before, "Pa-Shu-uben told me that Suti is dead. Do you understand now why I also wanted to die?!"

Buteh-Amun looked at his father, and when he received a sign of consent, he sat on the edge of the bed, took the girl's hand and, looking deep into her eyes, replied, "Amun wants you have to live and has torn you from death today. And a few months ago, he miraculously saved Suti-mes. Pa-nehsi sent him to death, and Pa-shu-uben apparently had to know about it, but your boyfriend didn't die. He is now at the side of Amen-hotep in Ipet-sut and, although there are enemies around, I believe that God will save him and someday unite with you, for he obviously loves you, since he miraculously saved both of you."

Henut listened in silence and only her eyes got bigger and bigger, then became glazed and once again that day tears began to flow from them; for the first time, however, these were tears of joy.

CHAPTER XI

By the end of the fourth month of Peret season, the patience of the besieging Ipet-sut had run out. Famine was prevailing throughout the City and its immediate surroundings, so General Pa-nehsi could not understand how many defenders of the temple, which became a fortress, could withstand.

"They obviously had to accumulate a lot of grain and other food, so Amen-hotep had predicted that he might be besieged," he finally concluded, and it upset him. In addition, Pa-Shu-uben showed him the letters he had received from the royal envoy who had come from Pi-Ramesse these days. One of them was addressed to the Chief of Police and His Majesty Ramesses, may he live, asked in it whether any of the desert attackers disturb the inhabitants of the City and whether the workers from the town regularly go to the Great Valley to work on the royal grave. The King emphasized that he had been waiting a long time for news in this matter and commanded that Pa-Shu-uben would not hesitate to answer. Other letters were addressed to the Vizier Un-nefer, to the Chief of Granaries Men-Maat-Re-nakht and to the High Priest Amen-hotep, and all these letters were expressing a deep concern at the lack of news and the King's clearly bad attitude to Pa-nehsi was evident, too. The Waset Secrets Inspector immediately responded in consultation with the General, assuring Pharaoh that the City, under the protection of his people, was flourishing and that everyone was living perfectly, and that the work on the tomb of His Majesty was moving quickly because no one threatens artisans. Admittedly, none of these sentences were true, but Pa-nehsi reassured that before the King finds out, the next months will pass, and at that time, perhaps, Pa-nehsi himself will "visit" Pi-Ramesse with his army while making appropriate proposals to Pharaoh. Either way, Pa-Shu-uben's answer was the only one to travel north, in the slowest boat, in order to make the journey at least 20 days long. After this date, the King, even if he calms down with good news about the progress of work on his grave, will probably be surprised that the messenger did not bring him an answer to other letters. A few days later, Pharaoh's astonishment could turn into anger, or – which Pa-nehsi was most afraid of – into the suspicion that it was not good in the City, which other generals, Pa-nehsi's rivals, and Heri-Hor, could easily suggest. Then the northern army corps could be mobilized and thwarted the plans of the "Governor of the Free Kush." However, the General knew Pharaoh well enough that he did not expect such a rapid action from him. He will probably send first, very angry letters, and only when he receives no answer, he will convene the royal council and ask for the opinion of generals. Pa-nehsi calculated that the whole Shemu season would thus pass, and only after the New Year the North would begin to prepare for war.

"Though even then," Pa-nehsi smiled at the thought, "The entire northern army will be weaker than the one with whom I will come. There are admitted troops from all over Kemet, as well as the terrible infantry of Sherdan's mercenaries[78], but the Kushite archers are incomparable and only the ones of Tjehenu could equal them in this respect. However, there are few mercenary Tjehenu troops and Ramesses he makes sure that there are not too many of them, because they could become dangerous; after all, their settlements are very numerous in the North..."

One thing was clear: the time for the final battle with Amen-hotep had just arrived, for another month of siege could ruin all plans. Pa-nehsi, therefore, sent another message in which, apart from the renewed proposal to Amen-hotep to surrender and thereby to save the destruction of "the holy sanctuary of our common father Amun," he expressed the promise that "all the faults would be forgiven those defenders who leave Ipet-sut voluntarily."

Amen-hotep guessed that the final assault was approaching, but did not understand how this "voluntary departure from Ipet-sut" would take place? His answer was as before: only the

---

[78] Appreciated mercenaries derived from the so-called The Sea Peoples with whom Egypt fought in the 13th and 12th centuries in BC At the time the novel takes place, they were used, among others, as an adjutant royal guard, and veterans were settled in Egypt and received land assignments.

abandoning of the siege can give Pa-nehsi a chance to get King's understanding, while the raising of his hand against Amun's house will be the beginning of his defeat. The High Priest expected that the next day the attack of the Kushite army would begin, and his people spent the night on the walls, ready to fight, however no storm took place. In the next morning, the siege troops standing in front of the Great Gate unexpectedly parted, and then all the free space between the walls of Ipet-sut and the Kushite army was filled with a crowd of women and children crying, and sometimes screaming with fear.

Then the trumpet's high voice broke through the tumult and a Kushite officer appeared at the Great Gate, who announced in a loud voice, "His Dignity The General, Vizier and Royal Son of Kush Pa-nehsi promised yesterday that to all those whom the great criminal Amen-hotep imprisoned in the walls of Ipet-sut and who would leave unarmed, he would give grace of forgiveness! Here are their women and their children. Those who leave, will regain their families and the *ankh* will appear on their houses. But all of you who will stay there, listen! Your children will be useful as slaves in the Kingdom of Kush, and your women will be useful to us even earlier. Decide today, because tomorrow it will be too late!"

When he finished, the lament of female and child voices increased again, and the defenders sitting on the walls could see the Kushite soldiers leading them beyond their lines again, often pushing, and sometimes even beating those who stopped, wanting to spot the walls of Ipet-sut their relatives: husbands, brothers or fathers.

"It is villainy how one can wage a war like that!" Amen-hotep thought. The High Priest had to admit that Pa-nehsi's cunning trick had put him in a very difficult position. Now, the sense of marking the houses of some inhabitants of the East and West Waset with the *ankh* has finally become clear. At night the besieging army was sent to pull women and children out of all the houses that did not have this sign, because women and children, because they were in some way associated with the defenders of Ipet-sut. Now, they became hostages and their fate was to depend on what Amen-hotep would do. If he wanted to save all those women and children, he should let most of the defenders do out of the walls, which would make the situation of the besieged even more difficult. Leaving everything unchanged could have resulted in the tragedy of many families. What the Kushite herald has announced was repeated from mouth to mouth, and soon reached all those who were in the temple precinct. Now many were waiting with great tension for what the First Servant of Amun would decide. He consulted with his closest advisers, led by Amen-em-Ipet. It was known that every solution was not good. Unfortunately, the danger seemed quite real that Pa-nehsi not only can commit the crime of rising hand against the temple of Amun and against the life of his servants, but also can take the innocent children into captivity.

Finally, it was decided that all priests who became amazed by the siege while being on their duty periodical service in the temple should remain here. This service, although extended many times, continued after all and could not be interrupted. Everyone else was given the freedom to choose to leave or stay:

"Let Amun, who has placed Maat in everyone's heart," the High Priest said, "Let everyone judge what is more valuable to him: protecting the family or serving the temple. We have an enemy in front of us who has already trodden all the rules of the art of war, so we do not know whether he will fulfill his promises, which he passed through the lips of the herald. But even if no one leaves Ipet-sut, the temple will fall under the overwhelming pressure of the army and then it is not known what will happen to the defenders. Therefore, let everyone make a choice and I will accept every decision without grudge. Already today, all who stayed here during the siege that is for the last six months, are heroes, have my gratitude and merits to God. Let Amun look after everyone and his women and children. The house of Amun once survived the attacks of his enemies and the time of destruction, so it will survive this war, too!"

Amen-hotep's decision immediately reached all the corners of Ipet-sut and for the next hours everyone asked his heart what to do. Many decided to stay and count on a miracle. Others did not expect a miracle but decided that to leave the House of Amun would be a sign of their weakness and a cause of shame the memory of which would not leave them until death, acting like a poison that would destroy all the joy of their lives. Still, others were talking about their destiny, about their attachment to Amen-hotep, about the dignity of serving God - they all decided to stay.

All those who decided to save their families and to trust in Pa-nehsi's promise for many hours until the dark were going out by a wicked in the Great Gate. They were to become convinced that

Pa-nehsi had fulfilled this promise only partially. When the defender of Ipet-sut crossed the lines of the Kushite army, it was immediately led to the place where women and children were gathered and the army scribe wrote his name there, after which those who belonged to his family were sought. At that time, there was usually a joyful greeting, but there were also such meetings as that Ta-shed-Mut gave her husband.

Instead of rejoicing, when she was called out of the crowd, she began to cry on the shoulder of her sister Bak-en-Mut, and when she saw the man, she came up to him and, taking off her sandal, hit him in the head, saying only, "You coward!" Other women were glad to see their loved ones, but the connection of each family lasted so short: the soldier escorted the woman and children of the Ipet-sut defender to the house where the *ankh* was now painted, but he was now led to a different place, where another scribe enrolled him as a recruit for Pa-nehsi's army, and if anyone refused to accept it, he was tied up. Squads of forced recruits were larger every day because Pa-nehsi announced the *medu-an* the forced recruitment to his troops[79]. The Kushite soldiers were now bringing here all the men who had not volunteered so far: shepherds, mockers, craftsmen from the town where they lived working on the royal tomb and, of course, all the *medjayu* who had protected the Great Valley and the City itself, except for those who remained at Pa-Shu-uben's disposal.

The night passed peacefully. In the morning, the High Priest could say that even thought there were fewer defenders, however

---

[79] This is confirmed in one papyrus, which is currently in the Liverpool City Museum.

still enough to ensure that the fortress could stand the first attack of the enemy. The High Priest himself climbed to the top of the Great Gate today, for he expected that whatever would happen would probably begin here. It happened as he thought, although neither he nor Amen-em-Ipet could predict how terrible a show Pa-nehsi prepared for them.

At first, everything was similar to the previous day. The line of the Kushite troops in front of the Gate parted, and after a while, among the laments, women ran in, some accompanied by children, this time pushed brutally by soldiers. Now here, in front of the defenders gathered on the walls, all the children were taken from their mothers and, among desperate screams, led to the harbor at the end of the avenue of lions, and there loaded onto a barge, which soon left somewhere. In its place a second one came and now every younger woman has been loaded to it. At the same time, from among those still standing in front of the Great Gate, five particularly pretty ones were selected, among them Bak-en-Mut, after which their robes were stripped off and they were brutally raped several times, as those who stood at the top of the gate and on the walls next to it could see everything. Bak-en-Mut and another woman tried to fight their persecutors and both finally broke free, but they could not take advantage of this temporarily acquired freedom. Surrounded from everywhere by overjoyed soldiers, they were running naked between them, trying to escape, and these were laughing and blocking their path until they were bored and killed the women with stabs of their spears.

"Forgive me Amun that I didn't protect them!" the pale High Priest whispered and added, "I saw and remembered everything. Maat is dead and it is necessary to create the world anew..."

"Will Your Grandness tell this to the King?" Amen-em-Ipet asked seriously.

"I will have to, although this King will not be able to make the Repeating of Births and will defend himself against this act," replied the First Servant and looked at Suti-mes standing next to him, who was watching with terror the scenes of the humiliation and killing of the women:

"Don't be afraid, she's not here. Her father joined Pa-nehsi from the beginning, so his house has an *ankh* sign that protects your girlfriend."

At this time, everyone standing on the walls saw a clear movement in the still peaceful troops besieging Ipet-sut. The soldiers lined up in battle formation, preparing their bows, and at the same time those who were supposed to put in front of the walls the giant shields protecting against the arrows, which were expected from there, came to the front. When some groups of strong half-naked men were also seen behind the line of archers holding high siege ladders, it became clear that the enemy was preparing to storm.

"And now is the time, Your Eminence!" Amen-em-Ipet said and put both hands on the heads of Amen-hotep and Suti-mes. "Let Amun look after you!"

"You too, my friend," the First Servant of Amun replied, and beckoning to Suti-mes, he walked toward the stairs leading down inside one of the towers of the Great Gate.

Hyenas & Lotuses

Soon the terrifying sound of trumpets gave the signal to attack. This time no teams of "breakers" were used; the fortified walls of Ipet-sut were only 12 cubits high, that is, one-third of what was the case of the fortress in Khefet-her-neb-es. Pa-nehsi decided to use here the method that was usually successful when it was necessary to attack the strongholds in the country of Retjenu. Archers thundered the tops of the walls with arrows, while heavy siege ladders were attached to them, followed by soldiers armed with spears and axes, covering themselves with shields. The first unfortunates selected for this task were condemned to death in advance because they were not able to cover themselves from all sides at once and were shot by defenders. Initially, they had the task easier, because there were so many attackers that almost every arrow released from the walls was accurate, while the shooters from below had to hit targets hiding behind various shields being part of the wall. However, the Kushite archers were excellent and after a few hours the number of defenders decreased significantly. That day, it was still possible to stop the storm troopers, but it was almost certain that the next day the fortress would fall. All who wielded weapons were preparing to die, and the priests made their last sacrifices in all the chapels dedicated to the various shapes and names of the One God under which he was traditionally worshiped in the main temples of the Both Countries. Their copies were gathered in Ipet-sut, so that the House of Amun was like a miniature of the entire land of Kemet.

Amen-em-Ipet made sure that all-important Amen-hotep's letters and documents that should be saved were well hidden. It wasn't even about them not falling into Pa-nehsi's hands, but they would not burn if the Kushite soldiers intentionally or accidentally started a fire.

Gold and silver liturgical items were locked in caches, but Amen-em-Ipet was afraid that at least some of them would be found. However, his greatest concern was to protect the holy statue of Amun in the sanctuary.

It was made of gold, but touching this statue, or even opening the chapel in which it stood, by barbarians, would mean that the whole world collapsed; there is nothing that protects it and at any moment the announcement of Atum can be fulfilled:

I will destroy everything, which I created and everything will return to the state it was at the beginning.[80]

Amen-em-Ipet swore that he would rather lay down his life than to allow this happens.

At dawn, the Kushites resumed their attack, and indeed around the noon in some places the first soldiers of Pa-nehsi managed to climb the wall from the siege ladders and to start a hand-to-hand combat there. When the defenders rushed to these places, weakening other positions, ladders were soon there and soon there were more attackers on the walls than defenders. A moment later, the guards defending access to the Great Gate were knocked out and it was opened from the inside. Now, the Kushite troops poured into the huge Hall of Appearance like a rushing river and rushed to the side gate, which led southwards,

---

[80] One of the religious texts in the *Book of the Dead* in which the Creator announces the end of the world and the return of water chaos. See the note 41 (Chapter IV).

constituting the beginning of the path for the procession going to Ipet-resit. Directly behind this gate was the courtyard in front of the palace of the First Servant of Amun, and it became now the main target of the attackers. The gate once made on the order of High Priest Amen-hotep, for which he was later awarded by His Majesty Ramesses Nefer-Ka-Re, was beautifully decorated, but it was intended for religious and not military purposes. Although it was covered with bronze, it could not resist for a long time the blows of a thick trunk of a freshly cut palm carried by twenty quickly running soldiers, who hit with it with great force the obstacle. Finally the Kushites broke into the courtyard and then into the rooms of the palace, killing the few guards and several other people found there. That is how the old doctor Sunu died who was living there for years and mistakenly thought that since he was always saving the lives of others, his own life was not threatened... All places of the palace were searched, but Amen-hotep was not found, so in helpless anger the soldiers began to destroy everything that was there, and the High Priest's personal furniture and things were thrown in the middle of the courtyard to a pile and burned. Fortunately, Pa-nehsi himself appeared and stopped his soldiers who were already trying to destroy the walls of the palace.

The General also saw a killed doctor, whom he knew from the old days when he did not yet feel hostility towards Amen-hotep and sometimes ate supper with him, also in the company of people closely associated with the High Priest, like Amen-em-Ipet, or even just killed now Sunu. Pa-nehsi flamed out with real anger, ordered to find the soldier who had killed the doctor and made sure that he was beheaded immediately.

This alleviated the bloodthirsty mood of his soldiers, whom the General forbade to kill anyone unless he wanted to fight. This order saved the lives of many other defenders who were still in Ipet-sut, as well as priests who were now in the depths of the temple, separated by still closed gates. Pa-nehsi, convinced that Amen-hotep is right there, ordered to check all the nooks and crannies around this area and then surrounded it with a tight ring of troops, so no one could sneak out. The night passed peacefully. The next day, the herald announced with the sound of a trumpet, which raised a multiplied echo in the great column hall that the General would speak to those who were hiding behind the closed gate on the eastern side of the Appearance Hall.

"Open the gate!" cried Pa-nehsi. "Nobody will be hurt if you stop protecting the great criminal Amen-hotep, who won't get out of the snare anyway! Otherwise, the gate will be open by force!"

The General's voice was reverberating from the roof of the Appearance Hall supported by 134 columns, some of which were 40 cubits high, erected there[81] and it returned with mighty echo. The defenders on the other side of the gate must have heard it well, but only silence answered him. Then, after a long moment, when Pa-nehsi was about to summon the soldiers carrying the palm trunk, both wings of the gate opened with the metallic

---

[81] The action takes place in the area known today as the Temple of Karnak and contains a reconstruction of the original appearance and functions of some fragments of this temple described here.

sound of the sliding staples. Pa-nehsi, followed by several of his officers, including Aa-neru, expected to enter an even darker room, which is usually found in the temples behind the Hall of Appearances, meanwhile they were struck by the glare of rays from high blue. They were again in the open courtyard, from which soaring skewers of obelisks were heading in the sky, and in the near distance, they saw another closed gate. Pa-nehsi and his officers approached it, expecting that it would also open immediately. However, before this happened, a voice so loud and clear that it was heard by everyone who was in the open space between the gates spoke up.

"You have come to a place where the path of those who do not know the secrets of earth, sky and the underground world ends. Here, even the Pharaoh's Majesty had to undergo a special cleansing ritual to get on! If you cross this gate, you will commit an *isefet* in the place of Maat and offend God with your filthiness! Bring yourselves to reason and turn back to avoid the Hidden punishment!"

The voice fell silent, and for a long moment, there was absolute silence in which they could hear the chirping of sparrows sitting on a tree, the crown of which protruded above the sidewall of the courtyard. Pa-nehsi was well aware that they had come to the intimate chambers of the House of Amun, those parts of the temple where only very few priests could enter on solemn occasions, with shaved heads, bodies bathed in the waters of the Holy Lake, robes without a trace of dirt, and additionally having been cleaned with natron, incense and special prayer. Yet he was standing here dirty and sweaty, and some of those who were with him had on their armors traces of freshly shed blood of the Ipet-sut defenders. At the same time, he had no doubt that Amenhotep was in the rooms hidden behind this gate, who, having no chance of escaping the army, decided to take advantage of his special religious privileges.

"Does he really think I'm so naive?" the General thought and was already turning to give the soldiers a sign to break the gate when, like the previous one, it opened for them. Pa-nehsi, Aa-neru and several other officers, followed by only a small part of those soldiers who stood in the courtyard entered the hall with a ceiling supported by stone columns in the shape of papyri stems tied together in bundles. It was a twilight here, only a scant light was oozing through a few small holes in the roof, extracting from the shadow the contours of Osiris statues standing along the walls. In the middle of the room, the tops of two obelisks could be seen, surrounded to a considerable height with walls covered with colorful reliefs. Only some 40 cubits from there was another gate, of course also closed. They approached it cautiously, but Aa-neru and two soldiers quickly traversed the entire hall from end to end, looking vigilantly behind each column. There was no one here, and yet a voice was heard again, coming from unknown source, being echoed in this dark mysterious space and filling the intruders with horror:

"Oh, unclean ones who uninvited dared to enter the House of God! Do you know that you are standing in the place where the crowns of the Both Countries were put on the Pharaoh's head so that he could stand with dignity before the Majesty of Amun? Move back as soon as possible to avoid His wrath!"

Pa-nehsi heard a rustle of footsteps from behind and while turning his head he saw some soldiers and even officers sneaking out of the dark room.

"Fools!" he thought, "How easy they are duped by these priestly tricks! It is good that at least this one is with me." He looked at Aa-neru with a pitying smile on his face: he had seen many temples and knew that no secret threats should be expected here. He also bravely headed towards the next gate, and then Pa-nehsi and several other Kushites also moved in this direction. The battering ram also proved unnecessary here; the gate opened, revealing the interior of an even darker room situated at a little higher level than the one where they were standing. A little to the right, a chapel emerged from the darkness, which even in this dimness was reflecting with a golden shine the faint light penetrating through the open gates. Aa-neru admired the walls and the floor covered with gold and electron. Nobody was found here once again. When their eyes got used to the deep twilight, they saw a bit further an offering altar and behind it another gate, also completely covered with gold, probably leading to the most sacred place in Ipet-sut.

"There will be wealth..." Aa-neru dreamed, sharing this expectation with the General, when the same voice intrusive as always interrupted their thoughts:

"You who do not know God and are heading towards your own perdition, learn that only the King's Majesty or the First Servant who substitutes him have the right to remain at this place having received Amun's blessing and to give him the due offerings. And what can you offer him besides your crimes? If you cross the gate, you'll be cursed forever!"

"Did you hear it?" Pa-nehsi turned to Aa-neru reassured that nothing bad had happened to them so far, "only Amun's First Servant has the right to be here and he probably is actually staying there. Let the soldiers come here and be ready, because the most faithful subjects of Amen-hotep may be lurking behind this door!"

At a given sign, a dozen soldiers of the General's guard armed with swords and spears stood in the front row, covering their leader and his officers. Then the gate began to open slowly. It turned out that Aa-neru was right.

Everyone entering this hall, dark like the previous one, was struck by the glow of gold. It was everywhere. Immediately behind the entrance they saw a tall bronze offering table with a burning oil lamp. Its light reflected a golden glow of the gilded walls and the floor, but everyone's eyes were caught by a richly covered festival barge – a magnificent User-hat, also resting on a gilded pedestal. From below the barge, to the left and right, numerous gilded spars made of valuable wood were protruding, rest on the shoulders of the priests carrying the barge during the procession. There was absolute silence in the room. There were no more noises from the world here as if it was non-existent. Here they were touching unknowingly the mystery of the act of creation, being in the depths of the primordial waters, where silence and darkness prevailed and where the Creator himself lived. Pa-nehsi and his men stood, shocked by this sight, and no one dared to break this silence that was hiding the sanctity, although some soldiers even began to stroke the gilded surfaces of the barge, and even check if the gold decorations could be easily torn off. Others checked, as before, all the nooks and crannies of this room and it turned out again that not only there were no armed defenders, but also no one other except for the gatekeepers, who, after having opened each subsequent gate, were standing by it, silent, more in the likeness of statues than human beings. There were only a few small rooms at the back of the Holy Barge Hall, and among them certainly was the Saint of Saints, or the chapel with the statue of Amun. The soldiers have not entered there yet and this was the right place where Amen-hotep must have been hiding.

"He probably wants to be arrested near the statue; he will then say that we have violated sanctity," Pa-nehsi smiled to his thoughts and, walking around the holy barge, went straight towards the vestibule of the sanctuary, which was only closed on a staple fastened in a door lined with gold. At that moment, another door opened that he had not even noticed before, and a white retinue of priests carrying Amun's holy emblems came out of the side room. They were led by Amen-em-Ipet, wearing the priestly robes and insignia at the moment, including a leopard skin and a special headgear made of gold metal, which, tightly adhering to the head, gave the impression that it was shaved, giving a noble glow. Walking slowly and reciting the hymn to Amun, the priests lined up in front of the entrance to the shrine's vestibule, turning their faces to Pa-nehsi. Everyone held an object representing Amun, usually carried in processions. After a few verses of the hymn, they fell silent and stood still as a living shield blocking the way to the holiest place in Ipet-sut and in the whole of the Southern Country. There was something so dignified in their attitude that for a long time there was silence again, which seemed to be the only proper atmosphere for this place.

Finally, Pa-nehsi interrupted it. "Do you think you have the right to oppose me?" he asked.

Amen-em-Ipet answered loudly and calmly, saying each sentence as if he was reciting the continuation of the hymn, "Our duty is to serve God and we are doing it right now. The power of the Vizier doesn't reach here, nor that of the Royal Son of Kush, nor that of the General. Even the Majesty of Pharaoh, when he arrives here, becomes the servant of God, for all the power, even the royal one, the more so yours one comes from Amun.

Just the fact that you came here and are standing in a place where only the Son of Re or the Servant of Amun acting on his behalf is allowed to act, being prepared for making offerings due to God and for uttering the right words foreseen in the course of these holy activities, is a crime against Maat, because you would never have the right to cross the threshold behind the Appearance Room.

The hands of the barbarians you direct unlawfully touch holy objects that only the Servants of God specially purified ones could approach. Now, you want to face Amun himself to do something unimaginable that no criminal has ever done before! However, before you do this, you must kill us. We are ready, remembering that death at the hands of those who are doing an iniquity is much better than living in the iniquity."

Throughout this speech, Pa-nehsi calmly waited for Amen-em-Ipet to finish, although he was not used to hear anyone talking to him like that. Something inexplicable, perhaps the uniqueness of this place made him listen to these words to the end.

"You're wrong, priest," he finally answered, "if you think that we want to kill you. We do not intend to raise our hands either against you or the more against Amun. He gave us victory over the one who brought all this misfortune to you. Don't protect your Amen-hotep who hid here like a rat and sent you to death!"

Amen-em-Ipet, looking straight into the General's eyes, calmly replied, "The Lord of All makes thousands unhappy and gives power to thousands, when he is in his hour.[82] Apparently it was his sentence that a misfortune fell upon the City, which would end one day. We are not to judge His decisions."

Pa-nehsi withstood the priest's eyes and repeated strongly, "The misfortune will end soon after Amen-hotep comes to me. I do not want to cross the threshold of the sanctuary, but if he is there, let him stop being a coward and show himself!"

"His Eminence of the First Servant of Amun is not in the Saint of Saints, nor in Ipet-sut at all. Can you not see that I am wearing High Priest's robes for him?" Amen-em-Ipet replied. "If you enter a holy chapel, you will commit a crime against God, although you will not find any human being there."

---

[82] These words repeat a fragment of the *Teachings of Amen-em-Ipet*. See the note 35 (Chapter III).

"Do you prefer, old man that I order to wall the entrance?" Pa-nehsi asked, still fighting with his gaze with Amen-em-Ipet's one.

"You can do it, General; then the holy statue will be safe," the priest answered, and Pa-nehsi looked down.

"Let ten men guard here," he decided, then turned back to the old priest, "I can't believe that Amen-hotep became like Amun and became invisible. We will keep looking for him, but you can do your service. None of us will cross the threshold of the sanctuary. However, you must know that I, the Royal Son of Kush, as well as all my soldiers who represent today the Free Kush army, think that this gold so much abundant here, which through pain and blood was once taken from the land of Kush, should not be present in the temple of the One who had created the Kushites. This is a bad offering, so we will remove it from the temple so that it couldn't offend the God!"

Without waiting for what Amen-em-Ipet could say now, the General turned and walked away along the path he had come here. He went through the Hall of the Barge, passing the magnificent User-hat as if escorted in a way by the gaze of a ram-headed Amun carved in its prow, and stopped only in the courtyard flooded with the light of Re. Many soldiers stood there who did not dare to cross the next gate. High above their heads magnificent obelisks rose, erected here almost 400 years ago. Their finials, forming the small pyramids, were covered with sheets of gold metal.

Pa-nehsi pointed at them and turned to Aa-neru, accompanying him like a shadow, "All the gold that you will find in the temple outside those rooms," - he pointed towards the Hall of the Barge and the Sanctuary, "recover and load on our boats!"

"Lord," the officer replied, "those rooms are exactly the place where the most of gold is gathered, as you have seen, and there is certainly a cache there... You have to check if a plate in the floor or in the wall is movable, or maybe Amen-hotep is sitting behind it?"

"Come on, Aa-neru!" Pa-nehsi looked at him with a pitying smile. "First, Ipet-sut is great and there is plenty of gold in it; you will have to work hard to remove it, even from all these obelisks. Secondly, I don't want to be considered an enemy of Amun now. Who knows, if I won't come back here in another role; much depends on the attitude of Ramesses. Thirdly, the gold that we saw even on the barge itself is easily accessible and the priests will not do anything with it, performing these ordinances...We will take it later if the talks at Pi-Ramesse would have brought no results. Anyway, there is another place in Waset, where at least the same amount of gold can be expected, and we will also take it..."

"True, other temples are full of it, I know something about it," Aa-neru chuckled.

"Well, they too..." Pa-nehsi added and he changed the topic: "I think that what Amen-em-Ipet was telling is true: Amen-hotep is not in Ipet-sut... I don't know how it is possible, but this old man just can't lie, and I looked him in the eye. Search for all caches throughout Ipet-sut, look into all nooks and crannies with statues, niches with the equipment necessary to celebrate all these sacrifices, libraries with papyri scrolls used during various ceremonies, also go to the rooftops, where everyday rituals; maybe we missed something..."

Aa-neru started eagerly to follow his superior's instructions. The great temple of Amun and all the chapels in its area, as well as the neighboring temple precincts of Montu and Mut, became plundered. The gold was "recovered" from the tops of obelisks, gates, walls of some rooms, it was torn off from large stelas displayed in the courtyards, the gilded surfaces of statues and of wooden chapels hiding various images of God were chopped off with axes. The "experienced" Aa-neru also discovered a dozen caches in which valuable items rested, having been used to perform religious ceremonies during various holidays: the vessels made of gold, silver and bronze, the censers, small images of boats and various sculptures, whose meaning was understood only by priests, but which were also made of precious metal. The whole area of the temple of Amun and other temples in the Eastern and Western City resembled the building site in these days, and this fact itself was not unusual: after all, almost in every temple, something was still added, changed or renovated, but it was always done in the name of the reigning King, for whom some work was a sacred duty. Now, the temples were stripped of their most precious ornaments, in the place of which nothing was planned. Moreover, the same team of "breakers" who participated in the attack on the fortress of His Majesty Ramesses User-Maat-Re Meri-Amun in Khefet-her-neb-es, now began, on Pa-nehsi's order to pull down, or actually to smash the great gate of Ipet-sut, as well to destroy the western gate of the fortress in Khefet-her-neb-es, along with large fragments of adjacent walls. In both cases, these were indeed barbarian activities, because both gates were beautifully decorated, and the western gate housed a rich palace with beautiful sculptures and so much decorative capitals of the column that it was difficult to find something equally wonderful in the entire City. This time, the work of „breakers", not disturbed by anyone, progressed quickly, but the hearts of the residents of Khefet-her-neb-es were becoming numb with sorrow when they saw the beautifully carved stone slabs falling from the upper floors of the gate[83] and smashing to a shapeless debris soon removed by other workers so that it would not interfere with the work of destruction.

The High Priest Amen-hotep was intensively sought all the time, but after a few days, it was recognized that he was probably not in Ipet-sut. Then Pa-nehsi decided to call the Necropolis Scribe Djehuty-mes, although he expected that this conversation would not be a pleasant one: the house of Djehuty-mes was standing near the ruined western gate.

"Chari, you have always been in such good relations with Amen-hotep that I suppose you are still in touch. How is he?" Pa-nehsi asked, not concealing his cynical tone.

"Your question is weird one," Djehuty-mes said. "Do you think that Amen-hotep may feel good after you armedly invaded Amun's House, of which he is the First Servant, after you deceived many people for whom the High Priest was a patron and father, while putting them against him, after you killed most of his servants and entered the temple, and after you plundered his

---

[83] Archeological research confirms that the western gate of this fortress was demolished from the top and not destroyed by warfare.

palace, as you are now plundering the holy buildings erected and decorated by numerous pharaohs? I assure you that the High Priest Amen-hotep feels very bad and that death would probably be better for him."

"Ah, so he lives!" Pa-nehsi exclaimed with hypocritical joy. - Your words, especially the news that he feels bad, are like a balm for my heart. You see, Chari, I rarely agree with you, but today I totally share your opinion that it would be better if Amen-hotep died and I would be ready to help him in this, but I can't meet him."

Djehuty-mes raised his voice, "You are a criminal, an enemy of Amun and an enemy of the Both Countries! I only expect evil from you. Did you bring me here to kill me?"

Pa-nehsi did not abandon the cynical tone: "No, Chari, you really underestimate me and my practical sense. What would it do to me if I killed an old man, so important for the City and for the King! It's a pity that you don't want to tell me what happened to Amen-hotep. But you probably know well where your son Buteh-Amun is, because, to my knowledge, he is absent from home, and he should take care of his old father, as well as his wife and child. Or maybe she will tell me more when she sees someone holding her baby by the foot above the well?"

Djehuty-mes looked at the General with the utmost contempt, "I knew you were a criminal and I know you could go so far as to kill an innocent child in front of his mother. Even then, she wouldn't tell you where Buteh-Amun is, because she doesn't know. I also don't know much more than that my son is doing the honorable service of protecting of that one whom you are persecuting. Buteh-Amun is where Amen-hotep is, but I don't know where they are; I only pray that Amun would protect them!"

Pa-nehsi decided that he would learn nothing more, so he suddenly changed the subject of the conversation, "I want you to know that I'm going on a long trip, maybe I can visit His King's Majesty whom I haven't seen for so long. I don't know how long it will take, but I hope you will do your duty well and guard the necropolis, especially the Great Valley. I ordered Pa-shu-uben to work at the western gate in this district; take care that no stone falls on your head there!"

Old Necropolis Scribe sensed both threat and mockery: he is to guard the necropolis in a situation when all the *medjayu* who guarded the royal tomb were conscripted, but at the same time he should not leave the house, because stones are now falling from above.

"Why are you doing this? Why are you destroying such a wonderful work of His Majesty Ramesses User-Maat-Re Meri-Amun, the pride of West Waset?" he asked quietly.

Pa-nehsi answered him with a mocking smile, "But the gate to my palace will remain untouched and it will continue to be the glory of Khefet-her-neb-es! Tell me, however, why such a powerful fortress in West Waset? I had a fight with it once, even though it was not defended by a decent army. I don't want to risk that somebody can be locked up again there when I am absent. Do you want to say goodbye to me with a good word?"

Djehuty-mes stood up and headed toward the exit. "I hope," he replied, already standing on the threshold, "that your expedition will end faster than you expect and that you will come back soon, fleeing!" Then he turned away, no longer hearing the quiet words of the General's answer, who watched him with hateful eyes.

"Ah, Chari, my debt to you increases, and I think I will pay it back soon... If Amen-hotep is still in the City," he thought, "this old man will certainly want to repeat him what I have told." He loudly commanded the soldier, "Follow him day and night!" However, two more days passed and people watching the house of the Necropolis Scribe said that the dignitary did not go anywhere and did not meet anyone, and those who were given the task of eavesdropping through the walls and roof of all conversations held in his house, reported that, apart from Djehuty-mes there are only two young women and a small child. "Two?" Pa-nehsi was surprised, "Does this old lecher sweeten his life with a lass? Anyway, what does it matter! Amen-hotep is not in Waset, and if so, he is certainly on his way to the King. How did he get out of Ipet-sut? On the morning of the assault day, I was assured that he was seen at the top of the Great Gate... Anyway, he doesn't go by the river, because the river and both its banks with all surrounding paths are closely guarded almost as far as to Abdju. So... it remains the only way, actually less patrolled, through the oases and the desert. It is probably that way the messenger used who reached the King and now the High Priest escapes[84]!"

Pa-nehsi immediately summoned Aa-neru and ordered him to capture the noble fugitive.

---

[84] The escape of the High Priest Amen-hotep from the besieged Thebes by desert way through oases is confirmed by sources.

"He's escaping through the oases, and Buteh-Amun is with him," the General explained. "The fast pursuit of a special horse troop should catch up with them before they reach Pa-im. It's best to kill them both because you have personal accounts with them. Then quickly return to the City, because here you will also have an important task: you will follow the paths of old Djehuty-mes, especially in the area of the Great Valley. Just don't hurt him because you would take away my pleasure!" he emphasized and patted his officer significantly on the shoulder.

Aa-neru took over a dozen of the fastest horses and an hour later set off in pursuit at the head of a small squad of armed Kushite messengers specialized in fast riding.

CHAPTER XII

Meanwhile, the three refugees were already quite far away, with a few days' advantage and all hopes that they would be able to reach Pi-Ramesse early enough for the northern part of the country to prepare for defense. It was the only hope of saving the kingdom, which for over a hundred years had not experienced the horror of war and seemed to be dozing in blissful peace. It is army was not only unprepared for defense against an attack by some foreign power (because, in fact, there was no such one nearby Kemet state), but it was also divided into many units located mainly along the long west and east borders. The High Priest Amen-hotep was aware of this danger, and he also knew that this situation was well known to Pa-nehsi. He, being a General and a close associate of the King, had participated in councils for years, at which Pharaoh heard reports about the state of security of the country and even if he had not been to Pi-Ramesse for a long time, he knew the content of these reports because his great friend, the General Pi-ankh equal to him in position, informed him of everything.

Amen-hotep knew that Ipet-sut could not withstand for a long time the pressure of an army composed of excellent Kushite soldiers and led by –he had to admit it – an equally excellent commander. He also assumed that over the next few days the conquerors would search all the corners of the temple and numerous buildings covering Ipet-sut, looking for him and that only then would they chase him, but the advantage obtained would allow the fugitives to reach Men-nefer or Iunu, from where they will safely and in good guards go to Pi-Ramesse. The plan was good, and it would certainly succeed, if a young man was in the High Priest's place, having been well trained in a fast horseback ride for hours. Unfortunately, Amen-hotep had never sat on a horse before, and besides, he was no longer young and he tired quickly, so the escape did not proceed as quickly as one would wish. And yet it all began so promising...

On the first day of escape, Amen-hotep with Suti-mes arrived in the evening as planned, to Sumenu. While walking on foot to Madu, and then riding on the donkeys along the edge of the desert to Djeret, they had to be very careful. In case if someone saw them they would pretend peasants who should not have aroused the slightest suspicion that they were running away from someone. There was a fear that Pa-nehsi's army or Pa-Shu-uben's guards could carry out forced recruitment into the army even in this area, and then they could be detained. Fortunately, it turned out that the Kushite units penetrating the area had been here two days earlier and took several villagers, about which a woman encountered along the way told them. The crossing from Djeret to Sumenu was easy; in this area there was, after all, the Crocodile Island and all the time someone was taking a boat in Djaret to sail there with some funeral retinue or to Sumenu itself, so the two men seeking for the opportunity to cross the river did not arouse anyone's suspicion. In Sumenu, very tired Amen-hotep and his companion arrived at Sobek's temple and here they could finally stop pretending to be someone else. When the *setem* priest in this temple saw the First Servant, he gave him a low bow, telling of the great honor to be host for the representative of Amun and assuring him of his readiness to give all the ministries that a distinguished newcomer may wish. This priest already knew that Amun's First Servant was on his way to Sumenu, because another young priest had arrived here an hour earlier and had told him about that. Hearing this, Amen-hotep breathed a sigh of relief, because it meant that Buteh-Amun was already here, but on the other hand, it seemed strange that it took him almost as much time to reach the straight road from the City as it did to them. It turned out that the house of Djehuty-mes was constantly watched and when Buteh-Amun went out to set off in his boat towards the river, he saw that a guard was coming behind him - one of the *medjayu* of Pa-shu-uben. In this situation, Buteh-Amon changed his mind and went to the Launderer's Bank, made some roam there and returned home, seeing the guard coming back after him. After waiting half an hour, Buteh-Amun left the house again, but everything recurred; this time, admittedly, the priest had something with him to "wash", but the guard was still accompanying him in this activity. Now, Buteh-Amon started playing with him: every half an hour he was repeating his route, still taking something out of the house that he allegedly washed; the guard continued to follow him until he finally gave up, seeing the priest walking slowly back towards Launderer's Banks with a tunic over his shoulder and a washing paddle in his hand. It was only then that Buteh-Amun got into the boat and rowed quickly into the river, then set sail and benefited from the successful afternoon wind two hours later arrived in Sumenu. Pa-nehsi's entire army was busy that day with the attack on Ipet-sut and the escape was successful, although the unfortunate guard probably had to confess to Pa-shu-uben that he had lost sight of Buteh-Amun, for which he undoubtedly received a flogging. Buteh-Amun told this at a meal prepared by the priest of the Sobek temple. Before they even sat down to eat, there was a joyful meeting of friends who had not seen each other for over a year. Suti-mes had to tell first of all about his previous mission and about his return with royal letters. When he got to the description of his arrival at Ipet-sut with the alleged letter of Pa-nehsi to Amen-hotep and told how he was unexpectedly attacked by the gatekeeper of the Great Gate, the High Priest jumped up, raising both hands up and shouted:

"So, it was Pen-nesti-tawy! Pa-nehsi's confidant and murderer in such an important position! I understand now why, in recent years, messengers with royal letters have come to me so rarely, and maybe others too! He was there almost until the end and only went out together with others on the eve of the assault!"

The First Servant was extremely agitated, but he finally decided that it did not matter now. When Suti-mes finished his story, he began to ask his friend if he had any news from Henut and, in turn he repeated the gesture of Amen-hotep almost exactly, when he learned that the girl was alive and lives in the house of Djehuty-mes. Now, Buteh-Amun had to tell him how he had saved Henut at the Crocodile Backwaters, but he did not have the courage to tell his friend how he found her there.

"She wanted to go to a crocodile because of hunger, like so many people from Khefet-her-neb-es," he explained. "It turns out that even service in Pa-nehsi's army does not protect the families of such volunteers as Djed-Mut-iuf-ankh, and he was so blind! If he knew what the situation in his house is now! Thanks to Amon, Henut survived the year of hyenas!"

"Thanks to Amun, but also thanks to you, my friend!" Suti-mes shouted, touched, "I will be in your debt for my whole life! She is like a lotus flower: beautiful and yet so delicate, and I can't do anything to protect her!"

"You are wrong, young man," Amen-hotep said, "right now you will be able to do a lot for your girlfriend, her loved ones, but also for everyone else in the City, and even for the whole Kemet! As the only one of the three of us, you have already made the same journey that lies ahead us and you have gained experience, which will be a treasure for us now. Therefore, from now on, you are the head of our group and I will follow your instructions; don't even protest!" he added, seeing the surprise on his servant's face.

"Yes, it is obvious," Buteh-Amun supported the High Priest, "Someone must guide us so that we don't waste time. So, what should we do now, boss?"

"Sleep," Suti-mes said, "Otherwise His Grandness will fall asleep on the way and may fall off his horse."

"Remember, I don't even know how to sit on it," Amen-hotep said, and Buteh-Amun admitted after a moment that he has never ridden a horse either. At this time, all three realized that in this situation they would be able to hit the road only after even a short lesson of this skill, and this somewhat reduced their advantage.

"I really don't know if we will succeed..." Suti-mes said to his friend when the High Priest fell asleep. "I remember that the road is very hard in places, you sleep under a tent, eat little and drink sparingly. The guide also had to teach me how to ride a horse, and it happened that I fell down. I don't know if Amen-hotep can handle it. Besides, when I was travelling to Pi-Ramesse, nobody knew about me, so they didn't chase me, and certainly the men who will pursuit us are masters of riding. May God look after us!"

The next day began with learning. Buteh-Amun quickly mastered the basic skills, while the High Priest had serious problems to stay on the horse's back and to keep properly the reins to guide the horse without disturbing him. Once, unfortunately, he made a mistake and fell, knocking his leg painfully. Finally, after several hours of rehearsals, they set out with their guide, because they could not afford to waste more time. Initially, they rode slowly. In the front, the guide led four additional horses, tied to his saddle with long straps, carrying water and food. Behind him the three priests rode side by side, while Suti-mes and Buteh-Amun led Amen-hotep among themselves, ready to support him at any time if he lost control of his horse. The High Priest tried very hard to follow all the recommendations, and after some time they could allow him to ride alone, so they moved a little faster. Every two hours they would take breaks, rest, and then change horses and ride on. Unfortunately, during the first days, they did not go more than four *iteru*[85] daily, realizing that the chase will go at least twice as fast. On the fourth day, they reached the first oasis. It was here that sometimes were brought under guard people unwanted in the City, mostly petty criminals or those who criticized Vizier's government too loudly[86]. There were a lot of date palms here, also acacias and sycamores and all vegetation known from Kemet, but this place, like other oases, was not included in the territory of the Both Countries. The local people also did not consider themselves residents of Kemet; while understanding their language they used another mother tongue to talk among themselves. The life in the oasis went on with its own leisurely rhythm, which is why the appearance of any newcomers was always an event that gathered a large group of curious people around them. Children came first, and these shouted to other residents who stopped all work and came running, expecting mostly a caravan of merchants or a unit of army leading prisoners sentenced to stay here for several years, with a ban on returning to Kemet. Four newcomers, whose equipment indicated that they are just passing through and for reasons known only to them are going deeper into the desert, while using a rarely frequented route, were less attractive, and a smaller number of onlookers gathered this time, making however

[85] A measure of length corresponding to approx. 10.5 km.

[86] Document from period not much later than the time of the novel's plot, talks about amnesty for the oppositionists sent ten years earlier to the oasis.

still considerable group of people. The guide showed them, saying to the priests, "They all have kept us perfectly in mind, and when the chase comes here, they will show exactly where we are or which way we went. We cannot avoid such places, because only there we can replenish our food and water supplies, but no oasis will shelter us. Similarly, on the desert trail, from which we cannot stray, because we could easily lose our way and fall victim to all the evil guards of the desert, we have no chance if they caught up with us..."

"What kind of desert guards were you talking about," Amenhotep asked as they had a break.

"There are many of them, Your Grandness," the guide said, sipping the water from the leather bag each had strapped on his back. Some are alive, like sand vipers or lions. But the animals rather run away from people, and the trail was also marked out to bypass their headquarters. If, however, you lose your way - and in the desert all the dunes and hills seem similar – you can find such a habitat. The worse guard is sand. There are places where you can fall down and never get out of it again, and they look innocent from afar. Sometimes, there is a great wind that carries a spinning pillar of sand. Where this pole falls, a hill arises and there is no rescue for those who are buried. You have to pray to Amun, who is in the wind, to avoid such storms! Lack of water is another threat, but we are protected. Time is our worst enemy. We have to go faster than before because we are still very far from Pa-im."

"What can we do?" Suti-mes asked, who remembered he had been here a day shorter before.

"The horse can sometimes run very quickly, but then you have to lie down on it and hold well," the guide said and immediately added, ahead of the next question of Suti-mes, "You can attach His Grandness to a horse, show how to hold reins and rush a horse. You just have to follow me to not get lost, but don't be afraid, because these horses will stick to the one who leads and will not get lost!"

Suti-mes was a little worried if the First Servant would agree to such a treatment, but Amen-hotep immediately suggested that they do it right away and set off on the trail the same day. This also happened and it turned out that even before the advent of the night it was possible to overcome the next two *iteru*.

After a short night spent in the tents, they moved on before dawn, immediately after the guide had decided that among the gray and deep shadows cast by the surrounding hills, he could find the right trail. They were going much faster now, and hope began to enter the hearts of refugees again. Between stops, there was now a change of fast and slow rides, the baits were shortened and they got up very early, and stopped to sleep late. The seventh day after leaving Sumen found them in the second oasis, but it was still only halfway. Amen-hotep said that according to his calculations today, and at the latest tomorrow the chase will set off after them, so they got up early again.

Already at the first stop, Buteh-Amun noticed, however, that the High Priest was very pale and shared this remark with Suti-mes. "We must slow down the pace and do a little longer rest, and at least one night we need to sleep normally, because His Grandness is very tired, although he will never say it himself," the head of the expedition decided and told the guide to lead so that the High Priest could not realize that they have slowed down for fear of his health. It turned out, however, that this part of the trail is extremely difficult, narrow, winding and requires increased attention so as not to get lost. It was told to Amen-hotep, who did not hide that he liked the slower ride.

"Unfortunately, I do not have your age, and this is probably the only thing I regret: old age is necessary, it brings experience, but it is harder to endure running," he added, laying down to rest.

The next days turned out to be even more difficult because they became unbearably hot, which was as difficult for people as for horses who refused to ride fast in these conditions. Moreover, after the heat of the day, which had to be borne without a bit of shade, the nights came, bringing a biting cold, against which there was not much to protect, and even woolen coverings were not sufficient. Suti-mes and Buteh-Amun discovered with horror that the High Priest had to catch a cold as he began to cough and have a fever. Fortunately, they reached the third oasis, where a man who knew an art of treatment, prepared a special drink to bring relief to the sick old priest. However, the man was clear on that the High Priest must lie in bed for two days, sweat and drink a lot of hot milk with honey and only then he can move on. Two days of forced rest were almost a sentence: they needed four more to reach Pa-im, where they could finally receive all help and protection from the pursuit. Both young priests were depressed about the situation, and the guide was wringing his hands. On the second day, he came to Suti-mes and said that they had to leave immediately, if they were to think about avoiding pursuit, "We have to go fast again, but the horses have rested, and the further route is quite wide and easy, so they should manage."

Suti-mes went into the room where Amen-hotep lay and found him in a much better mood; the fever dropped, even the cough calmed down considerably, although it harassed him still from time to time. The High Priest did not hesitate for a moment, "You will tie me up more than usual because I have weakened, but let's go if we need to!"

They moved an hour later, despite the protests of the doctor who announced that the disease could return. They were traveling now through such a beautiful desert that they regretted not having time to stop here and admire the strange creations of nature: white rocks rose from yellow sand, resembling large maces, heads of giant animals, or calyxes of developed flowers[87]. A little further they entered between the vast sandy hills, on which from time to time a plant was appearing that not only vegetated by some miracle in these waterless surroundings, but even bloomed. The color of the desert turned from yellow into black, its surface was covered with dark stones that formed also some pointed hills on the horizon. The road was clearly visible and flat, so they drove fast.

Unfortunately, two days later, when they reached the last oasis on the route, it turned out that the doctor's prediction came true: Amen-hotep again got a fever. There was no question of spending the next two days here: the pursuit had to be very close, so they only benefited from the unique gift of nature that this oasis was

---

[87] The phenomena described here occur in the so-called the White Desert between the oases of Farafra and Bahariya.

equipped with, and during the bait, in the shade of the palm trees they submerged in the hot water that gushed here from an underground source. This hot bath did very well to the patient, who again regained strength. They knew that the purpose of their escape was getting closer, so last night, unfortunately, very cold again, they shortened to a few hours only and set off before dawn. Amen-hotep felt bad, but everyone hoped that in Pa-im a local doctor would cure him again, and he would then continue his journey comfortably, mainly by boat.

It was approaching noon when they saw the towering pyramidal shape rising away from the plain, and soon afterward, the green fields and village houses, which heralded the dreamed end of the escape. They stopped under a group of trees to rest for a moment before the last short stretch of the ride. At that moment, the guide suddenly became motionless, he raised his finger in warning, then put his ear to the ground. He listened for a moment, suddenly jumped up and untied the horses in one move and having grabbed his whip with which he rushed them, with all his strength began to whip one horse after another so that they galloped freed from the weight of riders.

"To these bushes and to the ground!" he shouted and pointed to nearby scrubs.

They started running there and fell among the bushes growing on the roadside ditch.

"Did they have to be spiked bushes? I pricked myself..." the High Priest moaned, but fell silent like the others, because at that moment on the road they had recently traveled, they saw first a dust storm, and then a group of riders speeding in the same direction in which their own horses rushed.

"It was Aa-neru!" Buteh-Amun whispered, recognizing the rider leading the group. If we hadn't stopped, they would have caught up with us before the pyramid..."

"Now, at most, they will catch our horses up, and then they will have to recognize their defeat; they will not attack the whole village," added Suti-mes, looking towards the huts clearly visible from afar. "There are too few of them to take up the fight, and besides, the people here don't like the Kushites. But we must go to this village as soon as possible and move away from the road, because they will probably go this way again, looking for us!"

He stood up and reached out to Amen-hotep to help him up. Then he saw a terrible thing. The High Priest lay motionless, unnaturally pale, and his mouth was foaming saliva.

"Your Grandness!" the young priest shouted in terror and shook the lying one. Amen-hotep did not react; he was unconscious, though he was breathing.

"Look!" the guide, who was also leaning over the First Servant, showed them a large black scorpion right next to his leg. „His Grandness had to crush him; after all, he complained that he had pricked himself..."

There was no time to waste: they still had to race against death, and not just from the hands of Aa-neru. The bite looked bad, the scorpion was large and one of the most dangerous; only quick medical help gave hope for rescue. The guide ran first to prepare the villagers for the visit of a distinguished guest, and to warn them of the possible appearance of Kushites, and above all to find a doctor. Buteh-Amun and Suti-mes picked up the High Priest and started running toward the first visible hut. When they got there, they were in no much better condition than Amen-hotep. Half-conscious from fatigue, as soon as they laid him on a clay bench serving as a sleeping place in this hut, they fell to the ground themselves and for a long moment panted heavily, unable to speak. However, from the corner of their eye, they saw that the guide had accomplished his task perfectly, as a dozen or so men armed with arches and clubs had already gathered around the cottage, looking menacingly towards the road. After some time, a group of riders was actually noticed there, but they drove without stopping. The fugitives were saved. On the other hand, the situation of Amen-hotep looked very dangerous; he was still unconscious, but now he was moaning, and his body was shaking. The fetched man who did treatment in this village, put on the swollen leg a compress made of an ointment and leaves of a plant, then he incensed Amen-hotep, and began to dance, threateningly shaking the curved bone knife held in his hand, and uttered spells only partly understandable to both young priests:

Misery, misery! The scorpion has slipped under a tree, and its spike is raised to prick the strong one. Here is a spell for him, a spell over a cup of beer, as for everything that heals successfully: Adira! Adissana! Adirgaha! Adissana! Dewarhassa! Kina! Hama! Senenfteta! Batsit! Satita! Elhakati! Satita! Haballu! Haeri!

Seven children of Re are standing to protect you; they tie seven knots and put them on the one who was pricked, and he will stand up healthy on the ground, just as Horus stood the night he was pricked. The spell of Horus that protects is my protective spell!

Words of Horus overcome death, give life to those who suffocate. Horus's words quench the flame and his spells heal even the incurable. You, Poison! Flow out and step into the ground to rejoyce the hearts and to make Re still circling![88]

"Do you think these spells will help?" Suti-mes asked quietly, and Buteh-Amun replied equally quietly, "Doctors everywhere combine magical prayers with practical action. I hope that what is in the compress will help, but there is no harm in asking Amun for help, because you know that He, in whichever divine name will be called – as Djehuty, Bes or Isis – is able to change even that, which may seem hopeless to us."

They both fell silent and then were sitting next to the sick one for several hours. His condition seemed not to improve, and both men had less and less hope. Night has fallen. The First Servant stopped moaning, but now beads of sweat appeared on his face, neck and chest, and even on his hands. The young priests wiped them off immediately, but then new ones appeared in their place and it lasted for a long time. Then Amen-hotep opened his eyes, looked up consciously, and seeing both young men with him, smiled and weakly asked where they were and what about the pursuit?

After having heard their report, he raised eyes and was praying for a moment, then said, "Amun liked to save us, but I don't think I deserve to stand before the King in Pi-Ramesse and

---

[88] This is the authentic text of the spell against the scorpion prick, preserved on a papyrus from the Ramesside period, today in the Leiden Museum.

tell him what happened in Waset. You will have to do it for me because we are still racing against time and I am so weak that I can't even raise my hand. So, I won't write a letter, but I'll give you my ring. Just remember: don't look for Pi-ankh, just for Heri-Hor! Do you remember, Suti-mes, what I told you to tell him then?"

"Yes, Your Eminence: The Barge of Re no longer appears in the City and has disappeared on the western horizon," Suti-mes carried these words in his heart as if he had heard them yesterday.

"Very good!" the High Priest praised, "You will repeat it to him again. Don't forget about me, I hope we meet again..."

With difficulty he moved one hand towards the other one, then he removed the ring from his finger and handed it to Suti-mes, after that, exhausted by conversation, he sank into his sleeping place and closed his eyes. After a while, they stated that he had fallen asleep, so they also lay down to rest at least a bit before the further journey ahead.

CHAPTER XIII

Albeit they had little hope of recovering their horses and traveling luggage, they were pleasantly surprised in the morning. The guide brought all eight mounts, which, as it turned out, did not go very far. Having seen from the road a fertile meadow, where other horses were grazing, they joined the herd and started to search for the green delicacies they knew. Grazing calmly among the others, they did not pay attention to the chase group, despite the fact that they still had their panniers strapped. Apparently Aa-neru was watching the route, looking for fugitives on it. Besides, he probably decided that he would not catch up with them and determined to come back rather than risk a clash with the local people, who may could consider the armed dark Kushites as the attackers.

They set off early morning. Having reached the river, they crossed it, as there were many shoals and the water was shallow. On the east bank, they found a comfortable trail running in the same direction as Hapi was flowing.

Now, they moved quickly and scurried as before, and maybe even faster, because both young priests had already mastered the gallop technique. There was no one with them who could delay their ride and their luggage was much lighter, and finally, their horses were not only rested but even eager for quick ride. The road led between arable fields, where harvests were still going on here in the north, although they were clearly ending. During the stops, all three looked at the gold of the fields with joy, but also a hint of jealousy: this year Waset was deprived of such scenes. On the western horizon behind the river from time to time groups of dignified pyramids were appearing, after which the guide recognized where they were on the road. When they saw the unusual pyramid, as if made up of large platforms and towers stacked on top of each other, they recognized at once the oldest stone building resembling the primordial mound – a holy place where time began.[89]

"The pyramid of His Majesty Netjeri-khet! It must be really high!" Buteh-Amun exclaimed, who knew it shape because it was talked about at school, but he was never in this region and did not know if it was really as big as he had imagined.

"It's very big, but we'll see even bigger ones," the guide said. "We are close to Men-nefer, but because we are going to Iunu, I preferred to cross earlier and bypass such a big city, where we would be stopped at the entrance and exit, which would cause us to lose a lot of time."

---

[89] It is the so-called Step pyramid of Netjeri-khet (Djoser) in Saqqara.

An hour later, the guide finally saw what he expected most, "These are the houses of eternity of His Majesty Khufu justified and his son Khaf-Re, justified[90]," he said and added proudly in his voice, added proudly: "No man has ever built anything bigger: even the largest columns of the Hall of Appearances in Ipet-sut would be tiny when compared with them. For us it is a sign that we are approaching the goal. Now, these pyramids are ahead of us: when you have to look back to see them, we will be very close to Iunu, we will only have to travel a little more than one *iteru* of ride."

Although the great pyramids were still clearly visible, two hours passed before they saw the towering wall of the temple precinct in Iunu and the obelisks shooting up to the sky. They were at the destination of the first part of the journey. Guards at the gates, of course, stopped them, but the name of Amen-hotep – the First Servant of Amun of Waset worked like a magic wand and a moment later a priest appeared who introduced himself as Pa-di-Re, the servant of Heka-nefer – the Greatest of Seers of Re and Atum in Iunu and led the newcomers to a small room in the first courtyard, where they sat down to drink cool water with mint that was served to them. Pa-di-Re waited until they quench their thirst, and then asked, with which news were they coming from Amen-hotep.

"We did not come here with a message from His Grandness Amen-hotep, but we are going to His Majesty the King to Pi-Ramesse," Suti-mes said. "We were traveling with the High Priest,

---

[90] It's about the Pyramids of Kheops and Khefren at Giza (Western Cairo).

but a great scorpion stung him near Pa-im and His Grandness lies in a peasant's hut there. We have come to ask you to look after him, because these conditions are quite unworthy of his person and position."

Pa-di-Re listened to this attentively, but a great wonder bordering on disbelief appeared in his eyes:

"You say His Majesty Amen-hotep lies in the peasant hut in Pa-im. How is it possible that he even got there?!"

At the moment Buteh-Amun decided that they could not hide the worst news from this priest, "I know that it is hard to believe what we say, but something happened that the Both Countries have not known since the time of the forefathers. The house of Amun in Ipet-sut was invaded, besieged and certainly already captured by the army of the rebel Pa-nehsi, who declared war on the Both Countries on behalf of – as he calls it –"Free Kush." His Grandness Amen-hotep escaped and wanted to go to the King. Now, we're going there with his ring."

At that moment, Suti-mes took the gold Amenhotep's ring from a pocket in his tunic and offered it to Pa-di-Re so that he could read the inscription engraved on it.

The priest of Re was incapable of speaking for a moment, while looking only alternately at Suti-mes, at Buteh-Amun and at the ring.

"I must notify Heka-nefer immediately, forgive me," he finally said and left. He reappeared after a very short absence and now led both priests to the palace of the Greatest of Seers of Re and Atum.

The message they had to repeat again made a huge impression on Heka-nefer. However, it was clear that this man can make quick and accurate decisions and it was very good that they decided to come here.

"Tomorrow at the break of the day you will take my boat to Pi-Ramesse; you'll be there in three days," Heka-nefer was already giving orders. "Your guide will lead my people to His Grandness Amen-hotep and we will bring him here. I also recommend that the guards at the temple gates be vigilant!"

"They are always vigilant?" Buteh-Amon asked as they found themselves in the room, they were assigned to spend the night.

"It must have meant something special," Suti-mes said. "Amen-em-Ipet once told me that these guards on the high towers have some way of reporting particularly important news to each other. For example, one can read code word from an agreed signal: "It's coming", although I don't know if they use a trumpet, a torch, smoke or flashes of reflected light. Most often, in this case, it is a wave of flooding on the river at the threshold of the Akhet season. At other times, this may mean a visit by the King or an invasion of the enemy. Another signal that can be read as "gone" is sent when the King dies. Unfortunately, I don't know much about it, but I think Heka-nefer gave some wise command."

In the morning, the young men set off on a fast boat at the disposal of the High Priest from Iunu towards Pi-Ramesse. The canal from below the temple led to one of the branches into which the river was divided not far from here to flow towards the sea in the likeness of a large calyx of a lotus flower, each petal of which was separated by a stream of water giving life to the surrounding fields. They passed numerous villages booming at the harvest, which gave the impression that there were far more inhabitants here than in the Southern Country. On the third day in the evening, they finally arrived at the marina at Pi-Ramesse.

When they were on the main street leading to the royal palace, they had to admit that this City was very different from Waset. It was already dark, but there were so many lamps and torches on the street that one could see everything. Lamps were illuminating numerous elegant houses and palaces, and chariots were circling between these, with the servants running close to them and lighting the road with torches. There were also a lot of people walking alone or in groups on the street, clusters of customers were formed around boys selling cakes roasted on fire, and these clusters were complained about by those who rode chariots. In addition to an observation that a bigger number of people are living in Pi-Ramesse than in Waset, after which it was possible to recognize the capital, the newcomers also noticed many more foreigners, especially Tjehenu and Asians; only the *medjayu* had a dark skin of the Kushites, and these policemen were also more numerous here than in Waset.

"Do you remember where Heri-Hor lives?" Buteh-Amun asked, and Suti-mes became sad and had to admit that, unfortunately, he wasn't sure.

"Certainly on this street, because all the most important officials live here. I remember it was a palace, but now with these torches, all the larger houses look similar," he said, then pointed to one of the elegantly illuminated palaces in front of which a group of soldiers could be seen. "Maybe it's the one here?"

They approached the soldiers, among whom stood an officer wearing an elegant wig.

"Whose palace is this?" Buteh-Amun asked him.

The officer looked at the newcomers, but at that moment a chariot appeared in the gate of the courtyard, from which an older man in an equally elegant wig got out, wearing a red tunic. The soldiers, when they saw him, stood up and gave their respectful obeisance.

"This palace belongs to the noble Queen Tent-Amun," the officer answered only now, then apologized and, having approached his soldiers, also bowed. A man in a red tunic entered the palace.

"It was a general, judging by the dress and behavior of the soldiers," Buteh-Amun whispered, "Maybe it was Heri-Hor?"

"No, it wasn't Heri-Hor," Suti-mes said, but it could be Pi-ankh whom we should avoid. Maybe our polite officer will tell us?"

He just sat on the ground, like his soldiers, then took off the wig and began to brush his hair with his fingers; he apparently did not expect anyone important to appear again in the courtyard of the palace of the Queen Tent-Amun. Suti-mes came up to him and asked who the General was who had just arrived. The officer now looked more closely at the questioner, his white tunic, elegant papyrus sandals, and has recognized that he was dealing with someone worthy of conversation.

"I see," he replied, "that you do not live in Pi-Ramesse and you have probably come from afar since you do not know whose palace it is or who visits it at this time, because all the locals know it, and I think that everyone in North Country. I would like to tell you, but maybe you will invite me for a beer because I think you will have even more questions? I am Nakht, an officer in the service of General Nes-Ba-neb-Djedu, whom you have just seen and who will not leave this palace before the morning, so I have a lot of time..."

Suti-mes with Buteh-Amun willingly agreed to the unusual proposition, and when they introduced themselves as priests in the service of the High Priest Amen-hotep in Waset, Nakht whistled in surprise, "I see that in the Southern Country one knows very little about what is happening in Pi-Ramesse, and yet all the local beer houses like this are gossiping about it."

"About the visits of General Nes-Ba-neb-Djedu to the Queen?[91] The King doesn't know that?" Buteh-Amun asked.

"Maybe he knows, maybe he doesn't... The King himself has not been visiting his wife for a long time. She disappointed him, did not give him a son, but with respect to this, he did not get better with the harem wives. The King is aging and there is no heir to the throne."

"He seems to have a daughter," Buteh-Amun said again.

---

[91] Relationship of Queen Tent-Amon with Nes-ba-neb-Djedu is confirmed in the sources, and all of the characters listed below are authentic and they lived at the time when the novel is set.

"Yes, Princess Henut-tawy is a beautiful girl and it is time for her to share the bed with someone for the good of the Both Countries. The generals are closest to the King, there are four of them:" here Nakht spread his hand and began to count on his fingers, sipping beer on each name, "My boss, Nes-Ba-neb-Djedu is a good man, but he is interested in the mother, not the daughter, and besides, he comes from the Tjehenu tribes, and the King would never agree to him. There is a second General, very strong, Pa-nehsi," Suti-mes and Buteh-Amun exchanged quick glances, "and he certainly would have wanted her. He was here a long time ago, and Henut-tawy was still a child, but already then he looked at her like a cat on a sparrow, which everyone saw, because it was during some holiday and the family of the King and all the dignitaries were standing near the altar, and others could see them well. But Pa-nehsi is, like the Kushites, almost black one, so Ramesses probably won't accept him either. The third is Heri-Hor, aged already; this one, like Nes-Ba-neb-Djedu, comes from the people of Tjehenu, so he also has no chance, and besides, he looks at Nodjmet – the daughter of the fourth general, Pi-ankh. This one is at last a native inhabitant of Kemet, but the King Ramesses particularly hate him, maybe for his soldier's language and customs. And he is interested in Princess Henut-tawy, however he doesn't want her for himself, but for his son Pi-nodjem. This Pi-nodjem is a nice boy, maybe he would be a good King, and most importantly, Henut-tawy likes him, and maybe it is even something more than liking. But Ramesses would never agree to this marriage, because he would have accepted Pi-ankh in his family, and this is the last person whom Ramesses would like to see in his palace. So, it is not known what will happen to the throne. This poor King, he was left alone: a foreign wife, a foreign great dignitaries, even a foreign daughter because she rebels, knowing his father's dislike of Pi-ankh. And all around there are more and more of real foreigners, particularly Tjehenu. These are multiplying like rabbits and one day they may reach for power..."

Nakht yawned, so Suti-mes decided to ask the officer about how to meet the General Heri-Hor?

"There will be a meeting with the King tomorrow, on which occasion all the generals will be present, and also Heri-Hor will be there. If you want, I'll help you to meet him," said Nakht, pleased that he could talk and found listeners, and he drank beer at their expense. The young priests also felt that fortune follows them.

The next day, they waited for Nakht from the morning, but he did not have as much time today as the previous evening, because he had to be at the disposal of General Nes-Ba-neb-Djedu. It was only when the General went to the Pharaoh's palace for the council that Nakht could lead them to the house where Heri-Hor lived. However, they arrived too late, because Heri-Hor had already left for the King. In this situation, Nakht suggested that they should also go to the courtyard of the royal palace and wait there until the conference is over. When the time is right, he will notify one of Heri-Hor's men that messengers from Amen-hotep have arrived and then, who knows, maybe they will be able to stand not only before Heri-Hor, but maybe before Pharaoh himself?

Suti-mes and Buteh-Amon did as the officer proposed to them and went to the King's residence, located at the end of the main street of Pi-Ramesse and surrounded by a 10 cubits high wall on which armed guards were standing, set up densely.

The mighty gate was open and there was a lot of traffic. From time to time, a chariot would drive through it, carrying some dignitary, either going for a meeting to the Pharaoh or hurrying to one of the offices located near the palace. Those who had already done their matters, were heading the other way. In the depths of the courtyard, from the side of the palace, there was a second, internal wall with a gate, but this one was already closed. Only those, who was going to the King or to the rooms of the highest dignitaries placed in the palace building, was allowed trough the small wicket.

The young priests entered the courtyard and sat down in the shadow of the wall, having an entrance to the royal palace in view. Everyone had to go through this way, so also Heri-Hor. In anticipation their thoughts sought to penetrate the palace walls to answer the tormenting question: does the King already know what happened in Waset and is today's meeting even devoted to that? However, the walls of the residence of His Majesty Pharaoh were impervious and thanks to this their disappointment was spared to them, because this council was simply one of the monthly meetings at which the highest officials told the King first of all about what they had learned about Kemet's neighbors and whether something had happened unexpectedly that could endanger the interests of the Both Countries.

Ramesses did not expect anything like that. Minor problems in trade outside the eastern border did not obscure the fact that for 18 years since he sat on the throne of Geb, no foreign kingdom had grown enough for Kemet to fear. Some trouble could only arise in the future if any of the warlike peoples who lived today in the area of former Hatti power[92] conquered too much territory, or worse, chose a King to control them with a strong hand. Therefore, as every month, His Majesty Ramesses Men-Maat-Re Sechep-en-Ptah called as the first one the Vizier of the Lower Country and the Head of the Northern Lands, Ramesses-Nakht to submit the report.

"My King and Lord," the dignitary began, "Since God put an end to the life of the great Tiglat-Pileser, the land of Aa-sura[93] stopped growing south, and they had already reached Kadesh before. Now their new King, Ashur-bel-cala himself has trouble with the people of Aram, but their trouble is a good piece of news for the Pharaoh. So, the affairs of the countries between Iapu and Kadesh are also doing well." Ramesses-nakht confirmed what the Pharaoh had expected and therefore the King's face lit up. The dignitary continued: "There are many superiors of very small lands in this region, and everyone is doing what he supposes proper in his eyes.[94] At the same time, they constantly fight with each other and weaken each other. Only the people of Israel seem to be getting stronger and those who lead them are conquering more and more land. The worst thing was that they almost completely supplanted the Peleshet people[95], with which the Both

---

[92] This is the area of today's Syria; cf. a schematic map of the Middle East in the times when the novel takes place.

[93] The Kingdom of Assyria; cf. List of Geographical names.

[94] These words come from the biblical Book of Judges 21.25, which describes the same times as the novel.

Countries had agreements, according to which they passed us a part of the income from the trade routes running from the sea to the country of Aa-sura and the countries further away, in the mountains and in the valley of the great rivers. Unfortunately, it seems that the greatness of the Pharaoh's Majesty has been somewhat forgotten in some cities, like Djeden and Keben, whose princes are selling their goods including cedars more and more expensively for us," Ramesses-nakht ended.

"You said it right," Ramses praised him, "You will have to send letters to these princes reminding them that the Both Countries are still as strong as in the time of His Majesty Djehuty-mes Men-Kheper-Re, justified, or His Majesty Ramesses User-Maat- Re Sechep-en-Re, justified, and our army could remind them about that, but I trust that the name of Amun will have the same effect. To this leader of the people of Israel should be written that the heart of My Majesty is very joyful to see the happy development of his country and should also be added that I hope that this development will not interfere with our trade income that is ensured by our good contacts with Peleshet. We must also remind the new ruler of Aa-sura about our concern for him; it is good to have an ally on the other side of the land where these Israelites are doing so well. You need to strengthen contacts with him and send him something, some attractive gift, such as a live monkey and crocodile[96], which can only strengthen the favor of this King – what's his name?"

---

[95] It is about Philistines, known among others from the Bible.

[96] Assyrian sources confirm that King Ashur-bel-cala received such a gift from the Egyptian King "Mursi", which was undoubtedly Ramesses XI.

"Ashur-bel-cala, my King and Lord..."

"Well, strengthen his favor for the Both Countries. Did you remember everything?" the King ended with a question, and the dignitary bent in a low bow. Ramesses looked around and asked the next question to General Nes-Ba-neb-Djedu, "Are the districts on the western outskirts of the Northern Country not disturbed by the Tjehenu tribes?"

"No, my King and Lord," he replied and added: "On your borders there is peace, but I know that the elders from the tribes of Libu and Meshuesh[97] who reside, due to the royal grace, in large numbers in their settlements in the districts of the Northern Country, are not satisfied that they must still follow the instructions of the many sons of Kemet who do not understand their different way of life. Besides, Libu and Meshuesh look with a jealous eye at the privileges of such Sherdana who are not at all more combative but are far less numerous..."

"Well, Nes-Ba-neb-Djedu, the number of Sherdana is much smaller, and your tribesmen are still worryingly increasing. They all should, like you, live like the native inhabitants of Kemet, but they don't want to, they usually still live in tents, and while sleeping they have a bow at their fingertips. If we reduce our control and give them new privileges, we may have trouble with them: they will demand senior positions, and then, who knows, maybe also the throne. No, as long as I'm King, they won't get anything. They should be happy that they live in Kemet and thus have bread and beer, and their cattle and horses' fertile pasture.

---

[97] Meshuesh and Libu are the largest Libyan tribes to be found in Egypt.

Are those of the Nine Arches who have a home in the Both Countries missing something? I would love to hear the opinion of the Royal Son of Kush, but he is now far south. He hasn't written to me for a long time, but as I know, you are friends?" this question Pharaoh addressed to General Pi-ankh, who bowed low and confirmed.

"Yes, my King and Lord! As far as I know, the border in Abu is as safe as the borders in the west, and there is also no threat from desert bands in Waset, as Pa-Shu-uben wrote to me recently..."

"Yes, Pa-Shu-uben also wrote about it to me, but I am worried that I have since long had no letters from those who should write to me constantly and report because that's why they were sent there: from Un-nefer and from Men-Maat-Re-nakht. Immediately after arriving in Waset, they wrote to me that they had discovered many bad things that Pa-nehsi had done there; now they both fell silent. Pa-nehsi only once wrote that he complied with my orders, and Ines confirmed that Pa-nehsi and his army had found him in the region of Abu and that he remained there, but that was a long time ago. Even Amen-hotep is silent. I don't like it very much and I don't know if everything is in order in Waset, as it is shown by Pa-Shu-uben. New messengers must be sent there with a troop to protect them. I entrust this task to you," here he turned to General Heri-Hor, "Because, I think, Pi-ankh has too much confidence in Pa-shu-uben and also in Pa-nehsi. Who of your officers could leave for Waset today?"

"My Lord," the General said, "I have several people to whom I can entrust this task. Let me go out into the courtyard and in a moment I'll bring in front of you the one I have chosen."

King Ramesses gave a permissive hand gesture and Heri-Hor left the conference room, and then General Pi-ankh bowed to Pharaoh and asked for the right to speak.

"My King and Lord," he said, "I humbly accept your words of truth about my trust in the Waset Affairs Supervisor, but his numerous advantages have been described to me by my friend, General Pa-nehsi, who, after all, is a Fan Bearer and also enjoyed the grace of your favor. However, if it is the King's will to send a troop to Waset, please, Lord, remember that the inhabitants of the City may be very dissatisfied because of this, and besides, you can be sure that General Heri-Hor will send an officer there to whom he will order an excessive suspicion, which can easily create a new conflict in Waset."

Pharaoh looked reluctantly at Pi-ankh: this General dared again and in the presence of others critically assess his decisions, although he might have been a bit right... He wondered for a moment what to say to him, but at that moment Heri-Hor returned, whose absence was unusually short, and he returned alone, clearly excited, walking very quickly towards the royal throne.

"My Lord," he said excitedly, having only bowed, "I've just been told that the emissaries of Amun's First Servant Amen-hotep have come here and are waiting!"

"Let them come in, then," Ramesses commanded, and after a moment Suti-mes and Buteh-Amun appeared at the Reception

Hall, and fell on their faces having seen the King. Ramesses gestured impatiently for them to stand up and asked for a letter from the High Priest.

"We don't have a letter, Lord of the Both Countries," Buteh-Amon said, his words causing great surprise and agitation among all those present. "His Grandness Amen-hotep was coming here in order to stand before Your Majesty personally, but he was stung by an evil scorpion and when we said goodbye to him in Pa-im, he was so seriously ill that he was unable to write you a letter. Coming here, we asked His Grandness Heka-nefer of Iunu to look after our dear superior and this probably happened, but we do not know for sure whether Amun's First Servant is still alive. Instead of a letter, he ordered to give you, King and Lord, this sign," at that moment Suti-mes gave Pharaoh a ring of the High Priest.

Ramses examined it carefully and gave it to General Heri-Hor, who passed it on to Pi-ankh, and in this way all the dignitaries present in the room took it in turn and read the inscription on the underside of the image of the holy beetle with the title and name of Amen-hotep.

"I would not like to offend newcomer's self-respect," Pi-ankh said quietly, leaning toward the ear of Ramesses sitting on the throne, "but as long as it's probably a real Amen-hotep's ring, we don't know if it was taken from him insidiously. These young people have not even managed to say who they are, and we do not know their names..."

Pharaoh again confessed in mind, albeit reluctantly, that the General's suspicion could be justified. "Tell us your names!" Ramses ordered.

Buteh-Amun bowed and said, "Forgive me, Gracious King, for not doing it right away. My name is Buteh-Amun, I am the Father of God and a scribe in Khefet-her-neb-es, the son of the Royal Scribe of Necropolis, Djehuty-mes, who is called Chari."

The murmur of hushed voices that was now heard among those gathered testified that the name of Djehuty-mes, who was dignified and respected in the Both Countries, was very impressive. Now also Suti-mes repeated his friend's gesture and introduced himself, "I am Suti-mes, the God's Servant of Amun in Ipet-sut in the service of the noble Amen-hotep," after which he added: "I have come to Pi-Ramesse for the second time, carrying a message that my Supervisor told me to repeat now: the Barge of Re no longer appears in the City and has disappeared on the western horizon!" With that, Suti-mes turned his gaze toward General Heri-Hor, who also looked at him closely, and then said aloud:

"King and my Lord, he tells the truth! Indeed, he is the same man who previously brought the letter from Amen-hotep and who returned to Waset with your letters to the High Priest and to Pa-nehsi!"

"It was so," Suti-mes confirmed, "I delivered the letter personally to the General, and the High Priest himself found the letter addressed to him, as I was attacked at the Great Gate of Ipet-sut and the night came to me during the day. The God kept me alive, but I have evidence on my body that I am telling the truth!"

Now there was complete silence in the room, which only Pharaoh broke:

"Can you tell us what Amen-hotep meant when he told you to repeat the words about the barge of Re, which is no longer visible in Waset?"

"My King and Lord," the priest began, lowering his head before Pharaoh, "I would prefer it never to come to me that I should explain the meaning of these terrible words, because at the very recollection of what I saw, my heart stops in my chest and my lips refuse to obey. For six months, along with many of Amun's servants, I could not go beyond the walls of Ipet-sut, because hostile forces led by General Pa-nehsi, who shimmers with the Free Kush Lord, stood all around. His soldiers spent at the Great Gate of Ipet-sut women and children of those who serve Amun, took the children from their mothers and took them somewhere on their ships, then took women, and some of them raped and killed. This was happening before my eyes, and the High Priest Amen-hotep was also looking at it. Then the assault on the walls of Ipet-sut began and I do not know what was going on there, because then I went out from there by a secret exit, accompanying the First Servant and began to escape through the deserts and oases, and Amun in his grace prevented us from being caught by the pursuit unit under the command of the Kushite Aa-neru, the murderer."

There was still silence in the Reception Hall; everyone looked at each other with great surprise and disbelief at the same time, searching in the words they heard, any incoherence that would allow to reject this entire report.

"If Pa-nehsi has besieged Ipet-sut for half a year, it is explained why Amen-hotep did not send letters," Nes-Ba-neb-Djedu finally said, "but why did Un-nefer say anything?"

This question was directed properly to himself, because none of the dignitaries present here could answer it. But then Buteh-Amon spoke again, and his words were as difficult for the audience as the words of Suti-mes, "The dignified Vizier Un-nefer is dead; he was killed when Pa-nehsi's army captured the fortress temple of His Majesty Ramesses User-Maat-Re Meri-Amun in Khefet-her-neb-es. The Kushites took over Waset, took all the warehouses, and forced all tenants of Amun's land into their army. The fields in Waset were not sown during the Akhet season for the first time since their forefathers. Not only will the Great House not receive taxes due from the Waset District this year, but there is hunger in the Eastern and Western Cities and the need for urgent help for their residents. My King and Lord! We traveled here without rest, but we do not know if Pa-nehsi and his army are not on their way to the Lower Country now."

After these words, there was a strong commotion among the gathered, and only the presence of the King prevented everyone from shouting although almost everyone with intense gesticulation demanded taking the floor. But it was Ramesses himself who had to speak now. He first thanked Buteh-Amon and Suti-mes for their efforts to travel, and then instructed the unexpected newcomers to leave the Reception Hall, and when they did it, he turned to Pi-ankh with an angry face:

making you responsible for the proper preparation to confront the enemy!"

The meeting was over.

CHAPTER XIV

On the same day, the fastest messengers were sent to the troops stationed along the borders of the Northern Country with the order to take immediate march, and where possible – sailing on boats in the direction of Men-nefer, where the whole army was to gather. The abandoning of the borders was associated with a certain risk that groups of sheepherding people leading a nomadic life to the east and west of the fertile meadows and fields of the Black Country would pass the borders without obstacles, together with their herds, but such people were not posing at present a threat to the security of the country. Two major groups of military units of the Northern Country's army also set out towards Men-nefer, one from the vicinity of the ancient holy cities of Pe and Dep, and the other from the neighborhood of the residence of the King in Pi-Ramesse. It was from here that the greatest infantry units of the native inhabitants of Kemet went to the designated place. These consisted of powerfully built spearmen attired in leather armors, then soldiers armed with long swords or axes, finally archers and slingers. Warriors of Sherdana people, also greatly fighting with swords, were marching in separate units; these could easily be recognized from afar by their round shields, and especially by helmets topped with goat's horns and leather balls. The fair-skinned Tjehenu, who were the only ones who could match the Kushites in the art of archery, wore falcons or hawks' feathers put in their hair. There were several hundred chariots behind the infantry, each harnessed with two horses. Next to the coachmen native archers stood there native archers, the best of the best in Kemet, and the rumble of wheels produced a noise that announced the approaching of the army before anything could be seen.

Who saw the march of these troops, could become convinced that it was an invincible army, and so was it seen by the King Ramesses, who many times admired the Northern Corps parading in front of him. The generals looked at it differently. Heri-Hor, Pi-ankh and Nes-Ba-neb-Djedu could have many different interests, and especially the first two did not hide a certain rivalry, but in the assessment of the current military situation they agreed. Immediately after leaving the royal palace, they agreed that the next day, Heri-Hor and Nes-Ba-neb-Djedu would go to Pharaoh again to convince him to take up the necessary actions that would strengthen the army's power. Pi-ankh decided not to come and see the King, whom he clearly made nervous with his every appearance in the palace.

Ramesses received both commanders, although he was somewhat surprised that the very next day after the meeting, "where everything had been determined," they needed his instructions again. Knowing the King's irritability, Nes-Ba-neb-Djedu began to speak cautiously, emphasizing the uniqueness of the situation:

"It has never happened that any enemy army has gone so far into the country, or that the Kushites have moved in such numbers towards the Northern Country. What happened in Ipet-sut and the very fact that they are coming here means that they are ready for anything, and such soldiers fight twice as well. Our army will not have such stubbornness and may succumb to the opponent..."

Ramesses interrupted him with an angry gesture:

"What you are talking about will never happen!" The King was clearly nervous.

"Our troops are invincible and you as a General should know this best! How can you ever think of such a thing as a defeat!?"

Heri-Hor spoke up at that, "My King and Lord, Maat is in your mouth! Indeed, the army of the Both Countries has always been invincible and it would be so now, if it were complete, but another half of our magnificent army rebelled and evolved into enemies, they are led by a very good leader whom you made general for his ability. And, as Nes-Ba-neb-Djedu rightly said, they are going here driven by the thought that they are fighting for liberation, and this will double their strength. Our troops are great, but they don't even know what war is. Since the time of His Majesty Ramesses User-Maat-Re Meri-Amun, this army did not have to fight for independence, it was mainly a guardian of the safe borders..."

Pharaoh also interrupted this statement, and the expression on his face testified that his anger was rising.

"Are you cawing, too? What generals do I have! One is a friend of an approaching enemy, and two others are probably cowards! What exactly do you want from me?!" he shouted, and both commanders looked at each other eloquently; it was not a good day of the Pharaoh, and in this situation what they wanted to ask him seemed impossible, but they had to try...

"Lord of the Both Countries," said Nes-Ba-neb-Djedu, "It is very painful to hear from your mouth the suspicion that we are cowards. Yesterday you entrusted us with the task of relevant preparing to confront the enemy and we are fulfilling this task. All the troops of the northern corps are heading towards Men-nefer, but even if all of them arrive on time, because we don't know where Pa-nehsi is at the moment, there will be too few of us. There is only one chance to quickly supplement our ranks with a large number of valuable soldiers: the calling of the Tjehenu people who, after all, live in numerous settlements in the northern part of Kemet. They are actually ready, you said yesterday that when they sleep, they have a bow at their fingertips. We can easily get them to come with us, but we would have to promise them something, that is You, Lord, would have to show them your grace and announce some gift: a reduction of burdens, a granting of land, or the giving up of the control by our officials. Then they will go and fight very bravely, and, our Lord and King, they will love you. We ask you for advice what to do?"

This time Ramses listened to the end, but now he said something that surprised both of them:

"I understand why you came to me again today, although I said clearly yesterday that as long as I am the King, I will not agree to any privileges for Tjehenu. But you are also descendants of Tjehenu! Maybe you are plotting with them? I repeat: no exemption for Tjehenu! Do you want advice? Here you have it, persuade them, let them come with you and fight if they like it so much, but I will say again: our army is invincible and strong enough to deal with the rebels!"

"Oh, my Lord," Heri-Hor tried to speak once more to the King's imagination, "rebels are the most difficult opponent because they know what awaits them in case of a defeat..."

"That's enough!" Pharaoh shouted, "I said, and I will not change my mind. Our army will succeed, but it may be necessary to change its generals!" He signaled that the servants would come with a litter and carry to his private rooms. The hearing was over.

"You can see that we can't count on any help from this side," Nes-Ba-neb-Djedu looked resigned. "And also, those suspicions that we are in collusion with Tjehenu... Although the blood of the Meshuesh tribe flows in me, I cannot even speak the language of my ancestors. You have more vivid relation with them. Tell me, would you be able to persuade them to go with our army?"

"Yes," Heri-Hor replied, "But they must be given more independence, or they will not move from their settlements. When the enemy comes to them, they will defend themselves and sooner they will all die than give up but sending them to death without any promise will fail; they'll say it's a foreign war and

Heri-Hor's service suggested to him. He took one, then another quart of wine, and only then he spoke to the host sitting next to him in silence, "What happened to you inviting me for wine? Whenever I wanted to drink wine with you, you were weaseling out of this, while excusing yourself with duties!"

"Not true, Pi-ankh; I was refusing when you were dragging me to the house of wine and to the girls, but I always gladly come to you to your home," Heri-Hor replied. Pi-ankh took out the mouthpiece, leaned back on the back of the chair and started laughing loudly, "Ha Ha Ha! He gladly comes to me! To me! Maybe you are at my place with your body, you warm my chair with your butt, but your eyes are still running behind Nodjmet!"

"Are you surprised?" Heri-Hor blushed slightly, "I really like her and..."

"And you would like to have her in bed and have your twenty-fourth child with her![99] Really, you're a real child-maker! You didn't have many opportunities to prove your bravery on the battlefield, so you fight with a different weapon!" Pi-ankh laughed again and took a sip of wine, and Heri-Hor preferred not to respond to his colleague's comments in a typical style, but he gladly took the opportunity to leave, because just the sounds coming from the chambers in the front of the house testified that Nes-Ba-neb-Djedu arrived. When he also sat down in a comfortable chair, and the servants handed him a jug of wine, the

---

straight from the pitcher, a special mouthpiece should have been used to stop the pollution.

[99] It is known from sources that Heri-hor had 23 children from his first few marriages.

host closed the door of the chamber, announcing the servants not to be disturbed in conversation.

"Well, Pi-ankh," he began, "we wanted foremost to tell you about our visit to the King today. We informed him of a situation he apparently doesn't understand, and asked for his advice..."

"For advice? That fool?!" Pi-ankh exclaimed, taking out the mouthpiece for a moment, "And what brilliant advice did he give?"

"That only the generals should be changed, and our invincible army will deal with the rebels," Nes-Ba-neb-Djedu replied with sarcasm.

"Didn't I tell you before?" Pi- ankh exclaimed between one sip of wine and the other, "although our dear Ramesses, may he live in happiness and health! doesn't have time, to our luck, for such changes now, but as I know him, when only a threat to Pi-Ramesse ends, he will do it! Will he establish Tjehenu troops?"

"No," Heri-Hor replied, "Have you not heard that our army is invincible? Tjehenu are just waiting for new privileges to raise their heads, and besides, you probably don't know that the Pharaoh suspects that Nes-Ba-neb-Djedu and I have our own business and plot with them..."

"Well, then Ramesses will also start to dislike you and I will not be alone!" Pi-ankh murmured, trying to drain the wine from the mouthpiece that was clogged or pointed to the vanity of the pitcher. "An invincible army! Sure, just look at the carvings on the temple gates: Pharaoh alone is enough to defeat the enemy! Only, as far as I know, His Majesty is not going into the battle this time, but he commissioned it to us. How will we succeed without him?! If Pa-nehsi saw Ramesses on the chariot, he would have run away at his sight, but when he will see Heri-Hor... The wine has run out!"

"Maybe it's better, you've already drunk enough, or maybe too much," Heri-Hor said. "I appreciate your sense of humor, but now it's time for serious conversation and conclusions."

"The conclusion is self-evident," Pi-ankh firmly pushed the wine jug and leaned back comfortably, "either Ramesses and a defeat, or the lack of Ramesses..."

"...and also the defeat," Nes-ba-neb-Djedu finished, "At least ours, and certainly mine. I was thinking exactly the same a few hours ago, but Heri-Hor invited us here because he has some other suggestion."

"I have," Heri-Hor replied, "but before I present it, I would like you to look at this gift of nature..." He took out of the silver bowl which stood on a high support, filled with water and flowers, a wonderfully developed calyx of blue lotus.

"Its beauty results from the fact that the individual petals of the calyx, although each one is leaning out in a different direction, merge at the base, creating a perfect whole. If only one of these petals will be snatched out, this perfection and beauty will disappear, and no one girl will decorate her hair with such a damaged flower. The actions that must be taken to save the country must be designed such a way that by combining its various parts - its sanctity and traditionally sanctified offices - do not destroy any of them. I want to emphasize that the King in the Both Countries is a divine person and Majesty..."

"Come on!" Pi-ankh waved his hand.

"Please, don't interrupt me!" Heri-Hor's voice sounded resolute, "...the Majesty necessary for the normal functioning of this country. It has been like that since the time of our fathers and we cannot change it. We know that Ramesses is not ready to understand how shameful the situation of the Both Countries is, and he will not save them, but the King's person is to remain untouchable and this is the first petal of this flower. The next ones also apply to us. I mean the highest offices and those who manage them. Amun's first servant Amen-hotep is sick and defenseless; he can't save Kemet himself, though he can play a very important role. We know well the capabilities of officials, even the highest. Who among them has the chance to reverse the bad luck of the Both Countries? Only those who are present in this room because we have the army, but all three together," Heri-Hor strongly emphasized this word, "because we will achieve the goal, if we put aside the rivalry and while cooperating, we will help each other to fulfill our dreams," here the General looked eloquently on Pi-ankh, though he still didn't seem to understand what his colleague's speech was aiming for. "I emphasize again," continued Heri-Hor: "Each of us is such a petal: looks in a different direction, but something connects us." He showed the flower once more, then put it back into the bowl with water.

"You said nicely about the lotus," Nes-Ba-neb-Djedu said, "but I still don't understand what you actually want to do?"

"One more moment of patience," Heri-Hor returned to his place. "I was only talking about human parts of this entity that allows the Both Countries to live, and yet there exist even more important elements: the divine ones."

"I think it were you who had drunk too much wine," Pi-ankh growled, but he paused with further comment, dumbfounded by Heri-Hor's determined look.

"I will mention only two, but they contain almost everything. The first is Maat, without which nothing can work, neither in nature, nor in man, nor in the kingdom. Although the Pharaoh offers a Maat figurine to God every day, we know that Maat has been blinded or may have died: Pa-nehsi killed it by breaking into Ipet-sut with the Kushites. To get Maat back, the world must be created anew. Re-birth is necessary!" Heri-Hor suspended his voice, shifting his eyes from one of his guests to the other.

"I'm beginning to understand," Nes-Ba-neb-Djedu has liven up: "*uhem mesut* – "the Repeating of Births" – is this not a kind of the state of emergency that was once introduced in Kemet after the Great Heresy?"

"Of course, that's what I mean," Heri-Hor admitted and asked. "And do you remember from the military school, who then prepared *uhem mesut*?"

"If they talked about it at a military school, it must be army."

"Exactly, the army, the General Hor-em-heb, or rather His Majesty Hor-em-heb, justified," Heri-Hor nodded.

"If it was a king, unfortunately, nothing will come of it, because neither of us has the right to do so," Pi-ankh said, who was listening since a while to the conversation with great attention.

"I'm glad Pi-ankh that you have came back..." Heri-Hor said. "Of course, neither one of us as general nor the King Ramesses will do it, but someone who is more powerful than everyone: Amun. This is the second divine part I was talking about. Amun will announce the Repeating of Births through the lips of his High Priest."

"But Amen-hotep..." Pi-ankh started again.

Heri-Hor replied, "Not Amen-hotep, but the one that Amun chooses, or rather those whom Amun chooses. The Both Countries are vast and in the situation we have today we need two High Priests of Amun, and we need two places like Ipet-sut. A new Ipet-sut must be created in the North Country, but of course not here: Pi-Ramesse is over. Somewhere in the Lower Country a new town must be built, in a place where there was nothing like that before. Like the primeval hill used by Atum to create the world[100], this new town will be the place from where the future King will give his creative orders, in accordance with the newborn Maat!"

Heri-Hor finished and wiped the sweat from his face; he felt that a great deal of tension has abandoned him. For a moment, all three were sitting in an absolute silence, and Pi-ankh and Nes-Ba-neb-Djedu were analyzing what they had heard, asking inwardly many questions concerning the matters not yet mentioned. Nes-Ba-neb-Djedu has broken this silence as the first one:

---

[100] According to the creation myth, an island emerged from the chaos of water, on which the Creator - Atum stood, to continue the creative act.

"I see you have big plans. Do you know whom Amun will choose as his First Servant?"

"Here in the north, probably you," Heri-Hor replied. After all, you were born here and you are living your whole life here, and besides, you are very strongly associated with the royal house."

At that moment, Pi-ankh started laughing loudly. Nes-Ba-neb-Djedu slightly reddened, but turning to him, calmly replied, "Everyone knows that you too want to be connected to the same house. Think that maybe my connections might be useful to you if Amun chooses me as his High Priest. I must also tell you that I was talking with Tent-Amun today, and she has confirmed that Henut-tawy's heart was smiling at your Pi-nodjem. Moreover, the Queen is not against it. You know the position of Ramesses, but after the announcement of the Repeating of Births, he will not have much to say, while she still does."

Pi-ankh didn't laugh anymore. He looked at Nes-Ba-neb-Djedu for a moment, then said, "If you are serious, I assure you that I will do everything to make it happen!"

"I will help you too, Pi-ankh," Heri-Hor said, if Amun in Waset chooses me as his First Servant and if you give me your daughter as a wife."

Pi-ankh didn't know what to say. An hour ago he was mocking at Heri-Hor's considerable offspring and has not considered him as a good candidate for Nodjmet. This has, admittedly, not changed, however the circumstances have. He had to admit that the solution Heri-Hor had invented was excellent and fully suited his own plans. It would cost him nothing to gain support from Nes-Ba-neb-Djedu: what did he care about this man's relationship with the Queen, which had been going on since a long time? But Heri-Hor's support was also important, and here the price was high.

"However, it was worth paying it," Pi-ankh reflected, "since Heri-Hor would almost certainly become the High Priest". Yet, out of pure contrariness he said: "Maybe Amun will choose me?"

Heri-Hor smiled and replied, "You are younger than me, maybe you will still see it, and Pi-nodjem will certainly see it if the daughter of Ramesses will be by his side. Is that what you mean? Think about it, would you really rather be Amun's First Servant than a military leader? The army is your element. You will lead it against Pa-nehsi – we will give you the supreme command, and after that you will still continue to be the Head of the Army of the Both Countries. I think this would probably satisfy you?" Heri-Hor exchanged glances with Nes-Ba-neb-Djedu: they understood each other, and the outlined plan seemed really good, because if it is fulfilled everyone would get what was his secret desire.

Pi-ankh was still hesitating. Here, these two men wanted to share power in the Both Countries after the Repeating of Births, giving him an important but third function. But the marriage of his son with Princess Henut-tawy could in the future provide his home with lasting significance. He looked at Heri-Hor, who waited in suspense for what he would hear from him and said:

"I'm surprised myself, but I think you have convinced me. I will give you this girl because – I haven't tell you that – she also peeps at you, albeit I don't really understand what she can see in such an old man. But I lay down two conditions. The first one is that you will replace this empty pitcher of wine with a full one here. The second one is that we will write our contract in triplicate and everyone will take one, being a witness and a guarantor of its fulfillment. And woe to him who would cheat!"

"Do you always have to threaten, chief?" Heri-Hor smiled and, putting both hands on Pi-ankh's shoulders, added: "You can count on me!"

"Let's hurry, so that Pa-nehsi does not spoil everything," Nes-Ba-neb-Djedu decided to return to the specifics. "Do you already have a plan to defeat him?" he asked Pi-ankh while Heri-Hor prepared papyrus, feathers and ink.

"Yes, but you must provide me with your Tjehenu. Your problem, what and how will you promise them, but those whom Amun will choose as high priests must think up something."

After a while, all three sat on the floor, crossing their legs and, placing wooden boards on their knees, began to write the text of the contract in which they undertook to support each other's aspirations and lead to the announcement of the Repeating of Births. After having signed on all three pieces of papyrus, they hid them, aware that each of these documents was sufficient evidence to condemn them to death for the betrayal of the King.

CHAPTER XV

The next day, the generals set off towards Men-nefer, leading the remaining subordinate units, which were still stationing near Pi-Ramesse. Nes-Ba-neb-Djedu and Heri-Hor met again before marching out and after a short conversation, they have established that they would send fast horse messengers to all Tjehenu settlements scattered throughout the Northern Country, as well as those situated further in the south up to Pa-im. The messengers were to transmit the verbal order given allegedly on behalf of the King that the tribal elders from each settlement would immediately send their representatives to the meeting designated in the Men-nefer area, where all the troops gathered. When, after four days, the generals and their troops arrived at the place of the grouping, some of the tribal elders from the Tjehenu settlements nearest to Men-nefer were already waiting for them. Heri-Hor, who was to hold conversations with them, greeted them warmly in their native language, placed them in comfortable tents, and ordered the services to make sure that the guests had enough of everything. Every day new delegates were coming, but especially those were looked out for who lived in the area of Pa-im, because they were also expected to know something about the approaching army. When it turned out that they did not know what was going on, the generals took a breath, because it gave hope for a few extra days that could be devoted to preparations for the fight. When also the emissaries of the Tjehenu settlements situated furthest away from Men-nefer arrived, Heri-Hor with Nes-Ba-neb-Djedu gathered all the envoys and began the talks. Both generals dressed on that day in Tjehenu's traditional ceremonial robes and they stacked feathers in their hair. This gesture turned the gathered elders of the Libu and Meshuesh tribes very favorably, and when Heri-Hor recited in their dialect a prayer to Amun-Ash[101] he could be sure that he would be heard.

Heri-Hor began to talk about how happy years were given to Tjehenu living in the land of Kemet free from wars and famine, about which their forefathers could only dream in the past.

"Now, however, everyone can see that troops have gathered here because a common enemy of Kemet and Tjehenu is approaching from the south: the Kushites. Will the brave Tjehenu warriors want to join the assembled troops to face this enemy?"

Heri-Hor stopped speaking, which meant he was expecting an answer. Now, however, the gathered elders of Tjehenu began to

---

[101] The name of the Creator known from texts related to the Libyan Desert.

look at each other and it was clear that no one knew what to say. Finally, an old envoy from one of the villages on the eastern outskirts of the Lower Country rose, who introduced himself as Buyu-wawa[102] from the Meshuesh tribe, from the settlement at Per-Bastet. He said that since he can remember, and yet he came to the country of Kemet as child, no enemy dared to attack Pharaoh's land, for it is great.

"The army that has gathered here is also great," he said, "And the Kushites will not dare approach Men-nefer. If, however, it happened that they would appear where our settlements lie, then all Tjehenu would rise, and the strength of their bows will make Kushites flee like gazelles from a lion!"

Buyu-wawa stopped, and the murmur of recognition heard from everywhere testified that his words met with widespread support.

"Haven't I say?" Heri-Hor whispered to Nes-Ba-neb-Djedu, "They will not move without specific promises."

So, he got up and spoke again, "I do not doubt the bravery of the people of Meshuesh, whose blood also flows in my veins, as well as in the veins of General Nes-Ba-neb-Djedu sitting here, and I am sure that all the Tjehenu people would resist the Kushites if they appeared on the threshold of their settlements. But then it would be too late. Indeed, Buyu-wawa rightly compared his people to a lion, but he is wrong to compare

---

[102] This is the name, confirmed by sources, of a protoplast of the Libyan dynasty (so called 22nd Dynasty), which began of reigning in Egypt in the middle of the 10th century BC.

Kushites to gazelles. Rather, he should talk about a herd of hippopotami, which are very dangerous, do great harm and are rightly hated by the inhabitants of Kemet, but they are not afraid of the lion and could easily trample on his lair. The buffalo herd would do the same, but if such a herd sees many lions together, they will run away. We have to gather in large numbers because the army that is coming against us - and this is happening for the first time during Buyu-wawa's lifetime and during my lifetime - is huge and very dangerous."

The murmur again passed among the gathered, and some of them apparently began to consent to the words of Heri-Hor, because were nodding and lively discussing with others who were still not convinced. Buyu-wawa got up again and then all fell silent.

"General, your words have power and if the Kushites are really as dangerous as you say, they can also threaten our settlements. We must tell this to our brothers who sent us here and ask them what they advise us to do? We will go to our villages and will come back here in a half of the moon, and then we will meet again and tell you what the Tjehenu people think."

The words of Buyu-wawa were again well received by the gathered, and here and there were voices already saying: "Well said, let everyone know about it! Let's go and then we'll be back!" Heri-Hor silenced everyone again:

"Listen, Buy-wawa and all of you the brave Libu and Meshuesh warriors! You have gathered here because the fastest messengers had been sent for you. Time is running and the enemy may be nearby. You will go to your settlements, as you say, but you will return with your brothers ready to fight, like those of Tjehenu who are already serving in Pharaoh's army!"

Then Buyu-wawa jumped up immediately and uttered the words that the Generals actually expected from the beginning, "Will those Tjehenu who come here with their weapons to face the Kushites become part of Pharaoh's army, just like our brothers we met here? After returning home, will they get fields that give birth to grain, apart from the pastures they use? Will the heads of the settlements where Tjehenu are living be chosen from among Tjehenu? If this is the case, I assure you, General, that many warriors will come here, because the Tjehenu desire since years nothing but fighting for the Pharaoh!"

There were loud shouts of support, and some of the tribal elders jumped to their feet, ran to Buyu-wawa and began to embrace and kiss him. The turmoil continued for a long time, and although Heri-Hor had not promised anything yet, everyone presents at the assembly acknowledged that it would be just as the old Tjehenu asked, whom they now began to consider as their leader.

"You will have a difficult task," Heri-Hor murmured to Nes-Ba-neb-Djedu, seeing this enthusiasm, "because you will have to fulfill the promises we will give them now on behalf of Ramesses, but this is the only rescue for the country...", then signaled that he wanted to speak.

"Buyu-wawa," he said loudly to break through the hustle and bustle, "here you have just said what I was to convey as the message of His Majesty King Ramesses Men-Maat-Re, and may he live forever, to all Tjehenu. When the war is over, those warriors who take part in it will receive the fields in the same way that is used today in the Both Countries for Sherdana warriors and those of Tjehenu who are already serving in the army, and your brothers which you choose will be heads of the Tjehenu settlements! Go now and come back with the warriors as soon as possible!"

The hustle and bustle grew even bigger because everyone jumped up from their seats, embracing each other and shouting in honor of the King. Immediately they began to go to their villages to bring the good news to their fellows.

"I wonder what Ramesses would do if he were here now?" Nes-Ba-neb-Djedu asked this question more to himself than to Heri-Hor, for they both knew the answer very well.

"Do you have any doubts?" Heri-Hor's face expressed strong will and determination in action. "We have taken a path from which there is no turning back. I just hope that our colleague Pa-nehsi will not appear before our guests of today come back, because we would have to bar ourselves in the walls of Men-nefer, and as we know, he has recently specialized in conquering fortresses and uses villainy methods unbecoming to a soldier, but unfortunately effective ones. He certainly wouldn't spare women and children at Men-nefer. Let's go to report the results of our talks to whom we entrusted the command..."

Pi-ankh listened to the report with interest, but also with some reserve.

"I won't believe it until I see those Tjehenu. May we only don't see the Kushites first. Although..." Pi-ankh suspended his voice, "Pa-nehsi already knows that the Lower Country is expecting his army. He should have been here a few days ago and it may seem strange that he is still absent. One can see that my friend is not in hurry and I even think I know what he is going to do. Eventually, I drank enough wine with him to see trough him. I remember how he mocked Ramesses the Great at his unsuccessful expedition against Hatti, the one about which the bas-reliefs on our temples trumpet as a great victory[103]. Our army lost the battle then because our opponent chose her place and prepared well for it. A good leader should impose battle conditions on the enemy. Pa-nehsi said that if he were in Ramesses's place then he would look for a convenient place and wait for Hatti's army. He's unlucky now because I remember his words. I think he and his Kushites are waiting somewhere for us now. Let him wait, we will actually come, but there will be more of us than he thinks, provided, of course, that your Tjehenu really join us..."

Heri-Hor with Nes-Ba-neb-Djedu had to admit that Pi-ankh's behavior sometimes has been coarse one and he loved wine too much, but he mastered the military school well and felt great as a commander. He also ordered to watch out in the districts between Men-nefer and Pa-im, and now messengers came from there every day to inform the command of the situation there. Their reports, however, were invariably reassuring: no troops were noticed, indicating that Pi-ankh's suppositions were probably correct.

Meanwhile, three days after the meeting of the Generals with representatives of Tjehenu, the first of their armed groups began

---

[103] Allusion to the battle of Kadesh in 1275 BC (see footnote 72).

to arrive in the area of the grouping. Military scribes were registering the names of all warriors and officers of Heri-Hor and Nes-Ba-neb-Djedu were forming new units of them and were designating the place of stationing and an assignment to field bakeries and breweries. Every day new groups of volunteers were arriving and soon their number reached several thousand, which at the same time delighted the Generals, and on the other hand, showed the strength inherent in this soldierly and well-organized people.

"I am beginning to understand Ramesses's fears," Nes-Ba-neb-Djedu confided to Heri-Hor. "If Tjehenu receive land and new privileges, one day they may become stronger than the inhabitants of Kemet."

"I see it too," Heri-Hor replied, "but first of all it won't happen so soon, and it won't be a problem for our children's children, and probably also their children, and secondly, as we know, we have no choice. In addition, Tjehenu and Kemet residents can easily live in a big family, which we are an example."

The warriors of Libu and Meshuesh tribes were still coming and finally, Pi-ankh decided that the northern army was already strong enough to face the enemy. Nes-Ba-neb-Djedu was to stay in Men-nefer and continue to recruit volunteers and to form reserve troops of them, while Heri-Hor was to accompany Pi-ankh as his deputy. When Buteh-Amun and Suti-mes, who were in Heri-Hor's troops, serving as military scribes, learned that the supreme command rests with Pi-ankh, they did not hide their surprise and disappointment.

"Yet Pi-ankh is with Pa-nehsi in a good terms and now he is to fight him? I don't understand..." Suti-mes said to his friend.

"I am a bit worried about the outcome of such a fight," Buteh-Amun admitted, "but I have the impression that Pi-ankh as a commander gains, however, the ear of his subordinates who are afraid of him. Anyway, Heri-Hor is also here and since even he obeys Pi-ankh there must be some reasons. And we are now soldiers and we must follow the instructions of both of them..."

The time has come and finally, on the twentieth day of the third month of the Shemu-season, the army of the Northern Country set off from Men-nefer, beginning its march along the river and heading towards Pa-im. The main units were preceded by several groups of fast horseback scouts, who rode at clear intervals, advancing carefully and observing each other so that in case of any danger or trap that the enemy could set in front of them, subsequent groups could notice it and warn the approaching soldiers. The army was moving on a wide plain along the west bank of the river because on its other side the lofty desert began. Sometimes, however, arable fields were covering the area between the river and the vastness of sands. Then one or two groups of scouts were crossing the nearest ford to the other side and were penetrating such an area, examining whether the sly enemy wasn't hiding somewhere to move north only when the royal army will pass away, heading south. It was, admittedly, very unlikely because at this time of the year the fields were bare and covered only with a low yellow stubble creating a dry steppe that was as if dozing in a half-dead waiting for an invigorating flood. However, in some places, there were large and dense palm groves, and high clumps of papyrus also sometimes obstructed the field of vision. The scouts were galloping across the entire space separating the river from the desert, then returning, always bringing reassuring news: no trace of foreign troops.

The whole army was divided into two divisions, almost equal, in terms of the number of troops and their composition. In each division there were soldiers fighting with swords and spears, dressed in leather armors and carrying shields, half-naked slingers and archers, as well as chariot troops moving on the sides. The first part of the army was led by Heri-Hor, the second one by Pi-ankh. Both groups of combat troops were marching separated with a short distance only so that if the enemy attacked those coming in the front, the other group could enter the battle very quickly. Each division was also accompanied by a group of carts pulled by oxen carrying tents, while it was only at the rear behind the second part of the army that numerous pack donkeys carrying provisions for people and horses were kept. Everything was organized so that when the stop place was reached, the soldiers were pitching their tents and when the troops were already deployed, the supplies were arriving, and then the soldiers could have an evening meal. Because it was hot during the day at this time of year, every soldier was carrying water in a leather wineskin hanging over his shoulder, which he used to quench his thirst during stops. Every day, the army was covering about two *iteru* of the way only. Pi-ankh decided that since Pa-nehsi was not in a hurry to reach north, he would not torment soldiers with a too quick march in the opposite direction. Thus, two days after leaving Men-nefer, they found themselves at the height of the Pa-im oasis lying near the valley, and after two more days arrived at the walls of the fortress in Nen-ensu, guarding the ancient city and the holy lake at the temple of the ram-shaped Heri-shef. It housed the headquarters of the superior of the entire District of the Tree and also of Pa-im, who came surrounded by his entourage to warmly welcome the Generals and assure them of his readiness to provide all help. Pi-ankh immediately stated that the best expression of such kindness would be to provide a good meal for the tired army, because the soldiers certainly already longed for a piece of meat and fruit, and after all the tree bearing pomegranates is a symbol of this region. The mayor of Nen-ensu immediately invited both Generals to his palace for a rich meal, and at the same time issued an order to slaughter 100 cows from the royal and temple herds. The butchers began to work and soon the tasty scents of roasting began to spread from the numerous campfires lit in the camp. However, before that, at the request of the dignitary, Pi-ankh and Heri-Hor went in his company to the temple at the lotus-covered holy lake, where they were greeted by an aged High Priest who offered a burnt sacrifice on the altar and sang a hymn in honor of Osiris-Re-Amun-Heri-shef. The Generals, and especially Pi-ankh, attended this ceremony more out of duty than of willingness, but they had to appreciate that they were given the rare opportunity to see one of the most venerable sanctuaries in the whole country, and to the holy pond with lotuses only exceptionally anybody except for the High Priest could be admitted.

"Maybe they already know that you will be Amun's First Servant?" Pi-ankh asked mockingly as long prayers were coming to an end.

"Certainly not," Heri-Hor replied, "but they had to find out that the Kushites were on their way, and that their army wouldn't content itself to ask for 100 cows but would take all the cows they had and search the treasury of that temple. Besides, I have a suspicion that the local chief priest also comes, like me, from the people of Tjehenu, because his features testify to this, and he was smiling particularly warmly at me..."

It soon turned out that Heri-Hor was right. Not only the chief priest but also all his helpers belonged to the descendants of Tjehenu, whom His Majesty Ramesses User-Maat-Re Meri-Amun, justified, settled here as prisoners. At the urging of Heri-Hor, the old priest Heri-shef went to the Tjehenu volunteer troops who came here with the army and together with them, in their language led a prayer to Amun-Heri-shef who reigns in the sky as Re, and in the underground as the Osiris, and as the Creator brought to life all the people, including Tjehenu. Although Pi-ankh was shrugging at this, Heri-Hor was sure that this ceremony would have a very positive effect, making Tjehenu aware that they were being treated on an equal footing with the inhabitants of Kemet, their number was greater than they had imagined, and the enemy they were approaching, is a deadly threat to them all.

The next day, the army moved on. The fortress in Nen-ensu was already the last so strongly fortified place in this part of the Southern Country, that is why Pi-ankh has increased caution ever since; the enemy army certainly couldn't be far away. This was confirmed by conversations with the inhabitants of the villages passed, who apparently had already learned that a terrible enemy was coming from the south and who were welcoming their own army with real relief. The strip of fields between the river and the desert hills visible on the western horizon was now very wide, and groups of horseback scouts had to ride in a zigzag route, as far the only narrow branch of Hapi had created in the Both Countries and which flowed as far as Pa-im[104]. Sometimes they even had to cross it and then return to the river. After two more days of march, the army arrived near the city of Seper-meru in the Fish District, which now had to make an effort to feed the army. The mayor of Seper-meru said that it was a heavy duty for this city and the surrounding area, but he did not hide the joy that the first army that arrived here was the army of His Majesty Ramesses.

"Apparently," he said, "The city of Hor-di, the capital of the neighboring Dog District, must have been holding a similarly large army since the middle of the moon, whose arrival is like a locust for a field covered with fertile crops." This piece of news was brought by several fishermen who came here on the small river. I don't know if it's true, but every day when I wake up, I don't know if I'm going to see the evening. Let Amun bless your army for coming here first!"

The news obtained in Seper-meru were important and now the meeting with the enemy was to be expected at all times. The fact that they were not far away was evidenced by the groups of people, more and more often encountered now who, with their whole families, often rushing a cow or goat were following local roads leading north, apparently fleeing. Seeing the approaching

---

[104] It's about the so-called today Bahr Jussuf, flowing into Fayum.

army, these people sometimes panicked and ran somewhere sideways, and only when they realized that this army had no unfriendly intentions towards them, they stood waiting for the road to become free again. Asked who they were running from and to where?, they replied that they did not know where to, but they wanted to be as far as possible from those terrible black bandits who prowl in the Dog District, taking animals and grain from people, robbing houses, and raping all young women that fall into their hands. They kill those who defend their families and possessions, or capture them, binding and taking somewhere so that it is not known what is happening to them.

When in the late afternoon the army stopped for the night rest again, the Generals did not allow pitching of tents this time. Each unit was in combat readiness, and at night – so warm that it was possible to lie simply on the ground – only half of the soldiers slept, while the others watched to enter the battle immediately if necessary. It was not customary to conduct a battle at night, but Pa-nehsi managed to break so many rules during this war that Pi-ankh preferred not to risk. An evening was approaching and the camp was preparing for a night's rest when Heri-Hor, whose division was stationing more to the south. Once were reported that scouts had caught several suspicious refugees who were sneaking from the south near the river, and the detainees said they wanted to see the commander. Heri-Hor immediately remembered an old text that accompanied the numerous depictions of the battle of Kadesh at the largest temples and which was repeatedly discussed at a military school. Well, it also described how two scouts brought before the King Ramesses the Great two natives who pretended to be fugitives and misled the

King, falsely stating the place where the enemy army of Hatti was supposed to be.[105] Could this be a similar trick of Pa-nehsi? Prepared for this, the General ordered to bring these people and after a while saw five skinny, ragged, dirty and overgrown men, who were certainly the indigenous inhabitants of Kemet. Seeing the dignitary in front of them, these people bowed in a low bow, uttering the words of greeting.

"Who are you, where do you come from and why is your appearance so messy?" Heri-Hor asked.

The eldest of these men bowed again and replied, "Forgive me, dear Lord, that we stand before you in such a miserable condition that all meetings with people should be avoided but let me also say that the seeing of this army is like a lotus smell for us! Let Amun give you life, health and all good!"

Urged by the General's impatient gesture, he continued:

"I am Djed-Mut-iuf-ankh, a tenant of the land of Amun in the City, and with me are my kins whose fate joined with me in Waset when the Royal Son of Kush Pa-nehsi came with the army to besiege His Grandness the First Servant of Amun in Ipet-Sut. Just like them, I belonged to those fools who believed what Pa-nehsi and his men had told that it was Amen-hotep who ordered to pay six bags of grain instead of two, and our hearts were angry with him. We volunteered to help the Kushites in the siege and God rightly punished us. When Pa-nehsi conquered the walls of Ipet-sut, we could see how the hands of the infidels rip the walls,

---

[105] This episode is confirmed by sources, among others on the walls of the Ramesseum and Abu Simbel temples.

gates and obelisks of gold and destroy this holy place, although Amen-hotep was not there. But it was too late then! Although we had to serve the Kushites earlier, they treated us like free people and fed us well, but after capturing Ipet-sut they turned us into slaves and guarded us, and tied us up for the night, gave us anything to eat or nothing at all! Pa-nehsi then announced the *medu-an* conscription, and turned many residents of Waset and the surrounding area into prisoners of war. A month ago, when the moon was complete as it is today, he moved north with his army and he drove us, just like rush the cattle. For half a moon, making three *iteru* a day, we rode here, guarded by a Kushite troop, while the rest of Pa-nehsi's army, chariots and he himself sailed in boats. We came to Hor-di ten days ago and here we found the rest of his army. Since then, he has been there all the time, and the city and the surrounding area look as if there was no life in it at all. All of us who came from the City as slaves of the Kushites, were digging long ditches there and covering them with branches so that the chariots could not cross there, they always tied us up at night, but last night we found a knife and managed to hide it and cut the bonds, then we ran away and we have run all the day until your guards have found us. When we have seen the scouts, we were thinking it was a pursuit for us and we were saying goodbye to life...a hundred times, may Amun reward you and give you all strength!"

Heri-Hor listened carefully to the story and had to admit it sounded credible. If these people were telling the truth, the enemy was one day away, waiting for them in a place that he had prepared well for the battlefield and equipped with tricky traps to prevent the attack of the royal chariots. That would explain why they hadn't encountered him before. Also, the deplorable condition of the refugees was understandable if they were indeed treated as they describe. In no case, however, could Heri-Hor afford the sin of credulity.

"You know well," he said, "that we can force you to tell the truth, and if it turned out that you were lying, the end of your life would be terrible."

"Lord," Djed-Mut-iuf-ankh said, "Let Amun send me to death in an instant if I am not telling the truth! We may have deserved to die because we trusted the traitor Pa-nehsi, but now we could fight against him at best, if you agreed. How can I show that I really come from Waset, when only the soldiers from the Northern Country are in your army?"

At this moment, Heri-Hor has recalled something and, with a nod to one of the officers, gave him a silent command, and he addressed the prisoners this time in a gentle tone, "You will be able to prove what you said."

At that moment, an officer sent by Heri-Hor returned, leading Buteh-Amun and Suti-mes.

"This man claims he is coming from Waset..." the General said, indicating the captive with whom he had talked, but he could not finish the sentence yet, when the prisoner reached out his arms and called out, "Amun, you are Suti-mes, my daughter's beloved one, whom I threw out of the house in blind anger, while calling Seth! I was unjust and stupid. My son, forgive me! Maybe Seth will then forgive me, too, that I had called him in vain!" Djed-Mut-iuf-ankh fell to his knees, wanting to kiss the young man's feet. This lifted him immediately, embraced him, and said with a voice chopped because of emotion:

"Thanks be to Amun, Djed-Mut-iuf-ankh that he kept you healthy, although I can see that you have gone through a lot!"

This short scene provided Heri-Hor with the necessary proof that the captured people were telling the truth. He stood up and patted the shoulder of Djed-Mut-iuf-ankh, who was still standing in the arms of Suti-mes.

"Thank you, soldiers! If you really would like to fight with Pa-nehsi, you will have the opportunity tomorrow. Let your countrymen from the City take care of you and enroll you in my ranks. Give me a horse," he told one of the scouts, "I must personally inform the commander in chief of what I found out."

The General disappeared in the distance when Suti-mes, finally releasing Djed-Mut-iuf-ankh, dared to ask him the most important question: is he withdrawing his ban on marriage with Henut?

"My son," he answered, "may Amun give you happiness as I give my consent! However, I do not know what is happening to her, because the Kushites have never allowed me even a short visit to my own home. I hope she is alive and has not suffered any misfortune..."

"She was alive when I left the City, she was living in the house of my father Djehuty-mes, and this house was under special protection, like yours, where your wife and son live. Both of them were also healthy, at least that was three months ago," said Buteh-Amun, and when he saw two silent tears of joy flowing down the skinny and overgrown face of Henut's father, he quickly changed the subject and suggested that the weary runaways would clean, change into whole and clean kilts, go to the barber, finally eat something and lay down to rest before tomorrow that could bring the battle. He led them to the officer on duty, and having made sure that the newcomers were taken care of, he began looking for the friend whom he felt like hugging with joy. He saw, him kneeling with his hands raised in a gesture of adoration, facing the direction where Re's barge just disappeared over the horizon. Buteh-Amun thought he wouldn't interfere with the important conversation that Suti-mes certainly had just been having and withdrew discreetly.

Meanwhile, in Pi-ankh's division camp, both commanders held a council. When Heri-Hor told his colleague what he had heard from Djed-Mut-iuf-ankh, Pi-ankh shook his head in appreciation.

"I knew he would be waiting for us and the bastard, of course, chose the best place! I know those areas because I was once there, sent as a young military scribe for recruits. In the area around Hor-di the valley is still wide, but slightly further south it narrows quickly so that the distance between the great Hapi and the small river, diminishes only to half an *iteru* and if you subtract from this the area of swamp, reed fields and papyrus thickets, it remains little over 50 ropes of the hard ground only, and it is hard at this time of the year exclusively. We don't know where the boys dug these trap ditches, but I bet my friend is standing by the river and he will want to let us pass a bit, then to push us with a strong attack of his chariots towards this narrowing and to lock there like in a sack. That's why I think that next to Hor-di there are no such ditches because this way his chariots would run. If we want to use our chariots and the brave Tjehenu archers, we must stick to the river and approach Pa-nehsi as close as possible so that he does not succeed in the planned flanking maneuver. They will not move, so we will come near Hor-di tomorrow, but we will fight the day after tomorrow."

"I agree with your assessment," added Heri-Hor, "And I also think that due to the number of our archers, which should be a surprise to the Kushites, we should align our divisions in one line and create the longest possible front. I'm just wondering if Pa-nehsi is preparing a surprise for us yet..."

"Don't caw. I think we can handle any surprise," Pi-ankh concluded.

The next day, as planned, the royal army, proceeding cautiously and not too quickly, reached the place from which one could already see in the distance the houses in Hor-di.[106] Here it stood and stopped for the night, doing exactly the same as the previous evening, i.e. without pitching tents. Pi-ankh announced an early wake-up and soon after, as the sky in the east lit up with a red glow, the troops of the Heri-Hor's division, followed by Pi-ankh, set off in a compact formation towards Hor-di. This time the scouts were not only looking for the hostile army, but were attentively watching if there were any masked trenches in the ground, and the carts with tents and the pack donkeys remained

---

[106] Papyrus sources confirm that the battle between the royal army and Pa-nehsi rebels took place near this village, although its location has not yet been confirmed archaeologically. It was probably located near Sheh Fadl, about 40 km to the north of Minya.

at the last night's place, so as not to impede the movement of the armed troops.

The army had already passed the dormant and quiet as if deserted city and moved across the plain of fields, much expanded because the river made a bend here, moving eastwards. They were walking on for another hour when the scouts signaled that in that bend of the river, they saw from the distance flashes that could be caused by the rays of Re reflecting in chariots and spears. Then Heri-Hor's division stopped to let pass Pi-ankh's troops by and then a long line of royal troops with archers advancing in front and with chariots on both sides has turned to the river, while approaching with every step the troops standing there. From afar the ranks of black archers were already clearly visible, and on the left a great concentration of chariots.

"They are standing exactly as I thought," Pi-ankh has dropped a remark to Heri-Hor who was riding next to him. Both divisions stopped at the distance of two bow's shots from those soldiers. "You will have a hard time with these chariots because on this wing they have an advantage in this respect. They are probably weaker on another side. Blow!" he turned to the herald now, who picked up his trumpet and has blown a conventional melody announcing the arrival of a messenger.

One of the officers headed towards the Kushite line and, stopping a short distance away, shouted loudly, "His Grandness Pi-ankh, General of the troops of His Majesty the King of the Both Countries, Ramesses Men-Maat-Re, wants to talk with His Grandness the Royal Son of Kush, Pa-nehsi, and proposes that they meet on the ground that separates the two armies in halfway!"

For a while he waited until he heard someone responding: "His Grandness, the General of the Free Kush army, Pa-nehsi, agrees to meet with the General Pi-ankh!"

The officer turned back and told Pi-ankh what he had already heard. The General came out close by the front of his own ranks and stopped until he saw a single rider coming out from the other side. They both started moving slowly towards each other, as if suspiciously. Finally they came mutually up so close that they could recognize one another. They stopped the horses a few cubits from each other and looked closely. They haven't met long, but the time has not changed their appearance much. Only the situation in which they were to have the conversation changed. They were connected for many years with a relation that could be called friendship, although it was rather a kind of good camaraderie, seasoned with a certain amount of competition. Both of them reached the positions of army commanders, although they never had the opportunity to prove themselves in war conditions. Now, the life put them in a strange role of opponents who were to test their skills in the real battle, so even conversation, and even more the words of welcome were difficult for both.

They were silent for a long moment, and finally, Pi-ankh said, "Do I always have to save your ass? As long as you fought with Amen-hotep, I kept explaining to Ramesses that everything was fine in the City, and even once I was able to take over the letter that two *medjayu* carried from the First Servant to Pharaoh. But you had to attack Ipet-sut and we even know that you dragged women and kids into it. We were taught a little differently at a military school, so do not be surprised that Ramesses sends an army, not a messenger to meet you. You are unlucky and lucky that I am the commander in chief of this army. So, you are unlucky because I will not let you go further north, nor let you drive me between the two rivers, nor lead my chariots where you ordered to dig these ditches and mask them – as you can see, I know much more than you would like to. But you're also lucky because we've drunk too much wine together so that I'd destroy you now. I like you, so I'll give you a chance: retreat with your army to the south of Abu and sit there until the end of your days, and we'll leave you alone!"

Pi-ankh finished and waited for what Pa-nehsi would say, although he had no doubt that his offer would be denied; the opponent was too ambitious to give in without a fight to his colleague, whom he had competed with for years, so he was not surprised by what he heard.

"I like you, too, so you make me sad and disappointed that you do not even recognize me as the future King of Kush... You rather go back; I don't have anything against you. I just want to visit Ramesses and thank him that I became able to see the harm done to the lands of Wawat and Kush. Now, this harm is over, and we are only receiving what is due to us. Get out of my way because you know you have no chance; we both know that your army is now only a shadow and we will crush you!"

"You are very wrong," answered Pi-ankh, "We are stronger than you think, and besides, Heri-Hor is with me, and he doesn't like you and will want to prove he is brave."

"Well, it's a pity that we can't get through to us," Pa-nehsi answered. "I am stronger than you think, too. If Heri-Hor wants to prove something, he'll have the opportunity!"

They looked at each other for a moment, then each of them turned his horse towards his own ranks. The battle was about to start irrevocably. Pi-ankh gave Heri-Hor a brief account of the conversation:

"I do not know what is he threatening with and what is he plotting, but he probably doesn't know about our Tjehenu. We must be careful not to get pushed to the river because there they can attack us from their ships, so the chariots must secure our both wings. Take care!"

Pi-ankh drove away, after which the army began to take position as ordered by the commander-in-chief. They moved slowly, attentively watching the opponent. Finally, around the noon the royal army finally formed a fairly long line stretched over 20 ropes. The first five ranks were composed of the excellent Tjehenu archers – Pi-ankh counted most on this formation. The sling-holders followed, and only then the heavily armored soldiers fighting with spears, swords and axes, among them Sherdana's selected troops, which were actually a royal guard, which His Majesty Ramesses passed under the orders the Generals complaining about the weakness of the army. The battle tactics developed by Pi-ankh planned first a massive attack of archers, the number of which was to surprise Pa-nehsi. This attack should cause painful losses in the ranks of the enemy. After several series of shots, the archers were to let first the slingers pass in the front line, and then also the units of soldiers fighting hand-to-hand, while the archers were still to shoot from behind at the further ranks of enemies. The chariots were to ensure that the enemy did not attempt to invade the royal army from either side and in the later phase of the battle to launch an attack from the two sides and to cause the final crushing defeat.

Of course, at the same time, the opponent's troops were also moving, stretching their lines and moving mainly their chariots. Finally, the movements froze on both sides. It was already afternoon when Pi-ankh decided he should attack. At his signal, the trumpeters have blown a conventional signal, after which the entire line of the royal troops approached the enemy at a distance of a bow shot. Now, the trumpets sounded differently and then the archers tightened their bows and a cloud of several thousand arrows soared towards the opponents. At the same time the arriving enemy arrows have been seen. All the soldiers armed with shields have covered themselves with them, but not all of them were succeeded, and besides, not all of them had shields, so the first moans of the wounded joined the battle cries of Tjehenu shooters. Undoubtedly, the same happened among the opponents. After a while, the archers released another cloud of arrows, and simultaneously a second deadly cloud came from the opposite direction. Both armies were slowly approaching each other, so everything went as planned by Pi-ankh. Three more series of shots, and then both armies will clash in the hand-to-hand combat, and here the excellent Sherdana and equally excellent warriors from Kemet, dressed in leather armors, had no equals.

The first lines of the two armies were already at a distance of one rope from each other so that it was already possible to clearly distinguish individual soldiers and the Kushites could already see and recognize that the famous Tjehenu having feathers in their hair were standing against them. Suddenly a multitude of people who had no weapons at all ran out the parted ranks of the Kushites. Behind them the line of Pa-nehsi's chariots could be seen. All this mass of people and chariots was rushing straight into the royal ranks. After passing them, the Kushite archers once again closed their ranks, releasing another cloud of arrows above their chariots that took their bloody harvest. Meanwhile, Tjehenu archers did not know what to do. Half-naked people running towards them did not appear to be attackers, but rather they were chased by chariots themselves, and all those lagging behind were shot by the warriors riding on them.

"They are prisoners from Waset!!!" Buteh-Amun exclaimed standing near Heri-Hor at Sherdana's unit. Pa-nehsi's maneuver turned out to be just as villainy as effective. The army commanders had now only a short moment to make a decision.

"Stop shooting!" Heri-Hor shouted and Tjehenu on this wing lowered their bows. At the moment the first prisoners reached their ranks, and seeing the foreigners before them with feathers in their hair, panicked. Before and behind they had now armed warriors of the Nine Bows whom the inhabitants of the City always associated with the enemies annihilated and trampled by the King or portrayed as prisoners with their arms tied with ropes.

Some inhabitants of the City considered Tjehenu as bands that once attacked Waset from the desert and which were often called that. So now, expecting nothing but death, the terrified people were behaving variously. Some fell to their knees, begging for their lives, others threw themselves with their bare hands at the surprised archers, wanting to die in battle, and for some the view of Tjehenu was so terrifying that they turned back, to die a moment later with the spear blows inflicted on them by the Kushite soldiers from chariots. There were also those who ran on, breaking up the ranks of the royal soldiers. One effect was common to all of these behaviors: a chaos broke out in the ranks of both the archers and those standing behind them and all the plans that were discussed before the battle became an empty talk. At that moment the Kushite chariots arrived that impetuously burst into the ranks of Heri-Hor's division, spreading further confusion and death. The General himself stood far enough from this place that he could safely send a messenger to the commander of the royal chariot squad with the order to strike the side of the advancing Kushite chariots and to tie them with the fight, while the slingers were to focus on attacking the coachmen who led the first group of combat vehicles. All the dispersed archers were tried to be gathered again in a compact unit, but it was an extremely difficult task. Although the impetus of the Kushite attack was temporarily stopped, the infantry troops approached behind the chariots and again the Kushites gained the advantage pushing the royals towards the bend of the river, on which now Panehsi's boats filled with archers appeared that were so far in reserve. The specter of defeat hung over Heri-Hor's division. The General was ready for a crazy and desperate attack of the last Sherdana unit he had in reserve and was only considering in which direction to make the attack when the sounds of the enemy trumpets were heard, after which the Kushite units began to withdraw one by one. Although incomprehensible for Heri-Hor's dispersed troops, it was a real rescue. The Kushites were not hunted for, but the royal soldiers began to gather in a former order, and the condition of all the units of this division were reviewed now. The losses were very large, as more than 900 soldiers of all formations were killed. Of course, the opponent also left about 300 killed on this flank of the battlefield, and in addition, 40 chariots were captured, whose crews were killed and the retreating Kushites could not take them, all the more so that most of the horses were also killed. However, it turned out that Heri-Hor's decision to stop shooting so as not to kill the prisoners of Waset, meant that in the section where his division was fighting, most of them survived and Buteh-Amun with Suti-mes, who were given the task of registering them all, counted over 1000 saved men. When the first shock was over, they agreed to create a volunteer squad that was ready to fight tomorrow, giving the former captives the opportunity to avenge the times of adversity.

On the contrary, Pi-ankh's division fighting in another flank did not save even a hundred of the inhabitants of the City, because the battle on this wing was quite different. When Pa-nehsi's "live shield" of Waset prisoners threw itself at the royal line, Pi-ankh ordered the archers to shoot them as if they were attacking Kushites. Already the first series of deadly arrows released on them by the ranks of Tjehenu put half of the unfortunate in a row, the second almost completed the deadly harvest. Only a few of these people managed to reach the line of archers, and they were obviously let through to the rear without causing much confusion. In contrast, the pile of corpses lying in the foreground greatly slowed down the attack of the Kushite chariots, so that the archers still had time to send another cloud of arrows, this time directly at coachmen and warriors riding on chariots, as well as at horses. Dozens of chariots were instantly rendered harmless, becoming a barrier to the next who lost a line of battle and instead of attacking, were exposed themselves to the attack by the terrible Tjehenu archers. Seeing this, Pi-ankh sent into battle the best infantry troops including the most dangerous Sherdana. At the same time, royal chariots started from the right wing, slaughtering troops standing there. The terrible hand-to-hand battle lasted for an hour, but then Pa-nehsi saw that he was threatened with a complete defeat on this wing, because in addition to the chariots and Pi-ankh's heavily armed infantry, which gained a clear advantage, Tjehenu archers who regrouped into a powerful compact unit entered the action again, shooting at the rear of the Kushite troops. Then he signaled to stop the fighting and to retreat, although on the second wing his soldiers were prevailing. The fight was interrupted. The barge of Re was just disappearing on the horizon, passing into the kingdom of Osiris[107], and the purple sky was shedding bloody light on the

---

[107] It was believed that the world consists of two parts, each resembling a hemisphere. The upper one is the visible and luminous kingdom of Re, on the vault of which the sun barge flows through the day. The lower one is the dark and invisible kingdom of Osiris, around which the sun flows at night.

battlefield strewn with the dead. Pi-ankh with Heri-Hor and several officers were silently circling the areas where there was a fierce battle before two hours. After the arrangement of bodies lying on both sides, the corpses of horses and the abandoned chariots, the experienced eye of the commander could easily reconstruct the course of the battle.

"Let the donkey bang you!" Pi-ankh almost shouted at Heri-Hor, "How could you let to be driven back so much?! Have your Tjehenu forgotten what the bows are for?"

"I couldn't let them kill defenseless people, thanks to which many survived..." Heri-Hor tried to defend.

"Have you gone crazy?" Pi-ankh shouted. "Because of that more of your soldiers were killed! Indeed, you have proved that you are suitable for a procession as if you were already the First Servant in the City, but today you should be a general and not show that you are sentimental!"

"But the number of those I saved equalizes the number of dead and tomorrow my ranks will be more complete than yours," Heri-Hor retorted calmly. "We will smash them tomorrow, because Pa-nehsi has already used his secret weapon with which he has threatened, and our archers are better."

"We will not go further!" Pi-ankh made a decision, "Too bad for his people and ours, it was only one army recently. I think this fool has already understood that he will not win and will now step back."

"Do you want to release the entire rebel army, in addition under their own general?" Heri-Hor tried to convince a colleague,

"If you do this now, Kemet will get an enemy who will always be dangerous. We have to finish the work tomorrow!"

"If you still care about Nodjmet, don't try to oppose me," Pi-ankh said it in a low hissing tone, "Have you already forgotten what you have signed?"

To such an argument Heri-Hor answered nothing more.

The next morning the trumpeter announced that the General Pi-ankh was sending a messenger to the General Pa-nehsi. He was carrying a letter proposing a truce, provided that the Kushite forces immediately begin to retreat. In ten days, the royal army will move, and if it ever finds Pa-nehsi's army on the land of Kemet, it will crush it mercilessly, and Pa-nehsi himself will be imprisoned in Pi-Ramesse. The winner was speaking with such a language and Pa-nehsi had to admit that he underestimated the strength of the northern army. In short words he wrote back that he agreed. He also knew that if Pi-ankh's army leaves in ten days only, he will get twice as much time, because his army will use boats. And he needed that extra time very much.

That same day, the Kushites set off back south, and the royal army could rest: they were not in danger of an unexpected attack, though the guards watched as they had previously. Before the tents were pitched, there had been a sad ceremony of carrying the bodies from the battlefield, their identification, and then a joint soldier's funeral in the waters of the saint Hapi. This ceremony was commonly performed for all the fallen soldiers including the Kushites, as well as all prisoners from Waset who had died during the battle. Buteh-Amun and Suti-mes tried to register the names of all dead inhabitants of the City they could learn about from the survivors. Among the fallen ones they also discovered to their great regret the body of Henut's father, Djed-Mut-iuf-ankh.

"Look, he withdrew his curse, but he didn't conciliate Seth, and it still came true," Suti-mes nodded thoughtfully, "After all, he said that as long as he is alive, he will prevent our marriage... Poor Henut does not know that she lost her father!"

"You'll have to replace him now," Buteh-Amun replied, squeezing his friend's arm.

CHAPTER XVI

Djehuty-mes slowly climbed to the top of the rock ridge surrounding the Great Valley and sat in the shadow of a large stone, wiping with a sleeve of the tunic his sweated forehead and neck. There wasn an absolute silence all around, in which the hot air was trembling. High in the sky, a vulture was moving majestically, its nest was even not far from the place where the Necropolis Scribe was sitting. He was deeply concerned about the absence of all guards in the Great Valley. Since all the *medjayu* went with Pa-nehsi to the war in the north, the graves in this valley have been practically protected by no one. Admittedly, the thieves were probably conscripted into the Kushite army too, but someone from the area, knowing that no one was guarding the treasures hidden in the royal tombs, could now easily be tempted to break in. That is why the old Scribe of the Necropolis every two or three days was visiting the Great Valley, even though at his age it was a huge effort, especially now, when the rays of Re were smiting the earth mercilessly, the heated rocks were burning painfully at each touch, and in the valley itself surrounded by the lofty walls of the mountains was stuffy and hot, like in an oven.

Today, he also went there, setting off early in the morning through the mountains, when the temperature was still bearable, and when he reached the bottom of the Great Valley, he circled it thoroughly, looking into all the nooks and crannies. Apart from the tombs of the Ramesses family easily recognizable by their distinct gates cut in the rocks and visible from afar, also other graves were located there, well hidden under rock rubbles looking very naturally and undistinguished in the landscape. Djehuty-mes knew about them from his father, to whom his grandfather passed this knowledge, and now he nursed it, sharing it with his son Buteh-Amun, although in practice he has never seen most of these hidden entrances himself. However, every place visited by him today was looking as if nothing changed here since Atum and the First Time[108], and that meant that no thieves tried to get there. By the way, at most some equipment accumulated in the vestibules or halls accompanying the Sarcophagus Chamber could fall prey to them, because no one of these small burglars were able to overcome the protection of the royal mummies. These were secured by numerous walls of wooden and metal coffins, stone sarcophagi and thick wooden chapels surrounding these sarcophagi with fourfold protection. However, any burglary

---

[108] Time ran round for the Egyptian and every beginning of the period (New Year, new rule, morning of each day and so on) referred to the act of creating the world, which was referred to as the First Time.

would be a sacrilege, a violation of Maat, and the most sacred duty of Djehuty-mes, was to do everything possible to prevent it.

It was already noon, but the Scribe of the Necropolis deemed that before returning home and hiding in the salutary shadow of its walls, one more place should be checked. An access to the atypically high situated tomb of His Majesty Djehuty-mes Men-kheper-Re, justified, led not from the bottom of the Great Valley, but from above, through a small valley falling down with several slopes and protected by all means against the waters of a sudden downpour, which could sometimes fall here and what the City survived less than two years ago.

The old Scribe of Necropolis while sitting in a shadow was struggling with the overwhelming reluctance caused by a thought that he would again have to go out on a hot path not sheltered against the sun. Finally he sighed and started walking toward the small valley. Immediately before it a deep well was situated that would absorb most of the rain water that would running down here. Next was a thick wall made of very heavy stones that the water could not tear. Similar walls protected this valley from both sides.

For the water, which would overcome these protections, in the middle of the valley a pit waited filled with water-absorbing sand, then another wall and again a pit with sand. On the very end of the valley the last solid wall stood ready to keep the waters that would reach here, although such situation seemed difficult to imagine. Overcoming all these obstacles with great effort, Djehuty-mes reached the end of the valley and looked down: 20 cubits below there was a well-hidden entrance to the tomb, but those who did not know about it would not guess anything; this place looked as if no human had ever arrived here.[109] The satisfied Scribe of the Necropolis began slowly climbing up the valley.

He always had the greatest difficulty with the surmounting of the edge of a vertical rock fault above the lower of the two sand reservoirs; he had to stand here on a small ledge in the sidewall of the valley and pull himself up on his arms to reach the nearest horizontal surface with his knee. It would be a small thing for a young man, however it was always difficult for him.

He walked over to the rock and started looking for that rock ledge when he suddenly heard a voice above him, "Give me your hand, Chari, I will help you!"

Djehuty-mes reflexively looked up and became petrified: just above him was Aa-neru standing, his face contorted with a malicious smile."

"Aren't you glad that there is someone here who wants to help you?" Aa-neru was still outstretching his hand, but Djehuty-mes did not want to touch it: it was the hand of the killer and the old man imagined it clutching a stone that the same man dealt lethal blows to the unfortunate guard Nes-Amun. Aa-neru seemed to guess this thought because suddenly he himself began to talk about it.

"I have respect for old people, even those who spoke against me in court. Anyway, you rightly accused me then, because I actually had taken these few things from the temple of Seti Men-

---

[109] The description of the location of the Thutmose III tomb in the Valley of Kings and its original security features are accurate with reality.

Maat-Re. They were not needed by anyone there and I told this to this slow-witted Nes-Amun, but he insisted on defending them, and then in court, he was so silly and insisted in his accusations that I had no choice but to smash his stupid head... You must be surprised, why am I telling you this? Well, it doesn't matter anymore, you've all lost, and nobody will accuse me or judge me anymore, you won't either."

"So, you have come here to kill me and increase the number of your crimes?" the Necropolis Scribe asked calmly, albeit he was imagining that in a moment Aa-neru would jump down towards him and would push him towards the valley outlet, in order to throw him straight down to the place containing the royal grave, which would certainly bring the expected effect, while no one would find here for a long time his body.

"Of course not!" Aa-neru laughed loudly. "Killing the old man, you are would not increase my war merit, while giving me only a momentary pleasure. I hope to reap much more profit from leaving you alive. Well, you see, I'm interested in the tombs of the kings, but I didn't know where to look for some. I even thought about asking you, but you might not want to tell me. However, thanks to your trip today I learned a lot because I suspect that the places you have visited were not accidental? Thank you so much on behalf of the General and the future King of Kush, Pa-nehsi, to whom you have done a great service. You can go home with a sense of well-fulfilled duty...You see, I will do nothing to you, but I will tell you that I am pleased to see how helpless you are not having anybody to complain to, or anyone to warn!"

Again, the laughter that Djehuty-mes had already hated was heard, then Aa-neru turned and walked away, not in a hurry. The old man stood for a long time as if embedded in the ground. What has just happened was like a nightmare, and Aa-neru could appear as a specter born of a too intensive heat and fatigue. Yet it was happening in reality, and the silhouette of the criminal going away was still visible. Djehuty-mes understood that he had told him the cynical truth. Now, when there were no guards in the Great Valley, anyone could come here without being detained, then hide in one of the countless corners of the Great Valley and follow the typical round of the Necropolis Scribe. Indeed, he did not think about that... So, he, Djehuty-mes himself, the keeper of the secrets of this area, provided invaluable hints to the thief, and this robber will certainly want to take advantage of it! Fortunately, even this experienced burglar with his companions has no chance to get to the royal mummies, but he will certainly plunder several tombs, even taking advantage of Pa-nehsi's absence. But these words: "you all lost" and "Pa-nehsi – the future King of Kush" were even more disturbing: did he already know what was happening in the north? Could Pa-nehsi have triumphed? Such and similar sad thoughts accompanied the old man on his way back home. Today, he returned extremely late and Shed-em-dua and Henut were very anxious, and when they saw him, they immediately knew something had happened. Djehuty-mes did not even want to eat the meal they prepared, only sat down in his chair and spent a few hours in silence. Then he lay down and tried to fall asleep, but neither did he succeed: instead of sleep, he was overwhelmed by the recurring image of Aa-neru's face with a cynical smile. So, he got up and went to the room with the columns to drink water from the pitcher standing there and then he met both women who, too, unable to sleep, came here with the same purpose as he.

"What are you doing here?" he has blurted out, though he knew perfectly the reason of their insomnia. Not the first time the anxiety about their loved ones, growing with each passing day of lack of news have taken away their night rest, put their heads in their arms, squeezed tears of helplessness and invoked words of consolation, although it was based only on hope. Also now two friends sat close to each other and entrusted their beloved to the protection of the Creator, while ensuring each other that they would come back healthy. When she saw Djehuty-mes, Shed-em-dua said loudly what they were thinking during all the evening: "Father, we're worried about you! Tell us, at last, what happened?"

"I have seen a terrible man today," the Necropolis Scribe said, "He was telling me terrible things and laughing at it; it was like meeting with the disgusting hyena. I am living for a long time, but I don't remember such times, when I would associate this way so many people at once. Pa-nehsi, Pa-Shu-uben, that Aa-neru whom I met today, are like hyenas – the bloodthirsty beasts who like corpses, and when they laugh, you got chills. We live among hyenas and sometimes it seems that their laughter never stops. Fortunately, there are also lotuses like both of you: quiet once and bringing only the good, and at the same time beautiful and their view soothes every sorrowful heart." Djehuty-mes embraced both young women and added, "Even the darkest night must pass, though some nights are difficult and dragging out like this one."

Over the next three days, the old Necropolis Scribe did not leave the house; he was afraid that he would meet Aa-neru again, who would tell him something extremely disgusting. He was also afraid to go to the Great Valley again because even if he discovered traces of fresh burglary there or became an eyewitness of such activities, he would not be able to stop it or bring help.

"If something like this happens, I know who will be responsible today; the thief introduced himself," he thought, explaining to himself why he was neglecting his duty this time. He felt bad about it, but he was simply afraid for his life, and not just his own. If a robber pushes him off the rock, both young women living in his house and the small son of Buteh-Amun, Ankh-ef-en-Amun, will be deprived of any care, which in these terrible times could end tragically.

On the morning of the fourth day, a boy from the area arrived, bringing the news that apparently the ships with soldiers moored at the harbor of Khefet-her-neb-es, which meant that the Kushites had returned. Soon the approaching boat of Pa-nehsi appeared on a canal. Pa-Shu-uben was actually standing on the bank in front of his palace at the eastern gate of the fortress of Ramesses User-Maat-Re Meri-Amun to welcome him warmly. The One Who Knows the Secrets of Khefet-her-neb-es would be ready, after all, to open his arms to welcome also the royal army, for he did not lose the trust of the King Ramesses, but he did not hide the feeling that he was more pleased with the appearance of the Kushites.

"Did things go in the north as planned?" he asked. "I thought you were going to stay there a little longer."

"I thought so too," Pa-nehsi said, "but they got together with Tjehenu and the reaching Pi-Ramesse proved impossible. Actually, even better, we will return to our hometowns earlier and I think that nobody will be able to disturb us. I will create Free Kush; maybe you want to join me, I will gladly take you to organize for me the police, the prison and other matters that you know about? You just have to remember that we will establish there everything anew, and here you have this ready. Here you have a palace, whereas you will live in a tent there for a long time, it will be harder to get everything, also wine and women. Make you choice!"

The last two arguments finally convinced Pa-shu-uben that he should stay in the City.

"You're right," Pa-nehsi concluded. "You have the King's trust, you also enjoy the support of Pi-ankh, and he is the leader of the army and will probably rule here. Every authority needs police and security, and you have a lot of knowledge in this field, and some trusted people, even in Ipet-sut. Besides, whom would you fear here? That old man Djehuty-mes? Mayor Pa-uer-aa, whom you locked in his own house a long time ago? I will take real robbers, like Aa-neru, with me..." they both started laughing. "Right, get me Aa-neru now!"

Pa-Shu-uben did not have to look for the officer for a long time, because also that one has come to greet his leader and was standing nearby.

"How was your trip through the desert? I can see that the lions haven't eaten you?" Pa-nehsi asked with a broad smile.

"I succeeded," Aa-neru replied, "But I'm not sure whether they didn't eat Amen-hotep and Buteh-Amun, because I was chasing them all the way to Pa-im, not sparing horses, but I didn't catch them."

"Tough! But Amen-hotep, even if he survived, will never come back here, and Buteh-Amun..., well, we will facilitate his future task of protecting the royal tombs... Have you followed Djehuty-mes?"

"Yes, Lord," Aa-neru confirmed eagerly. "He can't live other way than by fulfilling his duties, so he was a grateful object of observation. I've followed him several times and I know where he went. There is even one grave there, which must be entered from above, not from below – I did not know that such a thing is in the Great Valley."

"You did excellent job! There is not much time left to me in the City, but I will use it so that the Kemet will never forget it. Tomorrow we'll start early, and we'll facing a battle with greater leaders than Pi-ankh or Heri-Hor. I wonder how all these great leaders: Djehuty-mes Men-kheper-Re or Ramesses User-Maat-Re Meri-Amun, not to mention Ramesses the Great[110] will defend themselves against my soldiers... So, see you tomorrow!"

Early in the morning, the Kushite troops crossed the river, then approached the residence of the General and stood in the order in which they were usually gathering before marching. So those inhabitants of the Western City who were staying here and now have taken to the streets of Khefet-her neb-es –mostly old

[110] The pharaohs mentioned: Thutmose III, Ramesses III and Ramesses II were among the greatest victorious rulers of ancient Egypt.

men, women, and children – could see the tight ranks of dark-skinned warriors. Nowhere was noticed a single man coming from this area and conscripted into the army when they were heading north, and they were not visible either on the boats on which Pa-nehsi arrived.

"Where are they?!" This question went from mouth to mouth and it was rising as a more and more heavy murmur. When the chariots with General Pa-nehsi, Pa-shu-uben and officers arrived in front of the army lines, an elderly woman broke free from the crowd, ran towards them and shouted desperately, "Where are my boys? What did you do with them?"

The coachman of the nearest chariot began to chase her away immediately with a whip, but then Pa-nehsi told him to stop and having turned towards the crowd staring hatefully at him, but now silent he cried loudly out: "City residents! Your sons are coming here safe and sound, but they will be here in a half moon!" Then he ordered the troops to move. Pa-Shu-uben drove his chariot to the General and asked silently: "Is it true that they will come back?"

"Maybe a few succeeded, but I had to calm down these people here, because this crowd looks unpleasantly, and I don't have time to suppress the riots. However, if they started to sauce, I leave you half of my archers here, and there are all chariots in the eastern City. The others go with me to the Great Valley; we will work there for two days. On the third morning, let the *medjayu* arrest Djehuty-mes and bring him there. On the evening of that day I will come to you for a farewell supper: prepare something suitable!"

The inhabitants of Khefet-her-neb-es were still standing for a long time, looking at the units moving away in the direction in which only the funeral processions rarely went. The sight was very strange, because here a noisy army even equipped with pipes and drums was going as if to war to the place over which Meretseger patronized, that is The One-Who-Loved-Silence. The soldiers were accompanied not only by numerous pack donkeys with water and supplies but also by a long row of carts. On several of these equipment used for the siege of fortresses could been seen: ladders, huge palm trunks serving as rams, huge hammers to break stone walls, thick copper crowbars, coils of ropes, on others many closed boxes where carried, yet the other carts were completely empty. The soldiers were also unusually "armed": only a few carried real weapons, while others instead of bows, spears, shields and swords carried hoes, wooden beams, copper poles and baskets. Everyone also had a leather skin bag with water. At the head chariots were moving with Pa-nehsi and several officers, among which Aa-neru was a guide. After two hours, the head of the wandering troops reached the last narrowing of the winding road leading between the hills, after which the road widened. Then the men in chariots and the first ranks of infantry could see on both sides the distinct gates cut in rock and their lintels covered with colorful reliefs. They were in the Great Valley, which everyone has heard about, but almost no one had the right to reach. They stood and for a moment were listening to the dignified silence of this place as if dumbfounded with amazement: it has never happened so many people to come here at once.

"Well, we're getting to work!" Pa-nehsi broke the silence. "Distribute people and equipment!" he ordered Aa-neru who started to follow this command with great energy. He was bringing two groups, each one composed of ten soldiers near each well visible gate leading to a tomb of a pharaoh of the Ramesses dynasty and then he was appointing a commander and was ordering others to bring palm trunk rams. The first task of such a team was to get inside the grave and soon hollow sounds of hitting the gates reverberated around various places of the Great Valley. The gates were yielding quickly; no one predicted that these graves would ever be besieged... The Kushite soldiers were entering the tombs "conquered" in this way and were standing there in a daze before the richness of colorful texts and images. A crowd of bizarre figures, boats or snakes spitting fire that terrified some and amused others was covering the walls and ceilings of the corridors and rooms. Everyone was looking, however, for what mainly brought them here: for the gold, and this was absent in the corridors leading deep into the rocks. Only far from the entrance, in the largest hall, was the golden glow noticed, emanating from the wall of a large wooden chapel, although this glow was only radiating by a thin layer of golden foil in which sacred texts and figures were imprinted. Now, hammers and axes were set in motion. The chapel was being broken into parts, and each of them was taken out of the grave to be given to other soldiers who were to chip the gilded surfaces away and put them into sacks. Each gilded part of a book about the Underworld that had accompanied the deceased king was greeted by the joyful and mocking laughter and applause of all who were still waiting for their assignment to an assault group. Such groups were led by Aa-neru to another place, where he expected to find the entrance to a tomb. Most often this was perfectly hidden and then the "diggers" started to work. Some soldiers were digging the whole "suspected" area through with hoes, others were carrying the sand and rocky debris hiding a secret away in baskets. It happened sometimes that after an hour only the entrance was found and then smashed with rams, but such a long and arduous work was often bringing no results, or only a grave-like hiding place was being found, in which only materials from the mummification of a pharaoh were stored. Sometimes hours of struggle with the rubble covering the entrance to the vertical shaft, and then emptying it of the stones and debris filling it were bringing the "discoverers" a huge disappointment: no King rested in the grave, but a dignitary undoubtedly honored by the ruler with the dignity of having his place of eternal rest at this royal cemetery. Admittedly, individual valuable items, such as furniture could be found in such tombs, but there was very little gold and the meager effect was not worth the huge effort. In one of these graves, several animal mummies were found that amused the soldiers; before leaving, they arranged these mummies as if they were talking to each other[111], someone suggested to put a jug of wine next to them, but then Aa-neru came and, seeing that the soldiers were playing with boredom, told them to dig elsewhere.

---

[111] In 1906, during excavations in the Valley of Kings for Theodor Davis, a tomb (today bearing the number KV 50) was discovered in which a monkey mummy "talking" to a dog mummy was found. Both animals probably belonged to King Amenhotep II. The unusual setting of the mummies was undoubtedly the work of ancient robbers.

Those who were assigned to the first tombs, those "with gates," were lucky: these graves were easy to access to empty and only slightly descended into the rocks. All the equipment that was placed in them with exception of the sarcophagi could easily be extracted from several rooms where they were closed. Not everything interested the "conquerors" there, so most of these things were simply left, and sometimes smashed against the walls or floor, as an expression of their disappointment. However, the treasures were also there. Some valuable, also golden objects were laying in chests, but the most valuable ones, including fabulously beautiful and precious royal jewelry, rested directly on pharaohs' mummies. To get to them, it was necessary not only to break down four wooden chapels with gilded walls but also to open two huge sarcophagi made of hard stone from around Abu[112]. This work lasted the longest and again required the use of the siege equipment, especially the heavy stone hammers. Sometimes a fire was lit right next to such a stone colossus, and the heated stone while poured with water was cracking so that it would be easier to break. Only after the removal of such an obstacle, gold began to shine from inside of the stone sarcophagi. There were two wooden coffins in the shape of Osiris, one inside the other, holding the scepters in their crossed hands. These coffins were covered with thick golden metal sheet, while the third, smallest coffin with the mummy of the King lying inside was made of gold and was very heavy. Such a golden casket at the explicit order of General Pa-nehsi was left closed and, after being removed from

---

[112] This means, of the red granite.

the grave, placed in a specially designated spot, in front of the chief's tent pitched in the most spacious central part of the Great Valley, from which narrower valleys departed in all directions, like the tentacles of a giant octopus.

Much harder work awaited those teams of soldiers that Aa-neru placed in the spots that Djehuty-mes had visited during his inspections. When it was finally possible to reach the walled-up entrance, after opening it usually a corridor was beginning, completely buried narrow and very steeply falling, and ended with another wall. Behind it a gaping hole of a deep well was lurking for the unprepared soldiers[113] behind which they could only see the smooth wall again. Several Kushite "conquerors" have fallen into such wells and have become the real victims of today's "battle" with the pharaohs. Since nothing was found in these wells, they were buried. Only when the opposite wall was crushed with rams the further path to the gold-bearing Sarcophagus Chamber could be found. Most often, this road was steep, too, the inside of the tomb was dark and uncanny heat was bursting from there. One had to work with torches here and only deep below the surface of the rock, sometimes at a distance of two ropes from the entrance, their light extracted golden flashes from the walls and chapels hiding stone sarcophagi. In these deep tombs, however, these sarcophagi were smaller and presenting not a major obstacle. Heavy copper crowbars were good enough to lift the lid and throw in on the floor, after which the lids of the mummy-shaped coffins were cut into pieces, to finally enable the

---

[113] In the older tombs in the Valley of the Kings, these wells served as protective reservoirs, collecting rainwater if it reached this point.

extracting of the most valuable treasure from inside: a pure gold casket with a pharaoh's mummy. This was carried out triumphantly and placed next to the others in front of the chief's tent, and then the fragments of two larger coffins were extracted one after the other, and as usual, the gilded foil was chipped from them. The deep tombs required more effort, but also provided many items that were covered with gold, but also fully retained their function as if they were placed in the grave only yesterday. Pa-nehsi and his officers were delighted to admire the wonderful gilded beds, chairs, thrones, stools, precious pharaoh's everyday equipment – their canes, bows and shields. Even richly gilded chariots dismembered into components were buried in these tombs; even tomorrow one could harness horses to them. The future ruler of the Free Kush was already weeing with his mind's eye all these items in his palace, and his pride grew.

Aa-neru himself decided to personally supervise the work of looking for the entrance and then digging up the grave, the place of which was seen by the old Necropolis Scribe, when they met a few days ago in that small ravine above the Great Valley. Aa-neru and the soldiers he selected lowered on ropes onto a small ledge of rock covered with debris, which they began to dig, throwing debris into the abyss below. Indeed, the entrance to the tomb was found, but this grave consumed, as many as five victims among those who intruded it. Three diggers fell from the ledge, one lost his life falling into the well already in the grave, and the last one fainted out of the heat and the stuffy air pervading in its depth and suffocated before he was taken outside.

"Who does this damn tomb belong to?" Aa-neru asked the oldest of the soldiers who was in this group and was called a "scribe" because he could read and write. The soldier looked at the signs surrounded by the sacred ring cut on the stone sarcophagi and said that it was probably His Majesty King of the Both Countries Men-kheper-Re, Son of Re Djehuty-mes, justified.

"Ah, this famous conqueror!" Aa-neru remembered and swore his personal revenge for the death of his subordinates.

Although the victims were few in total, the battle with the pharaohs proved to be very hard and exhausting. They worked tirelessly until the evening of the first day, and then throughout the next day from dawn to dusk. The morning of the third day, found soldiers resting, but having still ahead of them a difficult task of transporting the huge amount of valuable prey up to the distant harbor of Khefet-her-neb-es. Pa-nehsi also allowed himself a long sleep. He got up in a great mood, because he has foreseen a particularly attractive performance for today, with the start of which he waited only for the arrival of the *medjayu*, who were to bring the Scribe of Necropolis Djehuty-mes here. The barge of Re was already flowing high, when at the entrance to the Great Valley the sound of wheels rattled and a chariot carrying a distinguished detainee entered. The old man was standing tied between two *medjayu*, one of which was a coachman. This time Chari was sure that they were taking him to death, which would have some fancy character. But when they arrived, and the old man saw a series of golden coffins in the middle of the Great Valley, he understood that he would face a humiliation worse than death. He had devoted his whole life to guarding these relics, which were sacred to the whole Kemet, and now lay under the burning heat of Re's rays, deprived of any protection. On some coffins the remains of wreaths were still visible that had been laid on them on the day of the funeral, sometimes hundreds of years ago. However, the golden faces of the pharaohs carved in the lids of coffins, completely unaware of threats and frozen in dignity, were smiling cheerfully, while emanating with bright light, and the scepters kept in arms crossed on their chests were still a testimony to the greatness of these rulers. The half-naked dusty Kushite guards standing around them presented a sad contrast here, and a vivid denial of this splendor, which even already dead still aroused respect.

The chariot stopped in front of the tent from which Pa-nehsi came out. The General ordered the prisoner to be untied, and then greeted him with a cynical smile, "We were waiting for you, Chari, because the Royal Scribe of the Necropolis cannot miss on such an important day! Look, here are all the great ones whom you have guarded all your life and you haven't seen any of them! You now have the opportunity; you deserve it! As a scribe, you know the holy signs better than me, but I also tried to read the names written inside the holy rings and I think that only a few are missing. Where is, for example, Amen-hotep Djeser-Ka-Re? Such an important King, the patron of Khefet-her-neb-es, and he is not here. Right, Aa-neru?" here Pa-nehsi turned to the officer who has just approached them, "Ah, Aa-neru, I have forgotten to tell you that the eminent Djehuty-mes once asked about you; you see, Chari, he's here, safe and sound. Well, but the Amen-hotep isn't there, and you probably won't tell us where is he. Thought luck, I don't have time anymore, so I won't look for him, but you have to admit that my boys did their best – partly thanks to you – and hardly anyone is missing from those who were laid to rest in the Great Valley..."

Djehuty-mes decided not to speak at all. What he saw was terrible, but those people who did this terrible act were not worthy of speaking to them, and they probably could not understand much.

"You say nothing?" Pa-nehsi said with a pretended concern in his voice. "You must have been tired of traveling, so sit down!"

Djehuty-mes saw that they were offering him a beautiful gilded chair, certainly originated from one of the graves, and then he was forcibly seated on it. Pa-nehsi sat down on another similar throne.

"Give us water!" he shouted at the service, "We need to drink because we are going to have a long court session. You will now witness, Chari, how Maat should be done: the gold once taken by violence from the land of Kush will return to its owners. These Kings were thieves, so we will treat them like thieves. Take from them what they stole!" Pa-nehsi gave the order, and before the eyes of Djehuty-mes, for whom what was happening now exceeded all imagination, the soldiers armed with chisels, hammers and copper crowbars began to open the sarcophagi in turn, tearing off their lids. Now, with the help of the same crowbars, the mummies lying inside were jimmied and thrown out of the coffins. They were lying in their golden smiling masks, holding golden scepters, and the golden necklaces, golden hands, golden funnels on the toes of the legs, and a lot of other golden objects were emanating with a strong glow towards the sky. Crates were brought and the masks, jewelry and all items ripped off from the mummies were thrown into them. Unwrapped shrouds and bandages were thrown aside, removing everything that was found between them, and when a ring or bracelet could not be easily removed, the mummy was injured, while often breaking a finger or tearing off the whole arm.

Djehuty-mes sat pale, his eyes closed because he did not want to look at this cruel spectacle that was evidently amusing for the Kushite soldiers; laughter was bursting out among them every now and then. The terrible ceremony lasted for several hours, and finally, all the mummies, stripped of their valuables and bandages, were now black, naked and desperately defenseless among the shouting crowd of the Kushite soldiers. The Necropolis Scribe, who opened his eyes for a moment, seemed that this sight was the most terrible thing he could ever see. In a moment, it was to turn out that he was wrong.

Pa-nehsi settled himself on his throne and announced: "And now we will judge the greatest criminals who were destroying the land of Kush. Introduce the accused Djehuty-Mes Men-Kheper-Re!" After a while, two Kushites brought and laid his mummy only a few cubits from the sitting Pa-nehsi and Djehuty-mes.

"Ian-mes!" cried the General, raising peals of laughter among those who heard it.[114] "Do you admit that you have invaded,

---

[114] The Pharaoh's name Thutmose (III) contained the divine name Djehuty (Thot): "Thot is born", and this divine form was revered, among other things, as a baboon. The distorted royal name could be translated as "a monkey is born" in this case.

destroyed and looted the Kushite country and people? Are you not answering? Examine him with a stick and *menen*!"

Roaring with laughter, the soldier put wooden handcuffs on the mummy's dead crossed hands, then put a pole in it and began to twist it, while the other happily began to smash the dead body with a stick. After a short while a dry snap of cracking bones was heard.

"I'm condemning you to death!" Pa-nehsi announced, and the same soldiers now took the ax, then chopped the mummy, splitting it into three parts.[115]

"Take this carcass!" shouted the "president of the court". "Bring me the great criminal Ramesses User-Maat-Re Sechep-en-Re," he commanded, and the pathetic ceremony repeated.

When Ramesses the Great, beaten with sticks, also "pleaded not guilty," Pa-nehsi spoke again, "You had many children, and you showed great bravery in bed. For punishment, we will deprive you of the weapon you used so bravely!"

Some Kushites armed with axes amidst universal joy, began to cut the indicated part of the Ramesses' mummy.[116] At that moment, Aa-neru recalled his "promise" he made in the tomb of Djehuty-mes Men-kheper-Re, he walked over to his mummy previously chopped into pieces and rejected aside, stood over it

---

[115] This confirms the state of preservation of the Thutmose III mummy found in 1881 in the Royal Cache in Deir el-Bahari.

[116] The mummy of Pharaoh Ramesses II, found in 1881, is indeed without the abdomen, which could not in any case be a deliberate mummification procedure. The royal mummies were used to set up their members with bandages to resemble an erection.

and started to relieve himself on it, which aroused even greater enthusiasm of soldiers.

The act of Aa-neru has began to be widely imitated now, and there were those who also began to defecate, encouraging each other and calling for colleagues to follow in their footsteps.[117]

"Come here, relax, it's a unique opportunity!" some calls were heard.

"Or maybe you, Chari?"- Aa-neru exclaimed, then added, "Although you probably already got it under yourself!" he said with a loud chuckle.

The old man was sitting speechless, tears running down his cheeks.

"How could you fall so low!" he whispered, although the sitting next to Pa-nehsi did not know whether the Necropolis Scribe meant him or Aa-neru. Anyway, he was already disgusted by the behavior of his soldiers, and the terrible stench spreading around now, multiplied by heat caused the General to declare the "court" to be over.

"Enough!" he shouted and added: "Let's go! Then he has got up from his throne, which was immediately set on one of the carts. As part of the game, one of the soldiers has also pulled Djehutymes' throne from under him, so that the old man fell to the

---

[117] Such treatment of these mummies is indicated by the procedure confirmed by numerous protocols of repeated from time to time their ancient conservation. If the mummies had only been robbed, such a repeated inspection would not have been necessary; a single cleaning and wrapping in new bandages would have been enough. Clearly, it was feared that mummies that must have come into contact with moisture or unusual substances might decompose despite the new bandages.

ground. He expected to be killed in a moment, but he was left alone. The army stood in formation very smoothly and soon the whole procession moved, heading towards Kefet-her-neb-es. Long ranks of porters carrying various equipment taken from the tombs went first. They were followed by oxen-drawn carts, highly loaded with a pile of crates and sacks. On one of them the bodies of soldiers who lost their lives in an unusual "battle" were carried. The procession was closed by donkeys, now carrying the goods taken away from the Pharaohs in saddlebags. People, carts and animals have rushed out of the Great Valley, where absolute silence soon came again.

When the troops coming back with prey have already traversed most of the way, passing near the temples of Ta-Djeser visible from afar, Aa-neru looked in that direction, then said his coachman to go on his own and jumped off the chariot. He selected a group of soldiers who were carrying palm trees, stone hammers, hoes, axes, ropes and sacks and together with them began walking towards the temple of His Majesty Men-Kheper-Re Djehuty-mes, justified. Actually, it was no longer a temple, but the few remains of the ruins into which this once magnificent building was turned by falling rocks. The destruction was so great that it was decided not to rebuild the temple anymore, but to dismantle it using stone blocks for other purposes. Very few fragments of walls, columns or stone pavement were left on the site. But in one place, just a few cubits from the vertically cut rock on which the back wall of the temple once rested, Aa-neru saw a beautiful statue of the King Djehuty-mes sitting on the throne - the same King whose mummy he had recently personally defiled. The king's face carved in black stone was now looking with dignified focus, and Aa-neru had the unpleasant feeling that this pharaoh was looking at him as if he wanted to remember him.

In front of the statue there was a small offering table with the remains of bread. Nearby, to the left and right of Aa-neru, he saw as many as four guard booths; they were empty.

"They didn't just guard this statue, did they?" he thought, and when he saw that it was standing on a large stone slab, lying alone on the raw rock surface from which the temple floor was torn down, he smiled with malicious understanding.

On a given sign, his people pushed the statue down, knocking it over, and then hitting the slab with stone hammers. Underneath, a rectangular outline of the tomb shaft appeared. Now the hoes have started to move; here the work was easier than in the Great Valley, and the helpers of Aa-neru, who had gained experience there, moved quickly. Anyway, this shaft not only had even walls, but was surprisingly shallow, and only six cubits lower the "diggers" reached a horizontal corridor walled up with a stone wall covered with clay, on which several official seals were imprinted. Then the corridor was filled with rubble and it took an hour before they removed this obstacle. Now they came across a well, over which they tossed palm trunks and walked carefully over them to delve back into the darkness of the long corridor. At its end, in the light of the torch, they saw a chamber with a huge wooden sarcophagus, seven cubits long and completely covered with silver surface. Aa-neru undermined a lid and saw inside a small wooden coffin almost devoid of ornaments. It was taken outside and opened.

"You can chop off the silver ornaments from the great sarcophagus and share them as a reward that you helped me," Aa-neru threw to his people, "I must be alone with our holy patron Amen-hotep and thank him personally for such a successful day!"

When the others left, he took care of the mummy with great expectations, but soon he felt very disappointed. Compared to those he saw recently in the Great Valley, this mummy was very modestly equipped and did not even have a gold mask on its face. Unwrapping all the shrouds and bandages Aa-neru found some beautiful bracelets and necklaces made of gold and colored beads, a gold ring on his finger, and a precious dagger hanging on a string decorated with blue faience beads on Pharaoh's neck, but this was not the loot he expected. "I thought there was going to be more of this," he said, "but I won't give it up anyway. How good it is that the General has mentioned this king!" All the decorations taken off the mummy Amen-hotep packed into a bag, but after a while he took the dagger out of there again. Although his blade was made of silver and he noticed some gold ornaments, the whole handle was made of plain bronze, which he decided to get rid of.

It was already late in the afternoon, but the sun was still baking heavily at this time of year. Aa-neru looked around and, hoping to find a shady place, climbed the rocks and soon found what he was looking for: a wide gap in which he could sit down comfortably and take care of his work, at the same time well hidden from the gaze of some unexpected intruder. He began to dismantle the dagger into pieces and soon managed to recover all

Hyenas & Lotuses

the gold and silver. He put the unnecessary handle aside and then instinctively covered it with sand.[118]

It was already twilight, when he left Ta-Djeser.

At the same time, in the Great Valley, the dignified old man was still working hard, cleaning the royal mummies, one after the other, from feces, and then transferring them to one of the graves. All the tombs he entered were showing a terrible view. The stone sarcophagi lay shattered, mixed with the remains of wooden equipment chipped of the gold foil, as well as the scattered contents of the chests that the attackers did not take. Everywhere faience, stone or wooden figurines were lying around, which were supposed to do all the work for the dead in hereafter. Djehuty-mes was alone and he knew that no one would help him. His tears had long since dried up, he was working with stubborn persistence to save even these holy remains – he simply was fulfilling his duties as the Royal Necropolis Scribe. He was hungry and thirsty, but he did not even have time to look for some uneaten leftovers that Kushites could leave. The barge of Re was already disappearing on the western horizon when the last mummies rested in a temporary storage that the first corridor of one of the graves "with a gate" become for them.

Djehuty-mes fell to his knees, raised his hands to heaven, and began to pray to Atum when suddenly a ghostly laugh echoed

---

[118] On the rock shelf above the Hatshepsut temple in Deir el-Bahari, in 2000 the Polish Cliff Mission led by the author of this book discovered a bronze handle of a royal dagger from the early 18th dynasty and several faience beads. It is very likely that this dagger rested on the mummy of King Amenhotep I.

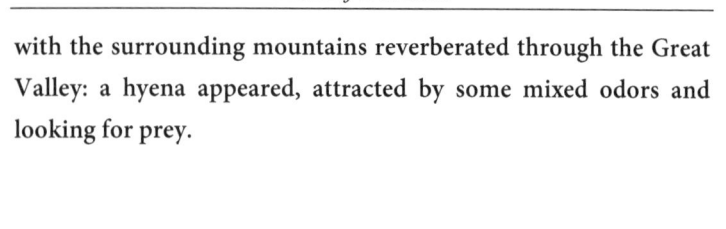

with the surrounding mountains reverberated through the Great Valley: a hyena appeared, attracted by some mixed odors and looking for prey.

CHAPTER XVII

Meanwhile, a mourning-like mood prevailed in the house of Djehuty-mes. Shed-em-dua had no doubts that the Necropolis Scribe was dead and wailed loudly together with the women who came from the neighborhood.

"Not only," was she explaining. "The *medjayu* took him from home, but also tied him up! But then again, all the time when Panehsi was waging war against Amen-hotep, and even after that, when he ordered the forced recruitment, the father could walk freely around the City and the Kushites have never arrested him, because there was an *ankh* sign on our house!"

"Come on," Henut said, "it was not always protecting; I know something about it myself... And if the Kushites wanted to kill the father, you or me, they could have done it a long time ago. As you know, Chari, is stubborn, maybe they came to him with a proposal, and he did not want to agree, so they tied him up. After all, they sent a chariot for him, and the convicts are unlikely be carried in a chariot. I think he is alive..."

"May Amun speak through you!" Shed-em-dua was calming down for a moment only, and then she was bursting into laments again. "What shall we do now?! We will both die and my little Ankhef too!" Her crying was joined by the neighbors, as well as by the small Ankh-ef-en-Amun and the laments were getting louder and louder, so those who heard them even from afar were also convinced that the Necropolis Scribe Djehuty-mes had died.

In the late afternoon, the Kushite troops appeared on the road leading from the old quarries, but also from the most distant parts of the necropolis. The inhabitants of Khefet-her-neb-es again took to the streets, but at the same time, some armed archers appeared, left here to maintain order, and they lined up along the entire route that the soldiers had to pass. Near the temple of His Majesty Amen-hotep Neb-Maat-Re the whole cortege turned towards the river. Although no one could come close, everyone saw that the soldiers were carrying large objects on their shoulders, including furniture that were glistening with gold ornaments. When the loaded carts as well as the pack donkeys were seen, everyone could easily guess that this must come from the tombs. Even though the hunger reigned in Waset, this message passed from mouth to mouth caused a murmur of indignation:

"How can one deprive the blessed dead of what they were once given for their eternal journey? Where is Maat?!"

General Pa-nehsi returned to his residence, but soon the sight of his servants and soldiers carrying various valuable equipment away from there was a foretoken of his preparations to leaving the City. According to the previous agreement, in the evening the Royal Son of Kush went to a farewell feast at the palace of Pa-shu-uben. The Chief of the Police prepared himself for this occasion exceptionally, and his chef showed an admirable mastery, especially in such difficult times. He prepared not only ducks stuffed with grapes but even a roasted ram, which completely surprised his distinguished guest.

"How did you get the ram when the dog is an extraordinary delicacy in this area?" Pa-nehsi asked.

Pa-Shu-uben laughed and said, "This ram was unlucky; it baa'd from a clever hideout where he was kept, just as my people controlling the stocks of the local peasants were passing by. And its owner had sworn a moment earlier that his family had nothing and was starving! Such are the peasants in Waset!"

"He probably defended himself against giving away such a treasure? Indeed, this ram is very tasty," the General has dropped a remark between bites.

"Apparently, shortly... The concealing of such a good towards the needs of the Royal Son of Kush is a crime that could only be punished in one way," Pa-Shu-uben explained, pulling another portion of meat from the ram with his hand.

"You will have to change such a reasoning. You will requisition another ram on your own," Pa-nehsi become sad. "I will miss you, and I will also pity you. You will again become an exemplary civil servant observing Maat and you will bow low to the First Servant of Amun, although just Pi-ankh will not hurt you... I have to visit Ipet-sut tomorrow and to say goodbye to

Amun himself, or rather to ask him to accompany me on my way to Kush."

"I haven't heard the last sentence..." Pa-Shu-uben reached for the fruits. "We must sweeten our parting, and figs and dates are the sweetest at this time of the year!"

The next day, from the early morning, the remaining military equipment, including chariots and horses, was loaded onto ships that one by one were leaving the harbors both on the east and on the west bank of the river, while heading south. Archers and infantry troops also departed in turn on boats, while accompanying the transport barges, on which sacks with the grain, jugs with oil, crates with linen canvas and with rolls of pure papyrus and with all the products of the metallurgical, glass, carpentry and other temple workshops were removed from the City. Pa-nehsi has thoroughly emptied the City's warehouses, although there was starvation. The General's ship departed as the last one from the harbor of Khefet-her-neb-es, however it didn't head south, but cut across the river, stopping at the harbor at Ipet-sut. Pa-nehsi, Aa-neru and a detachment of soldiers equipped with axes and sacks moved through the rooms and courtyards of the temple of Amun, stripped already of gold straight to the Saint of Saints. Since the capture of Ipet-sut, a Kushite infantry detachment has guarded it all days and nights. One didn't hinder priests the performing their liturgical duties, but one was closely watching whether no one emerges or whether anyone carries anything from the holiest room in Ipet-sut inaccessible to ordinary mortals. Those "guards" imposed by force, whose mere presence in this part of the temple was barbaric, could see every day two priests: the Servant of the God on duty and the lector accompanying him, entering the vestibule. The lector stayed there and read loudly technical remarks from the papyrus, while the main celebrant, following them began a sacrificial service in front of the holy statue which even the lector was not deserving to watch. The soldiers even heard the spoken texts and they got so used to these that they knew some of the spells already by heart and in their free time were "playing priests", while laughing at it loudly. No one, however, ever dared to enter the Saint of Saints; the soldiers were subconsciously afraid of the mysterious Force that could be revealed in such a situation, in order to punish the impudent ones. Today, however, Pa-nehsi and Aa-neru decided to violate the last sanctity.

"Since even the gates and obelisks were covered with gold, this statue must be made of pure gold," Aa-neru emphasized, though even his hand was trembling as he shifted the staple at the Gate of Heaven, as the entrance to the Saint of Saints was called.

However, already in the vestibule, there was an unpleasant surprise. On a simple bench lay the remains of old dry bread, a few simple clay dishes, besides, there were stone vases with natron balls, with incense, and sand next to it several scrolls of papyri lay. The only objects that could raise interest of robbers were a silver bowl, also another silver vase, and a silver bucket for water, as well as a bronze gilded censer in the shape of a human hand. On the sign of the leader, Aa-neru packed the four items into a sack, then pushed the staple of another door, this time covered with gold, as did the floor of this small room, which contained a granite chapel, also closed with a staple. Now even

Pa-nehsi hesitated: something was screaming in him that he would step back and not cross the last line; his blood was throbbing at his temples. He felt strangely hot, and at the same time he felt as if something was kneading his head. He stepped back into the vestibule and sat on the bench, gasping for breath.

"What is with you, Lord?" Aa-neru asked, concerned.

"Nothing, nothing, it will pass," the General answered and, in order not to show his strange weakness, gave a new command, "Go to the soldiers, and let them start working on the holy boat. I will come soon!"

Aa-neru carried out the order and after a while in the room preceding the vestibule of the Saint of Saints there were sounds of blows of axes: the magnificent User-hat barge was richly decorated with gold metal, just like the rich gilded poles of transport beams, which were carried by priests in time of processions and the gilded pedestal on which it rested. Aa-neru noticed that in this case, even the wood of which the User-hat barge was made - the noble cedar imported from Djeden and Keben - was of great value, so he ordered the soldiers to chop the barge into portable pieces rather than chipping it and to carry them straight to Pa-nehsi's ship. A few saws were brought additionally and thanks to that, the work progressed quickly. The barge was wasting away, and there were fewer and fewer soldiers. Those who previously served as guards here, as well as those who came here today with Pa-nehsi, were leaving one by one, carrying some parts of the holy barge. Finally, the boat disappeared, the walls of the pedestal were chipped of gold, and Aa-neru was just looking greedily at the floor, thickly covered with gold sheet metal. It would take several hours to remove it, and Aa-neru did not know if the General would allocate necessary time and people to this.

Because Pa-nehsi was still in the Saint of Saints, Aa-neru re-entered the vestibule to ask him for instructions. The General was not there, but Aa-neru has seen him in the room of the holy statue: Pa-nehsi was lying in front of the open chapel with the statue of Amun, just as the High Priest used to do when, after opening the Gates of Heaven, he falls on his face to "kiss the earth."

"Is he praying?" Aa-neru was surprised, but not wanting to disturb, he stopped in the doorway and looked into the open chapel. Yes, there was a small statuette whose head topped with a high double crown with a feather motif, was undoubtedly made of gold sheet, and the eyes of clear rock crystal, but the rest was made of wood and preserved in a terrible condition, half-eaten by moisture and time. Aa-neru felt a profound disappointment: there was much less gold he had expected here, though that head certainly had a value. However, Aa-neru had to wait with its detachment until Pa-nehsi would stand up because there was very little space in this room. At that moment, he heard the General's voice very much changed, resembling a gibberish rather than normal speech, and he could hardly understand what he was about to say to him.

"Help me...I can't!"

Aa-neru grabbed the boss by the shoulders and tried to lift, but Pa-nehsi weighed heavily; terrified eyes looked at him from an unnaturally red, even purple face drenched with sweat.

"It were you who have talked me into doing this. Take me away from here, quickly!" mumbled the Royal Son of Kush and Aa-neru has recognized that this man was in a serious condition. He called the last four soldiers who were still waiting in the Hall for the Barge and ordered them to take the General to the boat. He wanted to take right then that golden head of the statue of Amun, but he heard Pa-nehsi's mumbled order: "Leave it! I forbid!" So, though regretfully, he left the Saint of Saints, accompanying the soldiers carrying the sick one to the ship. There, the General was laid on the bed and the doctors took care of him immediately, while Aa-neru, who took over the command of the boat, ordered to leave. Soon the General's ship disappeared beyond the rivers bend, leaving the City forever.

There was silence in Ipet-sut, for the first time since that day when Pa-nehsi had broken into the Hall for Barge and left his soldiers here. And again, like then, in that very silence, the sounds of singing were heard, blurred at once, but with every moment taking on content and power. The procession of priests dressed in white with their heads shaved, was walking slowly from the Akh-menu - a magnificent temple erected here centuries ago by His Majesty King Djehuty-mes Men-kheper-Re, heading towards the holiest part of Ipet-sut. Amen-em-Ipet again wore a high-priestly outfit, and he carried a censer. A hymn to Amun which was filling the mutilated nooks of the temple, spoke of God's victory over enemies, of His omnipotence. When the procession reached the threshold of the Hall of the Barge, and the priests saw a terrible sight of a pedestal chipped of gold and carrying only a tragically eloquent emptiness, the words they recited could seem mocking, but the prayer was not interrupted.

Amen-em-Ipet has incensed the entrance three times and then he has walked around the empty pedestal three times, while cleansing with incense the place where the wonderful User-hat stood this morning. Without interrupting the hymn, the old priest now entered the open vestibule of the Saint of Saints, incensed the room, then turned toward the holy chapel and fell on his face, not daring to look there. Finally, he lifted himself remaining on his knees while reciting another verse of the hymn, and opened his eyes. He met Amun's eyes. Then the old man's face brightened up and tears of joyful gratitude started to flow from his eyes. He put the censer aside and moving on his knees, began to circle the chapel. Near its corner, he strongly pushed a fragment of the raw stone wall, which shifted, revealing a small hiding place. The golden statue of Amun the Lord of the Thrones of the Both Countries was there - the most venerable image of the Creator, for many generations being the object of everyday worship in Ipet-sut. Amen-em-Ipet kissed the floor before him, then took it out carefully, got up and carried it into its place inside the chapel, looking for a moment at the unusual scene of two Amuns standing next to each other: the gold one that should stand here and the wooden one, dating back to the times of the beginning of Ipet-sut that was long ago ritually buried in a cache, to which Amen-em-Ipet now carried it again.

"Forgive me, Amun, for making you even more hidden[119]..." he whispered. "I did it as a man of little faith, and you showed that I did it unnecessarily. Indeed, Your power is great!" He

---

[119] Name: "Amun" meant "Hidden".

closed the cache, returned on his knees in front of the open chapel and recited a few more verses of the hymn, then closed the Gates of Heaven and returned to the priests.

"Amun revealed His Power today," he said with a strong voice, "And will soon heal the wounds of Ipet-sut, the City and all of Kemet!"

However, meanwhile, the situation of the inhabitants of both parts of the City was tragic. For over half a year hunger reigned here and people have eaten what they had hidden for the worst time, and the Kushite army took away stock piles from others. There was no trace of the grain usually kept at this time of year in homes and intended for sowing, so there was no bread nor beer. The taste of meat was forgotten, almost all donkeys had already been killed, and to see a dog was also rare. Because it happened that someone had died outside the home, and it was almost impossible to organize funerals the wind was sometimes bringing the odor of the corpses that was luring hyenas, which themselves became the object of hunting now. A few vegetables from home gardens was the only salvation for the hungry people beside fruits; there were a lot of them on fig and sycamore trees, and dates were growing on the palms. The sudden departure of Pa-nehsi's army brought some relaxation, but it hasn't removed fear, because at night one could see bonfires and hear conversations of men whom it was better to never meet: they were local gangs of robbers who were now breaking into graves at the necropolis. For the time being, they did not attack the settlements, but in the stories told by old men images of bands were returning that had prowled in the area, invading villages and even murdering their residents. No one knew where the attackers were recruited from, but they were called "Tjehenu" and now there was a rumor that Tjehenu will come any moment to deal the final blow to the unfortunate City dwellers.

In this situation people in Khefet-her-neb-es were thinking with hope about Pa-Shu-uben, to whom a small group of *medjayu* was subject. Pa-Shu-uben himself did everything to show himself as a true guardian of the frightened inhabitants. As soon as the last Kushite boats disappeared on the southern horizon of the river, he immediately visited the house of the Mayor Pa-uer-aa, in which the former Head of Granaries Men-Maat-Re-nakht had also lived for many months, bringing them the joyful piece of news. "This terrible man, the enemy of God, Pa-nehsi has finally escaped with his army, so that all three of us are finally free, which should even be considered a miracle of Amun because during the whole terrible occupation there was no one day for me not to ask a question: will I stay alive until the dusk?"

Pa-Shu-uben also asked how the two dignitaries lived "so badly treated by this thug" while assuring of his readiness for all help and he proposed that without waiting for the royal army, each of them should restart their former duties in order to assess the situation properly. Thus, Men-Maat-Re-nakht could realize the condition of the warehouses, Pa-uer-aa could inspect the Western City, and he, Pa-Shu-uben would go to Ipet-sut and the East Waset. Both officials, who could not leave the house for many months and knew nothing about the course of the occupation or the situation in the City have well received this visit of the colleague allegedly not liked very much but having a reputation of an effective man and they agreed to his proposals, if only because that after long inactivity, every action was truly salutary for them. They got chariots and several *medjayu* at their disposal and the next morning they set off to find out what had changed in the City since the Kushite invasion. What they saw was beyond all comprehension. Men-Maat-Re-nakht went straight to the warehouses at the temple of His Majesty Ramesses the Great, to find that there is virtually nothing in them. Pa-uer-aa first went to the Vizier's Mansion in the temple precinct of His Majesty Ramesses User-Maat-Re Meri-Amun, to see the ruin at the site of the once magnificent fortress: all its western part did not exist. Shocked, he went to the house of Djehuty-mes, where he saw two torpid women overcome with mourning. When he learned that the army had taken the Necropolis Scribe, and then it was returning with great spoils from the side where the road to the Great Valley runs, he ordered to be taken there immediately. At the doorstep of one of the open tombs, he found a semi-conscious old man starving and exhausted, still guarding the naked mummies of the pharaohs. Pa-uer-aa left his *medjayu* in the Valley and immediately took Djehuty-mes to the house, where the mourning mood turned into frantic joy, albeit somewhat subdued by the fact that the old Necropolis Scribe returned sick: physically exhausted and completely mentally depressed. Lying in bed, he required intensive care, like a child, and at night he could not fall asleep, or falling into a shallow sleep, he shouted, often calling the name of Maat and violently protesting against something. He cried, "No! No!" He was often taking a seat on the bed drenched with sweat and was calling Buteh-Amun, and when Henut or Shed-em-dua came, who were sitting in turn at his bedside, he was looking at the woman as if he did not recognize her, and only after a moment he smiled and apologized for causing so much trouble. He didn't want to tell them anything, though it was obvious that he was carrying a heavy burden in his heart.

On the tenth day after the departure of the Kushite army, a rumor got around that evoked at first time panic among the inhabitants of Khefet-her-neb-es: "Tjehenu are coming!" And indeed, on the road running from the north on the west side of the river appeared regular troops of marching archers, whose skin was light, and in whose hair characteristic feathers were stuck. However, these soldiers did not give impression to be preparing to hunt for the inhabitants of the City, but after stopping they sat down and then began to pitch tents that soon arrived on carts. Now, soldiers were also seen, who undoubtedly originated from the land of Kemet, followed by chariots, and then it became clear that the City was not in danger of this army. Then hundreds of women and children rushed toward the upcoming troops that were still emerging from behind the bend of the road, finally wanting to welcome those whose coming had been announced by Pa-nehsi. The awaited squad of Waset residents who survived the battle at Hor-di came at last, but only now it turned out that only few joyful greetings would take place. A loud wailing of widows and mothers who had lost their husbands and sons swept unfortunate City, along with terrible curses now being thrown at Pa-nehsi and his army.

Among the lucky ones who could spend the today evening among their loved ones was Buteh-Amun, though his arrival, next to the frantic dance of joy performed by Shed-em-dua brought also tears of Henut, who learned of her father's death. When she saw that Buteh-Amun came alone, she thought immediately of Suti-mes and she was seeing spots before her eyes, but after a while that worry faded away. It turned out that just before leaving the area of Hor-di her beloved one received a message sent to him from Iunu that the sick High Priest Amen-hotep needed him and called him to come. So, both for Henut and Suti-mes the parting was not over yet, but it was only time what separated them now, because Djed-Mut-iuf-ankh's curse had been removed. Buteh-Amun even proposed that in this situation, the mother and brother of Henut could also live with her in the spacious house of the Necropolis Scribe, but of course, Djehuty-mes had to agree to it.

When Buteh-Amun returned, the old man was sleeping; the doctor gave him special herbs that made a healing sleep was coming to him often and lasted longer than usual. The sick man was slowly recovering from the illness, he was not shouting in his sleep anymore, but he still was calling his son sometimes. That was also the case that day, and Buteh-Amun who was sitting by the bed while holding his old father's hand, answered him, "I am here, father, did you call me?"

Djehuty-mes opened his eyes and did not react for a moment, probably thinking that it was still only a dream, but finally, his face lit up and he opened his arms wide with a loud cry,

"Son! Finally! Thank you, Amun!"

They talked until late at night. First, Buteh-Amun described his escape alongside Amen-hotep and Suti-mes, the arriving at

Pi-Ramesse and the meeting with His Majesty Ramesses, the preparations for a war expedition and the unexpected appearance of many Tjehenu who strengthened the ranks of the army and finally the march southwards. When he got to the description of the meeting with the father of Henut, who had given them valuable information about the opponent and then had asked Suti-mes for forgiveness, Chari was very delighted with this, and began then to praise Henut, whom he was already accustomed to treating as his own daughter. Of course, he praised the son's idea to bring her mother and brother here, especially since the poor Djed-Mut-iuf-ankh would no longer work in the fields of Amun because he went to the fields of Osiris.[120] Now, the conversation returned to the war again, because Djehuty-mes wanted to know about the fate of those numerous inhabitants of Waset, who were forcibly recruited into the Kushite army. Buteh-Amun had no choice but to tell his father about the vile trick of Pa-nehsi, who used the prisoners of Waset as a "living shield." He also saw that at the mention of the General's name Djehuty-mes' face froze and he clenched his fists.

"It's God's enemy and hell will consume him for sure!" he cried, "But probably also me because I helped him in doing *isefet*, even though I thought I was doing Maat! I was waiting for you, son, to tell you about this because I was at fault toward you!"

Here the old man began to reminisce about the terrible last days of the Kushites' stay. He accused himself that it happened

---

[120] It was believed that after death, man continued his earthly work, but by executing it for Osiris, king of the underground world.

through his fault that Aa-neru found all the hidden graves in the Great Valley.

"Father," Buteh-Amun said, "the thief always uses someone else's work; does one have to stop working because of it? They would have still break into all the graves with gates, and others may not be seen, but one can easily guess where they are. Your round could help them only a bit. Sleep now, please. I'll go there tomorrow and I'll see everything myself!" However, he had to admit that the story of Djehuty-mes had touched him so much that he could not fall asleep for long.

The next early morning, he went straight to General Heri-Hor to tell him what he had heard from his father. Heri-Hor has heard him, but then he has instantly admitted that he could not believe the story.

"Wasn't it Djehuty-mes' disease that set him such images?" he asked, but after some reflection he decided that both he and Pi-ankh should find out about it personally. Pi-ankh was even less inclined to believe the stories about judging mummies and profaning them.

"Chari is probably crazy, it happens to some old men," he said, "But if it's true, then Ramesses is over!" and he agreed to go to the Great Valley. After assigning a chariot to Buteh-Amun, they followed him along with Heri-Hor, taking Pa-uer-aa on their way, who confirmed that he had seen an open grave and some mummies but did not have time to look at them, because Djehuty-mes was in such condition that he was afraid if he would bring him home alive.

When they came to the Great Valley and entered the grave that Pa-uer-aa was talking about, they could see from the threshold that everything that Djehuty-mes passed on to his son was, unfortunately, true. A black cloud of flies rose to greet them from the grave in which the Necropolis Scribe laid profaned mummies. After several days of lying in the heat, the exposed bodies were covered with a stinky sticky gunge. Most of the impurities Djehuty-mes removed, albeit he could not take off everything.

"Good that he can't see them today," Pa-uer-aa murmured. "I don't know if these bodies can be saved..."

"They must be," Heri-Hor has spoken for the first time. "This will be the first task of the new High Priest. Pa-uer-aa didn't understand what Heri-Hor was talking about, but he didn't comment on.

They moved on, walking from tomb to tomb, seeing the shattered stone sarcophagi, sacred figures of divine images smashed against rock walls, scattered amulets everywhere, broken pitchers and chopped remains of coffins. When they returned, in the middle of the Great Valley, they saw piles of bandages stripped of mummies, lying next to some sticks, as well as an ax that was apparently forgotten.

"It was probably here that the "judgment" took place of which Djehuty-mes spoke," Buteh-Amun said.

"Yes," Heri-Hor confirmed, then added, "You, the Royal Necropolis Scribe Buteh-Amun, take the Mayor Pa-uer-aa with you and write down everything we have seen here, and also count the graves that were opened by the barbarians!"

Both officials bowed and left to carry out their tasks.

"Doesn't he speak like a King?" Pa-uer-aa murmured. Buteh-Amun didn't answer, though he had to admit he had the same impression.

Meanwhile, when the Generals were left alone, Heri-Hor looked at Pi-ankh and saw something in his face that he would never have expected of him: an expression of horror and humbleness.

"Do you doubt Maat is dead? We must do what we intended, not yet knowing what happened here."

Pi-ankh nodded silently.

"But you didn't have to let him leave," Heri-Hor added.

"I didn't want a bloodshed, and no one could expect that," Pi-ankh replied. "Either way, Ramesses will pay for all this now."

On the same day, both Generals went to Ipet-sut, where Amen-em-Ipet showed them around the mutilated temple. Standing in the place where Amun's barge had once rested, they then held a brief meeting.

"There is not a day to waste," the old priest admitted. "The First Servant must be elected immediately so that he can act, otherwise the inhabitants of the City – this Amun's herd – will not survive for long."

"The dead inhabitants of the Great Valley also don't," Heri-Hor added.

CHAPTER XVIII

The next day, the high distinctive sound of temple trumpets, which on a holiday usually announced the start of a solemn procession has caused that the inhabitants of the Eastern City left their homes. Some of them were very surprised and asked each other, isn't this a normal day for work? However, others were reasoning rightly that Amun had not appeared on the streets of Waset for almost a year, and he certainly wants to celebrate the departure of enemies. Isn't it enough reason to celebrate that the City is finally free and its inhabitants safe? Who knows? Will God not announce something important on this special occasion? This was what the most experienced people wondered, and it turned out that they were right. The procession was slowly moving along an avenue bordered by a long row of Pharaoh's-headed stone lions, going through the whole City towards the temple of Ipet-resit, as it did during the annual festival of Ipet. However, instead of the wonderful User-hat barge shining with gold from afar, the inhabitants of the City were looking with astonishment at the small, carried on six poles only and very modestly looking boat of Amun. It was, admittedly, decorated with typical ram's heads, but these were bearing very clear signs of time. Instead of gold sheet, the barge was adorned only with a thin layer of gilding, in many places even worn to bare wood, and the chapel containing the holy statue was cracked. The whole boat was very old and the oldest priests, and among them Amen-em-Ipet, who led the procession, did not remember that it was ever used. It has long been standing in one of the side chapels in Ipet-sut, where it was left as an unnecessary object, although still worshiped one. The ram's heads on the prow and stern were more recent than the rest of the boat, which meant that these parts of the boat had once been destroyed, and this could only have happened during the Great Heresy, almost 300 years ago. The old barge, even though there was still visible gilding, did not impress even the Kushites and they left it, busy with the tearing gold sheets off the walls and obelisks of the temple. Now, this ancient and poor boat, carrying the God stripped of all His riches, was traversing the wasted away City between the rows of hungry poor people who were today the inhabitants of the once proud royal capital. Yet wherever Amun was approaching, everyone was falling on his face as usual, and then was following the procession, joining in the hymn sung by the priests and repeating his every stanza.

A large altar was set up in front of the Great Gate of the temple in Ipet-resit, on which a pile of offerings was waiting to be set on fire. Near it all the most distinguished participants of this ceremony were standing: the highest dignitaries of the Eastern and Western City, each surrounded by his family, as well as the two Generals of the royal army with a group of officers. The procession led by a jackal-shaped figure of Up-uaut – the Opener of Ways has already approached the altar, and priests carrying various holy images began to set around it. Then something unexpected happened. Here is the holy barge, instead of going directly to the pedestal standing in front of the altar, on which the priests were to set it, unexpectedly turned towards the row of dignitaries and began to move right in front of them. Of course, when it approached someone, he was falling in front of it and kissing the earth, surprised by this closeness of God. However, when the retinue of the boat-carrying priests reached the place where Heri-Hor stood, the barge suddenly stopped and turned so that when the General having kissed the earth raised his head, he saw the ram's head end of the boat's prow above him, then a shrine shrouded in white veil hiding the holy image of Amun. There was no doubt that God had expressed in this way his will that the General kneeling before him would become his First Servant from now on. Still not rising from his knees, the dignitary raised both hands, and then Amen-em-Ipet approached him, who, having removed from his own head the golden High Priest's cap and put it on Heri-Hor's temples. At this sight, everyone who witnessed such an unusual oracle of Amun gave a cry of joy and this cry, carried along with the news of what happened passed through the entire City as if a refreshing wind, soon reaching the farthest alleys. Here, finally, after so many terrible months of ungodly violence, when hyenas and jackals were tearing Amun's heard apart, the shepherd reappeared and with him the hope.

Heri-Hor stood up and walked slowly toward the altar, before Amun's barge, which soon rested in its prepared place. The priests handed him the censer and the First Servant circled the barge three times, falling on his knees in front of her front, and then incensed the altar and all offerings made of meat, bread, vegetables and fruits, covered with a green carpet of aromatic herbs. Then he turned to the crowd that now surrounded the square in front of the temple on three sides, separated by the soldiers standing in a double row, and he delivered loudly a speech: "Oh, City dwellers, God has shown me his grace today and called me to be his First Servant in place of the venerable Amen-hotep, whom a serious illness didn't allow to come back to Waset. Now, as Amun's children, you are also my children. I promise you that from now on you will be safe in your homes, on the streets and on the roads leading from the City, and I will prevent you from being hungry. You will also get seed for sowing, and joy will return to your hearts. Maat will be in Waset soon again and everything will come back to the purity of the First Time. Call Amun together with me so that he would send life, prosperity and health to his First Servant Heri-Hor!"

Again, a joyful cry rolled through the City, and all, even those who only now have acquainted themselves with the name of their High Priest, brought in front of Amun's throne a request for strength and all good things for the one on whom they bestowed their great hope. Then Heri-Hor took a burning torch from one of the priests and set fire to the offering pyre, from which a strong smell spread soon through the surroundings. The hymn was sung to Amun, and then the procession set off on the way back to Ipet-sut.

The City dwellers were slowly moving to their homes, but with each step their joyful excitement was extinguishing as their pantries were empty and they had to find anything to eat. The highest hopes were put on trees on which fruits could be found. Some of the lucky ones had them in their gardens, but others made expeditions to the now arid fields, to the roads leading along the river, and even to the desert, where single palms, sycamores, the thorny trees bearing greenish elongated plums, or the *nebes* bushes with yellow balls of fruits, also protected by rough thorns[121] may sometimes grow. Of course, the trees growing in the vicinity have long been completely stripped of their fruits, so these trips were getting further and more difficult. Some people even dared to cut papyrus stems to get to their edible roots. In normal times it was forbidden, because the papyrus belonged to the King, however in these hard days of hunger no one obeyed too much such bans. Boats of fishermen and of those people who were hoping to catch a fish, although they have never done this before, were cruising about the river and backwaters. They all were disturbing each other and only rarely somebody has succeeded. Besides, this work was now especially dangerous because of the large number of crocodiles that were the only living creatures in Waset to thrive and

---

[121] The two types of fruit mentioned at the end were popular in ancient Egypt; today they are very rare. Their Latin botanical names, are: *Balanites aegyptiaca* and *Ziziphus spina-Christi*.

reproduce without hindrance. The City residents while returning from an unusual gathering were asking themselves, was it possible that the promises of the new High Priest could be fulfilled quickly? Many were openly saying that they have heard beautiful words many times already, however no good was born of these, and some others were still repeating that, after all, it was the previous First Servant of Amun who was guilty of their entire unhappy life, so the new one probably will change only a little, if at all.

Yet the miracle of change took place Nights changed first, because suddenly the bonfires disappeared together with all the groups of people holding at them suspected conversations, and the City dwellers stopped being afraid that robbers would invade them. *Medjayu* and sometimes soldiers watched order, as usual, and there were even rumors that Pa-uer-aa with Pa-Shu-uben prepared a list of suspects of burglary. However, the real miracle was noticed when numerous barges, mainly coming from the north, began to reach the harbors in the Eastern and the Western City, being laden with grain, oil, and then also with cows, sheeps, goats and birds. All this was being distributed among the impoverished families in Waset, which of course, temple and military scribes noted carefully. Amun's kingdom was vast, and it also possessed numerous fields and herds distributed in many districts that were not affected by war or hunger. The first thing the new High Priest did was to order that as many goods as possible be sent to the City from every Amun's estate in the Upper Country, as long as it could be allotted without harming its activities and safe duration. Grains also came to Waset, which at other times should have been sent to the royal warehouses at

Pi-Ramesse, and Heri-Hor knew well what the reaction of Pharaoh would be when he finds out, but here the grain was needed immediately. The water in the river has already begun to change its color and it was said that "Hapi is starting to envy a pregnant woman,"[122] the flooding was approaching, and soon after the sowing was to start. The First Servant, taking advantage of the presence of the army, directed his messengers to all tenants of the fields of Amun, to inquire about what everyone needed to return to normal work. People who had finally sated their hunger began to praise the new High Priest, and there was hardly anyone who would not recommend him to Amun in his daily prayers. Even those few, like Pa-Shu-uben, who had expected that someone else would become a First Servant, had to admit that there was a truly blessed change in the City, and now they were competing each other in service to ensure the new boss about their allegiance.

Pa-Shu-uben, who in normal times as the head of Secret Affairs of Waset and Police was subject to the Vizier, seeing the truly royal scope of Heri-Hor's orders, did not even dare to think that someone other than the High Priest would take the post of Vizier. In close cooperation with Pa-uer-aa whom he has recently imprisoned, he was scrupulously preparing a list of suspected of breaking into the temples in Khefet-her-neb-es. Buteh-Amun, who had completely replaced his old father in the activities of the Royal Necropolis Scribe, was given the difficult task of visiting all

---

[122] This saying appears in a certain Arabic agricultural calendar, but it was based on older local sources. The phenomenon described in this way occurred in June, a few weeks before the actual start of the flood.

corners of the extensive cemetery in the Western Waset and checking whose graves had been burglarized. During ten long days the young priest, from dawn to dusk, was traversing the paths in the necropolis, and the list being prepared by him of the houses of eternity where the thieves had invaded was steadily growing. In order not to miss any place, and not to lose his orientation where the entrances to the graves were hidden, Buteh-Amun was leaving his name, while incising it with a sharp stone on a rock or a large boulder, which he could easily recognize. Djehuty-mes was offering him help with his priceless tips, and several times he even went with his son to make a round among the places he knew better than the young man, but he has not recovered yet from his illness and each such trip was very exhausting for him. He told his son that he no longer wanted to approach the Great Valley so as not to refresh the terrible memories.

Meanwhile, in one of the tombs there, by Heri-Hor's order embalmer's workshop was organized and the best specialists in this art did everything to save the royal mummies. The High Priest promised them a special reward and he was sending his envoy to the Great Valley every day to learn about the progress of the work. The head of the embalmers' team, Itef-nefer-Amun was asserting that it has succeeded to protect the noble bodies from destruction, although in some of them voracious worms had already nested. The mummies were cleaned again, covered with oils and new bandages, but Itef-nefer-Amun argued that those found in the worst condition would need to be unrolled from time to time again and checked if any oversight had not been committed and the decay process wouldn't gnaw them.

One day, during a visit to the temple district of Ramesses User-Maat-Re Meri-Amun, whose western wall began to be partially rebuilt, Heri-Hor visited Djehuty-mes, promising him that soon the time would come when all the royal mummies, equipped with the appropriate amulets and golden masks would again be solemnly buried in their own tombs.

"This month, and with it all this awful year is coming to the end. After it, only five more days and a new life will come to the City. The King will not forget your merits, Chari," he said while preparing himself for leaving.

"Is Ramesses really going to come here?" Djehuty-mes asked, surprised, but the First Servant only smiled mysteriously and replied, "Amon is great!"

Finally the "days beyond the year" came. In the lists of favorable and unfavorable days these were always marked as particularly dangerous ones, that's why people spent them most often at home, refraining from all work. However, for Heri-Hor and his collaborators, it was a time of some intense preparations for the New Year's holiday, which was to be unique this time. Therefore, the reconstruction of the destroyed Ipet-sut began, but the piles of rubble originating from the destroyed gates, towering everywhere, some traces of fire and robbery left on the walls and obelisks by the destructive teams of the Kushite army evidenced that for a long time the temple of Amun could not provide any adequate housing for public ceremonies. Therefore, the decoration of the newly finished Hall of Appearances of the nearby temple of Khonsu was now completing at an accelerated pace. In the texts accompanying the images showing the performance of the holy ceremonies, sacred signs were carved from which the names of Ramesses and Heri-Hor could be read. In the area preceding the Hall of Appearances, the ceremony of the stretching the rope was carried out and the boundaries of the spacious square were marked, where a festive courtyard was to be built in the future. "Days out of the year" were still ongoing when, at the high gate of the temple in Ipet-resit, signs were noticed by the priests of the next temple further south, which were read as "Coming!" Because it was hard to expect a renewed General Panehsi's attack, it could only mean that the priests in the temple in Abu had found that the water level in the river had risen significantly, exceeding the conventional point on the wall where Hapi was recorded. The priests of the temple of Re in Ipet-sut observing the night sky also confirmed that they had seen the star Sopdet again, stunned before for over two months by the shine of Re.[123] These two signs: in the heaven and on the earth have confirmed that it is possible to start the celebration of the New Year.

Just before the dawn of the first day of the first month of the Akhet season, in the nineteenth year of the reign of His Majesty Ramesses Men-Maat-Re Sechep-en-Ptah, a ceremony was held in Ipet-sut to welcome the newborn Re. A small group of the highest rank priests including Heri-Hor and Amen-em-Ipet took the statuette of Amun the Lord of the Thrones of the Both Countries from the Saint of Saints and went with it to the roof.

---

[123] The astronomical phenomenon that coincided with the time of the flood was the reappearance before dawn of the star Sirius, previously invisible for about 70 days.

After a short time, it was seen how Reemerging from the primeval ocean on the eastern horizon of the sky caused golden flashes in the image of Amun.

The New Year has begun! Two hours later, the loud sounds of trumpets were heard again announcing an exceptionally solemn and joyful procession, which, as usual, set off along the main road between the stone lions towards Ipet-resit. This time, behind the standard of Up-uaut and a long line of girls shaking *sesh-sesh*, the First Servant of Amun walked solemnly in ceremonial robes covered with leopard skin and with the golden High Priest's cap on his head, followed by a series of holy barges carried by priests on transport poles. Today, the barge of Khonsu – the divine child and the patron of the moon and the protector of the time that has just begun again, was the first to go. It was only after it that Amun's barge, as well as that of Mut and various other were carried.

This time the crowd on the streets was really joyful, the more so because they were given sweet cakes, dates and everyone could drink beer. As usual, sacred ceremonies were held in the square in front of the temple in Ipet-resit, after which the sacred barges started to go back while the procession headed north again; this time they were carried in the reverse order.

Amon's barge was already moving toward Ipet-sut, when Heri-Hor suddenly stood in front of the boat with the holy image of Khonsu waiting for its turn and already held on the priests' shoulders.[124]

---

[124] The description of the oracle of Khonsu and Amun given below is

"Oh, Lord of eternal iterations, Lord of births, Ruler of time, Khonsu from Waset-Neferhotep!" he cried in a loud voice. "The misfortunes that hit the City have caused that Maat died, and the births must be repeated. Do you want this new time to be proclaimed and fulfilled by His Grandness the First Servant of Amun Amen-hotep in Your City?"

The barge of Khonsu didn't even flinch, and the priests carrying it seemed not have heard any question.

"So, do you wish," repeated Heri-Hor, "That the work of the world's renewal would announce and fulfill the dignified Pi-ankh in your City?"

The lack of any reaction indicated that God's response was negative.

"In that case, Lord, do you want me, Your First Servant, Heri-Hor, to provide life, happiness and all good things in Your City?"

At this moment, the priests took a step forward and the barge rocked: "God has chosen!"

"Oh, my Lord," continued Heri-Hor, "Since you tell me to give life, prosperity and all good in Your City, show me the time you will give me to achieve it. Is it 30 years?"

The barge has frozen again.

"I know that 30 years is a very long time. Will you give me 20 years to do this?"

Khonsu again took a step closer to Heri-Hor, and then the High Priest tossed up his hands in a gesture of joy. The news of

---

based on an authentic text carved on a limestone stela built into the wall of the column hall of the temple of Khonsu in Karnak.

the oracle quickly reached Amun's barge, which was a long distance away, before which Amen-em-Ipet was walking. Then he stopped the boat and asked God if he confirmed the person of Heri-Hor and the period of 20 years of extraordinary power for him brought by this extremely rare period of rebirth. When this divine image "very strongly" confirmed what Khonsu granted to Heri-Hor, Amen-em-Ipet headed toward the approaching High Priest, followed by Khonsu's barge. As both priests and both barges approached each other again, a loud sound of trumpets rang out and Amen-em-Ipet spoke, "Listen, all the inhabitants of Waset! God made the decision to repeat the birth of everything that exists, to re-create the world! Today, Maat is born again, and a new time is being born, according to which we will count the years.[125] Amun himself will be the King in the land of Kemet, just as he is the King in Ipet-sut. He decided today to make his First Servant Heri-Hor as son and co-ruler, whom he entrusted with full power in the City and the Upper Country for 20 years." Here the old priest interrupted and among the ovations of the crowds he fell before Heri-Hor on the face, and the High Priest-King raised him and embraced.

"It's a pity that Pa-nehsi can't see it..." Pi-ankh murmured to very subdue Pa-Shu-uben standing next to him, "He could only dream about it.

---

[125] Starting from the day of the New Year in the 19th year of the reign of Ramesses XI, the following years were dated according to the then introduced Renaissance period (in Egyptian: *uhem mesut*, or "Repeating of Births").

"And what does King Ramesses say about all this?" Pa-Shu-uben asked, who understood that he will have difficult times, but was still deluding himself that the Pharaoh could change this.

"Ramesses?" Pi-ankh smiled maliciously, "Forget about that old fool. He still thinks he is a powerful ruler, but he will soon find out how wrong he is..."

Indeed, this time was closer than Pa-Shu-uben could have imagined. The next day, a heavy traffic around the harbor announced that a large portion of the royal army, including all Tjehenu and Sherdana would leave the City, heading north. General Pi-ankh and Amen-em-Ipet who was the special envoy of the High Priest were sailing on the main boat. Heri-Hor escorted them all the way to the ship, where the Generals said each other goodbye very warmly, although Pi-ankh could not resist some caustic remarks:

"Your Grandness, High Priest, General, Vizier, Chief of the Granaries... Did I forget something?"

"You have forgotten the Royal Son of Kush," replied Heri-Hor with a smile.

"Well, what's about your majesty? Just don't expect me to kiss the ground in front of you," Pi-ankh added mockingly.

"Not yet, but next time you will fall before the King and his wife, your daughter. Send her to me quickly!" Heri-Hor slapped his friend on the shoulder, but he heard, "Would there a void get to you in bed?"

Half-moon later, the ships passed Men-nefer and stopped near Iunu, where Amen-em-Ipet sailed to on a smaller boat through a canal leading from the river. As a priest, Amen-em-

Ipet wanted to visit the ancient sanctuary of Atum-Re and thank him for the new time and the new creation of the world, as well as to meet his long-lost friend Heka-nefer, but of course, the main purpose of his visit was to meet Amen-hotep. When he was taken to the chambers of the sick High Priest, the first person he met was Suti-mes who was not abandoning his superior. The dignitary has not recovered yet from the scorpion's fatal sting, he was tired very quickly and complained of about the constantly repeated pain on the left side of the breast. He slept often, as he did now, so that the friends could converse longer.

The most important piece of news that Amen-em-Ipet brought to the young man was that Henut is healthy and she is living with her mother and brother, in the house of Djehuty-mes.

"As soon as you return, I'll marry you," the old priest promised, and Suti-mes just squeezed his hand gratefully, but said nothing, because they had just heard the voice of Amen-hotep who must have heard the last sentence as he added: "It's a pity that I won't be there then... I'd like to witness someone's joy. I have this very little here... Hello, my friend!" These words he addressed to Amen-em-Ipet and with difficulty he lifted himself up of bed. "You have never seen me in such condition... Damned scorpion. I'll never come back to Ipet-sut, although I am really going there every night, or maybe it is Ipet-sut that lives in me? I remember everything..."

"Then you are lucky," Amen-em-Ipet has broken into, "because I have, unfortunately, retained completely different picture..." He began to talk about what happened after the capture of the temple, how the Kushites stripped walls and obelisks of golden decorations, and finally on the last day they chopped the User-hat barge, but they didn't remove the holy statue, which the old priest considered to be a miracle. He also repeated what he had heard from Heri-Hor about the crime committed on the royal mummies and he ended with a description of the recent events: the election of Heri-Hor to the High Priest's post and the introduction of the Repeating of Births.

Amen-hotep was listening with attention while vividly and sorrowfully reacting to the terrible news. He took it with understanding a note of the election of a new High Priest that in the tragic situation of the City after the withdrawal of the Kushites was necessary as an immediate act. At the same time he expressed his satisfaction that it was Heri-Hor, not Pi-ankh, who became the First Servant. Amen-hotep admitted that it was the only reasonable solution although he recognized that the authority of the new High Priest after the introduction of the Repeating of Births – a religiously sanctioned state of emergency – became equal to the royal one.

"Unfortunately," he added sadly, "while it was an obviousness in the City because the famine had been there before, here in the north where the people didn't experienced war nor destruction and where the temples are untouched, an announcement of the Repeating of Births will be difficult. Ramesses would have to give voluntarily way to Amun, and this seems unlikely. I can write to him about this matter, but he used not to be concerned with my appeals..." he concluded, then sat down to write this letter, full of blessing for the Renaissance, which Amun announced through his oracle in the south of the country.

"Only," he wrote, "the repeating of this ceremony in the Northern Country will also allow to retain a unity of the country and to protect it against further misfortunes. After what happened in Ipet-sut and after the terrible events in the Great Valley, only the handing over the earthly authority to Amun – the King of Heaven will bring the necessary relief, and it will allow you, my Lord and King to avoid an accusation that you have committed some mistakes, to which as a human being you were entitled, but which would be incomprehensible at the divine Horus. I am begging you, deign to hear my voice, through which all my life experience speaks as well as my love for you and for this Country that feeds us! I have already resigned myself to my fate; do the same and you will keep your greatness and love of your subjects."

Amen-hotep finished, he read it aloud, then sealed the papyrus and gave it to Amen-em-Ipet. There was no time for further talks because Pi-ankh certainly was impatient that the visit to Iunu lasted so long. The friends hugged once more, for a long time not wanting to end the farewell which – they both knew it – was their last one. When finally, Amen-em-Ipet turned to Suti-mes to say goodbye to him, he had tears in his eyes and he did not try to hide them.

"You can see, young man, that even after having written a book about the life wisdom towards God, its author remains only a weak man..." he said, and he whispered in his ear, while embracing the young priest: "Come back healthy; more than one heart in the City will miss you!"

The further journey to Pi-Ramesse passed without obstacles and after four days of sailing along the calm branch of Hapi, the newcomers could exchange greetings with the General Nes-Ba-neb-Djedu, who was eagerly awaiting the news. Their initial lack, however, was a good piece of news itself, for it meant that the battle with Pa-nehsi, wherever and whenever it took place, was successful. In fact, a month after the royal army had left for the south, a small squad of Tjehenu arrived to Men-nefer, carrying several dozen of the tribesmen wounded in the battle at Hor-di, as well as a letter from Heri-Hor and Pi-ankh to Nes-Ba-neb-Djedu who learned from it of the retreat of the Kushites, but he did not know any further news. He suggested instantly that the eminent newcomers would go together with him to the palace of Tent-Amun and only then would talk about everything so as not to waste time for duplicating an account. This was a sensible resolution, as the Queen, with an exceptional acumen, which General Nes-Ba-neb-Djedu was somewhat lacking, was inquiring about the many details of both Amun's oracles, which made Heri-Hor the most powerful dignitary in the country at the moment. What happened in Ipet-sut, and especially the sacrilege committed on royal mummies, have deeply touched both Tent-Amun and the General.

"The Heri-Hor's plan to introduce the *uhem mesut* seemed to be the only solution even before, and now it is a necessity, especially since in the south time is already counted in relation to the Repeating of Births," Nes-Ba-neb-Djedu had no doubts.

"His Grandness Amen-hotep wrote the same in his letter to the King," Amen-em-Ipet added." In a few days the river will reach in the north a level which indicates the beginning of the new life for the fields; this is the best time to announce the Rebirth."

"So, do you guarantee that the King's person will remain untouchable?" Tent-Amun asked to be sure about this matter. "Yes, he will stayed alive," Pi-ankh answered. "But it depends on him, whether he also retains his full freedom, although he doesn't know it yet. So, let's go to him and find out which Ramesses will prevail in him: the Impetuous One or the Prudent One?"

An hour later, they were already sitting in the Reception Hall of the royal palace, waiting for the Lord of the Both Countries Men-Maat-Re Sechep-en-Ptah, Son of Re Ramesses Meri-amun, who, however, has not appeared for a long time. When the servants finally brought him in the litter, they all noticed immediately that the Pharaoh was in a bad mood today. He almost hasn't responded to their greeting and instantly after he had seated on the throne and the servants had carried the litter away, he addressed himself to Pi-ankh with a raised voice: "I have been reported that you already arrived several hours ago, but I see that the obligation to submit an immediate report to your Lord and ruler is not important to you. You probably don't care as well about the keeping the position of army commander. Have you forgotten," he turned to everyone here, "that all the dignities in the Both Countries depend entirely on my will?"

"Our Lord and King," Amen-em-Ipet spoke, seeing that both Generals hardly know what to say so as not to provoke Ramesses' wrath. "Maat lives in your heart and it directs you when you make your subordinates to be those who they are. However, it is

Amun who calls his First Servant. Something like this has recently happened in Waset – the City of Amun, and I came promptly to let you know about this. Here, the King of Gods Amun decided during his holy procession that his new First Servant would be the dignified Heri-Hor."

A huge surprise appeared on the King's face, "Heri-Hor is the High Priest? As far as I know, it is Amen-hotep... What does he say for that?"

"The dignified Amen-hotep, whom I visited on my way in Iunu is seriously ill, so he could not arrive in person, but he wrote a letter in which he explains everything," Amen-em-Ipet handed the sealed scroll to Ramesses, however, this one recommended that the priest would read it aloud. As Amen-em-Ipet was unveiling the secrets of the letter to the King, with which both Generals and the Queen were now acquainting themselves, too, his face changed and blushes appeared on it that heralded an outburst of anger.

"Amen-hotep must be crazy, that scorpion made him mad! What does he persuade me to do and how dare he to write to me so! What "terrible things" happened in the Great Valley and Ipet-sut to announce the Repeating of Births?"

"The holy barge of Amun User-hat was chopped and taken away, and Ipet-sut is so much damaged that all the greater ceremonies take place in the temple of Khonsu..." Amen-em-Ipet began to answer, and then Pi-ankh completed, "I saw your predecessors' mummies lying on the ground, stripped of their bandages, vilely contaminated with urine and barbarian excrements, some of them chopped with axes. For example one

Hyenas & Lotuses

has chopped Ramesses the Great off what Min boasts.[126] Everything that was in the graves, the Kushites took away!"

Without a word, Ramesses was shifting his sight from one to the other with fear and evident disbelief, as if expecting someone to deny the news.

"Your Majesty, Ipet-sut and the whole Country once experienced a similar situation during the Great Heresy, when a godless hand was raised on holy images, but even then the royal tombs remained intact. Maat has died and to restore it one has to repeat the births which has already happened in the City," Amen-em-Ipet returned to the topic about which the High Priest Amen-hotep wrote, but it only once again caused menacing flashes in the eyes of the Pharaoh, already cool and collected.

"Has Heri-Hor declared himself to be a King?" he asked briefly.

"No, Heri-Hor is depicted in reliefs on the walls of the temple of Khonsu - the only one he has decorated with inscriptions so far - as the High Priest and your faithful servant, but Amun entrusted him with the task of the healing of the City and restoring Maat while placing him above all," the priest replied, and Ramesses just smiled to himself and added:

"It means he will write his name in the holy ring, so for the people of Waset he will be the King, not me."

---

[126] An allusion to a phallus in a state of erection, with which Min - the patron of fertility and harvest - is presented in art.

"Our Lord, the only real King will be Amun, but this can only be announced by his new First Servant chosen by Amun..." Amen-em-Ipet replied.

Ramesses cut in on him again: "...and then this High Priest will declare himself King!"

Now, Queen Tent-Amun spoke for the first time: "Our King, may you live forever! That's what all your subjects say. However, you know that the last day will come also to you someday and you must have in mind just now that your blood would remain in the veins of the one who will sit on the throne of Geb. God did not give us a son, but we have a daughter and the one whom she will marry will be the King in the future. The heart of Henut-tawy has chosen long since and you must accept this for the good of the Both Countries. You know whom, I mean – we all mean," she repeated, pointing to the other participants in the conversation.

"And Pi-ankh probably the most!"

Ramesses, who listened to the words of the rejected spouse with growing nervousness, laughed ominously that was followed by a long rising explosion. "I will never agree!" he shouted, jumping from the throne and standing in front of his guests in an imperious attitude. "All of you wanted to entrap me, but I am Horus and Son of Re! I can't change Amun's decision regarding Heri-Hor, but it's me who appoints and dismisses all others!" As for you," he pointed his finger at Pi-ankh, "You are no longer a general because you were not able to defeat the Kushites and it was because of your fault that they plundered then the Great Valley! Nor are you," he turned to Nes-Ba-neb-Djedu, "because not only you haven't done anything at all, even not taking part in the battle, but against my orders you started here to fraternize with Tjehenu. Furthermore, do you think that I don't know that you are visiting every day my wife? Ex-wife!" The King's finger was pointed now at Tent-Amun, "I deprive you of the right to use the title of Queen, to live in the palace of the First Spouse. In general, I deprive you of everything you have! Guards!"

At this cry, armed soldiers appeared in the chamber. Ramesses has shown them his interlocutors, not even having noticed in his blindness that the dignified Amen-hotep's messenger Amen-em-Ipet was among them. "Arrest these people! A trial awaits them for betraying the King!" he shouted, when suddenly he noticed with immeasurable surprise that the armed men not only didn't follow this order, but have surrounded him himself.

Then Pi-ankh spoke: "As you can see, nobody is listening to you here anymore. Not me, neither Heri-Hor nor Nes-Ba-neb-Djedu are responsible for what happened in Waset, but you, because you trusted too much Pa-nehsi and showered him with titles. It happened for the first time since Atum that one official gained so much power! The Repeating of Births were already announced in Kemet and always then the Country regained its splendor. After the Great Heresy it was the army that helped to do this, and now it will also help. It will be done by those whom you wanted to downgrade and imprison. And be informed that from now on, not we but you will be under guard, although you will still be Pharaoh and you will live in your palace. I wanted you to give your daughter to my son Pi-nodjem and accept him as a son. You did not agree, but now Amun who will be King, will agree to this marriage, and the Queen will bless this relationship. The Queen whom we all love and whom no one will deprive of anything, neither of the palace nor of the title of King's Great Spouse. Take care of His Majesty," he turned to the soldiers, "that he would not lack anything. May you live in happiness and health!"

Pi-ankh bowed low before Ramesses. "Well, maybe not forever..." he added with a malicious smile.

Ramesses stood as if built into the palace's floor.

"It hurts me, Ramesses," Tent-Amun said now, "that you wanted to bring me to a trial even though you have long ceased to consider me to be your wife. It hurts me that you don't want to respect our daughter's feelings, but since you are no longer able to think about the future of the Country, I'll have, for the sake of Kemet, to make some decisions for you!" While saying this, she put her hand on the shoulder of Nes-Ba-neb-Djedu and they both left, following Pi-ankh. Amen-em-Ipet still remained for a moment, looking regretfully at Ramesses, who was standing motionless and speechless, certainly still not believing what has just happened here.

"Why did you set fire in your heart while opposing Amun? It wasn't Amen-hotep who has gone crazy, but you, King, have got blinded. Let Amun comfort you in this disease," he said, then bowed and left the Reception Hall.

On the next day, the oracle of Amun at Pi-Ramesse chose General Nes-Ba-neb-Djedu as a High Priest. The ceremony was rather of a local character: only the inhabitants of the district in which the temple of Amun was lying watched it, while in other parts of the city the principal places were occupied by the holy shrines of Ptah, Set and Re. However, the newly-elected High Priest of Amun immediately began talks with the First Servants of these cult statues, making them aware that a new time had come, in which Amun had the most important place, and that it is necessary that in a month only one common procession would cross Pi-Ramesse that would gather all residents. It was agreed that it would take place at the same time as in Waset the great marriage celebration of Amun, Ipet will be organized.

This year the holiday in the City was to have a particularly solemn course because, in addition to the symbolic ceremony of joining Amun with his wife Mut, a real wedding was to take place. Here, the daughter of General Pi-ankh, charming Nodjmet, who became the wife of the High Priest and King Heri-Hor came from Pi-Ramesse to the City. On the same day as the wedding, the coronation of the co-ruler of Amun took place, and Heri-Hor solemnly sat in a double pavilion, where he received signs of power in the Southern and Northern Countries. He also assumed like every pharaoh, five names, albeit the holy ring with his coronation's name only contained his title of the First Servant of Amun, which meant that in fact his royal dignity was symbolic only. For the inhabitants of the City, however, this dignity was very true and the crowds cheered the new King joyfully. For the first time since over 200 years the monarch was living in Waset once again, and not in the distant Men-nefer, or even more distant Pi-Ramesse.

Meanwhile, there, in Pi-Ramesse, the real Pharaoh could see from the windows of his palace an unusual celebration that took place after the end of the great procession in honor for Amun which the inhabitants of the capital had never seen before, and which had been prepared for a month. In the procession all the holy barges of the local sanctuaries participated, and long ranks of priests carrying various holy emblems, and women shaking *sesh-sesh* or striking tambourines accompanied them. On the streets decorated with greenery and flowers fruits and cakes were distributed, one could also have a drink of milk or even beer. That is why, since the trumpeters announced that the procession was going to start, the number of those who wanted to see it or participate in it was rising with each moment. A special elevation was erected near the royal palace, on which an offering altar and beside it two high thrones stood.

After the offerings were made, the trumpets sounded and the herald spoke in a loud voice: "Rejoice the inhabitants of the city, because Amun has shown his grace and has protected it from being destroyed by barbarians and from all terrible acts being committed as in Waset. There, in the south, Amun announced that the Repeating of Births began to restore the lost Maat. He will rule himself in Kemet now, and on His behalf the Northern Country will be governed by those whom he placed as his pillars here: the First Servant of Amun, Nes-Ba-neb-Djedu and the King's Great Spouse, Tent-Amun!"

At that moment, the two of them ascended the platform and appeared in front of the people, bringing about a great ovation, and then they sat on the prepared thrones. Now, the herald has announced that according to Amun's decision, in Djanet – a place where there was nothing so far a new city will be build.[127]

Like the Hill of the First Time for Atum, this city will constitute the place, where in a new great temple, which is to resemble Ipet-sut, Amun will make his creative decisions. The construction of this temple and City in Djanet will begin soon when the refreshing waters of Hapi flood the fields, and all the inhabitants of the Northern Country will participate in this work.

Finally, the herald announced one more joyful piece of news. Here, Henut-tawy, the daughter of His Majesty Ramesses – may he live! – is wedding Pi-nodjem, the son of General Pi-ankh!" Among the cheers, the young couple climbed the podium and came to Tent-Amun and Nes-Ba-neb-Djedu to receive their blessing on behalf of Amun.

Ramesses, standing in the window of his palace, watched all this and also heard the words of the herald and the cries of joy of the crowd. Perhaps for the first time during his 20-year reign, the Living Horus and Son of Re wept...

---

[127] This city was Tanis (today's San el-Hagar) - the capital city during the 21st dynasty - built in the wilderness in the northeastern Nile delta, about 20 km north of Pi-Ramesse.

CHAPTER XIX

Noon was approaching when Suti-mes standing on the prow of a boat bearing the colors of the High Priest of Amun, that was separating majestically the swollen waters of the river, has seen on the right side the characteristic outlines of the rocks he had missed so much during his six years long absence in the City. While the young priest was joyfully breathing in to the fullest the familiarly scented air, the rocks grew, revealing more and more well known to him details covered with the divine glow from the barge of Re, with which contrasted some mysterious nooks enveloped in perennial shade. A moment later Suti-mes could notice the magnificent group of temples built at the foot of the rock walls, to which Amun went every year in the second month of the Shemu season on the occasion of the Beautiful Feast of the Valley. It was the second month of the Akhet season now and the overflowing waters of Hapi covering the fields were to see another flotilla of colorfully decorated barges. Tomorrow in the first day of the great and joyful holiday of Ipet they would depart from the harbor in Ipet-sut towards Ipet-resit, constituting the wedding procession of Amun. The boat with Suti-mes has turned left and has sailed into the canal leading straight to the harbor in front of Ipet-sut, where all these barges were ready, washed and decorated with colorful ribbons, waiting only for the divine statues hidden in portable shrines. Of course, the largest one was Amun's barge decorated with ram's heads carved on the prow and stern. It was to take on the board the magnificent User-hat – the portable chapel also having the shape of a boat, carried by the priests during the processions. Right next to it the High Priest's and – being at the same time – royal boat was slightly rolling on the wave. The First Servant of Amun was to sail on it together with his retinue. This boat was furnishing a visible sign that Heri-Hor was present in his palace. Suti-mes checked spontaneously whether a pocket of his tunic still contains the letters from Nes-Ba-neb-Djedu and Tent-Amun addressed to Heri-Hor, and this action evoked the seven years old memories. It was then that he arrived at the same harbor in Ipet-sut with a royal letter to the High Priest Amen-hotep, but his path ended just after crossing the Great Gate. Now, Suti-mes was approaching this place again. The rebuilt gate looked magnificent, it was glistening with the white of limestone, the fresh colors of sacred signs and reliefs, even with a few gildings. Colorful ribbons fluttered from six high wooden masts attached to the walls and reaching almost the top of both towers of the gate, on which Suti-mes could see the figures of guards looking from the bottom so inconspicuously. In his mind's eyes another image from a few years ago appeared for a moment, when he stood next to the High Priest Amen-hotep on the top of the Great Gate, looking at the terrible scenes of violence taking place below. It was quiet here today, and there was a dignified calm in the clear air, making that tragedy almost impossible to imagine. However, Suti-mes was keeping this in memory, when, along with the ship's captain and two archers, he was traversing the distance from the harbor to the Great Gate, walking between the ram-headed lions – the stone guards of this place.

"The envoy of the First Servant of Amun Nes-Ba-neb-Djedu and the Great Royal Spouse Tent-Amun to His Majesty the First Servant and King Heri-Hor!" the captain shouted the guest's announcement at the feet of the Great Gate, and after a few moments, a small wicket was opened and a short, quite obese man with Kushite features stood there, at whose sight the worst reminiscence returned to Suti-mes: it was the same Pen-nesti-tawy who was to lead him then to the High Priest Amen-hotep! He has almost not changed, though he has gained some weight, and the red nose was still a very significant part of his face. Having bowed before the messenger, whom he obviously did not recognize, the Overseer of the Great Gate led the visitors through both wickets and then he headed towards the palace of the High Priest.

"So, this time we are going the shortest way. Won't you lead me around through that entrance?" – Suti-mes looked attentively at his guide, pointing at the wall next to the Great Gate.

Pen-nesti-tawy goggled, stared at the questioner, but still did not recognize him.

"Lord, I don't understand, what are you talking about?" he muttered.

"Well, I wouldn't understand either, if I were you," Suti-mes said. "But you see, you didn't kill me when Pa-nehsi commissioned you this, though I still have scars from your dagger."

Pen-nesti-tawy has paled. He squinted at the young priest, whose figure seemed to be familiar to him now, and then he suddenly bolted. The captain accompanying Suti-mes tried to hold him, but he has broken free. While running quickly he almost reached that passage in the wall through which one could easily get out of Ipet-sut, when an arrow shot by one of the archers hit him in the leg. Pen-nesti-tawy fell and after a while was caught by temple guards, who, alarmed by the captains' shouts and a noise unusual for this place, were running from all sides. Several priests on duty in the palace of the First Servant also appeared, and finally the superior of the High Priest's house, the eminent Pa-seba-kha-en-Ipet, came to find out the reasons for the incident, about which he had been informed. Pen-nesti-tawy lay pale and moaned quietly, but he didn't want to answer any questions. The dignitary heard the relation of Suti-mes and the captain, but he didn't hide his amazement. "I don't know you, Lord," he said to the young priest, "and though I have no reason not to believe you, your accusation is extremely puzzling. After the war, everyone who was to hold an important post in Ipet-sut, such as the Overseer of the Great Gate, had to show to the High Priest that someone significant in the City trusted in him. Thus, Pen-nesti-tawy surely obtained someone's opinion good enough to convince His Majesty King Heri-Hor. I am afraid he won't be happy because of what happened here, but you will tell him about that yourself. My only duty is to inform him of the event and announce your arrival with a letter. Let's go then!" he said to Suti-mes, and he ordered the guards to carry the wounded Overseer of the Great Gate to the temple custody and to call a doctor to dress his injured leg.

A moment later Suti-mes entered the Audience Hall of the palace, known to him for a long time, but now much more richly decorated than in the time of Amen-hotep. There was a throne here, absent before, set on a platform, and next to it Suti-mes saw beside the High Priest's symbols also royal ones: the huge vultures holding fans in their claws, painted on the wall. The canopy above the throne had the shape of a huge crown of the Both Countries, There were a few people standing in the room, but at first sight all of them seemed strangers to him, so he bowed only in their direction and stood aside, waiting for Heri-Hor. Then he heard a well-known voice, "Suti-mes, must always your arrival at the High Priest accompany some dramatic circumstances?" and he saw the open arms and the smile of an old friend. They greeted each other warmly and Amen-em-Ipet, taking Suti-mes by the hand, was about to introduce him to the audience when they heard the voice of the herald, "The First Servant of Amun ruling on His behalf in the Southern Country, the Son of Amun Heri-Hor!"

Suti-mes had to admit that since the time he had seen this dignitary as a general at Hor-di, he changed a lot: he gained weight, turned gray, his face looked tired. He seemed as if he felt unwell. He sat on the throne and looked around the room, and when he saw Suti-mes, he gestured for him to come up. The young priest knelt and kissed the High Priest's ring, and then, remembering that he was actually dealing with the King, he intended to fall on his face and "kiss the ground," but Heri-Hor stopped him, "Come on, young man! I had to accept these titles and crowns, but believe me that sometimes I find it very difficult and have fond recollections of the time when I was only a military commander... But, first of all, explain to me what all this confusion means: the Overseer of the Great Gate in Ipet-sut has been hurt and captured by the people who came here with you as guests... It is only me and my people for such actions here, no one else!" Heri-Hor's voice was firm.

"Lord, please forgive me!" Suti-mes replied quietly. "I gave no order and I'd not dare to act without your command. I have only recognized the man who wanted to kill me when I came here once with a royal letter to the First Servant Amen-hotep. I have asked why he was not leading me along the same path where he hit me with a dagger, when he started running away. The captain who accompanied me, hearing what I was saying, decided to prevent him from escaping."

There was a murmur of excitement among those gathered in the Audience Hall, and Heri-Hor himself was also extremely amazed. But before he posed another question, Amen-em-Ipet who had the privilege to speak in the presence of the King and High Priest even not being asked to, had said: "Let Your Dignity allow me to confirm the words of this young man, because I was then, as today, in the palace of the High Priest when a seriously wounded Suti-mes was brought here, in whose tunic we found a letter from the King. We barely succeeded to rescue him, but we had never recognized who the attacker was. Later, when Suti-mes got better, we were dealing with other attackers and that caused to be important. However, I must admit that I have never suspected Pen-nesti-tawy!"

"Nobody probably suspected him," Heri-Hor added. "After the war we were checking if anyone in Ipet-sut had been connected to Pa-nehsi's band. I hardly knew anyone here before, but I asked about everyone and I remember that Pen-nesti-tawy got personal support from Pa-Shu-uben, that's why he stayed here as Overseer of the Great Gate. I know," he turned to Amen-em-Ipet, "that you had some reservations about Pa-Shu-uben, although he proved to be very helpful in restoring order after the war, and his knowledge of the inhabitants of Waset is valuable. Still, I see that I will have to talk to Pa-Shu-uben soon, also about Pen-nesti-tawy, who will not run away anyway. But enough about that. Suti-mes, after all, you have brought me a letter from Nes-Ba-neb-Djedu, don't you?"

The young priest bowed and got a sealed scroll out the inside pocket of his tunic. Heri-Hor opened it and began to read. There was silence in the Audience Hall. Everyone was curious about the news from the North and knew that since they were invited here, the King would, according to his custom, share important news with them, and perhaps he would like to seek their advice? Finally, he paused and, still holding the papyrus, raised his head and said silently, as if to himself: "So, Amen-hotep is dead. This is a sad piece of news, though he couldn't return to the City as High

Priest, his heart was always here; I was hoping to see him again..."
Then, turning to Amen-em-Ipet, he continued, "It is my will because I valued him so much and loved him as a brother to tell in stone in the palace where he lived about him and his works.[128] It will be a permanent monument of our memory and in this way Amen-hotep, despite the fact that his mummy remained in the North, will also live in Ipet-sut, and his Ba will be able to come here whenever he wants and to see the places he loved. Suti-mes will help you in this work!"

Amen-em-Ipet bowed and said only, "It will happen!" Suti-mes felt that he had a great distinction and that the work he was commissioned to do would be a very grateful task.

Meanwhile, Heri-Hor plunged in the reading the letter again, then said loudly, this time addressing to all present ones, "Nes-Ba-neb-Djedu and Tent-Amun write to me about the difficulties that my envoy Wen-Amun had with buying cedar wood for the new User-hat barge and explain why it took so long.[129] Well, as it turns out, the thieves on his way to Keben took from him away all the gold and silver vessels that I had given him and it is not surprising that the local prince – Zakar-Baal, or what's his name – was not inclined to cut trees for the sole promise of payment. Fortunately, Nes-Ba-neb-Djedu did the job properly, but due to the storm and the threat from pirates, the transport was still

---

[128] In the area of the temple in Karnak near the former High Priest's Palace there is indeed such a text.

[129] The episode mentioned here refers to a literary work known as *Report of Wenamun* describing the adventures of Heri-Hor's envoy, who went to Byblos for cedar wood.

more delayed. Thank Amun! Undoubtedly it was His participation in it, that eventually the goods came on time and our craftsmen managed to make a barge before the holiday of Ipet. It is beautiful, you'll see it tomorrow," Heri-Hor turned his face to Suti-mes again. "Of course, you will stay with me today for supper, besides you must rest after the journey and prepare for tomorrow, because as a Servant of Amun you will go near His image."

Suti-mes made a gesture as if to say that he had planned differently this evening, but Heri-Hor has interpreted it at once properly:

"You don't probably want to offend me by refusing to eat the supper with me... I guess you have a girlfriend here, and very beautiful one – Buteh-Amun has even mentioned me that. But since you have waited seven years, you will wait one more day. I think you will meet in the procession tomorrow. I understand lovers. See, I belong to them too," the High Priest has clearly livened up. "You must know that my royal wife has recently given me a son who will be the Lord of the Both Countries in the future. After all, find it yourself!" He has signaled, and after a moment, Nodjmet entered with the baby in her arms. Suti-mes thought that this young woman who stood at the throne looked more like Heri-Hor's daughter than his wife. She was pretty, though chubby, with the face similar to her father Pi-ankh's features. The King has beamed, stretched out his arms and gently took the baby, but it almost immediately began to cry loudly and Nodjmet said, "Forgive me, my King and Lord, but Amen-em-ensu is hungry," and Heri-Hor, having kissed the child, gave it back to his mother, saying, "Of course, my love, this age also has its rights. But don't forget that it is my will that our son should also be carried in the procession tomorrow; let the inhabitants of the City see their future King!"

A grimace of pain appeared on his face at that moment; the High Priest began gasping for breath and clutching at his heart. Immediately the medic ran up and handed him a small vessel, the contents of which Heri-Hor drank, after which all bad symptoms subsided.

"It's okay," he said, trying to smile, "Sometimes something catches me, but it's okay."

"Lord," the medic turned to him seriously, strongly emphasizing every word, "It is necessary that you lie down and do not get up today. Tomorrow you will face a difficult day, full of emotions and effort!"

The hearing was over. Suti-mes went to his former seat in the wing of the High Priest's palace, escorted by Amen-em-ipet.

"I doubt whether this joint supper you have been invited to would take place at all; I think the King will soon lie down and fall asleep, especially after the medicine he received. But you can't leave Ipet-sut today, because it's not known if he won't ask you yet to him; he is very stubborn, and the medic complains that he is not listening to him and he should take care of himself. I'm worried about him because what you have seen is happening to him more and more often. Amun gave him 20 years, but I do not know if he..." the old priest suspended his voice. "And there is still so much to do here! But I'm glad you're finally back! You were missing here, especially for some people," he smiled eloquently, and Suti-mes smiled back.

"I don't think I need to explain to you what a torture these years were for me when looking after Amen-hotep. I could visit the City only in my thoughts during the day, in a dream at night, and of course, in letters! By return mail, I was receiving signs of love in the words of Henut dictated to Buteh-Amun, but that is not enough!"

"Your torture will end tomorrow!" summed up Amen-em-Ipet and left the young man alone. The barge of Re was still high, but Suti-mes felt sleepy. The tension that accompanied him during the entire journey has fallen away, and the large accumulation of emotions today caused that Heri-Hor's words that he should rest after the journey, which at first seemed excessive to him, suddenly gained value. After all, the tomorrow's day would require a great condition, both during and after the long procession. He lay down "for a while" on the bed and closed his eyes, and his imagination was suggesting various scenes of his dream meeting. Each vision was beautiful and gave way to another, equally charming, creating one series of pictures that at unknown moment turned into sleep.

On the next day, which was the 23rd day of the second month of the Akhet season Suti-mes got up before dawn and after having greeted, in a short prayer, Re on the eastern horizon, he began the necessary preparations for this special day he had dreamed of for so many years. Even ordinary everyday activities providing both cleanness and freshness was developing today into almost a ritual. There was no one at the Holy Lake, in a place intended for priestly ablutions, so he could wash slowly and thoroughly; a special paste made of natron mixed with ash was not only removing any impurities, all residues of sweat or cosmetic oil, but also it was setting freshness for the skin. The day was waking up quickly and it was quite brightly which made it possible to use the water's sheet of the lake as mirror at shaving. Suti-mes has returned to his apartment, has undressed and rubbed his whole body with a mixture of aromatic herbs, then he began to celebrate the putting on successive parts of the festive outfit that had been prepared since yesterday, glistening with fresh white. After having tied the underwear triangular loincloth[130] he put on a long tight fitting tunic with wide sleeves, made of the most delicate linen that was tightly clinging to his torso and hips, while falling in numerous folds almost to his ankles. It was so thin that his legs were completely visible, and his torso seemed bare. Now, Suti-mes put the elegant sandals braided of papyrus fiber, and he wrapped his hips in another densely pleated linen garment falling down to his knees and tied with a decorative scarf at his waist. At last he opened a small box with jewelry standing by the bed. He has he put on each arm two bracelets matching the necklace with the color and material. Finally he has taken out of the box an object that he could be proud of: a gold chain with three small artistically carved flies suspending from it and made of the same precious metal. It was an order given to war heroes, which was awakening a common admiration and respect for those few who had the honor to wear it. Suti-mes received it from Nes-Ba-neb-

---

[130] The equivalent of today's panties, a kind of big canvas diaper.

Djedu at the request of the High Priest Amen-hotep, but he has never put it on so far: today he was to do this for the first time. Additionally an elegant wig, the lappets of which were bordering his face with countless curls, girded with a blue band matching the necklace and bracelets, and now the Servant of Amun, Suti-mes, was ready to participate in the procession. The young man has smiled to himself: he knew that he looked great and should to appeal to the one and only person in the world who, perhaps like him, was not sleeping anymore and was preparing for the ceremony, which just for the two of them was a completely secondary event today; a day that started so brightly.

However, it was a special day for all the inhabitants of the City, and despite the early time, Suti-mes had seen feverish preparations for the procession everywhere. All the gates in the southern part of Ipet-sut, through which a large part of the divine images was to come out, were already wide open and the gatekeepers cleaned the passages from the sand blown by the winds, then poured water onto the floor to make the procession way spotlessly clean. Suti-mes has passed two such gates and has turned onto the path leading to the still-built temple of Khonsu in Waset-Nefer-hotep. He entered the courtyard, where the scaffoldings were still standing and the scenes on the walls were barely sketched, but looking at them, Suti-mes realized that their topic would be the wonderful Ipet feast, which was being prepared. The entrance to the Hall of Appearances was, exceptionally, open and so that he could see the glow of the fresh colors of the scenes painted on the walls and columns. Right at the entrance was a mighty stela covered with many lines of text telling how Heri-Hor had received 20 years of power from

Khonsu to carry out the Repeating of Births and how Amun subsequently approved it.

Suti-mes had not yet finished reading the text of this oracle, so important for the City, when he heard a choral recitation and after a moment saw in the depths of the Hall of Appearances two rows of the priests of Khonsu dressed in white. At the head the bearer of the sacred sign of Khonsu was strutting. The emblem looked a bit like a strangely formed pillow, yet it symbolized the placenta accompanying each birth; Khonsu was, after all, the patron of time, including the pregnancy and childbirth. It was followed by bearers of incense and censer as well as all the most important members of the holy staff of the House of Khonsu, and finally by the chief priest of that temple, Khonsu-mes, dressed in leopard pelt. Suti-mes knew him very well from school and liked him very much as a good friend. He also noticed the unexpected guest, and a real and joyful surprise appeared on his face, especially when he saw what adorns the chest of a long lost learning companion from Ipet-sut. However, unable to interrupt the recitation of the hymn, he greeted Suti-mes with a smile and gesture. Suti-mes had to kneel at the moment as the holy barge of Khonsu carried by eight priests was passing him. A group of Fathers of God on duty followed it. Suti-mes joined them, for the exit of this barge meant that it was time to go to the place of the grouping of priests, who were to accompany the main image of God carried in the magnificent User-hat-Amun. The Khonsu barge was leaving a little earlier because going now northwards it had to reach the Grand Courtyard before the barges of all other divine images inhabiting Ipet-sut would set off from the Great

Hall of Appearances of the House of Amun, heading in the opposite direction. Today, after all, the ceremony of repeating Amun's wedding took place. He himself, in the holy image placed on the User-hat barge, was to sail on his ship along the river towards the "wedding house" in the temple in Ipet-resit. Amun was to be accompanied by the boats of his mythical family: his consort Mut and his son Khonsu. All the other "wedding guests" that is all the sacred objects of worship from the Both Countries, the copies of which were gathered here in the City in the House of Amun in Ipet-sut, went towards Ipet-resit by a long avenue of lions. Suti-mes, following Khonsu's barge toward the harbor, passed the palace of the High Priest and turned toward the Great Gate. Among the columns of the Great Hall of Appearances, growing like a thicket of papyrus and lilies, he saw groups of white figures holding various holy signs and behind them the prows of barges decorated with the carved heads of divine images emerging from the shadow. The barges were resting on the shoulders of the priests, motionless as statues and waiting for a sign to move in a long path of the lions' avenue. Through the shapes of the sculptures Suti-mes was able to distinguish the barge of Atum wearing the crown of the Both Countries, the barge of Shu crowned with two high feathers, that of Horus with a head of falcon, and then a barge, the prow of which was decorated with woman's head crowned with a bunch of feathers.

"It is probably Anuket of Abu," the priest thought and began to wonder if he would be able to recognize all the divine images that are normally locked up in countless chapels in the vast territory of Ipet-sut. "It's probably impossible. How, without additional explanations engraved in sacred signs, to distinguish, for example, Ius-aas from Nebet-Hetepet, since they both look the same, they both come from Iunu and both are associated with Atum and his act of creating the world, and yet each of them has a separate holy image in the chapel and own priests? If someone can recognize and separate them, it's probably only Amen-em-Ipet who knows everything."

Thinking like that, Suti-mes went out into the courtyard and began looking for his colleagues with whom he was to go together in a procession, accompanying Amun's barge. He could see them easily, for they were the largest group, additionally characteristic because of the numerous holy emblems of Amun: pillars topped with a ram's head and a special decorative vase, which were also to be carried in the procession – and this one soon began. When all the barges with divine images awaiting in the Hall of Appearance already set off on the route running along the avenue of lions through the Eastern City towards Ipet-resit, the sounds of solemn fanfares rang out, and before the eyes of all those waiting in the courtyard a beautiful view unfolded of a retinue of the highest ranking priests preceding the group of the Pure Ones who carried the great User-hat barge. Heri-Hor walked right in front of it in the magnificent robes covered outside with the leopard pelt and wearing also a large golden necklace and the High Priest's golden cap decorated with the royal cobra above the front. He was supporting himself stately on a long richly decorated staff-scepter. On both sides of him two adjutant priests were walking who directed, with enormous fans made of feathers, the invigorating air towards him, as well as towards the head of Amun carved on the barge's prow. Suti-mes has entirely understood only now the words of Heri-Hor, who proudly told him yesterday about the latest wonderful work of artisans. Indeed, the barge looked impressive, made of precious cedar wood and covered with golden metal sheets, in which the shapes of sacred images were incised and filled with colored glass paste, for example the kneeling winged Hat-Hor – the mother of the Creator, and also of the King, embracing in a protective gesture the chapel covered with white veil, where during the procession the holiest statue of Amun lived.

The barge wrapped in the smell of incense, carried by 30 Pure Ones having their heads shaved moved majestically along the courtyard and the whole avenue of lions up to the harbor, where a high modulated scream issued by the women gathered there greeted it with the same sound they were greeting every young couple. At the same time each of them was shaking *sesh-sesh* making a joyful noise. With these sounds the message was carried over a considerable distance that Amun's dignified barge would sail away in a moment. The priests carefully brought the holy User-hat to the great boat. It looked very similar, having the ram-headed sculptures on the prow and stern, and the large chapel which housed the entire portable barge. However, the chapel on the great boat was preceded by miniature obelisks and masts with pennants which resembled the temple gate decorations, so that the boat carrying the holy barge with the statue became a floating temple. Preceded by the boats of Khonsu and Mut, and by several small auxiliary barges, the ship of Amun finally headed up the river. A large group of women holding *sesh-sesh* was moving along the banks followed by many priests among which also Sutimes was going. Together with several other persons he has been granted the honor of holding the ends of the ropes attached to a large boat that in symbolic way was helping it overcome the current of the river, being a God-fearing act. On the way the priests were reciting the subsequent phrases of a long hymn to Amun:

Greetings to you, Amun-Re, this image of the divine Power,
who came into being at the beginning of time!
Lord of Infinity, who created everything that is divine,
who created people and gave birth
to everything that lives!
You appeared as the Only One,
who was alone in Primeval Waters
with your father – the Earth
and your mother – the Heaven,
being Horus, who had illuminated the Both Countries
with his eyes, before Re appeared in the sky.
Your forehead reaches the sky,
when you take the form of This-One-In-High-Crown.
Remove all evil before the King...

The King and High Priest Heri-Hor, sailing on Amun's ship was kneeling in front of the chapel with the holy image, and rising his hands in a gesture of adoration. The Feast of Ipet was a renewal of Amun's wedding, but also the feast of every ruler who, as a legend recorded, among others in the temple of Ipet-resit, was born of the union of his royal mother with Amun. Thus, it was the day of confirmation of the relation between Amun and Heri-Hor and his family, and this year was special because the royal couple could boast the fruit of Amun's blessing. The small

Amen-em-ensu, according to the will of his father, was carried in the procession by Heri-Hor's eldest daughter, Shemet-sebeket, next to whom his three other daughters and 19 sons were going.[131] They also were holding the ropes of Amun's ship. The waves of the overflowing Hapi were carrying next stanzas of the hymn, while announcing to the crowds of residents gathered in the square in front of the Great Gate in Ipet-resit that the attractions they had been waiting for were approaching.

Finally, the ships arrived at the harbor, the Pure ones again took on their shoulders the magnificent User-hat and Amun preceded by all those who accompanied him on his way from Ipet-sut, headed towards the temple, again followed by a high wedding modulated shout of priestesses shaking *sesh-sesh*, but now multiplied because all the other women joined it. Other barges with divine images were already in place. In front of the Ipet-resit gate, between the two slender obelisks, a high pile of offerings was placed, before which three holy barges were to rest on pedestals: in the middle that of Amun, and on the sides those of Mut and Khonsu. The last two were already waiting there, surrounded by priests who were all facing the direction from which Amun was approaching. In front of the accumulation of offerings the Queen was waiting. Nodjmet was dressed in a long white, almost transparent robe, girded at the waist with a colorful ribbon and crowned with a colorful headgear used only on this occasion, consisting of feathers and faience balls stuck on flexible

---

[131] All the people mentioned here were depicted in the scenes of Ipet-feast of the 6th year of *uhem mesut*, which adorned the courtyard of the temple of Khonsu in Karnak.

gilded rods.[132] When the procession with the User-hat barge approached, the priestesses shaking their *sesh-sesh* surrounded Nodjmet, to which Heri-Hor now approached. The Queen, who was now both a priestess – the superior of the nurses of Mut and other women in the service of Amun – and the Great Spouse of the High Priest, took him by the hands, like a fiancée when she vows to her bridegroom. At this moment, an intense trill of wedding cry made by all women rose to the sky again. The royal couple turned to Amun's barge, which rested on a base prepared for it. At this moment, Shemet-sebeket, wearing the same crown as Nodjmet had, came up and handed small Amen-em-ensu to his mother, then Heri-Hor took him in his hands and raised him high, showing his son to both Amun and everyone gathered around. There was one great cry of joy: The City came alive under Amun and his governor, it had a King, and now his natural heir and successor appeared.

All barges were incensed, and a great fire was set to the offering pile: the flames shot into the sky, and the aromatic smell of burning herbs and incense spread around. At the moment, exotic bands of musicians and dancers entered the center of the square: the black newcomers from the Land of Punt dressed in animal pelts and the fair complexion Tjehenu shaking their heads dressed in ostrich feathers. With the sounds of drums, flutes, lutes, *sesh-sesh*, the rhythmic clapping and singing, several shapely young girl dancers appeared dressed only in short leather

---

[132] The appearance of this crown can be recreated from the image in the Temple of Khonsu.

skirts, open at the front. These girls began to perform acrobatic jumps and backward flips, while revealing their pubes, which caused a lively resonance and applause especially of young men watching this show.

After some time, the trumpets have sounded, the Great Gate of the temple was opened, and the three holy barges carried on the priests' shoulders in accompany of Nodjmet, Heri-Hor and his children, as well as the highest ranking priests went inside and disappeared from the eyes of the gathered people. At the same time, the other barges and symbols of the divine "wedding guests" set off back along the avenue of lions towards Ipet-sut. However, the crowd has not dispersed at once: dances and singing were continued, and now it was time to a feast: Amun and the King invited everyone to the wedding. Bread, beer, portions of roast sheep meat, wine, cakes and fruit were distributed in specially prepared places around the great square. Only when all these goods have been consumed, the people began to go home.

When the religious ceremonies were over, Suti-mes could start his searching for Henut. During all the celebrations he was separated from groups of women, now he finally ran towards them, but soon he realized how difficult task was ahead of him. There were plenty of women and all of them dressed in elegant long pleated robes, and on their heads almost the same fashionable wigs decorated with flowers. When such a woman stood with her back to the onlooker, it was impossible to recognize whether she was a young girl or a dignified older lady. The young servant of Amun completely forgot that as a bearer of the order of the golden flies he should behave with some seriousness and dignity. When he was founding in the crowd a woman's figure who seemed to him a bit similar to Henut, because of height, slimness or the way of movement, he was running to such a woman up, having a look into her face, and sometimes she was getting scared then. Seeing an elegant young man and not quite knowing what to do, the women accosted by Suti-mes were usually bowing, but often bursting then into laugh, seeing his surprised expression. This kind of a "hunt" lasted a long time and, worst of all, was completely ineffective. There were fewer and fewer people, and Suti-mes, looking helplessly in all directions, began to lose hope that he would meet the one he was thinking about during the whole ceremony.

"Or maybe something happened to her?" This unwanted thought appeared like an intruder whom he was unable to chase away. After some time he was almost certain that something terrible had to happen. Darker and darker images began to come to his mind, and finally, terrified with his own thoughts, he stood and having leaned against a tree, because he felt suddenly weak and helpless. Then he heard the voice that he had dreamed at nights during all these years spent in Iunu: "Is that you, my dear? I have found you at last! I have recognized you because you stood under the acacia, just like when you were waiting for me after the processions. If it weren't for that, maybe I wouldn't recognize you – you are so dignified and... Golden flies?"

Henut broke the stream of her words, nervously uttered as fast as arrows, incredulously looking at the badge of a supreme heroism, awarded for war merits. Is it possible? Is this the same boy whose robes were simple and woven from thick canvas and who could not afford sophisticated decorations? But here he was, after the first moment of infirmity that made him speechless, and caused by surprise and a sharp change in mood, when in one moment he traveled from the depths of the dark abyss of sadness to the luminous peak of joy, now he opened his arms wide and hugged the girl, kissing with abandon her eyes, nose and mouth, and when he paused to catch his breath, she began to kiss him. Suti-mes was feeling the tears of her happiness flowing down his face, and feeling himself close to crying, too, though he remembered that this would not be compatible with the golden flies order carrier. They were not saying anything for a long time, only every moment they were breaking away from each other to take in the sight, full of happiness, the beloved figure and face, and then they were again joining in a hug and kiss, only interrupting it from time to time with a single word: "my love", "only mine". At last they came to their senses and began to make sure that the long parting and longing no longer had any meaning and changed nothing in their mutual feelings. Then they started asking if their letters were coming? Henut was not able to write, but she was dictating her words to Buteh-Amun, who was also reading her what Suti-mes wrote.

The mention of Buteh-Amun made him realize that he has not thought of the friend so far, nor met him among the participants of the procession, just as he has not seen his father anywhere.

"What's up with Djehuty-mes?" he asked, and Henut became sad.

"He is very weak, he still has not completely recovered from that, he still has bad dreams and then screams at night, even though it has been so many years. He is already old and getting weaker and the doctor forbade him to prolong efforts, so he stayed today at home, and Buteh may have stayed with him. Let's go to them! When he sees you, the joy will definitely restore his strength," she suggested.

Clasping hands, they ran happily towards the harbor, where the traffic was very intensive today. Numerous smaller and larger boats were sailing across the river, bringing back the participants of the procession to Khefet-her-neb-es. The owners of larger barges very well disposed towards the whole world today were shouting that they still had free seats and inviting everyone who would like to cross the river, so that Henut and Suti-mes didn't have any difficulties to find such an opportunity, and soon sailed to the west bank with a few other people, among whom the view of the order of golden flies aroused obvious admiration. When the owner of the boat found out that his excellent passenger was going to the house of Djehuty-mes, he asked to say to the Necropolis Scribe the warm greetings from Pa-du-Amun, the brewery manager and the head of the house of beer, and he assured that "...Although this is not a place where such notable dignitaries as Chari come, their names are pronounced there with respect even by regulars."

The long road running through the fields overflown now was full of people who, individually or in small groups, were returning from the festivities. Some of them were turning soon, while continuing their walk on dikes to reach their houses situated on the ground elevations resembling islands lying among the fields under water. Such a house once belonged to Henut's father; now they passed its ruins seen from afar. That house, abandoned for several years, and also damaged by the last quite abundant flooding and not repaired, has already started to fall apart. Intuitively, they stopped and looked in this direction, where in every corner of this poor farmyard some personal memory was crouching. Henut could see the carefreeness of her childhood there, and then also the bliss of waiting for the visits of her beloved. She also could hear the voice and see the face of her father, whom she always had missing. In Suti-mes's mind it was the last meeting that has stuck at most, having brutally overshadowing the earlier positive images.

"It is good that Henut no longer lives here," he thought, and at the same time the question came back, never answered in letters. "How did it happen that she took up residence, first alone, and then with her mother and brother, in the rich house of Djehuty-mes, situated in the elite quarter of Khefet-her-neb-es?"

Buteh-Amun only mentioned once to him that he had saved the girl from the crocodile, but he has never come back to this topic. It seemed strange to Suti-mes, but he explained it with his friend's innate modesty. So now, holding the heroine of that event by the hand, he returned to this with a question, and he immediately sensed that he has touched a weak spot.

Henut became sad and her answer was also only an escape, "You know, Suti, it was a terrible memory and I have already thrown it out of my heart. Buteh-Amun simply came to the right place in the right time, and it was probably a miracle that Amun did. That's all, and because there was poverty then and my father was absent, your friend decided to help us and to take us into the family. Fortunately, it's been a long time ago and there is nothing to come back to. But you talk about yourself! I'm dying of curiosity; how did you get these golden flies? I always thought that only Kings get such an order, and you are not a King..." she smiled charmingly and flirtatiously, so Suti-mes replied, "But I am! I have you and you are my whole world, so I am the King of the world!" After this, he began to reminisce about his war deeds, albeit diminishing the importance of his order as much as he could. He talked about his escape with Amen-hotep through the desert, then about a visit to the King and his stay in General Heri-Hor's troops, about a war march and waiting for battle, and finally about how he met Henut's father. He developed this story, emphasizing that the escape of Djed-Mut-if-ankh from Pa-nehsi's camp was a real heroism, and the information provided about the enemy and the traps he set contributed to the victory.

"He," Suti-mes emphasized, "has deserved the golden flies, although he has not seen them because he died; but he died like a hero."

Meanwhile, they came to the house of Djehuty-mes.

"Look, father, whom I brought you!" Henut exclaimed happily, and the old man, who actually spent this day in bed, got up quickly and warmly welcomed "his daughter Henut and his son Suti-mes," in which they both sensed an allusion to their future relationship.

Seeing Suti-mes looking around, the old Necropolis Scribe immediately answered the unasked question, "He's not here; you had to pass each other. Buteh-Amun, Shed-em-dua and my already seven years old grandson Ankh-ef-en-Amun went to the Eastern City in the morning and have not returned yet. I preferred not to risk the emotions that acrobat women provide," he added with a smile. "At my age, it could be dangerous... for Nes-Mut, although he is 13 years old, in a sense, too, it was probably better that he stayed with his mother, who is also not feeling well lately, although she does not admit it; she won't deceive me, the old man..."

He was still saying these words when both of the just mentioned persons entered the room. Suti-mes noticed that Hereret - Henut's mother grew old very much, she turned gray and lost weight, though her eyes, just as black as those of her daughter, were shining with their former glow, and at that moment, they were beaming with joy. Immediately after the greeting, she turned to Suti-mes with the assurance that she knew the last will of her dead husband and joined it, agreeing to his marriage with Henut, "...if such a dignitary wants a poor girl," and she seriously added, not allowing him to protest: "I hope, my son, that you don't harbor a grievance against me, that I didn't defend you when my husband shouted against High Priest Amenhotep. We all believed in it then; after all, the dignitary Pa-Shuuben told us about it, whom even today everyone still believes and who is more powerful than then..."

Suti-mes took her hand and put it on his forehead, "I have long forgotten all about it, mother!"

"Gosh! Golden flies!" Nes-Mut's high-pitched voice suddenly sounded. "Can I touch them?" Only now Djehuty-mes noticed the order and his face beamed.

"I'm really happy, boy!" he said, watching as Suti-mes removed his order and hung it for a moment on Nes-Mut's neck, which turned red with pride. "You deserved these flies, like hardly anyone. How many times have you risked your life for Amen-hotep! Tell me if he..."Djehuty-mes has not finished, but without words he understood the answer. "I actually ask without sense if you came to the City. So, another friend left me, although we will probably meet soon on the Fields of Reeds[133], if God allows. Believe me, after what I had to experience here, I am actually waiting impatiently for the call up, but everyone around me explains that I am needed, and the Repeating of Births is not over yet ..."

"Me too, father, I could only repeat it: you are not only needed but even necessary. Buteh-Amun has told me more than once that there are still secrets of the necropolis that he is still learning from you, that he always feels small in comparison with you, and he would not be able to cope with all his duties without you, especially now. Tell me please, what is happening to the dignified mummies of Kings now?"

"They have all been embalmed and bandaged again, though from time to time they will have to be unrolled to check, if anything bad is happening to them. Let's hope that no one breaks down, even though this was the intention of the enemies. It is the

---

[133] One of the names of the ancient Egyptian paradise.

King's wish that they all should be reburied in their tombs and some repeated funerals even have already taken place. But it is proceeding slowly, because the restoring even of a small part of the equipment they had is very expensive. If all goes well, we will soon be preparing for the repeated funeral of His Majesty Amen-hotep Djeser-Ka-Re. Our family has always served him, so now Buteh-Amun will do it. Will you help him?" Djehuty-mes asked this question, knowing the answer.

"It will be an honor for me. Is he to be buried in the Great Valley?"

"No, he never lay there. He rested in the area of the Djeser-Akhet temple of His Majesty Djehuty-mes Men-kheper-Re, but this thug Aa-neru had to find out somehow about it, so that Amen-hotep Djeser-Ka-Re was pulled out of his grave and robbed."

"So, this is where the funeral will take place!" -Suti-mes guessed and was surprised when he heard the old Necropolis Scribe denied loudly as if reading his thoughts, "No, son. His Majesty Heri-Hor decided to keep this grave for himself and his son. But there is another older tomb once prepared for Amen-hotep's mother, Ah-mes-nefer-tari, situated not far away from Amen-hotep's tomb, just in the neighboring valley. Now, this grave will be used, and the son will repose beside his mother."

"Father," Henut interrupted the conversation, "you can tell Suti all this later. I don't want you to get tired. I'm taking him for a walk. Maybe we will meet Buteh-Amun?"

"Alright, children, go, but come back soon for a meal!" Chari smiled at this couple craving for being together and he thought that he unnecessarily disturbs their joy of meeting.

The young people clasped hands again and left. It was early afternoon when meals were eaten in many homes. Most of the inhabitants of the Western City have already returned from the procession and Buteh-Amun's family should also appear soon, if anything hasn't stopped them on the opposite bank. Initially, Henut and Suti-mes were going to meet them, but when, just behind the wall of the precinct also encompassing the house of Djehuty-mes, they have reached a junction with a road leading to the center of Khefet-her-neb-es, they changed plans. They would namely have to pass right next to the beer house, where from some unpleasant noises could be heard meaningfully telling that several guests of this place have overdone drinking beer and their sight and behavior did not encourage lovers to go in this direction. So, they went straight while passing a desert hill, behind which the cemetery began. A few ropes farther there was the beginning of the road going along the wall of the temple district of His Majesty Amen-hotep Neb-Maat-Re, justified, and heading as far as the harbor; they came from there today, and Buteh-Amun must have come back the same way. However, before they turned to that way, Suti-mes had stopped for a while, looking at the bright masonry of a huge walled house that certainly wasn't here years ago.

"Who ever built such a palace?" he asked, and not getting an answer looked at Henut and saw that she became pale.

"Let's go now," she took a brisk step toward the temple of Amen-hotep, pulling her boyfriend's hand. "Here someone lives who was serving to Pa-nehsi; many people had made fortunes then," she said finally.

"But who is that?" Suti-mes inquired, and now a little longer while passed before he heard: "I don't know" – Henut has turned now her beautiful face towards him and whispered, "Kiss me!" He did it eagerly once, twice, ten times... "Let's go for this walk at last!" Henut said it in such a way that Suti-mes followed her without resistance. Almost running and always clasping each other's hands they passed the Crocodile Backwaters and the harbor in front of the palace of His Majesty Ramesses User-Maat-Re Meri-Amun, and then they entered a side road shaded by palms. It was running towards the lake once dug here, as it was said, by the pharaoh Amen-hotep Neb-Maat-Re in love as a gift to his royal wife Ti. Almost no one ever was coming here and the reeds with decorative racemes grew so densely that they formed entire groves, among which one could hide completely. Suti-mes felt his temples throbbing while seeing that Henut was leading him there,

"I already know," he whispered, "why those who live on the Fields of Reeds are happy..."

"Are you happy?" the black-haired echo hugged to him asked.

"Are you still asking? Yes. I'm very happy! I love you and you are here with me. Re shines in the sky, there is no war nor hunger, the City revives, it is a joyful festive day, even these reeds are happy that we are here! One has just told me that... And you? Are you happy?"

"Yes, I am, Suti."

They stood completely hidden in the reeds and Suti-mes has again tasted the greatest flavor in the world. All the needs of love that were in him have awaken now; the dam has broken.

"I love you!" he repeated once more, hugging the girl and following her shapes through the dress. He has released the smooth girl's shoulders from the linen straps, and moved the heat of his mouth to her slender neck. For a moment, the girl seemed to give in to the caress that was certainly not indifferent for her, nor unwanted. However, she suddenly became as if stiffen and began to defend herself, and her mouth whispered with some desperate note that belied the whole situation: "No, please, no!"

Suti-mes interrupted the caress and he asked extremely surprised: "Why are you defending yourself from what we both are thinking about and what we are desiring?"

Henut looked at him with tears in her eyes, and suddenly she turned and started running away. Yet he has caught up her and took holding her hands. "Dearest Henut, what happened?

"I don't want you'd come to hate me!" she has dropped with changed voice, then she has broken free and started running toward the home, while crying loudly.

CHAPTER XX

For a long moment, Suti-mes stood motionless, more like a stone statue standing among reeds than a living man, and he felt half dead. This world which seems so friendly and joyful just a moment ago, suddenly began to collapse, but the reasons for this were inconceivable. What's with which he hurt his beloved girl? Didn't she bring them here, giving him signals of her readiness to cross the last border today, in front of which they were always stopping so far?

Didn't they promise themselves 100 times that as soon as the day comes, and conditions arise for them to unite, they will give themselves away to each other completely? This moment had just arrived: they enjoyed both Henut's parents' blessing, and Suti-mes finally had the position that provided him with the means to start a family. However, the most important was love, which did not expire in them - he was absolutely sure of this one thing. So, what is going on? Did Henut instantly decided to go to the temple first and to declare their will in the presence of the priest, and then to write the marriage papyrus? Suti-mes had reasons to doubt it. In the letters she sent to him during this long parting, Henut was leaving no doubts that she wanted him and intended to join him as soon as the separation would end. Buteh-Amun told him that sometimes he even had a blush on his cheeks when the girl in love was dictating with a passionate voice her letters to Suti-mes. No, it was certainly not the wedding formalities what was her point; after all, hardly any couple is waiting for papyrus to realize their passion. Anyway, if that was the case, she would simply say it to him directly. But Henut said something else…

What do these words mean, uttered with unconcealed despair in voice and with tears: "I don't want you would come to hate me"? How could he come to hate her? For what? What could she do? Maybe she hurt somebody? But it is unlikely, because there is only goodness in her…Or maybe she committed a crime? But what significance could it have for their love? He wouldn't stop loving her or wanting her, even if he knew she had killed someone. His love for Henut was no longer a lamp or even a torch that could be extinguished; it is a fire that will last in his heart as long as life! So, what happened, for Amun, in the heart of Henut?! Thoughts like lightning flashed through his mind, unanswered questions were multiplying.

Suti-mes started to walk slowly the same wat they came from. The living successive images were appearing before his eyes, in which he could initially only see his happiness. Here they were still running, and here Henut asked him to kiss her. He turned into the path they were following from the house of Djehuty-mes, and here, near the junction of the roads something told him to stop because a disturbing note began to fight in his memory for being taken into consideration. He closed his eyes, reproducing every word of his conversation with Henut, and then he suddenly realized that it was here, when he had asked her about the house visible from afar, partly obscured by the wall surrounding the great temple of His Majesty Amen-hotep Neb-Maat-Re; Henut reacted then somehow strangely. He directed his steps mechanically towards this very large and imposing residence, or rather a palace. As Suti-mes was approaching, the high whitewashed wall surrounding the yard, where palm trees grew was more and more obscuring the house and, finally, only the wall itself and the solid gate with as many as four *medjayu* were visible. Somebody very important had to live here.

Just as he approached, a small wicket in the gate opened, and a short man came out. He was dressed in an elegantly draped robe, as befits a holiday, but this was contrasted by the lack of a wig. In a sense, this lack deprived him of the dignity served by his robe, especially since the man had a bald head, and on its back a tuft of protruding hair, which gave him a ridiculous look.

Suti-mes came up, bowed and greeted the man, then asked: "Can you give me an information, Lord, who lives in this house?"

The man, who quite casually bowed back in greeting and made an impression that he was in a hurry somewhere, and no conversation interested him, has stopped now and a huge surprise combined with disbelief has been shown on his face. He narrowed his bulging eyes to better see the face of the questioner, almost learning it by heart, he was silent for a moment, and then answered with a question, "And who are you, young man, that you ask such a question?"

"I'm Suti-mes in the service of High Priest of Amun," the young man replied. "I haven't been in the City for a long time and I don't remember this house, hence my question, but if you find it tactless, I'm sorry."

"Of course, not! Your long absence in Waset perfectly explains why you don't know something that all locals know about! But where have you sojourned that you haven't been here for so many years?" the man asked another question, which Suti-mes answered again, not hiding some pride in his voice.

"I served the noble First Servant Amen-hotep, justified, and I was dogging his footsteps when he was in Iunu, and now that he's dead, I came back."

"So, he died... I didn't know that," the man's gaze now drifted from Suti-mes' face to his chest, where the golden flies were shown. "I can see that I am dealing with a hero. Could you repeat your name?"

"Suti-mes."

"Ah, right: Suti-mes," the mysterious man has recited, and only now he has deemed it appropriate to introduce himself, "I'm Pa-neb in the service of the venerable Pa-Shu-uben, in front of whose house you are standing. Will you come in? My master would certainly enjoy the visit of such a distinguished person..."

"No, Pa-neb, I can't do it now, maybe another time," the young priest replied, who only now realized that this Pa-neb had actually questioned him closely, as in an investigation. He has recalled his meeting with Pa-Shu-uben years ago, just before departure to Ipet-sut, where he was almost murdered. Then, he thought, Pa-Shu-uben served Pa-nehsi, and today he is still in his position, despite Pa-nehsi was regarded as an enemy of the Both Countries. Apparently, every authority needs such people. Now Pa-Shu-uben is probably the "ear" of Heri-Hor in his capacity as Vizier, while making sure that he knows everything that is happening in the City. In any case, Suti-mes did not miss a meeting with this not very cultural, but extremely cynical man, as he remembered him then.

He also quickly said goodbye to Pa-neb, who, admittedly, had been in a hurry, but now he was staying in front of the gate for a long time, watching which direction Suti-mes was headed, and then went back to Pa-Shu-uben's house. He walked quickly through the yard and came up to the *medjayu* guarding one of the entrances leading to the interior of the house.

"I have to see the venerable Pa-Shu-uben again," he said, then went in and then reached the first floor, while jumping over per two steps up the stairs. Breathless he walked up to the door, before which another pair of guards stood, and repeated the same sentence to them, and then one of them came in, and after a moment appeared again, indicating to Pa-neb with his head's movement that he could enter.

Pa-Shu-uben, who was sitting by the window, sipping a drink made of the *cucu* that is the *mama* palm's fruit, has eyed the entering man with a reluctant look, "Really, I don't have a moment of peace because of people like you... Did you forget something?" he dropped a question while looking through the window.

"Noble Pa-Shu-uben, I have just learned that the High Priest Amen-hotep is dead," Pa-neb quickly said the sentence, seeing that the dignitary was not very favorably disposed towards him.

"Finally!" Pa-Shu-uben murmured, always eyeing the courtyard of his home, "Who told you about that?"

"A given Suti-mes who served him!"

"Suti-mes?" Pa-Shu-uben turned his head to the speaker. He frowned and started rubbing his forehead with hand, as if trying to recall something. "There was once one, but he is dead. Another thing is that it may be someone with the same name. Pa-nebs, for example, are so numerous like dogs..." he dropped ironically a remark to his subordinate, who humbly bowed his head. Still, the message has sparked off a slight unease in the dignitary. "Where did you meet him?"

"Here, at the gate of your home. He hooked me up and asked who lived here which immediately seemed suspicious to me, and then he said that he had not been in the City for several years, only stayed in Iunu. Oh, one more thing: he was wearing the golden flies order!" Pa-neb noticed with satisfaction that his story intrigued the boss, who even got up and began to walk around the room.

"Golden flies, you say... Hmm, it's interesting, but does it matter? After the war, they were granting such orders, probably hardly anybody lacks it. But a few years of absence... Listen, you have to find him and bring him to me!"

"I tried to invite him, but he got away," said Pa-neb.

"If so, he probably doesn't want to meet me, and that's already interesting… If he's the same… No, it's rather impossible, but it is necessary to check it out; he could cause us a lot of harm…" Pa-Shu-uben was talking to himself as if Pa-neb was not here, but suddenly he stood in front of him, patted his shoulder and smiled, "Thank you for your vigilance. Follow him and my reward will not pass you by!" he said. Pa-neb beamed. He bowed in a low bow and left cheerful.

Pa-Shu-uben promised him a prize, and he needs it so badly! Having passed the gate, he started instantly walking quickly in the same direction as Suti-mes left. After a while, it seemed to him that he was seeing his silhouette. He started running and soon he had no doubt that the man walking ahead was the one he was about to follow. Than he slowed down.

Meanwhile, the young priest, walking slowly toward the house of Djehuty-mes, returned to his previous thoughts. He already knew that it was the house of Pa-Shu-uben or he himself that had caused the unpleasant memories to Henut…Then he has recalled another scene and he has clapped his hands with satisfaction that he solved the difficult puzzle." Of course! After all, it was the same man who had come to Henut's parents' home with the false news of Amen-hotep's alleged tax ordinance, which caused all the fatal exchange of opinions and the outbreak of Djed-Mut-iuf-ankh's anger. It was Pa-Shu-uben who made their separation! But why did Henut run away today? Trying to no avail to find any reasonable answer to this question, Suti-mes found himself again near the house which he and Henut have recently left in a cheerful mood.

"Hello Friend!" he heard the voice of Buteh-Amun and after a while became enveloped in his embrace. "My father told me that you went out to meet me; which way were you going?" he asked. "Or maybe you didn't want us to meet too soon?" Suti-mes saw a mischievous smile in his friend's eyes.

"But we really wanted to, we just decided to bypass the brewery, because it seemed there was unpleasant," Suti-mes explained, and Buteh-Amun confirmed it.

"Indeed, it was! You did well. When we were passing nearby, Pa-du-Amun, the owner of the pub, shouted terribly at several drunks and told them to clean up; the fight almost happened. It was then that we had to pass each other. But," Buteh-Amun lowered his voice almost to a whisper, "tell me, for Amun, what happened next? Henut came back from this walk crying and she is still sobbing, not wanting to talk to anyone. She locked herself in her room and not even Hereret or Shed-em-dua can get in. What did you do to her, Suti?"

"What did I do to her? I kept saying that I loved her and that I was happy, she was saying the same thing. It seemed to me that the sky was just opening for me, when she stiffened, pushed me away, started to cry and ran away, and additionally she told me that she didn't want that I would come to hate her! Do you understand anything of this because I can't? What did I do to hurt her?" Suti-mes looked straight into the friend's eyes, and his eyes were so honest that Buteh-Amun had no doubt he was telling the truth.

"I think, I do understand," he replied. "You didn't hurt her, but you have awaken very bad memory."

"Did she kill someone? Even then, I would love her the same..."

"She didn't kill, though maybe she should have to..." Buteh-Amun realized that he couldn't keep his friend in ignorance anymore. "I did not tell you everything, so, that you would not needlessly torment yourself, but I see that the old demons are still napping in Henut's memory. She has to bring them out and tell you about it herself and she will definitely do it because she really loves you. But give her some time and don't go to her today. Come back here tomorrow, Suti," Buteh-Amun put his both hands on his friend's shoulders, "preferably in the company of someone who is a "coming in" priest[134] and has the qualifications of a judge - you know many of these in Ipet-sut. You should get married with Henut as soon as possible, that's my heartfelt advice. Don't worry about her; I've been married for several years, so, I know women and their moods better than you. Everything will be fine, but don't delay!"

"Talking to you and your father is like medicine; you have to heal me for the second time," Suti-mes said, touched. "I will come for sure! And when you see her..."

"I probably won't see her today; she still has a large supply of tears..." the friend interrupted him. "I'll walk you a bit."

---

[134] Not all priests had the right to enter the sanctuary.

They headed toward the entrance to the district of His Majesty Ramesses, where once stood a great stone gate with a palace.

"Unfortunately, we will never rebuild it," Buteh-Amun pointed at the sad remains of the former fortress tower, and then he saw something strange. In their recess a man stood, pressed against the wall and hidden in the shade, whom they would have certainly not noticed, if Buteh-Amun had not started talking about the former Western gate ruined by Pa-nehsi. The man was no doubt looking at them before, though he turned his head now, and pretended to look at the sky. Buteh-Amun winced in disgust. "Do you know him?" he asked, pointing the man out with a movement of his head. Now Suti-mes looked at the man and recognized him instantly.

"Yes, this man, I think, Pa-neb, was talking to me today when I asked him who had built this new house behind the temple of Amen-hotep Neb-Maat-Re."

"Suti," Buteh-Amun became serious and lowered his voice, "stay away from this rat! He is a nasty type, a hunting dog in Pa-Shu-uben's service, and this one is the worst of all, but unfortunately, powerful one. Once he had gained the trust of King Ramesses, then he served Pa-nehsi, and now it seems that he is useful for Heri-Hor too. He has terribly "long hands" and it is better not to fall foul of him."

Suti-mes has recalled Henut pulling him away from Pa-Shu-uben's house and refusing to talk about him.

"Did this Pa-Shu-uben hurt Henut?" he asked, looking Buteh-Amun straight in the eye, and this one has nodded silently.

"I'll kill him!" Suti-mes has drawled his words, but the friend, taking his shoulders again and looking into his eyes, said very seriously, "Don't even think about it, he's too powerful. You guessed it, it's him who had did her wrong, but it was a long time ago. Now, leave the bills to God. The most important thing is that you met Henut and nothing shall separate you now!"

Suti-mes was not answering for a long moment, and there was a real fight in his mind. Finally, however, he smiled at his friend and said, "You are right; not all bills have to be settled on the earth. I don't care Pa-Shu-uben, it's important that Henut would want me! I will come back tomorrow, tell her that nothing in the world will change my heart, and... let her get ready for the wedding!"

He walked briskly toward the harbor without looking back. Buteh-Amun stood for a long moment and watched until his friend's silhouette disappeared around the bend. Then he saw Pa-neb again, who apparently followed Suti-mes.

"Why is he following him?" he murmured. "One thing is certain; he doesn't do it on his own. On his own initiative, he only goes to "sisters," he thought.

Pa-neb was a regular visitor to the house of prostitution in Khefet-her-neb-es. He was also the object of common mockery because in the beer house he used to boast about his night-time successes, telling in detail about these visits, which earned him the nickname "Bull." Some people expanded it maliciously, and knowing the function of Pa-neb were saying of him: "Mighty Bull Nasty in Waset"[135], as probably all men in the Western City knew except him. Now, he was toddling with small steps behind Sutimes while "walking" him to the harbor. The young priest went to the place where two boats belonging to Buteh-Amun swayed on the water, talked to the captain for a moment, then he got on and the boat, heading diagonally across the river, has sailed to Ipet-sut. Then Pa-neb returned to Pa-Shu-uben and gave him an account.

The dignitary pondered, "Since he is friend of Buteh-Amun, he may actually be the same man whom he, Pa-Shu-uben together with Pa-nehsi sent some time ago to the Great Gate Overseer, Pen-nesti-tawy, with an obvious command. How did it happen that he is alive? Did Pen-nesti-tawy fail then?" Pa-Shu-uben considered something for a moment, then wrote a few sentences on papyrus and handed it to unfortunate Pa-neb while ordering him to go a long way again to the harbor and to get to Ipet-sut. There he had to contact with Pen-nesti-tawy and to give him the letter and then to bring back the answer. It was getting dark when the tired Pa-neb reported again to his superior, while bringing him a surprising piece of news: he could not deliver the letter, because, as it turned out, the Overseer of the Great Gate had been arrested yesterday unexpectedly.

Pa-Shu-uben became very anxious about this. He was walking quickly around the room and was pondering on the recent events that had disturbed his comfortable and stable life. There was no

---

[135] An allusion to a well-known term from the Pharaoh's Thutmose III titulature: "Mighty Bull, Shining in Waset". There are known cases of occasional change of name; during the trial of people involved in the assassination of Ramesses III, the name of one of the defendants from "Shining in Waset" was changed to "Nasty in Waset".

doubt that the young priest who had come to the City was the same Suti-mes whom they with Pa-nehsi had decided to remove forever several years ago. In some incredible way this well-connected youngster stood alive. The Overseer's arrest is the best demonstration that he has a good memory, too. What happens, if Pen-nesti-tawy, while interrogated with a stick, also recalls who told him to "escort by an atypical way" some uncomfortable witnesses who were going to complain to Amen-hotep? And, if Suti-mes still confirms this, then…If he confirms…"

Pa-Shu-uben stopped in front of Pa-neb, who was standing humbly, waiting for a new command, and only secretly hoping that he would not have to go to the river for the third time today.

"You must make this Suti-mes arrested, for anything, such as taking part in a row. Let *medjayu* bring him to me then!" he said loudly, and in his mind he outlined the picture of further events until he smiled at these, although Pa-neb understood that the Boss was smiling at him, the more when he heard, "Pa-neb, I remember what I have told you about the reward. You really deserve a half of it just now. You will get the second half if you make me to see here this rascal, of whatever accused. I know you can handle it; I believe in your abilities!"

The low bow of the glad servant was accompanied by a warm assurance, "Thank you, Lord! I will do everything to please you!"

The darkness of the evening had fallen long since, so it was high time to go to the "sisters." Pa-neb lived near the house of Pa-Shu-uben, who after all wished to have him always at hand. It was a poor house, or rather a half-mud hut made of bricks, silt and palm trunks, covered with reeds. While entering, he stumbled, as usual, on the threshold and sweared, than lit a lamp. In the last room, where was the mat he used to sleep on, he knelt down and, just in a case, looked around as if fearing that someone might be watching. He rolled up the mat, and moved away a board covering a hole under the floor, then carefully took out a clay pot. Having taken off the lid, he looked around again, then spilled the contents of the pot onto the floor: there were three pairs of earrings and two copper bracelets, some *herset*-stone beads threaded on a string, a few rare shells, and a dozen small things: bone rings, faience amulets and some single beads, including two of blue *khesebedj*-stone[136] and even one of gold. For a long moment he was enjoying the sight of his treasure, but then he has got blue, as he had to make a choice, what to reduce it by.

"That's not good, I have less and less of it and the "sisters" are getting more and more demanding. Well, but Pa-Shu-uben will reward me soon," he muttered and finally he took one nice copper earring and a bead of the red stone, and having carefully collected everything else, he hid it in his secret place. He stroked his spiky hair with his hand and headed for the "sisters" house, which stood a bit out-of-the-way of Khefet-her-neb-es, on the road leading to the former craftsman's town, now deserted.

It was a two-story, quite prosperous building, located under a group of tall palm trees and partly built of large amphoras embedded in brick walls, which gave it a special, decorative appearance. In some windows, there were flashes of animal fat

---

[136] The ancient Egyptian names quoted here are relating to the valuable minerals: the red carnelian and the blue lapis-lazuli.

lamps, sometimes laughter was coming from there, and in one room someone was strumming the lute. Pa-neb opened the gate, entered the yard and pushed the low door leading to the narrow vestibule, behind which was a small internal courtyard with palm trees, under which there were several low tables and numerous mats. A few young women sat there, sipping wine and a cool drink from the *cucu* fruit and biting cookies filled with dates.

At the sight of the man coming in one of them - the oldest, characterized by very abundant shapes, apparently acting as superior, exclaimed, "look, girls, whom Hat-Hor sent us today! This is our friend Pa-neb! Today is a holiday, so, I guess you'll be particularly generous today, won't you?"

"Hello, Aset!" answered the slightly embarrassed guest, "Do you always have to make fun of the poor man, who is guided here only by the friendship reasons and the longing for yours and the sisters' beauty? I think that at such a holiday of love, when even Amun joins in bed with his wife, there are "sisters" who should be particularly generous and share their beauty for free..."

Aset and other girls burst out laughing, and Aset poured some wine into a cup and she said to Pa-neb, while handing it to him: "The wine is free today in the City, so it can't be differently here, but you have to pay for everything else!"

Pa-neb has drunk the contents of the cup, has wiped his mouth with his hand and has drawn out a red bead from his tunic pocket. "I have not forgotten you, Aset, please take this and join the other decorations of your beautiful neck!"

He handed her a bead and she smiled, because the *herset*-stone was highly valued and such a bead could be worth two *deben* of copper, but she made a grimace on her face and answered with a disappointment in her voice, "It's nice of you to remember about me and of course I will give you a girl, but if I were in her place, I could stroke your bald spot at most for this bead. I hope you have something special for her."

Pa-neb took a bundle out of his pocket, but he did not show its contents, only made a sly face and said, "How could you doubt? When she sees it, she won't stop loving me all night! Is Nofret free?"

"Undoubtedly she is waiting for you from the morning," Aset murmured and left, and after a while came back with a black-haired girl with curls, large eyes and eyelashes painted thickly black.

"Nofret, here is your admirer who promised to make you happy on this special day," said Aset, but the girl didn't seem to be particularly pleased.

"Come!" she has dropped a short remark and started going up the creaking stairs to the first floor, without looking back at Pa-neb. In a small room they had entered, apart from the low wide bed in the middle, there were only a few appliances. In the corner was a pitcher of water and a bowl, and in another corner a small stove with glowing coals. Nofret, right after entering the room, threw off her dress, so that bracelets, a necklace of a single string of faience beads and the wig only remained on her naked body. "Wash yourself!" she instructed Pa-neb, pointing to him the corner with the bowl and the water jug. She took with fire tongs a few red glowing coals, put these on a copper bowl, and then threw a handful of herbs at them, which began to smoke, filling the room with a thick fragrance. Now, she put on the bowl a clay vessel resembling an inverted funnel with a hole at the very top through which the smoke began to come out. She crouched as if bestriding its pointed end so that the smoke started to enter her interior. Then she took a mirror and lipstick and while she was fumigated for a long while, she painted her lips.[137] Finally, she got up and walked up to Pa-neb.

"What do you have for me?" she asked briefly, and he took out the copper earring and gave her it with a smile; he knew that she would like this gift. Indeed, Nofret smacked her lips with satisfaction, though she added: "It's nice, but only one, so I don't think I can use it."

"You'll get a second one tomorrow," said Pa-neb, "If you are pleasant to me today!"

"How should I be pleasant to you?" she asked while stowing the earring away.

"On the chariot..." he expressed his hidden desire and she laughed. Indeed, down stairs in the inner courtyard, was an old broken chariot standing in the corner, which from time to time became the object of interest for the customers of this house, bored with the uniformity of experiences and seeking original sensations.[138]

---

[137] This is documented with a scene on the so-called *Erotic Papyrus* preserved in the Egyptian Museum in Turin. It seems that the procedure described here had for purpose the contraception.

[138] The drawing showing the couple copulating on the chariot is on the *Erotic Papyrus*, stored in the Egyptian Museum in Turin.

"On the chariot only when you bring me a second earring" she said.

"You're cruel!" Pa-neb groaned, but at the moment he would agree to everything, so without extending the waiting time, he pushed Nofret towards the bed.

Meanwhile, Suti-mes returned to Ipet-sut with a firm resolution that he should take Buteh-Amun's advice absolutely. He has to persuade a priest having permission to enter the sanctuaries and to confirm the will being expressed in the face of God to go with him to the West City tomorrow and to witness a vow of loyalty to each other, which he and Henut were to take. He had no doubt that he would convince his girlfriend of the strength and stability of his feelings, he only was not sure who would be willing to go with him to Khefet-her-neb-es. He decided, as usual, to ask Amen-em-Ipet for advice, but the old priest was very busy today, and when Suti-mes arrived to his house at the High Priest's palace, he didn't catch the dignitary in. He was told that Amen-em-Ipet was at Heri-Hor, but several hours elapsed before the old priest appeared. It was obvious that he was tired and subdued, and had Suti-mes not greeted him loudly, he would probably not have noticed him at all

"Ah, it's you, my friend!" Amen-em-Ipet replied and a smile lit up his furrowed face. „How was your day? I don't notice a joy in your eyes, and yet you have been waiting for this holiday with great hopes."

"I see that nothing can be hidden from you. Indeed, unexpected clouds obscured my clear sky and I hope you will help me to disperse them. But before I'll tell you about my troubles, please, disclose me the reason for your concern, which is painted in your eyes and on your face," Suti-mes took the old priest's hand, looking at him anxiously.

"Well," Amen-em-Ipet nodded, "I think I wasn't the only one who took away a concern from the royal palace today. Heri-Hor is seriously ill, that we have observed for some time. After returning from today's procession, he had another similar attack of breathlessness and pain that you witnessed yourself yesterday. This time, unfortunately, it lasted much longer, and this attack was probably the strongest one since the disease came to light. The doctor absolutely tells him not to leave his bed for at least 10 days, until the beginning of the third month, when the second part of the ceremony will take place and Amun will return to Ipet-sut. But the High Priest is stubborn, he says as always that it's just a temporary indisposition, and he doesn't like to stay in bed. I am afraid that we won't be able to keep him lying for the entire ten days, especially since the guests from Djanet announced their arrival: Pi-nodjem – the brother of the Queen Nodjmet with his wife Henut-tawy and two children. Of course, they would understand the situation, but Heri-Hor will definitely want to show them everything personally, to boast of how much has already been rebuilt. That is what I am afraid of: he will fully re-enter all activities and the doctor's recommendations will remain only a wish... Anyway, although he keeps saying that 'the City residents must see him as full of strength and healthy', I forced him today into the shortening of the ceremonies on the day of the great return from Ipet-resit; maybe he'll get a little less tired thanks to this. Well, but now that you already know the reasons for my clouds, explain to me yours. I guess, it's a girl, isn't it? Would it have been that, contrary to what you expected, her feeling for you lost its power?"

"Thanks to Amun, nothing like that happened. She loves me and I love her, but something else must have happened: some clouds have appeared in her heart, too. She wanted to be with me - I know that for sure - but she unexpectedly ran away crying, telling me something that makes no sense at all, namely that she doesn't want me to come to hate her... I lay down my life for her... I love her like Hat-Hor, like Maat. Buteh-Amun told me that she had suffered some harm from Pa-shu-uben, but I don't care about this jerk... I want to give her my heart, joy and home, but how can I do it away from her? I want to marry her right now, tomorrow, and Buteh-Amun is also urging me to do this, but he tells me to bring someone to Khefet-her-neb-es for this. Could you recommend someone to me and support my request that he would cross over there with me tomorrow and go to her home, that is, to the house of Djehuty-mes? There, we'd write the wedding papyrus and I'd declare my love in a temple in his presence. I am begging you, my friend, help me, my life is a stake here! You surely know someone like that!" Suti-mes stopped talking and as if in a silent begging he has sunk his sight into the wrinkled face of Amen-em-Ipet.

The old priest smiled, but his face remained morose. "I know someone like that," he said after a moment's reflection. His name is Amen-em-Ipet and he disposes of all the permissions..."

Suti-mes did not believe his own ears. "You, my friend, would make me such a grace yourself, despite the fact how busy you are and how much the King needs you?" he asked quietly, at the same time feeling unspeakable joy and relaxation, which filled his heart like a balm.

"That's true," Amen-em-Ipet said, "I have many duties, and Heri-Hor may need me, but not tomorrow because he was given a strong medicine and will sleep all the day. For the sake of my friendship with you, and also of the memory of my friendship with Amen-hotep, justified, for whom you have done so much, I'll go to Khefet-her-neb-es and will marry you, because I promised you that when we saw each other in Iunu. Could you have had a worse memory than is mine? On that occasion I'll pay a visit to another my old friend - Djehuty-mes, because I haven't seen him for a long time. Finally, I'll do it yet for another reason. If, as I heard, Pa-Shu-uben is somehow involved in it, then it may actually your life be a stake here, although differently than you think. It was him who, before Heri-Hor, vouched for Pen-nesti-tawy that he was a good and honest man and that one, at the same time, wanted to kill you. Perhaps Pa-Shu-uben had something to do with that assassination attempt, so he shouldn't find out about that you are safe and sound. Your every trip to the Western City is risky for you, remember that! But as I see that nothing in the world can stop you from visiting this girl, so indeed, it would be the best if you are married and live together preferably on this side of the river. In Ipet-sut, of course, it's impossible, but we'll find something for you, although it will probably take a few days."

Suti-mes grabbed the old man's hand and pressed it to his forehead and heart. "How will I return the favor" he whispered, being moved.

"Have you already forgotten that you are to help me at the monument for Amen-hotep? Compose a text that, to your mind, should be engraved there, think about its arrangement, and in this way, you will help me a lot."

Suti-mes embraced his friend and gave him a warm hug, "You are like a father and a mother in one person for me! They are both already in the Fields of Offerings.[139] I'll write a letter to them still today and I'll tell them about it!"

In fact, right after returning to his apartment, Suti-mes took a scroll of blank papyrus, he cut off a piece of it and having taken his scribe's palette wrote a letter. The title and all the names mentioned there, as well as the last sentences were written in red ink, while the remaining text he wrote in black.

To the Akh[140] of the noble Pa-di-Amun and the Akh of the noble Ankh-iri from their son, the Servant of Amun in Ipet-sut, Suti-mes. Greetings to you! May the offerings that the King gives to Osiris the First of the Western Ones, to Anubis on His Mount and to all the divine images in the south, north, west and east come also to you from them! Let them give you thousands of loaves, jugs of beer, beef, poultry, robes, fragrant oils, and let these offerings be multiplied during all holidays! Let your Ba go out freely to see how well your son is doing, who thinks about you every day! Behold, love is in my

---

[139] Another name for paradise.

[140] The term defines a blessed deceased who, being a divine form, shines like the sun. The text of Suti-mes letter has been arranged in the shape of a letter to the deceased, also containing one of the versions of the so-called offering formula, found in tombs and on various objects of grave equipment.

heart! I love Henut – the daughter of Djed-Mut-iuf-ankh, justified, and of Hereret. Henut is a good girl. Give your protection for her and for me! Make also that the health and prosperity do not leave the noble Amen-em-Ipet, the Second Servant of God in Ipet-sut, neither Buteh-Amun, the Necropolis Scribe, nor his father Djehuty-mes, nor his wife Shed-em-dua, nor his children, nor Nes-Mut - the brother of Henut, nor her mother!*

Suti-mes put the feather aside, read everything again, then rolled up the papyrus and put it into a small vessel he had prepared in purpose to take with him tomorrow and to place it at his parents' grave. He recited now a hymn to Osiris – the Lord of the night sky, because it was already night, and then he went to bed with his heart filled with hope again.

CHAPTER XXI

Pa-neb woke up late. The barge of Re has almost reached the highest point in the sky, where not even a smallest cloud appeared, it was also hot. His head ached and he was feeling a terrible thirst. He was barely getting out of memory the images of the previous day, and especially of the last night. Some of these memories were pleasant: Nofret paid him back generously for that copper earring, and even gave him an advance for the second one, he promised to bring her tonight. Her body was supple and was adapting easily to the most elaborate postures, and she promised him a chariot... But in addition to these good things, also worse were remembered, and the picture when he is lying on the floor completely exhausted, and Nofret mocks his inability[141] while laughing at him, Pa-neb, whom people call "Bull" was

---

[141] This is a description of yet another illustration from the Turin *Erotic Papyrus*.

stinging him with a painful shame. When he decided to get stronger through wine, which was free yesterday, he quickly lost all his strength and he remembered little what happened later. He awoke in the yard, lying next to the chariot and, like it, unable to ride. From there he somehow dragged himself home, but he must have fallen down on the way, because his leg hurt, and he discovered that he had a huge bruise on his thigh.

Damning his fortune, Pa-neb headed straight to the beer house. He had to have a drink to put out the heat in his stomach and of course, he knew that he had to do it in moderation, because the main purpose of the visit was different, after all. At this time, when no reasonable person drinks beer, in the beer house mainly the people could be met, who were hardly leaving this place, every day passively waiting for an event that would diversify their drab existence and to which they could return later with a short recollection. Pa-neb cared about meeting such people; he remembered perfectly what a commission he had received from Pa-Shu-uben. When he entered the dark room, where the overwhelming aroma of beer was mixed with the smell of roasted barley pies, a few heads turned to him, and he heard words of greeting: "Hello, Bull! What are you doing here so early?"

He had not yet answered, when someone else, who was undoubtedly familiar with his lifestyle, asked directly about what Pa-neb used to brag of, although he would rather not talk about it today.

"How many times have you been a bull that night?"

Pa-neb emptied the mug of beer, then grinned and replied, "I don't remember: four or five times…"

"Oh, not bad, can you tell us more?" pushy person asked.

"Why, do you envy me? You could also try someday," Pa-neb retorted, but then he heard another voice he knew, "For what? I can hardly afford a beer!"

Pa-neb moved closer to the one who uttered the last sentence – a strong and well-muscled man and he intentionally lowered his voice, "I'd have a gravy for you, Arsu! My lord Pa-Shu-uben always pays well."

"Is that so?" answered the other one, "Would your master, whom everyone knows well, not have enough servants for such tasks? I am not going to beat or kill anyone!"

"But who's talking about such things?" Pa-neb felt his bait start working, "To beat? To kill? What came into your head, Arsu? It's just a matter of jogging someone and then shouting - the *medjayu* will appear immediately to arrest him: he is a very dangerous criminal, the enemy of our King!"

At that moment, another pub guest interrupted, who was sitting in a corner of the room, but who could hear everything perfectly.

"Arsu, don't be stupid! If that's the point, as the Bull says, then I'll do it, too, even though I don't have your muscles."

Pa-neb immediately picked up the thread, "Of course, you both are great, and you can both earn if you want to go to the "sisters" once!"

Arsu very much wanted to go to the "sisters", and, at the same time did not want that his friend would consider him stupid. Besides, what Pa-neb wanted from him actually seemed easy and it didn't conflict with Maat. That he would push someone? A lot of people can jostle someone in the crowd, especially on such occasions as a holiday or a trading day? That he will scream? What's wrong with that! Many people scream. He shrugged, finished his beer and said in a firm voice, "Well, I'm coming with you!"

"Me too!" added his companion.

Both of them were ready to act immediately, and Pa-neb had to reassure them now that he did not yet know where and when they would take action.

"Stay here, drink beer and wait for me to come for you" he said, then came over to the innkeeper and whispered that for those two, Pa-Shu-uben will pay for beer, provided that they won't get too much beer and won't get drunk. He went out and sat in the shade under the wall of the temple of Ramesses User-Maat-Re Meri-Amun, while beginning to watch closely the entrance to the house of Djehuty-mes. He did not know how long it would take him to wait, but he was convinced that he would not wait pointlessly.

Suti-mes did not sleep well that night if one could say at all that he was sleeping. All the time the images of the previous day were appearing before his eyes, he relived every moment, he heard every word of Henut and his own so that everything was arranged, like a charming dream animated by the sight of the figure of Henut, the smell of her hair, the touch of her hand, the taste of her mouth and sound of her love spells. But this beautiful image, full of light and color - the image that Suti-mes understood well, always turned into a shapeless, sinister shadow, from which only the crying of the beloved girl came, and this one, completely incomprehensible, meaningless sentence: "I don't want you would come to hate me". Then Henut was running away, Suti-mes was trying to follow her, but he was unable to move. After a while as resulting from a touch of a magic wand, everything was beginning again. In this way, this night, throwing him between feelings of happiness and despair an infinite number of times was a kind of torture and the dawn became a real salvation.

He cleaned quickly up and dressed in a clean new tunic, put on sandals and a wig. For a moment, he hesitated if he should adorn himself with his gold flies' necklace today, but he came up with an idea and put on not only flies but also a gold bracelet with red *herset*-stone decorations, he had been once given by Amen-hotep. He looked not only festively now, but also quite richly, and so he appeared at Amen-em-Ipet, who shook his head and said he had never seen such a chic young man.

"There is no solemn procession, and you look like you are going to the royal court."

"My friend," Suti-mes gave him a broad smile, "This day is for me a thousand times more important than a visit to the royal palace, and after all, we will go to the temple: is not marriage also a meeting with God and His daughter Maat?"

"And these adornments?" – Amen-em-Ipet was not convinced. "Is your love and the white of tunic not enough? You will be different from all the people in Khefet-her-neb-es, and in your situation, as I told you, it's even a little risky."

"Ah, dear friend, let me enjoy them once again only for a few hours," Suti-mes asked, and the old priest just smiled.

"At young people the head and heart aren't a pair so often..."

They boarded soon Suti-mes's boat and crossed the river, then slowly set off into a long walk on a road running among the fields. Few people only were them passing today. All residents of both parts of the City still enjoyed the holiday of Ipet and the opportunity to rest at home. Amen-em-Ipet, who was entitled to both a litter and an accompanying servant with an umbrella, deliberately resigned from both, as well as from his barge, so as not to catch the eye of the services of Pa-Shu-uben, who would otherwise certainly immediately notice the arrival of someone significant and inform him about it. Going on foot they were standing out to a smaller extend, although their white tunics vividly contrasted with the simple hip bands of most men in Khefet-her-neb-es. They looked like priests – after all, they were them – and because there were a dozen or so temples here, they seemed as if they were visiting one of them. Therefore, being not disturbed by anyone, they arrived at the house of Djehuty-mes. Pa-neb obviously noticed their coming; He recognized Suti-mes easily but couldn't remember if he had ever seen another guest coming with him. He decided to keep waiting because he knew that even the longest visit would also end.

"The most important thing is that the bird flew in," he murmured to himself.

Meanwhile, a real holiday reigned in the house of the old Necropolis Scribe. Admittedly, Buteh-Amun told his father that he expected the arrival of Suti-mes in the company of another priest, but no one thought that this guest would be the dignified Amen-em-Ipet himself who was now the Second Servant of Amun!! In addition, such a high temple dignitary, who was only a little younger than Djehuty-mes, came here on foot, neither using the official boat, or even a litter! The hosts' surprise and amazement gave way to their great joy. The chamber with columns, where four men sat down, sipping a cool drink of the *cucu*-fruit and gnawing sweet cookies with dates, since a long time had not heard such a portion of cheerfulness, nor saw so many heartfelt smiles. Djehuty-mes every now and then was shaking hands of his long unseen old friend, repeating how happy he was because of his arrival and that such a visit was like a real medicine for him, after which he immediately felt better. When the conversation turned to the matter of health, Amen-em-Ipet shared his concerns about the condition of Heri-Hor, as well as about the fate of the little Amen-em-ensu, if something happened to his father.

"Pi-ankh hates him, despite the fact that he is his grandson, seeing him as a future rival for his second beloved grandson Ma-sa-harti, son of Pi-nodjem. I don't really know, why he is such an evil man, but luckily his children are more reasonable than him."

"Remember," he said to Suti-mes and Buteh-Amun, "If one day Heri-Hor would die, you can trust both Nodjmet and Pi-nodjem!"

Suti-mes felt like he was sitting on a burning embers during entire conversation. He understood that his friends had not seen each other for a long time, and the visit of such an outstanding guest as Amen-em-Ipet - was an honor for the home and an opportunity to discuss important matters, but the purpose of his visit was still hidden in the depth of this house. Did Henut recover from yesterday's events, is she willing to see him at all, to talk to him, and, most important, will she dare to say the few words about which they both were dreaming for years? That is why he leaned over to Buteh-Amun and, taking advantage of the fact that Amen-em-Ipet and Chari were lively discussing the situation in the City, asked him in a whisper, how does Henut feel and does she know that Amen-em-Ipet is here?

Buteh-Amun brightened his face. "She certainly awaits you. Yesterday she was crying for many hours that is during the first hours she was crying over her old memories, and then only because she was afraid that you would not come back after what she had told you. Of course, she doesn't know that Amen-em-Ipet is here. Come, I will lead you to her!"

Both young men left, followed with the old men's eyes, full of understanding. They entered a small yard in the back of the house, and then went up the stairs to the first floor, where several rooms were located, occupied by women and children. In front of one of the doors Buteh-Amun stood and asked, knocking: "Are you there, Henut-netjeru?"

At the same time, the door opened, and the girl stood there, beautiful as always but now being pale, with dark circles under her eyes as a result of a long crying and with her long black hair falling down in unruly curls on her cheeks. When she saw Suti-mes, in her eyes appeared at the same time the unhidden happiness, and at the same time a confusion that both men, dressed in festive robes, and especially extremely chick Suti-mes, saw her in such a condition. A blush of shame covered her face, she tried to say something as justification, but Suti-mes didn't let her to do.

"Henut, my love – I've never seen you more beautiful!" he said, and without waiting for a reaction and ignoring the presence of Buteh-Amun, he grabbed her head with both hands and began to kiss her eyes in which there were still traces of recent despair. She didn't defend herself much, but a grunting of Buteh-Amun has called them both to order.

"I have brought to you this culprit - wasn't it because of him that you had cried all the night? You have to explain something to each other. But let your "conversation," this word he clearly emphasized, "does not last too long, because our distinguished guest will not wait forever," he added and left.

"What..." Henut began, but Suti-mes did not let her finish, while kissing until the breathlessness, when he had to take a gasp of fresh air again. Henut already knew that his feelings had not changed, but the awareness that she must finally confess to him the reason for her yesterday's behavior removed again from her face the expression of joy that had already managed to appear there for a moment. Suti-mes noticed it immediately and began to speak quickly as if he was afraid that she would run away again, although in these conditions it was not possible.

"Dearest, I know everything, I even know the name of the one who hurt you. God knows my heart in which I swear my revenge to him. But what happened then is insignificant for me now, can you hear it? I love you and I want to be with you until the end of my days. This is the only thing that matters. If you want the same thing, we will become brother and sister today, we'll go to the temple and we'll tell God that we want to be together. There is someone here who has the right to enter and knows the secrets of heaven, earth and the underworld. He came here especially for you and me. Henut, I am begging you, do not refuse my love! I won't let you escape anymore! And don't tell me things like yesterday: I will love you even if I knew you had hurt someone badly!"

"Suti, my love," the girl said in a very serious voice, not looking at him and staring at the floor. "I know that you would forgive me if I hurt a stranger, but I did something worse: I hurt you and that's why all my misfortunes happened to me later. I... I..."

She swallowed hard, finally she stopped looking at the floor and threw out a desperate confession, as if she was jumping into the abyss, "I went under the sycamore trees!" Then she added in a whisper, "I was hungry, my mother and brother were hungry..." and she covered her face with her hands, bursting into tears again.

Suti-mes hugged her and waited for a moment, stroking her hair, "Honey, it was a long time ago, there was a war..."

"I thought you were dead, everyone was thinking so, and he confirmed it," Henut whispered, still sobbing.

Suti-mes understood right now something that had been a mystery to him so far. He already knew why this poor girl who had experienced so many terrible moments was looking for a crocodile herself. After this confession she became even dearer for him. But once Pa-Shu-uben said he knew that he, Suti-mes had been dead, it means that he sent him straight to death at the hands of Pen-nesti-tawy, so Amen-em-Ipet was right! It is obvious that now the living Suti-mes is a dangerous witness to this villain. Suti-mes noticed that this still powerful dignitary, who for incomprehensible reasons always enjoys the trust of the most important people in the City, constitutes a deadly threat to him, and perhaps also to Henut. But he will not tell her about it, especially on such a day. Determination and energy have suddenly possessed the young man: they must be in a hurry, get married and leave to stay possibly farthest from here.

"Henut, look at me," he said with a firm voice, and the girl obediently raised her tearful eyes, which now expressed an anxiety, as the eyes of the accused in court and waiting for the sentence. "Do you really judge me so badly, thinking that I could stop loving you and turn my back on you just because you became a victim of war? On the contrary, I love you even more, I respect you and understand and even I am full of praise for you: I was not hungry not even for one day during the war!"

"So, you really can forgive me that?" Henut felt that her life was coming back to her, just like on that terrible day when she wanted to die, having no hope, and then she learned that her beloved had not died. "So you're not even angry?" she asked, though she already knew the answer.

Now, however, Suti-mes frowned, setting a fake harsh tone to his voice. "I'll get angry soon if you don't quickly get yourself ready for going down to meet Amen-em-Ipet who came here to see you, but smiling one, not in tears!"

"Amen-em-Ipet!" Only now Henut understood who the mysterious guest was. She has never seen him from close range, but she knew perfectly well that he was one of the highest temple dignitaries, the deputy of King Heri-Hor, radiant with the heroic act of defending the sanctuary in Ipet-sut against the revolted Kushite soldiers - everyone in Waset was talking about this for years! It was precisely this great man who came here especially for her and was waiting?

Henut grabbed the mirror, looked and screamed in horror, "How will I show to him up? For Hat-Hor! I have to change, to comb my hair..." Suddenly, she looked at Suti-mes, "But I won't need you for this. Go to him, apologize and wait...brother!"

Suti-mes felt the sky opened for him on the earth: so, she agreed!

"I love you, Henut, my sister!" he shouted so loudly that certainly all the inhabitants of this house could hear it. He grabbed the girl's face again with both hands and sunk into her mouth, then ran out of the room. In two jumps he overcame the stairs, shot across the yard and fell into the chamber with columns. He only calmed down here, while seeing the dignified old men and Buteh-Amun still engaged in the conversation, who interrupted it at the moment, and looked at him.

"One can see that Re looks from your face!" Amen-em-Ipet commented. "You've chosen a good time for your wedding – while imitating Amun. Have you also hired the dancing girls?"

"Only one, but it will not be a public show," the young man replied, causing widespread cheerfulness. Suddenly, Suti-mes became serious, "I have to ask you for advice while she's not here yet. Well, Pa-Shu-uben told her that I was dead. How did he know that? He was the one who sent me to the one who wanted to kill me, so he was a partner of Pa-nehsi. What should I do in this situation?"

"You start thinking like a man finally, because you were just a silly boy until now," Amen-em-Ipet nodded. "I've already told you that every visit you make to this side of the river is risky. One must talk to Heri-Hor about it as soon as possible. It is high time to stop the ruling of Pa-Shu-uben here. But now don't think about him, but about what to tell to your fiancée when you stand in front of the statue."

"She seems to be ready now; she had to be in a hurry," Djehuty-mes added, hearing the voices of several women coming. Indeed, a moment later Henut entered the room, and together with her also her mother Hereret, her brother Nes-Mut and Shed-em-dua - Buteh-Amun's wife, followed by small Ankh-ef-en-Amun.

"Here's what a love spell can do!" Buteh-Amun exclaimed at the sight of Henut, who looked completely different from the moment he saw her upstairs.

Her eye-lashes were painted black, which effectively hid traces of all-night cry. Her own hair fell on the sides of her head with two braids, but on this, she had a wig consisting of small wavy strands, girded over her forehead, she also had a scarf made of very delicate canvas on her elegant robe. Three beautiful lotus flowers adorned her above her forehead,

"She looked so gorgeous that old Djehuty-mes has dropped a remark: "Oh, what a beautiful lifetime is the youth!"

Suti-mes beamed, Amen-em-Ipet and Buteh-Amun did not hide their admiration.

"Dear friend, this is the destiny of my life!" Suti-mes took Henut's hand and led her to the old priest, and Amen-em-Ipet stroked her cheek, saying to the betrothed couple:

"You both have to thank Amun, who tried and rewarded you. Man's destiny always has two faces, and once we see our wrong destiny Shai, and sometimes good one – Renenet. You have already met with your Shai several times, but today, you undoubtedly have the right to talk about Renenet, although only God knows when we will see and which side of what is intended for us. Fortunately, we are not completely powerless towards our Shai and we can fight that it would be as little as possible sensible in our lives, using the prayer as a shield and the love as a spear. I think, children, you won't miss this weapons!"

Henut took the old man's hand and pressed it to her forehead, only able to say with emotion, or rather to whisper, "Thank you!" and Suti-mes, equally moved, repeated the same gesture and word.

"Let's go then!" Buteh-Amun suggested, and they left all together. Pa-neb hidden in the shadow of the temple, has damned silently, seeing how many people accompanied Suti-mes. After all, he decided not to leave his position:

"If this old man is also going with them, they'll probably be back soon," he thought, yawning.

After leaving the gate, they headed the same road heading towards the necropolis. They passed the desert slopes of the hills densely covered with tombs, whose courtyards, shadowy column porticos, white pyramids and colorful carvings were clearly distinguished from the yellow-gray background of sand. When they came to the place where, by the road at the foot of the Hill of Wedding Rites, some large vessels placed on racks and containing always cool water were waiting for the passers-by, they stopped to refresh themselves. Now Henut, accompanied by the other women, climbed a steep path to the top of the hill that she was to encircle three times, and when she did so and made a lettuce offering in the Osiris-Min chapel, Hereret and Shed-em-dua issued this characteristic high modulated sound,[142] which also accompanied yesterday's ceremonies at Amun's barge going to his wedding to Ipet-resit.

At the same time, Suti-mes also climbed the slope of the Hill of Wedding Rites, and at the foot of his parents' grave he placed a vessel with the letter written to them yesterday. He took it out and read it aloud, after which he poured some water on an offering table and he repeated again the wish that Amun would give them life.

"It is a pity that you cannot enjoy my happiness on earth today, but you certainly know that I am happy!" he sighed, then returned to the men and boys waiting below, and after a while women also appeared.

""Look what I have found!" Henut cried out while showing Suti-mes the fossilized mussel's shell brought from above.

---

[142] The wedding custom described here takes place even today on the hill of Sheikh Abd el-Qurna, near Deir el-Bahari. It stems from the local tradition and can go back to ancient times.

"It's life enchanted in stone: it will be a good souvenir of today!" Amen-em-Ipet commented and everyone headed towards the nearby temple of His Grandness Mentu-hotep Neb-hepet-Re and Amen-hotep Djeser-Ka-Re. Temple guards stopped them at the entrance, but when they saw Amen-em-ipet and Djehuty-mes, they greeted them in a friendly manner. Djehuty-mes was well known to them, so when he introduced his distinguished colleague as the one who knows the secrets of heaven, earth and the underworld, they bowed respectfully. Now, Amen-em-Ipet revealed the purpose of his visit, introducing a couple of young people who were going to declare their love before the holy image, which he was to witness. The guards bowed again and let the three of them in, but before they allowed them to cross the small wavy brick wall that marked the boundaries of the sanctified area, the duty priest poured water on their feet and hands to remove the uncleanness of the secular world they came from.

"You are clean, go in peace!" he said and only now Amen-em-Ipet, holding Henut and Suti-mes by hands, started walking towards the temple garden.

On both sides of the ramp leading to the main part of the building crowned with a large pyramid numerous tamarisks and sycamores grew in deep pits cut in the rocky ground. One of the sycamore trees, exceptionally patulous one, was their first target. They knelt and raised their hands in a gesture of adoration, and Amen-em-Ipet said a short prayer:

Hail, Maat, Lady of the North Wind, who lets the breathing of the noses of those who live on earth! Hail, Nut in your sycamore, who feeds those who come to you![143] Oh, Mother Nut, spread

Hyenas & Lotuses

your protective wings over these children: Henut and Suti-mes, and let them never be in short of air, water and food!

They stood up and walked through the trees to a small pavilion composed of three parallel chapels joined by common walls and open towards the garden. In each of them stood a small wooden statue, in front of which they also knelt, begging with Amen-em-Ipet's mouth for protection and support on their common path ahead of them. These sacred images depicted the patron of the western City, His Majesty Amen-hotep Djeser-Ka-Re, justified (popularly called here "Amen-hotep from the Garden"), then his mother – the pious Queen Ah-mes-nefertari, as well as his wife, Queen Merit-Amun.

Now all three turned back and climbed the ramp to the platform on which the temple of His Majesty Mentu-hotep Neb-hepet-Re, justified, was erected, and after passing the pyramid they came to the small temple hidden under the rocks devoted to Hat-Hor – the patron of love and all people in love. In the twilight that covered the main room, they saw the outlines of a wooden statue in the shape of a cow. They fell to their knees again, and Amen-em-Ipet, closing his eyelids, chanted, with a slightly trembling voice, a fragment of the hymn[144]:

Hello, Great Lady of Heaven
who give birth to Re in the morning,

---

[143] This is an authentic text of the prayer to Maat and Nut, known from several sources, including the Hor-em-heb stela at the British Museum in London.

[144] The text presented here is based on the hymn to Hat-Hor, preserved on papyri in the Trinity College library in Dublin, Ireland.

and at dusk you take Atum into your inside,
Mother of every King,
Lady of the West,
Carer of those who live,
those who have not yet been born,
and also those who have rested in peace in You!
Lady who give love
and who surround with love all the people in love,
which you give them life
and make them create a new life,
Good Mother!
Cover with your love and care your children:
Suti-mes and Henut,
who came to you to become brother and sister!

They stood up and Amen-em-Ipet turned to the young ones, "Now join hands and here, before Hat-Hor, and so before the One who is Invisible and in my presence as the one who testifies your words, promise the love to yourself!"

Henut and Suti-mes solemnly took each other's hands and, looking mutually with great affection in each other's eyes, said - each in a slightly different way - what the priest asked for.

"Sister," Suti-mes said, "You know that you are the dearest to me in the world, you are the fulfillment of my dreams and my love, which was not changed by time or distance between Waset and Iunu. I want to be with you for the rest of my life and I want you to give birth to my children. I will always love you and look after you. Amun, you heard!"

"Brother," Henut answered like an echo, "I will always love you too, even if you went as far as Iunu again. I want to be the mother of your children and your wife until the end of my days on earth, and longer. Amun, you heard!"

Amen-em-Ipet approached them, embraced them fatherly and added, "I heard it too. Let it come true!" They returned to those waiting outside the temple.

"Here are the brother and the sister!" Amen-em-Ipet announced and the young people became enveloped in hugs.

"Let's go back!" Djehuty-mes said and went first towards the house.

Pa-neb, who was already starting to worry seriously if it was the right decision not to follow them, heaved a sigh of relief. "They'll probably eat something now, lucky ones," he thought, "but then this young man will finally come out, and the women, kids and this old Djehuty-mes will definitely stay home. I think it's time..." and he quickly went to the beer house, where Arsu and his colleague were still eager for the beer they didn't have to pay today, albeit the innkeeper was rationing it out sparingly.

Meanwhile, at the Necropolis Scribe's house, as Pa-neb had predicted, the women bustled with the meal, while the men surrounded the young spouse who wrote on papyrus that from today everything that he, Suti-mes owns, is also owned by Henut-netjeru. Amen-em-Ipet and Chari signed this document as witnesses. Henut was called and Suti-mes read the wedding papyrus, then removed his gold bracelet from his hand and the gold flies from his neck and adorned his wife with them, said, "Let them serve you from today, sister! This bracelet looks much better on your hand than on mine, and this order - well, I got it, although I wasn't in the first row of those fighting in the battle near Hor-di. It would be due rather to your father, but also to you and your mother, because you were living here during the "year of hyenas", while I have never lacked bread."

"That's very noble of you, Suti-mes," Amen-em-Ipet said, "but don't be so modest! Several times you risked your life for Amen-hotep, and once you only miraculously escaped death; you also deserve the golden flies!"

Henut didn't know what to say; for the first time in her life she wore a gold bracelet, and the gold flies order itself presented a considerable fortune. That day was definitely the happiest in her life and her emotion made her to be on the brink of tears. She was sitting at the meal next to Suti-mes, whom she looked at with great joy and pride every now and then.

However, it got late and Amen-em-Ipet could not postpone his return to Ipet-sut.

"Re is already low and will soon reach the horizon," he said while rising. "I have to come back, because tomorrow I will probably have a busy day. I suppose that our guests from Djanet will reach the City tomorrow, and I do not know what plans Heri-Hor has in connection with their visit and to what extent he will be able to participate in their implementation. I have to be ready for everything. I think, Chari, that you too will be asked to accompany Pi-nodjem when, for example, he wants to go to the Great Valley. I don't mention your son, because it is obvious that he will also be asked for help. It seems that only this lucky Suti-mes can devote himself to his new duties. Just don't lose yourself in them to keep your strength for the second part of the Ipet celebration and remember that Henut also needs to have the strength to hold *sesh-sesh*," he added with a smile, looking at the girl who blushed and lowered her eyes.

"I'll walk you a bit, my friend!" Suti-mes said, and Buteh-Amun also decided to walk. Amen-em-Ipet and Chari said goodbye to each other cordially, after which the three men left and headed to the harbor. At this time a lot of people were again hanging around on the streets of Khefet-her-neb-es, after a period of usual break, most often devoted to an afternoon nap and various market stalls operated again. A barber placed a chair for his customers under a palm tree, a fruit seller, a potter, a milkman also drew up in a line on the main street, and a boy squatting on the ground next to a seller of honey and sweet pies was broiling these pies on the glow while warding off with a fan flies lured by a tasty fragrance. The beer house was very much frequented at this time. The stalls spreading out on the ground and the increased number of passers-by who were stopping by them and bargained for prices meant that the street became narrow in places and only one person could hardly walk there.

Buteh-Amun was going as the first, paving the way for Amen-em-Ipet, by whom Suti-mes was walking. In one of such narrow passages near the beer house, from where several men have just come out, Suti-mes had to stop for a moment because there was no room for the two of them. Amen-em-Ipet has already passed and Suti-mes followed him, when a heavily built man suddenly rolled out straight on him, pushing him so hard that Suti-mes almost fell, bumping into a slim man standing near to him, who smelled of beer drunken in large quantities.

"Forgive me, Lord, I did not want..." Suti-mes said, but the man grabbed his stomach with both hands, and began to moan and to shout loudly that he had been beaten. Suti-mes wanted to pass by him, but at this moment the same broad-shouldered man who almost knocked him down, grabbed him by the tunic and also shouted, "Don't try to run, you rascal! Do you think that when you dressed so elegantly, you are allowed to beat other people?"

Suddenly two tall *medjayu* popped up next to Suti-mes who took his hands and began to lead him sideways. All this happened so quickly that Suti-mes did not even have time to say anything. Anyway, the *medjayu* seemed as if they did not want to hear anything. One of them took wooden stocks from a bag slung over his shoulder and put one Suti-mes's hand in it. When he wanted to put in the second one, the young man began to defend himself, which immediately provoked a second policeman. He strongly pushed Suti-mes, brutally twisting his hand, which he also placed then in stocks.

"You hit people first, then you fight the police?" Pa-neb said who appeared as if out of the blue near Suti-mes. Then, while twisting his face in a cynical smile, he hissed, "You're under arrest for disturbing order during the Ipet Feast."

"Pa-neb, I guess you are not supposing..." Suti-mes began to talk, but Pa-neb was already ordering the *medjayu* to lead the detainee to Pa-shu-uben's house.

At that moment, they heard a loud and firm command, "Stand still! No step!" Amen-em-Ipet, who at first did not realize the situation and went after Buteh-Amun, wanted to say something to Suti-mes, or rather express his surprise that suddenly it got so strangely crowded in this place. He turned but did not see the young man, however noticed that everyone he was passing: sellers, buyers, a barber and even a boy baking pies, stopped their activities and stared somewhere back. Above their heads, Amen-em-Ipet saw policemen and the worst concerns seized him. He pushed the onlookers apart and went forward, where he saw Suti-mes with his hands in wooden stocks, led by two large Kushites; beside him he saw Pa-neb walking with an expression of great joy on his face and then he understood everything.

"Free this man immediately! He is with me and serves me!" he said with a firm voice.

"And who are you, Lord, that you have the right to order policemen who perform their duties?" Pa-neb asked, who had never seen Amen-em-Ipet from close range; he only could observe him sometimes from a distance. He would never have come up with the idea that such a dignitary could go on foot in a narrow street near the beer house in Khefet-her-neb-es.

"This is the dignified Amen-em-Ipet, Second Servant of Amun and the mouth of His Majesty King Heri-Hor!" the loud words of Buteh-Amun sounded, who appeared at that moment, having heard Amen-em-Ipet's voice. Everyone gathered there gave a murmur of surprise and great interest:

"Amen-em-Ipet! So, this is the hero and sage! What is he doing here? What does he look like? Amen-em-Ipet!" The comments were spreading around.

Pa-neb goggled his bulging eyes; the well-thought-out plan began to get unexpectedly complicated: "Forgive me, Lord," he said to the old priest, "But I have never had the luck to see you here. Could I be granted an honor to see – I mean to kiss your ring?"

"I am surprised by your request, Pa-neb. Don't you really know me? I thought you knew all the City's residents. But since you insist – see!" Amen-em-Ipet replied and put under Pa-neb's nose his ring, where his title and name were clearly seen, engraved in hieroglyphs. Pa-neb understood his tactlessness and the sweat suddenly sprinkled his brow. He grabbed the priest's hand to kiss the ring, but Amen-em-Ipet snatched it from him in disgust and again ordered the policemen, "What are you waiting for? Set him free!"

The *medjayu* glanced at Pan-neb, but he looked so terrified that there was no doubt that it was not him, but the old man whom they should listen to, so they removed the stocks from Suti-mes and bowed low, placing their hands on their hearts.

"Let's go!" Amen-em-Ipet dropped briefly and headed towards the harbor, and the two young men on both sides of him. This time they did not need to squeeze by, because the crowd of onlookers parted before them, still whispering admiringly the name of the Second Servant.

"I'm afraid, Suti-mes, you'll have to spend your wedding night alone in Ipet-sut, where you are safe," Amen-em-Ipet said, and turning to Buteh-Amun, he added, "Come back and explain to Henut that the young man did not run away from her. They'll see each other as soon as we arrange a flat on the east bank for them; it will take a day or two."

Buteh-Amun returned home, where a difficult and thankless mission awaited him, and Amen-em-Ipet and the very sad Suti-mes arrived without further adventures to the harbor and then to the great temple of Amun in Ipet-sut.

Meanwhile, the gathering slowly dissolved on the street next to the beer house. For some time, people were still standing in larger and smaller groups, discussing the unusual event and wondering what prompted the great dignitary to come to Khefet-her-neb-es without the litter and servants carrying the sun cover over him. However, they returned slowly to the interrupted activities of selling, buying, shaving and baking pies.

Pa-neb was sneaking home. The horror that he had fell afoul of such a great person as Amen-em-Ipet was slowly giving way to simple anger: what would Pa-shu-uben say? Of course, the award will pass him by, and this Suti-mes will now be on his own guard and it will not be easy to arrest him.

Suddenly someone grabbed his arm. Pa-neb saw Arsu followed shadow-likely by his second companion from the beer house. "We did everything as you ordered. We want our payment!"

"Off with you!" Pa-neb said furiously. "You fouled up the job; you won't get anything!"

"What?!" Arsu shouted. "Did we foul up? Did not you want us to hook him? Has he not been arrested? But people like you are liars! If you come to the beer house again, I will piss to your beer!"

Pa-neb shook for a moment, imagining how heavily muscled Arsu was fulfilling his threat. He wouldn't even have a chance to disturb him... "A terrible day!" he thought. "And I still have to take other earring today to Nofret, because if I lose the sisters' confidence, too, my life will lose the rest of the charm..." and to sweeten today's defeats with something more pleasant, he began to imagine how he would trifle with Nofret on the chariot.

CHAPTER XXII

Very busy days drew on for Amen-em-Ipet. When, after returning from Khefet-her-neb-es, he went to his chambers tired, dreaming only of laying down and sleeping off the exhausting and nervous last few hours he had spent in the Western City, in the vestibule he found a messenger who arrived on horseback from the Min temple in Gebtu, bringing news for King Heri-Hor. The High Priest's servants, following the doctor's instructions, did not allow him to go to the ill man but sent him to the Second Servant of Amun. Amen-em-Ipet expected this messenger, while hoping that he would arrive at least one day later... The envoy confirmed that the distinguished guests: Pi-nodjem – the Queen's brother, and his noble consort, this is the noble wife Henut-tawy and their underage children: Ma-sa-harti and his sister Maat-Ka-Re – are approaching the City, and tonight they have exercised the hospitality of the temple in Gebtu. The old priest just sighed, and on the next morning the preparations for the visit began, which in other circumstances would probably only be a pleasure.

Amen-em-Ipet liked Pi-nodjem very much, although he never had an opportunity to meet in person his wife – the beautiful daughter of Ramesses. Most of the matters related to the guests were to be discussed with Queen Nodjmet: Heri-Hor received strong medications from the doctor, after which he usually slept. Amen-em-Ipet had to admit that the Queen had a very sharp mind and was able to pull out the most important content from each conversation or letter, focusing only on them, and skipping the rest while ensuring that the interlocutor felt not be offended by anything. When she learnt that the guests would be arriving in a few hours, she immediately gave the appropriate orders to the servants, and then began to tick out on her fingers the places in the City and in the surrounding area where to lead the newly arrived so that they could best assess Heri-Hor's several years long regime, and who should be their guide there. Amen-em-Ipet got impression that she was going to spare him, and when he insisted that she would be willing to share her responsibilities with him to a larger extend, she replied that she had reserved the most difficult task for him. "You will be a guide and caregiver of the children of Pi-nodjem, who will definitely perform important functions in the City and Ipet-sut in the future and it would be good if their first contact with this temple and its secrets took place under the guidance of a real master." Having said this she covered with a broad smile her unspoken concern that the old priest would not become tired too much in chariot expeditions, especially in Khefet-her-neb-es. On the one hand, Amen-em-Ipet felt his gratitude, however, on the other one some anxiety, as he had never the opportunity to look after children.

However, it turned out that the unusual task was not as difficult as he thought, nor unrewarding. On the second day of the visit, Nodjmet and her brother and his wife crossed to the opposite shore to see the area of the district of His Majesty Ramesses the Great, now renovated and to Heri-Hor's order, enlarged by numerous new warehouses, while Amen-em-Ipet took five-year old Ma-sa-harti and his two years younger sister Maat-Ka-Re for a walk around Ipet-sut.

First, they went to the great Holy Lake surrounded by trees and bushes, some of which were covered with colorful flowers, among which numerous birds were flying.

"It's so pretty here," the girl's face expressed nothing but admiration, "And we don't have neither such trees nor so many flowers... I would like to live here."

"But this lake is small, and ours near Djanet is large one, and geese are there" – Ma-sa-harti protested. "And grandfather said that when we would grow up, it will be just in Djanet as in the City!"

"But it's cold there while it's warm here," Maat-Ka-Re persisted.

"We've barely left, and I've learnt so much from you about Djanet," Amen-em-Ipet said. "Please, tell me how it is there because I've never been there."

The children began to describe to him, one by one, the scenes they watched every day, and from these small, disorderly sentences the image of the being built city slowly emerged. There were a lot of transport ramps, people carrying baskets of sand walked on them. The construction sites were surrounding by opaque walls. The screams of supervisors accompanying the crews of workers pulling wooden sleighs with stone blocks were heard. Dust was floating everywhere. There was still a lack of the dignified beauty of the lofty temples, and the gardens established only recently on this vast empty hill, surrounding the newly built palaces and houses did not impress with the lush greenery of the slender trees.

"Maybe Pi-ankh is right that in ten or twenty years a large city resembling Waset will be there?" – Amen-em-Ipet thought, and he headed for the Great Hall of Appearances. The children fell silent, and their wide-open eyes and mouths were meaning everything. When they found themselves between the rows of central columns, from above which a scant light was oozing through narrow window openings unable to light up this huge space, filled with columns and dark, by which it seemed even larger, the little Ma-sa-harti asked shyly: "Did God build this house himself?"

Amen-em-Ipet replied seriously, "No, boy, people did it, but they did it for God, and that's why they succeeded." At the same time, he thought that a similar question might have been asked by ambassadors of foreign powers, whom the great pharaohs had previously entertained in the same place. They passed through the Hall of Appearances, and the guards of the gate bowed only in respect, while seeing the Second Servant and let them pass. They were dazzled with daylight again, so that the children narrowed their eyes, but just behind two high obelisks and another gate they found themselves again in the dense twilight lit only by the flickering flame of two lamps standing in front of yet another closed door. There were also guards standing, but again one gesture of Amen-em-Ipet's hand was enough for the door open silently. The small people who liked it very much that subsequent gates were actually "opening themselves" in front of them, now stood and at the same time gave a cry in which delight was mixed with some fear: just before them a huge ram's head wearing a crown emerged from the darkness, being the decoration of the prow of the magnificent User-hat barge shining with gold. Maat-Ka-Re instinctively grabbed the old priest's hand and snuggled into his robe, and he stroked her head, saying reassuringly: "You don't have to be afraid of Amun or of anything that depicts him. You will see in a few days, when the priests will carry this boat on their shoulders that everyone will enjoy it just as people are pleased with a wedding, or when children are born. The Aunt Nodjmet will happily welcome Amun, because it will be his feast."

"Is Aunt Nodjmet the wife of Amun or of Heri-Hor?" Ma-sa-harti asked unexpectedly, and Maat-Ka-Re almost at the same time asked an even more difficult question. "Will Aunt Nodjemet have a baby?"

Amen-em-Ipet was glad that it was dark inside the Barge Hall, for he felt a blush of embarrassment pour over his cheeks. He was a sage, bore the title "the one who knows the secrets of heaven, earth and the underworld," and felt that he was unable to answer these simple questions. Which words should be used so that these smart, but after all young children could understand all the intricacies of religious connections between the celebration of the renewal of life in nature and the renewal of the royal power, to which purpose the legend of the love relationship of Amun and the Queen was serving?"

"These are very difficult matters..." he began, but at the same moment the girl added one more sentence, which was not only a disembarrassment for Amen-em-Ipet, but also an important explanation of her question, and at the same time a piece of news.

"...because my mother will have a baby."

"Ah, that's great news, are you happy?" the old priest eagerly changed the subject, and when he heard the children's affirmation, he leaned toward them and whispered: "We are very close to Amun here, ask him so that your brother or sister would be born healthy!" and was touched while hearing the small voices repeating this request.

"Let's go now, I will show you yet something interesting" Amen-em-Ipet announced, after which they retreated outside the door that was closed "themselves" again behind them.

They now walked along a long wall until the next entrance visible in the distance, which led to a large building with a very complicated layout. When they entered the large hall filled with pillars and columns, little Ma-sa-harti asked, "Is this a tent?"

"You noticed it very well" the priest answered, looking approvingly at the boy. "Yes, this room is a bit like a tent, yet it is made of stone.[145] Special ceremonies are held here in honor of the

---

[145] This is the so-called Jubilee Temple called Ah-menu, erected in Karnak

King, but also in honor of Amun, who comes out of the Land of the Dead and makes everything coming alive and flourishing all over the world."

They just entered a long room with several columns; on its walls, the children saw beautiful, colorfully painted plants, flowers and fruits, which they had never seen before, and among these plants, unknown birds were walking.

"What is this?" Ma-sa-harti asked again, and Maat-Ka-Re began to stroke all these flowers with her hand and even pressed her little nose to the wall to check if they smelled.

"Once upon a time," Amen-em-Ipet began to speak as if he were telling a story, "was the great King Men-kheper-Re who was fighting against Kemet's enemies in the land of Retjenu. In this land, such plants grew, and the King liked it so much that when he returned from his expedition and decided to build the temple in which we are now, he ordered to carve and paint everything he saw there. But the land of Retjenu was far away and the road to it was long and dangerous and the artists were worried about how to fulfill the royal order? Then the news spread that a prince ruling the city of Iapu at the coast of Retjenu rebelled against Pharaoh's rule. When the King sent against him warships and the army commanded by General Djehuty, the Vizier agreed that a talented artist Min-nakht would be sent there with the army, just to draw on papyrus various plants, flowers and fruits and even birds from the land of Retjenu. The war expedition was successful. The clever General Djehuty first captured the prince of the city of

---

by King Thutmose III.

Iapu, and then hid his soldiers in large baskets and ordered others to take these baskets to the City, saying that they were gifts from Pharaoh. When the gullible guards opened the gates, the soldiers jumped out of the baskets and easily captured the city.[146] In this way, also the artist Min-nakht found himself in Retjenu. He immediately began to draw various plants and trees, but then he saw that some of them not only have no fruit yet, but also no flowers and even no leaves. You know that it can be sometimes cold during the Peret season, even here in the City, and in Djanet, as Maat-Ka-Re said it is even colder and it rains. In Retjenu, however, it is so much cold that small white stars can fall sometimes instead of water from the sky, that the inhabitants of Retjenu call *selg*. This *selg* when touched, first burns like fire, although it leaves no traces, and then turns into water. During the cold season the trees in Retjenu stand sad, leafless, and that's how it was then. The patient Min-nakht stayed in Retjenu for the whole year, because he waited for, that in the Akhet season each plant in this land will produce its flowers and each tree its fruits. Min-nakht also learnt what the seeds of all these plants look like, and at the same time, he wandered around Retjenu and constantly drew on papyrus everything he saw and accurately described all the colors. Finally, one day, he returned with the merchants to the City and showed his work to the King, whose heart was very happy. Thanks to this King and this artist, we can,

---

[146] The plot of a narrative created in the New Kingdom known as *The capture of Joppa* preserved on the so-called Harris 500 papyrus in the British Museum, London, is used here.

while standing here, get to know a distant land and admire how beautiful and interesting the world created by Amun is."

Amen-em-Ipet finished speaking, and then little Maat-Ka-Re asked, "Will you show us other such nice pictures?"

"Yes, I promise I will show you very nice colorful paintings on the other side of the river, if of course your Daddy agrees," the old priest answered seriously, and Ma-sa-harti assured:

"He'll agree, I will ask him!"

"Me too!" his sister added.

"Then let's go and ask him," Amen-em-Ipet summed up, "Maybe your parents are back."

On the same day, in the evening, Pi-nodjem invited the old priest for wine.

"The children are already asleep, and Henut-tawy went to Nodjmet for a women's chat," he explained. "Do you already know?"

"That you'll be a father again?" Amen-em-Ipet cut in on his words. "I know, your small daughter told me about this today. I am happy with you, because if all your children will be so nice and also smart, then you should have as many of them as possible. I admit that I was really afraid that day – I have unfortunately never had children, but I hope I passed the exam as a caregiver?"

"You passed it perfectly, my friend," Pi-nodjem grabbed his hand and met his eyes warmly. "Thank you; the children were delighted, they said that you had told them a fairy tale."

"Ah, it's probably about the history of capturing Iapu; you probably also read it at school. But I must tell you that I also received a lesson today and I think that the time of changes in the organization of the holiday of Ipet and even changes in the structures of the State of Amun is approaching. Well, your son asked me if Nodjmet was the wife of Heri-Hor or of Amun and I admit that I did not know what to answer. Such questions can be asked at the holiday of Ipet by many, especially those not very favorably disposed to Heri-Hor, and yet, we know that there are also those in the City. Long ago, when a pharaoh lived here constantly, his divinity and sanctity of Amun were obviously complementary: God the Father in heaven and the Son of God on earth were worshiped without reservation, and the queen was the only woman who naturally fulfilled the role of the divine mother, especially that her son was to be the next Horus and Son of Re. Today, High Priest of Amun is only playing a role of a king, despite the fact that he has full royal titles, and it is not known at all whether his son will ever be a pharaoh; after all, in Pi-Ramesse there is still another King who has never come to terms with his current situation. The wife of Amun's First Servant does not suit the role of Amun's consort. I think that a separate office of the Divine Spouse of Amun should be created that is of a woman whose dignity would be equal to that of the High Priest, but who wouldn't be married to anyone on earth..."

Amen-em-Ipet looked piercingly at the young man who was to become king one day, as Heri-Hor, Pi-ankh and Nes-Ba-neb-Djedu established in Pi-Ramesse. Pi-nodjem wasn't answering for a long time, sipping slowly wine, and gathering his thoughts. He was agreeing with what Amen-em-Ipet meant, but was imagining that someday his lovely wife Henut-tawy would also play the role of a priestess at the festival of Ipet.

"Undoubtedly, Maat speaks through you, my friend!" he replied finally, "And your wisdom will not find an equal anywhere. Perhaps it will be necessary to establish the office of the Divine Spouse, or better, The Divine Adoratrice of Amun,[147] but not yet. The period of the Repeating of Births will be over one day, and everything will be back to normal, and only one person will bear the royal titles. For many reasons, the King should stay closer to our borders in the north and the east, because news are still coming from there, to which he must react quickly, so someday his main place will be in Djanet. Here, in the City only the First Servant of Amun will remain. However, I don't know when this happens. And to complete those "20 years" that Amun gave Heri-Hor there are still many missing, and besides we should bear the King Ramesses in mind."

"How is he?" Amen-em-Ipet changed the subject.

"You know, sometimes I feel sorry for him. He lives alone in the City, from where most of the residents have already moved to Djanet, and half of the temples have already been demolished and the stone material derived from them was transported to Djanet, where it is used for new buildings. As you know, there are no stone deposits in the north and you have to bring it even if from around Men-nefer; for this purpose very old tombs are pulled down even there. Ramesses always sees official delegations of foreign monarchs, but also less and less often since they realized that Nes-Ba-neb-Djedu and Tent-Amun are more important now.

---

[147] Such an office has been introduced about 15 years after the time of the novel. The first priestess to hold this dignity was Maat-Ka-Re, daughter of Pi-nodjem.

The worst thing is that the old King was uncompromising in his anger and he doesn't even want to see his daughter. Henut-tawy tried to see him several times, but he never received her, he didn't even want to see his grandson. My father got very irritated then and to spite Ramesses he forced Henut-tawy to name the little one Ma-sa-harti."

"Yes, I even wanted to ask you about it: this is a typical name for Tjehenu," Amen-em-Ipet raised his eyebrows with a look of surprise in his eyes.

"That's what Pi-ankh's point," Pi-nodjem answered. "The first grandson of the great King Ramesses, an opponent of Tjehenu, who fought against all attempts to grant those privileges, bears a name derived from this people! It must have been very painful for this old man. At the same time, however, my father and also Nes-Ba-neb-Djedu gained even greater favor among the Meshuesh and Libu tribes. Old Buyu-wawa, when he learned about it, began to cry with emotion, and now Tjehenu is in perfect relations with them, thanks to which Nes-Ba-neb-Djedu gained workers to build the City of Djanet, which in this wasteland was of great importance."

"I got the impression that your kids, especially little Maat-Ka-Re, don't really like this land," Amen-em-Ipet mentioned the first sentences he exchanged with his little guests today.

"That's true," Pi-nodjem sighed. "Not only few people live there, but also even drinking water had to be, at the beginning, brought from the river until we dug a new canal. We also have a big lake nearby, but its water is salty, like in the sea. In addition, it often rains there and in the Peret season is cold and there are so many clouds that Re is often not visible at all. Who once saw Waset, has difficulty with getting accustomed to live in Djanet. I don't like it as Henut-tawy or Pi-ankh either, and we all want to move to the City. I will definitely build a palace here; I have even talked about this with Pa-uer-aa and Pa-Shu-uben. This one, by the way, is a very unpleasant character, although he certainly knows a lot about the City..."

"Far too much..." Amen-em-Ipet murmured. "There are some things that should be clarified in conversation with Heri-Hor, but we have to wait for him to recover."

Now, they began to talk about the illness of the High Priest, and soon Henut-tawy appeared, who also heartily thanked the old priest for today's tour of Ipet-sut.

"I promised the kids that I would show them some grave chapels in the western City, of course with your permission. Maybe the day after tomorrow? I will send a letter to Buteh-Amun to send his boat for us."

The conversation ended there and Amen-em-Ipet returned home, but again, as a few days ago, he found Suti-mes waiting for him, this time joyfully excited.

"I arranged a flat for Henut and myself!" he informed him at the doorstep as soon as they exchanged greeting words. "The *setem*-priest in the temple of Khonsu and my good friend from the school, Khonsu-mes, and his wife Mut-em-Ipet will give us a part of their apartment and their house is near Ipet-sut!" Suti-mes spoke quickly, throwing out the words of happiness.

"It is fortunate, because I am about to write a letter to Buteh-Amun, who should appear the day after tomorrow at Ipet-sut harbor with his boat; maybe he'll bring you an urgent shipment" – the old priest replied with a smile, and Suti-mes grabbed his hand and pressed it to his forehead.

Five days later, the day came, which all residents of the City were eagerly waiting for. Those who wanted to take the best places to watch from close range the expected attractions of the second part of the Ipet-feast celebration were gathering from the early morning hours in front of the Great Gate of the temple in Ipet-resit. More and more boats were arriving to the nearby harbor bringing people from Khefet-her-neb-es, but also from the neighboring villages located both up and down the river. Whole families were getting out of them and heading for the temple. Elegantly dressed women and girls gathered there in a separate place, and some officer priestesses distinguished by long colorful sashes decorating their white dresses were giving them *sesh-sesh* or *menit*.[148] Women for whom the instruments have run out were to go in procession while clapping hands and singing. Elsewhere, slightly closer to the gate, priests gathered in white tunics, sometimes girded with colored ribbons, which meant a higher rank in the hierarchy. Some had wigs, while the Fathers of Gods and Clean Ones on duty, who were to carry a barge or various holy emblems had their heads shaved carefully. All free places except of the avenue of lions and the ceremonial square in front of the Great Gate, surrounded by the army and the *medjayu*

---

[148] A kind of rattle in the shape of a decorative necklace.

were crowded with more and more big number of the passive participants of the ceremony waiting for its start. Everybody watched as in the designated places on the outskirts of the square the soldiers were preparing piles of fruits, sweet cakes, and large vessels with wine, water and *cucu* juice. As before, the inhabitants of both parts of the City and the surrounding area were, after all, Amun's wedding guests, although it was His First Servant, King Heri-Hor who invited them to the wedding.

Litters and chariots bringing dignitaries began to appear, which meant that the beginning of the ceremony was approaching. Finally, there was a hum among the gathered people: the royal cortege was approaching from Ipet-sut, and after a while, His Majesty Heri-Hor and his wife Nodjmet got out of the chariots and walked into the temple, followed by priests. The gates were closed behind them, but very soon after, with loud sounds of trumpets, they were opened again and in the distance a procession preceded by the jackal-shaped Up-uaut appeared. A dozen high-ranking priests walked just before the King and Queen, followed by the priests carrying the great barge of Amun User-hat, decorated with numerous wreaths of fragrant lotus. The more and more distinct sounds of the joyful hymn to Amun, rhythmically recited by a large group of *hesiyu* - singing priests following the barge, were reaching the ears of all gathered people.

Here Amun appeared in his boat like Re in the sky;
The whole Country rejoices to see his rays.
They emanate from the User-hat, just like
from the barge of Re in the sky,

The whole country sings and dances
on this beautiful day of Ipet.
Here the Lord of Life comes
from the place where he appeared for the first time.
Amon, give life and health to his son Heri-Hor![149]

Finally, the procession stopped and the Clean Ones carefully placed the barge on a special pedestal constructed here yesterday of boards and covered with a purple fabric. The hymn was completed, and at that time Heri-Hor incensed the barge, circling it three times, each time wearing a different headgear. After that, Heri-Hor gave back the censer, and having put the white crown of the Southern Country on his head, he picked up an oar and shouted, standing in front of the barge's prow:

I am hurrying to You, Amun,
to bring you a river that you will sail on,
while your son will row,
that you would enjoy this view!

Than he started to trot, while circling Amun's boat again. Returning to the starting point he put aside the paddle, and took two slender vases partially filled with water, one with each hand and – now wearing the red crown of the Lower Country – started running again around the User-hat. This second ceremonial was

---

[149] The texts quoted here are mostly fragments of authentic records of words spoken during the Ipet-feast, preserved on the walls of the temple in Luxor.

more difficult, because the priest had both hands occupied, and the objects he was carrying were heavier. When Heri-Hor finally stood in front of the offering altar to pour the contents of both vases onto it, it was obvious that he was tired and had to catch his breath before saying the next formula:

Take these vessels containing cold water,
which I brought you, running through the whole country!
Receive these two vases
filled with the divine seed!
Now, he took a bowl filled with lettuce
and placing it on the altar, turned again to Amun:
Oh, Amun, how wonderful that you have begotten Your Son!
Oh, City dwellers, rejoice!

Then Nodjmet carrying the little son Amen-em-ensu in her arms appeared next to the High Priest, while showing everyone this small, today woefully crying living proof that Amun became father and that he took up residence in the King (which the name: Amen-em-ensu literally meant). The crowd waved and greeted the child – perhaps the future king – with a loud ovation. At that moment pipes, flutes, tambourines rang out, and from behind an artificial curtain a group of the same acrobats ran out as during the first part of the ceremony ten days ago: the actually naked girls who were wearing only wigs, bracelets and short hips covers open in the front. The copper-gold shapely bodies began to perform ecstatic jumps and bends, and all the gathered people also began to clap their hands rhythmically, and women were again uttering a high modulated characteristic wedding shout.

While everyone was watching the performances of the dancers, Heri-Hor and Nodjmet got into the chariots and surrounded by a group of courtiers drove to the harbor by a special processional route prepared for this purpose, then boarded the royal ship and sailed to Ipet-sut. The next part of the ceremony was celebrated by Amen-em-Ipet. When the dance group finished the performance, further acts of offering took place. Among the offerings special high floral bouquets consisting of many types of flowers attached to a long bunch of papyrus stems could be distinguished. Finally, Amun's barge, which was still incensed, followed the royal couple. Just before it, two priests walked, carrying bucket-like round vessels filled with milk. They poured it on the road with small spoons, thus giving another sign that a new life had appeared. At one point, Amen-em-Ipet, who preceded them by a few cubits, stopped, turned towards the barge and raised his hand so that everyone felt silent, then posed loudly a question to Amun, asking for being heard. The Clean Ones made a single step forward without a word: God agreed. Amen-em-Ipet expressed his joy that once again as in the past, the great User-hat barge traverses the City, while filling the hearts of the residents of Kemet with happiness.

"But now," he continued, "when the traces of the past war are rarer and the City is flourishing, the time has come to thank the one who was like a shepherd for his sheeps, and whom the enemy forced to leave to Iunu, and an unexpected illness struck down so that he couldn't return: His Grandness First Servant of Amun, Amen-hotep, justified!"

Amen-em-Ipet uttered the name loudly, and the crowd responded with a favorable shout. There was no one anymore who wouldn't have remembered this High Priest well, and wouldn't have compared his time to paradise in comparison with the hell of the later Kushite rule. Therefore, when Amen-em-Ipet asked now, if God would agree that the person and deeds of Amen-hotep will be commemorated in stone in Ipet-sut, which Amun "confirmed very strongly" again with a clear movement of his barge, everyone also began to shout that they loved Amen-hotep.

The procession continued, and soon the User-hat-barge was deposited on its great ship, which, now driven only by rowers, set off majestically along the river towards Ipet-sut. Along the shore, it was accompanied by a colorful procession, in which not only groups of priests reciting hymns and women making noise with *menit* and *sesh-sesh* were going, but also various troops of soldiers joyfully waving with palm branches, above all the music and dance groups composed of exotic performers: the black newcomers from Punt and Tjehenu adorned with feathers. While the loud and joyful gathering was slowly moving away heading towards Ipet-sut, others made use of free refreshments and soon everything that was accumulated for this purpose was consumed and the inhabitants of both parts of the City also began to head for their homes.

Amen-em-Ipet envied them all in his heart. Several hours passed since the ceremony began and the old priest was very tired and hungry. Today was unusually stuffy and hot. When Amen-em-Ipet was finally able to head towards his apartment near the palace of the First Servant, he saw a dozen of people there: some servants, as well as several priests standing in the courtyard and looking up at the sky. It was only now that he could see what has been the object of observation of others for a long time, and he became overcome with feelings of surprise, mixed with a strange fear, but also with delight. Here, from the west, extremely black clouds were approaching, the same as those from which huge amounts of water could pour out, or fire could flare, carrying terror and sometimes destruction. Now, one could see the constant flashes of lightning, but although the clouds were approaching very quickly, Amen-em-Ipet did not hear the slightest roar of the storm: the flashes of lightning were firing only between one cloud and the other. It looked as if the mighty celestial armies were fighting each other, sending fiery arrows, but completely ignoring the earth and all its inhabitants, who watched this spectacle of Nature with pious fear.[150] Amen-em-Ipet has never seen anything like it, even though his age has furrowed his face.

"You are inscrutable, Great God!" he thought. "Do you want to reveal something to us in this way? Your anger or warning?"

He stared at the unusual phenomenon for a long time, then thoughtfully directed his steps towards the Heri-Hor's palace.

Suti-mes, who came with the same procession and, as the Servant of Amun, accompanied God until the Hall of

---

[150] The Author had occasion to observe a similar phenomenon in 2008 in Luxor.

Appearances in Ipet-sut, just wanted to refresh himself, to change his clothes and then to go to the house of Khonsu-mes as soon as possible to continue the celebrating in Henut's accompany.

"The girl has probably already managed to get there, having given back the organizers the *sesh-sesh*," he thought.

When he went to the Holy Lake to wash himself, he also saw that everyone was looking up and after a while, he was watching, too the amazing battle of clouds that was taking place in the sky. After some time, he went to his lodging and began to change, but the dangerous and mysterious sight he had just witnessed returned to him. It occurred to him that a similar fight was going on in his heart for several days. Terrible anger was burning in him against the one who had hurt his beloved girl, and now was persecuting him, too, only because he had not managed to kill him before. At the same time, he felt that the thunders he threw at Pa-Shu-uben in his mind were strangely silent, for he had no means to effectively reach his enemy. There was no doubt that the powerful Chief of Police wouldn't give up capturing him, and now, when he united with Henut, the shadow of danger also rested on her. The thought that it was he, led by love and longing, could bring a danger to her, filled him with horror, and at the same time, he felt happy for several days. The House of Khonsu-mes was hospitable and they could feel safe in it, for the time being. Preparations for today's holiday, as well as the visit of distinguished guests from Djanet meant that Pa-shu-uben had other things to worry about, and he and Henut successfully got out of the sight of Pa-neb and similar to him other servants of the One Who Knows the Secrets of the City, but for how long? The holiday has already taken place, the guests will leave, and then Pa-Shu-uben will resume his search and find them sooner or later. Suti-mes remembered what Amen-em-Ipet advised him, and indeed this old man is right in everything he says. So, if he thinks that it is good to go to Heri-Hor himself with a complaint about Pa-shu-uben, he will do so, but what exactly should he tell the First Servant? Suti-mes began to compose his speech and found it a very difficult task. It cannot be a simple accusation of hit order, because he disposes only of assumptions, nor a general suspicion, too delicate and veiled one, because the King may consider this not worth of the interest. He cannot show that he is afraid, because such a behavior is unbecoming of the gold flies order's owner and priest... Should he mention about what Henut told him? Then he would have to reveal her painful secret... Maybe it's better to confine himself to yesterday's event: the attempt to arrest him was clearly organized by Pa-neb who is at Pa-Shu-uben's service. After all, he should, as usual, consult Amen-em-Ipet; maybe they could go to Heri-Hor together?

At that moment, Suti-mes heard somebody running across the courtyard toward his apartment. The whole area was lined with stone slabs and every step could be easily heard. There was no doubt: someone was hurrying here. Suti-mes opened the door and left, almost colliding with the one he has just thought about. Amen-em-Ipet's face changed; the run tired him clearly. A sight of this old priest running was so much atypical that Suti-mes sensed immediately that something unusual had happened.

"Friend, what happened?" he broke out, though he knew he would find out in a moment. And indeed, Amen-em-Ipet gasping for breath, sputtered an intermittent sentence, from which even in today's heat Suti-mes got cold:

"King... Heri-Hor... is dead!"

CHAPTER XXIII

Suti-mes was sitting on a stone at the bank of the river descending toward the harbor in Sunu, while looking towards the Island of Abu and its temples founded on granite rocks. The barge of Re was already quite low, and the sky beyond the island grew golden and red, embracing several purple clouds. The plumes of the palms stood out with dark green, almost black pattern against this colorful background. In the distance behind the island the second high bank of the river loomed, while hiding in its yellow and black slopes some long ramps leading to the tombs built here in the time immemorial. The great pharaohs were reigning then, who were building artificial mountains of the pyramids at the opposite end of this long country stretching along Hapi in the region of Men-nefer. For Suti-mes it was a time immersed in legend: so distant that it was inconceivable.

The oldest houses of God on the island of Abu were built just then, although they were not as beautiful and extensive as the temple of Khnum, which reigns here today. Its mighty rock-based walls also provided hospitality for the sanctuaries of many other forms of God, just like the walls of the Amon Temple in Ipet-sut. But in the City Amon was a host, and here only a visitor to the house of Khnum and his tabernacle was small. There was only one Servant of God here who had been Suti-mes for three years.

The young priest shifted his eyes closer to river's bank, where bonfires burned in several places, and flickering lights also marked human homes centered both on the island to the north from the temple, and on the eastern bank, in Sunu. From the place where he sat, the entire harbor could be seen clearly, where various boats moored, while directing towards the sky a forest of skewed masts. Still nearer, several rows of houses were standing, and among them several larger, wealthier ones. Suti-mes was intrigued by both the harbor and these wealthier houses.

One of them belonged to Khnum-nakht, the captain of a transport barge who was bringing from the north grain, oil and all things necessary for the temple in Abu, especially for the House of Khnum. This cooperation of the temples with the captain Khnum-nakht lasted for many years, much longer than the entire, three-year stay of Suti-mes on the island. It so happened, however, that after his arrival at Abu the local priests began to complain that they were running short of grain, which never happened before. It was decided to count the stocks in the warehouse and then it turned out that there were much less sacks of grain than expected. The priests were terrified: if anyone would find out, they would be the first suspects because they had access to the temple's warehouse. Seriously, they began to expect an investigation, and it could be painful. Suti-mes stood, at first, away from all this, but seeing the great concern in the eyes of his colleagues, with whom he has already established friendly relations, he became soon involved in an explanation of the riddle. He asked by letter his friend Buteh-Amun to check at the first opportunity how many bags would be loaded in the City on a barge intended for the temples of Abu. When he got an answer a month ago, he managed to be present at the unloading of the barge that brought this grain. When the unloaded sacks were counted, it turned out that four were missing compared to the number provided by Buteh-Amun. Suti-mes was watching then the Captain Khnum-nakht closely. The behavior of the last one, his insolent self-confidence, a brutal treatment of boys carrying sacks from the hold, sharp shouting and urging, supported by intensive use of the whip, aroused in him a distinct dislike of this never-before-seen man. He suspected that the barge had actually arrived earlier at the harbor in Abu, and that some sacks were secretly unpacked. The young priest decided to check if his suspicions were correct. Because tomorrow the boat was expected to arrive again with another grain transport, so Suti-mes decided to wait for this boat near the harbor to see when it really would arrive and if nothing suspicious would happen with it. He came here especially early, sat on a stone and soon became a part of the landscape. He had a few hours of waiting ahead.

Using the last hour of light before dark, Suti-mes took out from his tunic pocket a letter that he had received a few days ago. It was, as always, a dearest amulet for him, and also the source of all energy, of which he began to be already short in this unusual exile. The letter was written by Buteh-Amun's hand, but a considerable part of it was, as usual, dictated by Henut.

Every day I am asking Amun, Re, Horus on both Horizons, when he appears and disappears, to give you health, happiness and people's respect! My beloved One, your sister feels good and assures you of her constant love. When will Amun finally make you come and console my heart that lusts for you like the dry earth for a flooding! Every morning I wake up with your name on my lips and I fall asleep thinking about your love. You come back to me every night, but when I open my eyes you are gone again...

Your son is starting to run a lot and I have to be very careful that he does not fall down the stairs. I taught him your name and we utter it together. We call: "Suti! Suti!" and he laughs loudly. I'd like rather to cry, but he wouldn't understand it, so only my heart cries and calls: come to me! Don't worry, my dear, everything will be fine. I am lucky I have friends here who must replace you and my father and mother. Nes-Mut goes to school in Ipet-sut and Amen-em-Ipet arranged for him an apartment there. Djehuty-mes is fine, although he walks less and less slowly. Buteh-Amun, Shed-du-dua and the children are wonderful. Dear, do you have to be so far away? Your enemy probably has already forgotten about you, because neither Pa-neb nor others are standing by the house long since, and I think I can go out freely and sometimes I do, although Chari is always angry then. I have to finish now, because Buteh-Amun will be angry, in turn. Do men still have to get angry? I love you and kiss you, and our little son Pen-Amun too.

Suti-mes rolled up the papyrus and put it back again. He closed his eyes and was moved for a moment. He imagined how the little Pen-Amun is uttering his name, how he laughs... he has never seen his son.

Three years have already passed, and the memories of those days were still as vivid as if it had all happened yesterday. Heri-Hor's death surprised everyone. Some asked themselves, how is it possible that after only six years the one died whom Amun promised 20 years of rule? Others were saying that those 20 years were a period of renewal, which, after all, did not end, because in the City documents were still dated according to the Repeating of Births. In the seventh year of the *uhem mesut* Amun appointed a new High Priest during the oracle; Pi-ankh became him. Earlier, however, there was a time of mourning. All music stopped, even the beer house was closed, men grew their beards, and women stopped plaiting braids, or put on elegant clothes. Men avoided contact with their wives and even "sisters" did not accept any clients. Everyone was sad but also calm, so the *medjayu* had seldom occasion to intervene. Some people left Waset and went to their estates situated away, because they couldn't withstand the gloomy waiting of the King's funeral for over two months. Perhaps they wished to avoid therefore the temporary rule of Amen-em-Ipet who was very accurate in executing the obedience toward the state of the mourning. Among such "temporary refugees" was also Pa-Shu-uben with a group of his closest associates, including Pa-neb, for whom staying in the City with the closed house of the "sisters" was difficult to imagine. Thanks to this, for Suti-mes this period was a time of peace because his persecutors were meanwhile far away, but also of very difficult abstinence, which encompassed all priests, and which for him – the newly married spouse – was a kind of particular torture. In this situation, together with Henut, they decided that they would resign from the hospitality of Khonsu-mes, and Suti-mes would return to his lodging in Ipet-sut, while Henut to the house of Djehuty-mes in Khefet-her-neb-es, all the more because her mother wasn't feeling well and needed care. From then on, throughout the mourning period, they saw each other rarely, meticulously counting those ritual 70 days, during which the body of the deceased was subjected to the necessary procedures, and which were passing especially slowly for them.

Finally, the funeral's day came, preceded by some ceremonies that took place at the royal palace of Heri-Hor in Ipet-sut. The golden casket of the High Priest lay on a "lion's bed," surrounded by flowers and lamps, and at its both ends two kneeling young girls recited mourning formulas of lamentation, playing the characters of Isis and Nephthys – the sisters of the dead Osiris, Lord of the Underground. The coffin was then taken round the palace, and it even was rowed across the Holy Lake on the boat. In this way, the deceased was saying goodbye to his earthly apartment and all the servants were saying goodbye to him. Finally, the ceremonial retinue left the Heri-Hor's palace and went to the other side of the river, escorted by actually all residents of the City; only the sick ones, the women in childbirth, the newborn babies and the doddering old people remained in the Eastern Waset. From the harbor in Khefet-her-neb-es, the route of a slowly progressing funeral procession went through the whole Western City, while visiting subsequent temples, by where the retinue was always stopping, and the Sons of Horus were taking the coffin on their shoulders and were carrying it into the internal halls, where offerings were laid before it. All the time, priests recited holy formulas written on papyri. However, the most important ceremonies took place in Djeseru, where the procession visited all the holy shrines: that of the patron of the necropolis, His Majesty Amen-hotep Djeser-Ka-Re of the Garden, that of the caregiver and feeder of all the dead Hathor embodied in the form of a cow, as well as that of the heavenly mother Nut residing in the sycamore, and finally, various parts of the magnificent Djeser-Djeseru temple rising with terraces, where hymns were sung to both forms of God appearing on the eastern and western horizon at the altar of Re. Also in Djeser -Djeseru area, next to the chapel of the jackal-headed Anubis, an exceptionally long Judgment of the Dead ceremony was held. Through the mouth of a priest the deceased assured the divine judges of the Tribunal of Osiris about his innocence, after which Anubis the Great of Secrets carried out the weighing of the heart. Because both scales appeared on an equal level, which meant that Maat lived in the heart of the deceased, he received a justification. In the end, the chief priest proceeded the Opening the Mouth ceremony, while touching the mouth of the lid of the vertically placed coffin with various instruments, and delivering appropriate spells. Nodjmet - the unhappy widow, weeping buckets, knelt at the feet of the gilded, Osiris-shaped coffin while embracing it. Finally, the time of parting came for her, too. The participants of the ceremony after a funeral banquet consumed in Djeseru, returned home. Only priests and guardians of the necropolis stayed in the temple, who were to take the coffin to the place of actual burial in the old tomb of the King Amen-hotep Djeser-Ka-Re, the funerary chapel of which was towering over the whole of Djeseru. From there the deceased King Heri-Hor was to send blessings to the entire City.

At that moment, the period of mourning was over, and at the same time preparations began for a great ceremonial procession, during which the oracle of Amun was to indicate who would become his new First Servant. Since the time of the funeral, however, many people have already guessed that it would be Pi-ankh, because he was the main celebrant.

When the mourning was over, Suti-mes and Henut spent some really wonderful days. However, this beautiful time was short, because Amen-em-Ipet invited Suti-mes to announce him a surprising piece of news: "Soon, when Pi-ankh is chosen, my influence in the City will decrease, in contrast to the possibilities of Pa-Shu-uben, who is on friendly terms with the General. Knowing the Chief of the Police, I presume that this villain will want to reach you and I'm afraid that in the City you wouldn't have had the chance to avoid his tentacles. The only advice I give you as a friend is that you should leave immediately. On the island of Abu the servant of Amun has just died, who was responsible for daily offerings in Amun's chapel in the House of Khnum. So long as I can decide, I appoint you as his successor. In Abu, Pa-Shu-uben's power no longer reaches, and he doesn't even have to find out where you went. I will purposely announce that I sent you to Iunu.

When, on the next day, Suti-mes ready for the travel went for Henut to the house of Djehuty-mes, the bad news fell on him like a bolt from the blue: her mother suddenly became seriously ill and the girl could not leave her in this situation. The Amen-em-

Ipet's boat was to depart on the same day and only on its board Suti-mes could feel safe and imperceptibly leave the City. So, he sailed away with a heavy heart, hoping that his wife would follow him a few days later. Unfortunately, Hereret, who was still on the verge of death, a month later crossed this threshold. So, again the period of mourning began, this time in family circle, and for the next two months, Henut could not sail to Abu. When the day of the funeral came, Henut who had been very exhausted and for some time strangely pale, fainted and fell during the ceremonies in the necropolis. Doctors from the temple of Khonsu, whom Amen-em-Ipet sent, said that Henut would become a mother, but only on the condition that she would lie flat from now on and wouldn't carry out any onerous work. Of course, Djehuty-mes with Buteh-Amun and Shed-em-dua were looking after her with utmost care, but the time of reunion of the married couple was again delayed. Suti-mes finally got a letter from which he learnt that Henut happily gave birth to a son and, as they agreed earlier, she named him Pen-Amun. At the same time, with this joyous piece of news, Buteh-Amun sent a second one, much worse. He namely observed that some people were always standing in front of his house, and because he saw Pa-neb among them several times, he guessed that they were at Pa-Shu-uben's service. It was not clear whether they waited until Suti-mes would appear at home one day, or maybe Henut was the object of their interest? This supposition frightened the young father at most, but his friend assured him that they were watching that the girl would never leave alone.

Further months passed, but all the subsequent letters were always revealing that the house of Djehuty-mes, as well as practically every step of its inhabitants, were still under observation. In this situation, it was obvious that Suti-mes could not return to the City, and Henut's trip with a small child to Abu would also be immediately noticed. There was nothing else to do but wait that maybe Pa-Shu-uben would lose his position or give up prosecuting Suti-mes. Did Henut's words from the last letter really indicate that the recently unseen persecutors had ceased observing the Necropolis Scribe's house? The most worrying thing was that Henut herself, as she admitted, was not always careful...

Suti-mes was roused from meditations because he noticed a movement on the river enlightened with moonshine. A transport barge very quietly, almost noiselessly was reaching port at Sunu, and Suti-mes seemed to recognize it. He has frozen. The place where he was sitting was now completely dark and invisible from this part of the harbor where the boat had moored. On the contrary, he had good conditions to make observations. After a while, two people came out of the barge who placed a wooden pier between the boat and the bank of the river, and then a third man came out of the boat. Undoubtedly this was the Captain Khnum-nakht, for he was limping slightly, as Suti-mes remembered from his previous encounter with this man. The captain stood on the shore but did not leave; he gave both men some vigorous signs. They climbed back onto the boat, and after a while, appeared again on the pier, carrying sacks on their shoulders. The captain led the way and led them to one of the wealthier houses in the first row near the harbor. For a long time, no one was visible, then the three men reappeared, returned to the boat and in a moment took more sacks from it. The whole operation was repeated now, but then only two people left the captain's house, who returned to the barge. Khnum-nakht stayed at his home.

Thus, the whole mysterious story became clear and the puzzle was already properly solved: from each transport, Captain Khnum-nakht stole several sacks of grain[151], and because he was trusted one, no one checked whether the quantity of the goods corresponded to what was undoubtedly enumerated on the bill of lading. It is strange that no one has noticed it so far and only recently the action of checking the stock showed such a difference.

This was so much significant that in a case of an official control, it would be certainly noticed and the priests from the temple in Abu would probably be accused.

Suti-mes got up and went to the other end of the harbor, where a small boat stood moored. He got on it and rowed to the island, then went to his apartment, having spoken for a long time with the night guards of the gate and with their superiors.

As was expected by the young priest, on the next day, as soon as it became quite brightly and the night guards were preparing

---

[151] On one of the papyri in the Egyptian Museum in Turin there is an extensive text of the report, on the basis of which it is possible to determine the course of events conventionally referred by Egyptologists as the *The Elephantine scandal*. One of its negative characters is Captain Knum-nacht. The real scandal took place during the reign of Ramesses V, so only a few decades earlier than the time of the novel's plot, but it illustrates well the corrupt arrangements of the entire late Ramessid period in Egypt.

for the change, the boat of the Captain Khnum-nakht reached port at the temple harbor on Abu.

He himself, as he used to always, shouting at his people, scolding them for no reason and rushing with his whip, ordered the sacks of grain to be taken out of the hold and stacked on the bank, from where another group of porters – temple workers – were to transfer them to warehouse. Usually both activities were performed simultaneously, and no one counted the goods, but today, exceptionally, at Suti-mes' command, the temple group waited until all the sacks were on the bank.

"Why don't you take your grain? Would you have too much of it?" the Captain asked surprised. "I think it is necessary to inform the Vizier in the City about that, because he is always urging me to hurry to you so that I sail day and night, and here, there is no rush nor joy that you will have something to fill your bellies!"

"Did you also sail to us this time at night?" Suti-mes asked the Captain this question, not expecting an answer, but, strangely enough, he received it immediately:

"Of course, I arrived only an hour ago and did not even have my morning meal!"

"It's strange, Captain, that your family doesn't have the habit of preparing you a breakfast... As far as I know, you slept in your home today," Suti-mes said in a slightly amused tone.

But the Captain flushed with anger and shouted loudly so that everyone would hear him. "What?! How dare you, the cub, to speak to me like this?! I was bringing grain here when you were still a kid with a bare butt, and I got a gold chain from Vizier as a reward!"

"Are you talking about Vizier Pa-nehsi?" Now Suti-mes' voice sounded serious. "The fact alone that you are older than me doesn't entitle you to insult me. I am a priest in this temple, which you seem to be deceiving for years. You probably have a bill of lading – let me check how many sacks of grain you were supposed to deliver to us and then we count the ones that are lying here. If everything is correct, I will ask you for forgiveness and you can punish me for my suspicions!"

Khnum-nakht was speechless for a moment, then flushed with anger, and finally shouted even more loudly, "You insolent whippersnapper, did His Grandness Pi-ankh authorize you to read my bill of lading? I won't show you anything! Who are you at all? May the donkey rape you for daring to talk to me like that! What is your name, and maybe you are ashamed to reveal it to me, and rightly so, because your accusations bring shame to your name!"

The young priest turned pale of indignation, "I am not ashamed of my name, Khnum-nakht; I am Suti-mes, Servant of Amun at the House of Khnum. However, your name will soon be infamous. Tonight, along with your servants, you walked twice between this barge and your home, and I am sure there are at least four sacks of grain missing, as were in the previous month and two months ago. You are a liar and you should be arrested by *medjayu*. Here they come back from visiting your home. What did you find at Khnum-nakht?" this question Suti-mes addressed to the temple guards, who in the company of the *medjayu* appeared at the harbor right now.

"Lord, according to the agreement and with the permission of the Mayor of Abu, we entered the house of Khnum-nakht when he arrived here. In the chamber behind the house, we found 16 sacks of wheat and eight sacks of barley, and at home four more sacks of wheat."

"These are the sacks he took yesterday and couldn't hide" – thought Suti-mes, while the Captain screamed, "It's all mine! You have entered my house, while making *isefet*, you will pay me for it!" He turned and got into the boat and ordered to set sail. The guards did not stop him, because they received permission from the Mayor to check if there were any suspicious bags with grain in Captain's house, but there was no one who could order to arrest him. Meanwhile, the news spread quickly, other priests came and began to thank Suti-mes for solving the mystery tormenting them and praising his acumen. The hero himself slowly calmed down after the strong agitation caused by the offensive words of Khnum-nakht, but at the same time he realized that he did not do it well, revealing his name. This man was once rewarded by the infamous Pa-nehsi, who before the revolt of the Kushite troops, was among others Vizier, who knows, if Khnum-nakht has no connections with those who were looking for Suti-mes? "Too bad", he thought, "it happened, but I did something very important today and while doing well I multiplied Maat."

His heart overwhelmed with joy.

CHAPTER XXIV

Pa-neb entered quietly and stood on the threshold of Pa-Shu-uben's room. He did not know why he was summoned, but another trusted man of the dignitary encountered on Pa-neb's way warned that the boss was in a bad mood, which never boded well. Pa-Shu-uben was, as usual, sitting in a comfortable chair with footrest, while looking through the window. He could observe from there a large fragment of the area, up to the temple of His Majesty Ramesses User-Maat-Re Meri-Amun, including the busiest part of Khefet-her-neb-es. He was holding a scroll of papyrus

Pa-neb said quietly, "You called me, Lord, so I am."

It seemed to Pa-neb that the One Who Knows the Secrets of Waset has not noticed his entry. However, after a while, he slowly turned his head towards the door and looked at the subordinate standing in them. Then he unrolled the papyrus and began to look alternately at Pa-neb and at this manuscript, as if there was a connection between them. After some time he rolled up the scroll again and suddenly threw it under Pa-neb's feet, with a short question asked in a very unpleasant tone, "What is this?!"

Pa-neb bent down, picked up the scroll, unrolled it, and an indescribable amazement appeared on his face. An unknown artist - apparently a very talented draftsman - placed here a series of strange illustrations drawn next to each other, which represented some typical scenes that could be found in tombs or temples, but where the role of people was unexpectedly played by animals. Here the army is attacking the fortress, but the cats are the defenders, the mice are the attackers, and the mouse king is running in a chariot drawn by dogs. Close by, a donkey wearing a priestly dress stands at the offering table. Near a cat grazes the ducks, and above the musicians stand: a donkey plays the harp, a lion the lyre, a crocodile the lute and a monkey the flute[152].

Pa-neb has never seen anything like this. The scenes were funny and could only cause dignitary's amusement, not anger. „So, why..."Pa-neb, embarrassed, asked in mind, and unrolled this papyrus a little more. Then he saw something that might have cheered someone up, but certainly not him. Here the main "hero" of several scenes was Pa-neb, easily recognizable by his bald head with an addition of a tuft of hair sticking out in disarray at the back, as well as by the rounded belly. These scenes clearly illustrated his adventures in the house of the "sisters",

---

[152] Two papyri with such scenes have been preserved. One is located in the British Museum, while the other is the above-mentioned *Erotic Papyrus* from Turin, some of which contain satirical scenes with animals.

adorned with a few short comments. In addition to the images illustrating his possibilities, which he was so proud of, he also noticed others, by no means glorifying him. Here he lies under the bed, complaining that "he is sick," while the girl stretches out her arms towards him, saying: "My bed is empty", and a little further the "sisters" carry him away, the drunk one, which actually happened to him sometimes, though he wasn't going to brag about it.

"I don't know what that means," Pa-neb mumbled, "or where it came from..."

"Where did it come from?!" – Pa-Shu-uben roared – "It was sent to me today from the office of the General himself! The whole City laughs at you and everyone I meet, "congratulates" me on such a servant. You make fun of yourself and of me. What for such a fool to me who can't follow anyone, but who can "fight" only with women and those who don't defend themselves!"

"I try, Lord, to carry out all your orders..." Pa-neb murmured, terrified that he would be thrown out soon and lose his only source of income.

"You are trying to? But you are not trying hard! Do you remember Suti-mes? You were to arrest him, and you failed, then he disappeared, and you were to find out where he was, but you also did not succeed! You prated that Amen-em-Ipet had sent him to Iunu, yet "our friend" found himself in Abu! Captain Khnum-nakht I know, has just told me about it. This Suti-mes, let donkey rape him, made a row about some stupid sacks of grain! And there he and his family are really safe, and I will do nothing to them!"

"Lord, if you say that this priest is on Abu, then he certainly is, but his woman still lives in Khefet-her-neb-es, in the house of Djehuty-mes!" Pa-neb sputtered the words quickly as if feeling that this was for him the last resort from the consequences of Pa-Shu-uben's anger.

The dignitary who was actually about to tell Pa-neb that he was dismissing him, has paused, was thinking for a moment, and then he has dropped the sentence: "If so, I'll reach him differently...You have proven that you are only suitable for dealing with women. So, deal with this, what's her name?"

"Henut-netjeru."

"...right. Fix her ultimately. I don't care how you'll do it... I want that the Captain Khnum-nakht would bring Suti-mes a piece of news on his next visit to Abu... let's say about an unfortunate accident. I wonder if he will be then equally so inquisitive when counting sacks... And by the way, find out who painted you so beautifully, he is a talented man and deserves a reward..."

Pa-neb sensed the mockery in Pa-Shu-uben's last words, but without a word he bowed and left, taking the papyrus.

"It is a pity that such nice drawings would perish; just watching them evokes pleasant memories", he thought. "So, again I got a task to do and if I try hard, it can be even nice! This girl is not bad at all...It's certain that I can't disappoint Pa-Shu-uben again!"

Without wasting time, as soon as he took the papyrus home, he left again and went to observe the house of Djehuty-mes.

The days that have now come, have brought a considerable animation to the City and have provided the inhabitants of both banks with unforgettable sensations. A flotilla of ships and transport barges moored to the eastern bank and all military equipment was loaded there: parts of chariots, siege ladders, rams, huge shields for archers, and above all large numbers of arrows, bows, spears and shields. Other vessels were to transport large supplies of food - dried meat, dates, *cucu* fruit, onions, as well as sacks with grains, jugs with oil and everything necessary for the production of bread and beer, that is, the most important things for everyone.

Numerous troops were moving to the City, among which Tjehenu with their feathers stuck in hair and Sherdana wearing the characteristic helmets ended with balls were easily distinguishable. This time the Kushite squads were absent, because the General and High Priest Pi-ankh didn't want to take with his army even those few Kushites who remained in Kemet after the last war, for fear that they might decide to come over to the side of the enemy. The City was preparing for a military expedition against Pa-nehsi's forces, the strength of which – as the scouts reported – was also growing. Pi-ankh, after all, was not going to bring about a decisive confrontation; the Egyptian army was too weak for this and the outcome of an eventual battle was uncertain. The real purpose was to demonstrate to the Kushites, who certainly had their scouts in Kemet, too, that the State of Amun is aware of the threat and is by no means passive. Pi-ankh hoped that such a manifestation of strength would facilitate negotiations that were his main goal. For the residents of the City, quite differently, everything that was happening was understood as a clear sign that, as it happened many times in the past, the army of the Both Countries is again setting out to suppress the Nine Bows. It was clear to everyone that this time the Kushites were precisely meant under this general designation, and the memory of them was still fresh here. Therefore they reacted with unbelievable enthusiasm to this accumulation of troops which were now supposed going to avenge the victims of the long occupation, fear and hunger and all who died in the battle at Hor-di. It was difficult to meet a family in the City which didn't lose somebody next of kin at that time.

When the time came for the flotilla to sail towards Abu, horses were loaded onto the barges and subsequent units were taking their assigned places on the boats. Virtually all the City residents gathered on both banks, while greeting the soldiers and wishing them a successful return soon. The General didn't make any speeches: he was not a good speaker and didn't like official ceremonies. For the period of his absence, he left the temple matters – and only these – in the hands of his son Pi-nodjem, who was assisted by the old Amen-em-Ipet. With all the other tasks he entrusted Pa-Shu-uben whom he liked and sensed him as kindred spirit. He spent a lot of time in his company, especially at wine, which they both didn't avoid. If he hadn't the son, Pi-nodjem, whose career he had long prepared, he would probably make Pa-Shu-uben as his successor. However, knowing the ambitions of the Chief of the Police, Pi-ankh has decided to make his daughter Nodjmet, the widow of Heri-Hor, as a kind of controller and advisor for Pa-Shu-uben. He knew, of course, very well that the two of them hated each other.

Old Djehuty-mes was clearly nervous since Pi-ankh and the army went towards Abu. Admittedly he didn't like the General, who in no way was suitable for the role of High Priest, and whose attitude to temples, priests and most likely to the faith itself left much to be desired, but his presence in the City was giving some feeling of safety and protection against the unlawful activities of his subordinates. Now, however, the real power was in the hands of the one who had been the persecutor of their friend and his family for a long time. Djehuty-mes had no illusions that Pa-Shu-uben would forget about Suti-mes, but since this one was safe at the moment, the old Necropolis Scribe was thinking with all the greater anxiety about Henut. Pa-Shu-uben has already hurt her once, so he certainly won't hesitate to do it again. Yet Henut naively believed that since she doesn't do anything wrong to anyone, the evil will pass her by. She was leaving the house more and more often, while walking with little Pen-Amun. Chari was always then scolding, but the young woman obviously underestimated a danger. Therefore, he decided to protect her differently. Among the *medjayu* who guarded the Necropolis, were two war veterans, particularly devoted to Djehuty-mes: Kari and Kasaya, the same men who were once sent with a letter to King Ramesses. Their mission was not quite successful at that time, however they revealed that they were fully reliable. At the same time, they were exceptionally fortunate people, because they both survived the battle of Hor-di.

When the two dark-skinned servants arrived summoned by Djehuty-mes, he first began a general conversation with them about guarding the tombs, but having winked at Buteh-Amun, he sent him for Henut, "...to bring fresh water to drink." After a while, the young woman came in carrying the jug; her little son Pen-Amun has run into the room behind his mother, while loudly demanding to be carried.

Everyone, of course, was watching the scene for a while, and when Henut met her son's requirements, and left, apologizing for the disruption of the conversation, the old Necropolis Scribe again turned to both *medjayu*, "I am very happy that you could have a good look at this woman and this child, because, to tell you the truth, that's why I called you. You once undertook a very difficult mission of carrying a letter to the King so that no one in the City would have noticed you. Today, I would like to entrust you with an even more difficult task: I want you to watch over the safety of these two, but also so that neither she nor anyone else finds out. I think she is in danger, but this young woman does not believe it, she goes more and more often for long walks and especially likes to walk along this old canal running to the former lake and this old house by the water, where it is difficult to meet somebody. I have a very bad feeling about this, and my feelings usually don't deceive me. Protect her, please, because she is like a daughter for me!"

Kari and Kasaya bowed respectfully and, putting their hands on their hearts, promised that they would do their best to secure that nobody harms a hair on the heads of these two. However, neither they nor Djehuty-mes suspected that the premonition of the old Necropolis Scribe was to be fulfilled just on the next day.

Pa-neb has known for a long time where Henut usually goes after leaving the temple precinct within the walls of which the house of Djehuty-mes stood. If she was going shopping, she was turning right and visited then the bakery and the shoppers in the busiest part of Khefet-her-neb-es; there was no chance to surprise a woman without witnesses, and this was what Pa-neb intended to do. But Henut also liked walking along the canal shaded by numerous trees and partly overgrown with reeds, which was begun south of the haven before the eastern gate of the precinct and ran towards the old port built in the days of King Amenhotep Neb-Maat-Re. This port didn't fulfill its function anymore since long and was overgrown with rushes so that it resembled a pond. Besides, Henut liked to walk there also because among these reeds memories of that day came alive when she led Sutimes there and although she ran away from herself then, this place was always associated with the feeling of happiness offered by the closeness of the beloved boy regained after years of longing. Now she was missing him, too, but the noise of the reeds, from which she was catching his passionate words whispered to her then, let create a short-lived oblivion to everyday worries. Henut used to walk slowly here, while enjoying the shadow and silence that were lacking in Khefet-her-neb-es. She was taking with her the small Pen-Amun sometimes, but then she had always to carry him during the return journey, which was exhausting, therefore she usually waited until the little one fell asleep and then went out to meet her memories.

Pa-neb was lurking, usually hidden in the shadow of the temple, while waiting for the day when Henut would go on such a lonely walk. When the General left and full power was vested in Pa-Shu-uben, the best time occurred for implementing the plan. Initially, Pa-neb considered whether to just run to the woman walking and stab her with a dagger, but first of all, he has never killed anyone and was not sure if his hand wouldn't shake at the last moment. Secondly, at the sight of gushing blood, he was coming over dizzy, even if it was the blood of a ram or a duck. Finally, thirdly (or maybe firstly?) Pa-neb liked young women too much, and Henut was extremely pretty. Therefore, he made a different resolution, wanting not only to fulfill the order of Pa-Shu-uben, but also to have some pleasure: he would stun the woman with a club, then take her, and after that drown her in the canal. He prepared his very hard wooden cane, which in normal circumstances could be a sign of dignity; almost all the officials were carrying such objects on everyday occasions so that the cane itself didn't arouse anyone's suspicion. He practiced various ways of striking for a long time, while placing clay jugs filled with water or sand at the height of the head of an adult man, which he was running up to and striking with all his strength. Finally he gained such a skill that he was smashing a pitcher with every blow, regretting the loss he suffered, but promising himself a purchase of new and better vessels, whenever he receives the prize from Pa-Shu-uben.

On that day the expected moment came at last. It was a late afternoon. Henut appeared at the gate of the temple precinct alone and turned left, so she was going for her walk. Kari and Kasaya who were to follow her discretely, according to the promise made to Djehuty-mes, were just going to set off behind her, heading for the old canal, when they suddenly noticed something strange. From below the temple wall, not far from the place, where they were standing, a man sitting there so far stood up and started going in the same direction as the woman. He was behaving strangely from the beginning, because he looked around as if to make sure that no one was following him.

Kari took a closer look at him and said quietly to Kasaya:

"Listen, isn't this Pa-neb, who has nickname "Bull"?

"This one from the papyrus?"

They both started laughing: the pictures showing Pa-neb at the house of the "sisters" before reaching the General himself had been spreading among practically the entire male community in Khefet-her-neb-es, being shown in a beer house, being viewed by street vendors, barbers, medics, *medjayu,* temple guards and cleaners of the streets, and apart from the official elite only Pa-neb was not aware of the existence of this papyrus, until he was given it by Pa-Shu-uben.

"Look how dignified he presents himself: have you ever seen him with a cane?" Kari added, and Kasaya, looking more accurately at Pa-neb's behavior, asked: "Doesn't he, by any chance, follow the daughter of Djehuty-mes?"

They both fell silent because they were approaching the canal, along which only one narrow road was running, completely shaded by trees, and they had to start sneaking, if they didn't want to be noticed. Henut was walking slowly, lost in reverie, and surrounded by silence. A few dozens steps behind her, Pa-neb silently moved, while slowly approaching the woman. He knew this road perfectly and didn't expect that anyone may appear here at this time. Although he looked back several times, he made this not enough accurately to notice the two other "walkers" who were trying hard not to become visible. At every moment when he began to turn his head, Kasaya and Kari instantly were becoming motionless under the nearest tree. However, the unexpected appearance of Pa-neb caused that they were walking at quite a long distance from Henut, and Kasaya noticed this at one point, while whispering to his companion: "We were supposed to protect her, and now we are too far away, and if "Bull" would like to hurt her, what will we do? Look, he is clearly chasing her..."

Indeed, Pa-neb decided that it was time to swing into action, because Henut might soon want to turn back. All the houses of Khefet-her-neb-es already disappeared completely behind the trees, and only a distant dogs' bark could be heard. Thus, Pa-neb stopped looking around, he grabbed his cane at the base, and in a few leaps he reached the walking woman. He took a violent swing. At the same moment he heard screams from behind: "Stop! Henut, watch out!"

The young woman turned away, but she couldn't avoid the blow anymore, she only mechanically covered her head with her left arm, on which a terrible cane blow came down at the same time. Henut firstly heard the unpleasant sound of bones breaking, then she felt awful pain, and collapsed unconscious to the ground. Pa-neb imagined this moment just like that, but he couldn't proceed according to his plan, because Kari and Kasaya reached him at the same time and twisted his hands.

"Ah, you're such a bull! Wait, you won't get away with it! Oh, a bastard, with a club to a defenseless woman?" Kari sputtered sentences one after another without concealing his terror. Here a young woman whom Djehuty-mes loved as a daughter and entrusted to his protection, lay now without senses.

"Save her, Kasaya!" he dropped a plea to his companion, "and I'll deal with this crud!"

Then he twisted Pan-nebe's hand even harder, and with his other one grasped him by the rare shags sticking out behind his head, and said briefly: "Go and don't try to run, otherwise I'll break your arm!" and began to lead the prisoner towards Khefet-her-neb-es.

Pa-neb, of course, recognized the two *medjayu* and decided to defend himself in his own way.

"You fool, you don't know what this one is? This woman has long been wanted and accused of helping a criminal! You've interrupted my arrest; my lord will repay you accordingly! Let me free, because only then you may save your heads!"

"Don't talk nonsense!" Kari spot out: "We know this woman; if it was as you say, you could have arrested her a long time ago. But you wanted to do something different with her, that's why we'll hand you over to the City guards! And don't scare us with your master, because we personally know General Pi-ankh, who is the superior of Pa-Shu-uben!"

"You miserable servant of the necropolis, do you still have the audacity to lie like that?!" Pa-neb shouted with squeaky voice. "Do you personally know His Grandness High Priest?"

"Yes, we know each other from the old days when he was not a High Priest yet. We gave him a letter from the First Servant of Amun Amen-hotep to His Majesty the King!" Kari was outraged. This vile rat Pa-neb, whom they just captured when he wanted to commit a crime, accuses him of lying! Now Pa-neb was silent, though he remembered every word of the black policeman perfectly. He did not even resist when Kari led him to the *medjayu* post in Khefet-her-neb-es where told about what had happened on the canal. Policemen put the prisoner in the wooden stocks, and while thanking the brave man, they promised that "bull" would be sent to the custody at Pa-Shu-uben's palace today.

"We thought that he only bravely deals with "sisters," but we can see that he decided to expand his contacts. He cannot be sent to Kush now, so one should cut off his nose and ears, and maybe not only that... It would be the best punishment for him," added Kari and went quickly to the house of Djehuty-mes, where he found everyone gathered around a makeshift bed arranged in a room where guests were received. Henut, whom Kasaya had just brought, was laid there, already awaken, but now moaning and shading tears of pain. Her left arm was swollen, bloodstained, and here and there purple one: Pa-neb's cane not only broke both forearm bones, but caused a huge bruise. The doctor, called hurriedly, has examined the arm thoroughly, while mumbling the magic texts of spells, and then he ordered to pour a large amount of cold water on it, and into the mouth of the woman the entire content of a large cup of wine mixed with herbs. Then he committed the men being present here to hold Henut firmly so that she couldn't move, and having grabbed her sick arm he began to press it, while putting the broken bones in place. In consequence of the awful pain, Henut fainted again. After some time, the medic, while still holding the ill arm, asked for two small flat pieces of wood, which he laid on both sides of the arm, and wrapped everything around with a strong bandage.

"You should give her wine and these herbs continually; she must sleep a lot making no moves with this arm. If Khonsu wants, in two months everything will go back and she may be able to perform normal activities, but you have to pray a lot because it was a bad blow," he said while leaving.

Djehuty-mes, who had almost fainted himself, when Kasaya brought in Henut hanging listlessly from his hands, was only repeating during all the medic's actions: "I knew, I knew it would happen, I had a bad feeling". After the medic had left, he got up and prepared to leave as well.

"Where do you want to go, father?" Buteh-Amun asked, "It is already getting dark."

"There is no time to lose. These villains are ready to come even here: Henut must find better protection."

"Is it possible? Will it be better to her anywhere than with us?"

"You can see it yourself. We did everything, but even Kari and Kasaya didn't preserve her from this terrible adventure, although they certainly saved her life. Now, they may become suspects themselves, and maybe they will be persecuted, because Kari told Pa-neb unnecessarily about this old story with a letter. I am old, you have many duties and you are rarely present at home. Who will defend Henut, if this rat Pa-neb or another rogue comes here with evil intentions? To whom will you complain? To Pa-Shu-uben? Even Pi-ankh doesn't guarantee that he will respect Maat. There is only one person whom Henut can find a safe shelter, together with her son: this is Nodjmet and I am going to her."

Although he was walking little, the old Necropolis Scribe immediately set off to a nearby harbor in front of the eastern gate of the precinct of Ramesses Meri-Amun, where his boat with faithful crew was always ready to depart, and his arrival was soon reported to the daughter of the High Priest.

Nodjmet received him all the more warmly since they have not seen each other for a long time, although she did not hide her surprise that the old and sick official came to her personally. When she found out what brought him, she immediately ordered that a litter should be sent, along with Djehuty-mes, when he would return to Khefet-her-neb-es. In this litter Henut and little Pen-Amun were to be transported from the Western City to Nodjmet's palace in Ipet-sut.

"I'll include her in the group of my personal servants," she said. "Of course, I'll provide her with care and the best medic, and I will not let her work until she is fully recovered. If I knew what threatened her, I would have done it before, but who could suppose that this nasty Pa-Shu-uben would seek revenge on a defenseless girl? General Pi-ankh is my father, but we don't understand with my brother what he sees in this villain? Although..." Nodjmet suspended her voice, "The power of Pa-Shu-uben will not last long... I know, Chari, that you can keep secret what someone entrusts to you, so I tell this only you, that my father is seriously ill, although he doesn't let feel it. When he was leaving, he bid me farewell for an exceptionally long time, and he mentioned to Pi-nodjem something about the grave in which he would like to rest... I'm afraid that I may not see him again, especially since he was going to war. I love him..." Nodjmet wiped a tear furtively.

CHAPTER XXV

Still on the same day Pa-Shu-uben learnt about the arresting of Pa-neb, but he did not rush to any intervention. He was mad at his subordinate and decided to keep him in prison for some time. Finally, after 10 days he has called a prisoner who stood before him starving and sleepy, actually half dead and brimming with fear because he didn't know if Pa-Shu-uben wouldn't want to treat him this time as a criminal, since he didn't respond to repeated pleas for release from the custody.

"Well, how do you like my prison?- Pa-Shu-uben greeted him harshly, looking with disdain and also with disgust at the shrunken figure standing in the doorway, from which very unpleasant whiffs were coming through the entire length of the chamber. "But you are stinking, I wonder if the "sisters" would welcome you today... I see that you didn't become accustomed to live in such conditions, but maybe it is worth getting used to?

One more assault on a woman and you will spend the rest of your life there, which, I think, wouldn't last too long."

Pa-neb was almost speechless with surprise, "Lord, you have ordered me…"

"I have ordered something completely different. If you had stabbed her with a dagger, it would have been all over now, and even her defenders wouldn't have been in time to save her."

"You said you don't care how I do it," Pa-neb defended himself.

"Well, I have forgotten that you have only one thing in mind when it comes to women. Now, she is living in the palace of Nodjmet, and we will not get there. Suti-mes is also safe, and it's all because of you, jackass!" Pa-Shu-uben has turned red with anger and Pa-neb understood that the last moment has come to save himself.

"Lord, Suti-mes is far away, but those who arrested me, the people of Djehuty-mes, are here and they know some things too. One of them mentioned that they had once been sent to the King with a letter from High Priest Amen-hotep and that they gave this letter to General Pi-ankh, so they know him personally and will complain to him about you!"

Pa-Shu-uben has knitted his brows while rubbing his forehead. He didn't remember this case or never heard of it. Could such a talk of ordinary *medjayu* be harmful to Pi-ankh's authority? But since they are in the service of Djehuty-mes, then one could, by the way, direct the General's suspicion against him and muddle thereby this awfully clear water around all those obnoxious virtuous ones, including his daughter..."

"I think I have to write to him about it," he murmured, and Pa-neb has almost interrupted him:

"And Lord, ask His Grandness to send an answer through Suti-mes - after all, as High Priest of Amun, he has power over the people of Amen-em-Ipet!"

"Sometimes even a fool has flashes of right senses", Pa-Shu-uben thought and smiled for the first time since many days.

Suti-mes was going through a hard time. A month elapsed since General Pi-ankh had arrived in Abu, and Suti-mes has not received any letter from Henut since then, even though on account of the stay of the head of the State of Amun here boats were coming from the City virtually every day, bringing besides supplies also couriers who were usually going straight to the palace of the Administrator of the First District of the South, where Pi-ankh was stationed. War preparations were visible everywhere. The dismembered chariots were unloaded from the ships and they again took the form of dangerous armors vehicles, and horses brought on other barges, were grazing on a riverside meadow behind a firm fence. The desert on the east bank, near Sunu, was covered with a multitude of tents, and the military units were making daily trainings. The flotilla carrying a siege equipment could also gain the respect of the enemy. Pi-ankh had no doubt that Pa-nehsi was constantly informed about what was happening in and around Abu, so he was to receive a clear message that the Both Countries were preparing for an expedition against Kush.

Finally, after nearly two months long break, Suti-mes received the so much expected letter from Buteh-Amun, and only then he understood why he had not heard from Henut for so long. Buteh-Amun wrote that only now, after another medical check they got the news good enough: the broken bones were healing well and Henut could move all fingers and the whole arm without pain.

We were so far simply afraid to tell you about what had happened, because who knows if you wouldn't have gone home then, perhaps at your own undoing, and besides we didn't know whether Henut would regain an absolute use of her wounded arm. Now we know that your wife will regain her health entirely, so I can describe what happened to her. Then came a colorful description of the whole event. *The worst is that Pa-neb despite the fact that he was given to the guards and arrested is still being seen in the City that is he has not suffered any punishment for his assault. As you can see, Pa-Shu-uben rules here now, and as long as it will be like that, Maat will be absent here.* Farther in the letter, Suti-mes finally got the words dictated, as usual, by Henut, who greeted him, while assuring of her love and her good health. *My arm is almost perfectly healthy, and the medic said that he would take my bandages off in a few days. I won't be able only to carry anything heavy, nor to work hard. Most of all I feel sorry for our little Pen-Amun who often wants me to carry him in my arms, and when I don't take him, he cries bitterly. Our son is growing fast, I hope that you will find this yourself soon. I am now completely safe at Nodjmet, for whom I work in the palace for the time being I dust furniture in her rooms, and we'll see later what will happen. Dear, tell me why some people were so hard on us: you and me? What wrong have we done to them?*

There was also a short note of Buteh-Amun in the lower part of the papyrus, but this amazed Suti-mes most of all. Buteh-Amun, no less astonished, reported that General Pi-ankh suddenly summoned the old Djehuty-mes to come to Abu *...who is of such an age that he is unfit to participate in the war.*[153] *Nobody knows Pi-ankh's intentions, but we're all worried about my father's health, so we entrust him to your protection. His boat should reach Abu in three or four days.*

Suti-mes finished reading, but he couldn't deny himself the pleasure of repeating it. He could finally do not worry about his wife and son: they lived in a safe place, where not only Pa-neb or another scoundrel on his sort couldn't reach them, but also where the power of Pa-Shu-uben didn't extend. Suti-mes felt his surging gratitude to Queen Nodjmet. She was at Henut's age, having a son only a little less than two years older than Pen-Amun, so she understood well all the problems of motherhood, and as a widow as well those of feminine longing, and at the same time she was kind-hearted. Suti-mes imagined that the two boys may play with each other. "In that case", he thought, "the more so Henut and Pen-Amun are really safe. But why does Pi-ankh call Djehuty-mes

---

[153] Several museums and libraries (in Berlin, Geneva, Leiden, London, Paris and Turin) contain a set of letters written on papyri in the 10th year of the *uhem mesut* by Amon's High Priest Pi-ankh and officials of his administration. These letters mainly concern the period when Pi-ankh was in Elephantine, from where he travelled to Nubia, also taking the very old Necropolis scribe Djehuty-mes, about whom the family was worried. The sentence quoted here is a literal quote from one of Buteh-Amon's letters.

to Abu? To what purpose does he need an old man who is close to his grave?" These considerations were interrupted by a priest Suti-mes knew from the temple of Khnum, one of those who emphasized their gratitude to Suti-mes at every step after he has unraveled the riddle of grain.

"Suti," he said, while stopping at the door, "you are looked for. Apparently, Pi-ankh wants you to come to him, and the matter is apparently very urgent one".

"What may Amun's First Servant want from me?" Suti-mes could not hide his surprise, but having put aside the precious papyrus, he hurried to the palace of the District Administrator of Abu, transformed temporarily into the residence of the High Priest. Dimness pervaded in the chamber, where he was led to, and his eyes had first to get used to it to see the figure of the General wandering back and forth in the room.

"Your Grandness have called me," Suti-mes said quietly, and Pi-ankh stopped and looked in his direction, then called out to the servants and ordered that lighted lamps should be brought. In their light, Suti-mes could look from close range at the figure of the General, whom he had previously seen only once in passing years in Pi-Ramesse. The first thing that struck him was Pi-ankh's face: red and tumid, as if as a result of a bee sting, deep in which the eyes were shining disproportionately small in relation to this huge face, as if belonging to another person. Pi-ankh was also looking at a young man whom he obviously didn't remember, and about whom he learnt from the letter of Pa-Shu-uben that he was the former trusted servant of the High Priest Amen-hotep, and a strong opponent of him, Pi-ankh. "He was wanted since long," Pa-Shu-uben wrote, "…for matters that I'll pass over, not wanting to bother Your Grandness. Besides, here in the City, he left his wife with a small child who are living in poverty, while he leads a life of luxury in Abu. By sending him here, you will help his family, because I'll try to make them reunite". After such a description, Pi-ankh imagined the young priest quite differently. He wondered what kind of doing mentioned by Pa-Shu-uben he had on his conscience, but eventually, he decided to leave this thread.

"I have heard a lot about you," the General said finally, "you have a faithfully served His Grandness Amen-hotep justified?"

"It was a great happiness for me, Lord," he heard in reply, so he added:

"You probably know that a monument for his Ka was erected in the temple of Amun in Ipet-sut?"

"Yes, I had been granted myself the honor of arranging the text, which was carved on it," he answered, which caused the General's surprise.

"Ah, you were the author? I thought it was done by Amen-em-Ipet… It doesn't matter. I am sending you with important letters. First: I stress "first," you will go to Pa-Shu-uben, and then to Her Royal Highness Nodjmet. Wait in the next room until I write these letters."

Pi-ankh turned and walked towards the stool, while sitting on which he used to write his letters, but when he sat down, he saw that Suti-mes was still standing.

"Do you have a request for me?"

"Yes, Lord, I dare to ask you for the grace of intervention against a certain Pa-neb who brutally assaulted my wife, but Maat didn't meet him, and therefore he can be dangerous again."

"Pa-neb? This scoundrel?" Pi-ankh was clearly surprised, but he immediately recalled the papyrus with drawings of scenes in which "the Bull" played the main role and smiled honestly.

"I can see, after all, that your wife isn't indifferent to you... Well, I mention about that in a letter to Pa-Shu-uben," the General answered and reached for a scroll of papyrus, which meant that the audience was over. Suti-mes bowed and left, wondering what Pi-ankh's words might mean? Would have Henut been indifferent to him? What did the smile on the face of the dignitary mean when he mentioned Pan-neb? One thing was certain: Pa-neb wasn't Pi-ankh's favorite. Perhaps he will, after all, be arrested?

Meanwhile, Pi-ankh quickly wrote a few words to Nodjmet:

General of the army of Pharaoh, may he live in happiness and health, to the Chief of the Women's Service of Amun-Re, King of Gods, the noble Lady Nodjmet, may she live in prosperity, health and in the favor of Amun-Re, King of Gods! Every day I tell to all the images of God by whom I pass to cause you to live and to be in health and to let me see you when I come back and to fill my eyes with the sight of you. I have noted all matters about which you have written to me. As for these two medjayu and for what they had said, join with Pa-Shu-uben and the Scribe Chari, then bring them to my house, order them briefly to tell what their words had to mean, and, if you find it's true, after that kill them, then place them in two sacks and throw them by night into the water. Write me, how are you? Keep well.[154]

He rolled up the papyrus without reading, then began to write to Pa-Shu-uben:

I am sending you, as you wanted, this Suti-mes. He looks like a decent man and it turns out that he is concerned about his wife. I have heard that Pa-neb did something wrong to her; doesn't that jackass distinguish anymore between "sisters" and honest housewives? You should dismiss him because he is a disgrace to you. Place him in the new craftsmen's town[155]*, where the guards will keep an eye on him; he may be suitable perhaps for handing tools and water, and you will have one more ear there. And now, another matter.*[156] *As for these two medjayu you wrote to me about while quoting their words, join up with Nodjmet and the Scribe Chari, and send and have them brought to my house and get to the bottom of their words in short order, and if you find it's true, slay them, then place them in two sacks and throw them into this water by night. But do not let anybody of this land find out about them.*

Pi-ankh finished writing, sealed both papyri with clay, sealed them with his ring, and then called Suti-mes again.

---

[154] This is a literal translation of Pi-ankh's entire letter to his daughter Nodjmet, with a short supplement quoted from Pi-ankh's letter to Djehuty-mes; both letters are kept today in the Papyri Collection of the Egyptian Museum in Berlin.

[155] During the turbulent times of riots during the reign of Ramesses XI, a group of craftsmen who carried out work on the necropolis, moved from the former town (Deir el-Medina) to the area where the seat of the administrative authorities in Thebes (Medinet Habu) was located.

[156] From this point on, the contents of Pi-ankh's letter to Pa-Shu-uben shall be identical to the authentic document, as keeping in Berlin too.

You will leave with these letters tomorrow at dawn with my boat. I want them to reach the addressees as soon as possible, and you probably want to see your wife and child. Go!

Suti-mes came out joyful. He is to go to the City as an official messenger of the High Priest himself! What can Pa-Shu-uben do to him? Anyway, he won't stay in his palace for a long time, but he will go right after to Nodjmet, where he will see his loved ones! This thought delighted him so much that he could not sleep at night while waiting impatiently the dawn's advent. When he arrived in the harbor, it turned out that one was only waiting for him and the boat departed immediately. While sitting on the prow and absorbing the fresh breeze coming from the river, Suti-mes was looking at the palm groves and the fields passed by, over which sweeps with clay pots hanging were leaning from time to time. People were almost absent, even the peasants had not left for work yet. Re was just rising with his large bloody ball, half-obscured by a band of gray clouds. Suti-mes' thoughts, as usual, soared to his loved ones, and then he realized that as followed from the last Buteh-Amun's letter, the old Djehuty-mes was on his way to Abu, where Suti-mes was to protect him. In this situation, there could be no option to do that. This impossibility of acting on his friend's request has saddened Suti-mes. For a long moment he was considering what he could do, and finally he found a solution.

He took out his scribe's palette, and in a few words wrote a letter to Shed-su-Hor – a Hat-Hor's priest he knew and who was an officer in the army that came from the City:

I pray to Amun that he may give you health, prosperity and the favor of the General and that he will let you return home. Well, Pi-ankh sent me unexpectedly to the City and I am on my way, but at the same time my and your good friend, the Scribe of Necropolis Chari will come soon to Abu, and I won't be able to take care of him. Please, help him! You know that he is a man who doesn't have his strength at all, for he never before made the journey, on which he is. Assist him in the boat. Look with vigilance in the evening as well. And be a pilot for him, then Amun shall be a pilot for you[157].

The only Suti-mes's problem remaining now was how he will forward this letter to the island of Abu. Djehuty-mes should also be notified that Suti-mes wouldn't wait for him in Abu. The priest looked at the river that was not as wide here as near Waset, and thought that by no means one can overlook a boat coming from the north, so that their boats should pass each other at some point. He decided to reveal to the Captain his plans to meet Djehuty-mes, to whom, as he emphasized,..."I'd like to convey important information intended for the High Priest Pi-ankh, and I know that the Necropolis Scribe will go straight to him.

The Captain agreed without hesitation; he was a faithful servant of the General, so he recognized that he should certainly help a man who is sailing on the General's boat with General's letters. He even promised to stop all the official boats at the disposal of the Chief of the State of Amun sailing in the opposite direction.

---

[157] The last sentences are authentic quotations from two letters conserved in the British Museum, London, and in the National Library in Paris, both addressed to Shed-su-Hor and concerning, among others, the care due to the old Necropolis Scribe Djehuty-mes.

Suti-mes was pleased. He calculated that the meeting of the boats could take place tomorrow afternoon, however still the same day before dusk they noticed a rapidly approaching boat *tjesem* and it turned out that in fact there was Djehuty-mes on its board, The young priest was surprised that the meeting took place so quickly and that the Necropolis Scribe was on the boat of the High Priest, and not on his own, which, after all, was constantly at his disposal, but he learnt that Pi-ankh had sent his fast boat especially for Djehuty-mes, who, sailing in the meantime on his own boat, has reached Behdet town. From there the *tjesem* boat, using the favorable wind, and special sails was moving very quickly so that both ships met above the city of Nebit. Chari was just dozing in the boat's cabin when Pi-ankh's servant at his disposal entered there, introducing an unexpected guest.

"I thought I was still asleep; where did you come from, my friend?! Wouldn't it be enough if you greeted me just at Abu?" Djehuty-mes spread his arms and gave the young priest a warm hug.

"Unfortunately!" Suti-mes did not hide the bitterness, "I will not be there when you arrive, and I do not know if I will be in time back before your departure... I am on my way to the City, where the General sent me with his letters. That's why I absolutely wanted to meet you on the way, and I succeeded!"

At that moment, the Captain of Suti-mes' boat entered the cabin, bowed before the old man, but turned to Suti-mes. "Forgive me, Lord, but we've only stopped for a moment so that you can pass on the letter you mentioned. His Grandness the General insisted on rush, so we must move on."

"Of course, Captain, but let me at least say goodbye, because I was just saying hello, and the Royal Necropolis Scribe also has important news for me," Suti-mes said, looking eloquently at his friend.

"That is true, Captain," the old priest nodded, "This is confidential, so give us a moment; otherwise the General would not be pleased." The Captain, though showing clear signs of impatience, bowed again and said, "Please, hurry up. I am waiting on my boat!" then left the cabin, leaving friends alone.

"What letter was he talking about?" Djehuty-mes asked silently, fearing that the Captain might step back and hear a fragment of their conversation.

"Here is the letter!" Suti-mes has uttered the sentence loudly, and clearly. "Please, hand it over to General's officer, Shed-su-Hor who will hand it over to the General!" Quieter he added: "It is just a letter to Shed-su-Hor who will replace me in my duties towards you. I wanted to ask you about so many things... How are Henut, Pen-Amun, Buteh-Amun, Shed-em-dua, the children...? However, as you can see, they won't even let us enjoy our company."

"To all your questions about the family, thank God, I have only one answer: good! You know that Henut is now in the palace of Nodjmet, among her adjutant servants, where she is safe and I know that she and the daughter of Pi-ankh got like to each other, and their children are still playing with each other."

Suti-mes smiled broadly and he said while looking cordially at his friend: "I am going with a letter to Nodjmet, so I will see them soon, just after I give another letter to Pa-Shu-uben, to whom the General ordered me to go first."

"For Amun-Re-Hor-akhty, Montu and Sekhmet! My friend, don't do it!" Facial expression of Djehuty-mes' has suddenly changed. "Under no circumstances and regardless of any future consequences, you cannot start with a visit to Pa-Shu-uben, because you can never leave his house: remember that there is a prison and that precisely in that home this villain hurt Henut!" Djehuty-mes was quickly throwing the words of warning, "Swear to Hat-Hor and to your love that you'll go to Nodjmet first!"

Suti-mes was surprised by the words of his friend; he was raging with contradictory feelings. He was obliged to fulfill the order of Amun's First Servant, and, after all, was the mere fact that he fulfills the mission with which he sends him not offering sufficient protection? The old man probably exaggerates. But when he looked again at the pale and truly terrified face of Djehuty-mes and recalled that this man's intuition towards Henut had once proved to be accurate, he put his hand on his heart and said seriously, "If you demand that from me, I swear!" and he embraced the old man warmly. "I hope we will see each other soon!" he added.

"Yes, let Amun do it!" Chari answered a little calmly down. "But go now, because your Captain will start to suspect that we are plotting something..."

"And he would be right a little," Suti-mes laughed and, jumping into his boat, he shouted out loudly: "Let Maat lead you!"

Both boats began to move away from each other quickly, and soon Suti-mes, who was still watching from the stern the departing ship with his friend on board, could only see the tall sail disappearing against the background of the sky still enlightened with the afterglow, but already darkening. Soon it also turned into a black spot, to vanish after a while on the river's horizon.

CHAPTER XXVI

Shed-su-Hor, to whom Djehuty-mes was led shortly after the boat carrying him moored to the harbor in Abu, warmly greeted the guest, surprised only that instead of Suti-mes whom he expected to see at the old man's side, only a letter was handed to him. Of course, he took care of the old man like a son.

He placed him in the comfortable room of Suti-mes, cushioned his bed with additional pillows, chose the right headrest so that the guest could sleep comfortably and provided the newcomer with all the food and drink, as well as fresh fruit in such abundance that Djehuty-mes protested, joking that the greatest danger of this far trip is not an inconvenience and fatigue, but the overeating.

Shed-su-Hor also immediately provided that Chari wouldn't be disturbed by anyone until the end of that day, also addressing to General Pi-ankh, along with an information about the arrival of the Necropolis Scribe, a personal request that he would receive the guest only the next day, taking into account the need of the old man to rest after the travel. The First Servant of Amun agreed with these arguments and it was only the next day that he sent his officer for an aged guest, who took Djehuty-mes to the chambers of the General.

Chari didn't know why he was called to Abu and he was very much curious indeed, about what he would hear, but at the same time also slightly worried, because he was never concealing his dislike of today's Chief of the State of Amun.

He was afraid a little of his impetuosity, which in combination with the widely known lack of good manners of this dignitary usually created problems for almost every interlocutor.

However, when he saw the High Priest, his appearance terrified him very much. Admittedly, he had not seen Pi-ankh for a long time, but the changes visible on his face and the pervasive swelling left no doubt that his illness was very serious.

"Please, Chari, don't say anything; I know what I am looking like" he said as a greeting when the old man entered the room. "You will soon have a new High Priest, and also probably a new King as well. It was reported to me that Ramesses was seriously ill. Although I also have heard other rumors that he was going personally to come to the south. This is obviously nonsense.

How could the King, may he live in happiness and health, come here? And in general, for whom this King may he live in happiness and health, is a superior?[158] Under no circumstances,

---

[158] The last two sentences are literal quotations from one of Pi-ankh's

he should not be let out from Pi-Ramesse, even though the Repeating of Births lasts already 10 years. Even only his mummy brought to the City would bring back bad memories. His grave, one of the first ones visible when you enter the Valley... excuse-me, Chari, I have forgotten to whom I say this – is actually ready, but it will have a different owner... I have ordered to open it and to prepare for myself, and I wrote to Buteh-Amun about it. After all, the kings are not the only ones who rest in the Valley. And my son, I think, will be King, maybe we can rest together; there is quite spaciously, ha, ha!"

A loud chopped laughter filled the room for a moment, and Djehuty-mes thought, not without some admiration, that since the General could really laugh by saying such a thing, he kept his old sense of humor and at least in these matters reasonably measures proportions, but of course, he said loudly, "Your Eminence, I can't listen to it calmly and my heart rebels against what you say about yourself. Nobody knows tomorrow, it's veiled to a man, so even you can't know when you will stand in the Two Maats Hall."[159]

---

letters to Djehuty-mes from Elephantine; the document is today at the Egyptian Museum in Berlin.

[159] According to the Egyptian religious ideas, this was the place where the court over the deceased took place. The term: two Maat refers to the principle of heart weighing illustrated by a popular scene. On one of the scales there is a symbol of God's law - Maat, on the other there is the heart of the deceased, in which Maat should also live; in this way both scales are balanced.

"Come on, Chari!" Pi-ankh rarely used beautiful names[160] in official conversations, and it was such a name of the old Necropolis Scribe that he now used, which meant that he treated the conversation as a private meeting. "Sometimes, unfortunately, one knows when it may happen. For example, the sentenced to death also know it. I brought you here just for you to help me to make Maat. Recently, I'm a bit touchy. Maybe I'm too nervous, or possible that I want to cheat the time, knowing how bad is my condition. For example, I have recently convicted to death two *medjayu* – your people – because Pa-Shu-uben wrote to me that they were gossiping about me. I have even sent you a letter on this issue, forgetting that you would not receive it because I had called you here before, and you are on the way... You see, Chari, I regret it now, because, as I know Pa-Shu-uben, he already carried out the sentence."

"It worries me, General, about what you have told me. Since you have called me to help you to make Maat, please, listen to my advice: don't trust Pa-shu-uben because he is a bad man who sometimes persecutes completely innocent people. It was even necessary to hide one of them from him here on Abu, and your noble daughter took care of his wife."

"Are you talking about Suti-mes?!" Pi-ankh asked, and his face became serious.

"Yes, I'm talking about him; we met on the way because you sent him with some letters..."

---

[160] In addition to his official name, the Egyptian often had another, so-called "small" or "beautiful" name, which was used, it seems, primarily among his closest friends.

"For Set!" Pi-ankh did not hide his anger, "I see that I did it stupid again because I told him to go straight to Pa-shu-uben. This one, let a donkey rape him, wrote to me that this Suti-mes had abandoned his wife and left his family in poverty! I meant well..."

"I hope so," Djehuty-mes cut in on him, "that in the last case, I helped you: I asked Suti-mes to go with another letter first; if he listened to me, maybe he is still alive. I don't know a more loving spouse like Suti-mes. You can see that Pa-Shu-uben is a liar."

Pi-ankh walked nervously around the chamber in silence, finally stood in front of the old man and said, "I want you to know, Chari... Everyone sometimes commits evil deeds and makes bad choices. Once, I trusted Pa-Shu-uben because we had similar assessments of the way of exercising power. I liked, of course for a time, the way Pa-nehsi ruled in the City For some early years, an order pervaded there, and only later the Kushite soldiers deemed themselves to be allowed everything. He probably also thought that he was standing above the law, and his wife strengthened him in this conviction. He got too many titles from the King, and some people seem to lose their senses then. Heri-Hor, I must admit, was different in this respect. But I considered Heri-Hor to be a rival for a long time, and I was friends with Pa-nehsi, supported him and sometimes even covered up for him...I would take it all back today. A lot of harm happened later and it's partly my fault. I hope that my son will correct my errors, but I also have to do something to make things easier for him. I want pass away while leaving behind a safe border which allows the peaceful development of the Land of

Amun. So long as Pa-nehsi hasn't grown too strong yet, and his kingdom is still under construction, I want to show that we are not afraid of him. I will sail up the river with the army to meet Pa-nehsi where he is[161] but not to fight him, because we are too weak for that now, but to talk and to get what is possible to stop the outbreak of the new war. I want to take you, Chari, to the south so that you were next to me when I'd have to write a letter to him. You can see that I am often directed by a fire in my heart. I want you to be like cold water for me, which will extinguish this fire when needed. I hope you won't refuse me?"

Pi-ankh turned a questioning look to the old man. He was, admittedly, the superior of the Necropolis Scribe and could command him, but he felt that now he was expecting help from his subject, whose experience and good judgment evoked high regard in the Both Countries. In addition, he was feeling a great and previously unknown need to confide in someone his thoughts, confess his doubts, and even admit his mistakes of the past. He has already begun to talk about it and now he was afraid that Djehuty-mes would reject him. But the old priest, albeit completely surprised by the course of this conversation, and seriously scared by the prospect of a distant journey beyond the borders of Kemet, also sensed that his presence alongside this seriously ill and changed dignitary is now needed and may be important for the Both Countries.

---

[161] This sentence is also a literal quotation from Djehuty-mes' letter to Buteh-Amon, in which the old Necropolis Scribe repeats Pi-ankh's words. This document is today in the Egyptian Museum in Turin.

He looked piercingly in General's eyes, and, seeing the human fear in them, smiled soothingly and said, "If you think that such an old, bent down and half rotten tamarisk may still be useful in your garden, and if the Kingdom of Amun needs it, you can count on me."

"Thank you!" Pi-ankh felt great gratitude to the old man. "You won't run out of bread or beer at me. Rest now, sleep as much as you like. We are leaving in two or three days!"

On the fifteenth day of the first month of the Shemu season, when all work on the grain and flax harvest was completed in the fields around Abu and Sunu, numerous residents of this district and soldiers of Pi-ankh's army began the pulling the fleet ships by means of ropes through the water surf south of Abu, formed by a swift river's stream squeezing here between countless rocks and surmounting five rocky chutes even one cubit high. The boats that had already overcome the cataract, were moored in the calm waters of the river at both its banks, where they waited for the end of the entire operation. It lasted all day long, and the next day, after the last night spent in the tents and quarters of Abu and Sunu, the soldiers loaded all the equipment and food supplies on the boats, after which subsequent troops under the command of their officers took places in the assigned ships and began to sail upriver. Chariots and wheeled carts, drawn by oxen, moved along the west side of the river, though the road running there was sometimes going far away from the river, bypassing some rocky hills sticking out as if black granite lumps over yellow sandy spaces. The troops of horseback scouts were considerably preceding the army and fleet, ready to send a warning in time if an enemy army was seen. However, Pi-ankh did not expect the surprise, at least in the first phase of the expedition, because from scouts sent to the south earlier, he got an assertion that at least to the vicinity of the Baki fortress, guarding the road leading to the gold mines, not only no foreign troops were seen, but not even any natives.

Indeed, the first days of the expedition confirmed that all the local population apparently abandoned their homes and fled as far as possible from Abu, where the Southern Country of Kemet began. This was mainly evidenced by the fields that bordered on the river with very narrow strips, sometimes not exceeding the width of one rope. These fields were not sown this year at all, and individual ears grown here from once lost grains have already become gold, showing proudly their mature shapes, as if demanding a harvest. The motionless sweeps leaned over these plots and farther some empty clay huts covered with branches stood among the palm coppice. Everything together made a sad impression, and when, after a few hours of traveling, the rocks visible from a distance approached the river while squeezing it with gray walls, it became gloomy, despite the undisturbed blue on which the barge of Re was visible straight above as if flowing exactly above the heads of those who imitated it while sailing on an earthly river.

Soon they stopped for a night's rest. A temple was visible nearby, cut in the rocks, but with some additional frontal rooms built of stone. Djehuty-mes went in that direction, wanting to take a walk before sleep. Close to the temple a house stood, different in size from the nearby mud huts and preceded by a fairly large yard, on which several *mama* palm trees grew.

The house certainly belonged to the priest who served the temple and the Necropolis Scribe thought for a moment that maybe this man, probably originating from Kemet, was present. However, when he reached the door, he saw two strings hanging from it: it was closed, but the "key" was ready. It seemed as if the host had gone out for a moment and was nearby, but no one answered the call.

A terrible idea occurred suddenly to Djehuty-mes, and having manipulated the strings, he opened the door, ran through the yard and opened another, also closed door of the house. He came in and looked into all the rooms in turn, then went upstairs. There was no doubt: the house was empty and there was no indication that any violent scenes might have taken place there.

The old priest, not yet believing it, left the house, closing the two doors behind him, and entered the temple confines where he reached the last room cut in the rock.[162] It was dim. Djehuty-mes looked around carefully, and only now sighed with relief: nowhere had he seen what he was most afraid to find...

"He isn't here," he said to himself in an undertone, "Probably Pa-nehsi ordered him to be abducted."

---

[162] The description here corresponds to a temple that was located near the village of Beit el-Wali. Saved in the 1960's during the so-called Nubian Action (moving monuments threatened with flooding by the waters piled up by the construction of the Great Aswan Dam), today it is located near Aswan.

The Necropolis Scribe's eyes have already got used to the twilight here. Just before him three statues stood, before which the priest should make daily offerings; their remnants were visible here on a bowl placed in front of the central statue.

Djehuty-mes looked at these divine images: Amun - the incarnation of the heavenly Hidden God – was visible on the left, Re –the incarnation of the Visible God in heaven - on the right, and between them King Ramesses the Great – Son of God on earth stood. The priest stepped back a little bit, then knelt down and, placing both hands on the floor, touched it with his forehead and mouth.

"May you make, Amun-Re," he whispered, "that I will happily return home from a trip to this wild land where the fate dumped me too!"

He stood up and looked again at the figure of Ramesses. It was just this king who had ordered that this temple was built, he thought, and he ordered to be presented himself as equal to God.

He looked around the temple and saw that other scenes on the walls of this room also represented Ramesses the Great as breast-fed by Isis, and also by Anuket, Lady of Abu. In the adjacent transverse room the ceiling of which was supported by two columns, Ramesses User-Maat-Re-Sechep-en-Re could be seen again everywhere, surrounded by divine figures. Djehuty-mes could not remove from his memory the image that was coming to him in his nightmares, of the Kushite soldiers delivering blows of sticks on the mummy of this earthly deity, and then chopping his abdomen with axes...

"Why did they hate him so much?" he asked himself a question, and after a while, as he passed through the long vestibule that was the first room of this temple, he thought that maybe the scenes shown here contain a partial answer. Along the entire southern wall of this hall a series of events were represented that may have actually taken place in this region many times. Here the king – again Ramesses the Great, accompanied by his sons – is attacking on his chariot a group of black Kushites trying to run to their village hidden under palm trees. In the next scene, Ramesses sits on the throne, and in his direction a procession is coming, carrying the booty originated from the local, already conquered land. One can see the bound dark-skinned prisoners, also women and children taken captive. Soldiers are carrying valuable goods – gold, ebony wood, ivory fangs, leopard skins, ostrich feathers and eggs, and finally the cattle which once belonged to the inhabitants of Kush, as some Kushite heads and hands depicted on cows' heads symbolized. Admittedly, on the opposite wall, similar scenes of conquest showed the triumph of the Pharaoh over Tjehenu and the inhabitants of the lands of the East, but for the inhabitants of Kush watching these images this was probably not a great consolation. Djehuty-mes lowered his head and returned to his boat depressed.

He had seen the same scenes many times in various temples in the City, but he never wondered how they had to act on those who saw in them themselves, and their mud huts, their cattle and yet were supposed to recognize that the one who took them all this was divine and reverent...

"I learned a lot today", he thought and lay down, but several more hours passed before he finally fell asleep.

The following days brought no change except for the landscape: the wild rocks moved away from the river again, and the green groves and fields filled the whole area. These fields had been even sown, and their crops harvested, but those who did it disappeared without a trace. The subsequent villages and temples that were passed by stood empty, but the archers were standing now on each boat with bows ready to use. The place was approached where the water inlet was guarded from both sides by the walls of the mighty fortresses. These seemed extremely menacing already from a distance like two crouching great beasts only pretending to be asleep, to suddenly catch the passing ships in their terrible claws and crush them. Yet, it turned out that these fortresses were abandoned, too, though they could probably resist any army for a long time. This emptiness and silence began to be alarming: did the enemy prepare a deadly trap for them? This atmosphere of tension and horror was further enhanced by the sight of the vicinity, because the bare rocks again narrowed the river, while hiding on the left side, among their mysterious recesses dozens of small coves that were suddenly appearing before the boats. If hidden ships with the Kushite archers were waiting in such a place, they could easily surprise Pi-ankh's fleet. It was already a region patronized by Horus of Baki and Horus of Miam, although in the temples passed by, which all stood empty, reliefs and sacred texts on the walls also evoked other images of God, more familiar to the newcomers from the Both Countries, and among them almost everywhere the figures of the King Ramesses the Great were shown, whose divinity was emphasized here particularly clearly. The tension felt by the soldiers who did not let their arches out of their hands increased even more when, after the next bend of the river, another pair of fortresses were seen in the distance. These were built on the rocks situated opposite each other and embracing an extremely narrow water passage with the arms fatal for all unwanted guests. It was the fortress of Miam, which made Djehuty-mes aware that the distance from Abu, from where they had set sail a few days ago was over 20 *iteru* long. As they were floating between the gloomy gray walls, the archers have put their bows aside, while grabbing their shields and huddled beneath them, expecting that in a moment deadly arrows may fall from above, or stones which could have been equally dangerous here. However, Miam fortress was silent: it was also abandoned. The tension subsided and rowers began conversations, and laughter heard now and then was evidence that everyone's urge to live have returned. The landscape itself has also softened. The rocky horizon receded, and greenery appeared again.

The next day before dusk, the shapes of a huge temple, completely cut out inside the rock were seen in the distance[163]. The entrance to this temple was guarded by four large statues of the sitting pharaoh, reaching a height of 44 cubits. Djehuty-mes has never seen such a huge thing before, although Ramesses the Great who liked emphasizing his own greatness, also ordered two giants to be erected in front of his temple in the Western City. When the boats came closer, a second, slightly smaller temple

---

[163] It is about the Great Temple in Abu Simbel.

appeared, decorated with standing sculptures of the royal family. The sight of such huge houses of God in the middle of this seemingly extinct land filled with spaces of yellow sand, rocky hills and deserted villages among palm groves was so amazing that everyone looked in silence and with admiration at these human works while convicted that they were rather a product of divine forces; the pharaoh who realized something like this in this wildness had to be greater than a human being...

Boats began to moor around the bay, in the depths of which the rocks hid both temples, also probably, as it was thought – empty. Yet, to a complete surprise of all, a wicket in the gate between the sitting Ramesses suddenly opened and a dozen men in white priestly robes came out. When they saw the similarly dressed Djehuty-mes, who had already got off his boat, they headed towards him. From a distance, the Necropolis Scribe noticed that these people were emaciated, and when they came closer, he inferred from their appearance that they were on the verge of death by starvation, with deeply sunken cheeks and glistening eyes that seemed unnaturally large. Without waiting for their explanations, the essence of which was guessed by the old priest, he immediately ordered to bring dried bread, water and dates, and watching them eating greedily.

"You saved our life, Lord, when we were all preparing us to pass the last threshold," one of them said who introduced himself as Amun-nakht, a servant from the House of Serkit. As Djehuty-mes supposed, all priests serving the temples south of Abu were taken three months ago by Kushite soldiers and brought here to the House of Ramesses-Beloved-by-Amun, where they were released and joined by four other priests who served here. Only some food was left to them, and because the local people were told to leave their homes and move south, they did not even have a chance to replenish their supplies. They had already eaten all the fruits growing on the neighboring trees, and there was no other food here, or they were not able to get it, having no suitable equipment. Only once they were succeeded in hooking a fish. Initially, they still fulfilled their daily duties before the divine images in the local temples, while giving them modest, but due offerings, but later they stopped even these, and what's worse, they ate the breads and vegetables intended for a gift to God, which is incompatible with Maat and is a sin. At the court of Osiris, they will no longer be able to say: "I didn't reduce the offerings of food in the temples," or: "I did not damage the bread belonging to God." They have not eaten anything at all for 10 days, they only drank water from the river. Asked if they knew where Pa-nehsi was, they answered with a conviction that they did not, but probably not far, since he left them here, and did not take to south, where there are also temples and priests from the Both Countries.

It was getting dark when a fast small sailing *tjesem* boat arrived at the place of stationing of Pi-ankh's fleet prepared to a night's stop, with a messenger with letters on board. To Djehuty-mes' great joy, he also received news from his family. He immediately decided to write back because he learnt that tomorrow or the day after, that messenger, named Djehuty-hotep, would set off on the return journey. The old priest envied him this: he was fed up with this trip, and he was not feeling well, and was even afraid that a disease was starting to reveal itself. So, he sat on the side of the boat and began to write, while using an animal fat lamp to get some light.

Royal Scribe of the great and noble Necropolis of Millions of Years, Djehuty-mes to the Necropolis Scribe, Buteh-Amun, the musician of Amun Shed-em-dua and her children, may they live in health, prosperity and in the favor of Amun-Re – King of Gods, Mut, Khonsu and all divine images in the City! I tell Horus of Baki, Horus of Miam and Atum – Lord of all the earth, to give you life, happiness and health, longevity and the attainment of a good ripe old age and to let Amun my good Lord of Thrones of the Both Countries bring me back alive from this place where I am abandoned in this far-off land where the fate has dumped me, and let fill my embrace with you! This letter of you reached me by the hand of the messenger Djehuty-hotep in the tenth year of the Repeating of Births, in the first month of the third season, on day 25. I received it and inquired him about you, and he said to me that you were healthy, and all matters were going well. My heart became alive, my eyes opened, and I raised my head because I had been ill. Everything is going well between me and my superior, he doesn't neglect me. He ordered me to be given a large pitcher of beer once every five days and five normal breads a day... And this beer has removed the illness which was in me! Don't worry about me because I know it is so; I know the nature of your hearts! Everything will be fine, but ask Amun, Amen-hotep, Ah-mes-Nefertari, as well as the One-Who-Loves-the-Silence and Amun from the Holy Place to bring me back alive...[164]

---

[164] This is another fragment of the authentic text of the letter written by Necropolis Scribe Djehuty-mes to Buteh-Amon of Nubia in the year 10

Chari stopped writing and thought that he would ask the General to let him return to Abu with Djehuty-hotep. He blew out the lamp and after entering his cabin, lay down, wrapped himself in sheepskins, and fell asleep.

He slept for a very long time and only the boat captain woke him, saying that Pi-ankh asks him to come. The General didn't leave his ship during the whole journey from Abu, and now Djehuty-mes saw him standing ashore surrounded by his officers. Before them, at some distance, a Kushite messenger was standing who had just arrived here with a message from Pa-nehsi, and a bit further at the side Djehuty-mes saw a group of a dozen teenagers of the age of about 11-12, dressed as Kushites, but with faces bearing clear features of the residents of Kemet.

"You finally got up, I thought that maybe you got drunk because you don't lack beer!" Pi-ankh greeted the old man in a way typical for him, but without waiting for an answer he continued: "Look at these youths! They are the inhabitants of the City, the sons of the defenders of Ipet-sut whom Pa-nehsi took away from their mothers during his war with Amen-hotep. Now, he gives them back to us, admittedly not all of them, but it is great on his part, I didn't expect that of him... Here is the letter he sent to me; read it and then tell me if I think correctly while planning my answer." And the General handed him a papyrus with a longer text:

Prince of Wawat and Kush, General of the Kush Army, Pa-nehsi to the First Servant of Amun in Waset, General Pi-ankh. I know

---

uhem mesut. This letter is now in the British Museum in London.

about your war intentions and I know all the movements of your fleet and your chariots. However, I am not your enemy and I do not want to fight against the Both Countries. As you can see, you have traveled the whole country of Wawat and I did not attack you, although you could lose many soldiers already in Baki and Miam. I left your priests from the temples in Wawat alive, though I could kill them. Other priests are also alive and can continue their offerings in Kush, they are safe. I am sending you, as a sign of my good intentions, those children that I took away from the City, because their fathers preferred to be with Amen-hotep than with their sons. These children were growing up in my care and they didn't suffer any hurt, and some other are still with me and don't want to go back to Kemet, like their sisters who have already become mothers themselves. They feel good. I did all this to make peace between us. If you choose it - you are wise, and if you choose war, you will not win it and your army will die here. Don't try to go further, because Horus of Behen protects my people well. Go back to Abu and don't cross the cataract with the army anymore, because you'll never manage to reach such a distant place as you did now. I am waiting for your answer. Send a letter by the same man.

Djehuty-mes handed over the letter. "What are you going to do, General?" he asked. "I don't think we have the strength enough to attack the fortress in Behen and all the others that are swarming in that area?"

"Sure not," Pi-ankh replied. "There is actually all in this letter I was going to achieve, and these boys are a real surprise. But apparently, Pa-nehsi is not as strong as it would seem, since he has retreated much. I must take advantage of it. Come to me in an hour, then I'll show you my answer," the General stepped back into his barge.

The Necropolis Scribe was curious as to what the army leader would think up, who apparently felt to be the master of the situation. The hour mentioned was dragging by long time, and Djehuty-mes reported to the High Priest much earlier, yet Pi-ankh was already waiting for him. As soon as the priest entered the cabin, he handed him the letter he had prepared. The letter should start with the sender's and recipient's titles, but Pi-ankh concluded that it is still too early to confirm that he had recognized his former colleague as "Prince of Wawat and Kush," so he omitted the heading, going straight to negotiations:

Listen, I appreciate your gestures, it's good that you gave those boys back, though it's a pity that just few. There are more mothers in the City who miss their kids. It's good that you don't want the war, because I don't want it, either, and I propose that we get along with each other and make a truce for many years. If you meet my conditions, I won't start a war now, and also later my troops won't exceed the cataract beyond Abu. You can't cross it either; you know that if you wanted to break the truce, we would crush you. But you also need to understand - and these are my conditions - that I cannot give up the use of the title of Royal Son of Kush and all my successors will wear it, too. You have to offer me something to lend sense to it. Second thing: what you did in Ipet-sut with the holy barge and then in the Great Valley with the royal mummies – this is the greatest crime and nobody in the City will forget it; someone should end on a stake for it. Many people would like you to be there, but if you don't want (and probably you don't) – maybe you could find a deputy?

Remember that I don't want to fight with you, because I pity the wine we drank together. Let's be old friends – that's my suggestion.

"Does Your Grandness really think that Pa-nehsi will give us his companion? I think this is an impossible condition, but one can write something like this in a letter of this type. The first condition is a good move," Djehuty-mes said, while returning the papyrus.

"Because this is the only condition," Pi-ankh came to his words. "The second one is only to offer him something to reject, with which I'll finally agree. You see, Chari, these negotiations turned out to be much easier than I thought. It's good that I came here with the troops, but I think, I needlessly bothered you. I have to wait for his reply now, though it will take some time again, but you can return with this messenger to Abu, if you want, but wait there for my return. I'd like that you take with you these boys Pa-nehsi gave back. Let them recall the smell of their homeland as soon as possible," Pi-ankh added. The old priest was very happy that he didn't have to ask the General for permission to leave these parts where he felt uncomfortable. He immediately carried his belongings to Djehuty-hotep's boat and made sure that a second boat was prepared, on which the recovered Pa-nehsy's former prisoners were to be transported.

When both boats have already set off and sailing quickly with the tide of the river left the site of the great temples, Djehuty-mes took out his letter that he has begun to write to Buteh-Amun, and added two sentences:

> *There are children here with me who have returned from Pa-nehsi's captivity. Find mothers in the City who are still mourning them, and announce that a joy lies ahead some of them.*

He has also recalled some other matters about which he wanted to write to his son. At the end, he took a small stick out of his tunic pocket. He received it in the last letter as an amulet from his three years old grandson Neb-hepet, and put it into the folded letter, while adding:

> *As for the stick you put in my letter, I am sending it to you because it has done its job well. I think I'll be back, fortunately.*[165]

Four days later a messenger from Pa-nehsi arrived, bringing Pi-ankh a reply to his letter, which confirmed that the Kushite army was nearby, indeed. Pi-ankh didn't conceal his surprise when he saw who the messenger was, because he has seen this officer occasionally, and even more often has heard about him: it was Aa-neru! Pi-ankh first asked him about Pa-nehsi's health and then he learnt that the Prince of Wawat and Kush since he had returned from Kemet 10 years ago couldn't walk and was carried everywhere in a litter, but Aa-neru couldn't explain what happened, anyway. Pi-ankh told the messenger to wait, offering him a pitcher of beer. He went to his cabin because he wanted to be alone while reading this much expected letter. He regretted now a bit that he had sent back Djehuty-mes. He was not sure, how did Pa-nehsi react to the conditions set for him? However,

---

[165] This is an authentic addition to the above quoted letter from Djehuty-mes.

already the beginning of the letter forecasted that Pa-nehsi would accept the truce proposed to him:

You old bastard, may a donkey rape you! You know me well! I also remember this wine and it is a pity that we cannot drink together again: I – the head of the independent Land of Kush and you, the head of the State of Amun. Who would have thought that you would be a High Priest; as far as I remember, you were not very much interested in the temples. But now when you're asking me, I can say that I don't care much about someone in Kemet claiming to be the "Royal Son of Kush" – this title means today as much as your King, so nothing. But if you want to feel to be superior of anything in my country, I can only offer you what you once haven't like: the temples. As you know, there are many of them here and they are served by priests, who are still formally subject to the High Priest of Amun, so actually to you. You can keep this title and the authority over these priests and temples[166] – I'll do no harm to them. You can send new priests and supplies for them over here, but remember that they cannot be accompanied by any armed men. If more than 50 people in a group cross my border, they'll be considered as attackers. I don't want a war with you, but you have to remember that my people are very happy now. They are living in an independent country and have regained the pride of being Kushites. We will defend this pride at all costs and any war caused by the Both Countries will end in your defeat. But at the same time, I assure you,

---

[166] Amun's High Priests in Thebes still 100 years later used the title of the Royal Son of Kush. A similar title was even held by Nesi-Khonsu - the wife of the High Priest Pi-Nodjem II around 970 BC, which should be understood as the titular authority over the Egyptian temple staff in the country of Kush, independent from Egypt.

while swearing by Amun and Horus of Behen, Miam and Baki, that we will not attack you first: what I wanted, I have already taken...

You have rubbed my nose in this barge and these mummies. You will believe it or not, but I can tell you today that I regret doing that. You probably don't know that on the day I opened the chapel with the statue of Amun in Ipet-sut and let Aa-neru chopping this barge, a curse fell on me: I lost my ability to walk and I will never get on the horseback again. You can announce it in the City: they will be happy there: God's revenge has caught up with me! In the Great Valley, too, things went too far, and I was unable to stop the fools who had relieved themselves on the mummies, and I was even sorry to see what they were doing. The main instigator of these events, Aa-neru, who first had begun to defile these mummies, and then had persuaded me to open the chapel with the statue in Ipet-sut, I have just sent you with my letter. He always liked robbery and he carried out many such actions without my knowledge, and my misfortune is also caused by him. I am giving him to you, you can arrest him and do whatever you want with him. Are you satisfied? If I don't get a new letter from you, I assume that we have got along with us, and I conclude a truce; there is a bit too early for the treaty. Build your State of Amun calmly, we'll not disturb you, you have my word!

Pi-ankh finished reading, and a feeling of great relaxation was overwhelming him. He has achieved not only a guarantee of a peace on the border, but also a formal right to use the title of the Royal Son of Kush, thus everything he intended to get. As a matter of fact, from a powerful head of the entire territory south of the cataract beyond Abu, he became barely an inspector of a dozen of temples... On the other hand, he can boast of capturing the one who desecrated the royal mummies. Pi-ankh has read the letter once again, wondering if there was anything written "between the lines" that he might have overlooked or misunderstood, but found nothing like that. Therefore, he summoned several officers, read aloud the appropriate fragment of Pa-nehsi's letter and ordered them to bring Aa-neru waiting for an answer. The soldiers have brutally pulled the messenger away from the beer he was enjoying, then took him under his arms and brought him to the General.

"Your Grandness, do you allow such a treatment of a messenger?" Aa-neru's indignation was boundless. "I'll complain to my Lord!"

"You won't complain to anyone, rat," Pi-ankh said between his teeth. "Your Lord has just allowed me to arrest you. A trial awaits you, and it seems that you had become famous for many deeds that even Pa-nehsi has condemned. You can only guess what fate awaits you, but you will still have some time for these meditations." With one hand's movement he indicated to the soldiers to place a bound prisoner under the deck of the boat, on which the High Priest himself was to return to Abu.

Aa-neru turned pale, as if all the blood drained away his face. In a silent dullness he allowed to be tied up and pushed into a cramped room under the floor of the ship, where he could at best expect the company of rats.

"How could Pa-nehsi treat me so?!" he was repeating in his mind as the wet darkness of a temporary prison surrounded him.

CHAPTER XXVII

Meanwhile, Suti-mes after the meeting on the river with the old Necropolis Scribe reached the City, sailing on a fast boat of the High Priest, while making only a few short stops. To Captain's astonishment, when Suti-mes saw that the boat begins to moor to the harbor of the west bank, gave the order to proceed on toward the harbor at Ipet-sut on the other side of the river. As the messenger of the Chief of State of Amun, Suti-mes was obviously the most important on the boat and the sailors immediately complied with his ordinance. However, the Captain asked Suti-mes to enter his cabin for a moment and posed him a question, if he was not mistaken, because, as far as the Captain knows, they were first to go to Pa-Shu-uben in Khefet-her-neb-es.

"I can see, Captain, that you know a lot indeed, but all this concerns everyday affairs, on which we humans can only have proper influence, provided that God directs the helm of our boat. I am priest of Amun, and I am obliged to go to Him first, thanking for the successful journey, and only then to pass the letters, for which one hour of delay makes no difference. We could have run aground or have a less favorable wind and then your ship would have been still far from the City, despite having such an excellent Captain."

The Captain didn't find any argument to persuade Suti-mes to change his mind, he only shook his head, but immediately after he had dropped the young priest at the harbor in front of the great temple, he turned the boat to Khefet-her-neb-es to inform the people of Pa-Shu-uben that the General's messenger with the letters was already in the City.

Suti-mes felt as happy as on the day when he was promising Henut his love at the Hat-Hor shrine. For the three years he spent on Abu, he was corroded by a longing not only for his beloved woman and friends, but also for his hometown, temples in Ipet-sut and Khefet-her-neb-es, for this characteristic landscape with the majestic line of mountains closing the west horizon, even for the air which was also smelling differently here. He inhaled it now to the fullest, while looking around. Not much has changed here over these three years. The Great Gate rebuilt by Heri-Hor shone as before with the white stone, fresh colors of paintings and a few gildings, and the colorful ribbons fluttered in the wind on the masts, which already from a distance resembled the holy sign *netjer* announcing the presence of God, while standing out against the background of the pristine blue of the sky, not disturbed by a smallest cloud.

Suti-mes reached the temple guards at the harbor and ordered to be led to the main gate. Here, as required by the regulations, he was asked to wait for the Gate Overseer. Suti-mes as always has recalled himself his encounters with Pen-nesti-tawy serving here formerly, and he couldn't overcome the strange feeling of expecting that in a moment the same man would appear again... Soon the Overseer of the Gate arrived, who was Pa-neb-Montu known to Suti-mes from the old school years. He was pleased to see the long unseen guest, greeted him warmly in words full of joy, but also of the respect due to the messenger of the High Priest, and they started to move through the shadowed Great Column Hall towards the High Priest's Palace, where Nodjmet now lived.

"I thought Pen-nesti-tawy would welcome me again, as before," Suti-mes said. "What's with him?"

"He's been dead since a long time," answered Pa-neb-Montu. "He died in the temple custody, where he was imprisoned when it came out that he wanted to murder you. He was to be tried, but Heri-Hor died, the case dragged on, and it turned out that the wound the archer had inflicted on him became inflamed, went bad and no one noticed it. Apparently, Pen-nesti-tawy concealed it; probably he expected that he would be sentenced to death and die in greater torment. Actually, it was almost certain, because, after all, during the Repeating of Births there is no other punishment for murders. One day, when the food was brought to him, it turned out that he was lying unconscious and the medic could do nothing. Pen-nesti-tawy meted out Maat to himself, and Amen-em-Ipet, who replaced Heri-Hor, was probably glad that everything ended that way."

"How is my friend Amen-em-Ipet?" Suti-mes asked again, when the Overseer of the Great Gate led him into the courtyard of the High Priest's palace.

"Very well for his age. His Grandness General Pi-ankh didn't spare him the allocation of bread and beer due to the dignified old man. He now lives in the palace we are going to, because the noble Lady Nodjmet entrusted him with bringing up her son."

Nothing could please Suti-mes more: he was going with a letter to Nodjmet, and in her palace he had the chance to see not only his wife, longed for so much, and his son whom he had never seen, but also his old friend!

"You made me happy with such news, Pa-neb-Montu!" Suti-mes beamed with joy. "My heart is so much filled with gratitude to Amun that I must tell Him about it. Let me go to His statue first and stay there for a moment!"

Suti-mes really felt the need to talk to God, and besides, didn't he tell that to the Captain who apparently directed him right into the hands of Pa-shu-uben?

On the eastern side of the Great Hall of Appearances just next to the high wall of another gate, several statues were showing different faces of God. Suti-mes came to one of them, representing Amun-Re, Lord of the Thrones of the Both Countries, wearing a high crown, accompanied by his divine consort Mut, then he prostrated and kissed the floor in front of the base on which Amun stood.

"Thank You, God hidden in Your visible form, who are omnipresent and who also protected me in the House of Khnum on Abu! Thank You for saving me and my family and saving us from our enemies, for letting me return to the City and make my heart happy while seeing it and for giving us all health! Please, keep us prosperous and give us a good day!"

Remained in a prayer posture he was looking at Amun's slightly smiling face; he might have the impression that the smile was directed at him. He kissed the floor again, got up and returned to the waiting Pa-neb-Montu. Together, they headed now straight towards the palace of the High Priest. Pa-neb-Montu introduced Suti-mes to the guards standing there as a messenger with a letter from General Pi-ankh to the Royal Spouse Nodjmet and also as a friend of Amen-em-Ipet, after which he said goodbye and Suti-mes was introduced to this part of the palace, which he did not know before, always staying only in the High Priest's chambers; women lived here. The guard handed the guest over to one of the room servants, who led him to a spacious room, the walls of which were covered with painted garden and banquet scenes, showing, among others, a group of young musicians, feasting guests, then a pool surrounded by bushes and garden trees. There were comfortable chairs standing by the walls and low benches surrounded by pillows, so probably all social gatherings were held in this room, probably also with the assistance of music. Here, probably, the arriving guests were also waiting for an audience at the Royal Spouse. A servant asked Suti-mes to rest, then he brought a jug of cool water, a mug and a moment later a bowl of grapes, bowed, and before leaving the room, he informed that Lady Nodjmet was not in the palace now, but she would be back soon.

Suti-mes reached for fruit, drank some cool water, and then he felt a relaxing sleepiness overwhelming him. He closed his eyes and, not knowing when, he lost contact with reality. As usual, Henut appeared before him in a moment, and together with her a series of scenes recalling some events experienced long ago, which were staying alive in his memory sometimes, and were returning in his dreams, while arranging themselves in an unreal sequence of phantasms. Here he was walking next to Henut, but when he wanted to embrace her, she ran away, crying: "I don't want you would come to hate me!" When he wanted to chase her, Pa-neb stood in his way, whispering in his ear with a sneering smile: "You are under arrest!" Fortunately, the picture has changed, and the richness of colors, among which he was living in recent years have appeared: the vastness of the blue sky, and below it the green of trees and shrubs, and the gray of granite blocks sticking out of the water, which could resemble a herd of elephants at a water hole. And here again a change, and the water blue turns into the gold of ripe wheat ears, among which Suti-mes and Henut are walking, holding hands. Suddenly he became overwhelmed by the irresistible need to hug this beloved being, so he embraced her with his arm, while beginning to kiss and they slowly started to lower into the golden curtains. Then he heard a voice saying: "Somebody is here!" which interrupted this intimate moment of closeness.

"Somebody is here!" A dream's mist slowly dispersed but the voice remained; actually a thin and high children's voice, and here Suti-mes identified its source: a small boy was standing before him, having the face of fair complexion and the head covered with curls. He was holding a toy-bow.

Suti-mes immediately came to his senses and stared at the boy, absorbing every fragment of the small figure. Would it be just him? "Pen-Amun?" he dared to ask the question at last, and then saw that the boy shook his head.

"I'm Ameni and here is Pen-Amun!" Suti-mes, following the movement of the little finger, saw that another boy was standing behind, a little smaller, but darker on his face. In this, especially in the pair of large and coal-black eyes, Suti-mes immediately saw a resemblance to Henut. His son! Never seen but loved so much! Pen-Amun had a small imitation of a shield in one hand, and a stick undoubtedly imitating a spear in the other one. The boys were playing soldiers, maybe scouts, who unexpectedly discovered the presence of a stranger. Will he become an element of their fun? Suti-mes decided to help them with this.

"Who are you looking for, noble warriors?" he asked, and Ameni, undoubtedly the son of Heri-Hor and the companion of Pen-Amun, often mentioned in letters from Henut, immediately answered resolutely:

"We're looking for those who come from Ta-Seti, spies of evil Pa-nehsi!"

Suti-mes wanted to laugh: he was coming from the south, actually...

"Let it be far from me, nobler soldiers! Admittedly, I have come from Ta-Seti, actually from Abu, but I have nothing to do with Pa-nehsi!" he explained, placing his hand on his heart.

"All the spies say so," little Ameni said. "If you are coming from Ta-Seti, we must arrest you and lead you to the General! Take him!" he gave the order and little Pen-Amun only now dared to come closer, while raising his "spear" and even hitting with it several times the "prisoner" whom Suti-mes has become from that moment.

"I am begging you, soldiers, don't beat me, I will go wherever you want..." Suti-mes was amused by the situation: here his own son began his contacts with his father by hitting him with a stick.

He stood up and started to go, assisted by the little warriors, through a series of rooms. Finally in one of these they found an old man sitting on a chair, at the sight of whom Suti-mes beamed.

"General, we brought a captive who claims to be coming from Abu. Is it a spy or an ally?"

Amen-em-Ipet only now looked carefully at the entrant, "For Amun!" he shouted, leaping up, "I thought I fell asleep and it was a dream!" Turning to the little ones, he said, "It's an ally, you don't even know how a great ally! But I must praise you for your vigilance!"

"You should appoint them officers," Suti-mes said, but immediately heard the protests of all three.

"They are officers already, of course. Let me introduce them. Here is the Captain of Archers of His Majesty Pharaoh, Amen-em-ensu, beloved bodily son of the King Heri-Hor, justified, and this is the Head of the Royal Guard, Pen-Amun, the son of a certain Servant of Amun, whom I could just a moment ago still think that he is in Abu. And this, noble soldiers, is my great friend and companion of numerous adventures..."

"Suti-mes!!!???" a cry in a high-pitched female voice, in which a surprise mixed with joy, and so intense one that it frightened a hoopoe perching on the window sill, rang suddenly out from the side door. Henut was entering with a bowl and a pitcher of water for Amen-em-Ipet to refresh him after a walk with the boys, from where he has just returned. Having freed her hands, the young woman stretched them out towards her husband, who grabbed them as a dearest treasure while looking at his wife in silence for a moment. He felt that he could burst into tears at the first word, but he was aware of the presence of the little witnesses who were watching this scene with great interest: they have never seen anything like that before.

Finally, Suti-mes took a step towards Henut and, hugging to his shoulder her head shaken with a silent sob, stroked her hair, repeating only, "My beloved, my dearest," unable to say anything else. Suddenly, little Pen-Amun, seeing that his mother was crying, ran up to Suti-mes and began to hit him with his "spear" again, repeating menacingly, "Leave her; this is my mother!"

They both came to their senses. Henut has squatted, looked at her son with love and said, "Honey, this is your daddy, this is Suti! Every day you ask Amun for health for him and for him to come back and you see? Your request has been heard! Suti is with us!"

Pen-Amun hugged his mother, but was still looked distrustfully at his father, "I don't want you to cry!"

"A happy age in which everything is unambiguous and who doesn't know yet that a pain may be good, and tears may be a sign of happiness," Amen-em-Ipet said. "It's a while before Pen-Amun will get used to you, it's obvious. But don't let us wait any longer for your story: how did it happen that you came here?"

Suti-mes began to talk about how he was summoned by Pi-ankh and sent with letters to Pa-Shu-uben and Nodjmet, how he met Djehuty-mes on the way and how warned by him, he took his first steps here, and after that was "arrested" by little "officers."

"Good that only by them," Amen-em-Ipet had no doubt. Something similar could happen in Khefet-her-neb-es, but for real. "It is interesting why the General just chose you as a messenger and how he found out that you were there. All this looks like Pa-Shu-uben's doing. I wonder what's in those letters anyway."

Suti-mes was, of course, also curious, and his curiosity was soon to be partly satisfied. Suti-mes didn't even have time enough to enjoy the family, nor to learn what happened to them during his absence, when a chamber servant announced that Her Majesty Queen Nodjmet had returned and wanted to see him. Suti-mes had previously only once the opportunity to meet the Queen shortly before that unlucky day, when Heri-Hor returned to the palace after the procession on the occasion of the holiday of Ipet and got an attack of his illness which he didn't survive. Small, today almost four years old Amen-em-ensu was a baby at the breast then. The Queen hasn't changed much since then, although she clearly gained weight. When the young priest entered, she was sitting at a small table with a bowl filled with grapes.

"So, you're Suti-mes I've heard so much about... Have we ever met?" she asked.

"A few years ago, His Majesty King Heri-Hor honored me with showing his loved ones when the holiday of Ipet was approaching, and I came to him with a letter from Nes-Ba-neb-Djedu and Tent-Amun. Maybe then your eye, Lady, saw me among those who were there."

"So, you saw me when I was still happy... A woman, even a queen, needs someone who loves her, and a child, even a future King – a father who can take him in his arms. As you know, we both with Amen-em-ensu, don't have anyone like that. "You know, I looked many times with jealousy at your wife and your son, and thought that I'd willingly change the roles with Henut, although she didn't have an easy life, either, and both of you have your own persecutors."

"Lady," said Suti-mes, "Let me first deny your words that there would be no one who loves you, because there are many of such people. Secondly, it is difficult for me to express in words, how great is my gratitude, combined with adoration, for you, Lady, for your heart and for the help you have shown to my beloved ones in their difficult situation. I would be happy if I could be of any help, if I could serve you. And my happiness would be immeasurable if I could stay in Waset – here is everything I love and everyone I love, though with one, Djehuty-mes, I passed by on the river. Your father, Lady, the dignified Pi-ankh called him to Abu, as he sent me here. Carrying letters has become an important part of my life, although sometimes I was bringing terrible secrets... I hope that this time I am not a messenger of bad news, but only of greetings from the one who loves you."

Nodjmet looked carefully at Suti-mes, and a kind of smile appeared in her eyes, though it was not a smile of pure joy.

"You are a noble man, Suti-mes, but as I see, you are far from politics, so naive one. Of course, my father loves me, but he would not write a letter to express it to me, at least not only to do that. I suppose, as always, he wants me to find out something that I can't control. Or maybe he just recommends your services to me? Is this the only letter he sent you with?"

"No, Lady, I am still carrying a letter to Pa-Shu-uben and I even confess to you that I have abused the will of your father who wanted me to go with this second letter as first one... However, the winds were favorable, and we reached Waset earlier, so I dared to go to the temple for prayer first, and since you and my loved ones live at the House of Amun..."

"I understand you perfectly, you have done well, but let us not waste time, since you have one more task to do. Give me that letter!"

The Queen took the papyrus scroll, read the seal on the clay sticking to it, and having broken it, she unrolled the papyrus. She read intently for a moment, but soon Suti-mes noticed that the content of the letter has moved her. Blushes appeared on her face, and her eyes were no longer smiling but were sending flashes that heralded a storm. Nodjmet finished reading, then rolled up the papyrus again and, holding it in her left hand, covered her face with her right hand, as if to hide her overly readable reactions. She sat there silently for a long moment, and Suti-mes did not dare to speak. The letter must have included matters that were not easy for this woman, after all so high in the hierarchy of the entire population of the Both Countries. Suti-mes also sensed that this letter was to some extent important to him and felt like a man standing in front of the tribunal awaiting the sentence of a judge.

A fly appeared on the back of the chair on which Nodjmet was sitting, certainly attracted by the smell of grapes, and was preparing for the next part of its flight... Does the Queen intend to send him to Pa-Shu-uben indeed? Djehuty-mes and Amen-em-

Ipet warned that he might be arrested there... The fly moved closer to the tray with grapes and made quick movements of the front limbs, giving the ridiculous impression of "rubbing its hands" with joy...What did Nodjmet's words mean that Pi-ankh wanted to inform her about something, she couldn't control? Is the Queen really so helpless? The fly flew up and then sat on the fruit, but at the same moment another fly came flying and sat on the first one. For a split second the insects struggled with each other in the fusion, after which the "striker" broke away and flew off, while leaving a grape amateur... A thought crossed Suti-mes' mind that this insects' world reduced to meeting the basic instincts is easier than a complicated system of entangled human affairs. Years passed since he was with his wife for the last time. Won't his fate after he saw her again today take him away from her anew, this time forever? Will he have to take the letter to his pursuer? What if he dies? Why is the Queen silent? Suti-mes stared at the Queen's face, still partially obscured, while biting his lips so as not to blurt out with the question imposing itself: what would await him in the coming hours? Nodjmet probably sensed this tension, exposed her face, and now she seemed to Suti-mes perfectly calm, though her eyes expressed cold determination.

"The dignified Pi-ankh does not say a word about you, so it is probably the second letter you brought that has something to do with you since he has chosen you as a messenger. Tell me, do you know anything about some two *medjayu* about whom my father is writing to me?"

"Your Majesty, there are 60 *medjayu* in Waset. I have been to Abu in the recent years, where are others. I haven't heard of any case of *medjayu* in Abu, but my friend Buteh-Amun wrote to me in a recent letter about Kari and Kasaya – the *medjayu* in the service of Djehuty-mes for years: they saved Henut from the death at the hands of Pa-neb. As far as they are concerned, they probably have a well-deserved reward."

"The reward..." Nodjmet repeated the word and a short sarcastic smile flashed across her face. "Okay then, it will happen as you wish. I take you into a difficult service – I hope that Amen-em-Ipet will forgive me that he will again have to find someone in your place at the House of Amun in Abu... Don't thank me, Suti-mes," she added, seeing great joy in eyes of the man standing before her, "because this service is a risk to you. It would be for you, maybe also for your family, much safer if you sat in Abu several months longer. Yes, I think it's a matter of months, maybe even weeks..."

Nodjmet suspended her voice while biting her lips, and Suti-mes could now see a truly profound sadness in her eyes.

"Give me that second letter; someone else will take it to Pa-Shu-uben!" – Nodjmet held out her hand. Suti-mes took out the scroll, knelt, put it in the Queen's hand, but for a moment he held it and pressed his forehead against it.

"I'll be in your debt until my death, Lady," he whispered.

The Queen smiled sincerely and cordially this time, "May I have this debtor for a long time... Go back now to Henut and your son, enjoy them and wait for my call; a very difficult test awaits you soon."

Suti-mes bowed and left, but just outside the door of the chamber of Nodjmet, he forgot about the dignity of the priest and servant of the Queen, as well as the high standing of the royal palace at the House of Amun, and he performed a crazy dance of joy without thinking about the words he heard, and which undoubtedly contained some mysterious warning.

Meanwhile, after his departure, Nodjmet read the received letter again, then threw it on the floor and began to trample over it furiously.

"How can you do this to me?! Is this what can be called love? You are asking God for favors for me, and at the same time you want that I have my hand in the murder? Was this villain completely addled you? Can't you see that it is a hyena that is just waiting for your death? Near death? No, I won't let your heart be blamed when the Hall of the Two Maats is perhaps close on your path!" While throwing out more sentences, at the same time she was reaching for the fruits of grape and was putting them into the mouth, several at a time. She swallowed them greedily, just like a hungry wanderer who after a long walk through the desert meets a vineyard with the life-saving nectar. Finally, she calmed down, then opened the side door of the chamber and called for a servant.

"Go and get my brother here," she ordered, then returned to the tray with grapes. When Pi-nodjem appeared shortly thereafter, Nodjmet was just eating the last fruits.

"Look, I am getting more and more fat, but when I'm nervous, I can't control my desire to eat. Just a few months more of Pa-Shu-uben's intrigues and I'll have trouble walking through the door!" she said in greeting.

"What did our noble father thought up this time?" Pi-nodjem had no doubt, what the reason for the summoning him by his sister might have been.

"Really, this time he surpassed himself, maybe it was in result of this disease? Read!" And Nodjmet handed him the papyrus she had previously trampled. Pi-nodjem quickly ran his eyes over the content of the letter and became amazed no less than Nodjmet before.

"Who are the people he commands to kill and why he involves you in this, and not me, for example? These are not the things to be done by a woman."

"You will soon be High Priest, and when Ramesses, may he live forever, dies in his loneliness, you will also be King someday – you must have clean hands. I am here officially serving as the deputy and confidante of our father, but something like that would cast a shadow on Heri-Hor's memory and could also harm our son. Maybe this is precisely Pa-Shu-uben's point, who will not hesitate to spread the whole matter as soon as our father dies, and we know that it will happen soon. Also note that during this quasi-judgment, 'I am to connect with the Scribe Chari.' After all, he is not here – our father called him to Abu, but those two *medjayu* are his people. Pa-Shu-uben also wants to ruin his reputation at one go. Then he will say that "he was only the executor of our orders."

"Where do you know from that these men are the servants of Djehuty-mes?"

"Suti-mes has just told me about it. He is the young priest whose wife was recently injured and whom Amen-em-Ipet hid from Pa-Shu-uben on Abu. This villain Pa-Shu-uben had to find out somehow about this and persuaded our father to send him here with letters, recommending that he should visit Pa-Shu-uben first. Fortunately, he is not stupid, and at the same time his heart was rushing towards his wife and son, who, as you know, are under my protection and he came with the first letter to me. I think that otherwise, he would never have left Pa-Shu-uben's house, and I probably would never have received this letter. Pa-Shu-uben would have killed these wretches, and we would not only have learnt everything after the fact, but we could not even defend ourselves, because Pa-Shu-uben would keep this letter as evidence against me, Djehuty-mes, and who knows if not against you, too."

"I do not know what's going on with these *medjayu*, what did they say?"

"Unfortunately, I do not know; I suspect it's some old thing from the war with Amen-hotep. You know that our father competed then with Heri-Hor, towards whom he probably always felt inferior and at the same time he sympathized with Pa-nehsi. His soft spot for Pa-Shu-uben also originates from those days. Maybe we'll learn something more from the main author of this plot? Take to him the letter that Suti-mes brought. I bet there is exactly the same order to kill the *medjayu* – someone was supposed to "take care of it" and it was known that it would not be me, nor even more so Djehuty-mes who does not know anything at all and is far away. You must find out where exactly and when Pa-Shu-uben will want to "talk" with those *medjayu* and say that, according to the will of our father, I'll also be present at this "talk".

Pi-nodjem smiled at his sister, put his arm around her and kissed her on the forehead, "Well, I didn't expect you to go so far. I really admire you, because it's a risky undertaking. If Pa-Shu-uben really kills them, and he certainly doesn't lack the willingness or people to do it, you will indeed become an accomplice."

"I know that and I'm afraid, but I have to take the risk. Only being there I will be able to do something to save those people from death, and the City from the power of an exceptional villain."

"Perhaps Pa-Shu-uben will get the same command from another messenger, so we must hurry."

"So, I am going, and you don't eat grapes anymore, because Kemet will run out of wine!" Pi-nodjem said and dodged to avoid being hit by a sandal his sister threw at him.

CHAPTER XXVIII

It was almost noon when Pa-Shu-uben was reported on the arrival of the son of His Grandness, the High Priest of Amun and General Pi-ankh, the spouse of the royal daughter of His Majesty King Ramesses, may he live forever, noble Pi-nodjem. Pa-Shu-uben was surprised; he was expecting not this visit and it was not because of this guest that the soldiers were hidden in a side chamber, who had been commanded to wait for a sign to capture the person with whom he would end the conversation. At first, he thought that maybe Pi-nodjem was arriving with another matter, and only by accident he disturbed the course of this so much expected day.

Therefore, while pretending to be cordial, he asked with a broad smile: "What favorable winds have brought the son of my Lord to my humble port? You are doing honor to me, my dignified, long gone visitor! Tell me what I can do for you?"

"Ah, Pa-Shu-uben" – Pi-nodjem answered with equally feigned affection – "It's nice of you to declare your willingness to cooperate, on which I and my sister, the first among the noble ones, Nodjmet, reliably are counting. It is she who sends me to you because she came into possession of a letter that our father, His Grandness Pi-ankh sent to you. He has chosen an unfortunate messenger, a dumb young priest who also brought a letter from our father to Nodjmet and handed her both of them – he probably didn't read well, because the addresses on the letters were different. He has been scolded and certainly won't make a career in the temple hierarchy anymore. I was there when he arrived and I decided to bring you myself a letter written by my father's dear hand. I hope, you have no hard feelings toward me about that?"

Pi-nodjem, saying this, looked straight into the eyes of Pa-Shu-uben, enjoying the view of the pretended indifference of the dignitary, although the words of the newcomer fell on him like a bolt from the cloudless blue: the whole intricately woven plan collapsed and Suti-mes slipped out of another trap set for him.

Unable to control himself completely, Pa-Shu-uben turned slightly red and said without a smile: "I am extremely pleased that you have come to me, although for such an offense this young man should at least have got the lashing; send him to me, please, that I may punish him in an exemplary way, using my right to control the obedience to Maat in the City."

"Don't bother, Pa-Shu-uben, about such a small thing. Your respect for Maat is widely known, but there are, I believe, more dangerous criminals to be punished – my sister said something to me that the General wrote to her and, as the letter implied, he probably wrote to you as well about that. Do you know anything about it?"

The dignitary felt really surprised: it happened for the first time that this youngster, who was the son and probably the successor of General Pi-ankh, knew about something unknown to him who, after all, was responsible for the security in almost the entire south of the country... Not only Pi-nodjem did know about a secret, but apparently was now waiting for an answer. In an instant, Pa-Shu-uben stopped thinking about Suti-mes, while searching intensively the recesses of his memory and looking for something that would lead him to the right track. Criminals? He couldn't remember anyone like that, but he pretended that this was not new to him.

He grunted and assured, "Of course, you are right. I'm on their trail. Let me read the General's words and see if we are thinking of the same people."

He quickly broke the seal while damaging and tearing the papyrus, then began to read. The first words of Pi-ankh's letter about Suti-mes made him mad, but he had to control it, though he turned red and the beads of sweat densely covered his forehead. It was only the further part of the letter that made him recall that Pa-neb actually had told him about two *medjayu,* and that even he had himself mentioned it to the General, although he didn't expect that such an incriminating letter – one of many similar ones written to Pi-ankh almost every day – would provoke such a reaction from the Chief of the State of Amun. Pi-ankh completely surprised him. However, he immediately remembered that when writing about this to the General, he consciously involved in the matter the name of Nodjmet who allegedly knew everything about it. Now, with a real satisfaction he noticed that the High Priest accepted it without reservations, since he recommended that his own daughter and Queen would be a witness of what Pa-Shu-uben would do with these policemen. "The General gave me a real present," he thought, "Though on the other hand, maybe it would be better if this woman was not there; they tend to be so sensitive..." Something had to be answered to Pi-nodjem.

"Indeed, it is as I thought; they are the same people, and I have scheduled to arrest and interrogate them tomorrow."

"You give me real relief with this assurance," Pi-nodjem replied, "But please tell me where it will take place so that my sister can participate in it as the dignified Pi-ankh wishes?"

"But, Pi-nodjem, interrogation of dangerous criminals can be brutal; this is not a show for a lady like Nodjmet. I will tell her exactly what they say."

"However, my sister insists; even though she is a lady and queen, she used to obey her father, and he wants her to be with you," Pi-nodjem insisted, and Pa-Shu-uben according to a behavior typical for him immediately revealed a suspiciousness.

"I see, Pi-nodjem that you know well the content of the letter Pi-ankh wrote to me; it's very puzzling..."

"Pa-Shu-uben, I think you're exaggerating with your distrust: doesn't spring it to your mind that my father wrote two similar letters? I know the content of one, and your words only confirm that I'm right. I am surprised that a woman got such an order, but it is the will of the High Priest, and it is not proper, neither to you nor to me to call it into question. So, where and exactly when are these two *medjayu* supposed to be brought?"

Pa-Shu-uben has fallen silent. There was no doubt that Pi-ankh had sent two similar letters; otherwise, Pi-nodjem wouldn't have known that it was about two policemen. There was no point in pretending that it was a misunderstanding, nor in changing the subject, because the priest may even be ready to complain to his father that the Controller of the City's Secret Affairs was obstructing the fulfillment of his orders.

"Well, Pi-nodjem," he stressed sarcastically, "I didn't know your sister from this side; I see that she likes painful performances. The General purposely chose a place far enough away from Khefet-her-neb-es that no one would hear anything. Do you know this lonely old palace once erected by His Majesty King Amen-hotep Neb-Maat-Re at his Great Lake? Your father as you know has commanded to renew it and to deepen the canal so that the water could get there again, and one could go boating. Tomorrow, when Re descends low to the ground, my people will bring these two *medjayu* there. I will ask them a few questions, probably the Queen too, and then..."

"Then Maat's time will come," Pi-nodjem finished and left the house of Pa-Shu uben quite coldly.

The sunset of the next day turned exceptionally bloody, spilling into the entire horizon with red, and further spaces of the sky with all shades of pink and purple, while giving the same colors also to a few clouds that decorated this colorful space here and there with undulating and alternating shapes. Dark plumes of date palms unset in motion by the slightest breeze, were stuck in this background constantly changing its shades from warm to more and more cold, as mainstays of durability. They resembled columns crowned by Nature with rich capitals supporting the blue vault itself, without a need of architraves.

"It is a pity that today's architects only rarely use the shapes of palm trees to crown their columns; they have been enchanted by the lotuses, but these direct our eyes downwards, luring with their beauty on the water surfaces, while the palms invite the eyes to the sky, so they look more like roof supports," Nodjmet was considering, whose litter carried by four men was approaching the Palace on the Water.

It was the residence almost forgotten of a pharaoh in love – Amen-hotep Neb-Maat-Re – who ordered to build it as a stunning gift for his wife Ti, still before the period of great madness that directed his son Akh-en-Aton to raise a godless hand against God's images. Over the next decades, the palace stood as a defiant monument of the superfluous luxury. Large crowds of people were engaged to create it along with a huge artificial lake. The level of the ground was lowered so that the water of the river, especially at the time of flooding, could fill this reservoir, enabling the King to make pleasant boat trips, after all, not always in the accompany of the one whom he had offered the work. There were exceptionally many beauties in Amen-hotep's harem, also originating from exotic countries.

"Nodjmet wondered if, against all appearances this didn't indicate the loneliness of the King, whose own son during just a dozen years had to destroy the power of the country that he had inherited. An escape into loneliness – it was also the life of her father, Pi-ankh. When he became unexpectedly, after Heri-Hor's death, the First Servant of Amun, he didn't move into the Palace of the High Priest in Ipet-sut, but chose other residences, especially those where he was living as a general for years. Her mother was dead for a long time, and Pi-ankh had only few friends, which was due to his difficult character and rather not much courtly manners, which were perhaps seemly among officers but were offending priests and members of many old noble families. Pi-ankh knew that he was not popular and with time he was retiring into himself more and more, and even began to shun people. The old palace, almost resembling a ruin, has become a place where he liked to stay more and more often. At his command a part of the old palace was rebuilt, and the damage done by time and especially by rains ruthless for the sun dried mud brick of which the building had been erected was repaired. A fragment of the lake at the palace itself was also reconstructed by deepening and connecting to a canal (the same at which Pa-neb attacked Henut), so that a small basin was here created, having a length of one rope, where a sailing boat stood moored.

When the Queen's litter reached the palace, Nodjmet got out and taking with her one of the servants who had carrying her before she entered the building. The room on the first floor to which the servants led them was furnished very modestly; there were only several chairs and small tables with a bowl and a jug of water, a cup and a tray with dates. The window in front of the main entrance faced the lake directly, while smaller entrances on both sides of the main room led to small windowless dens. In one of these was a bed, in another one along the walls only a few baskets; the only larger piece of furniture was here a large chest. The Queen pointed to her attendant the room with the bed, and when he entered there she closed the door and bolted the staple. Having found out that she was alone, she looked curiously into the chest in the second room and found there two large linen sacks and some cords. She winced at the very thought of the contents of Pi-ankh's letter..."It's for them," she concluded. "Thus, the crime is to take place in this room. I wondered, if I'd wait long?"

As if in answer to this silent question, she heard the steps and voices of a number of people just entering the palace. Soon the stairs began to crackle under somebody's weight, and Pa-Shu-uben entered the room. He wore a light tunic girt with a leather belt with a dagger stuck behind it. The huge, bulky figure of the dignitary, illuminated by the red glow of the western sky, seemed almost supernatural, more like a statue than a human being. Strength and terror emanated from this figure; no wonder that he was widely feared. Seeing Nodjmet seated, Pa-Shu-uben greeted her with a bow, and a sneering smile appeared on his obese face.

"I see, Lady, that you were in a hurry to take part in this evening rite, to which your father has summoned both of us," he said.

"He has summoned three of us," Nodjmet corrected "probably in the letter written to you the name of Djehuty-mes called Chari was also mentioned as it was in mine. In his absence, the "rite" as you were kind to call the murder planned here cannot take, as I think, place."

"You amaze me, Lady. Would you accuse your own father of an intention to commit a crime? I think, it is improper neither for the daughter nor for the Queen. His Grandness General will be worried indeed about hearing that you are protecting criminals."

"Before you dare to utter your threat to me for a second time – indeed, my father will be worried about hearing that you have threatened his daughter whom he appointed his deputy during his absence – think, if you are capable of, that you are harming the noble Pi-ankh. Can't you really see that it is just to prevent this lynching that he called Djehuty-mes to Abu? These people belong to the servants of Djehuty-mes and it is him who should speak out in this case. Secondly, from where does my father know that these people are criminals, if not from your letters? He probably trust in you very much since he gave credit to your incriminating letter, but as he wrote, we are first to find out if they really said something that is worthy of death penalty, and only then to pass a sentence. Yet, we haven't asked any question, and the sentence has already been prejudged and there are prepared sacks in the chest. Where is Maat in this case?!"

"I see that you didn't waste time while waiting for me." The cynical smile not for an instant disappeared from Pa-Shu-uben's face. "But now, we are both wasting time. Who is the highest authority in the State of Amun? His First Servant and it is him who passed the sentence you know. It is Repeating of Births and the courts are working fast. Yes, indeed, the General trusts me. These people were threatening him, there is no place for them among the living ones!"

"Pa-Shu-uben, I remind you that the highest authority in the State of Amun is Amun himself and he also gives judgments in the oracles. You have to turn to the oracle of God..."

Pa-Shu-uben laughed crudely. "You have amused me, woman. Don't you really know how oracles are created, or do you pretend to be so naive? By the time Amun sets off in the barge to announce the oracle, everything is already well researched and prepared, including the judicial matters: many people work on it for a long time!"

"Exactly! Many people, and for a long time, and in the heart of each of them Maat lives, the daughter of God. Amun gives them knowledge necessary to establish the truth, so it is Him who makes decisions; the ritual for the observers is secondary. You have said: many people study each case for a long time, and you were the only one person here. Are you infallible like God? Just be careful what you'll answer now so that you wouldn't blaspheme!"

Pa-Shu-uben stopped smiling.

"Of course, I'm fallible," he said. "I was wrong while letting you to come here. Or maybe I came too late: by the time you would have entered here, the sacks should have already been full. But this can be corrected. My people are holding those damn *medjayu* downstairs. All I have to do is to order them. Decide now, do you want to attend the interrogation, or will you just help me in putting the bodies in the sacks, according to your father's order? I don't have time, Re is getting lower!"

Nodjmet understood that she had lost this part of the battle. "Let them be lead in!" she said with resignation.

"At last! Hey, give me those villains here!" Pa-Shu-uben shouted and after a while four soldiers brought in the pale detainees whose hands were tied with cords on their backs. "Wait downstairs, I'll call you," Pa-Shu-uben winked knowingly at the soldiers who perfectly understood what they have to wait for."

Kari and Kasaya stood terrified, looking at the huge figure of the one who was about to give an order – they had no doubts which one. They were surprised by the presence of an elegant woman, completely incompatible with this situation and surroundings.

But it was she who asked the question, "Is it true that you threatened the High Priest Pi-ankh?"

The *medjayu* looked at each other in disbelief.

"Let Amun be my witness," Kari said, "that we have never said a bad word about the First Servant in our lives! I only threatened "Bull" after he had attacked Suti-mes's wife that I'd accuse him before the General."

At that moment, Pa-Shu-uben's fist big like a melon landed on the speaker's stomach, who shouted and bent in half.

"How dare you to lie so, dog" – the torturer roared – "My soldiers heard that you said that you knew the General personally and you'd kill him if he hadn't kill Pa-neb! You rat! You said that you met the General when you were going to him with some letters? What letters?!"

"The dignified Amen-hotep sent us with a letter to His Majesty King Ramesses when Pa-nehsi was plundering the houses of God in Ipet-sut and Khefet-her-neb-es!" Kasaya shouted, but Pa-Shu-uben now also hit him.

"Keep silent! What a liar! Do you dare to say that you also personally knew the High Priest Amen-hotep, justified, and that he sent such a worm with his letter to His Majesty?"

"The noble Djehuty-mes sent us!" Kari had groaned, before another blow fell this time on his head."

"Oh, Djehuty-mes! Now, that's just great!" Besides all his rage, Pa-Shu-uben was clearly delighted with these words.

"Stop beating them immediately, Pa-Shu-uben! Do you want them to talk or do you rather make everything so that they couldn't say anything?!" Nodjmet shouted sharply. "Don't you remember anymore how it was in Waset in Pa-nehsi's time, or do you rather prefer not to remember?"

"Enough of this!" Pa-Shu-uben decided to end this unnecessary interrogation, which, especially in the presence of Nodjmet, started to turn for a less favorable course for him.

"Get in there!" he screamed and shoved both of them into the room with the chest, then made a move towards the stairs, apparently to call his soldiers.

"Halt!" Nodjmet shouted even louder. "You want to kill them because they remember your doings from the time of the "year of hyenas". You were ordering assassinations and you colluded with this killer Pen-nesti-tawy!"

Pa-Shu-uben's face from red turned purple – "How dare you to make such accusations against me! Who will confirm these?!"

"Him!" Nodjmet jumped up from the chair, pushed the bolt of the door leading to the room with the bed and opened it wide.

Suti-mes came out of the room and, looking straight into the eyes of the Controller of Secret Affairs in Waset, confirmed calmly and loudly, "Yes, I can confirm that. You gave Pen-nesti-tawy an order to kill me and then you told people that you knew I was dead!"

Pa-Shu-uben became speechless. He was staring in disbelief alternately at Nodjmet and at Suti-mes, and at the same time he knew that the whole shouted exchange of ideas was heard not only by Kari and Kasaya hugged to the wall in the room with the chest, but also by his own soldiers. However, he was slowly regaining his self-control and self-confidence. Among all the people gathered here only Nodjmet was inviolable. The soldiers obedient to him can kill both prisoners and Suti-mes; later he'll remove these killers themselves as inconvenient witnesses, and Nodjmet, let her shout and protest: after all, he has a letter from Pi-ankh with a sentence on the *medjayu* and giving him Suti-mes…Pa-Shu-uben's face has just reddened again and a venomous smile returned to it.

"Ah, what a beautiful day, we are meeting again! So, that's an explicit conspiracy against me! This coward who had the order to give me a letter from the General hid behind a woman, and now he has emerged like a cockroach from a hole and is still daring to insult me with silly accusations! Just an objection to the will of the High Priest and the General during the Repeating of Births is worthy the death penalty, and this nonsense even more. To whom would I allegedly have said that you were dead?"

"To my wife whom you cruelly hurt!"

"Me? Did I hurt your wife? It was Pa-neb who attacked her – he likes women," the One Who Knows the City's Secrets replied, still smiling, but Suti-mes instantly replied:

"Pa-neb did it with your consent; he is too stupid to act alone. But I'm not talking about this assault, but about another harm: you raped her and beat her with a whip; then you said that I was dead!"

Pa-Shu-uben hesitated for a moment, but his memory immediately prompted him with a well-remembered picture. "Ah, so this cheap bitch from under the sycamores, was it her?"

At that moment, Suti-mes jumped towards Pa-Shu-uben, and he grabbed his tunic with both hands, while shouting loudly: "I'm warning you! One hair from her wig is much more valuable than your mean person, your position and your whole property!"

"Come on, Suti-mes, it's not worth it!" Nodjmet whispered, but at the same time Pa-Shu-uben grabbed Suti-mes with his huge paws by the throat and while choking him, he began to hiss through his clenched teeth:

"You dirty dog, so to me? Well, find out before you'll die that I had her twice: from the front and from the back, I had the pleasure of chopping her bare stomach and breasts with a whip and all I regretted was that you didn't see it, and I regretted you didn't see how my soldiers raped her one by one and she screamed bound while helplessly writhing under them, and..."

A throaty roar, followed by an incomprehensible bubbling came out from Pa-Shu-uben's mouth along with a fountain of blood spurting from the stabbed artery, when Suti-mes in a desperate reflex pulled the dagger out of his belt and struck his neck several times. The grip of Pa-Shu-uben's hands became limp and Suti-mes was finally able to tear them off, catching the life's breathe. Pa-Shu-uben's big body fell to the floor; his eyes were expressing an unbelievable surprise for a few moments, then froze.

Everything lasted so shortly that Nodjmet managed only to run up to the fighters and to take hold of Pa-Shu-uben, while trying to pull him away from Suti-mes, though she was too fragile, and her intervention would probably be to no avail. Now, she was standing over the corpse of Pa-Shu-uben, not knowing what to do. For a moment, she pieced together the fact that in the chest next to which Kari and Kasaya stood scared sacks intended for bodies lay, and the instruction from Pi-ankh's letter. Were there not those soldiers downstairs. She leaned with disgust over the corpse and pulled out the dagger still stuck in his neck, then cut the bindings of the hands of both *medjayu*. Then she called the soldiers.

"Your Lord is dead, now you are to follow my orders," she said seeing that she was inspiring their respect, but also terror.

"Unfortunately, Suti-mes, you won't pass over the trial and you have to wait for it in a custody, but you'll be safe there. Let them tie you up. Take the prisoner to the custody at the Amun's House in Ipet-sut," she instructed the soldiers. "The body of this one here hand over to the embalmers in Khefet-her-neb-es. And these people," she pointed to both policemen, "turned out to be innocent and they are free!"

In less than one hour later, the Palace on the Water became empty.

CHAPTER XXIX

Both boats which set sail on day 26 of the first month of the Shemu season from before the great House of Ramesses-Beloved-by-Amun, heading to Abu moved quickly, carried by the swift current of the river and with favorable wind from the north, lightly sighing their sails. The main trouble of the captains was to bypass the numerous underwater rocks and sandbanks that lurked on careless sailors, especially around the fortress of Miam, and later near the cataract, where the wild bare rocks were pressing against the river from the eastern side. Knowing that nothing else threatens the boats and their passengers, and no hostile archers are hiding in the recesses of passed by rocks, Djehuty-mes could admire now with great pleasure the surrounding landscapes, delighting with the unique color saturation. The sky was bluer here than wherever else, the sands of the desert were intensely yellow, the green of the palm trees in the clear air was extremely rich, and the water in the river was so much transparent that it was possible to see the bottom, albeit separated by several cubits from the onlooker. The Necropolis Scribe could also enjoy a sleep at any time, and all this caused that the disease he was afraid of didn't develop. On the contrary, its symptoms subsided and after four days of travel, when they arrived to Abu, Djehuty-mes felt better than on the day he came from the City.

Shed-su-Hor, whom Suti-mes asked to look after his aged friend was very delighted with the successful return of the old priest. Now, he made sure that the old man hadn't out of anything, and he sent promptly a letter to Buteh-Amun that his father returned from Wawat safe and sound. The messenger, Djehuty-hotep, after a short stop in Abu, sailed to the City, carrying the General's last orders, as well as all the good news, including the unexpected joyful one, of the recovery from the Kushite captivity of 12 boys deported more than a decade ago by Pa-nehsi. While awaiting a response, Djehuty-mes hoped that all these boys would return to their own families, although some of them were so small at the time of tearing them off from their mothers that they didn't remember their own names.

The eldest boys, at that time four or five years old, remembered that many children and one continuous cry, as well as fear were on the boats, on which they were transported. A terrible reminiscence embedded in the memory of one of them, when the Kushite supervisor wanting to calm down the little prisoners screaming after their mothers, who with a vigorous use of his whip tried to silence them unsuccessfully, finally grabbed the most loudly crying little one, maybe one and a half year old boy and just threw him into the river's whirlpools near the cataract. A childhood spent with strangers, among soldier families, especially in the fortress of Behen, was also sad, full of work, sometimes over the child's strength, which for many prisoners turned out to be too difficult and ended tragically:

during a few years of their stay there their number decreased considerably. Even the games were bringing to their minds memories of sometimes even cruel treatment by the Kushite peers, for whom the boys from Kemet were always inferior. Such terms as "dirty dog" usually replaced their names. Some recent years have been a bit easier, although completely filled with military exercises that would make them full-fledged soldiers. However, it was apparently noticed that some of these recruits had too much sadness in their faces and could not forget their country of origin, so Pa-nehsi decided that it would be better to send them back, thus gaining a better position during negotiations with the Kingdom of Amun.

Now, their fortune changed from day to day, resembling a good end of a fairy tale: everyone around was smiling at them and taking care both of their bodily needs (they got new clothes, were well fed), and the spiritual ones. Not only they could see the richly decorated temples in Abu, much richer than the rather severe chapels at Behen, but Djehuty-mes also drove them to the quarry near Sunu, in which a huge obelisk lay, left here in their great grandfathers times (or maybe even before?), being a sign of the power of the Both Countries capable of producing such great works. Joy returned to the boy's faces, accompanied by the hope of a close reunion with their families.

However, before the answer came from the City, the horizon on the river filled up with the approaching ships of the returning Pi-ankh's fleet. The chariots were still far away, but the boats with infantry soldiers carried by fast current have already reached Abu. The General himself also arrived, who immediately after reaching his palace ordered to call the Necropolis Scribe. However, the officer who led Djehuty-mes to the High Priest warned that his Lord was very unwell, he had terrible attacks of pain and it is not known if he could talk at all. When the old man entered the shady chamber, he found the General resting in his bed, pale and with his brow wet with beads of sweat, and next to him a medic who was pouring some infusion into his mouth. Seeing the priest coming in the medic only looked at him and shook his head in silence.

At the same time Pi-ankh spoke: "Stay, Chari; it's good that you came. Let the medic stay, too. You see, I am in a serious condition; this disease is making progress faster than I thought and my passage through the snake's mouth is also approaching[167]. But not only mine. Imagine that Pa-nehsi accepted both my conditions and gave us this robber, Aa-neru. He is waiting here for a trial in which you will be an important witness. As it turns out, in one of the units a young scribe, Aha-nefer-Amun called Pa-khar is also here, who came from the City. He is son of Nes-Amun, the doorkeeper from the temple of His Majesty Seti Maat-men-Re, whose father was found dead after the trial of Aa-neru. He will also be a witness. As for Aa-neru, I can say that I know rather well the day he will stand at the Hall of Two Maats, and I think, I also know, in this case, the judgment of the Osiris Court..."

---

[167] The spherical time was imagined as a snake that eats its own tail. While the body of the snake symbolized the duration or course of time, the mouth marked every beginning or end of any period. Here it is an allusion to death.

"No one can know that, General," the Necropolis Scribe answered seriously. "Maybe Aa-neru also has his Maat box?[168] It is indeed a unique villain and it is good that he will appear before court, although I was hoping I would never see him again."

"You'll see him the day after tomorrow, just after the tenth-day festival, because there is no need to postpone this process since you are already here. See you the day after tomorrow!" Pi-ankh called for a servant and ordered him to escort the old man to his quarters. "Everyone has the Maat box," Djehuty-mes thought when he was already at home. "Pi-ankh, this formerly primitive man has recently said a lot of things I'd never expect of him. Indeed, sometimes the shadow of death brings blessed results, though I would not expect it from Aa-neru... I will again have to look at his disgusting mug," Djehuty-mes moaned and reached for a pitcher with beer.

In the northern part of the temple precinct on the island of Abu was a small Maat's temple, in the courtyard of which trials were held sometimes. That day, so many people gathered here that they had hardly room enough. A part of this courtyard was occupied by a series of chairs, where the tribunal members sat, a place beside was reserved for scribes who squatted while recording the proceedings. On a special sanded place to the side the soldiers stood guarding the order, and ready to use, if necessary, the tools to interrogate the villains. The main

---

[168] According to Egyptian beliefs, at the Osiris Court, a man presented his collection of good deeds committed in life. In the famous heart weighing scene, a box topped with a Maat head is often depicted next to the scale - probably the "container" of good deeds.

participants of the court came in. Pi-ankh sat in a central place, and on his sides the Mayor of Abu, Khnum-hotep, two high army officers, the First Servant of the temple of Khnum and Djehuty-mes took the places. Before the session began, the priest of Maat, on the altar in front of Maat's statue standing in the small sanctuary adjacent to it, made offerings, while chanting the hymn:

Greetings to You, the Eye of Re,
thanks to which He lives every day,
Serpent, You who came out of his forehead!
You are the light that leads Him,
Law that directs the One with Hidden Names,
Lady of fear, of great dignity,
Justice because of which Re enjoys,
whom You enjoy in the Both Countries,
while ordering the divine actions.
You who dismiss the evil and reject wrong doing,
who satisfy the hearts of the Nine,
You are the balance of the Lord of Both Banks...[169]

The pile of offerings was set on fire and soon the smell of the burning mixed with that of herbs and incense filled the whole temple courtyard. When the last words of the hymn to Maat died away and the offerings burned down, the priest performed the ritual of cleansing the room where the trial was to take place with water and incense. Now everyone who was supposed to speak on that day: the judges and witnesses put their tongues out and the priest sketched on everyone's tongue the shape of the feather of

---

[169] This is a fragment of the hymn to Maat written in the tomb of Ramesses VI in the Valley of Kings.

Maat with a natron ball. The priest recited the last prayers and left, then the judges sat down and Pi-ankh opened the session. He started with saying that justice was done, because ten years after the terrible events related to the "year of hyenas", the war and the rebellion of the Kushite mercenaries under the command of Pa-nehsi – the enemy of God – the bringing before the court became possible today of one of the greatest criminals: Aa-neru. A murmur passed through the crowd at the mention of this name. Some remembered this officer, but most of the gathered people heard the name only from stories.

"We have no conditions today, nor the time to judge this criminal in the City where he committed most of the crimes," Pi-ankh continued, "but the witnesses of his crimes came to us, especially the dignified Djehuty-mes, the Royal Necropolis Scribe who had many occasions, to see the effects of this man's terrible activities." The crowd murmured again, this time repeating the name of the old man, much more known than the name of the tried criminal.

Pi-ankh gave a sign, and after a while two soldiers brought in the bound prisoner His arms and hands were tied on the back so that they touched each other from wrists to elbows, which must have been great torture. Around the neck Aa-neru had a rope, with which he was led. His face was gray and covered with deep furrows, but what for some of the people was most surprising was that his hair was snow-white.

"Is that him? Djehuty-mes asked an officer sitting next to him. "I have difficulty with recognizing him, though his face has haunted me for years!"

"Me too," the officer said, "but mainly because he turned gray. When he came to us as messenger of Pa-nehsi he had no gray hair, and that was only a few days ago..."

"What's your name?" Pi-ankh turned to the prisoner with a question that usually began court sessions.

"You know my name, so why are you asking?" the accused replied, and only now Djehuty-mes recognized that this man was really Aa-neru.

"Don't put my patience to the test, because we can force you in a different way to answer us, and you probably don't want it?" Pi-ankh has brought under control his agitation. "So, what's your name?"

Aa-neru was still silent. Pi-ankh waited for a long moment, then beckoned to the soldiers. They knocked the prisoner down on the sand and began to beat him with sticks, mainly on the twisted and tied hands. After several hits, Aa-neru shouted, "Stop it! I'll say!"

Pi-ankh signaled that the beating should be stopped, but the lying one had not yet been raised, because the "stick test" might be resumed if necessary.

"What's your name?" Pi-ankh asked for the third time and then everyone heard a reply more whispered than spoken: "Aa-neru."

"Who were you in the City?"

"Officer of General Pa-nehsi."

"Let him stand up!" Pi-ankh ordered, then turned to the prisoner again:

"Then, Aa-neru, listen to what a man you know well accuses you of, whose presence you probably didn't expect here: the dignified Royal Necropolis Scribe Djehuty-mes!"

Aa-neru looked at the old man who was just getting up from the chair, and a huge surprise appeared in his eyes.

"I see that you are surprised, Aa-neru, with my sight," the priest began his speech. "You probably thought that I was already dead? However, I am here, and my memory has preserved some images that I wouldn't rather like to remember, although they are with me and sometimes disturb my sleep. I remember as during the war, when Pa-nehsi went north, you met me while I was making the round in the Great Valley. Then you told me about some things, while thinking that these would never be revealed. You confessed to having stolen some pieces of equipment from the temple of His Majesty Seti Maat-men-Re, justified, because, as you said 'They were not needed by anyone there'. So many years have passed, and I still remember your cynical words about the temple guardian, Nes-Amun. You called him 'slow-witted' because he defended himself and then accused you in the court. You said then: 'I had no choice but to smash his stupid head'. You also said: 'You have all lost and nobody will accuse me or judge me anymore, you won't either.' You see, Aa-neru, Maat, in whose house we are now, caused you to be tried, and I am among the judges, and Nes-Amun's son Pa-khar is also with us. You also told me that you were interested in royal tombs, and later these tombs were all looted. I also know that you were the leader of those who stripped the temple of Amun in Ipet-sut of gold and robbed the temple caches. But the picture that haunts me at night in bad reams is the "process" you and Pa-nehsi organized for the royal mummies. You made me look at what you did with them. You beat the holy mummies of His Majesty Djehuty-Mes Men-kheper-Re justified, and of His Majesty Ramesses the Great, justified. You even used *menen,* because the mummies didn't answer your questions, and then you broke their hands. After that the Kushite soldiers chopped them with axes, and they cut down the lower abdomen of His Majesty Ramesses while laughing at the same time. But you did the worst thing - you urinated on the already chopped mummy of King Djehuty-Mes Men-kheper-Re and you prompted others to do similar acts. Do you remember how you then dared blasphemously to ask me, if I'd join you? I could never forget that. You are worthy of the death penalty for each of these crimes. How could you lead such a life? Did you think you would run away from Maat?"

Djehuty-mes finished and sat down tired; this speech, combined with the revival of all the terrible memories, was very difficult for him. There was absolute silence in the temple despite the crowd. Even those who only knew these terrible events by hearing were impressed by the words of the old Necropolis Scribe. The prisoner stood with his head down.

"Aa-neru, do you confess to all the crimes you have been charged with?" Pi-ankh asked and Aa-neru no longer refused to answer.

"Do you admit the stealing of the equipment from the temple of His Majesty Seti and the killing the temple guardian, Nes-Amun?"

"Yes."

"Do you admit that you took part in robbing temples and royal tombs?"

"Yes."

"Do you admit that you have profaned the mummy of His Majesty Djehuty-mes Men-kheper-Re, justified, by peeing on it?"

"Yes."

"So, great criminal, I condemn you to the great death penalty, and it is only unfair that you can only suffer it once. The penalty will be executed immediately. Let Aha-nefer-Amun called Pa-khar, son of the murdered guard Nes-Amun, come here; he will be among those who will perform Maat on you. Know also that your body will be burned later, and your name will never live. I said! Amun, you heard!"

The court was over. A side gate from the courtyard of the temple of Maat gave access to the execution site. There was a small platform constructed above the precipice. About six cubits below it a sharpened wooden stake made of freshly cut, not very thick acacia tree was dug deep and strengthened with stones.

"Give me that villain!" Pa-khar said while taking place on the platform. Soldiers led there the convict, then knocked him down and brought him to the very edge of the platform.

"Do you remember my father? Do you remember how you smashed his head with a stone when he lay sore after the court interrogation?" Pa-khar looked at Aa-neru hatefully. "Look, what is down there waiting for you and think about how nice it will be for you to recall your crimes when you are already get impaled on this stick!"

"Please forgive me, please!" Aa-neru knew that he could not say much more, so he was talking quickly. "Forgive me, Djehuty-mes, forgive me priests, and forgive me the First Servant Pi-ankh..."

"Move him a little more towards me, a little more" Pa-khar assessed the position of the body against the stake below. "Now!" he gave the command.

"Forgive me Amuuuun!!!" Aa-neru's scream filled the small amount of time that was covering the distance between the platform edge and the wooden skewer, then turned into a monstrous roar in which no words could be distinguished. After a few moments, this roar changed into steady, quieter wheezing, interrupted only by involuntary gasping for breath that was prolonging the suffering.

Djehuty-mes came up to Pi-ankh.

"Do you think, he'll suffer for a long time?"

"It depends on where the point will stick in. Sometimes it tears apart the spine and then the dying man doesn't feel pain any more, but this happens very rarely. Usually it lasts a few hours, but when the stake sticks in so that the heart can continue its work and the blood leaks out slowly, it happens that it lasts even two days. I don't know how he fell here."

"He was a real criminal, no doubt, but I have to say, I don't feel satisfaction." Djehuty-mes sighed deeply. "I was wishing him the death for years, now this wish has come true, and I have a strange feeling as if I contributed to something bad. Did you hear what he said before he has been thrown down? He asked the forgiveness – the people's forgiveness, yours and mine, but he also asked God's forgiveness, and he didn't believe in him... Pakhar didn't forgive him, he was cruel to the end. I... I already did it. And Amun? Can we say something about it? Has this death which we, convincedly, committed as consistent with Maat changed anything of what he had done? Did it improve anything? Or maybe he will have his Maat box, when he arrives at this Hall today, tomorrow, or – if he was unlucky – the day after tomorrow? I am old, General, and maybe I grew gentler, but I have more doubts today than ever."

"What do you want me to tell you?" Pi-ankh stared straight ahead with motionless eyes. "He was worthy of death more than others, but he did speak to Amun, and the last word he was able to utter was His name. In addition, he asked His forgiveness. I have never heard anything like that from the convict's lips, and I have participated in such executions many times. Is an ask for God's forgiveness directed to Him before the death placed by Him into the Maat box? Can it balance the scales at the court of Osiris? I am Amun's First Servant, and I know so little about Him... I asked you to participate in this process to give relief for your heart, and you tell me now that you don't feel it. But your presence and everything you told me was important to me. Maybe I learnt something today, too? I'll also stand before this court soon and I must think about my Maat box. Does a confession and a plea for forgiveness complete it? If so, I am asking your forgiveness. I have already told you that I ordered to kill these two *medjayu*, your servants, and they probably are already dead. Do you know why I gave such an order? Because they once came to me to Pi-Ramesse bringing a letter from His

Grandness Amen-hotep, justified, to His Majesty King Ramesses, may he live! And I then thought that Amen-hotep complained of Pa-nehsi, whom I liked very much at that time, because of pure jealousy and destroyed this letter. Now I have learnt that they were speaking about that meeting and a fire appeared in my heart that removed Maat. I wrote letters ordering to kill these people and I even mentioned you in them, so that one would think that it was done with your knowledge. I'll not correct this evil that I have done to these policemen, but may you forgive me, please, and keep good thoughts about me."

Chari was completely surprised by the unexpected confession revealing this secret that had been hidden for years and guarded by the First Servant so much that its defense has prompted him to commit a crime. Now, the same man not only entrusted it to the old Necropolis Scribe, but he also asked his forgiveness! Djehuty-mes thought for a moment what to say and already opened his mouth, but at that moment a young officer, clearly tired of the fast march, approached them, handing Pi-ankh a roll of papyrus.

"Captain Djehuty-hotep has just returned from the City and he passed it on, saying that it was a very urgent matter," he said, gasping for breath.

"There are no other matters here, nor a place where one could hide from them," Pi-ankh murmured with dissatisfaction, then tore the seal and began to read. After a moment, Djehuty-mes noticed that the letter caused a strong agitation of the General, and after a while he heard his outraged voice: "Pa-Shu-uben is dead, your Suti-mes killed him! Regardless of how we assessed the Chief of the Police in the City, he was my deputy during my absence. In this situation it's almost a coup! And what should I do now?!"

Djehuty-mes knew that in a moment Pi-ankh's mouth could give another death sentence today, so he took his hand and began to say quickly, "Please, General, don't act on the spur of the moment! You already know what the fire in your heart can do! You asked me for help in exercising Maat, so take my advice! Something terrible must have happened there because it is completely unlike Suti-mes; you must know the whole truth and listen to all sides; I will gladly help you if you let me!"

Pi-ankh shook his head, fought with his thoughts for a moment, and then finally decided, "Well, come back to the City, I'll give you a fast boat. Find out what happened there and prepare a court session. I'll be back in a few weeks and will judge him. But don't promise yourself too much, because it is a murder case, of a dignitary, and you know by which sentence such cases usually end. We still have the Repeating of Births, remember that!"

"Unfortunately, I know that," the Necropolis Scribe answered quietly and lowered his head.

That same evening, after saying goodbye to the General and to Shed-su-Hor, the old priest set off on his way back to the City. Unfortunately, the boat on which Djehuty-hotep arrived had an accident and had to be repaired, and all the other fast boats were on the way, therefore Djehuty-mes had to settle for an ordinary boat, which was much slower. This time the trip was a nightmare for him because the wind was almost imperceptible, and instead of moving north quickly, the boat was zigzagging from one riverbank to the other so that a man walking quickly along the shore would not have difficulty in overtaking it. To make matters worse, during one of these maneuvers, the boat ran aground, its rudder was damaged, and the captain had to spend many hours repairing it.

Four days later, they were only halfway to the City, passing only by the quarries at Khenu. During that time, the old man could hardly fall asleep at all, and various thoughts were occurring to him. The death of Pa-Shu-uben was a good piece of news, because with him the rule of violence, incriminating letters and assassinations in the City ended, about which Djehuty-mes learnt in recent years extremely often. Also the period of threat and uncertainty for Henut ended, but at the same time, another dark cloud hung over Suti-mes.

Djehuty-mes did not know how it was even possible that the short and slim Suti-mes could kill the huge Pa-Shu-uben; in any duel, the young priest would not have the slightest chance. So, did he surprise him from the ambush? Did he organized an attack on this, after all, a high dignitary who almost never moved without a guard? In this case, the term "coup d'état" used by Pi-ankh would be justified and the death penalty certain. Djehuty-mes thanked God in his mind that a letter with the information about the death of Pa-Shu-uben and some participation of Suti-mes in this event had reached Pi-ankh at the time of such an atypical conversation. Perhaps a few hours earlier, the General, known for his violent character, would grab a reed and from the fire in his heart would produce a deadly spark while ordering to kill Suti-mes instantly, as he had done to the poor *medjayu*. It is good that he decided to organize a court and that he would participate in it himself. Maybe there are some circumstances, witnesses who will defend Suti-mes? Maybe after the court of Aa-neru, the General will be more restrained in passing the sentence, and if Suti-mes would be convicted, maybe he would get the grace to execute himself, like those accused of magical practices in the trial after the death of His Majesty Ramesses Meri-Amun, about which Chari read from one of the old papyri kept in the archive in his own house?

All these sad thoughts depressed the old man, who even didn't feel like food. The boat captain, seeing this, became very anxious and finally dared to tell the Necropolis Scribe about it, "Lord, please don't hurt me, what have I done to you? We are sailing so slowly because the wind is not favorable to us, but tomorrow we will be in Behdet, where your own boat awaits, better than this. You have been entrusted to my protection and it is my duty to bring you in good health to the City. And how can I do it when you don't sleep nor want to eat? You are already old and close to the grave, the more so you have to eat and rest, otherwise you will faint and die on this trip, on my boat, and then I'll be accused, and they cut my head off!"

Old Necropolis Scribe had to agree that the Captain was right, so he promised him that he would eat and lie down to sleep. Indeed, he slept for a long time, and when he woke up, he found that the rocking of the boat stopped and they were standing again.

"Have we run aground again?" he asked the Captain.

"No, Lord, we are in Behdet and I waited for you to wake up so that we could change to your boat, which you left here on the way to Abu," the sailor said and began to prepare a hot meal, so that Djehuty-mes would eat something before continuing his journey. The luggage was already moved and an hour later the priest changed to his well-known boat, where he felt much better. The Captain also changed and was about to sail away when he noticed that a fast boat was approaching from the south, one of those that Pi-ankh had at its disposal. It had to leave Abu two days before when the shipping conditions improved, and thanks to its speed it managed to catch them up. The captain of that boat also noticed them and started to give signs with his hand, to wait. Soon, he moored right next to Djehuty-mes's boat. He leaped nimbly over the board onto its deck and bowed low before the Necropolis Scribe.

"I am Keni-Khnum in the service of General Pi-ankh. Lord, on my boat you will reach the City faster, and your Captain will escort your boat there."

"I am grateful to you, Keni-Khnum, because Amun made us sail very slowly and we lost a lot of time. Do you have any news from Abu?"

"Yes, Lord, but unfortunately very bad ones. The eminent General Pi-ankh is very sick and I heard that the medic who examined him said that this is a disease he will not treat. Immediately after your departure, the High Priest got terrible pains again and even lost consciousness for some time. Attacks of pain come back more and more often, and he no longer leaves the bed and cannot even eat, because everything returns immediately. At the time between the pains, he wrote a few more letters, including one for you," here Keni-Khnum handed a papyrus to

Djehuty-mes, on which, after opening, the Necropolis Scribe found several lines written with an uncertain, trembling hand; some words were barely legible.

To the Royal Necropolis Scribe, Chari. Every day I am praying to Amun for your health and for you to return home safely. I am thanking to Amun for your stay in Abu, for what you told me, and for what I was able to tell you so that my Maat box would become more complete. The Hall of Two Maats is closer to me than I thought; it's a matter of a few days. I wrote to my children Pi-nodjem and Nodjmet. I hope that Amun will agree with Pi-nodjem's choice as his First Servant. He will judge Suti-mes then, but help him the establishing Maat.

The last word was written in one big zigzag, taking up most of the papyrus card; presumably as he wrote it, a new paroxysm of pain caught him.

"So, with this word, you said goodbye to me and to the world, my friend whom until recently I was afraid and didn't like, and whom I'll miss now," Djehuty-mes said quietly, rolling up the papyrus.

CHAPTER XXX

The courtyard and main hall of the Maat temple in the northern district of Ipet-sut, where the lawsuits of the City's residents were held, was slowly filling up. This was the first time for ten years, because until recently, when the strict rules of the Repeating of Births period were still in force, the court rarely allowed anyone to enter except those who had to appear as defendants or witnesses. Not only did it debated in a narrow circle, but also quickly - the army officers in the service of the First Servant of Amun, who conducted the trials, did not have time for long meetings. The penalties were severe and very often the sessions ended up with taking the defendant to a nearby riverside area where death sentences were carried out. Maat in the years of the Repeating of Births, a period of restoring order after the terrible events of the years of war, hunger and lawlessness, was often showing the dangerous face of a lioness and much less often that of a cat[170], so her temple aroused fear.

Today, however, cheerful people gathered here, with smiles on many faces. There were several soldiers and the *medjayu* lined up around the hall to keep order; however white priestly tunics

---

[170] The lioness symbolized Sekhmet - the personification of the dangerous power of God, while the cat - Bastet - the personification of His gentleness.

dominated, and women's dresses were also seen. Both the appearance of the visitors and the cheerful tone of their conversations, which Maat in her statue seemed to listen to without indignation on her stony face, provided an unusual background for the murder trial to take place today. It was to be the first court hearing since His Majesty Horus, Beloved-by-Re, the Lord-whose-power was-strengthened by-Amun-to-exalt-Maat, the King of the Southern and Northern Country: Of-glorious-form like-Re, chosen-by-Re, Son of Re: Nes-Ba-neb-Djedu was seated on the throne of Geb in Kemet.

It was his first year of reign and at the same time the first year no longer counted according to *uhem mesut*. The third month of Akhet's season began and the river, spilled widely in the surrounding fields, began to fall slowly. Here and there, small black islets appeared above the surface of the water, attracting waterfowl, which eagerly used these places to observe the river, where it now was swarming with fish. In the houses of the City's inhabitants who were doing agriculture, preparations for ploughing and sowing took place. While repairing the ploughs, if necessary, or checking that the grain baskets were not punctured, one mentioned in talks the wonderful return of the Ipet-resit procession and the milk sprinkling of the route that Amun's barge followed during the feast, which ended two days ago. Now that everything was returning to its daily routine, it was time to judge Suti-mes. It were his friends and people he knew who filled the trial room in the Maat temple today, as His Grandness the First Servant of Amon, Pi-nodjem, son of Pi-ankh, justified, allowed.

In the fourth month of the Shemu season, in the tenth year of the Repeating of Births, the General rested in the tomb once provided for His Majesty Ramesses Men-Maat-Re Sechep-en-Ptah in the Great Valley. The next day the great barge of Amun User-hat set off in the procession from the House of Amun in Ipet-sut towards the House of Khonsu in Waset Nefer-hotep. Although the distance between these temples is small, the ceremony lasted a long time, because the procession was stopping many times to repeat the offerings, to sing subsequent phrases of the hymn to Amun and also to ask Amun for the oracles given in public. The ceremony had a particularly solemn setting. Old Amen-em-Ipet, who as the Second Servant led the procession, stood before the barge and, as usual, asked if he could ask God a question, and the priests carrying the User-hat barge took one step forward. Then Amen-em-Ipet asked, if God can agree that in a difficult situation of the southern part of the Kingdom of Amun after the death of the First Servant Pi-ankh his successor would be chosen. Again, the barge carried by the priests moved forward.

"Will you agree, the Great God," Amen-em-Ipet asked, "that Ser-Amun, the protector of Your holy pole, would become the new High Priest in the City?"

A beautifully carved and gilded pole ended with ram's head – the holy emblem of Amun was always carried in processions near the holy barge User-hat itself, and Ser-Amun was a highly respected priest and had a deep knowledge of the secrets of heaven, earth and the underground world, but Amun's barge remained motionless at the sound of this noble name.

"So," the celebrating priest asked again, "Will the Great God agree that Amen-em-Ipet be elected as the First Servant?"

Amen-em-Ipet was not only a sage and author of the book in which he wrote his thoughts about God and life, but he was also a hero of the war with the Kushites, he was not only a known person but also very much loved by the people of the City. However, the User-hat barge made no move again.

"So, do you want to agree, Lord, that Pi-nodjem, son of Pi-ankh, justified, would be Your First Servant in your City?" Amen-em-Ipet asked, and then the priests carrying the holy boat took a step forward. This meant that "God confirmed very strongly," which was later written on the walls of the temple. Pi-nodjem then stepped out of the row of priests who accompanied the procession, and Amen-em-Ipet put on his shoulders a ceremonial leopard pelt, and on his head the golden cap. It was a public sanctioning of the new function, signifying Amun's approval.

This instant, Pi-nodjem entered the hall with a vigorous step. He wasn't wearing any High Priest's distinctions, or even a wig, which, admittedly, he didn't need. His own hair was carefully cut above forehead and fell down on the sides and back of the head in a slightly wavy black thicket, which perfectly resembled it. Pi-nodjem first fell on his knees in front of the Maat statue, prayed for a while, and then sat on a high chair set up against the wall to serve the chairman. On the sides some similarly elegant pieces of furniture stood, on which other distinguished members of the tribunal were to sit, and then a dozen smaller stools for lower-rank officials. All of these were respected citizens of the City, invited today by Pi-nodjem to participate in the process, as was the case in the old days, before the "order" of the dictator Panehsi came here. All of them, while coming in, first bowed deeply, knelt or even kissed the ground in front of the statue, and then solemnly were taking their seats, proud of the honor they had received.

When the old Amen-em-Ipet came in, some people stood up and did not dare to sit down until he took a seat next to the High Priest. After a while, the same people stood up again, because Djehuty-mes entered the room slowly, led from both sides by the arms of *medjayu* Kari and Kasaya. The royal Necropolis Scribe Buteh-Amun was walking next to him. The old Djehuty-mes hardly ever was leaving the house. The unexpected trip to Wawat and the intense experience have weakened his health. On his return from Abu, he immediately went to Pi-nodjem to talk about Suti-mes. He knew the case very well, because his sister was telling him about it, so he calmed down the old man and advised him to postpone the trial until the laws of the Repeating of Births cease to apply. Djehuty-mes was afraid that he would not live long enough to see this moment, as he felt weaker every day. However, it turned out that he was to wait for a little while only.

Since the election of Pi-nodjem to the position of High Priest, important events in Kemet followed one after another. First, the news came from the north of the country, which many expected. The old King Ramesses Men-Maat-Re Sechep en-Ptah, who had long been removed from power, died in his palace in Pi-Ramesse. While the King's body was still resting in Wabet[171], the day of the

---

[171] "Clean Place" (rather: the place of cleansing) - the name of the embalming workshop.

New Year came. Ten years have just passed since the introduction of the *uhem mesut*, and it was a good time to end the period of the Repeating of Births. It was also then that a solemn procession took place in Djanet with Amun's oracle, who agreed that the next King would be the former First Servant of Amun in Djanet, Nes-Ba-neb-Djedu. The widowed Queen Tent-Amun, who ten years ago left Ramesses's Palace and accompanied Nes-Ba-neb-Djedu in Djanet, now officially became Queen again.

One had to wait with the coronation of the new king until the funeral ceremonies of Ramesses were completed, which took place in the second month of Akhet. The High Priest Pi-nodjem went to Djanet for the coronation ceremony and with the new King he concluded then an important agreement which was to ensure long lasting peaceful development of the Both Countries. According to this, Nes-Ba-neb-Djedu was to bear the royal titles, and the years of his reign were to be recognized also in the City, but he had no children and, as long ago it was agreed, the heir to the throne was to be Pi-nodjem's son. The High Priest already had three sons: ten years old Ma-sa-harti, five years old Pa-seba-kha-en-Niut, and Men-kheper-Re, who was one year younger.

It was too early to decide which one of them would wear the crown,[172] but it was agreed that after fifteen years Pi-nodjem would also accept the royal titles to ensure that the heir to the

---

[172] The successor of Nes-Ba-neb-Djedu (usually referred to in textbooks under the Greek version of the name: Smendes) was Pa-seba-kha-en-Niut-"The Star that appeared in the City" - known from royal letters under the Greek version of the name as Psusennes I, son of Pi-nodjem (I). Ma-sa-harti and Men-kheper-Re successively took the position of Amun's High Priest in Thebes.

throne would be King's son. Of course, only a few people knew about these plans, and Djehuty-mes was one of them.

Today was a joyous day for him for many reasons. He did not doubt even for a moment how the judgment on Suti-mes would end, moreover, he had the opportunity to meet his old friend Amen-em-Ipet again, and finally he went to Ipet-sut in the company of his faithful servants, sentenced by Pi-ankh to death and miraculously saved from the hands of Pa-Shu-uben. As soon as he greeted Pi-nodjem and Amen-em-Ipet, he sat next to him and began a conversation with that event.

"What a wonderful surprise! When Kari and Kasaya came to me the same day I came back from Abu, I was so moved that I cried with joy, just like a child. As you can see, this is proof that I'm entering this age again..."

"Chari, that's more like pride! Being an old man and a child at the same time is a divine feature and only Re can do[173]... Anyway, it's not so bad with you, because I don't see you holding a finger in your mouth. But speaking of children, look who's coming here! Not long ago, I told him a fairy tale..."

Nodjmet was entering the room, and Ma-sa-harti was walking by her - not tall but hubby-cheeked boy. His presence in this room indicated that he was already ten years old. He walked slowly, like adults, and tried to imitate them, pretending to be serious and dignified, but when the old priest smiled at him, the boy ran up to him and cried joyfully:

---

[173] Sun-God Re was depicted at dawn as a small child with a finger in his mouth and at dusk as a bent old man leaning on a cane.

"Amen-em-Ipet!"

All turned their heads towards him, and he was ashamed and has dropped his gaze.

"Hello, future priest!" Amen-em-Ipet answered. "This is the courtroom, but we are in the temple, and he who has hot blood in the house of God is like a tree that has grown in the forest...[174] How is your sister?"

Ma-sa-harti red on his face was glad that the old priest changed the subject. He raised his head and asked:

"Which one?"

"I forgot you already have two," the priest admitted. "Aset-em-Akhbit is still tiny, but Maat-Ka-Re is already eight years old. It was her I was thinking about, I remember when we visited Ipet-sut together when you were here for the first time. And now you live in the City. Are you happy?"

"Very much," the boy said, "and Maat-Ka-Re is fine. I'll tell her that you asked for her."

They couldn't continue this conversation because Pi-nodjem got up and it was known that he was about to start court proceedings. So Ma-sa-harti went to Nodjmet, next to whom he was supposed to sit in the chair, and Amen-em-Ipet only managed to whisper to Djehuty-mes:

---

[174] Words from the *Teachings of Amen-em-Ipet*, 21st dynasty (XI-X century BC). The end of the thought contained there is as follows: ...it quickly loses its branches and finds its end in the fire. A truly silent man who keeps himself out of the way is like a tree growing in a garden, greens and multiplies his fruit.

"This girl, Maat-Ka-Re, when she grows up, will be the Divine Spouse of Amon. It's already set.[175]"

In the meantime, all the conversations have quietened, and everyone's eyes have turned to Pi-nodjem who spoke:

"The noble priests," he has nodded his head towards both old men, "the noble Clean Ones, the Fathers of God, and the scribes who make up the great company of the tribunal today, as it was at the time of the "corner" of the forefathers[176], and all of you residents and inhabitants of the City! We are gathered here before the face of Atum's daughter for the first time since the Repeating of Births, which brought her back to the world. No one is hungry anymore and no enemy threatens the City, Hapi has come in his time and dimension, and all faces turn with joy to Amun-Re, who has just been born[177] who is great and merciful. The time has come to judge the act of the Servant of God Suti-mes. Six months ago, when an expedition to Kush, led by my pious father the First Servant and General Pi-ankh, justified, was still going on, he raised his armed hand and killed the General's deputy in the City, the Chief of the Secret Affairs of Waset, Pa-Shu-uben. Suti-mes will no longer be able to stand before the Lords of Eternity in the Hall of Two Maats and say, "I have not killed any man," but we must decide whether he will be able to say,

---

[175] Maat-Ka-Re, daughter of Pi-nodjem I, is attested as the first priestess bearing this title.

[176] The Egyptian word for court: *kenebet* also means "corner" and is defined by a hieroglyph in the shape of a corner. Probably at first the court gathered in a specially designated corner of the temple hall where the trials were held.

[177] References to the Nile's flood and the Ipet-feast.

"I have not unjustifiably killed anyone unless his crime was obvious[178]. Let the court proceed according to Maat! Bring in the accused!"

Pi-nodjem sat down. The murmurs of silent conversations filled the room again for a while, but they fell silent when the *medjayu* leading Suti-mes appeared. The young priest had wooden stocks on his hands, and those who saw him only after a long break could see that he had lost weight and was pale - even the good conditions of the temple's custody that were provided for him left their mark on the prisoner. However, he walked vigorously, and while passing the statue of Maat, he fell on his face in front of it and remained in a prayerful position for a while, then he got up and walked to the designated place, looking brightly at the members of the tribunal sitting before him.

"Who are you?" A ceremonial question was asked, and when he answered it, he was asked a second:

"Do you admit that you killed Pa-Shu-uben, Chief of Police and Secret Service in the City?"

"Yes," answered the priest loudly and a wave of murmur ran through the hall. Suti-mes continued:

"God is the one who does righteousness, and his destiny will also come to the one who is evil. Man does not know what tomorrow will be like. There is no one perfect in the hand of God, but also nothing that is crippled will stand before Him. Sin belongs to God, it is sealed with His finger[179]. I know that I have

---

[178] This is a source-confirmed version of one of the spells of the so-called declaration of innocence in the 125th "chapter" of the *Book of the Dead*.

sinned, and double that. Not only did I kill Pa-Shu-uben, but before that, I had repeatedly flamed in my heart against him, even though it never happened without a reason. It was him who gave me a letter to the Great Gate Keeper at Ipet-sut, Pen-nesti-tawy, and sent me to him for death when I returned from the legation to the King, with which I was sent by the First Servant Amen-hotep, justified. Amun saved me, so Pa-Shu-uben later sought vengeance on me and my wife. He was the one who sent his helper Pa-neb on her.

The brave *medjayu* Kari and Kasaya saved her, so Pa-Shu-uben decided to take revenge on them too. When accompanying as a servant, the noble Nodjmet, I found myself in a house on the water where these people were to be killed, Pa-Shu-uben threw himself at me and wanted to strangle me. In defending myself, I wounded him with his own dagger, but I didn't even know exactly what I was doing at the time, as it began to take over me night at day. I swear on Amun that everything I said was true, and everyone I mentioned can confirm it."

The young priest finished, and the hall came alive again with whispering conversations. In this trial, the accused was Suti-mes, but it was the other people mentioned here by name who should have taken his place. Many of those present in this room had painful memories of not only Kushites' violence - these were already obliterated - but also of the recent time when Pa-Shu-uben took advantage of his position to continue committing crimes. But he had already paid for them, while his assistant and

---

[179] Excerpt from the Doctrine of Amen-em-Ipet, 21st Dynasty (XI-X century BC).

faithful servant Pa-neb still held a clerical position in the City. It was at this very moment that this name was called by Pi-nodjem.

"Let the craftsman scribe, Pa-neb, stand here as a witness."

Everyone, not excluding Suti-mes, was surprised. Djehuty-mes leaned towards his son:

"Pa-neb a witness? He doesn't know what it is truth..."

"It seems to me, father," Buteh-Amun said "that's what Pi-nodjem is about"

After a while, the guards brought the summoned witness, who looked exceptionally dignified today, in a festive robe, though as usual without a wig. He must have been informed beforehand that he would be an important witness in the trial of his superior's killer and considered it an exceptional honor. He walked slowly, looking around and looking for people he knew, but he encountered faces full of contempt or derision everywhere. When he reached the place where Suti-mes stood, he took on the expression of condemnation and superiority, not without satisfaction. Finally, the one he tried to capture several times stood in front of the court in the stocks, while he, Pa-neb, was a free witness!

"What is your name?" he heard Pi-nodjem's voice.

"Don't you know me, Lord?" he said, but seeing the judges' unfavorable looks and the general stir in the hall, he quickly added: "I'm Pa-neb, the scribe at the craftsmen's estate."

"Pa-neb, you seem never to be in the courtroom and you don't know the customs here. On entering, you passed the statue of Maat indifferently, you did not even bow before her, and so you must take an oath. Swear that you will speak Maat and complete it with the right formula," seriously said Pi-nodjem.

"Of course I will speak Maat, that's clear."

"I see you don't know the formula, so repeat: "I swear to say only Maat. Otherwise, let them send me to the oasis".

Pa-neb murmured the words of the formula, in which the inaccessible place of exile, which for centuries was Kush, was turned into an oasis. He lost his self-confidence. His court appearance was, for the time being, completely different from what he had imagined. Only after a while did he hear another question from the President, and only then did it seem reasonable to him.

"Do you recognize the accused?"

"Yes," Pa-neb nodded and added: "he's the one who killed my Lord, the Chief of Police, Pa-Shu-uben!"

"How do you know that, Pa-neb? Were you present at this yourself?"

"I wasn't, but I heard others talking about it."

"Who was talking about it? Where and when?" Pi-nodjem inquired, and Pa-neb felt a trickle of sweat running down his back.

"Well, everybody was talking, in the beer house..."

There was a lot of laughter in the hall, and someone in the back filled in:

"At the "Sisters"!"

Pi-nodjem had a hard time controlling himself, so as not to laugh along with almost the whole room.

"I ask you to be serious in the Maat house!" he called, and addressed another question to the witness."

"How do you know the accused?"

"He's been planning to assassinate Pa-Shu-uben for a long time. He was hanging around his palace, asking me about him, but when I wanted to arrest him, I wasn't allowed to..." Pa-neb fixed his angry eyes on Amen-Ipet, which he saw right next to the High Priest.

"Who told you to arrest Suti-mes and for what?"

"He beat up a man at the beer house, so I..."

"So you decided to arrest him?"

"Not me... I mean, I just had... But he beat up..." Pa-neb started to get tangled up, and his face was blushing.

"Someone gave you an order, and you were supposed to follow it. Who gave you that order and why?"

"Pa-Shu-uben, but I don't know why. He said he was a great criminal."

"Was Suti-mes's wife a big criminal because you wanted to arrest her too?" Pi-nodjem was well prepared for this trial, and Pa-neb didn't know what to answer, so he kept quiet.

"Pa-neb, one should answer the court by saying Maat. Why did you assault Henut-netjeru? Did anyone ordered you to do?"

Pa-neb was still silent. He understood that from the witness he became an accused.

"Are you deaf? Shall we examine you with a stick?"

That sentence reached Pa-neb with all its horror. After all, in court, the witness could also expect to be flogged in case he'd lie.

So he started to talk fast, disorderly, and certainly more than he wanted.

"It was Pa-Shu-uben who ordered me, because she was the wife of this criminal Suti-mes, she certainly knew where he was hiding, so I was supposed to stop her and bring her into custody."

"I guess, rather to carry her in after you hit her with a baton. You arrested a lot of different people, sometimes they were strong men, but you handled things differently. Did you have to use a cane for a woman? Is that what Pa-Shu-uben told you? Just tell the truth!"

Pa-neb was so scared that he answered this time faster than he thought:

"He told me to use a dagger, but I don't like blood, so I wanted to stun her, and after... then to drown her in the canal."

"After what?"

"Well, after the... the hearing."

Pa-neb's last sentences have strongly moved everyone. Both the deceased Police Chief and his assistant were well known in the City and they were widely disliked, but the details of the planned crime brought to light here were shocking. At the same time, they were the best evidence of Pa-Shu-uben's accusation and Suti-mes' defense. Pi-nodjem quietly exchanged a few remarks with the closest members of the tribunal, and they passed them on. For a long time, the consultations of the judges lasted, dying in the midst of the general bustle of the public. Finally Pi-nodjem raised his hand and silence fell.

"Pa-neb, you were lucky that *medjayu* Kari and Kasaya did not let you finish what you were going to do. Today you tried to conceal the truth here. That is why you will face the punishment you chose for yourself by taking an oath. You will be sent to an oasis and spend the rest of your days there as a scribe at the service of the *medjayu*, who will also watch over you. Just remember that men living in the oasis can guard their women well! Let the *medjayu* Kari and Kasaya come here!"

They came out of the crowd filling the hall and approached the place where Suti-mes and beside him Pa-neb, petrified with fear stood.

"Do you confirm what the accused Suti-mes said about the situation in which he killed Pa-Shu-uben?" the High Priest asked.

"Yes, Your Grandness!" answered Kari, who was more eloquent than his colleague. "This scoundrel Pa-Shu-uben, who is surely already walking upside down with his head cut off and heart ripped out[180], grabbed this young priest by the throat and was saying terrible things to him, and then suddenly he started to growl and fell. We two saw it, and Her Royal Highness Lady of Both Countries Nodjmet too!"

"It was so!" Nodjmet spoke without moving, and her testimony was received with a friendly rustle in the hall.

"Therefore, let the *medjayu* release Suti-mes, who is no longer the accused, and put on the stocks of Pa-neb, who is no longer an inhabitant of the City and of all Kemet![181]"

---

[180] This typical image of a man condemned in the Judgment of the Dead – an equivalent of a vision of the hell – can be found in some royal tombs in the Valley of the Kings.

Kari and Kasaya were happy to carry out the order and all those present applauded the court's ruling. However, before the court session ended, Pi-nodjem once again silenced the gathered by raising his hand.

"Suti-mes!" he said loudly. "The House of Amun and the whole City are grateful to you for what you have done. As a reward, I make you the head of all scribes writing down God's offerings in Ipet-sut![182] It is completed!" he ended and stood up, which was a signal to the others that the court meeting was over.

The *medjayu* have escorted Pa-neb, who still could not understand what actually happened. Everyone now was approaching Suti-mes, while greeting him, praising and congratulating on the high position he has just obtained in the temple hierarchy.

Finally, Henut also managed to approach his husband and to hug him, and he embraced her gently, as the figure of his wife indicated that she would be mother again.

"How did you do this while you were in custody?" Pi-nodjem asked when he noticed this.

"I let Henut bring supplies for the prisoner from time to time," Nodjmet explained, freeing both young people from the awkward situation.

Pi-nodjem smiled and blinked to Suti-mes in a communicative way, peeking at Henut's pretty face, on which

---

[181] Oases, with the exception of Fayum, were treated as foreign territory, not belonging to Egypt, though subordinate to it.

[182] This is one of the titles that appears on the coffins of Suti-mes, which are today in the Louvre Museum in Paris.

blushes appeared. Maybe they were caused by Re's rays, which fell through the ajar door of the temple hall, along with a reviving breeze from the widely spilled river, together carrying the announcement of the new life.

Geographical ethnic and local names

appearing in the book

Aa-sura – Assyria, a kingdom in the northern Mesopotamia (between the Euphrates and Tigris rivers), in today's Iraq.

Abdju – Abydos, an important religious center arranged around the temple of Osiris, in the 8th District of the Southern Country.

Abu – Elephantine island, the pharaonic Egypt's border town, the capital of the 1st District of the Southern Country.

Akh-menu – jubilee temple built by Thutmose III in Karnak.

Aramu – Arameans: militant Semitic tribes spreading in the region of Northern Syria and Mesopotamia, and in the 11th cent. BC threatening Assyria.

Asheru – the precinct of the Mut temple in the Eastern City, today in Luxor.

Baki - Quban fortress in the Lower Nubia, controlling the access to the nearby gold mine; today in the area flooded by the Nasser's Lake in the southern Egypt.

Behdet – Edfu, an important city and the capital of the 2nd District of the Southern Country.

Behen - Buhen fortress near the 2nd Nile cataract, today in the area flooded with the waters of the Nasser's Lake in the northern Sudan.

Black Country – cf. Kemet.

Both Countries – the official name of the Egyptian state, consisting of the Southern and the Northern Countries; this duality was emphasized by many symbols, among others two plants (lily and papyrus), two divine patrons (vulture and cobra), two royal crowns (white and red).

City – the ancient Egyptian name of Thebes (today's Luxor), used interchangeably with the name Waset; the most important center of the Southern Country, located in the 4th District.

Crocodile Island – an island on the Nile between the South Iunu and Sumenu, ca 15-20 km upstream the Nile of the City.

Dep – the second (next to Pe) part of the double city of Buto, an important religious center located in the 4th District of the Northern Country, in the northwest of the Nile Delta.

District – the administrative unit of the territorial division of Egypt, usually referred to by the Greek term: nome; the whole country was divided into 42 districts, with the Southern Country covering 22 of them, counted from the south of the Nile Valley, and the Northern Country consisting of 20 districts, counted from the south and the west of the Nile Delta.

Djanet – Tanis, a city founded in the times of the Repeating of Births, ca 1080 BC in the Northern Country to replace the old Pi-Ramesse residence, located in the same 19th District, about 20 km further south, in the eastern part of the Nile Delta.

Djedu – a city known by the later Greek name as Busiris, an important religious center in the Northern Country, in the 9th District, in the central part of the Nile Delta.

Djeret – a town located on the east bank of the Nile about 20 km south of Luxor, near today's village of Tod.

Djeser-Akhet – "holy horizon" – first it was the name of a slope of the Theban mountains, partly identical with the southern part of today's Deir el-Bahari, encompassing the small temple of Hathor and the tomb of Amenhotep I; after the erection of a temple by king Thutmose III there in the 15th century BC, the same name was taken over by this temple, then replacing the greater part of the former slope, removed to make room for the new structure.

Djeser-Djeseru – "holy (place) of the holiest" – the name of the temple erected by Hatshepsut in the 15th century BC in the West City, in the area known today as Deir el-Bahari, north of the place called Djeser-Akhet.

Dog District – the name of the 18th District of the Southern Country, with the capital in Hor-di.

Fish District – the name of the 19th District of the Southern Country.

Gebtu – a town known by the Greek name Koptos (today's Qift), an important city in the 5th District of the Southern Country, about 40 km downstream the Nile of Luxor.

Great Green – an ancient Egyptian term for the sea, especially the Mediterranean Sea.

Great Valley – a part of the royal necropolis in the West Thebes, located west of Ta-Djeser, surrounded by high cliffs, encompassing the best protected group of tombs, today known by the commonly used name Valley of the Kings. Its ancient name is uncertain; "Great Valley" is the name given by the author.

Hapi – the ancient Egyptian name of the river Nile.

Hatti – the former Hittite kingdom with which Egypt competed in the 13th century BC for dominion over the area of the present Syria; it no longer existed in the time, the novel's action goes on.

Hill of Wedding Rites – a hill in the central part of Theban necropolis, today referred to as Shekh Abd el-Qurna; its ancient name is unknown; the name given by the author refers to the contemporary rites practiced by Muslim women observed there that may be of ancient origin.

Hor-di – an important center in the 18th District of the Southern Country, known by the Greek name as Kynopolis.

Iapu – the Egyptian name of the port town and fortress at the eastern sea-shores of the Mediterranean Sea; in the antiquity it remained in the zone of the Egyptian influence; on its territory Tel-Aviv is situated today.

Ipet-resit – the ancient Egyptian name of the temple in Luxor.

Ipet-sut – the ancient Egyptian name of the temple complex in Karnak.

Israel – the name of the Semitic tribes confirmed in the Egyptian sources; in the period of the novel's action (11th cent. BC) they were conquering the area of the Palestine, fighting, among others, with the Philistines (see Peleshet); according to the biblical history, it was Judges' period.

Iunu – one of the most important religious centers of Egypt, the worship center of the Sun, hence the Greek name: Heliopolis; it was located in the 13th District of the Northern Country; its today's ruins are located in the east Cairo

Kadesh – a town and fortress on the Orontes river in Syria; in the 5th year of the reign of Ramesses the Great, ca 1275 BC a great battle between the Egyptian and the Hittite armies took place there.

Keben – a city and an important port on the Mediterranean Sea coast (the area of today's Lebanon), with which Egypt made trade, bringing from there, among others, the cedar wood; the Greek name: Byblos.

Keftiu- a population living in Crete in the 3rd and 2nd millennium BC, with whom Egypt made trade, especially in the 15th and 14th centuries BC.

Kemet – "Black Country" – the ancient Egyptian name of the territory of the land of the pharaohs, referring in particular to the fertility of the arable lands.

Khefet-her-neb-es – "The one who is in front of her Lord" (i.c. in front of the temple of Amun in Karnak) – the name of the Western City, today's West Luxor, the former Qurna and Bairat villages.

Khemenu – an important city in the 15th District of the Southern Country, named by Greeks Hermopolis Magna (due to the temple of Thoth identified by Greeks with Hermes).

Khenu – the sandstone quarries on the west bank of the Nile, today known as Gebel el-Silsila, about 65 km north of Aswan.

Kush – the general name of the areas located south of the 1st cataract (later usually referred to as Nubia), inhabited by dark-skinned people (Kushites); in the narrower sense, the term refers to the area south of the 2nd cataract (while the area between the 1st and the 2nd cataracts was named Wawat).

Libu – one of the most important tribes among the Tjehenu people; hence the name: Libyans.

Madu – a village located ca 8 km north-east of Luxor; today's town Medamud.

Medjayu – one of the Kushite tribes of which many mercenaries in the Egyptian army originated; in the New Kingdom the term was used to define the policemen.

Men-nefer – the city known by the Greek name: Memphis, one of the main centers in Egypt, the capital of the 1st District of the Northern Country, ca 20 km south of Cairo.

Meshuesh – one of the main Tjehenu tribes; many settlers originating from this tribe, similar to those of the Libu tribe, lived in Egypt in the time of the novel's going on.

Miam – a city and fortress, the capital of the Wawat region, known in modern times as Aniba.

Nebit – a city in the 1st District of the Southern Country, called by the Greeks: Ombos; today's Kom Ombo.

Nefer-hotep – the precinct of the Khonsu temple in Ipet-sut, a part of today's Karnak.

Nen-ensu – an important center in the 20th District of the Southern Country, known by the Greek name: Herakleopolis.

Nine Bows – a general name of the potentially hostile peoples surrounding Egypt from the south (Kushites), west (Libyans) and north-east (Asians).

Northern Country – the northern part of Egypt including the northernmost part of the Nile Valley and the whole Nile Delta; today it is referred to as the Lower Egypt.

Pa-im – the Fayum oasis located in the Western Desert, at the height of the 20th and 21st Districts of the Southern Country, near the Nile Valley; it was the only oasis considered to be a part of Egypt, while other oasis were regarded as situated beyond its borders.

Pe – the second (next to Dep) part of the double town of Buto, an important religious center in the 6th District of the Northern Country, in the northwest part of the Nile Delta.

Peleshet – Philistines, in the 11th century BC inhabiting the area of Palestine, one of the belligerent so-called Sea peoples that in the 12th century BC defeated the kingdom of the Hittites and settled in the Near East. Egypt concluded an agreement with them and at the price of peace on its eastern border used them as intermediaries in trade with further located countries.

Per-Bastet – a town known by the Greek name as Bubastis, located in the 18th District of the Northern Country, in the eastern part of the Nile Delta.

Pi-Ramesse – a large city and at the time of the novel's action, the pharaoh's residence, i. e. the capital of Egypt, located in the 19th District of the Northern Country, in the eastern part of the Nile Delta.

Punt – a land located in the eastern Africa, in the region of the present day Sudan, Somalia and Ethiopia, to which the pharaohs organized trips for African exotic products such as ebony, ivory, leopard skins, or valuable incense.

Retjenu – a land located east of the Mediterranean Sea on the area of today's Syria; the aim of the Egyptian policy was to preserve its dominance there, mainly to control the trade routes crossing this area.

Seper-meru – a town in the 19th District of the Southern Country, ca 40 km south of Nen-ensu.

Sherdana – the name of the belligerent tribe belonging to the so called Sea peoples that invaded Egypt in the 13th century BC; at the time of the novel's action many mercenaries from this tribe served in the Egyptian army.

Southern Country – the southern part of Egypt, covering the most of the Nile Valley, from the first cataract south of the Elephantine island (Abu) to almost the base of the Nile Delta; today its territory is usually referred to as the Middle Egypt (its northern part) and the Upper Egypt.

South Iunu – a religious center south of Thebes, today's Armant, about 15 km of Luxor.

Sumenu – a village located on the west bank of the Nile, ca 22 km upstream the Nile of Khefet-her-neb-es (West Luxor); today's Rizeikat lies there; a desert route running through the oases in the Western Desert begins there.

Sunu – the present day town Aswan, a city in the 1st District of the Southern Country on the east bank of the Nile, opposite the Elephantine Island (Abu).

Ta-Djeser – an important temple area located in the Western City, where the temples of Mentuhotep, Hatshepsut and Thutmose III were situated; today this place is referred to as Deir el-Bahari.

Ta-mehu – cf.: Northern Country.

Ta-seti – the designation of the areas of the 1st District of the Southern Country as well as those located directly south of the 1st Nile cataract.

Ta-set-neferu – a part of the Theban necropolis, mainly devoted to the tombs of royal spouses and children of the New Kingdom period; today it is referred to as the Valley of the Queens.

Ta-shema – cf.: Southern Country.

Tjehenu – the ancient Egyptian general designation of the Libyans – the western neighbors, also partly settled in Egypt, especially in the Northern Country.

Tree District – the name of the 20th District of the Southern Country.

Waset – another term for Thebes (the City), as well as for the entire 4th District of the Southern Country.

Wawat – the area between the 1st and the 2nd Nile cataracts, later referred to as Lower Nubia.

Divine names

mentioned in the book, with explanations

According to the ancient Egyptian theologians, at the time when the action of the novel goes on, that is in the 11th century BC, one God existed, who created the world and "made millions of himself", which means that in every particle of reality, with which the human being meets, a divine element is embedded. The divinity that permeates the whole created world and every individual creature is, additionally, comparable to the idea of the Trinity. The most vivid image of God the Father was the Sun, named Re. The Son of God present on the earth was identified with the king, and God's law that permeated everything was known as Maat. God was called by many names and represented in many forms. Sometimes these characters and names are derived from an ancient tribal tradition, older than the unified state. Many separate tribal organisms inhabited the territory on the Nile, and each of them worshipped the Creator-God while imagining and naming it somewhat differently. Other divine figures found in texts and images are sanctified concepts related to the king, yet others were created to express only a feature of God or to illustrate a sacred episode of mythical tradition; we call such divine characters personifications or incarnations. They are not separate "deities", but images of the One God expressing a given aspect which in prayers or hymns was mentioned depending on the need arising from the circumstances. The word:

"gods" which can be found in various texts, most often refers to the statues in temples.

The following list of the various divine names that appear in the book is, therefore, a list of various concepts related to the idea of the One God who is invisible (expressed by the word: Amun), but who was worshipped in various visible forms.

Akh -"luminous spirit" - a designation of the deceased who obtained justification during the Judgment of the Dead, that is, the right to live in paradise, and thus it possess a kind of a divine status.

Amun - "invisible, hidden One" - the most commonly used term for God, ubiquitous in nature (among others in air, light, wind), as well as in all divine images, whatever they depict and whatever their name would be.

Anubis - a guardian of the dead and cemeteries, and the patron of the mummification, depicted as a jackal or king with a jackal's head, especially worshipped in the 17th District of the Southern Country, from where it may originate.

Anuket - a patron of the area around the first cataract, depicted as a woman wearing a crown of feathers.

Ash - a divine name popular in the circles of Tjehenu (Libyans).

Atum - the name of the Creator meaning "Everything" (in Him) and at the same time "Nothing" (outside Him). According to the myth, Atum first brought to life the first pair of his "children": Shu (air, light) and Tefnut (moisture) that is the necessary conditions for the emergence of the life. A version of this myth replaces Shu and Tefnut with another pair of terms: Life and Maat. Then came the sky (Nut) and earth (Geb).

Ba - the name of one of the spiritual elements of man, associated with the upper (visible) half of the world (the Kingdom of Re), i.e. the "solar soul" of a man, depicted as a bird with a human head. The connection of Ba with another spiritual element: Ka (the "Osirian soul") meant the (cyclical) resurrection (every night for one hour).

Bes - one of the divine names expressing great magical power; a protector ("guardian") of the sleep, of pregnant women, of childbirth, as well as a guardian of the mysterious changes of the Sun ("born" at dawn, "aging" during the day, and "rejuvenating" at night). His appearance was supposed to deter the evil powers, so he was depicted as a dwarf (or "old child") with a naked hairy body, protruding tongue, a beard, lion's ears, mane and tail, often armed with a knife.

Djehuty - the Egyptian version of the divine name known as Thoth, the guardian of all science, the writing, the calendar, as well as the patron of the magical knowledge and all rituals. Perhaps he was originally worshipped in the central part of the country (15th District of the Southern Country with a center in Khemenu); from the beginning of the unified state was closely associated with the king, probably as a deified form of the divine wisdom as pharaoh's attribute. In the art depicted as an ibis, a baboon or the king with the head of ibis, holding a scribe's palette in his hand, and having two forms of the Moon represented on his head.

Ennead - a designation of all the cult statues and objects worshipped in a given temple, town or region, as well as the set of divine names occurring in a myth (for example, the creation myth); the name expresses the idea of "plurality" of pluralities" (i. e. 3 x 3).

Geb - the personification of the Earth as one of the sources of life; in the myth depicting the history of the creation of the world, Geb and Nut (heaven) are (after the Creator Atum and his first "children": Shu and Tefnut, that is, air and water, and according to another version: Life and Maat) "the third generation" of the divine creative work, or of an imitative "divine dynasty"; every Egyptian king as "a descendant" of this dynasty was "sitting on the throne of Geb".

Hat-Hor - "House of Horus" - the designation of the womb of the mother of the king, as well as the mother of the Sun, the personification of many aspects of the divine power and protection. In the afterlife beliefs, she appeared as a guardian and feeder of all the dead, lavishing maternal care on them and guaranteeing a new life; as a life-giver she patronized the love and marriage. In the art she is depicted as a cow emerging from the Western Mountain (Theban necropolis), as a sycamore or a woman appearing at the tree, watering and feeding the souls of the deceased; she often has a sun disc on her head placed between cow's horns, which identifies her with Isis.

Heri-shef - "The One who is at his lake" - the name of the ram-shaped patron of the 20th District of the Southern Country, with the center in Nen-ensu.

Horus - "The one who is above" - one of the names of the Great Sun-god as well as the divine name of each king as the successor of the mythical ruler of the world - Osiris (and Isis). In the art is usually depicted as a falcon or as king with the head of a falcon. Each local cult form of God could be referred to as Horus, which was the rule in the area south of Egypt, in Kush (Horus from Baki, Horus from Miam, Horus from Behen).

Iah - the personification of the Moon; the name was often encountered in the theophoric names of the people living in the area of Waset (4th District of the Southern Country).

Ini-heret - "The one who brought back the (female) One who left" - the construction of this name refers to several myths associated both with the Nile flood (awaited very much in the end of the Shemu season) and the Sun (the myth of the "lost" eye of Re). In the art he is often unified with Shu and is wearing a crown consisting of four high feathers. Onuris – as sounded the Greek form of his name – was the patron of hunters and travelers.

Isis - the personification of the royal throne, the mythical wife of Osiris and mother of Horus, that is a king; in this role Isis is very similar to Hat-Hor (she even has the same crown consisting of the sun disc between cow's horns); Isis is a guardian of the dead and a donor of life; she was considered as an incarnation of the divine magical power capable of effective protection, both of Re during his night journey through the underground land and of her son Horus, finally of every deceased.

Ius-aas - the personification of the hand of Atum thanks to which, according to one of the versions of the creation myth through the act of God's masturbation the first pair of divine works appeared: Shu (air, sunlight) and Tefnut (water) which are the factors necessary for the development of life; this deified element of the myth was depicted in the form of a female figure being an object of worship particularly in Iunu (Heliopolis) but also in Ipet-sut (Karnak).

Ka - one of the spiritual elements of a human being, associated with the lower part of the world – the kingdom of Osiris and Osiris himself; this can be therefore recognized as "Osirian soul"; during a man's life his (or her) Ka is looking after its owner from outside, providing him with food and being a carrier of genetic traits which he inherits from his parents; after the death the Ka is living in his mummy, provided that the man obtained justification at the Court of Osiris, becoming a hypostasis of Osiris; the Osirian soul Ka was supposed to unify every night with another spiritual element – the "solar soul" Ba, and this union meant the temporary resurrection for one hour; Ka was usually depicted in the art identically to a living person, but also as a pair of arms stretched in a gesture of embracing.

Khnum - personification of a creative union, the patron of fertility, birth and the beginning of life; as a guardian of the life-giving flood of the Nile Khnum was worshipped on the Elephantine island, where the onset of the rising level of the river's waters was first observed; in the art Khnum was depicted as a ram or a king with ram's head.

Khonsu - "the one who traverses" (the sky) - the patron of the Moon and all the manifestations of life related to the passing of time or associated with the lunar cycle (including pregnancy, birth, youth, renewal (also posthumous one), and king's reign; Khonsu was depicted in art as a mummy wrapped in bandages, holding royal scepters; on his head is the so-called children's lock represented, and it is crowned with the images of Moon in its two different phases (as a disc and a crescent); a delivery room operated at his temple in Karnak, and medical advice for pregnant women was given related to an oracle.

Maat - the basic concept that regulates the operation of the world, the state and the human life, it can be compared to the idea of the Holy Spirit that is omnipresent, defining the laws of the cosmos and nature, the principles of the society's functioning, and the human behavior; the word can be translated, depending of the situation, as God's law, truth, justice, righteous conduct, etc.; it was left untranslated in the book. According to one version of the creation myth, Maat belonged, alongside Life to the first pair of the Creator's works; a special significance of Maat is reflected by the Judgment of the Dead idea where Maat becomes a symbolic measure of human life's balance: only Maat's presence "in the heart" of the deceased ("put" on one scale) and meaning the necessary amount of good deeds ensures an equilibrium with another scale, where Maat is represented (as a woman or as a feather), and in consequence the positive judgment of Osiris's court.

Meret-seger - "the one who loves silence" - the personification of the Theban necropolis and of the highest peak of the rocks surrounding it, i.e. the pyramid shaped el-Qurn.

Min - the personification of the forces of fertility and abundance, usually identified with Amun (which is emphasized by Amun's crown Min wears) as well with Osiris (with whom he shares the symbolic black color); perhaps originally worshipped in the 5th District of the South Country with its center in Gebtu (Koptos). In the art Min is depicted as a mummy with an erected phallus and one hand raised in a magical gesture; the another hand is usually not depicted or is shown as performing the act of masturbation, which testifies to Min's relation to Atum as the creator of life.

Montu - the ancient patron of the 4th District of the Southern Country with the centers in the City (Thebes) and in South Iunu (Armant), as well as in Madu (Medamud); Montu was patron of king's war deeds; his symbolic animal was a bull.

Mut - "mother" - the personification of the divine motherhood, associated mainly with the City, where she was worshipped in a separate temple precinct as the mythical wife of Amun and mother of king; a special relationship existed linking Mut with the myth of the "divine birth" of the ruler and the Ipet-feast; Mut was considered the patron of pregnant women, and (like Khonsu) she was giving them oracles.

Nebet-hetepet - "Lady of contentment" - just like Ius-aas she was a deified element of the creation myth, a personification of the result of the act done by the hand of Atum; she was worshipped in Iunu, as well as in the Ipet-sut.

Nephthys - "Lady of the Palace" - the personification of the sanctity of the royal residence; according to the creation myth, she was daughter of Nut and Geb (therefore the sister of Isis, Osiris and Seth) representing the first stage of the earthly history; often represented together with Isis as a weeper by the mummy of Osiris; hence her role as a guardian of the deceased.

Nine - cf. Ennead

Nun - the incarnation of mythical primordial ocean, or a divine primordial substance filling chaotically the universe before the act of creation, and afterwards surrounding the already created world; Nun was associated with the cyclical character of the natural phenomena (like the sunrise and the sunset) and the beginning and the end of the human life, while explaining them by the repeated immersion into, and the emergence from the primeval waters.

Nunet - the underground Nut, or a "lower sky" invisible but imagined as symmetrical towards the "upper" sky.

Nut - the personification of the visible sky in the upper part of the world, on which the sun flows in his barge during the day; it was sometimes presented in the art as a naked woman symbolizing both the solar daily path and the mother of Re who "was swallowing" him at sunset and "was giving birth to him anew at dawn; while identified with Hat-Hor, Nut was worshipped as the guardian and feeder of the dead, often identified with the personification of the sycamore.

Osiris - one of the most important names of God making Him the lord of the lower half of the universe or the underworld referred to as the "kingdom of Osiris" and being understood to be the source of new life; he was venerated as a protector of the vegetation and fertility, as well as the patron of the world of the dead. According to the well-known myth, Osiris was a good ruler of the world, reigning together with his wife Isis, but he was killed by his jealous brother Set; the dismembered and drowned body of Osiris was reunited as the first mummy and brought to life thanks to the efforts of Isis and Anubis; the resurrected Osiris became the father of Horus who later won a lawsuit against Set in the process for the domination over the world (of the living), while Osiris became the king of the world of the dead; each deceased, after the justification obtained during the judgment of the dead was becoming a hypostasis of Osiris; the traditional centers of the worship of Osiris were: Djedu (Busiris) in the Northern Country and Abdju (Abydos) in the South.

Ptah - one of the most important names of God and the Creator, worshipped especially in Men-nefer (Memphis) and associated with the person of the king; as the patron of the royal workshops, Ptah was the care-giver of the artists; the living form of Ptah was the Apis bull; the Memphite doctrine of Creation emphasized that Ptah created the world through the Creative Word, but he was also worshipped as a form of the primordial mound "the Earth that is rising", which identifies him with Atum; in the art, Ptah is usually depicted as a standing mummy, holding with both hands various scepters and wearing a characteristic cap tightly fitting the skin; the high priest of Amun in the City also wore a similar headwear.

Re - the most important visible divine form, the Sun; not considered to be a celestial body by the ancient Egyptians, but as God, hence the position of Re in the sky is repeatedly referred to in the book as a daytime designation; Re was commonly imagined as flowing in a barge, because the blue sky was interpreted as water; the name of Re was combined with other divine names, for example with Amun as Amun-Re (an idea of the invisibility of the

God as contrasted with the sunlight resulted in the meaning of this combined name as the Invisible One in His Visible Form), or with Horus as Re-Horakhty (meaning: Re-Horus on the Both Horizons, i.e. appearing at the sunrise and disappearing at the sunset); Re was worshipped in every temple, his sanctuary was often situated on the roof; the dazzling effect of Re's glare resulted in the creation by the artists of a number of imaginary, most fanciful shapes that were symbolizing the different appearances of Re at different stages of his journey on the sky; in the royal tombs a composition can be seen showing 75 forms of Re, and on the funerary papyri and some coffins yet other shapes of Re were painted; Re was understood as the Lord of the upper half of the Universe that he circled during the day, while becoming Osiris at the sunset; at the sunrise Osiris was becoming Re anew.

Renenet - the personification of man's good destiny, a prognostication of what positive would await him or her while "feeding" the man and enriching his life; together with Shai – a bad destiny – it was a preview of what could be expected by the man in his life as a divine gift or try.

Renenutet - "The one who feeds" - the embodiment of an abundance, depicted in the art in the form of a serpent; the feast of Renenutet in the first days of the first month of the Shemu season was similar to "harvest festivals" nowadays.

Sekhmet - "Powerful One" - the personification of the menacing divine force that can be used as a weapon carrying death, destruction, disease or plague, but also for magical protection against them; Sekhmet was imagined in the form of a woman with a head of lioness (not lion, because the grammatical gender of this word was feminine one), sometimes topped with a solar disk; Sekhmet was the theological opposite of the aspect of the divine gentleness personified by Bastet, imagined as a woman with the head of cat.

Serket - "The one who lets breathe" - one of the female divine forms embodying a protective and defensive character both towards the king and towards the deceased; she is represented in the art as a woman with a scorpion on her head.

Set - the personification of the wild destructive force coming from the outside, inherent potentially both in the nature (for example as the desert, the sandstorms) as well as in foreign countries surrounding Egypt; Set also personified the desert itself that was furnishing numerous goods (stones, minerals), therefore Set was also seen as one of the patrons of the country; the myth making him the killer of Osiris and a rival of Horus for ruling the world, caused that in the Late Period when Egypt was dependent on foreign occupiers, Set was blamed for all evil; however, in the periods when Egypt was still independent (thus also in the period, when the action of the novel goes on), Set was considered only to be a symbol of a brute force that could be used in combat; in the art Set was imagined as an unidentified or fabulous animal with high ears, a protruding tail and a long-snouted muzzle.

Shai - the personification of the bad destiny; cf. Renenet.

Shu - the personification of the sun light and air, both filling the space between the sky and the earth; according to the creation myth, Shu together with Tefnut were the first pair of beings made by the Creator Atum; in one text the name of Shu was replaced with "Life".

Sobek - one of the most popular divine forms embodying the power inherent in water and the floods of the Nile; worshipped in the form of crocodile, often depicted with a crown consisting of the solar disc, two ostrich feathers and ram's horns; the cult of Sobek was alive throughout Egypt, especially in the areas comprising backwaters and lakes, but also in the City and south of in, in Sumenu, as well as in Nebit; the crocodile, associated with water, and therefore also with Nun, was considered to be a guardian of the dead, because the death meant a return to the primordial waters; hence the importance of the crocodiles for the funeral ceremonies of those who were not mummified nor had any grave; the crocodiles devouring the dead bodies, made the waters of the Nile clean, hence their great importance also to everyday life in ancient Egypt.

Sons of Horus - the personification of the four cardinal points and the supports of the sky, as well as Anubis's mythical helpers during the mummification of Osiris and at his burial ceremonies; in the everyday life in Egypt the designation "Sons of Horus" was applied to the priests who assisted the main celebrant of the burial rites; they were also regarded as divine guardians of the embalmed intestines put in the course of the mummification into four vessels usually referred to as "canopic vases".

Sopedet - the name of the star Sirius appearing before dawn, with exception of the period of 70 days when the glow of the Sun (from May to July) was obscuring its light; the reappearance of Sopedet in the sky coincided with the beginning of the flood of the Nile and was a sign of the New Year; in the art Sopedet appears as a woman wearing a solar crown combined with the horns of antelope and a star.

The One Who Loved Silence - cf. Meret-seger.

Thoth - cf. Djehuty.

Wepwawet - "Opener of the Ways" – a representation of a jackal carried on a high pole which preceded each procession; perhaps he was originally worshipped in the 13th District of the Southern Country with the center in Saut (today's Asyut).

Outline of the chronology of ancient Egypt

Includes only the rulers mentioned in the novel

Old Kingdom (dynasties 3rd - 8th) - ca 28th-22nd cent. BC among others:

Netjeri-khet - ca 2690-2670.

Khufu - ca 2620-2580.

Khaf-Re - ca 2570-2550.

I Intermediate Period and Middle Kingdom (dynasties 9th – 12th) - ca 22nd - 18th cent. BC among others:

Mentu-hotep Neb-hepet-Re - ca 2050-1990.

II Intermediate Period (dynasties 13th-17th) - 18th-16th cent. BC among others: kings who erected in the City tombs crowned with pyramids.

New Kingdom (dynasties 18th-21st) – 16th – 10th cent. BC among others:

18th dynasty:

Amen-hotep Djeser-Ka-Re (= Amenhotep I) – ca 1525-1504.

Djehuty-mes Aa-kheper-Ka-Re (= Thutmose I) – ca 1504-1492.

Djehuty-mes Men-kheper-Re (= Thutmose III) – ca 1479-1425.

Hat-shepsut Maat-Ka-Re (regency and kingship) – ca 1479-1457.

Amen-hotep Neb-Maat-Re (= Amenhotep III) – ca 1388-1350

Akh-en-Aton (= Amenhotep IV, later Akhenaton) – ca 1350-1334.

Hor-em-heb (earlier general) – ca 1319-1292.

19th dynasty:

Seti Maat-men-Re (= Seti I) – ca 1290-1279

Ra-mes-su User-Maat-Re Sechep-en-Re (= Ramesses II – ca 1279-1213.

Ta-useret – ca 1193-1186.

20th dynasty:

Ra-mes-su User-Maat-Re Meri-Amun (= Ramesses III) – ca 1183-1152.

Ra-mes-su Nefer-Ka-Re (= Ramesses IX) – ca 1125-1108.

Ra-mes-su Kheper-Maat-Re (= Ramesses X) – ca 1108-1099.

Ra-mes-su Men-Maat-Re Sechep-en-Ptah (= Ramesses XI – ca 1099-1070.

Repeating of Births period – ca 1080-1070.

Heri-Hor Sa-Amen (earlier general) – ca 1080-1074.

21st dynasty:

Nes-Ba-neb-Djedu (= Smendes) [in Tanis] – ca 1070-1045.

Pi-nodjem (= Pinodjem I) [in Thebes] – ca 1055-1035.

Pa-seba-kha-en-Niut (= Psusennes I) [in Tanis] – ca 1045-995.

Amen-em-ensu Nefer-Ka-Re (= Neferkheres) [in Thebes] – ca 1045-1041.

Pharaohs and high priests

Names of pharaohs and of Amun's high priests in Thebes and their spouses mentioned in the book

Ah-mes-Nefertari – mother of Amenhotep I, she held regency during the first years of his reign (ca 1525-1515; he was a small child at the time); her posthumous worship, running parallel to that of her son, continued throughout the New Kingdom. Her tomb has been recently identified as the so-called Royal Cache at Deir el-Bahari, where her mummy and coffin were found.

Akh-en-Aton – king of the 18th dynasty, son of Amenhotep III, ascended the throne as Amenhotep (IV), then changed his name to Akhenaton; reigned ca 1350-1334; the so-called Akhenaton's reform led the country to civil war and severely weakened it; the destruction of all divine images in temples, tombs, archives, etc. was the reason for the announcement of the so-called Repeating of Births, or a kind of a martial law explained in religious terms as the ritual re-creation of the world, resulting in numerous changes, among others of the ruling dynasty, and in the construction of a new capital (Pi-Ramesse); this period formally announced by Seti I was actually prepared and begun by Horemheb.

Amen-em-ensu – son of Herihor and Nodjmet, he exercised the royal power as a co-ruler of Psusennes I in four first years of his reign, ca 1045-1041 while residing in Thebes; perhaps he is buried in Herihor's tomb, still in search.

Amen-hotep – high priest of Amun during the reigns of Ramesses IX, Ramesses X and Ramesses XI, ca 1125-1080; in the temple in Karnak, both scenes showing the rewarding of Amenhotep by Ramesses IX and a text commemorating his life and works are represented, also mentioning a siege of Karnak for several months by hostile troops, after which Amenhotep had to flee across the desert to the north of the country, where he died after a few years long stay in the temple in Iunu (Heliopolis).

Amen-hotep Djeser-Ka-Re – Amenhotep I, king of the 18th dynasty, one of the creators of Egypt's power during the New Kingdom; he reigned ca 1525-1504; in the first part of this period he was replaced by his mother, Ahmes-nefertari; he was worshipped together with her, especially in Thebes, as the patron of the City and of the Theban necropolis. His mummy has been found in the Royal Cache, but his tomb is always looked for; most probably it is situated under the ruins of the temple of Thutmose III at Deir el-Bahari.

Amen-hotep Neb-Maat-Re – Amenhotep III, king of the 18th dynasty; on his reign ca 1388-1350 the peak of Egypt's prosperity and great construction investments in Thebes fall; the temples in Karnak (Ipet-sut) and Luxor (Ipet-resit) were considerably enlarged at that time; on the west bank an artificial lake of huge size was built, with a port and a palace complex next to it, as well as a great temple dedicated, among others, to the pharaoh's posthumous cult (two large statues of the king known as the Colossi of Memnon can always be seen there along other remains of the temple excavated in the recent years by a German mission).

Aset-em-Akhbit – one of the daughters of Pi-nodjem I, sister and wife of the high priest Men-kheper-Re, she held a high office of the superior of the priestesses in the City in the second half of the 11th century BC. Her mummy and coffins were found in the Royal Cache.

Djehuty-mes Aa-kheper-Ka-Re – Thutmose I, king of the 18th dynasty, successor of Amenhotep I, he reigned in the years 1504-1492 and is considered to be one of the creators of the power of Egypt; during his reign the areas from the Euphrates (in the east) to the 4th Nile cataract (in the south) were subordinated to Egypt.

Djehuty-mes Men-kheper-Re – Thutmose III, king of the 18th dynasty, ruled ca 1470-1425 (although during his first 22 years the real rule was held by Hatshepsut); he strengthened the power and prosperity of the country as a great conqueror who confirmed the reign of Egypt in the area from Syria (in the north-east) to the 4th cataract of the Nile (in the south), and also a great builder (among others, Akh-menu in Karnak and the temple in Deir el-Bahari).

Hat-shepsut – daughter of Thutmose I, stepmother and aunt of Thutmose III, who around 1479 took power as a regent during his minority, but ruled as king until her death ca 1457; she erected a great temple (Djeser-Djeseru) in West Thebes (at Deir el-Bahari).

Henut-tawy – Daughter of Ramesses XI and Tent-Amun, ca 1080 she married Pi-nodjem I; their children (Ma-sa-harti, Maat-Ka-Re, Pa-seba-kha-en-Niut, Men-kheper-Re, Aset-em-Akhbit) held key positions during the early 21st dynasty (1st half of the 11th cent. BC).

Heri-Hor – high official and general in the time of Ramesses XI, probably of foreign (Libyan) origin; after the civil war caused by the rebel of the Kushite corps of the Egyptian army under the command of general Pa-nehsi, he introduced a state of emergency or martial law in the upper Egypt, called the Repeating of Births (from the religious point of view it was a renewed creation of the world, and the power in Egypt was wielded by Amun himself); as a co-ruler of Amun he accepted full royal titles; he reigned ca 1080-1074 BC; the search for his tomb is still underway, however it is possible that he was buried in the old tomb of Amenhotep I.

Hor-em-heb – high official and general during the last kings of the 18th dynasty (Akhenaton, Smenkh-Ka-Re and Tut-ankh-Amun); after the civil war related to Akhenaton's reform (referred to as the Amarna period, and in the novel as a great heresy) prepared the Repeating of Births, starting the construction of a new capital (in Pi-Ramesse) and sat on the throne while preparing the new dynasty.

Khaf-Re – Khefren, one of the rulers of the 4th dynasty, son of Khufu, builder of the second largest pyramid (today on the outskirts of Cairo, in Giza)

Khufu – Kheops, one of the rulers of the 4th dynasty, the builder of the largest pyramid (today in Giza).

Maat-Ka-Re – daughter of Pi-nodjem (I) and Henut-tawy; in the early 21st dynasty she was the first Amun's Divine Adoratrice – a priestess performing the ritual function of his wife. Her mummy and coffins were found in the so-called Royal Cache at Deir el-Bahari.

Ma-sa-harti – son of Pi-nodjem (I) and Henut-tawy, in the years ca 1055-1045 BC he was high priest of Amun. His mummy and coffins were found in the so-called Royal Cache at Deir el-Bahari.

Men-kheper-Re – son of Pi-nodjem (I) and Henut-tawy; he was high priest of Amun during almost 50 years, ca 1045-995 BC; during last two years of his pontificate he accepted royal titles as co-ruler of his brother Psusennes I.

Mentu-hotep Neb-hepet-Re – king of the 11th dynasty who brought about the reunification of the state after the period of its breakup during the so-called I Intermediate Period; he ruled ca 2050-1990; he built a great temple connected to his tomb in Ta-Djeser (Deir el-Bahari).

Merit-Amun – queen, wife of Amenhotep I; her grave and mummy were found in Deir el-Bahari.

Nefertari – queen, wife of Ramesses II (the Great), 13th century BC; her grave with magnificent paintings is located in the Valley of the Queens in the West Thebes; Ramesses built a temple for her (today it is the so-called small temple in Abu Simbel).

Nes-Ba-neb-Djedu – known by the Greek name as Smendes, the first ruler of the 21st dynasty, ca 1070-1045 BC; his tomb was in Tanis.

Netjeri-khet – king of the 3rd dynasty, usually referred to as Djoser, the builder of the first great (so-called step) pyramid; reigned ca 2690-2670 BC.

Nodjmet – daughter of Pi-ankh, wife of Herihor and mother of Amen-em-ensu; her mummy was found in the Royal Cache at Deir el-Bahari.

Pa-seba-kha-en-Niut – known by the Greek name as Psusennes (I), son of Pi-nodjem (I), he was the second king of the 21st dynasty, reigned ca 1045-995 BC; his tomb partly intact was discovered in Tanis.

Pi-ankh – high official and general during the reign of Ramesses XI; father of Pi-nodjem (I) and Nodjmet; after the death of Heri-Hor he became ca 1074 high priest of Amun; in several museums his letters are preserved written ca 1070 on the Elephantine island during the expedition against Kush. His mummy hasn't been discovered so far.

Pi-nodjem – son of Pi-ankh and his successor in the position of the high priest of Amun in Thebes since ca 1070; he held this post for 15 years, when ca 1055 he assumed the royal titles, becoming a co-ruler of Smendes, while transferring his high priest's function to his son Ma-sa-harti. Pi-nodjem's mummy buried in the re-used coffin of the king Thutmose I was discovered in the Royal Cache.

Ramesses the Great – see Ra-mes-su User-Maat-Re Sechep-en-Re.

Ra-mes-su Kheper-Maat-Re – king Ramesses X, reigned ca 1108-1099 BC. A tomb was made for him in the Valley of the Kings.

Ra-mes-su Men-Maat-Re Sechep-en-Ptah – king Ramesses XI, the last king of the 20th dynasty, reigned ca 1099-1070 BC; in the 18th year of his reign a corps of the Egyptian army consisting of the Kushite mercenaries under the command of a high dignitary and general Pa-nehsi revolted that led to a civil war which brought, among others, a partial destruction of the temple in

Karnak and the fortress in West Thebes (around the temple of Ramesses III in Medinet Habu), as well as the complete plunder of the Valley of the Kings; then the king was removed from power by the army, among others by the generals Herihor and Pi-ankh, and a martial law was introduced in the whole Egypt known as the Repeating of Births that lasted until the death of the pharaoh; his tomb in the Valley of the Kings was never used for him; probably Pi-ankh (temporarily) and later Pi-nodjem, Henut-tawy and Nodjmet were buried there; the novel's action goes on during the reign of this king.

Ra-mes-su Nefer-Ka-Re - Ramesses IX, king of the 20th dynasty, reigned ca 1125-1108 BC; his tomb is in the Valley of the Kings; a group of documents written on papyrus have survived, relating, among others, to the trial of a royal grave robber in the West Thebes.

Ra-mes-su User-Maat-Re Meri-Amun - Ramesses III, king of the 20th dynasty, the last great warrior and builder of the New Kingdom; he ruled ca 1183-1152 BC; on that time victorious wars with invaders from Libya and with the so-called Sea People fall; he built a large temple in Western Thebes (today's Medinet Habu) that he surrounded with gigantic walls, thus creating a fortress; this fortress was destroyed in the 11th cent. BC, probably during the civil war with the Kushite rebels.

Ra-mes-su User-Maat-Re Sechep-en-Re Ramesses II, king of the 19th dynasty, reigned ca 1279-1213; he was son and successor of Seti I; during his long reign he confirmed Egypt's rule over the lands south of Egypt, until the 4th Nile cataract, and was struggling with another power of those days – the kingdom of the

Hittites - with which Egypt competed for the control over the trade routes in Syria; in his 5th year he made a military expedition against the Hittites that brought about the battle at Kadesh; the battle ended in failure but it was later glorified on monuments as a great victory; Egypt's position was strengthened in his year 21 with the signing of the peace treaty with the Hittites; during the long reign a great number of temple buildings was erected in the whole Egypt, among which the best known are: (in East Thebes) the Great Column Hall of the temple of Amun-Re in Karnak, and the front part of the temple in Luxor, (in West Thebes) the so-called Ramesseum, and in the territory of Kush the two temples in Abu Simbel, as well as several smaller temples like that in Beit el-Wali.

Seti Maat-men-Re - Seti I, king of the 19th dynasty, father of Ramesses the Great; he reigned ca 1290-1279 BC; he formally counted the years of his reign as a period of Repeating of Births after the Amarna period, although changes began already under Horemheb; under Seti's reign the symbolism of the recreation of the world was emphasized, among others by the construction of a special temple in Abydos, as well as in the architecture of his tomb in the Valley of the Kings; in the West Thebes another large temple erected by this king can be seen.

Ta-useret - the queen and the last king of the 19th dynasty; she began her rule after the death of her husband, Seti II, ca 1193, as a regent during the minority of her son Si-Ptah, and after his death she remained on the throne until ca 1186 BC. Her tomb is in the Valley of the Kings.

Tent-Amun - queen, wife of Ramesses XI; after his death wife of Smendes, with whom she shared power before, during the Repeating of Births in Tanis; she was mother of Henut-tawy

Ti - queen, wife of Amenhotep III, mother of Akhenaton; from the time of Amenhotep III a group of interesting texts written on large scarabs are preserved; one of these informs that king Amenhotep ordered the building of the so-called lake of pleasure, the traces of which are still visible in West Thebes, not far from today's Medinet Habu.

Andrzej Niwinski

MAPS

Map 1

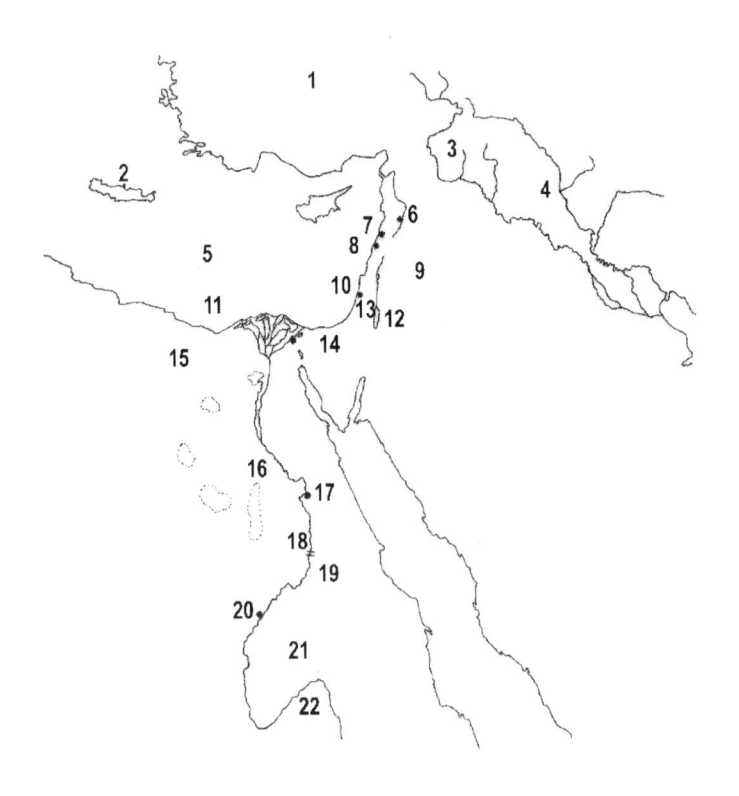

Map 1 description

1 - Hatti

2 - Keftiu

3 - Aramu

4 - Aa-sura

5 - Great Green

6 - Kadesh

7 - Keben

8 - Djeden

9 - Retjenu

10 - Iapu

11 - Northern Country (Ta-mehu)

12 - Israel

13 - Peleshet

14 - Pi-Ramesse

15 - Meshuesh (Libu)

16 - Southern Country (Ta-shema)

17 - City (Waset)

18 - Abu

19 - Wawat (Ta-seti)

20 - Behen

21 - Kush

22 - Hapi

Map 2

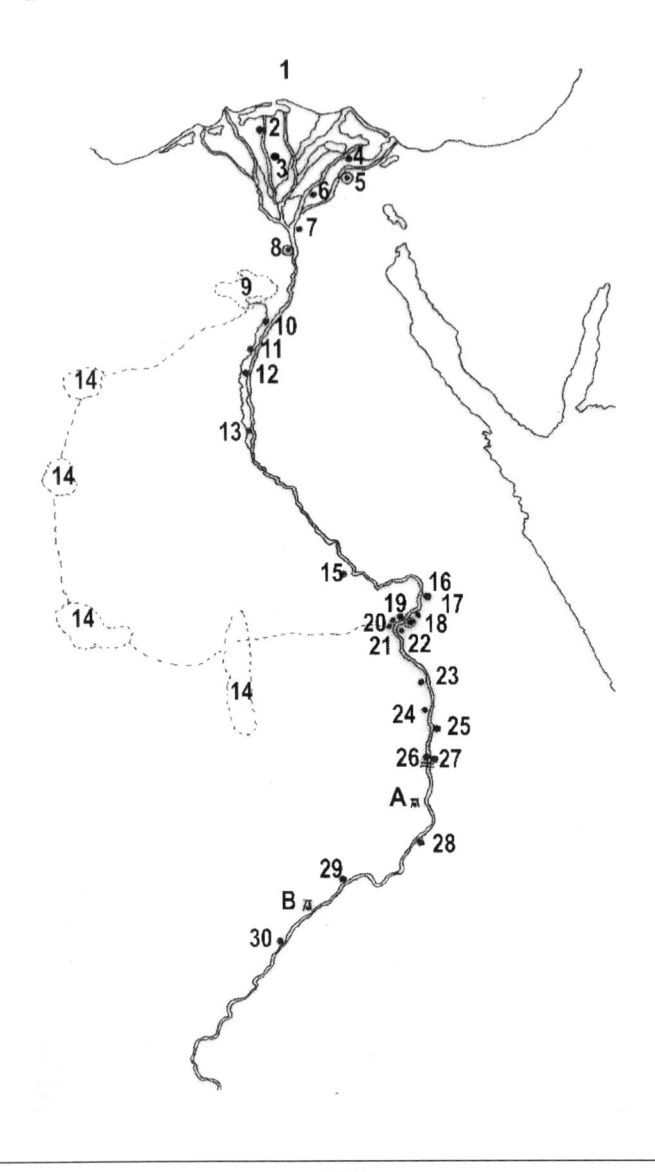

Map 2 - description

A - Temple of Beit el-Wali
B - Temple of Abu Simbel
1 - Great Green
2 - Pe/Dep
3 - Djedu
4 - Djanet
5 - Pi-Ramesse
6 - Per Bastet
7 - Iunu
8 - Men-nefer
9 - Pa-im
10 - Nen-ensu
11 - Seper meru
12 - Hor-di
13 - Khemenu
14 - Oasis
15 - Abdju
16 - Gebtu
17 - Madu
18 - City (Waset)
19 - Khefet-her-neb-es
20 - South Iunu
21 - Sumenu
22 - Djeret
23 - Behdet
24 - Khenu
25 - Nebit
26 - Abu
27 - Sunu
28 - Baki
29 - Miam
30 - Behen

Map 3

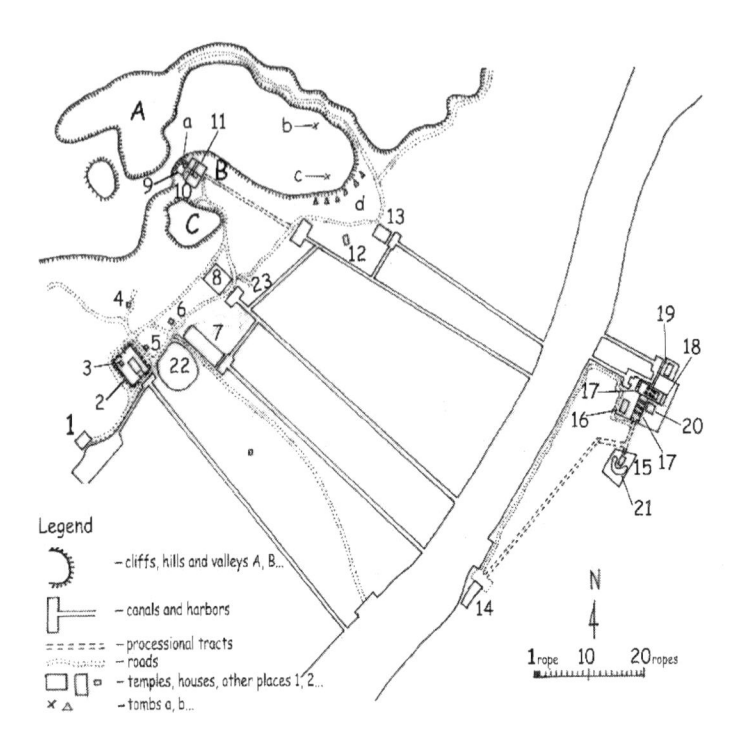

Legend

- cliffs, hills and valleys A, B...
- canals and harbors
- processional tracts
- roads
- temples, houses, other places 1, 2...
- tombs a, b...

1 rope 10 20 ropes

Map 3 description

A - Great Valley
B - Ta-Djeser
C - Hill of Wedding Rites
a - the tomb of Amenhotep Djeser-Ka-Re and Heri-Hor
b - the old tomb (inspected by Djehuty-mes and Buteh-Amun)
c - old tomb of Amen-hotep Djeser-Ka-Re and Ahmes-Nefertari
d - old royal tombs with the pyramids
1 - the old palace of Amen-hotep Neb-Maat-Re (palace by the water)
2 - temple precinct and fortress of Ramesses User-Maat-Re
3 - house of Djehuty-mes and Buteh-Amun
4 - house of "sisters"
5 - beer house
6 - house of Pa-Shu-uben
7 - temple of Amen-hotep Neb-Maat-Re
8 - temple of Ramesses the Great
9 - temple of Men-kheper-Re Djehuty-mes (Djeser-Akhet)
10 - temple of Mentu-hotep and Amen-hotep of the Garden
11 - temple of Hatshepsut (Djeser-Djeseru)
12 - temple of Amen-hotep of the Court
13 - temple of Seti Maat-men-Re
14 - temple Ipet-resit
15 - temple of Mut Lady of Asheru
16 - temple of Khonsu Nefer-hotep
17 - temple of Amun (Ipet-sut)
18 - Akh-menu
19 - temple of Montu and Maat
20 - sacred lake in Ipet-sut
21 - sacred lake in Asheru
22 - Crocodiles'Backwater (Launderers' Bank)
23 - sycamores

ABOUT THE AUTHOR

Professor Andrzej Niwinski was born in 1948 in Warsaw, where he lives and where he accomplished his education. Under the direction of the famous creator of the Polish School of Mediterranean Archaeology, prof. Kazimierz Michalowski, he graduated and wrote a doctorate (in 1979). He wrote the postdoctoral dissertation 10 years later at the University of Warsaw, and soon after he got a post of professor in the Institute of Archaeology of the Warsaw University. Actually he is retired, but still is actively participating in the research, while directing the so-called the Cliff Mission at Deir el-Bahari (Upper Egypt, Luxor region).

In the recent years the works of this mission have brought some sensational results and contributed to the solution of several great archaeological puzzles of Egyptian history, concerning, among others the location of the tombs of King

Amenhotep I, probably re-used for Heri-Hor (both tombs have been intensively sought by archaeologists for a hundred years, and now their uncovering is only a matter of time). The evidence has been furnished that this tomb, in which probably even more royal burials can be expected, was protected in the 21st Dynasty by an enormous artificial "slope of the mountains" that once covered completely the whole southern part of Deir el-Bahari, including the ruins of two temples: to make such a thing a work had been done comparable with the buildings of the pyramids...

During the last season a royal deposit of King Thutmose II (Hatshepsut's husband) was found by the Cliff Mission that without any doubt leads to a discovery of yet another royal tomb, probably intact one, as well.

Professor Niwinski is considered to be an international authority in the field of research on the 21st Dynasty (11th-10th centuries BC), as well as in the field of research on Egyptian coffins and funerary papyri. Actually he is directing a new large-scale project related to the incredibly rich iconography of the coffins of the 21st Dynasty period.

Professor Niwinski is the author of about 220 publications including 15 books both scientific and popular ones.

Table of contents

INTRODUCTION..7
CHAPTER I..10
CHAPTER II...30
CHAPTER III..54
CHAPTER IV..82
CHAPTER V..114
CHAPTER VI...131
CHAPTER VII..158
CHAPTER VIII...170
CHAPTER IX...193
CHAPTER X..209
CHAPTER XI...234
CHAPTER XII..262
CHAPTER XIII 278
CHAPTER XIV..301
CHAPTER XV...319
CHAPTER XVI..351
CHAPTER XVII...379
CHAPTER XVIII..397
CHAPTER XIX...424
CHAPTER XX..456
CHAPTER XXI...479
CHAPTER XXII..505
CHAPTER XXIII..528
CHAPTER XXIV..542
CHAPTER XXV...558

CHAPTER XXVI..573

CHAPTER XXVII...597

CHAPTER XXVIII...615

CHAPTER XXIX..631

CHAPTER XXX...650

GEOGRAPHICAL ETHNIC AND LOCAL NAMES........................668

DIVINE NAMES..677

OUTLINE OF THE CHRONOLOGY..689

PHARAOHS AND HIGH PRIESTS..693

MAPS...702

ABOUT THE AUTHOR..708

Printed in Great Britain
by Amazon